D1499658

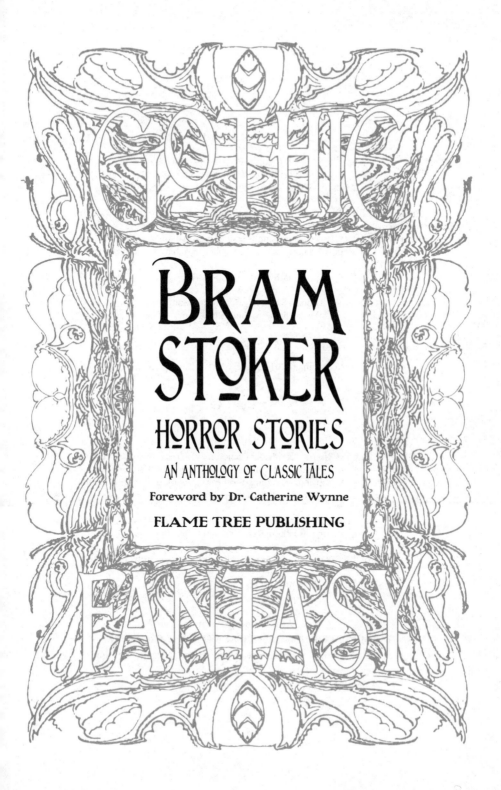

GOTHIC

BRAM STOKER

HORROR STORIES

AN ANTHOLOGY OF CLASSIC TALES

Foreword by Dr. Catherine Wynne

FLAME TREE PUBLISHING

FANTASY

This is a FLAME TREE Book

Publisher & Creative Director: Nick Wells
Project Editor: Laura Bulbeck
Editorial Board: Gillian Whitaker, Josie Mitchell, Catherine Taylor

FLAME TREE PUBLISHING
6 Melbray Mews, Fulham,
London SW6 3NS, United Kingdom
www.flametreepublishing.com

First published 2018

ISBN: 978-1-78664-783-2

A copy of the CIP data for this book is available from the British Library.

Printed and bound in China

And Coming Soon
FLAME TREE PRESS | FICTION WITHOUT FRONTIERS
New and original writing in Horror, Crime, SF and Fantasy

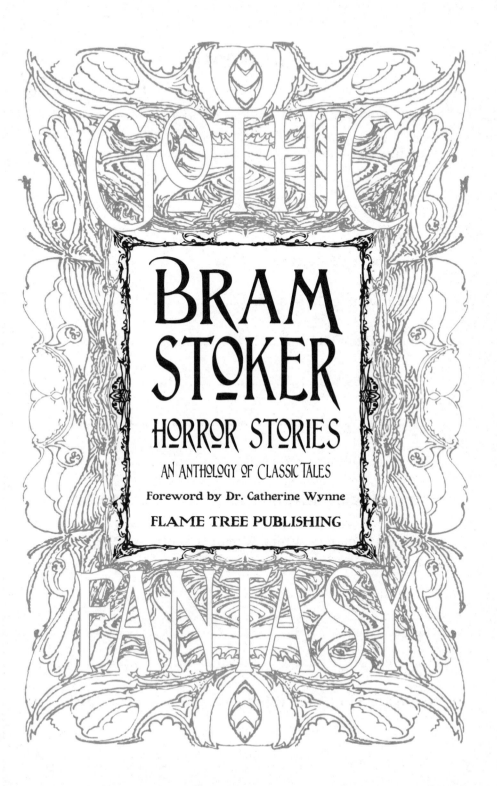

GOTHIC

BRAM
STOKER

HORROR STORIES

AN ANTHOLOGY OF CLASSIC TALES

Foreword by Dr. Catherine Wynne

FLAME TREE PUBLISHING

FANTASY

Contents

Supernatural Foes

Murder & Revenge

Love & Tragedy

Foreword: Bram Stoker Horror Stories

WHEN BRAM STOKER published *Dracula* in 1897, his mother, Charlotte, compared him to Edgar Allan Poe. Indeed, Poe, she declared, was 'nowhere.' A reading of her son's other fictions published in this anthology would have revealed to Charlotte an imagination fuelled by a range of Gothic terrors.

Born in Dublin in 1847 – the worst year of the Irish Famine – Stoker entered a world of the living dead. He then spent the first seven years of his life bedridden by a mysterious illness. His mother's tales of folklore and her account of a cholera epidemic experienced in her youth developed her son's interest in the supernatural, the Gothic and the catastrophic.

Charlotte related the story of man who was informed that his wife had died of cholera. Seeking confirmation, he went to see for himself and discovered her still alive amongst a pile of corpses. He rescued her and she survived. Such tales of love and loss, and of events beyond rational explanation, infuse Stoker's early Gothic tales.

In 'The Crystal Cup' love and tragedy are combined in the tale of an artist, separated from his wife by a cruel king who forces him to make a crystal cup. The artist, longing for his love, infuses the cup with his soul but dies before he can be released from his captivity. In 'The Chain of Destiny' a woman is threatened by the sight of a supernatural monster as her lover tries to save her from the demonic vision. In 'The Castle of the King' a man traverses a threatening landscape to attempt to be reunited with his love. Stoker also explores love betrayed. In 'The Secret of Growing Gold' a murdered wife takes revenge on her husband when her golden hair grows up out of the floorboards.

The second formative influence on Stoker's Gothic imagination was the theatre. Stoker was a theatre critic in Dublin before becoming the business manager of the actor Henry Irving's Lyceum theatre, London's home of Gothic melodrama, in 1878. The theatre is the setting for the carpenter's fall in *The Primrose Path* (he falls off a stage trap used to propel actors to the stage and sinks into degradation). The story is Othello-like.

Stoker's most gruesome stories are collected here. The horror of 'The Judge's House' lingers long after the story is read. In 'The Star Trap' the mangled body of an acrobat horrifies. 'The Squaw' combines a vengeful cat with the medieval torture device, an Iron Virgin, with devastating consequences for an American tourist in Nuremberg [Nurnberg]. But Stoker titillates as well. In *The Lady of the Shroud* the hero is not quite sure whether the woman he loves is a vampire or not. *The Lair of the White Worm* echoes *Dracula* with its snake woman who threatens to consume.

This anthology reveals a writer who should not be limited by the achievement of *Dracula* or by comparison to anyone else. His stories reveal that Bram Stoker was in his own right a master of the gruesome, the grotesque and the uncanny. Bram Stoker will haunt you.

Dr. Catherine Wynne
Author of *Bram Stoker, Dracula and the Victorian Gothic Stage* (2013)

Publisher's Note

BRAM STOKER is of course best-known as the creator of *Dracula*, one of the most iconic horror stories of all time. His horror fiction does not start and end there however – lurking within these pages are some of his most chilling works, from ancient curses to bloodcurdling acts of revenge from beyond the grave and gothic tragedies which Edgar Allan Poe would be proud of. Collected in this fantastic new anthology are stories you may know and love alongside some of his lesser-known, but wonderfully atmospheric tales, which deserve to be read. We have organized the works by theme; arranging them here in a way we hope is both interesting and forms a natural fit – although of course no story has only one layer to it, and several could be argued to fit into more than one category. Therefore at the end of every piece we also offer recommendations for two other stories – not always within the same theme – which you might like to try next.

As with many of our collections, we have included some novel extracts, and all of these come with a link to download the full novel for free from our website. The main extract from *The Lair of the White Worm* comes from the end of the book, which may seem like an odd choice. This was done for two reasons: this is where the horror itself really builds and so we believe is the most deserving of inclusion here; and it also has the extra benefit of avoiding parts of the text with much of the more uncomfortable language and attitudes towards race that can sometimes be found in late Victorian/ early Edwardian works. The latter is always a difficult balance for us when considering classic fiction, and we felt that *The Lair of the White Worm* ought to be included as part of Stoker's horror canon, but without wishing to cause too much offence for the modern reader. We truly hope this *Bram Stoker Horror Stories* collection will be one to treasure on your bookshelves for years to come.

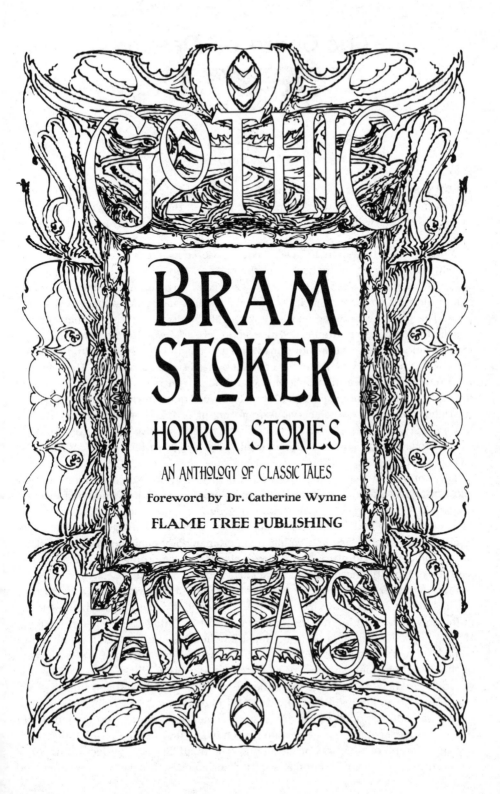

GOTHIC

BRAM STOKER

HORROR STORIES

AN ANTHOLOGY OF CLASSIC TALES

Foreword by Dr. Catherine Wynne

FLAME TREE PUBLISHING

FANTASY

The Chain of Destiny

Chapter I
A Warning

IT WAS SO LATE in the evening when I arrived at Scarp that I had but little opportunity of observing the external appearance of the house; but, as far as I could judge in the dim twilight, it was a very stately edifice of seemingly great age, built of white stone.

When I passed the porch, however, I could observe its internal beauties much more closely, for a large wood fire burned in the hall and all the rooms and passages were lighted. The hall was almost baronial in its size, and opened on to a staircase of dark oak so wide and so generous in its slope that a carriage might almost have been driven up it. The rooms were large and lofty, with their walls, like those of the staircase, panelled with oak black from age. This sombre material would have made the house intensely gloomy but for the enormous width and height of both rooms and passages. As it was, the effect was a homely combination of size and warmth. The windows were set in deep embrasures, and, on the ground story, reached from quite level with the floor to almost the ceiling. The fireplaces were quite in the old style, large and surrounded with massive oak carvings, representing on each some scene from Biblical history, and at the side of each fireplace rose a pair of massive carved iron fire-dogs. It was altogether just such a house as would have delighted the heart of Washington Irving or Nathaniel Hawthorne.

The house had been lately restored; but in effecting the restoration comfort had not been forgotten, and any modern improvement which tended to increase the homelike appearance of the rooms had been added. The old diamond-paned casements, which had remained probably from the Elizabethan age, had given place to more useful plate glass; and, in like manner, many other changes had taken place. But so judiciously had every change been effected that nothing of the new clashed with the old, but the harmony of all the parts seemed complete.

I thought it no wonder that Mrs. Trevor had fallen in love with Scarp the first time she had seen it. Mrs. Trevor's liking the place was tantamount to her husband's buying it, for he was so wealthy that he could get almost anything money could purchase. He was himself a man of good taste, but still he felt his inferiority to his wife in this respect so much that he never dreamt of differing in opinion from her on any matter of choice or judgment. Mrs. Trevor had, without exception, the best taste of any one whom I ever knew, and, strange to say, her taste was not confined to any branch of art. She did not write, or paint, or sing; but still her judgment in writing, painting, or music, was unquestioned by her friends. It seemed as if nature had denied to her the power of execution in any separate branch of art, in order to make her perfect in her appreciation of what was beautiful and true in all. She was perfect in the art of harmonising – the art of every-day life. Her husband used to say, with a far-fetched joke, that her star must have been in the House of Libra, because everything which she said and did showed such a nicety of balance.

Mr. and Mrs. Trevor were the most model couple I ever knew – they really seemed not twain, but one. They appeared to have adopted something of the French idea of man and wife – that they should not be the less like friends because they were linked together by indissoluble bonds – that they should share their pleasures as well as their sorrows. The former outbalanced the latter, for both husband and wife were of that happy temperament which can take pleasure from everything, and find consolation even in the chastening rod of affliction.

Still, through their web of peaceful happiness ran a thread of care. One that cropped up in strange places, and disappeared again, but which left a quiet tone over the whole fabric – they had no child.

> *They had their share of sorrow, for when time was ripe*
> *The still affection of the heart became an outward breathing type,*
> *That into stillness passed again,*
> *But left a want unknown before.*

There was something simple and holy in their patient endurance of their lonely life – for lonely a house must ever be without children to those who love truly. Theirs was not the eager, disappointed longing of those whose union had proved fruitless. It was the simple, patient, hopeless resignation of those who find that a common sorrow draws them more closely together than many common joys. I myself could note the warmth of their hearts and their strong philoprogenitive feeling in their manner towards me.

From the time when I lay sick in college when Mrs. Trevor appeared to my fever-dimmed eyes like an angel of mercy, I felt myself growing in their hearts. Who can imagine my gratitude to the lady who, merely because she heard of my sickness and desolation from a college friend, came and nursed me night and day till the fever left me. When I was sufficiently strong to be moved she had me brought away to the country, where good air, care, and attention soon made me stronger than ever. From that time I became a constant visitor at the Trevors' house; and as month after month rolled by I felt that I was growing in their affections. For four summers I spent my long vacation in their house, and each year I could feel Mr. Trevor's shake of the hand grow heartier, and his wife's kiss on my forehead – for so she always saluted me – grow more tender and motherly.

Their liking for me had now grown so much that in their heart of hearts – and it was a sanctum common to them both – they secretly loved me as a son. Their love was returned manifold by the lonely boy, whose devotion to the kindest friends of his youth and his trouble had increased with his growth into manhood. Even in my own heart I was ashamed to confess how I loved them both – how I worshipped Mrs. Trevor as I adored the mother whom I had lost so young, and whose eyes shone sometimes even then upon me, like stars, in my sleep.

It is strange how timorous we are when our affections are concerned. Merely because I had never told her how I loved her as a mother, because she had never told me how she loved me as a son, I used sometimes to think of her with a sort of lurking suspicion that I was trusting too much to my imagination. Sometimes even I would try to avoid thinking of her altogether, till my yearning would grow too strong to be repelled, and then I would think of her long and silently, and would love her more and more. My life was so lonely that I clung to her as the only thing I had to love. Of course I loved her husband, too, but I never thought about him in the same way; for men are less demonstrative about their affections to each other, and even acknowledge them to themselves less.

Mrs. Trevor was an excellent hostess. She always let her guests see that they were welcome, and, unless in the case of casual visitors, that they were expected. She was, as may be imagined, very popular with all classes; but what is more rare, she was equally popular with both sexes. To be popular with her own sex is the touchstone of a woman's worth. To the houses of the peasantry she came, they said, like an angel, and brought comfort wherever she came. She knew the proper way to deal with the poor; she always helped them materially, but never offended their feelings in so doing. Young people all adored her.

My curiosity had been aroused as to the sort of place Scarp was; for, in order to give me a surprise, they would not tell me anything about it, but said that I must wait and judge it for myself. I had looked forward to my visit with both expectation and curiosity.

When I entered the hall, Mrs. Trevor came out to welcome me and kissed me on the forehead, after her usual manner. Several of the old servants came near, smiling and bowing, and wishing welcome to "Master Frank." I shook hands with several of them, whilst their mistress looked on with a pleased smile.

As we went into a snug parlour, where a table was laid out with the materials for a comfortable supper, Mrs. Trevor said to me:

"I am glad you came so soon, Frank. We have no one here at present, so you will be quite alone with us for a few days; and you will be quite alone with me this evening, for Charley is gone to a dinner-party at Westholm."

I told her that I was glad that there was no one else at Scarp, for that I would rather be with her and her husband than any one else in the world. She smiled as she said:

"Frank, if any one else said that, I would put it down as a mere compliment; but I know you always speak the truth. It is all very well to be alone with an old couple like Charley and me for two or three days; but just you wait till Thursday, and you will look on the intervening days as quite wasted."

"Why?" I inquired.

"Because, Frank, there is a girl coming to stay with me then, with whom I intend you to fall in love."

I answered jocosely:

"Oh, thank you, Mrs. Trevor, very much for your kind intentions – but suppose for a moment that they should be impracticable. 'One man may lead a horse to the pond's brink.' 'The best laid schemes o' mice an' men.' Eh?"

"Frank, don't be silly. I do not want to make you fall in love against your inclination; but I hope and I believe that you will."

"Well, I'm sure I hope you won't be disappointed; but I never yet heard a person praised that I did not experience a disappointment when I came to know him or her."

"Frank, did I praise any one?"

"Well, I am vain enough to think that your saying that you knew I would fall in love with her was a sort of indirect praise."

"Dear, me, Frank, how modest you have grown. 'A sort of indirect praise!' Your humility is quite touching."

"May I ask who the lady is, as I am supposed to be an interested party?"

"I do not know that I ought to tell you on account of your having expressed any doubt as to her merits. Besides, I might weaken the effect of the introduction. If I stimulate your curiosity it will be a point in my favour."

"Oh, very well; I suppose I must only wait?"

"Ah, well, Frank, I will tell you. It is not fair to keep you waiting. She is a Miss Fothering."

"Fothering? Fothering? I think I know that name. I remember hearing it somewhere, a long time ago, if I do not mistake. Where does she come from?"

"Her father is a clergyman in Norfolk, but he belongs to the Warwickshire family. I met her at Winthrop, Sir Harry Blount's place, a few months ago, and took a great liking for her, which she returned, and so we became fast friends. I made her promise to pay me a visit this summer, so she and her sister are coming here on Thursday to stay for some time."

"And, may I be bold enough to inquire what she is like?"

"You may inquire if you like, Frank; but you won't get an answer. I shall not try to describe her. You must wait and judge for yourself."

"Wait," said I, "three whole days? How can I do that? Do, tell me."

She remained firm to her determination. I tried several times in the course of the evening to find out something more about Miss Fothering, for my curiosity was roused; but all the answer I could get on the subject was – "Wait, Frank; wait, and judge for yourself."

When I was bidding her good night, Mrs. Trevor said to me:

"By-the-bye, Frank, you will have to give up the room which you will sleep in tonight, after tomorrow. I will have such a full house that I cannot let you have a doubled-bedded room all to yourself; so I will give that room to the Miss Fotherings, and move you up to the second floor. I just want you to see the room, as it has a romantic look about it, and has all the old furniture that was in it when we came here. There are several pictures in it worth looking at."

My bedroom was a large chamber – immense for a bedroom – with two windows opening level with the floor, like those of the parlours and drawing rooms. The furniture was old-fashioned, but not old enough to be curious, and on the walls hung many pictures – portraits –

the house was full of portraits – and landscapes. I just glanced at these, intending to examine them in the morning, and went to bed. There was a fire in the room, and I lay awake for some time looking dreamily at the shadows of the furniture flitting over the walls and ceiling as the flames of the wood fire leaped and fell, and the red embers dropped whitening on the hearth. I tried to give the rein to my thoughts, but they kept constantly to the one subject – the mysterious Miss Fothering, with whom I was to fall in love. I was sure that I had heard her name somewhere, and I had at times lazy recollections of a child's face. At such times I would start awake from my growing drowsiness, but before I could collect my scattered thoughts the idea had eluded me. I could remember neither when nor where I had heard the name, nor could I recall even the expression of the child's face. It must have been long, long ago, when I was young. When I was young my mother was alive. My mother – mother – mother. I found myself half awakening, and repeating the word over and over again. At last I fell asleep.

I thought that I awoke suddenly to that peculiar feeling which we sometimes have on starting from sleep, as if some one had been speaking in the room, and the voice is still echoing through it. All was quite silent, and the fire had gone out. I looked out of the window that lay straight opposite the foot of the bed, and observed a light outside, which gradually grew brighter till the room was almost as light as by day. The window looked like a picture in the framework formed by the cornice over the foot of the bed, and the massive pillars shrouded in curtains which supported it.

With the new accession of light I looked round the room, but nothing was changed. All was as before, except that some of the objects of furniture and ornament were shown in stronger relief than hitherto. Amongst these, those most in relief were the other bed, which was placed across the room, and an old picture that hung on the wall at its foot. As the bed was merely the counterpart of the one in which I lay, my attention became fixed on the picture. I observed it closely and with great interest. It seemed old, and was the portrait of a young girl, whose face, though kindly and merry, bore signs of thought and a capacity for deep feeling – almost for passion. At some moments, as I looked at it, it called up before my mind a vision of Shakespeare's Beatrice, and once I thought of Beatrice Cenci. But this was probably caused by the association of ideas suggested by the similarity of names.

The light in the room continued to grow even brighter, so I looked again out of the window to seek its source, and saw there a lovely sight. It seemed as if there were grouped without the window three lovely children, who seemed to float in mid-air.

The light seemed to spring from a point far behind them, and by their side was something dark and shadowy, which served to set off their radiance.

The children seemed to be smiling in upon something in the room, and, following their glances, I saw that their eyes rested upon the other bed. There, strange to say, the head which I had lately seen in the picture rested upon the pillow. I looked at the wall, but the frame was empty, the picture was gone. Then I looked at the bed again, and saw the young girl asleep, with the expression of her face constantly changing, as though she were dreaming.

As I was observing her, a sudden look of terror spread over her face, and she sat up like a sleep-walker, with her eyes wide open, staring out of the window.

Again turning to the window, my gaze became fixed, for a great and weird change had taken place. The figures were still there, but their features and expressions had become woefully different. Instead of the happy innocent look of childhood was one of malignity. With the change the children had grown old, and now three hags, decrepit and deformed, like typical witches, were before me.

But a thousand times worse than this transformation was the change in the dark mass that was near them. From a cloud, misty and undefined, it became a sort of shadow with a form. This gradually, as I looked, grew darker and fuller, till at length it made me shudder. There stood before me the phantom of the Fiend.

There was a long period of dead silence, in which I could hear the beating of my heart; but at length the phantom spoke to the others. His words seemed to issue from his lips mechanically, and without expression – "Tomorrow, and tomorrow, and tomorrow. The fairest and the best." He looked so awful that the question arose in my mind – "Would I dare to face him without the window – would any one dare to go amongst those fiends?" A harsh, strident, diabolical laugh from without seemed to answer my unasked question in the negative.

But as well as the laugh I heard another sound – the tones of a sweet sad voice in despair coming across the room.

"Oh, alone, alone! Is there no human thing near me? No hope – no hope. I shall go mad – or die."

The last words were spoken with a gasp.

I tried to jump out of bed, but could not stir, my limbs were bound in sleep. The young girl's head fell suddenly back upon the pillow, and the limp-hanging jaw and wide-open, purposeless mouth spoke but too plainly of what had happened.

Again I heard from without the fierce, diabolical laughter, which swelled louder and louder, till at last it grew so strong that in very horror I shook aside my sleep and sat up in bed. listened and heard a knocking at the door, but in another moment I became more awake, and knew that the sound came from the hall. It was, no doubt, Mr. Trevor returning from his party.

The hall-door was opened and shut, and then came a subdued sound of tramping and voices, but this soon died away, and there was silence throughout the house.

I lay awake for long thinking, and looking across the room at the picture and at the empty bed; for the moon now shone brightly, and the night was rendered still brighter by occasional flashes of summer lightning. At times the silence was broken by an owl screeching outside.

As I lay awake, pondering, I was very much troubled by what I had seen; but at length, putting several things together, I came to the conclusion that I had had a dream of a kind that might have been expected. The lightning, the knocking at the hall-door, the screeching of the owl, the empty bed, and the face in the picture, when grouped together, supplied materials for the main facts of the vision. The rest was, of course, the offspring of pure fancy, and the natural consequence of the component elements mentioned
acting with each other in the mind.

I got up and looked out of the window, but saw nothing but the broad belt of moonlight glittering on the bosom of the lake, which extended miles and miles away, till its farther shore was lost in the night haze, and the green sward, dotted with shrubs and tall grasses, which lay between the lake and the house.

The vision had utterly faded. However, the dream – for so, I suppose, I should call it – was very powerful, and I slept no more till the sunlight was streaming broadly in at the window, and then I fell into a doze.

Chapter II
More Links

LATE IN THE MORNING I was awakened by Parks, Mr. Trevor's man, who always used to attend on me when I visited my friends. He brought me hot water and the local news; and, chatting with him, I forgot for a time my alarm of the night.

Parks was staid and elderly, and a type of a class now rapidly disappearing – the class of old family servants who are as proud of their hereditary loyalty to their masters, as those masters are of name and rank. Like all old servants he had a great loving for all sorts of traditions. He believed them, and feared them, and had the most profound reverence for anything which had a story.

I asked him if he knew anything of the legendary history of Scarp. He answered with an air of doubt and hesitation, as of one carefully delivering an opinion which was still incomplete.

"Well, you see, Master Frank, that Scarp is so old that it must have any number of legends; but it is so long since it was inhabited that no one in the village remembers them. The place seems to have become in a kind of way forgotten, and died out of people's thoughts, and so I am very much afraid, sir, that all the genuine history is lost."

"What do you mean by the genuine history?" I inquired.

"Well, sir, I mean the true tradition, and not the inventions of the village folk. I heard the sexton tell some stories, but I am quite sure that they were not true, for I could see, Master Frank, that he did not believe them himself, but was only trying to frighten us."

"And could you not hear of any story that appeared to you to be true?"

"No, sir, and I tried very hard. You see, Master Frank, that there is a sort of club held every week in the tavern down in the village, composed of very respectable men, sir – very respectable men, indeed – and they asked me to be their chairman. I spoke to the master about it, and he gave me leave to accept their proposal. I accepted it as they made a point of it; and from my position I have of course a fine opportunity of making inquiries. It was at the club, sir, that I was, last night, so that I was not here to attend on you, which I hope that you will excuse."

Parks's air of mingled pride and condescension, as he made the announcement of the club, was very fine, and the effect was heightened by the confiding frankness with which he spoke. I asked him if he could find no clue to any of the legends which must have existed about such an old place. He answered with a very slight reluctance:

"Well, sir, there was one woman in the village who was awfully old and doting, and she evidently knew something about Scarp, for when she heard the name she mumbled out something about "awful stories," and "times of horror," and such like things, but I couldn't make her understand what it was I wanted to know, or keep her up to the point."

"And have you tried often, Parks? Why do you not try again?"

"She is dead, sir!"

I had felt inclined to laugh at Parks when he was telling me of the old woman. The way in which he gloated over the words 'awful stories,' and 'times of horror,' was beyond the power of description; it should have been heard and seen to have been properly appreciated. His voice became deep and mysterious, and he almost smacked his lips at the thought of so much pabulum for nightmares. But when he calmly told me that the woman was dead, a sense of blankness, mingled with awe, came upon me. Here, the last link between myself and the mysterious past was broken, never to be mended. All the rich stores of legend and tradition that had arisen from strange conjunctures of circumstances, and from the belief and imagination of long lines of villagers, loyal to their suzerain lord, were lost forever. I felt quite sad and disappointed; and no attempt was made either by Parks or myself to continue the conversation. Mr. Trevor came presently into my room, and having greeted each other warmly we went together to breakfast.

At breakfast Mrs. Trevor asked me what I thought of the girl's portrait in my bedroom. We had often had discussions as to characters in faces for we were both physiognomists, and she asked the question as if she were really curious to hear my opinion. I told her that I had only seen it for a short time, and so would rather not attempt to give a final opinion without a more careful study; but from what I had seen of it I had been favourably impressed.

"Well, Frank, after breakfast go and look at it again carefully, and then tell me exactly what you think about it."

After breakfast I did as directed and returned to the breakfast room, where Mrs. Trevor was still sitting.

"Well, Frank, what is your opinion – mind, correctly. I want it for a particular reason."

I told her what I thought of the girl's character; which, if there be any truth in physiognomy, must have been a very fine one.

"Then you like the face?"

I answered:

"It is a great pity that we have none such now-a-days. They seem to have died out with Sir Joshua and Greuze. If I could meet such a girl as I believe the prototype of that portrait to have been I would never be happy till I had made her my wife."

To my intense astonishment my hostess jumped up and clapped her hands. I asked her why she did it, and she laughed as she replied in a mocking tone imitating my own voice:

"But suppose for a moment that your kind intentions should be frustrated. 'One man may lead a horse to the pond's brink.' 'The best laid schemes o' mice an' men.' Eh?"

"Well," said I, "there may be some point in the observation. I suppose there must be since you have made it. But for my part I don't see it."

"Oh, I forgot to tell you, Frank, that that portrait might have been painted for Diana Fothering."

I felt a blush stealing over my face. She observed it and took my hand between hers as we sat down on the sofa, and said to me tenderly:

"Frank, my dear boy, I intend to jest with you no more on the subject. I have a conviction that you will like Diana, which has been strengthened by your admiration for her portrait, and from what I know of human nature I am sure that she will like you. Charley and I both wish to see you married, and we would not think of a wife for you who was not in every way eligible. I have never in my life met a girl like Di; and if you and she fancy each other it will be Charley's pleasure and my own to enable you to marry – as far as means are concerned. Now, don't speak. You must know perfectly well how much we both love you. We have always regarded you as our son, and we intend to treat you as our only child when it pleases God to separate us. There now, think the matter over, after you have seen Diana. But, mind me, unless you love each other well and truly, we would far rather not see you married. At all events, whatever may happen you have our best wishes and prayers for your happiness. God bless you, Frank, my dear, dear boy."

There were tears in her eyes as she spoke. When she had finished she leaned over, drew down my head and kissed my forehead very, very tenderly, and then got up softly and left the room. I felt inclined to cry myself. Her words to me were tender, and sensible, and womanly, but I cannot attempt to describe the infinite tenderness and gentleness of her voice and manner. I prayed for every blessing on her in my secret heart, and the swelling of my throat did not prevent my prayers finding voice. There may have been women in the world like Mrs. Trevor, but if there had been I had never met any of them, except herself.

As may be imagined, I was most anxious to see Miss Fothering, and or the remainder of the day she was constantly in my thoughts. That evening a letter came from the younger Miss Fothering apologising for her not being able to keep her promise with reference to her visit, on account of the unexpected arrival of her aunt, with whom she was obliged to go to Paris for some months. That night I slept in my new room, and had neither dream nor vision. I awoke in the morning half ashamed of having ever paid any attention to such a silly circumstance as a strange dream in my first night in an old house.

After breakfast next morning, as I was going along the corridor, I saw the door of my old bedroom open, and went in to have another look at the portrait. Whilst I was looking at it I began to wonder how it could be that it was so like Miss Fothering as Mrs. Trevor said it was. The more I thought of this the more it puzzled me, till suddenly the dream came back – the face in the picture, and the figure in the bed, the phantoms out in the night, and the ominous words – "The fairest and the best." As I thought of these things all the possibilities of the lost legends of the old house thronged so quickly into my mind that I began to feel a buzzing in my ears and my head began to swim, so that I was obliged to sit down.

"Could it be possible," I asked myself, "that some old curse hangs over the race that once dwelt within these walls, and can she be of that race? Such things have been before now!"

The idea was a terrible one for me, for it made to me a reality that which I had come to look upon as merely the dream of a distempered imagination. If the thought had come to me in the darkness and stillness of the night it would have been awful. How happy I was that it had come by daylight, when the sun was shining brightly, and the air was cheerful with the trilling of the song birds, and the lively, strident cawing from the old rookery.

I stayed in the room for some little time longer, thinking over the scene, and, as is natural, when I had got over the remnants of my fear, my reason began to question the genuineness – vraisemblance of the dream. I began to look for the internal evidence of the untruth to facts; but, after thinking earnestly for some time the only fact that seemed to me of any importance was the confirmatory one of the younger Miss Fothering's apology. In the dream the frightened girl had been alone, and the mere fact of two girls coming on a visit had seemed a sort of disproof of its truth. But, just as if things were conspiring to force on the truth of the dream, one of the sisters was not to come, and the other was she who resembled the portrait whose prototype I had seen sleeping in a vision. I could hardly imagine that I had only dreamt.

I determined to ask Mrs. Trevor if she could explain in any way Miss Fothering's resemblance to the portrait, and so went at once to seek her.

I found her in the large drawing room alone, and, after a few casual remarks, I broached the subject on which I had come to seek for information. She had not said anything further to me about marrying since our conversation on the previous day, but when I mentioned Miss Fothering's name I could see a glad look on her face which gave me great pleasure. She made none of those vulgar commonplace remarks which many women find it necessary to make when talking to a man about a girl for whom he is supposed to have an affection, but by her manner she put me entirely at my ease, as I sat fidgeting on the sofa, pulling purposelessly the woolly tufts of an antimacassar, painfully conscious that my cheeks were red, and my voice slightly forced and unnatural.

She merely said, "Of course, Frank, I am ready if you want to talk about Miss Fothering, or any other subject." She then put a marker in her book and laid it aside, and, folding her arms, looked at me with a grave, kind, expectant smile.

I asked her if she knew anything about the family history of Miss Fothering. She answered:

"Not further than I have already told you. Her father's is a fine old family, although reduced in circumstances."

"Has it ever been connected with any family in this county?
With the former owners of Scarp, for instance?"

"Not that I know of. Why do you ask?"

"I want to find out how she comes to be so like that portrait."

"I never thought of that. It may be that there was some remote connection between her family and the Kirks who formerly owned Scarp. I will ask her when she comes. Or stay. Let us go and look if there is any old book or tree in the library that will throw a light upon the subject. We have rather a good library now, Frank, for we have all our own books, and all those which belonged to the Scarp library also. They are in great disorder, for we have been waiting till you came to arrange them, for we knew that you delighted in such work."

"There is nothing I should enjoy more than arranging all these splendid books. What a magnificent library. It is almost a pity to keep it in a private house."

We proceeded to look for some of those old books of family history which are occasionally to be found in old county houses. The library of Scarp, I saw, was very valuable, and as we prosecuted our search I came across many splendid and rare volumes which I determined to examine at my leisure, for I had come to Scarp for a long visit.

We searched first in the old folio shelves, and, after some few disappointments, found at length a large volume, magnificently printed and bound, which contained views and plans of the house, illuminations of the armorial bearings of the family of Kirk, and all the families with whom it was connected, and having the history of all these families carefully set forth. It was called on the title-page *The Book of Kirk*, and was full of anecdotes and legends, and contained a large stock of family tradition. As this was exactly the book which we required, we searched no further, but, having carefully dusted the volume, bore it to Mrs. Trevor's boudoir where we could look over it quite undisturbed.

On looking in the index, we found the name of Fothering mentioned, and on turning to the page specified, found the arms of Kirk quartered on those of Fothering. From the text we learned that one of the daughters of Kirk had, in the year 1573, married the brother of Fothering against the united wills of her father and brother, and that after a bitter feud of some ten or twelve years, the latter, then master of Scarp, had met the brother of Fothering in a duel and had killed him. Upon receiving the news Fothering had sworn a great oath to revenge his brother, invoking the most fearful curses upon himself and his race if he should fail to cut off the hand that had slain his brother, and to nail it over the gate of Fothering. The feud then became so bitter that Kirk seems to have gone quite mad on the subject. When he heard of Fothering's oath he knew that he had but little chance of escape, since his enemy was his master at every weapon; so he determined upon a mode of revenge which, although costing him his own life, he fondly hoped would accomplish the eternal destruction of his brother-in-law through his violated oath. He sent Fothering a letter cursing him and his race, and praying for the consummation of his own curse invoked in case of failure. He concluded his missive by a prayer for the complete destruction, soul, mind, and body, of the first Fothering who should enter the gate of Scarp, who he hoped would be the fairest and best of the race. Having despatched this letter he cut off his right hand and threw it into the centre of a roaring fire, which he had made for the purpose. When it was entirely consumed he threw himself upon his sword, and so died.

A cold shiver went through me when I read the words 'fairest and best.' All my dream came back in a moment, and I seemed to hear in my ears again the echo of the fiendish laughter. I looked up at Mrs. Trevor, and saw that she had become very grave. Her face had a half-frightened look, as if some wild thought had struck her. I was more frightened than ever, for nothing increases our alarms so much as the sympathy of others with regard to them; however, I tried to conceal my fear. We sat silent for some minutes, and then Mrs. Trevor rose up saying:

"Come with me, and let us look at the portrait."

I remember her saying the and not that portrait, as if some concealed thought of it had been occupying her mind. The same dread had assailed her from a coincidence as had grown in me from a vision. Surely – surely I had good grounds for fear!

We went to the bedroom and stood before the picture, which seemed to gaze upon us with an expression which reflected our own fears. My companion said to me in slightly excited tones: "Frank, lift down the picture till we see its back." I did so, and we found written in strange old writing on the grimy canvas a name and a date, which, after a great deal of trouble, we made out to be 'Margaret Kirk, 1572.' It was the name of the lady in the book.

Mrs. Trevor turned round and faced me slowly, with a look of horror on her face.

"Frank, I don't like this at all. There is something very strange here."

I had it on my tongue to tell her my dream, but was ashamed to do so. Besides, I feared that it might frighten her too much, as she was already alarmed.

I continued to look at the picture as a relief from my embarrassment, and was struck with the excessive griminess of the back in comparison to the freshness of the front. I mentioned my difficulty to my companion, who thought for a moment, and then suddenly said:

"I see how it is. It has been turned with its face to the wall."

I said no word but hung up the picture again; and we went back to the boudoir.

On the way I began to think that my fears were too wildly improbable to bear to be spoken about. It was so hard to believe in the horrors of darkness when the sunlight was falling brightly around me. The same idea seemed to have struck Mrs. Trevor, for she said, when we entered the room:

"Frank, it strikes me that we are both rather silly to let our imaginations carry us away so. The story is merely a tradition, and we know how report distorts even the most innocent facts. It is true that the Fothering family was formerly connected with the Kirks, and that the picture is that of the Miss Kirk who married against her father's will; it is likely that he quarrelled with her for so doing, and had her picture turned to the wall – a common trick of angry fathers at all times – but that is all. There can be nothing beyond that. Let us not think any more upon the subject, as it is one likely to lead us into absurdities. However, the picture is a really beautiful one – independent of its being such a likeness of Diana, and I will have it placed in the dining-room."

The change was effected that afternoon, but she did not again allude to the subject. She appeared, when talking to me, to be a little constrained in manner – a very unusual thing with her, and seemed to fear that I would renew the forbidden topic. I think that she did not wish to let her imagination lead her astray, and was distrustful of herself. However, the feeling of constraint wore off before night – but she did not renew the subject.

I slept well that night, without dreams of any kind; and next morning – the third tomorrow promised in the dream – when I came down to breakfast, I was told that I would see Miss Fothering before that evening.

I could not help blushing, and stammered out some commonplace remark, and then glancing up, feeling very sheepish, I saw my hostess looking at me with her kindly smile intensified. She said:

"Do you know, Frank, I felt quite frightened yesterday when we were looking at the picture; but I have been thinking the matter over since, and have come to the conclusion that my folly was perfectly unfounded. I am sure you agree with me. In fact, I look now upon our fright as a good joke, and will tell it to Diana when she arrives."

Once again I was about to tell my dream; but again was restrained by shame. I knew, of course, that Mrs. Trevor would not laugh at me or even think little of me for my fears, for she was too well-bred, and kind-hearted, and sympathetic to do anything of the kind, and, besides, the fear was one which we had shared in common.

But how could I confess my fright at what might appear to others to be a ridiculous dream, when she had conquered the fear that had been common to us both, and which had arisen from a really strange conjuncture of facts. She appeared to look on the matter so lightly that I could not do otherwise. And I did it honestly for the time.

Chapter III
The Third Tomorrow

IN THE AFTERNOON I was out in the garden lying in the shadow of an immense beech, when I saw Mrs. Trevor approaching. I had been reading Shelley's *Stanzas Written in Dejection*, and my heart was full of melancholy and a vague yearning after human sympathy. I had thought of Mrs. Trevor's love for me, but even that did not seem sufficient. I wanted the love of some one more nearly of my own level, some equal spirit, for I looked on her, of course, as I would have regarded my mother. Somehow my thoughts kept returning to Miss Fothering till I could almost see her before me in my memory of the portrait. I had begun to ask myself the question: "Are you in love?" when I heard the voice of my hostess as she drew near.

"Ha! Frank, I thought I would find you here. I want you to come to my boudoir."

"What for?" I inquired, as I rose from the grass and picked up my volume of Shelley.

"Di has come ever so long ago; and I want to introduce you and have a chat before dinner," said she, as we went towards the house.

"But won't you let me change my dress? I am not in correct costume for the afternoon."

I felt somewhat afraid of the unknown beauty when the introduction was imminent. Perhaps it was because I had come to believe too firmly in Mrs. Trevor's prediction.

"Nonsense, Frank, just as if any woman worth thinking about cares how a man is dressed."

We entered the boudoir and found a young lady seated by a window that overlooked the croquet-ground. She turned round as we came in, so Mrs. Trevor introduced us, and we were soon engaged in a lively conversation. I observed her, as may be supposed, with more than curiosity, and shortly found that she was worth looking at. She was very beautiful, and her beauty lay not only in her features but in her expression. At first her appearance did not seem to me so perfect as it afterwards did, on account of her wonderful resemblance to the portrait with whose beauty I was already acquainted. But it was not long before I came to experience the difference between the portrait and the reality. No matter how well it may be painted a picture falls far short of its prototype. There is something in a real face which cannot exist on canvas – some difference far greater than that contained in the contrast between the one expression, however beautiful of the picture, and the moving features and varying expression of the reality. There is something living and lovable in a real face that no art can represent.

When we had been talking for a while in the usual conventional style, Mrs. Trevor said, "Di, my love, I want to tell you of a discovery Frank and I have made. You must know that I always call Mr. Stanford, Frank – he is more like my own son than my friend, and that I am very fond of him."

She then put her arms round Miss Fothering's waist, as they sat on the sofa together, and kissed her, and then, turning towards me, said, "I don't approve of kissing girls in the presence of gentlemen, but you know that Frank is not supposed to be here. This is my sanctum, and who invades it must take the consequences.

But I must tell you about the discovery."

She then proceeded to tell the legend, and about her finding the name of Margaret Kirk on the back of the picture.

Miss Fothering laughed gleefully as she heard the story, and then said, suddenly, "Oh, I had forgotten to tell you, dear Mrs. Trevor, that I had such a fright the other day. I thought I was going to be prevented coming here. Aunt Deborah came to us last week for a few days, and when she heard that I was about to go on a visit to Scarp she seemed quite frightened, and went straight off to papa and asked him to forbid me to go. Papa asked her why she made the request, so she told a long family legend about any of us coming to Scarp – just the same story that you have been telling me. She said she was sure that some misfortune would happen if I came; so you see that the tradition exists in our branch of the family too. Oh, you can't fancy the scene there was between papa and Aunt Deborah. I must laugh whenever I think of it, although I did not laugh then, for I was greatly afraid that aunty would prevent me coming. Papa got very grave, and aunty thought she had carried her point when he said, in his dear, old, pompous manner, 'Deborah, Diana has promised to pay Mrs. Trevor, of Scarp, a visit, and, of course, must keep her engagement. And if it were for no other reason than the one you have just alleged, I would strain a point of convenience to have her go to Scarp. I have always educated my children in such a manner that they ought not to be influenced by such vain superstitions; and with my will their practice shall never be at variance with the precepts which I have instilled into them.'

"Poor aunty was quite overcome. She seemed almost speechless for a time at the thought that her wishes had been neglected, for you know that Aunt Deborah's wishes are commands to all our family."

Mrs. Trevor said:

"I hope Mrs. Howard was not offended?"

"Oh, no. Papa talked to her seriously, and at length – with a great deal of difficulty I must say – succeeded in convincing her that her fears were groundless – at least, he forced her to confess that such things as she was afraid of could not be."

I thought of the couplet:

> *A man convinced against his will*
> *Is of the same opinion still,*

but said nothing.

Miss Fothering finished her story by saying:

"Aunty ended by hoping that I might enjoy myself, which I am sure, my dear Mrs. Trevor, that I will do."

"I hope you will, my love."

I had been struck during the above conversation by the mention of Mrs. Howard. I was trying to think of where I had heard the name, Deborah Howard, when suddenly it all came back to me. Mrs. Howard had been Miss Fothering, and was an old friend of my mother's. It was thus that I had been accustomed to her name when I was a child. I remembered now that once she had brought a nice little girl, almost a baby, with her to visit. The child was her niece, and it was thus that I now accounted for my half-recollection of the name and the circumstance on the first night of my arrival at Scarp. The thought of my dream here recalled me to Mrs. Trevor's object in bringing Miss Fothering to her boudoir, so I said to the latter:

"Do you believe these legends?"

"Indeed I do not, Mr. Stanford; I do not believe in anything half so silly."

"Then you do not believe in ghosts or visions?"

"Most certainly not."

How could I tell my dream to a girl who had such profound disbelief? And yet I felt something whispering to me that I ought to tell it to her. It was, no doubt, foolish of me to have this fear of a dream, but I could not help it. I was just going to risk being laughed at, and unburden my mind, when Mrs. Trevor started up, after looking at her watch, saying:

"Dear me, I never thought it was so late. I must go and see if any others have come. It will not do for me to neglect my guests."

We all left the boudoir, and as we did so the gong sounded for dressing for dinner, and so we each sought our rooms.

When I came down to the drawing room I found assembled a number of persons who had arrived during the course of the afternoon. I was introduced to them all, and chatted with them till dinner was announced. I was given Miss Fothering to take into dinner, and when it was over I found that we had improved our acquaintance very much. She was a delightful girl, and as I looked at her I thought with a glow of pleasure of Mrs. Trevor's prediction. Occasionally I saw our hostess observing us, and as she saw us chatting pleasantly together as though we enjoyed it a more than happy look came into her face. It was one of her most fascinating points that in the midst of gaiety, while she never neglected anyone, she specially remembered her particular friends. No matter what position she might be placed in she would still remember that there were some persons who would treasure up her recognition at such moments.

After dinner, as I did not feel inclined to enter the drawing room with the other gentlemen, I strolled out into the garden by myself, and thought over things in general, and Miss Fothering in particular. The subject was such a pleasant one that I quite lost myself in it, and strayed off farther than I had intended. Suddenly I remembered myself and looked around. I was far away from the house, and in the midst of a dark, gloomy walk between old yew trees. I could not see through them on either side on account of their thickness, and as the walk was curved I could see but a short distance either before or behind me. I looked up and saw a yellowish, luminous sky with heavy clouds passing sluggishly across it. The moon had not yet risen, and the general gloom reminded me forcibly of some of the weird pictures which William Blake so loved to paint. There was a sort of vague melancholy and ghostliness in the place that made me shiver, and I hurried on.

At length the walk opened and I came out on a large sloping lawn, dotted here and there with yew trees and tufts of pampass grass of immense height, whose stalks were crowned with large flowers. To the right lay the house, grim and gigantic in the gloom, and to the left the lake which stretched away so far that it was lost in the evening shadow. The lawn sloped from the terrace round the house down to the water's edge, and was only broken by the walk which continued to run on round the house in a wide sweep.

As I came near the house a light appeared in one of the windows which lay before me, and as I looked into the room I saw that it was the chamber of my dream.

Unconsciously I approached nearer and ascended the terrace from the top of which I could see across the deep trench which surrounded the house, and looked earnestly into the room. I shivered as I looked. My spirits had been damped by the gloom and desolation of the yew walk, and now the dream and all the subsequent revelations came before my mind with such vividness that the horror of the thing again seized me, but more forcibly than before. I looked at the sleeping arrangements, and groaned as I saw that the bed where the dying woman had seemed to lie was alone prepared, while the other bed, that in which I had slept, had its curtains drawn all round. This was but another link in the chain of doom. Whilst I stood looking, the servant who was in the room came and pulled down one of the blinds, but, as she was about to do the same with the other, Miss Fothering entered the room, and, seeing what she was about, evidently gave her contrary directions, for she let go the window string, and then went and pulled up again the blind which she had let down. Having done so she followed her mistress out of the room. So wrapped up was I in all that took place with reference to that chamber, that it never even struck me that I was guilty of any impropriety in watching what took place.

I stayed there for some little time longer purposeless and terrified. The horror grew so great to me as I thought of the events of the last few days, that I determined to tell Miss Fothering of my dream, in order that she might not be frightened in case she should see anything like it, or at least that she might be prepared for anything that might happen. As soon as I had come to this determination the inevitable question 'When?' presented itself. The means of making the communication was a subject most disagreeable to contemplate, but as I had made up my mind to do it, I thought that there was no time like the present. Accordingly I was determined to seek the drawing room, where I knew I should find Miss Fothering and Mrs. Trevor, for, of course, I had determined to take the latter into our confidence. As I was really afraid to go through the awful yew walk again, I completed the half circle of the house and entered the backdoor, from which I easily found my way to the drawing room.

When I entered Mrs. Trevor, who was sitting near the door, said to me, "Good gracious, Frank, where have you been to make you look so pale? One would think you had seen a ghost!"

I answered that I had been strolling in the garden, but made no other remark, as I did not wish to say anything about my dream before the persons to whom she was talking, as they were strangers to me. I waited for some time for an opportunity of speaking to her alone, but her duties, as hostess, kept her so constantly occupied that I waited in vain. Accordingly I determined to tell Miss Fothering at all events, at once, and then to tell Mrs. Trevor as soon as an opportunity for doing so presented itself.

With a good deal of difficulty – for I did not wish to do anything marked – I succeeded in getting Miss Fothering away from the persons by whom she was surrounded, and took her to one of the embrasures, under the pretence of looking out at the night view. Here we were quite removed from observation, as the heavy window curtains completely covered the recess, and almost isolated us from the rest of the company as perfectly as if we were in a separate chamber. I proceeded at once to broach the subject for which I had sought the interview; for I feared lest contact with the lively company of the drawing room would do away with my present fears, and so breakdown the only barrier that stood between her and Fate.

"Miss Fothering, do you ever dream?"

"Oh, yes, often. But I generally find that my dreams are most ridiculous."

"How so?"

"Well, you see, that no matter whether they are good or bad they appear real and coherent whilst I am dreaming them; but when I wake I find them unreal and incoherent, when I remember them at all. They are, in fact, mere disconnected nonsense."

"Are you fond of dreams?"

"Of course I am. I delight in them, for whether they are sense or gibberish when you wake, they are real whilst you are asleep."

"Do you believe in dreams?"

"Indeed, Mr. Stanford, I do not."

"Do you like hearing them told?"

"I do, very much, when they are worth telling. Have you been dreaming anything? If you have, do tell it to me."

"I will be glad to do so. It is about a dream which I had that concerns you, that I came here to tell you."

"About me. Oh, how nice. Do, go on."

I told her all my dream, after calling her attention to our conversation in the boudoir as a means of introducing the subject. I did not attempt to heighten the effect in any way or to draw any inferences. I tried to suppress my own emotion and merely to let the facts speak for themselves. She listened with great eagerness, but, as far as I could see, without a particle of either fear or belief in the dream as a warning. When I had finished she laughed a quiet, soft laugh, and said:

"That is delicious. And was I really the girl that you saw afraid of ghosts? If papa heard of such a thing as that even in a dream what a lecture he would give me! I wish I could dream anything like that."

"Take care," said I, "you might find it too awful. It might indeed prove the fulfilling of the ban which we saw in the legend in the old book, and which you heard from your aunt."

She laughed musically again, and shook her head at me wisely and warningly.

"Oh, pray do not talk nonsense and try to frighten me – for I warn you that you will not succeed."

"I assure you on my honour, Miss Fothering, that I was never more in earnest in my whole life."

"Do you not think that we had better go into the room?" said she, after a few moment's pause.

"Stay just a moment, I entreat you," said I. "What I say is true. I am really in earnest."

"Oh, pray forgive me if what I said led you to believe that I doubted your word. It was merely your inference which I disagreed with. I thought you had been jesting to try and frighten me."

"Miss Fothering, I would not presume to take such a liberty.

But I am glad that you trust me. May I venture to ask you a favour?

Will you promise me one thing?"

Her answer was characteristic:

"No. What is it?"

"That you will not be frightened at anything which may take place tonight?"

She laughed softly again.

"I do not intend to be. But is that all?"

"Yes, Miss Fothering, that is all; but I want to be assured that you will not be alarmed – that you will be prepared for anything which may happen. I have a horrid foreboding of evil – some evil that I dread to think of – and it will be a great comfort to me if you will do one thing."

"Oh, nonsense. Oh, well, if you really wish it I will tell you if I will do it when I hear what it is."

Her levity was all gone when she saw how terribly in earnest I was. She looked at me boldly and fearlessly, but with a tender, half-pitying glance as if conscious of the possession of strength superior to mine. Her fearlessness was in her free, independent attitude, but her pity was in her eyes. I went on:

"Miss Fothering, the worst part of my dream was seeing the look of agony on the face of the girl when she looked round and found herself alone. Will you take some token and keep it with you till morning to remind you, in case anything should happen, that you are not alone – that there is one thinking of you, and one human intelligence awake for you, though all the rest of the world should be asleep or dead?"

In my excitement I spoke with fervour, for the possibility of her enduring the horror which had assailed me seemed to be growing more and more each instant. At times since that awful night I had disbelieved the existence of the warning, but when I thought of it by night I could not but believe, for the very air in the darkness seemed to be peopled by phantoms to my fevered imagination. My belief had been perfected tonight by the horror of the yew walk, and all the sombre, ghostly thoughts that had arisen amid its gloom.

There was a short pause. Miss Fothering leaned on the edge of the window, looking out at the dark, moonless sky. At length she turned and said to me, with some hesitation, "But really, Mr. Stanford, I do not like doing anything from fear of supernatural things, or from a belief in them. What you want me to do is so simple a thing in itself that I would not hesitate a moment to do it, but that papa has always taught me to believe that such occurrences as you seem to dread are quite impossible, and I know that he would be very much displeased if any act of mine showed a belief in them."

"Miss Fothering, I honestly think that there is not a man living who would wish less than I would to see you or anyone else disobeying a father either in word or spirit, and more particularly when that father is a clergyman; but I entreat you to gratify me on this one point. It cannot do you any harm; and I assure you that if you do not I will be inexpressibly miserable. I have endured the greatest tortures of suspense for the last three days, and tonight I feel a nervous horror of which words can give you no conception. I know that I have not the smallest right to make the request, and no reason for doing it except that I was fortunate, or unfortunate, enough to get the warning. I apologise most sincerely for the great liberty which I have taken, but believe me that I act with the best intentions."

My excitement was so great that my knees were trembling, and the large drops of perspiration rolling down my face.

There was a long pause, and I had almost made up my mind for a refusal of my request when my companion spoke again.

"Mr. Stanford, on that plea alone I will grant your request. I can see that for some reason which I cannot quite comprehend you are deeply moved; and that I may be the means of saving pain to any one, I will do what you ask. Just please to state what you wish me to do."

I thought from her manner that she was offended with me; however I explained my purpose:

"I want you to keep about you, when you go to bed, some token which will remind you in an instant of what has passed between us, so that you may not feel lonely or frightened – no matter what may happen."

"I will do it. What shall I take?"

She had her handkerchief in her hand as she spoke. So I put my hand upon it and blessed it in the name of the Father, Son, and Holy Ghost. I did this to fix its existence in her memory by awing her slightly about it. "This," said I, "shall be a token that you are not alone." My object in blessing the handkerchief was fully achieved, for she did seem somewhat awed, but still she thanked me with a sweet smile. "I feel that you act from your heart," said she, "and my heart thanks you." She gave me her hand as she spoke, in an honest, straightforward manner, with more the independence of a man than the timorousness of a woman. As I grasped it I felt the blood rushing to my face, but before I let it go an impulse seized me and I bent down and touched it with my lips. She drew it quickly away, and said more coldly than she had yet spoken: "I did not mean you to do that."

"Believe me I did not mean to take a liberty – it was merely the natural expression of my gratitude. I feel as if you had done me some great personal service. You do not know how much lighter my heart is now than it was an hour ago, or you would forgive me for having so offended."

As I made my apologetic excuse, I looked at her wistfully. She returned my glance fearlessly, but with a bright, forgiving smile.

She then shook her head slightly, as if to banish the subject.

There was a short pause, and then she said:

"I am glad to be of any service to you; but if there be any possibility of what you fear happening it is I who will be benefited. But mind, I will depend upon you not to say a word of this to anybody. I am afraid that we are both very foolish."

"No, no, Miss Fothering. I may be foolish, but you are acting nobly in doing what seems to you to be foolish in order that you may save me from pain. But may I not even tell Mrs. Trevor?"

"No, not even her. I should be ashamed of myself if I thought that anyone except ourselves knew about it."

"You may depend upon me. I will keep it secret if you wish."

"Do so, until morning at all events. Mind, if I laugh at you then I will expect you to join in my laugh."

"I will," said I. "I will be only too glad to be able to laugh at it." And we joined the rest of the company.

When I retired to my bedroom that night I was too much excited to sleep – even had my promise not forbidden me to do so. I paced up and down the room for some time, thinking and doubting. I could not believe completely in what I expected to happen, and yet my heart was filled with a vague dread. I thought over the events of the evening – particularly my stroll after dinner through that awful yew walk and my looking into the bedroom where I had dreamed. From these my thoughts wandered to the deep embrasure of the window where I had given Miss Fothering the token. I could hardly realise that whole interview as a fact. I knew that it had taken place, but that was all. It was so strange to recall a scene that, now that it was enacted, seemed half comedy and half tragedy, and to remember that it was played in this practical nineteenth century, in secret, within earshot of a room full of people, and only hidden from them by a curtain, I felt myself blushing, half from excitement, half from shame, when I thought of it. But then my thoughts turned to the way in which Miss Fothering had acceded to my request, strange as it was; and as I thought of her my blundering shame changed to a deeper glow of hope. I remembered Mrs. Trevor's prediction – "From what I know of human nature I think that she will like you" – and as I did so I felt how dear to me Miss Fothering was already becoming. But my joy was turned to anger on thinking what she might be called on to endure; and the thought of her suffering pain or fright caused me greater distress than any suffered myself. Again my thoughts flew back to the time of my own fright and my dream, with all the subsequent revelations concerning it, rushed across my mind. I felt again the feeling of extreme terror – as if something was about to happen – as if the tragedy was approaching its climax. Naturally I thought of the time of night and so I looked at my watch. It was within a few minutes of one o'clock. I remembered that the clock had struck twelve after Mr. Trevor had come home on the night of my dream. There was a large clock at Scarp which tolled the hours so loudly that for a long way round the estate the country people all regulated their affairs by it. The next few minutes passed so slowly that each moment seemed an age.

I was standing, with my watch in my hand, counting the moments when suddenly a light came into the room that made the candle on the table appear quite dim, and my shadow was reflected on the wall by some brilliant light which streamed in through the window. My heart for an instant ceased to beat, and then the blood rushed so violently to my temples that my eyes grew dim and my brain began to reel. However, I shortly became more composed, and then went to the window expecting to see my dream again repeated.

The light was there as formerly, but there were no figures of children, or witches, or fiends. The moon had just risen, and I could see its reflection upon the far end of the lake. I turned my head in trembling expectation to the ground below where I had seen the children and the hags, but saw merely the dark yew trees and tall crested pampass tufts gently moving in the night wind. The light caught the edges of the flowers of the grass, and made them most conspicuous.

As I looked a sudden thought flashed like a flame of fire through my brain. I saw in one second of time all the folly of my wild fancies. The moonlight and its reflection on the water shining into the room was the light of my dream, or phantasm as I now understood it to be. Those three tufts of pampass grass clumped together were in turn the fair young children and the withered leaves and the dark foliage of the yew beside them gave substance to the semblance of the fiend. For the rest, the empty bed and the face of the picture, my half recollection of the name of Fothering, and the long-forgotten legend of the curse. Oh, fool! fool that I had been! How I had been the victim of circumstances, and of my own wild imagination! Then came the bitter reflection of the agony of mind which Miss Fothering might be compelled to suffer. Might not the recital of my dream, and my strange request regarding the token, combined with the natural causes of night and scene, produce the very effect which I so dreaded? It was only at that bitter, bitter moment that I realised how foolish I had been. But what was my anguish of mind to hers?

For an instant I conceived the idea of rousing Mrs. Trevor and telling her all the facts of the case so that she might go to Miss Fothering and tell her not to be alarmed. But I had no time to act upon my thought. As I was hastening to the door the clock struck one and a moment later I heard from the room below me a sharp scream – a cry of surprise rather than fear. Miss Fothering had no doubt been awakened by the striking of the clock, and had seen outside the window the very figures which I had described to her.

I rushed madly down the stairs and arrived at the door of her bedroom, which was directly under the one which I now occupied. As I was about to rush in I was instinctively restrained from so doing by the thoughts of propriety; and so for a few moments I stood silent, trembling, with my hand upon the door-handle.

Within I heard a voice – her voice – exclaiming, in tones of stupefied surprise:

"Has it come then? Am I alone?" She then continued joyously, "No, I am not alone. His token! Oh, thank God for that. Thank God for that."

Through my heart at her words came a rush of wild delight. I felt my bosom swell and the tears of gladness spring to my eyes.

In that moment I knew that I had strength and courage to face the world, alone, for her sake. But before my hopes had well time to manifest themselves they were destroyed, for again the voice came wailing from the room of blank despair that made me cold from head to foot.

"Ah-h-h! Still there? Oh! God, preserve my reason. Oh! For some human thing near me." Then her voice changed slightly to a tone of entreaty: "You will not leave me alone? Your token. Remember your token. Help me. Help me now." Then her voice became more wild, and rose to an inarticulate, wailing scream of horror.

As I heard that agonised cry, I realised the idea that it was madness to delay – that I had hesitated too long already – I must cast aside the shackles of conventionality if I wished to repair my fatal error. Nothing could save her from some serious injury – perhaps madness – perhaps death; save a shock which would break the spell which was over her from fear and her excited imagination. I flung open the door and rushed in, shouting loudly:

"Courage, courage. You are not alone. I am here. Remember the token."

She grasped the handkerchief instinctively, but she hardly comprehended my words, and did not seem to heed my presence. She was sitting up in bed, her face being distorted with terror, and was gazing out upon the scene. I heard from without the hooting of an owl as it flew across the border of the lake. She heard it also, and screamed:

"The laugh, too! Oh, there is no hope. Even he will not dare to go amongst them."

Then she gave vent to a scream, so wild, so appalling that, as I heard it, I trembled, and the hair on the back of my head bristled up. Throughout the house I could hear screams of affright, and the ringing of bells, and the banging of doors, and the rush of hurried feet; but the poor sufferer comprehended not these sounds; she still continued gazing out of the window awaiting the consummation of the dream.

I saw that the time for action and self-sacrifice was come.

There was but one way now to repair my fatal error. To burst through the window and try by the shock to wake her from her trance of fear.

I said no word but rushed across the room and hurled myself, back foremost, against the massive plate glass. As I turned I saw Mrs. Trevor rushing into the room, her face wild with excitement.

She was calling out:

"Diana, Diana, what is it?"

The glass crashed and shivered into a thousand pieces, and I could feel its sharp edges cutting me like so many knives. But I heeded not the pain, for above the rushing of feet and crashing of glass and the shouting both within and without the room I heard her voice ring forth in a joyous, fervent cry, "Saved. He has dared," as she sank down in the arms of Mrs. Trevor, who had thrown herself upon the bed.

Then I felt a mighty shock, and all the universe seemed filled with sparks of fire that whirled around me with lightning speed, till I seemed to be in the centre of a world of flame, and then came in my ears the rushing of a mighty wind, swelling ever louder, and then came a blackness over all things and a deadness of sound as if all the earth had passed away, and I remembered no more.

Chapter IV
Afterwards

WHEN I NEXT BECAME CONSCIOUS I was lying in bed in a dark room. I wondered what this was for, and tried to look around me, but could hardly stir my head. I attempted to speak, but my voice was without power – it was like a whisper from another world. The effort to speak made me feel faint, and again I felt a darkness gathering round me.

* * *

I became gradually conscious of something cool on my forehead. I wondered what it was. All sorts of things I conjectured, but could not fix my mind on any of them. I lay thus for some time, and at length opened my eyes and saw my mother bending over me – it was her hand which was so deliciously cool on my brow. I felt amazed somehow. I expected to see her; and yet I was surprised, for I had not seen her for a long time – a long, long time. I knew that she was dead – could I be dead, too? I looked at her again more carefully, and as I looked, the old features died away, but the expression remained the same. And then the dear, well-known face of Mrs. Trevor grew slowly before me. She smiled as she saw the look of recognition in my eyes, and, bending down, kissed me very tenderly. As she drew back her head something warm fell on my face. I wondered what this could be, and after thinking for a long time, to do which I closed my eyes, I came to the conclusion that it was a tear. After some more thinking I opened my eyes to see why she was crying; but she was gone, and I could see that although the window-blinds were pulled up the room was almost dark. I felt much more awake and much stronger than I had been before, and tried to call Mrs. Trevor. A woman got up from a chair behind the bed-curtains and went to the door, said something, and came back and settled my pillows.

"Where is Mrs. Trevor?" I asked, feebly. "She was here just now."

The woman smiled at me cheerfully, and answered:

"She will be here in a moment. Dear heart! but she will be glad to see you so strong and sensible."

After a few minutes she came into the room, and, bending over me, asked me how I felt. I said that I was all right – and then a thought struck me, so I asked, "What was the matter with me?"

I was told that I had been ill, very ill, but that I was now much better. Something, I know not what, suddenly recalled to my memory all the scene of the bedroom, and the fright which my folly had caused, and I grew quite dizzy with the rush of blood to my head. But Mrs. Trevor's arm supported me, and after a time the faintness passed away, and my memory was completely restored. I started violently from the arm that held me up, and called out:

"Is she all right? I heard her say, 'saved.' Is she all right?"

"Hush, dear boy, hush – she is all right. Do not excite yourself."

"Are you deceiving me?" I inquired. "Tell me all – I can bear it. Is she well or no?"

"She has been very ill, but she is now getting strong and well, thank God."

I began to cry, half from weakness and half from joy, and Mrs. Trevor seeing this, and knowing with the sweet instinct of womanhood that I would rather be alone, quickly left the room, after making a sign to the nurse, who sank again to her old place behind the bed-curtain.

I thought for long; and all the time from my first coming to Scarp to the moment of unconsciousness after I sprung through the window came back to me as in a dream. Gradually the room became darker and darker, and my thoughts began to give semblance to the objects around me, till at length the visible world passed away from my wearied eyes, and in my dreams I continued to think of all that had been. I have a hazy recollection of taking some food and then relapsing into sleep; but remember no more distinctly until I woke fully in the morning and found Mrs. Trevor again in the room. She came over to my bedside, and sitting down said gaily:

"Ah, Frank, you look bright and strong this morning, dear boy. You will soon be well now I trust."

Her cool deft fingers settled my pillow and brushed back the hair from my forehead. I took her hand and kissed it, and the doing so made me very happy. By-and-by I asked her how was Miss Fothering.

"Better, much better this morning. She has been asking after you ever since she has been able; and today when I told her how much better you were she brightened up at once."

I felt a flush painfully strong rushing over my face as she spoke, but she went on:

"She has asked me to let her see you as soon as both of you are able. She wants to thank you for your conduct on that awful night.

But there, I won't tell any more tales – let her tell you what she likes herself."

"To thank me – me – for what? For having brought her to the verge of madness or perhaps death through my silly fears and imagination. Oh, Mrs. Trevor, I know that you never mock anyone – but to me that sounds like mockery."

She leaned over me as she sat on my bedside and said, oh, so sweetly, yet so firmly that a sense of the truth of her words came at once upon me:

"If I had a son I would wish him to think as you have thought, and to act as you have acted. I would pray for it night and day and if he suffered as you have done, I would lean over him as I lean over you now and feel glad, as I feel now, that he had thought and acted as a true-hearted man should think and act. I would rejoice that God had given me such a son; and if he should die – as I feared at first that you should – I would be a prouder and happier woman kneeling by his dead body than I would in clasping a different son, living, in my arms.

Oh, how my weak fluttering heart did beat as she spoke. With pity for her blighted maternal instincts, with gladness that a true-hearted woman had approved of my conduct toward a woman whom I loved, and with joy for the deep love for myself. There was no mistaking the honesty of her words – her face was perfectly radiant as she spoke them.

I put up my arms – it took all my strength to do it – round her neck, and whispered softly in her ear one word, 'mother.'

She did not expect it, for it seemed to startle her; but her arms tightened around me convulsively. I could feel a perfect rain of tears falling on my upturned face as I looked into her eyes, full of love and long-sought joy. As I looked I felt stronger and better; my sympathy for her joy did much to restore my strength.

For some little time she was silent, and then she spoke as if to herself – "God has given me a son at last. I thank thee, O Father; forgive me if I have at any time repined. The son I prayed for might have been different from what I would wish. Thou doest best in all things."

For some time after this she stayed quite silent, still supporting me in her arms. I felt inexpressibly happy. There was an atmosphere of love around me, for which I had longed all my life. The love of a mother, for which I had pined since my orphan childhood, I had got at last, and the love of a woman to become far dearer to me than a mother I felt was close at hand.

At length I began to feel tired, and Mrs. Trevor laid me back on my pillow. It pleased me inexpressibly to observe her kind motherly manner with me now. The ice between us had at last been broken, we had declared our mutual love, and the white-haired woman was as happy in the declaration as the young man.

The next day I felt a shade stronger, and a similar improvement was manifested on the next. Mrs. Trevor always attended me herself, and her good reports of Miss Fothering's progress helped to cheer me not a little. And so the days wore on, and many passed away before I was allowed to rise from bed.

One day Mrs. Trevor came into the room in a state of suppressed delight. By this time I had been allowed to sit up a little while each day, and was beginning to get strong, or rather less weak, for I was still very helpless.

"Frank, the doctor says that you may be moved into another room tomorrow for a change, and that you may see Di."

As may be supposed I was anxious to see Miss Fothering. Whilst I had been able to think during my illness, I had thought about her all day long, and sometimes all night long. I had been in love with her even before that fatal night. My heart told me that secret whilst I was waiting to hear the clock strike, and saw all my folly about the dream; but now I not only loved the woman but I almost worshipped my own bright ideal which was merged in her. The constant series of kind messages that passed between us tended not a little to increase my attachment, and now I eagerly looked forward to a meeting with her face to face.

I awoke earlier than usual next morning, and grew rather feverish as the time for our interview approached. However, I soon cooled down upon a vague threat being held out, that if I did not become more composed I must defer my visit.

The expected time at length arrived, and I was wheeled in my chair into Mrs. Trevor's boudoir. As I entered the door I looked eagerly round and saw, seated in another chair near one of the windows, a girl, who, turning her head round languidly, disclosed the features of Miss Fothering. She was very pale and ethereal looking, and seemed extremely delicate; but in my opinion this only heightened her natural beauty. As she caught sight of me a beautiful blush rushed over her poor, pale face, and even tinged her alabaster forehead. This passed quickly, and she became calm again, and paler than before. My chair was wheeled over to her, and Mrs. Trevor said, as she bent over and kissed her, after soothing the pillow in her chair:

"Di, my love, I have brought Frank to see you. You may talk together for a little while; but, mind, the doctor's orders are very strict, and if either of you excite yourselves about anything I must forbid you to meet again until you are both much stronger."

She said the last words as she was leaving the room.

I felt red and pale, hot and cold by turns. I looked at Miss Fothering and faltered. However, in a moment or two I summoned up courage to address her.

"Miss Fothering, I hope you forgive me for the pain and danger I caused you by that foolish fear of mine. I assure you that nothing I ever did –"

Here she interrupted me.

"Mr. Stanford, I beg you will not talk like that. I must thank you for the care you thought me worthy of. I will not say how proud I feel of it, and for the generous courage and wisdom you displayed in rescuing me from the terror of that awful scene."

She grew pale, even paler than she had been before, as she spoke the last words, and trembled all over. I feared for her, and said as cheerfully as I could:

"Don't be alarmed. Do calm yourself. That is all over now and past. Don't let its horror disturb you ever again."

My speaking, although it calmed her somewhat, was not sufficient to banish her fear, and, seeing that she was really excited, I called to Mrs. Trevor, who came in from the next room and talked to us for a little while. She gradually did away with Miss Fothering's fear by her pleasant cheery conversation. She, poor girl, had received a sad shock, and the thought that I had been the cause of it gave me great anguish. After a little quiet chat, however, I grew more cheerful, but presently feeling faintish, was wheeled back to my own room and put to bed.

For many long days I continued very weak, and hardly made any advance. I saw Miss Fothering every day, and each day I loved her more and more. She got stronger as the days advanced, and after a few weeks was comparatively in good health, but still I continued weak. Her illness had been merely the result of the fright she had sustained on that unhappy night; but mine was the nervous prostration consequent on the long period of anxiety between the dream and its seeming fulfilment, united with the physical weakness resulting from my wounds caused by jumping through the window. During all this time of weakness Mrs. Trevor was, indeed, a mother to me. She watched me day and night, and as far as a woman could, made my life a dream of happiness. But the crowning glory of that time was the thought that sometimes forced itself upon me – that Diana cared for me.

She continued to remain at Scarp by Mrs. Trevor's request, as her father had gone to the Continent for the winter, and with my adopted mother she shared the attendance on me. Day after day her care for my every want grew greater, till I came to fancy her like a guardian angel keeping watch over me. With the peculiar delicate sense that accompanies extreme physical prostration I could see that the growth of her pity kept pace with the growth of her strength. My love kept pace with both. I often wondered if it could be sympathy and not pity that so forestalled my wants and wishes; or if it could be love that answered in her heart when mine beat for her. She only showed pity and tenderness in her acts and words, but still I hoped and longed for something more.

Those days of my long-continued weakness were to me sweet, sweet days. I used to watch her for hours as she sat opposite to me reading or working, and my eyes would fill with tears as I thought how hard it would be to die and leave her behind me. So strong was the flame of my love that I believed, in spite of my religious teaching, that, should I die, I would leave the better part of my being behind me. I used to think in a vague imaginative way, that was no less powerful because it was undefined, of what speeches I would make to her – if I were well. How I would talk to her in nobler language than that in which I would now allow my thoughts to mould themselves. How, as I talked, my passion, and honesty, and purity would make me so eloquent that she would love to hear me speak. How I would wander with her through the sunny-gladed woods that stretched away before me through the open window, and sit by her feet on a mossy bank beside some purling brook that rippled gaily over the stones, gazing into the depths of her eyes, where my future life was pictured in one long sheen of light. How I would whisper in her ear sweet words that would make me tremble to speak them, and her tremble to hear. How she would bend to me and show me her love by letting me tell her mine without reproof. And then would come, like the shadow of a sudden rain-cloud over an April landscape, the bitter, bitter thought that all this longing was but a dream, and that when the time had come when such things might have been, I would, most likely, be sleeping under the green turf. And she might, perhaps, be weeping in the silence of her chamber sad, sad tears for her blighted love and for me. Then my thoughts would become less selfish, and I would try to imagine the bitter blow of my death – if she loved me – for I knew that a woman loves not by the value of what she loves, but by the strength of her affection and admiration for her own ideal, which she thinks she sees bodied forth in some man.

But these thoughts had always the proviso that the dreams of happiness were prophetic. Alas! I had altogether lost faith in dreams. Still, I could not but feel that even if I had never frightened Miss Fothering by telling my vision, she might, nevertheless, have been terrified by the effect of the moonlight upon the flowers of the pampass tufts, and that, under Providence, I was the instrument of saving her from a shock even greater than that which she did experience, for help might not have come to her so soon. This thought always gave me hope. Whenever I thought of her sorrow for my death, I would find my eyes filled with a sudden rush of tears which would shut out from my waking vision the object of my thoughts and fears. Then she would come over to me and place her cool hand on my forehead, and whisper sweet words of comfort and hope in my ears. As I would feel her warm breath upon my cheek and wafting my hair from my brow, I would lose all sense of pain and sorrow and care, and live only in the brightness of the present. At such times I would cry silently from very happiness, for I was sadly weak, and even trifling things touched me deeply. Many a stray memory of some tender word heard or some gentle deed done, or of some sorrow or distress, would set me thinking for hours and stir all the tender feelings of my nature.

Slowly – very slowly – I began to get stronger, but for many days more I was almost completely helpless. With returning strength came the strengthening of my passion – for passion my love for Diana had become. She had been so woven into my thoughts that my love for her was a part of my being, and I felt that away from her my future life would be but a bare existence and no more. But strange to say, with increasing strength and passion came increasing diffidence. I felt in her presence so bashful and timorous that I hardly dared to look at her, and could not speak save to answer an occasional question. I had ceased to dream entirely, for such day-dreams as I used to have seemed now wild and almost sacrilegious to my sur-excited imagination. But when she was not looking at me I would be happy in merely seeing her or hearing her speak. I could tell the moment she left the house or entered it, and her footfall was the music sweetest to my ears – except her voice. Sometimes she would catch sight of my bashful looks at her, and then, at my conscious blushing, a bright smile would flit over her face. It was sweet and womanly, but sometimes I would think that it was no more than her pity finding expression. She was always in my thoughts and these doubts and fears constantly assailed me, so that I could feel that the brooding over the subject – a matter which I was powerless to prevent – was doing me an injury; perhaps seriously retarding my recovery.

One day I felt very sad. There had a bitter sense of loneliness come over me which was unusual. It was a good sign of returning health, for it was like the waking from a dream to a world of fact, with all its troubles and cares. There was a sense of coldness and loneliness in the world, and I felt that I had lost something without gaining anything in return – I had, in fact, lost somewhat of my sense of dependence, which is a consequence of prostration, but had not yet regained my strength. I sat opposite a window itself in shade, but looking over a garden that in the summer had been bright with flowers, and sweet with their odours, but which, now, was lit up only in patches by the quiet mellow gleams of the autumn sun, and brightened by a few stray flowers that had survived the first frosts.

As I sat I could not help thinking of what my future would be.

I felt that I was getting strong, and the possibilities of my life seemed very real to me. How I longed for courage to ask Diana to be my wife! Any certainty would be better than the suspense I now constantly endured. I had but little hope that she would accept me, for she seemed to care less for me now than in the early days of my illness. As I grew stronger she seemed to hold somewhat aloof from me; and as my fears and doubts grew more and more, I could hardly bear to think of my joy should she accept me, or of my despair should she refuse. Either emotion seemed too great to be borne.

Today when she entered the room my fears were vastly increased. She seemed much stronger than usual, for a glow, as of health, ruddied her cheeks, and she seemed so lovely that I could not conceive that such a woman would ever condescend to be my wife. There was an unusual constraint in her manner as she came and spoke to me, and flitted round me, doing in her own graceful way all the thousand little offices that only a woman's hand can do for an invalid. She turned to me two or three times, as if she was about to speak; but turned away again, each time silent, and with a blush. I could see that her heart was beating violently. At length she spoke.

"Frank."

Oh! What a wild throb went through me as I heard my name from her lips for the first time. The blood rushed to my head, so that for a moment I was quite faint. Her cool hand on my forehead revived me.

"Frank, will you let me speak to you for a few minutes as honestly as I would wish to speak, and as freely?"

"Go on."

"You will promise me not to think me unwomanly or forward, for indeed I act from the best motives – promise me?"

This was said slowly with much hesitation, and a convulsive heaving of the chest.

"I promise."

"We can see that you are not getting as strong as you ought, and the doctor says that there is some idea too much in your mind – that you brood over it, and that it is retarding your recovery. Mrs. Trevor and I have been talking about it. We have been comparing notes, and I think we have found out what your idea is. Now, Frank, you must not pale and red like that, or I will have to leave off."

"I will be calm – indeed, I will. Go on."

"We both thought that it might do you good to talk to you freely, and we want to know if our idea is correct. Mrs. Trevor thought it better that I should speak to you than she should."

"What is the idea?"

Hitherto, although she had manifested considerable emotion, her voice had been full and clear, but she answered this last question very faintly, and with much hesitation.

"You are attached to me, and you are afraid I – I don't love you."

Here her voice was checked by a rush of tears, and she turned her head away.

"Diana," said I, "dear Diana," and I held out my arms with what strength I had.

The colour rushed over her face and neck, and then she turned, and with a convulsive sigh laid her head upon my shoulder. One weak arm fell round my waist, and my other hand rested on her head. I said nothing. I could not speak, but I felt the beating of her heart against mine, and thought that if I died then I must be happy for ever, if there be memory in the other world.

For a long, long, blissful time she kept her place, and gradually our hearts ceased to beat so violently, and we became calm.

Such was the confession of our love. No plighted faith, no passionate vows, but the silence and the thrill of sympathy through our hearts were sweeter than words could be.

Diana raised her head and looked fearlessly but appealingly into my eyes as she asked me:

"Oh, Frank, did I do right to speak? Could it have been better if I had waited?"

She saw my wishes in my eyes, and bent down her head to me. I kissed her on the forehead and fervently prayed, "Thank God that all was as it has been. May He bless my own darling wife for ever and ever."

"Amen," said a sweet, tender voice.

We both looked up without shame, for we knew the tones of my second mother. Her face, streaming with tears of joy, was lit up by a sudden ray of sunlight through the casement.

If you enjoyed this, you might also like...
'The Judge's House,' see page 47
'The Coming of Abel Behenna', see page 408

The Invisible Giant

TIME GOES ON in the Country Under the Sunset much as it does here.

Many years passed away; and they wrought much change. And now we find a time when the people that lived in good King Mago's time would hardly have known their beautiful Land if they had seen it again.

It had sadly changed indeed. No longer was there the same love or the same reverence towards the king – no longer was there perfect peace. People had become more selfish and more greedy, and had tried to grasp all they could for themselves. There were some very rich and there were many poor. Most of the beautiful gardens were laid waste. Houses had grown up close round the palace; and in some of these dwelt many persons who could only afford to pay for part of a house.

All the beautiful Country was sadly changed, and changed was the life of the dwellers in it. The people had almost forgotten Prince Zaphir, who was dead many, many years ago; and no more roses were spread on the pathways. Those who lived now in the Country Under the Sunset laughed at the idea of more Giants, and they did not fear them because they did not see them. Some of them said:

"Tush! What can there be to fear? Even if there ever were giants there are none now."

And so the people sang and danced and feasted as before, and thought only of themselves. The Spirits that guarded the Land were very, very sad. Their great white shadowy wings drooped as they stood at their posts at the Portals of the Land. They hid their faces, and their eyes were dim with continuous weeping, so that they heeded not if any evil thing went by them. They tried to make the people think of their evil-doing; but they could not leave their posts, and the people heard their moaning in the night season and said:

"Listen to the sighing of the breeze; how sweet it is!"

So is it ever with us also, that when we hear the wind sighing and moaning and sobbing round our houses in the lonely nights, we do not think our Angels may be sorrowing for our misdeeds, but only that there is a storm coming. The Angels wept evermore, and they felt the sorrow of dumbness – for though they could speak, those they spoke to would not hear.

Whilst the people laughed at the idea of Giants, there was one old man who shook his head, and made answer to them, when he heard them, and said:

"Death has many children, and there are Giants in the marshes still. You may not see them, perhaps – but they are there, and the only bulwark of safety is in a land of patient, faithful hearts."

The name of this good old man was Knoal, and he lived in a house built of great blocks of stone, in the middle of a wild place far from the city.

In the city there were many great old houses, storey upon storey high; and in these houses lived many poor people. The higher you went up the great steep stairs the poorer were the people that lived there, so that in the garrets were some so poor that when the morning came they did not know whether they should have anything to eat the whole long day. This was very, very sad, and gentle children would have wept if they had seen their pain.

In one of these garrets there lived all alone a little maiden called Zaya. She was an orphan, for her father had died many years before, and her poor mother, who had toiled long and wearily for her dear little daughter – her only child – had died also not long since.

Poor little Zaya had wept so bitterly when she saw her dear mother lying dead, and she had been so sad and sorry for a long time, that she quite forgot that she had no means of living. However, the poor people who lived in the house had given her part of their own food, so that she did not starve.

Then after awhile she had tried to work for herself and earn her own living. Her mother had taught her to make flowers out of paper; so that she made a lot of flowers, and when she had a full basket she took them into the street and sold them. She made flowers of many kinds, roses and lilies, and violets, and snowdrops, and primroses, and mignonette, and many beautiful sweet flowers that only grow in the Country Under the Sunset. Some of them she could make without any pattern, but others she could not, so when she wanted a pattern she took her basket of paper and scissors, and paste, and brushes, and all the things she used, and went into the garden which a kind lady owned, where there grew many beautiful flowers. There she sat down and worked away, looking at the flowers she wanted.

Sometimes she was very sad, and her tears fell thick and fast as she thought of her dear dead mother. Often she seemed to feel that her mother was looking down at her, and to see her tender smile in the sunshine on the water; then her heart was glad, and she sang so sweetly that the birds came around her and stopped their own singing to listen to her.

She and the birds grew great friends, and sometimes when she had sung a song they would all cry out together, as they sat round her in a ring, in a few notes that seemed to say quite plainly:

"Sing to us again. Sing to us again."

So she would sing again. Then she would ask them to sing, and they would sing till there was quite a concert. After a while the birds knew her so well that they would come into her room, and they even built their nests there, and they followed her wherever she went. The people used to say:

"Look at the girl with the birds; she must be half a bird herself, for see how the birds know and love her." From so many people coming to say things like this, some silly people actually believed that she was partly a bird, and they shook their heads when wise people laughed at them, and said:

"Indeed she must be; listen to her singing; her voice is sweeter even than the birds."

So a nickname was applied to her, and naughty boys called it after her in the street, and the nickname was 'Big Bird.' But Zaya did not mind the name; and although often naughty boys said it to her, meaning to cause her pain, she did not dislike it, but the contrary, for she so gloried in the love and trust of her little sweet-voiced pets that she wished to be thought like them.

Indeed it would be well for some naughty little boys and girls if they were as good and harmless as the little birds that work all day long for their helpless baby birds, building nests and bringing food, and sitting so patiently hatching their little speckled eggs.

One evening Zaya sat alone in her garret very sad and lonely. It was a lovely summer's evening, and she sat in the window looking out over the city. She could see over the many streets towards the great cathedral whose spire towered aloft into the sky higher by far even than the great tower of the king's palace. There was hardly a breath of wind, and the smoke went up straight from the chimneys, getting further and fainter till it was lost altogether.

Zaya was very sad. For the first time for many days her birds were all away from her at once, and she did not know where they had gone. It seemed to her as if they had deserted her, and she was so lonely, poor little maid, that she wept bitter tears. She was thinking of the story which long ago her dead mother had told her, how Prince Zaphir had slain the Giant, and she wondered what the prince was like, and thought how happy the people must have been when Zaphir and Bluebell were king and queen. Then she wondered if there were any hungry children in those good days, and if, indeed, as the people said, there were no more Giants. So she went on with her work before the open window.

Presently she looked up from her work and gazed across the city. There she saw a terrible thing – something so terrible that she gave a low cry of fear and wonder, and leaned out of the window, shading her eyes with her hands to see more clearly.

In the sky beyond the city she saw a vast shadowy Form with its arms raised. It was shrouded in a great misty robe that covered it, fading away into air so that she could only see the face and the grim, spectral hands.

The Form was so mighty that the city below it seemed like a child's toy. It was still far off the city.

The little maid's heart seemed to stand still with fear as she thought to herself, "The Giants, then, are not dead. This is another of them."

Quickly she ran down the high stairs and out into the street. There she saw some people, and cried to them:

"Look! Look! the Giant, the Giant!" and pointed towards the Form which she still saw moving onwards to the city.

The people looked up, but they could not see anything, and they laughed and said, "The child is mad."

Then poor little Zaya was more than ever frightened, and ran down the street crying out still:

"Look, look! The Giant, the Giant!" But no one heeded her, and all said, "The child is mad," and they went on their own ways.

Then the naughty boys came around her and cried out:

"Big Bird has lost her mates. She sees a bigger bird in the sky, and she wants it." And they made rhymes about her, and sang them as they danced round.

Zaya ran away from them; and she hurried right through the city, and out into the country beyond it, for she still saw the great Form before her in the air.

As she went on, and got nearer and nearer to the Giant, it grew a little darker. She could see only the clouds; but still there was visible the form of a Giant hanging dimly in the air.

A cold mist closed around her as the Giant appeared to come onwards towards her. Then she thought of all the poor people in the city, and she hoped that the Giant would spare them, and she knelt down before him and lifted up her hands appealingly, and cried aloud:

"Oh, great Giant! Spare them, spare them!"

But the Giant moved onwards still as though he never heard. She cried aloud all the more:

"Oh, great Giant! Spare them, spare them!" And she bowed her head and wept, and the Giant still, though very slowly, moved onward towards the city.

There was an old man not far off standing at the door of a small house built of great stones, but the little maid saw him not. His face wore a look of fear and wonder, and when he saw the child kneel and raise her hands, he drew nigh and listened to her voice. When he heard her say, "Oh, great Giant!" he murmured to himself:

"It is then even as I feared. There are more Giants, and truly this is another." He looked upwards, but he saw nothing, and he murmured again:

"I see not, yet this child can see; and yet I feared, for something told me that there was danger. Truly knowledge is blinder than innocence."

The little maid, still not knowing there was any human being near her, cried out again, with a great cry of anguish:

"Oh, do not, do not, great Giant, do them harm. If someone must suffer, let it be me. Take me, I am willing to die, but spare them. Spare them, great Giant and do with me even as thou wilt." But the giant heeded not.

And Knoal – for he was the old man – felt his eyes fill with tears, and he said to himself:

"Oh, noble child, how brave she is, she would sacrifice herself!"

And coming closer to her, he put his hand upon her head.

Zaya, who was again bowing her head, started and looked round when she felt the touch. However, when she saw that it was Knoal, she was comforted, for she knew how wise and good he was, and felt that if any person could help her, he could. So she clung to him, and hid her face in his breast; and he stroked her hair and comforted her. But still he could see nothing.

The cold mist swept by, and when Zaya looked up, she saw that the Giant had passed by, and was moving onward to the city.

"Come with me, my child," said the old man; and the two arose, and went into the dwelling built of great stones.

When Zaya entered, she started, for lo! the inside was as a Tomb. The old man felt her shudder, for he still held her close to him, and he said:

"Weep not, little one, and fear not. This place reminds me and all who enter it, that to the tomb we must all come at the last. Fear it not, for it has grown to be a cheerful home to me."

Then the little maid was comforted, and began to examine all around her more closely. She saw all sorts of curious instruments, and many strange and many common herbs and simples hung to dry in bunches on the walls. The old man watched her in silence till her fear was gone, and then he said:

"My child, saw you the features of the Giant as he passed?"

She answered, "Yes."

"Can you describe his face and form to me?" he asked again.

Whereupon she began to tell him all that she had seen. How the Giant was so great that all the sky seemed filled. How the great arms were outspread, veiled in his robe, till far away the shroud was lost in air. How the face was as that of a strong man, pitiless, yet without malice; and that the eyes were blind.

The old man shuddered as he heard, for he knew that the Giant was a very terrible one; and his heart wept for the doomed city where so many would perish in the midst of their sin.

They determined to go forth and warn again the doomed people; and making no delay, the old man and the little maid hurried towards the city.

As they left the small house, Zaya saw the Giant before them, moving towards the city. They hurried on; and when they had passed through the cold mist, Zaya looked back and saw the Giant behind them.

Presently they came to the city.

It was a strange sight to see that old man and that little maid flying to tell people of the terrible Plague that was coming upon them. The old man's long white beard and hair and the child's golden locks were swept behind them in the wind, so quick they came. The faces of both were white as death. Behind them, seen only to the eyes of the pure-hearted little maid when she looked back, came ever onward at slow pace the spectral Giant that hung a dark shadow in the evening air.

But those in the city never saw the Giant; and when the old man and the little maid warned them, still they heeded not, but scoffed and jeered at them, and said:

"Tush! There are no Giants now"; and they went on their way, laughing and jeering.

Then the old man came and stood on a raised place amongst them, on the lowest step of the great fountain with the little maid by his side, and he spake thus:

"Oh, people, dwellers in this Land, be warned in time. This pure-hearted child, round whose sweet innocence even the little birds that fear men and women gather in peace, has this night seen in the sky the form of a Giant that advances ever onward menacingly to our city. Believe, oh, believe; and be warned, whilst ye may. To myself even as to you the sky is a blank; and yet see that I believe. For listen to me: all unknowing that another Giant had invaded our land, I sat pensive in my dwelling; and, without cause or motive, there came into my heart a sudden fear for the safety of our city. I arose and looked north and south and east and west, and on high and below, but never a sign of danger could I see. So I said to myself:

'Mine eyes are dim with a hundred years of watching and waiting, and so I cannot see.' And yet, oh people, dwellers in this land, though that century has dimmed mine outer eyes, still it has quickened mine inner eyes – the eyes of my soul. Again I went forth, and lo! this little maid knelt and implored a Giant, unseen by me, to spare the city; but he heard her not, or, if he heard, answered her not, and she fell prone. So hither we come to warn you. Yonder, says the maid, he passes onward to the city. Oh, be warned; be warned in time."

Still the people heeded not; but they scoffed and jeered the more, and said:

"Lo, the maid and the old man both are mad"; and they passed onwards to their homes – to dancing and feasting as before.

Then the naughty boys came and mocked them, and said that Zaya had lost her birds, and gone mad; and they made songs, and sang them as they danced round.

Zaya was so sorely grieved for the poor people that she heeded not the cruel boys. Seeing that she did not heed them, some of them got still more rude and wicked; they went a little way off, and threw things at them, and mocked them all the more.

Then, sad of heart, the old man arose, and took the little maid by the hand, and brought her away into the wilderness; and lodged her with him in the house built with great stones. That night Zaya slept with the sweet smell of the drying herbs all around her; and the old man held her hand that she might have no fear.

In the morning Zaya arose betimes, and awoke the old man, who had fallen asleep in his chair.

She went to the doorway and looked out, and then a thrill of gladness came upon her heart; for outside the door, as though waiting to see her, sat all her little birds, and many, many more. When the birds saw the little maid they sang a few loud joyous notes, and flew about foolishly for very joy – some of them fluttering their wings and looking so funny that she could not help laughing a little.

When Knoal and Zaya had eaten their frugal breakfast and given to their little feathered friends, they set out with sorrowful hearts to visit the city, and to try once more to warn the people. The birds flew around them as they went, and to cheer them sang as joyously as they could, although their little hearts were heavy.

As they walked they saw before them the great shadowy Giant; and he had now advanced to the very confines of the city.

Once again they warned the people, and great crowds came around them, but only mocked them more than ever; and naughty boys threw stones and sticks at the little birds and killed some of them. Poor Zaya wept bitterly, and Knoal's heart was very sad. After a time, when they had moved from the fountain, Zaya looked up and started with joyous surprise, for the great shadowy Giant was nowhere to be seen. She cried out in joy, and the people laughed and said:

"Cunning child! She sees that we will not believe her, and she pretends that the Giant has gone."

They surrounded her, jeering, and some of them said:

"Let us put her under the fountain and duck her, as a lesson to liars who would frighten us." Then they approached her with menaces. She clung close to Knoal, who had looked terribly grave when she had said she did not see the Giant any longer, and who was now as if in a dream, thinking. But at her touch he seemed to wake up; and he spoke sternly to the people, and rebuked them. But they cried out on him also, and said that as he had aided Zaya in her lie he should be ducked also, and they advanced to lay hands on them both.

The hand of one who was a ringleader was already outstretched, when he gave a low cry, and pressed his hand to his side; and, whilst the others turned to look at him in wonder, he cried out in great pain, and screamed horribly. Even whilst the people looked, his face grew blacker and blacker, and he fell down before them, and writhed a while in pain, and then died.

All the people screamed out in terror, and ran away, crying aloud:

"The Giant! The Giant! He is indeed amongst us!" They feared all the more that they could not see him.

But before they could leave the market-place, in the centre of which was the fountain, many fell dead and their corpses lay.

There in the centre knelt the old man and the little maid, praying; and the birds sat perched around the fountain, mute and still, and there was no sound heard save the cries of the people far off. Then their wailing sounded louder and louder, for the Giant – Plague – was amongst and around them, and there was no escaping, for it was now too late to fly.

Alas! In the Country Under the Sunset there was much weeping that day; and when the night came there was little sleep, for there was fear in some hearts and pain in others. None were still except the dead, who lay stark about the city, so still and lifeless that even the cold light of the moon and the shadows of the drifting clouds moving over them could not make them seem as though they lived.

And for many a long day there was pain and grief and death in the Country Under the Sunset.

Knoal and Zaya did all they could to help the poor people, but it was hard indeed to aid them, for the unseen Giant was amongst them, wandering through the city to and fro, so that none could tell where he would lay his ice-cold hand.

Some people fled away out of the city; but it was little use, for go how they would and fly never so fast they were still within the grasp of the unseen Giant. Ever and anon he turned their warm hearts to ice with his breath and his touch, and they fell dead.

Some, like those within the city, were spared, and of these some perished of hunger, and the rest crept sadly back to the city and lived or died amongst their friends. And it was all, oh! so sad, for there was nothing but grief and fear and weeping from morn till night.

Now, see how Zaya's little bird friends helped her in her need.

They seemed to see the coming of the Giant when no one – not even the little maid herself – could see anything, and they managed to tell her when there was danger just as well as though they could talk.

At first Knoal and she went home every evening to the house built of great stones to sleep, and came again to the city in the morning, and stayed with the poor sick people, comforting them and feeding them, and giving them medicine which Knoal, from his great wisdom, knew would do them good. Thus they saved many precious human lives, and those who were rescued were very thankful, and henceforth ever after lived holier and more unselfish lives.

After a few days, however, they found that the poor sick people needed help even more at night than in the day, and so they came and lived in the city altogether, helping the stricken folk day and night.

At the earliest dawn Zaya would go forth to breathe the morning air; and there, just waked from sleep, would be her feathered friends waiting for her. They sang glad songs of joy, and came and perched on her shoulders and her head, and kissed her. Then, if she went to go towards any place where, during the night, the Plague had laid his deadly hand, they would flutter before her, and try to impede her, and scream out in their own tongue:

"Go back! Go back!"

They pecked of her bread and drank of her cup before she touched them; and when there was danger – for the cold hand of the Giant was placed everywhere – they would cry:

"No, no!" and she would not touch the food, or let anyone else do so. Often it happened that, even whilst it pecked at the bread or drank of the cup, a poor little bird would fall down and flutter its wings and die; but all they that died, did so with a chirp of joy, looking at their little mistress, for whom they had gladly perished. Whenever the little birds found that the bread and the cup were pure and free from danger, they would look up at Zaya jauntily, and flap their wings and try to crow, and seemed so saucy that the poor sad little maiden would smile.

There was one old bird that always took a second, and often a great many pecks at the bread when it was good, so that he got quite a hearty meal; and sometimes he would go on feeding till Zaya would Shake her finger at him and say:

"Greedy!" and he would hop away as if he had done nothing.

There was one other dear little bird – a robin, with a breast as red as the sunset – that loved Zaya more than one can think. When he tried the food and found that it was safe to eat, he would take a tiny piece in his bill, and fly up and put it in her mouth.

Every little bird that drank from Zaya's cup and found it good raised its head to say grace; and ever since then the little birds do the same, and they never forget to say their grace – as some thankless children do.

Thus Knoal and Zaya lived, although many around them died, and the Giant still remained in the city. So many people died that one began to wonder that so many were left; for it was only when the town began to get thinned that people thought of the vast numbers that had lived in it.

Poor little Zaya had got so pale and thin that she looked a shadow, and Knoal's form was bent more with the sufferings of a few weeks than it had been by his century of age. But although the two were weary and worn, they still kept on their good work of aiding the sick.

Many of the little birds were dead.

One morning the old man was very weak – so weak that he could hardly stand. Zaya got frightened about him, and said:

"Are you ill, father?" for she always called him father now.

He answered her in a voice alas! hoarse and low, but very, very tender:

"My child, I fear the end is coming: take me home, that there I may die."

At his words Zaya gave a low cry and fell on her knees beside him, and buried her head in his bosom and wept bitterly, whilst she hugged him close. But she had little time for weeping, for the old man struggled up to his feet, and, seeing that he wanted aid, she dried her tears and helped him.

The old man took his staff, and with Zaya helping to support him, got as far as the fountain in the midst of the market-place; and there, on the lowest step, he sank down as though exhausted. Zaya felt him grow cold as ice, and she knew that the chilly hand of the Giant had been laid upon him.

Then, without knowing why, she looked up to where she had last seen the Giant as Knoal and she had stood beside the fountain. And lo! as she looked, holding Knoal's hand, she saw the shadowy form of the terrible Giant who had been so long invisible growing more and more clearly out of the clouds.

His face was stern as ever, and his eyes were still blind.

Zaya cried to the Giant, still holding Knoal tightly by the hand:

"Not him, not him! Oh, mighty Giant! Not him! Not him!" and she bowed her head and wept.

There was such anguish in her heart that to the blind eyes of the shadowy Giant came tears that fell like dew on the forehead of the old man. Knoal spake to Zaya:

"Grieve not, my child. I am glad that you see the Giant again, for I have hope that he will leave our city free from woe. I am the last victim, and I gladly die."

Then Zaya knelt to the Giant, and said:

"Spare him! Oh! Spare him and take me! But spare him! Spare him!"

The old man raised himself upon his elbow as he lay, and spake to her:

"Grieve not, my little one, and repine not. Sooth I know that you would gladly give your life for mine. But we must give for the good of others that which is dearer to us than our lives. Bless you, my little one, and be good. Farewell! Farewell!"

As he spake the last word he grew cold as death, and his spirit passed away.

Zaya knelt down and prayed; and when she looked up she saw the shadowy Giant moving away.

The Giant turned as he passed on, and Zaya saw that his blind eyes looked towards her as though he were trying to see. He raised the great shadowy arms, draped still in his shroud of mist, as though blessing her; and she thought that the wind that came by her moaning bore the echo of the words:

"Innocence and devotion save the land."

Presently she saw far off the great shadowy Giant Plague moving away to the border of the Land, and passing between the Guardian Spirits out through the Portal into the deserts beyond – for ever.

If you enjoyed this, you might also like...
'Crooken Sands,' see page 59
'The Shadow Builder,' see page 382

The Judge's House

WHEN THE TIME for his examination drew near Malcolm Malcolmson made up his mind to go somewhere to read by himself. He feared the attractions of the seaside, and also he feared completely rural isolation, for of old he knew its charms, and so he determined to find some unpretentious little town where there would be nothing to distract him. He refrained from asking suggestions from any of his friends, for he argued that each would recommend some place of which he had knowledge, and where he had already acquaintances. As Malcolmson wished to avoid friends he had no wish to encumber himself with the attention of friends' friends, and so he determined to look out for a place for himself. He packed a portmanteau with some clothes and all the books he required, and then took ticket for the first name on the local time-table which he did not know.

When at the end of three hours' journey he alighted at Benchurch, he felt satisfied that he had so far obliterated his tracks as to be sure of having a peaceful opportunity of pursuing his studies. He went straight to the one inn which the sleepy little place contained, and put up for the night. Benchurch was a market town, and once in three weeks was crowded to excess, but for the remainder of the twenty-one days it was as attractive as a desert. Malcolmson looked around the day after his arrival to try to find quarters more isolated than even so quiet an inn as 'The Good Traveller' afforded. There was only one place which took his fancy, and it certainly satisfied his wildest ideas regarding quiet; in fact, quiet was not the proper word to apply to it – desolation was the only term conveying any suitable idea of its isolation. It was an old rambling, heavy-built house of the Jacobean style, with heavy gables and windows, unusually small, and set higher than was customary in such houses, and was surrounded with a high brick wall massively built. Indeed, on examination, it looked more like a fortified house than an ordinary dwelling. But all these things pleased Malcolmson. "Here," he thought, "is the very spot I have been looking for, and if I can get opportunity of using it I shall be happy." His joy was increased when he realised beyond doubt that it was not at present inhabited.

From the post-office he got the name of the agent, who was rarely surprised at the application to rent a part of the old house. Mr. Carnford, the local lawyer and agent, was a genial old gentleman, and frankly confessed his delight at anyone being willing to live in the house.

"To tell you the truth," said he, "I should be only too happy, on behalf of the owners, to let anyone have the house rent free for a term of years if only to accustom the people here to see it inhabited. It has been so long empty that some kind of absurd prejudice has grown up about it, and this can be best put down by its occupation – if only," he added with a sly glance at Malcolmson, "by a scholar like yourself, who wants its quiet for a time."

Malcolmson thought it needless to ask the agent about the 'absurd prejudice'; he knew he would get more information, if he should require it, on that subject from other quarters. He paid his three months' rent, got a receipt, and the name of an old woman who would probably undertake to 'do' for him, and came away with the keys in his pocket. He then went to the landlady of the inn, who was a cheerful and most kindly person, and asked her advice as to such stores and provisions as he would be likely to require. She threw up her hands in amazement when he told her where he was going to settle himself.

"Not in the Judge's House!" she said, and grew pale as she spoke. He explained the locality of the house, saying that he did not know its name. When he had finished she answered:

"Aye, sure enough – sure enough the very place! It is the Judge's House sure enough." He asked her to tell him about the place, why so called, and what there was against it. She told him that it was so called locally because it had been many years before – how long she could not say, as she was herself from another part of the country, but she thought it must have been a hundred years or more – the abode of a judge who was held in great terror on account of his harsh sentences and his hostility to prisoners at Assizes. As to what there was against the house itself she could not tell. She had often asked, but no one could inform her; but there was a general feeling that there was something, and for her own part she would not take all the money in Drinkwater's Bank and stay in the house an hour by herself. Then she apologised to Malcolmson for her disturbing talk.

"It is too bad of me, sir, and you – and a young gentlemen, too – if you will pardon me saying it, going to live there all alone. If you were my boy – and you'll excuse me for saying it – you wouldn't sleep there a night, not if I had to go there myself and pull the big alarm bell that's on the roof!" The good creature was so manifestly in earnest, and was so kindly in her intentions, that Malcolmson, although amused, was touched. He told her kindly how much he appreciated her interest in him, and added:

"But, my dear Mrs. Witham, indeed you need not be concerned about me! A man who is reading for the Mathematical Tripos has too much to think of to be disturbed by any of these mysterious 'somethings', and his work is of too exact and prosaic a kind to allow of his having any corner in his mind for mysteries of any kind. Harmonical Progression, Permutations and Combinations, and Elliptic Functions have sufficient mysteries for me!" Mrs. Witham kindly undertook to see after his commissions, and he went himself to look for the old woman who had been recommended to him. When he returned to the Judge's House with her, after an interval of a couple of hours, he found Mrs. Witham herself waiting with several men and boys carrying parcels, and an upholsterer's man with a bed in a car, for she said, though tables and chairs might be all very well, a bed that hadn't been aired for mayhap fifty years was not proper for young bones to lie on. She was evidently curious to see the inside of the house; and though manifestly so afraid of the 'somethings' that at the slightest sound she clutched on to Malcolmson, whom she never left for a moment, went over the whole place.

After his examination of the house, Malcolmson decided to take up his abode in the great dining-room, which was big enough to serve for all his requirements; and Mrs. Witham, with the aid of the charwoman, Mrs. Dempster, proceeded to arrange matters. When the hampers were brought in and unpacked, Malcolmson saw that with much kind forethought she had sent from her own kitchen sufficient provisions to last for a few days. Before going she expressed all sorts of kind wishes; and at the door turned and said:

"And perhaps, sir, as the room is big and draughty it might be well to have one of those big screens put round your bed at night – though, truth to tell, I would die myself if I were to be so shut in with all kinds of – of 'things', that put their heads round the sides, or over the top, and look on me!" The image which she had called up was too much for her nerves, and she fled incontinently.

Mrs. Dempster sniffed in a superior manner as the landlady disappeared, and remarked that for her own part she wasn't afraid of all the bogies in the kingdom.

"I'll tell you what it is, sir," she said; "bogies is all kinds and sorts of things – except bogies! Rats and mice, and beetles; and creaky doors, and loose slates, and broken panes, and stiff drawer handles, that stay out when you pull them and then fall down in the middle of the night. Look at the wainscot of the room! It is old – hundreds of years old! Do you think there's no rats and beetles there! And do you imagine, sir, that you won't see none of them? Rats is bogies, I tell you, and bogies is rats; and don't you get to think anything else!"

"Mrs. Dempster," said Malcolmson gravely, making her a polite bow, "you know more than a Senior Wrangler! And let me say, that, as a mark of esteem for your indubitable soundness of head and heart, I shall, when I go, give you possession of this house, and let you stay here by yourself for the last two months of my tenancy, for four weeks will serve my purpose."

"Thank you kindly, sir!" she answered, "but I couldn't sleep away from home a night. I am in Greenhow's Charity, and if I slept a night away from my rooms I should lose all I have got to live on. The rules is very strict; and there's too many watching for a vacancy for me to run any risks in the matter. Only for that, sir, I'd gladly come here and attend on you altogether during your stay."

"My good woman," said Malcolmson hastily, "I have come here on purpose to obtain solitude; and believe me that I am grateful to the late Greenhow for having so organised his admirable charity – whatever it is – that I am perforce denied the opportunity of suffering from such a form of temptation! Saint Anthony himself could not be more rigid on the point!"

The old woman laughed harshly. "Ah, you young gentlemen," she said, "you don't fear for naught; and belike you'll get all the solitude you want here." She set to work with her cleaning; and by nightfall, when Malcolmson returned from his walk – he always had one of his books to study as he walked – he found the room swept and tidied, a fire burning in the old hearth, the lamp lit, and the table spread for supper with Mrs. Witham's excellent fare. "This is comfort, indeed," he said, as he rubbed his hands.

When he had finished his supper, and lifted the tray to the other end of the great oak dining-table, he got out his books again, put fresh wood on the fire, trimmed his lamp, and set himself down to a spell of real hard work. He went on without pause till about eleven o'clock, when he knocked off for a bit to fix his fire and lamp, and to make himself a cup of tea. He had always been a tea-drinker, and during his college life had sat late at work and had taken tea late. The rest was a great luxury to him, and he enjoyed it with a sense of delicious, voluptuous ease. The renewed fire leaped and sparkled, and threw quaint shadows through the great old room; and as he sipped his hot tea he revelled in the sense of isolation from his kind. Then it was that he began to notice for the first time what a noise the rats were making.

"Surely," he thought, "they cannot have been at it all the time I was reading. Had they been, I must have noticed it!" Presently, when the noise increased, he satisfied himself that it was really new. It was evident that at first the rats had been frightened at the presence of a stranger, and the light of fire and lamp; but that as the time went on they had grown bolder and were now disporting themselves as was their wont.

How busy they were! And hark to the strange noises! Up and down behind the old wainscot, over the ceiling and under the floor they raced, and gnawed, and scratched! Malcolmson smiled to himself as he recalled to mind the saying of Mrs. Dempster, "Bogies is rats, and rats is bogies!" The tea began to have its effect of intellectual and nervous stimulus, he saw with joy another long spell of work to be done before the night was past, and in the sense of security which it gave him, he allowed himself the luxury of a good look round the room. He took his lamp in one hand, and went all around, wondering that so quaint and beautiful an old house had been so long neglected. The carving of the oak on the panels of the wainscot was fine, and on and round the doors and windows it was beautiful and of rare merit. There were some old pictures on the walls, but they were coated so thick with dust and dirt that he could not distinguish any detail of them, though he held his lamp as high as he could over his head. Here and there as he went round he saw some crack or hole blocked for a moment by the face of a rat with its bright eyes glittering in the light, but in an instant it was gone, and a squeak and a scamper followed. The thing that most struck him, however, was the rope of the great alarm bell on the roof, which hung down in a corner of the room on the right-hand side of the fireplace. He pulled up close to the hearth a great high-backed carved oak chair, and sat down to his last cup of tea. When this was done he made up the fire, and went back to his work, sitting at the corner of the table, having the fire to his left. For a little while the rats disturbed him somewhat with their perpetual scampering, but he got accustomed to the noise as one does to the ticking of a clock or to the roar of moving water; and he became so immersed in his work that everything in the world, except the problem which he was trying to solve, passed away from him.

He suddenly looked up, his problem was still unsolved, and there was in the air that sense of the hour before the dawn, which is so dread to doubtful life. The noise of the rats had ceased. Indeed it seemed to him that it must have ceased but lately and that it was the sudden cessation which had disturbed him. The fire had fallen low, but still it threw out a deep red glow. As he looked he started in spite of his sang froid.

There on the great high-backed carved oak chair by the right side of the fireplace sat an enormous rat, steadily glaring at him with baleful eyes. He made a motion to it as though to hunt it away, but it did not stir. Then he made the motion of throwing something. Still it did not stir, but showed its great white teeth angrily, and its cruel eyes shone in the lamplight with an added vindictiveness.

Malcolmson felt amazed, and seizing the poker from the hearth ran at it to kill it. Before, however, he could strike it, the rat, with a squeak that sounded like the concentration of hate, jumped upon the floor, and, running up the rope of the alarm bell, disappeared in the darkness beyond the range of the green-shaded lamp. Instantly, strange to say, the noisy scampering of the rats in the wainscot began again.

By this time Malcolmson's mind was quite off the problem; and as a shrill cock-crow outside told him of the approach of morning, he went to bed and to sleep.

He slept so sound that he was not even waked by Mrs. Dempster coming in to make up his room. It was only when she had tidied up the place and got his breakfast ready and tapped on the screen which closed in his bed that he woke. He was a little tired still after his night's hard work, but a strong cup of tea soon freshened him up and, taking his book, he went out for his morning walk, bringing with him a few sandwiches lest he should not care to return till dinner time. He found a quiet walk between high elms some way outside the town, and here he spent the greater part of the day studying his Laplace. On his return he looked in to see Mrs. Witham and to thank her for her kindness. When she saw him coming through the diamond-paned bay window of her sanctum she came out to meet him and asked him in. She looked at him searchingly and shook her head as she said:

"You must not overdo it, sir. You are paler this morning than you should be. Too late hours and too hard work on the brain isn't good for any man! But tell me, sir, how did you pass the night? Well, I hope? But my heart! Sir, I was glad when Mrs. Dempster told me this morning that you were all right and sleeping sound when she went in."

"Oh, I was all right," he answered smiling, "the 'somethings' didn't worry me, as yet. Only the rats; and they had a circus, I tell you, all over the place. There was one wicked looking old devil that sat up on my own chair by the fire, and wouldn't go till I took the poker to him, and then he ran up the rope of the alarm bell and got to somewhere up the wall or the ceiling – I couldn't see where, it was so dark."

"Mercy on us," said Mrs. Witham, "an old devil, and sitting on a chair by the fireside! Take care, sir! Take care! There's many a true word spoken in jest."

"How do you mean? 'Pon my word I don't understand."

"An old devil! The old devil, perhaps. There! Sir, you needn't laugh," for Malcolmson had broken into a hearty peal. "You young folks thinks it easy to laugh at things that makes older ones shudder. Never mind, sir! Never mind! Please God, you'll laugh all the time. It's what I wish you myself!" and the good lady beamed all over in sympathy with his enjoyment, her fears gone for a moment.

"Oh, forgive me!" said Malcolmson presently. "Don't think me rude; but the idea was too much for me – that the old devil himself was on the chair last night!" And at the thought he laughed again. Then he went home to dinner.

This evening the scampering of the rats began earlier; indeed it had been going on before his arrival, and only ceased whilst his presence by its freshness disturbed them. After dinner he sat by the fire for a while and had a smoke; and then, having cleared his table, began to work as before. Tonight the rats disturbed him more than they had done on the previous night. How they scampered up and down and under and over! How they squeaked, and scratched, and gnawed! How they, getting bolder by degrees, came to the mouths of their holes and to the chinks and cracks and crannies in the wainscoting till their eyes shone like tiny lamps as the firelight rose and fell. But to him, now doubtless accustomed to them, their eyes were not wicked; only their playfulness touched him. Sometimes the boldest of them made sallies out on the floor or along the mouldings of the wainscot. Now and again as they disturbed him Malcolmson made a sound to frighten them, smiting the table with his hand or giving a fierce "Hsh, hsh", so that they fled straightway to their holes.

And so the early part of the night wore on; and despite the noise Malcolmson got more and more immersed in his work.

All at once he stopped, as on the previous night, being overcome by a sudden sense of silence. There was not the faintest sound of gnaw, or scratch, or squeak. The silence was as of the grave. He remembered the odd occurrence of the previous night, and instinctively he looked at the chair standing close by the fireside. And then a very odd sensation thrilled through him.

There, on the great old high-backed carved oak chair beside the fireplace sat the same enormous rat, steadily glaring at him with baleful eyes.

Instinctively he took the nearest thing to his hand, a book of logarithms, and flung it at it. The book was badly aimed and the rat did not stir, so again the poker performance of the previous night was repeated; and again the rat, being closely pursued, fled up the rope of the alarm bell. Strangely too, the departure of this rat was instantly followed by the renewal of the noise made by the general rat community. On this occasion, as on the previous one, Malcolmson could not see at what part of the room the rat disappeared, for the green shade of his lamp left the upper part of the room in darkness, and the fire had burned low.

On looking at his watch he found it was close on midnight; and, not sorry for the divertissement, he made up his fire and made himself his nightly pot of tea. He had got through a good spell of work, and thought himself entitled to a cigarette; and so he sat on the great oak chair before the fire and enjoyed it. Whilst smoking he began to think that he would like to know where the rat disappeared to, for he had certain ideas for the morrow not entirely disconnected with a rat-trap. Accordingly he lit another lamp and placed it so that it would shine well into the right-hand corner of the wall by the fireplace. Then he got all the books he had with him, and placed them handy to throw at the vermin. Finally he lifted the rope of the alarm bell and placed the end of it on the table, fixing the extreme end under the lamp. As he handled it he could not help noticing how pliable it was, especially for so strong a rope, and one not in use. "You could hang a man with it," he thought to himself. When his preparations were made he looked around, and said complacently:

"There now, my friend, I think we shall learn something of you this time!" He began his work again, and though as before somewhat disturbed at first by the noise of the rats, soon lost himself in his propositions and problems.

Again he was called to his immediate surroundings suddenly. This time it might not have been the sudden silence only which took his attention; there was a slight movement of the rope, and the lamp moved. Without stirring, he looked to see if his pile of books was within range, and then cast his eye along the rope. As he looked he saw the great rat drop from the rope on the oak arm-chair and sit there glaring at him. He raised a book in his right hand, and taking careful aim, flung it at the rat. The latter, with a quick movement, sprang aside and dodged the missile. He then took another book, and a third, and flung them one after another at the rat, but each time unsuccessfully. At last, as he stood with a book poised in his hand to throw, the rat squeaked and seemed afraid. This made Malcolmson more than ever eager to strike, and the book flew and struck the rat a resounding blow. It gave a terrified squeak, and turning on his pursuer a look of terrible malevolence, ran up the chair-back and made a great jump to the rope of the alarm bell and ran up it like lightning. The lamp rocked under the sudden strain, but it was a heavy one and did not topple over. Malcolmson kept his eyes on the rat, and saw it by the light of the second lamp leap to a moulding of the wainscot and disappear through a hole in one of the great pictures which hung on the wall, obscured and invisible through its coating of dirt and dust.

"I shall look up my friend's habitation in the morning," said the student, as he went over to collect his books. "The third picture from the fireplace; I shall not forget." He picked up the books one by one, commenting on them as he lifted them. "Conic Sections he does not mind, nor Cycloidal Oscillations, nor the Principia, nor Quaternions, nor Thermodynamics. Now for the book that fetched him!" Malcolmson took it up and looked at it. As he did so he started, and a sudden pallor overspread his face. He looked round uneasily and shivered slightly, as he murmured to himself:

"The Bible my mother gave me! What an odd coincidence." He sat down to work again, and the rats in the wainscot renewed their gambols. They did not disturb him, however; somehow their presence gave him a sense of companionship. But he could not attend to his work, and after striving to master the subject on which he was engaged gave it up in despair, and went to bed as the first streak of dawn stole in through the eastern window.

He slept heavily but uneasily, and dreamed much; and when Mrs. Dempster woke him late in the morning he seemed ill at ease, and for a few minutes did not seem to realise exactly where he was. His first request rather surprised the servant.

"Mrs. Dempster, when I am out today I wish you would get the steps and dust or wash those pictures – specially that one the third from the fireplace – I want to see what they are."

Late in the afternoon Malcolmson worked at his books in the shaded walk, and the cheerfulness of the previous day came back to him as the day wore on, and he found that his reading was progressing well. He had worked out to a satisfactory conclusion all the problems which had as yet baffled him, and it was in a state of jubilation that he paid a visit to Mrs. Witham at 'The Good Traveller'. He found a stranger in the cosy sitting-room with the landlady, who was introduced to him as Dr. Thornhill. She was not quite at ease, and this, combined with the doctor's plunging at once into a series of questions, made Malcolmson come to the conclusion that his presence was not an accident, so without preliminary he said:

"Dr. Thornhill, I shall with pleasure answer you any question you may choose to ask me if you will answer me one question first."

The doctor seemed surprised, but he smiled and answered at once, "Done! What is it?"

"Did Mrs. Witham ask you to come here and see me and advise me?"

Dr. Thornhill for a moment was taken aback, and Mrs. Witham got fiery red and turned away; but the doctor was a frank and ready man, and he answered at once and openly.

"She did: but she didn't intend you to know it. I suppose it was my clumsy haste that made you suspect. She told me that she did not like the idea of your being in that house all by yourself, and that she thought you took too much strong tea. In fact, she wants me to advise you if possible to give up the tea and the very late hours. I was a keen student in my time, so I suppose I may take the liberty of a college man, and without offence, advise you not quite as a stranger."

Malcolmson with a bright smile held out his hand. "Shake! As they say in America," he said. "I must thank you for your kindness and Mrs. Witham too, and your kindness deserves a return on my part. I promise to take no more strong tea – no tea at all till you let me – and I shall go to bed tonight at one o'clock at latest. Will that do?"

"Capital," said the doctor. "Now tell us all that you noticed in the old house," and so Malcolmson then and there told in minute detail all that had happened in the last two nights. He was interrupted every now and then by some exclamation from Mrs. Witham, till finally when he told of the episode of the Bible the landlady's pent-up emotions found vent in a shriek; and it was not till a stiff glass of brandy and water had been administered that she grew composed again. Dr. Thornhill listened with a face of growing gravity, and when the narrative was complete and Mrs. Witham had been restored he asked:

"The rat always went up the rope of the alarm bell?"

"Always."

"I suppose you know," said the Doctor after a pause, "what the rope is?"

"No!"

"It is," said the Doctor slowly, "the very rope which the hangman used for all the victims of the Judge's judicial rancour!" Here he was interrupted by another scream from Mrs. Witham, and steps had to be taken for her recovery. Malcolmson having looked at his watch, and found that it was close to his dinner hour, had gone home before her complete recovery.

When Mrs. Witham was herself again she almost assailed the Doctor with angry questions as to what he meant by putting such horrible ideas into the poor young man's mind. "He has quite enough there already to upset him," she added. Dr. Thornhill replied:

"My dear madam, I had a distinct purpose in it! I wanted to draw his attention to the bell rope, and to fix it there. It may be that he is in a highly overwrought state, and has been studying too much, although I am bound to say that he seems as sound and healthy a young man, mentally and bodily, as ever I saw – but then the rats – and that suggestion of the devil." The doctor shook his head and went on. "I would have offered to go and stay the first night with him but that I felt sure it would have been a cause of offence. He may get in the night some strange fright or hallucination; and if he does I want him to pull that rope. All alone as he is it will give us warning, and we may reach him in time to be of service. I shall be sitting up pretty late tonight and shall keep my ears open. Do not be alarmed if Benchurch gets a surprise before morning."

"Oh, Doctor, what do you mean? What do you mean?"

"I mean this; that possibly – nay, more probably – we shall hear the great alarm bell from the Judge's House tonight," and the Doctor made about as effective an exit as could be thought of.

When Malcolmson arrived home he found that it was a little after his usual time, and Mrs. Dempster had gone away – the rules of Greenhow's Charity were not to be neglected. He was glad to see that the place was bright and tidy with a cheerful fire and a well-trimmed lamp. The evening was colder than might have been expected in April, and a heavy wind was blowing with such rapidly-increasing strength that there was every promise of a storm during the night.

For a few minutes after his entrance the noise of the rats ceased; but so soon as they became accustomed to his presence they began again. He was glad to hear them, for he felt once more the feeling of companionship in their noise, and his mind ran back to the strange fact that they only ceased to manifest themselves when that other – the great rat with the baleful eyes – came upon the scene. The reading-lamp only was lit and its green shade kept the ceiling and the upper part of the room in darkness, so that the cheerful light from the hearth spreading over the floor and shining on the white cloth laid over the end of the table was warm and cheery. Malcolmson sat down to his dinner with a good appetite and a buoyant spirit. After his dinner and a cigarette he sat steadily down to work, determined not to let anything disturb him, for he remembered his promise to the doctor, and made up his mind to make the best of the time at his disposal.

For an hour or so he worked all right, and then his thoughts began to wander from his books. The actual circumstances around him, the calls on his physical attention, and his nervous susceptibility were not to be denied. By this time the wind had become a gale, and the gale a storm. The old house, solid though it was, seemed to shake to its foundations, and the storm roared and raged through its many chimneys and its queer old gables, producing strange, unearthly sounds in the empty rooms and corridors. Even the great alarm bell on the roof must have felt the force of the wind, for the rope rose and fell slightly, as though the bell were moved a little from time to time and the limber rope fell on the oak floor with a hard and hollow sound.

As Malcolmson listened to it he bethought himself of the doctor's words, "It is the rope which the hangman used for the victims of the Judge's judicial rancour," and he went over to the corner of the fireplace and took it in his hand to look at it. There seemed a sort of deadly interest in it, and as he stood there he lost himself for a moment in speculation as to who these victims were, and the grim wish of the Judge to have such a ghastly relic ever under his eyes. As he stood there the swaying of the bell on the roof still lifted the rope now and again; but presently there came a new sensation – a sort of tremor in the rope, as though something was moving along it.

Looking up instinctively Malcolmson saw the great rat coming slowly down towards him, glaring at him steadily. He dropped the rope and started back with a muttered curse, and the rat turning ran up the rope again and disappeared, and at the same instant Malcolmson became conscious that the noise of the rats, which had ceased for a while, began again.

All this set him thinking, and it occurred to him that he had not investigated the lair of the rat or looked at the pictures, as he had intended. He lit the other lamp without the shade, and, holding it up went and stood opposite the third picture from the fireplace on the right-hand side where he had seen the rat disappear on the previous night.

At the first glance he started back so suddenly that he almost dropped the lamp, and a deadly pallor overspread his face. His knees shook, and heavy drops of sweat came on his forehead, and he trembled like an aspen. But he was young and plucky, and pulled himself together, and after the pause of a few seconds stepped forward again, raised the lamp, and examined the picture which had been dusted and washed, and now stood out clearly.

It was of a judge dressed in his robes of scarlet and ermine. His face was strong and merciless, evil, crafty, and vindictive, with a sensual mouth, hooked nose of ruddy colour, and shaped like the beak of a bird of prey. The rest of the face was of a cadaverous colour. The eyes were of peculiar brilliance and with a terribly malignant expression. As he looked at them, Malcolmson grew cold, for he saw there the very counterpart of the eyes of the great rat. The lamp almost fell from his hand, he saw the rat with its baleful eyes peering out through the hole in the corner of the picture, and noted the sudden cessation of the noise of the other rats. However, he pulled himself together, and went on with his examination of the picture.

The Judge was seated in a great high-backed carved oak chair, on the right-hand side of a great stone fireplace where, in the corner, a rope hung down from the ceiling, its end lying coiled on the floor. With a feeling of something like horror,

Malcolmson recognised the scene of the room as it stood, and gazed around him in an awestruck manner as though he expected to find some strange presence behind him. Then he looked over to the corner of the fireplace – and with a loud cry he let the lamp fall from his hand.

There, in the Judge's arm-chair, with the rope hanging behind, sat the rat with the Judge's baleful eyes, now intensified and with a fiendish leer. Save for the howling of the storm without there was silence.

The fallen lamp recalled Malcolmson to himself. Fortunately it was of metal, and so the oil was not spilt. However, the practical need of attending to it settled at once his nervous apprehensions. When he had turned it out, he wiped his brow and thought for a moment.

"This will not do," he said to himself. "If I go on like this I shall become a crazy fool. This must stop! I promised the doctor I would not take tea. Faith, he was pretty right! My nerves must have been getting into a queer state. Funny I did not notice it. I never felt better in my life. However, it is all right now, and I shall not be such a fool again."

Then he mixed himself a good stiff glass of brandy and water and resolutely sat down to his work.

It was nearly an hour when he looked up from his book, disturbed by the sudden stillness. Without, the wind howled and roared louder than ever, and the rain drove in sheets against the windows, beating like hail on the glass; but within there was no sound whatever save the echo of the wind as it roared in the great chimney, and now and then a hiss as a few raindrops found their way down the chimney in a lull of the storm. The fire had fallen low and had ceased to flame, though it threw out a red glow. Malcolmson listened attentively, and presently heard a thin, squeaking noise, very faint. It came from the corner of the room where the rope hung down, and he thought it was the creaking of the rope on the floor as the swaying of the bell raised and lowered it. Looking up, however, he saw in the dim light the great rat clinging to the rope and gnawing it. The rope was already nearly gnawed through – he could see the lighter colour where the strands were laid bare. As he looked the job was completed, and the severed end of the rope fell clattering on the oaken floor, whilst for an instant the great rat remained like a knob or tassel at the end of the rope, which now began to sway to and fro. Malcolmson felt for a moment another pang of terror as he thought that now the possibility of calling the outer world to his assistance was cut off, but an intense anger took its place, and seizing the book he was reading he hurled it at the rat.

The blow was well aimed, but before the missile could reach him the rat dropped off and struck the floor with a soft thud. Malcolmson instantly rushed over towards him, but it darted away and disappeared in the darkness of the shadows of the room. Malcolmson felt that his work was over for the night, and determined then and there to vary the monotony of the proceedings by a hunt for the rat, and took off the green shade of the lamp so as to insure a wider spreading light. As he did so the gloom of the upper part of the room was relieved, and in the new flood of light, great by comparison with the previous darkness, the pictures on the wall stood out boldly. From where he stood, Malcolmson saw right opposite to him the third picture on the wall from the right of the fireplace. He rubbed his eyes in surprise, and then a great fear began to come upon him.

In the centre of the picture was a great irregular patch of brown canvas, as fresh as when it was stretched on the frame. The background was as before, with chair and chimney-corner and rope, but the figure of the Judge had disappeared.

Malcolmson, almost in a chill of horror, turned slowly round, and then he began to shake and tremble like a man in a palsy. His strength seemed to have left him, and he was incapable of action or movement, hardly even of thought. He could only see and hear.

There, on the great high-backed carved oak chair sat the Judge in his robes of scarlet and ermine, with his baleful eyes glaring vindictively, and a smile of triumph on the resolute, cruel mouth, as he lifted with his hands a black cap. Malcolmson felt as if the blood was running from his heart, as one does in moments of prolonged suspense. There was a singing in his ears. Without, he could hear the roar and howl of the tempest, and through it, swept on the storm, came the striking of midnight by the great chimes in the market place. He stood for a space of time that seemed to him endless still as a statue, and with wide-open, horror-struck eyes, breathless. As the clock struck, so the smile of triumph on the Judge's face intensified, and at the last stroke of midnight he placed the black cap on his head.

Slowly and deliberately the Judge rose from his chair and picked up the piece of the rope of the alarm bell which lay on the floor, drew it through his hands as if he enjoyed its touch, and then deliberately began to knot one end of it, fashioning it into a noose. This he tightened and tested with his foot, pulling hard at it till he was satisfied and then making a running noose of it, which he held in his hand. Then he began to move along the table on the opposite side to Malcolmson keeping his eyes on him until he had passed him, when with a quick movement he stood in front of the door. Malcolmson then began to feel that he was trapped, and tried to think of what he should do. There was some fascination in the Judge's eyes, which he never took off him, and he had, perforce, to look. He saw the Judge approach – still keeping between him and the door – and raise the noose and throw it towards him as if to entangle him. With a great effort he made a quick movement to one side, and saw the rope fall beside him, and heard it strike the oaken floor. Again the Judge raised the noose and tried to ensnare him, ever keeping his baleful eyes fixed on him, and each time by a mighty effort the student just managed to evade it. So this went on for many times, the Judge seeming never discouraged nor discomposed at failure, but playing as a cat does with a mouse. At last in despair, which had reached its climax, Malcolmson cast a quick glance round him. The lamp seemed to have blazed up, and there was a fairly good light in the room. At the many rat-holes and in the chinks and crannies of the wainscot he saw the rats' eyes; and this aspect, that was purely physical, gave him a gleam of comfort. He looked around and saw that the rope of the great alarm bell was laden with rats. Every inch of it was covered with them, and more and more were pouring through the small circular hole in the ceiling whence it emerged, so that with their weight the bell was beginning to sway.

Hark! It had swayed till the clapper had touched the bell. The sound was but a tiny one, but the bell was only beginning to sway, and it would increase.

At the sound the Judge, who had been keeping his eyes fixed on Malcolmson, looked up, and a scowl of diabolical anger overspread his face. His eyes fairly glowed like hot coals, and he stamped his foot with a sound that seemed to make the house shake. A dreadful peal of thunder broke overhead as he raised the rope again, whilst the rats kept running up and down the rope as though working against time. This time, instead of throwing it, he drew close to his victim, and held open the noose as he approached. As he came closer there seemed something paralysing in his very presence, and Malcolmson stood rigid as a corpse. He felt the Judge's icy fingers touch his throat as he adjusted the rope. The noose tightened – tightened. Then the Judge, taking the rigid form of the student in his arms, carried him over and placed him standing in the oak chair, and stepping up beside him, put his hand up and caught the end of the swaying rope of the alarm bell. As he raised his hand the rats fled squeaking, and disappeared through the hole in the ceiling. Taking the end of the noose which was round Malcolmson's neck he tied it to the hanging-bell rope, and then descending pulled away the chair.

* * *

When the alarm bell of the Judge's House began to sound a crowd soon assembled. Lights and torches of various kinds appeared, and soon a silent crowd was hurrying to the spot. They knocked loudly at the door, but there was no reply. Then they burst in the door, and poured into the great dining-room, the doctor at the head.

There at the end of the rope of the great alarm bell hung the body of the student, and on the face of the Judge in the picture was a malignant smile.

If you enjoyed this, you might also like...
'The Chain of Destiny,' see page 10
'The Burial of the Rats,' see page 347

Crooken Sands

MR. ARTHUR FERNLEE MARKAM, who took what was known as the Red House above the Mains of Crooken, was a London merchant, and being essentially a cockney, thought it necessary when he went for the summer holidays to Scotland to provide an entire rig-out as a Highland chieftain, as manifested in chromolithographs and on the music-hall stage. He had once seen in the Empire the Great Prince – 'The Bounder King' – bring down the house by appearing as 'The MacSlogan of that Ilk,' and singing the celebrated Scotch song, 'There's naething like haggis to mak a mon dry!' and he had ever since preserved in his mind a faithful image of the picturesque and warlike appearance which he presented.

Indeed, if the true inwardness of Mr. Markam's mind on the subject of his selection of Aberdeenshire as a summer resort were known, it would be found that in the foreground of the holiday locality which his fancy painted stalked the many hued figure of the MacSlogan of that Ilk. However, be this as it may, a very kind fortune – certainly so far as external beauty was concerned – led him to the choice of Crooken Bay. It is a lovely spot, between Aberdeen and Peterhead, just under the rock-bound headland whence the long, dangerous reefs known as The Spurs run out into the North Sea. Between this and the 'Mains of Crooken' – a village sheltered by the northern cliffs – lies the deep bay, backed with a multitude of bent-grown dunes where the rabbits are to be found in thousands. Thus at either end of the bay is a rocky promontory, and when the dawn or the sunset falls on the rocks of red syenite the effect is very lovely.

The bay itself is floored with level sand and the tide runs far out, leaving a smooth waste of hard sand on which are dotted here and there the stake nets and bag nets of the salmon fishers. At one end of the bay there is a little group or cluster of rocks whose heads are raised something above high water, except when in rough weather the waves come over them green. At low tide they are exposed down to sand level; and here is perhaps the only little bit of dangerous sand on this part of the eastern coast. Between the rocks, which are apart about some fifty feet, is a small quicksand, which, like the Goodwins, is dangerous only with the incoming tide. It extends outwards till it is lost in the sea, and inwards till it fades away in the hard sand of the upper beach.

On the slope of the hill which rises beyond the dunes, midway between the Spurs and the Port of Crooken, is the Red House. It rises from the midst of a clump of fir-trees which protect it on three sides, leaving the whole sea front open. A trim old-fashioned garden stretches down to the roadway, on crossing which a grassy path, which can be used for light vehicles, threads a way to the shore, winding amongst the sand hills.

When the Markam family arrived at the Red House after their thirty-six hours of pitching on the Aberdeen steamer *Ban Righ* from Blackwall, with the subsequent train to Yellon and drive of a dozen miles, they all agreed that they had never seen a more delightful spot. The general satisfaction was more marked as at that very time none of the family were, for several reasons, inclined to find favourable anything or any place over the Scottish border. Though the family was a large one, the prosperity of the business allowed them all sorts of personal luxuries, amongst which was a wide latitude in the way of dress. The frequency of the Markam girls' new frocks was a source of envy to their bosom friends and of joy to themselves.

Arthur Fernlee Markam had not taken his family into his confidence regarding his new costume. He was not quite certain that he should be free from ridicule, or at least from sarcasm, and as he was sensitive on the subject, he thought it better to be actually in the suitable environment before he allowed the full splendour to burst upon them. He had taken some pains, to insure the completeness of the Highland costume. For the purpose he had paid many visits to 'The Scotch All-Wool Tartan Clothing Mart' which had been lately established in Copthall-court by the Messrs. MacCallum More and Roderick MacDhu. He had anxious consultations with the head of the firm – MacCallum as he called himself, resenting any such additions as 'Mr.' or 'Esquire.' The known stock of buckles, buttons, straps, brooches and ornaments of all kinds were examined in critical detail; and at last an eagle's feather of sufficiently magnificent proportions was discovered, and the equipment was complete.

It was only when he saw the finished costume, with the vivid hues of the tartan seemingly modified into comparative sobriety by the multitude of silver fittings, the cairngorm brooches, the philibeg, dirk and sporran that he was fully and absolutely satisfied with his choice. At first he had thought of the Royal Stuart dress tartan, but abandoned it on the MacCallum pointing out that if he should happen to be in the neighbourhood of Balmoral it might lead to complications. The MacCallum, who, by the way, spoke with a remarkable cockney accent, suggested other plaids in turn; but now that the other question of accuracy had been raised, Mr. Markam foresaw difficulties if he should by chance find himself in the locality of the clan whose colours he had usurped.

The MacCallum at last undertook to have, at Markam's expense, a special pattern woven which would not be exactly the same as any existing tartan, though partaking of the characteristics of many. It was based on the Royal Stuart, but contained suggestions as to simplicity of pattern from the Macalister and Ogilvie clans, and as to neutrality of colour from the clans of Buchanan, Macbeth, Chief of Macintosh and Macleod. When the specimen had been shown to Markam he had feared somewhat lest it should strike the eye of his domestic circle as gaudy; but as Roderick MacDhu fell into perfect ecstasies over its beauty he did not make any objection to the completion of the piece. He thought, and wisely, that if a genuine Scotchman like MacDhu liked it, it must be right – especially as the junior partner was a man very much of his own build and appearance. When the MacCallum was receiving his cheque – which, by the way, was a pretty stiff one – he remarked:

"I've taken the liberty of having some more of the stuff woven in case you or any of your friends should want it." Markam was gratified, and told him that he should be only too happy if the beautiful stuff which they had originated between them should become a favourite, as he had no doubt it would in time. He might make and sell as much as he would.

Markam tried the dress on in his office one evening after the clerks had all gone home. He was pleased, though a little frightened, at the result. The MacCallum had done his work thoroughly, and there was nothing omitted that could add to the martial dignity of the wearer.

"I shall not, of course, take the claymore and the pistols with me on ordinary occasions,' said Markam to himself as he began to undress. He determined that he would wear the dress for the first time on landing in Scotland, and accordingly on the morning when the *Ban Righ* was hanging off the Girdle Ness lighthouse, waiting for the tide to enter the port of Aberdeen, he emerged from his cabin in all the gaudy splendour of his new costume. The first comment he heard was from one of his own sons, who did not recognise him at first.

"Here's a guy! Great Scott! It's the governor!" And the boy fled forthwith and tried to bury his laughter under a cushion in the saloon. Markam was a good sailor and had not suffered from the pitching of the boat, so that his naturally rubicund face was even more rosy by the conscious blush which suffused his cheeks when he had found himself at once the cynosure of all eyes. He could have wished that he had not been so bold for he knew from the cold that there was a big bare spot under one side of his jauntily worn Glengarry cap. However, he faced the group of strangers boldly. He was not, outwardly, upset even when some of the comments reached his ears.

"He's off his bloomin' chump," said a cockney in a suit of exaggerated plaid.

"There's flies on him," said a tall thin Yankee, pale with sea-sickness, who was on his way to take up his residence for a time as close as he could get to the gates of Balmoral.

"Happy thought! Let us fill our mulls; now's the chance!" said a young Oxford man on his way home to Inverness. But presently Mr. Markam heard the voice of his eldest daughter.

"Where is he? Where is he?" and she came tearing along the deck with her hat blowing behind her. Her face showed signs of agitation, for her mother had just been telling her of her father's condition; but when she saw him she instantly burst into laughter so violent that it ended in a fit of hysterics. Something of the same kind happened to each of the other children. When they had all had their turn Mr. Markam went to his cabin and sent his wife's maid to tell each member of the family that he wanted to see them at once. They all made their appearance, suppressing their feelings as well as they could. He said to them very quietly:

"My dears, don't I provide you all with ample allowances?"

"Yes, father!" they all answered gravely, "no one could be more generous!"

"Don't I let you dress as you please?"

"Yes, father!" – this a little sheepishly.

"Then, my dears, don't you think it would be nicer and kinder of you not to try and make me feel uncomfortable, even if I do assume a dress which is ridiculous in your eyes, though quite common enough in the country where we are about to sojourn?' There was no answer except that which appeared in their hanging heads. He was a good father and they all knew it. He was quite satisfied and went on:

"There, now, run away and enjoy yourselves! We shan't have another word about it." Then he went on deck again and stood bravely the fire of ridicule which he recognised around him, though nothing more was said within his hearing.

The astonishment and the amusement which his get-up occasioned on the *Ban Righ* was, however, nothing to that which it created in Aberdeen. The boys and loafers, and women with babies, who waited at the landing shed, followed *en masse* as the

Markam party took their way to the railway station; even the porters with their old-fashioned knots and their new-fashioned barrows, who await the traveller at the foot of the gang-plank, followed in wondering delight. Fortunately the Peterhead train was just about to start, so that the martyrdom was not unnecessarily prolonged.

In the carriage the glorious Highland costume was unseen, and as there were but few persons at the station at Yellon, all went well there. When, however, the carriage drew near the Mains of Crooken and the fisher folk had run to their doors to see who it was that was passing, the excitement exceeded all bounds. The children with one impulse waved their bonnets and ran shouting behind the carriage; the men forsook their nets and their baiting and followed; the women clutched their babies, and followed also. The horses were tired after their long journey to Yellon and back, and the hill was steep, so that there was ample time for the crowd to gather and even to pass on ahead.

Mrs. Markam and the elder girls would have liked to make some protest or to do something to relieve their feelings of chagrin at the ridicule which they saw on all faces, but there was a look of fixed determination on the face of the seeming Highlander which awed them a little, and they were silent. It might have been that the eagle's feather, even when arising above the bald head, the cairngorm brooch even on the fat shoulder, and the claymore, dirk and pistols, even when belted round the extensive paunch and protruding from the stocking on the sturdy calf, fulfilled their existence as symbols of martial and terrifying import! When the party arrived at the gate of the Red House there awaited them a crowd of Crooken inhabitants, hatless and respectfully silent; the remainder of the population was painfully toiling up the hill. The silence was broken by only one sound, that of a man with a deep voice.

"Man! But he's forgotten the pipes!"

The servants had arrived some days before, and all things were in readiness. In the glow consequent on a good lunch after a hard journey all the disagreeables of travel and all the chagrin consequent on the adoption of the obnoxious costume were forgotten.

That afternoon Markam, still clad in full array, walked through the Mains of Crooken. He was all alone, for, strange to say, his wife and both daughters had sick headaches, and were, as he was told, lying down to rest after the fatigue of the journey. His eldest son, who claimed to be a young man, had gone out by himself to explore the surroundings of the place, and one of the boys could not be found. The other boy, on being told that his father had sent for him to come for a walk, had managed – by accident, of course – to fall into the water butt, and had to be dried and rigged out afresh. His clothes not having been as yet unpacked this was of course impossible without delay.

Mr. Markam was not quite satisfied with his walk. He could not meet any of his neighbours. It was not that there were not enough people about, for every house and cottage seemed to be full; but the people when in the open were either in their doorways some distance behind him, or on the roadway a long distance in front. As he passed he could see the tops of heads and the whites of eyes in the windows or round the corners of doors.

The only interview which he had was anything but a pleasant one. This was with an odd sort of old man who was hardly ever heard to speak except to join in the 'Amens' in the meeting-house. His sole occupation seemed to be to wait at the window of the post-office from eight o'clock in the morning till the arrival of the mail at one, when he carried the letter-bag to a neighbouring baronial castle. The remainder of his day was spent on a seat in a draughty part of the port, where the offal of the fish, the refuse of the bait, and the house rubbish was thrown, and where the ducks were accustomed to hold high revel.

When Saft Tammie beheld him coming he raised his eyes, which were generally fixed on the nothing which lay on the roadway opposite his seat, and, seeming dazzled as if by a burst of sunshine, rubbed them and shaded them with his hand. Then he started up and raised his hand aloft in a denunciatory manner as he spoke:

"'Vanity of vanities, saith the preacher. All is vanity.' Mon, be warned in time! 'Behold the lilies of the field, they toil not, neither do they spin, yet Solomon in all his glory was not arrayed like one of these.' Mon! Mon! Thy vanity is as the quicksand which swallows up all which comes within its spell. Beware vanity! Beware the quicksand, which yawneth for thee, and which will swallow thee up! See thyself! Learn thine own vanity! Meet thyself face to face, and then in that moment thou shalt learn the fatal force of thy vanity. Learn it, know it, and repent ere the quicksand swallow thee!" Then without another word he went back to his seat and sat there immovable and expressionless as before.

Markam could not but feel a little upset by this tirade. Only that it was spoken by a seeming madman, he would have put it down to some eccentric exhibition of Scottish humour or impudence; but the gravity of the message – for it seemed nothing else – made such a reading impossible. He was, however, determined not to give in to ridicule, and although he had not yet seen anything in Scotland to remind him even of a kilt, he determined to wear his Highland dress. When he returned home, in less than half-an-hour, he found that every member of the family was, despite the headaches, out taking a walk. He took the opportunity afforded by their absence of locking himself in his dressing-room, took off the Highland dress, and, putting on a suit of flannels, lit a cigar and had a snooze. He was awakened by the noise of the family coming in, and at once donning his dress made his appearance in the drawing-room for tea.

He did not go out again that afternoon; but after dinner he put on his dress again – he had, of course dressed for dinner as usual – and went by himself for a walk on the sea-shore. He had by this time come to the conclusion that he would get by degrees accustomed to the Highland dress before making it his ordinary wear. The moon was up and he easily followed the path through the sand-hills, and shortly struck the shore. The tide was out and the beach firm as a rock, so he strolled southwards to nearly the end of the bay. Here he was attracted by two isolated rocks some little way out from the edge of the dunes, so he strolled towards them. When he reached the nearest one he climbed it, and, sitting there elevated some fifteen or twenty feet over the waste of sand, enjoyed the lovely, peaceful prospect. The moon was rising behind the headland of Pennyfold, and its light was just touching the top of the furthermost rock of the Spurs some three-quarters of a mile out; the rest of the rocks were in dark shadow. As the moon rose over the headland, the rocks of the Spurs and then the beach by degrees became flooded with light.

For a good while Mr. Markam sat and looked at the rising moon and the growing area of light which followed its rise. Then he turned and faced eastwards and sat with his chin in his hand looking seawards, and revelling in the peace and beauty and freedom of the scene. The roar of London – the darkness and the strife and weariness of London life – seemed to have passed quite away, and he lived at the moment a freer and higher life. He looked at the glistening water as it stole its way over the flat waste of sand, coming closer and closer insensibly – the tide had turned. Presently he heard a distant shouting along the beach very far off.

"The fishermen calling to each other," he said to himself and looked around. As he did so he got a horrible shock, for though just then a cloud sailed across the moon he saw, in spite of the sudden darkness around him, his own image. For an instant, on the top of the opposite rock he could see the bald back of the head and the Glengarry cap with the immense eagle's feather. As he staggered back his foot slipped, and he began to slide down towards the sand between the two rocks. He took no concern as to falling, for the sand was really only a few feet below him, and his mind was occupied with the figure or simulacrum of himself, which had already disappeared.

As the easiest way of reaching *terra firma* he prepared to jump the remainder of the distance. All this had taken but a second, but the brain works quickly, and even as he gathered himself for the spring he saw the sand below him lying so marbly level shake and shiver in an odd way. A sudden fear overcame him; his knees failed, and instead of jumping he slid miserably down the rock, scratching his bare legs as he went. His feet touched the sand – went through it like water – and he was down below his knees before he realised that he was in a quicksand. Wildly he grasped at the rock to keep himself from sinking further, and fortunately there was a jutting spur or edge which he was able to grasp instinctively. To this he clung in grim desperation. He tried to shout, but his breath would not come, till after a great effort his voice rang out. Again he shouted, and it seemed as if the sound of his own voice gave him new courage, for he was able to hold on to the rock for a longer time than he thought possible – though he held on only in blind desperation. He was, however, beginning to find his grasp weakening, when, joy of joys! his shout was answered by a rough voice from just above him.

"God be thankit, I'm nae too late!" and a fisherman with great thigh-boots came hurriedly climbing over the rock. In an instant he recognised the gravity of the danger, and with a cheering "Haud fast, mon! I'm comin'!" scrambled down till he found a firm foothold. Then with one strong hand holding the rock above, he leaned down, and catching Markam's wrist, called out to him, "Haud to me, mon! Haud to me wi' ither hond!"

Then he lent his great strength, and with a steady, sturdy pull, dragged him out of the hungry quicksand and placed him safe upon the rock. Hardly giving him time to draw breath, he pulled and pushed him – never letting him go for an instant – over the rock into the firm sand beyond it, and finally deposited him, still shaking from the magnitude of his danger, high upon the beach. Then he began to speak:

"Mon! But I was just in time. If I had no laucht at yon foolish lads and begun to rin at the first you'd a bin sinkin' doon to the bowels o' the airth be the noo! Wully Beagrie thocht you was a ghaist, and Tom MacPhail swore ye was only like a goblin on a puddick-steel! 'Na!' said I. 'Yon's but the daft Englishman – the loony that had escapit frae the waxworks.' I was thinkin' that bein' strange and silly – if not a whole-made feel – ye'd no ken the ways o' the quicksan'! I shouted till warn ye, and then ran to drag ye aff, if need be. But God be thankit, be ye fule or only half-daft wi' yer vanity, that I was no that late!" and he reverently lifted his cap as he spoke.

Mr. Markam was deeply touched and thankful for his escape from a horrible death; but the sting of the charge of vanity thus made once more against him came through his humility. He was about to reply angrily, when suddenly a great awe fell upon him as he remembered the warning words of the half-crazy letter-carrier: "Meet thyself face to face, and repent ere the quicksand shall swallow thee!"

Here, too, he remembered the image of himself that he had seen and the sudden danger from the deadly quicksand that had followed. He was silent a full minute, and then said:

"My good fellow, I owe you my life!"

The answer came with reverence from the hardy fisherman, "Na! Na! Ye owe that to God; but, as for me, I'm only too glad till be the humble instrument o' His mercy."

"But you will let me thank you," said Mr. Markam, taking both the great hands of his deliverer in his and holding them tight. "My heart is too full as yet, and my nerves are too much shaken to let me say much; but, believe me, I am very, very grateful!" It was quite evident that the poor old fellow was deeply touched, for the tears were running down his cheeks.

The fisherman said, with a rough but true courtesy:

"Ay, sir! Thank me and ye will – if it'll do yer poor heart good. An' I'm thinking that if it were me I'd be thankful too. But, sir, as for me I need no thanks. I am glad, so I am!"

That Arthur Fernlee Markam was really thankful and grateful was shown practically later on. Within a week's time there sailed into Port Crooken the finest fishing smack that had ever been seen in the harbour of Peterhead. She was fully found with sails and gear of all kinds, and with nets of the best. Her master and men went away by the coach, after having left with the salmon-fisher's wife the papers which made her over to him.

As Mr. Markam and the salmon-fisher walked together along the shore the former asked his companion not to mention the fact that he had been in such imminent danger, for that it would only distress his dear wife and children. He said that he would warn them all of the quicksand, and for that purpose he, then and there, asked questions about it till he felt that his information on the subject was complete. Before they parted he asked his companion if he had happened to see a second figure, dressed like himself on the other rock as he had approached to succour him.

"Na! Na!" came the answer, "There is nae sic another fule in these parts. Nor has there been since the time o' Jamie Fleeman – him that was fule to the Laird o' Udny. Why, mon! Sic a heathenish dress as ye have on till ye has nae been seen in these pairts within the memory o' mon. An' I'm thinkin' that sic a dress never was for sittin' on the cauld rock, as ye done beyont. Mon! But do ye no fear the rheumatism or the lumbagy wi' floppin' doon on to the cauld stanes wi' yer bare flesh? I was thinking that it was daft ye waur when I see ye the mornin' doon be the port, but it's fule or eediot ye maun be for the like o' thot!"

Mr. Markam did not care to argue the point, and as they were now close to his own home he asked the salmon-fisher to have a glass of whisky – which he did – and they parted for the night. He took good care to warn all his family of the quicksand, telling them that he had himself been in some danger from it.

All that night he never slept. He heard the hours strike one after the other; but try how he would he could not get to sleep. Over and over again he went through the horrible episode of the quicksand, from the time that Saft Tammie had broken his habitual silence to preach to him of the sin of vanity and to warn him. The question kept ever arising in his mind: "Am I then so vain as to be in the ranks of the foolish?" and the answer ever came in the words of the crazy prophet: "'Vanity of vanities! All is vanity.' Meet thyself face to face, and repent ere the quicksand shall swallow thee!" Somehow a feeling of doom began to shape itself in his mind that he would yet perish in that same quicksand, for there he had already met himself face to face.

In the grey of the morning he dozed off, but it was evident that he continued the subject in his dreams, for he was fully awakened by his wife, who said:

"Do sleep quietly! That blessed Highland suit has got on your brain. Don't talk in your sleep, if you can help it!" He was somehow conscious of a glad feeling, as if some terrible weight had been lifted from him, but he did not know any cause of it. He asked his wife what he had said in his sleep, and she answered:

"You said it often enough, goodness knows, for one to remember it – 'Not face to face! I saw the eagle plume over the bald head! There is hope yet! Not face to face!' Go to sleep! Do!" And then he did go to sleep, for he seemed to realise that the prophecy of the crazy man had not yet been fulfilled. He had not met himself face to face – as yet at all events.

He was awakened early by a maid who came to tell him that there was a fisherman at the door who wanted to see him. He dressed himself as quickly as he could – for he was not yet expert with the Highland dress – and hurried down, not wishing to keep the salmon-fisher waiting. He was surprised and not altogether pleased to find that his visitor was none other than Saft Tammie, who at once opened fire on him:

"I maun gang awa' t' the post; but I thocht that I would waste an hour on ye, and ca' roond just to see if ye waur still that fou wi' vanity as on the nicht gane by. An I see that ye've no learned the lesson. Well! The time is comin', sure eneucht! However I have all the time i' the marnins to my ain sel', so I'll aye look roond jist till see how ye gang yer ain gait to the quicksan', and then to the de'il! I'm aff till ma wark the noo!"

And he went straightway, leaving Mr. Markam considerably vexed, for the maids within earshot were vainly trying to conceal their giggles. He had fairly made up his mind to wear on that day ordinary clothes, but the visit of Saft Tammie reversed his decision. He would show them all that he was not a coward, and he would go on as he had begun – come what might. When he came to breakfast in full martial panoply the children, one and all, held down their heads and the backs of their necks became very red indeed. As, however, none of them laughed – except Titus, the youngest boy, who was seized with a fit of hysterical choking and was promptly banished from the room – he could not reprove them, but began to break his egg with a sternly determined air. It was unfortunate that as his wife was handing him a cup of tea one of the buttons of his sleeve caught in the lace of her morning wrapper, with the result that the hot tea was spilt over his bare knees. Not unnaturally, he made use of a swear word, whereupon his wife, somewhat nettled, spoke out:

"Well, Arthur, if you will make such an idiot of yourself with that ridiculous costume what else can you expect? You are not accustomed to it – and you never will be!" In answer he began an indignant speech with: "Madam!" but he got no further, for now that the subject was broached, Mrs. Markam intended to have her say out. It was not a pleasant say, and, truth to tell, it was not said in a pleasant manner. A wife's manner seldom is pleasant when she undertakes to tell what she considers 'truths' to her husband. The result was that Arthur Fernlee Markam undertook, then and there, that during his stay in Scotland he would wear no other costume than the one she abused. Woman-like his wife had the last word – given in this case with tears:

"Very well, Arthur! Of course you will do as you choose. Make me as ridiculous as you can, and spoil the poor girls' chances in life. Young men don't seem to care, as a general rule, for an idiot father-in-law! But I must warn you that your vanity will some day get a rude shock – if indeed you are not before then in an asylum or dead!"

It was manifest after a few days that Mr. Markam would have to take the major part of his outdoor exercise by himself. The girls now and again took a walk with him, chiefly in the early morning or late at night, or on a wet day when there would be no one about; they professed to be willing to go out at all times, but somehow something always seemed to occur to prevent it. The boys could never be found at all on such occasions, and as to Mrs. Markam she sternly refused to go out with him on any consideration so long as he should continue to make a fool of himself. On the Sunday he dressed himself in his habitual broadcloth, for he rightly felt that church was not a place for angry feelings; but on Monday morning he resumed his Highland garb. By this time he would have given a good deal if he had never thought of the dress, but his British obstinacy was strong, and he would not give in. Saft Tammie called at his house every morning, and, not being able to see him nor to have any message taken to him, used to call back in the afternoon when the letter-bag had been delivered and watched for his going out. On such occasions he never failed to warn him against his vanity in the same words which he had used at the first. Before many days were over Mr. Markam had come to look upon him as little short of a scourge.

By the time the week was out the enforced partial solitude, the constant chagrin, and the never-ending brooding which was thus engendered, began to make Mr. Markam quite ill. He was too proud to take any of his family into his confidence since they had in his view treated him very badly. Then he did not sleep well at night, and when he did sleep he had constantly bad dreams. Merely to assure himself that his pluck was not failing him he made it a practice to visit the quicksand at least once every day; he hardly ever failed to go there the last thing at night. It was perhaps this habit that wrought the quicksand with its terrible experience so perpetually into his dreams. More and more vivid these became, till on waking at times he could hardly realise that he had not been actually in the flesh to visit the fatal spot. He sometimes thought that he might have been walking in his sleep.

One night his dream was so vivid that when he awoke he could not believe that it had only been a dream. He shut his eyes again and again, but each time the vision, if it was a vision, or the reality, if it was a reality, would rise before him. The moon was shining full and yellow over the quicksand as he approached it; he could see the expanse of light shaken and disturbed and full of black shadows as the liquid sand quivered and trembled and wrinkled and eddied as was its wont between its pauses of marble calm. As he drew close to it another figure came towards it from the opposite side with equal footsteps. He saw that it was his own figure, his very self, and in silent terror, compelled by what force he knew not, he advanced – charmed as the bird is by the snake, mesmerised or hypnotised – to meet this other self. As he felt the yielding sand closing over him he awoke in the agony of death, trembling with fear, and, strange to say, with the silly man's prophecy seeming to sound in his ears: "'Vanity of vanities! All is vanity!' See thyself and repent ere the quicksand swallow thee!"

So convinced was he that this was no dream that he arose, early as it was, and dressing himself without disturbing his wife took his way to the shore. His heart fell when he came across a series of footsteps on the sands, which he at once recognised as his own. There was the same wide heel, the same square toe; he had no doubt now that he had actually been there, and half horrified, and half in a state of dreamy stupor, he followed the footsteps, and found them lost in the edge of the yielding quicksand. This gave him a terrible shock, for there were no return steps marked on the sand, and he felt that there was some dread mystery which he could not penetrate, and the penetration of which would, he feared, undo him.

In this state of affairs he took two wrong courses. Firstly he kept his trouble to himself, and, as none of his family had any clue to it, every innocent word or expression which they used supplied fuel to the consuming fire of his imagination. Secondly he began to read books professing to bear upon the mysteries of dreaming and of mental phenomena generally, with the result that every wild imagination of every crank or half-crazy philosopher became a living germ of unrest in the fertilising soil of his disordered brain. Thus negatively and positively all things began to work to a common end. Not the least of his disturbing causes was Saft Tammie, who had now become at certain times of the day a fixture at his gate. After a while, being interested in the previous state of this individual, he made inquiries regarding his past with the following result.

Saft Tammie was popularly believed to be the son of a laird in one of the counties round the Firth of Forth. He had been partially educated for the ministry, but for some cause which no one ever knew threw up his prospects suddenly, and, going to Peterhead in its days of whaling prosperity, had there taken service on a whaler. Here off and on he had remained for some years, getting gradually more and more silent in his habits, till finally his shipmates protested against so taciturn a mate, and he had found service amongst the fishing smacks of the northern fleet. He had worked for many years at the fishing with always the reputation of being 'a wee bit daft,' till at length he had gradually settled down at Crooken, where the laird, doubtless knowing something of his family history, had given him a job which practically made him a pensioner. The minister who gave the information finished thus:

"It is a very strange thing, but the man seems to have some odd kind of gift. Whether it be that 'second sight' which we Scotch people are so prone to believe in, or some other occult form of knowledge, I know not, but nothing of a disastrous tendency ever occurs in this place but the men with whom he lives are able to quote after the event some saying of his which certainly appears to have foretold it. He gets uneasy or excited – wakes up, in fact – when death is in the air!"

This did not in any way tend to lessen Mr. Markam's concern, but on the contrary seemed to impress the prophecy more deeply on his mind. Of all the books which he had read on his new subject of study none interested him so much as a German one *Die Döppleganger*, by Dr. Heinrich von Aschenberg, formerly of Bonn. Here he learned for the first time of cases where men had led a double existence – each nature being quite apart from the other – the body being always a reality with one spirit, and a simulacrum with the other.

Needless to say that Mr. Markam realised this theory as exactly suiting his own case. The glimpse which he had of his own back the night of his escape from the quicksand – his own footmarks disappearing into the quicksand with no return steps visible – the prophecy of Saft Tammie about his meeting himself and perishing in the quicksand – all lent aid to the conviction that he was in his own person an instance of the döppleganger. Being then conscious of a double life he took steps to prove its existence to his own satisfaction. To this end on one night before going to bed he wrote his name in chalk on the soles of his shoes. That night he dreamed of the quicksand, and of his visiting it – dreamed so vividly that on walking in the grey of the dawn he could not believe that he had not been there. Arising, without disturbing his wife, he sought his shoes.

The chalk signatures were undisturbed! He dressed himself and stole out softly. This time the tide was in, so he crossed the dunes and struck the shore on the further side of the quicksand. There, oh, horror of horrors! he saw his own footprints dying into the abyss!

He went home a desperately sad man. It seemed incredible that he, an elderly commercial man, who had passed a long and uneventful life in the pursuit of business in the midst of roaring, practical London, should thus find himself enmeshed in mystery and horror, and that he should discover that he had two existences. He could not speak of his trouble even to his own wife, for well he knew that she would at once require the fullest particulars of that other life – the one which she did not know; and that she would at the start not only imagine but charge him with all manner of infidelities on the head of it. And so his brooding grew deeper and deeper still.

One evening – the tide then going out and the moon being at the full – he was sitting waiting for dinner when the maid announced that Saft Tammie was making a disturbance outside because he would not be let in to see him. He was very indignant, but did not like the maid to think that he had any fear on the subject, and so told her to bring him in. Tammie entered, walking more briskly than ever with his head up and a look of vigorous decision in the eyes that were so generally cast down. As soon as he entered he said:

"I have come to see ye once again – once again; and there ye sit, still just like a cockatoo on a pairch. Weel, mon, I forgie ye! Mind ye that, I forgie ye!" And without a word more he turned and walked out of the house, leaving the master in speechless indignation.

After dinner he determined to pay another visit to the quicksand – he would not allow even to himself that he was afraid to go. And so, about nine o'clock, in full array, he marched to the beach, and passing over the sands sat on the skirt of the nearer rock. The full moon was behind him and its light lit up the bay so that its fringe of foam, the dark outline of the headland, and the stakes of the salmon-nets were all emphasised. In the brilliant yellow glow the lights in the windows of Port Crooken and in those of the distant castle of the laird trembled like stars through the sky.

For a long time he sat and drank in the beauty of the scene, and his soul seemed to feel a peace that it had not known for many days. All the pettiness and annoyance and silly fears of the past weeks seemed blotted out, and a new holy calm took the vacant place. In this sweet and solemn mood he reviewed his late action calmly, and felt ashamed of himself for his vanity and for the obstinacy which had followed it. And then and there he made up his mind that the present would be the last time he would wear the costume which had estranged him from those whom he loved, and which had caused him so many hours and days of chagrin, vexation, and pain.

But almost as soon as he arrived at this conclusion another voice seemed to speak within him and mockingly to ask him if he should ever get the chance to wear the suit again – that it was too late – he had chosen his course and must now abide the issue.

"It is not too late," came the quick answer of his better self; and full of the thought, he rose up to go home and divest himself of the now hateful costume right away. He paused for one look at the beautiful scene. The light lay pale and mellow, softening every outline of rock and tree and house-top, and deepening the shadows into velvety-black, and lighting, as with a pale flame, the incoming tide, that now crept fringe-like across the flat waste of sand. Then he left the rock and stepped out for the shore.

But as he did so a frightful spasm of horror shook him, and for an instant the blood rushing to his head shut out all the light of the full moon. Once more he saw that fatal image of himself moving beyond the quicksand from the opposite rock to the shore. The shock was all the greater for the contrast with the spell of peace which he had just enjoyed; and, almost paralysed in every sense, he stood and watched the fatal vision and the wrinkly, crawling quicksand that seemed to writhe and yearn for something that lay between.

There could be no mistake this time, for though the moon behind threw the face into shadow he could see there the same shaven cheeks as his own, and the small stubby moustache of a few weeks' growth. The light shone on the brilliant tartan, and on the eagle's plume. Even the bald space at one side of the Glengarry cap glistened, as did the cairngorm brooch on the shoulder and the tops of the silver buttons. As he looked he felt his feet slightly sinking, for he was still near the edge of the belt of quicksand, and he stepped back. As he did so the other figure stepped forward, so that the space between them was preserved.

So the two stood facing each other, as though in some weird fascination; and in the rushing of the blood through his brain Markam seemed to hear the words of the prophecy: "See thyself face to face, and repent ere the quicksand swallow thee." He did stand face to face with himself, he had repented – and now he was sinking in the quicksand! The warning and prophecy were coming true.

Above him the seagulls screamed, circling round the fringe of the incoming tide, and the sound being entirely mortal recalled him to himself. On the instant he stepped back a few quick steps, for as yet only his feet were merged in the soft sand. As he did so the other figure stepped forward, and coming within the deadly grip of the quicksand began to sink. It seemed to Markam that he was looking at himself going down to his doom, and on the instant the anguish of his soul found vent in a terrible cry. There was at the same instant a terrible cry from the other figure, and as Markam threw up his hands the figure did the same.

With horror-struck eyes he saw him sink deeper into the quicksand; and then, impelled by what power he knew not, he advanced again towards the sand to meet his fate. But as his more forward foot began to sink he heard again the cries of the seagulls which seemed to restore his benumbed faculties. With a mighty effort he drew his foot out of the sand which seemed to clutch it, leaving his shoe behind, and then in sheer terror he turned and ran from the place, never stopping till his breath and strength failed him, and he sank half swooning on the grassy path through the sandhills.

* * *

Arthur Markam made up his mind not to tell his family of his terrible adventure – until at least such time as he should be complete master of himself. Now that the fatal double – his other self – had been engulfed in the quicksand he felt something like his old peace of mind.

That night he slept soundly and did not dream at all; and in the morning was quite his old self. It really seemed as though his newer and worser self had disappeared for ever; and strangely enough Saft Tammie was absent from his post that morning and never appeared there again, but sat in his old place watching nothing, as of old, with lack-lustre eye. In accordance with his resolution he did not wear his Highland suit again, but one evening tied it up in a bundle, claymore, dirk and philibeg and all, and bringing it secretly with him threw it into the quicksand. With a feeling of intense pleasure he saw it sucked below the sand, which closed above it into marble smoothness. Then he went home and announced cheerily to his family assembled for evening prayers:

"Well! my dears, you will be glad to hear that I have abandoned my idea of wearing the Highland dress. I see now what a vain old fool I was and how ridiculous I made myself! You shall never see it again!"

"Where is it, father?" asked one of the girls, wishing to say something so that such a self-sacrificing announcement as her father's should not be passed in absolute silence. His answer was so sweetly given that the girl rose from her seat and came and kissed him. It was:

"In the quicksand, my dear! And I hope that my worser self is buried there along with it – for ever."

* * *

The remainder of the summer was passed at Crooken with delight by all the family, and on his return to town Mr. Markam had almost forgotten the whole of the incident of the quicksand, and all touching on it, when one day he got a letter from the MacCallum More which caused him much thought, though he said nothing of it to his family, and left it, for certain reasons, unanswered. It ran as follows:

The MacCallum More and Roderick MacDhu.
The Scotch All-Wool Tartan Clothing Mart.
Copthall Court, E.C.,
30th September, 1892.

Dear Sir,

I trust you will pardon the liberty which I take in writing to you, but I am desirous of making an inquiry, and I am informed that you have been sojourning during the summer in Aberdeenshire (Scotland, N.B.). My partner, Mr. Roderick MacDhu – as he appears for business reasons on our bill-heads and in our advertisements, his real name being Emmanuel Moses Marks of London – went early last month to Scotland (N.B.) for a tour, but as I have only once heard from him, shortly after his departure, I am anxious lest any misfortune may have befallen him. As I have been unable to obtain any news of him on making all inquiries in my power, I venture to appeal to you. His letter was written in deep dejection of spirit, and mentioned that he feared a judgment had come upon him for wishing to appear as a Scotchman on Scottish soil, as he had one moonlight night shortly after his arrival seen his 'wraith'.

He evidently alluded to the fact that before his departure he had procured for himself a Highland costume similar to that which we had the honour to supply to you, with which, as perhaps you will remember, he was much struck. He may, however, never have worn it, as he was, to my own knowledge, diffident about putting it on, and even went so far as to tell me that he would at first only venture to wear it late at night or very early in the morning, and then only in remote places, until such time as he should get accustomed to it.

Unfortunately he did not advise me of his route so that I am in complete ignorance of his whereabouts; and I venture to ask if you may have seen or heard of a Highland costume similar to your own having been seen anywhere in the neighbourhood in which I am told you have recently purchased the estate which you temporarily occupied. I shall not expect an answer to this letter unless you can give me some information regarding my friend and partner, so pray do not trouble to reply unless there be cause. I am encouraged to think that he may have been in your neighbourhood as, though his letter is not dated, the envelope is marked with the postmark of 'Yellon' which I find is in Aberdeenshire, and not far from the Mains of Crooken.

I have the honour to be, dear sir,
Yours very respectfully,
Joshua Sheeny Cohen Benjamin
(The MacCallum More.)

If you enjoyed this, you might also like...
The Jewel of Seven Stars, see page 117
'The Gipsy Prophecy,' see page 296

Dracula's Guest

WHEN WE STARTED for our drive the sun was shining brightly on Munich, and the air was full of the joyousness of early summer. Just as we were about to depart, Herr Delbruck (the maitre d'hotel of the Quatre Saisons, where I was staying) came down bareheaded to the carriage and, after wishing me a pleasant drive, said to the coachman, still holding his hand on the handle of the carriage door, "Remember you are back by nightfall. The sky looks bright but there is a shiver in the north wind that says there may be a sudden storm. But I am sure you will not be late." Here he smiled and added, "for you know what night it is."

Johann answered with an emphatic, "Ja, mein Herr," and, touching his hat, drove off quickly. When we had cleared the town, I said, after signalling to him to stop:

"Tell me, Johann, what is tonight?"

He crossed himself, as he answered laconically: "Walpurgis nacht." Then he took out his watch, a great, old-fashioned German silver thing as big as a turnip and looked at it, with his eyebrows gathered together and a little impatient shrug of his shoulders. I realized that this was his way of respectfully protesting against the unnecessary delay and sank back in the carriage, merely motioning him to proceed. He started off rapidly, as if to make up for lost time. Every now and then the horses seemed to throw up their heads and sniff the air suspiciously. On such occasions I often looked round in alarm. The road was pretty bleak, for we were traversing a sort of high windswept plateau. As we drove, I saw a road that looked but little used and which seemed to dip through a little winding valley. It looked so inviting that, even at the risk of offending him, I called Johann to stop – and when he had pulled up, I told him I would like to drive down that road. He made all sorts of excuses and frequently crossed himself as he spoke. This somewhat piqued my curiosity, so I asked him various questions. He answered fencingly and repeatedly looked at his watch in protest.

Finally I said, "Well, Johann, I want to go down this road. I shall not ask you to come unless you like; but tell me why you do not like to go, that is all I ask." For answer he seemed to throw himself off the box, so quickly did he reach the ground. Then he stretched out his hands appealingly to me and implored me not to go. There was just enough of English mixed with the German for me to understand the drift of his talk. He seemed always just about to tell me something – the very idea of which evidently frightened him; but each time he pulled himself up saying, "Walpurgis nacht!"

I tried to argue with him, but it was difficult to argue with a man when I did not know his language. The advantage certainly rested with him, for although he began to speak in English, of a very crude and broken kind, he always got excited and broke into his native tongue – and every time he did so, he looked at his watch. Then the horses became restless and sniffed the air. At this he grew very pale, and, looking around in a frightened way, he suddenly jumped forward, took them by the bridles, and led them on some twenty feet. I followed and asked why he had done this. For an answer he crossed himself, pointed to the spot we had left, and drew his carriage in the direction of the other road, indicating a cross, and said, first in German, then in English, "Buried him – him what killed themselves."

I remembered the old custom of burying suicides at cross roads: "Ah! I see, a suicide. How interesting!" But for the life of me I could not make out why the horses were frightened.

Whilst we were talking, we heard a sort of sound between a yelp and a bark. It was far away; but the horses got very restless, and it took Johann all his time to quiet them. He was pale and said, "It sounds like a wolf – but yet there are no wolves here now."

"No?" I said, questioning him. "Isn't it long since the wolves were so near the city?"

"Long, long," he answered, "in the spring and summer; but with the snow the wolves have been here not so long."

Whilst he was petting the horses and trying to quiet them, dark clouds drifted rapidly across the sky. The sunshine passed away, and a breath of cold wind seemed to drift over us. It was only a breath, however, and more of a warning than a fact, for the sun came out brightly again.

Johann looked under his lifted hand at the horizon and said, "The storm of snow, he comes before long time." Then he looked at his watch again, and, straightway holding his reins firmly – for the horses were still pawing the ground restlessly and shaking their heads – he climbed to his box as though the time had come for proceeding on our journey.

I felt a little obstinate and did not at once get into the carriage.

"Tell me," I said, "about this place where the road leads," and I pointed down.

Again he crossed himself and mumbled a prayer before he answered, "It is unholy."

"What is unholy?" I enquired.

"The village."

"Then there is a village?"

"No, no. No one lives there hundreds of years."

My curiosity was piqued, "But you said there was a village."

"There was."

"Where is it now?"

Whereupon he burst out into a long story in German and English, so mixed up that I could not quite understand exactly what he said. Roughly I gathered that long ago, hundreds of years, men had died there and been buried in their graves; but sounds were heard under the clay, and when the graves were opened, men and women were found rosy with life and their mouths red with blood. And so, in haste to save their lives (aye, and their souls! – and here he crossed himself) those who were left fled away to other places, where the living lived and the dead were dead and not – not something. He was evidently afraid to speak the last words. As he proceeded with his narration, he grew more and more excited. It seemed as if his imagination had got hold of him, and he ended in a perfect paroxysm of fear – white-faced, perspiring, trembling, and looking round him as if expecting that some dreadful presence would manifest itself there in the bright sunshine on the open plain.

Finally, in an agony of desperation, he cried, "Walpurgis nacht!" and pointed to the carriage for me to get in.

All my English blood rose at this, and standing back I said, "You are afraid, Johann – you are afraid. Go home, I shall return alone, the walk will do me good." The carriage door was open. I took from the seat my oak walking stick – which I always carry on my holiday excursions – and closed the door, pointing back to Munich, and said, "Go home, Johann – Walpurgis nacht doesn't concern Englishmen."

The horses were now more restive than ever, and Johann was trying to hold them in, while excitedly imploring me not to do anything so foolish. I pitied the poor fellow, he was so deeply in earnest; but all the same I could not help laughing. His English was quite gone now. In his anxiety he had forgotten that his only means of making me understand was to talk my language, so he jabbered away in his native German. It began to be a little tedious. After giving the direction, "Home!" I turned to go down the cross road into the valley.

With a despairing gesture, Johann turned his horses towards Munich. I leaned on my stick and looked after him. He went slowly along the road for a while, then there came over the crest of the hill a man tall and thin. I could see so much in the distance. When he drew near the horses, they began to jump and kick about, then to scream with terror. Johann could not hold them in; they bolted down the road, running away madly. I watched them out of sight, then looked for the stranger; but I found that he, too, was gone.

With a light heart I turned down the side road through the deepening valley to which Johann had objected. There was not the slightest reason, that I could see, for his objection; and I daresay I tramped for a couple of hours without thinking of time or distance and certainly without seeing a person or a house. So far as the place was concerned, it was desolation itself. But I did not notice this particularly till, on turning a bend in the road, I came upon a scattered fringe of wood; then I recognized that I had been impressed unconsciously by the desolation of the region through which I had passed.

I sat down to rest myself and began to look around. It struck me that it was considerably colder than it had been at the commencement of my walk – a sort of sighing sound seemed to be around me with, now and then, high overhead, a sort of muffled roar. Looking upwards I noticed that great thick clouds were drafting rapidly across the sky from north to south at a great height. There were signs of a coming storm in some lofty stratum of the air. I was a little chilly, and, thinking that it was the sitting still after the exercise of walking, I resumed my journey.

The ground I passed over was now much more picturesque. There were no striking objects that the eye might single out, but in all there was a charm of beauty. I took little heed of time, and it was only when the deepening twilight forced itself upon me that I began to think of how I should find my way home. The air was cold, and the drifting of clouds high overhead was more marked. They were accompanied by a sort of far away rushing sound, through which seemed to come at intervals that mysterious cry which the driver had said came from a wolf. For a while I hesitated. I had said I would see the deserted village, so on I went and presently came on a wide stretch of open country, shut in by hills all around. Their sides were covered with trees which spread down to the plain, dotting in clumps the gentler slopes and hollows which showed here and there. I followed with my eye the winding of the road and saw that it curved close to one of the densest of these clumps and was lost behind it.

As I looked there came a cold shiver in the air, and the snow began to fall. I thought of the miles and miles of bleak country I had passed, and then hurried on to seek shelter of the wood in front. Darker and darker grew the sky, and faster and heavier fell the snow, till the earth before and around me was a glistening white carpet the further edge of which was lost in misty vagueness. The road was here but crude, and when on the level its boundaries were not so marked as when it passed through the cuttings; and in a little while I found that I must have strayed from it, for I missed underfoot the hard surface, and my feet sank deeper in the grass and moss. Then the wind grew stronger and blew with ever increasing force, till I was fain to run before it. The air became icy-cold, and in spite of my exercise I began to suffer. The snow was now falling so thickly and whirling around me in such rapid eddies that I could hardly keep my eyes open. Every now and then the heavens were torn asunder by vivid lightning, and in the flashes I could see ahead of me a great mass of trees, chiefly yew and cypress all heavily coated with snow.

I was soon amongst the shelter of the trees, and there in comparative silence I could hear the rush of the wind high overhead. Presently the blackness of the storm had become merged in the darkness of the night. By-and-by the storm seemed to be passing away, it now only came in fierce puffs or blasts. At such moments the weird sound of the wolf appeared to be echoed by many similar sounds around me.

Now and again, through the black mass of drifting cloud, came a straggling ray of moonlight which lit up the expanse and showed me that I was at the edge of a dense mass of cypress and yew trees. As the snow had ceased to fall, I walked out from the shelter and began to investigate more closely. It appeared to me that, amongst so many old foundations as I had passed, there might be still standing a house in which, though in ruins, I could find some sort of shelter for a while. As I skirted the edge of the copse, I found that a low wall encircled it, and following this I presently found an opening. Here the cypresses formed an alley leading up to a square mass of some kind of building. Just as I caught sight of this, however, the drifting clouds obscured the moon, and I passed up the path in darkness. The wind must have grown colder, for I felt myself shiver as I walked; but there was hope of shelter, and I groped my way blindly on.

I stopped, for there was a sudden stillness. The storm had passed; and, perhaps in sympathy with nature's silence, my heart seemed to cease to beat. But this was only momentarily; for suddenly the moonlight broke through the clouds showing me that I was in a graveyard and that the square object before me was a great massive tomb of marble, as white as the snow that lay on and all around it. With the moonlight there came a fierce sigh of the storm which appeared to resume its course with a long, low howl, as of many dogs or wolves.I was awed and shocked, and I felt the cold perceptibly grow upon me till it seemed to grip me by the heart. Then while the flood of moonlight still fell on the marble tomb, the storm gave further evidence of renewing, as though it were returning on its track. Impelled by some sort of fascination, I approached the sepulchre to see what it was and why such a thing stood alone in such a place. I walked around it and read, over the Doric door, in German:

COUNTESS DOLINGEN OF GRATZ
IN STYRIA
SOUGHT AND FOUND DEATH
1801

On the top of the tomb, seemingly driven through the solid marble – for the structure was composed of a few vast blocks of stone – was a great iron spike or stake. On going to the back I saw, graven in great Russian letters: 'The dead travel fast.'

There was something so weird and uncanny about the whole thing that it gave me a turn and made me feel quite faint. I began to wish, for the first time, that I had taken Johann's advice. Here a thought struck me, which came under almost mysterious circumstances and with a terrible shock. This was Walpurgis Night!

Walpurgis Night was when, according to the belief of millions of people, the devil was abroad – when the graves were opened and the dead came forth and walked. When all evil things of earth and air and water held revel. This very place the driver had specially shunned. This was the depopulated village of centuries ago. This was where the suicide lay; and this was the place where I was alone – unmanned, shivering with cold in a shroud of snow with a wild storm gathering again upon me! It took all my philosophy, all the religion I had been taught, all my courage, not to collapse in a paroxysm of fright.

And now a perfect tornado burst upon me. The ground shook as though thousands of horses thundered across it; and this time the storm bore on its icy wings, not snow, but great hailstones which drove with such violence that they might have come from the thongs of Balearic slingers – hailstones that beat down leaf and branch and made the shelter of the cypresses of no more avail than though their stems were standing corn. At the first I had rushed to the nearest tree; but I was soon fain to leave it and seek the only spot that seemed to afford refuge, the deep Doric doorway of the marble tomb. There, crouching against the massive bronze door, I gained a certain amount of protection from the beating of the hailstones, for now they only drove against me as they ricocheted from the ground and the side of the marble.

As I leaned against the door, it moved slightly and opened inwards. The shelter of even a tomb was welcome in that pitiless tempest and I was about to enter it when there came a flash of forked lightning that lit up the whole expanse of the heavens. In the instant, as I am a living man, I saw, as my eyes turned into the darkness of the tomb, a beautiful woman with rounded cheeks and red lips, seemingly sleeping on a bier. As the thunder broke overhead, I was grasped as by the hand of a giant and hurled out into the storm. The whole thing was so sudden that, before I could realize the shock, moral as well as physical, I found the hailstones beating me down. At the same time I had a strange, dominating feeling that I was not alone. I looked towards the tomb. Just then there came another blinding flash which seemed to strike the iron stake that surmounted the tomb and to pour through to the earth, blasting and crumbling the marble, as in a burst of flame. The dead woman rose for a moment of agony while she was lapped in the flame, and her bitter scream of pain was drowned in the thunder-crash. The last thing I heard was this mingling of dreadful sound, as again I was seized in the giant grasp and dragged away, while the hailstones beat on me and the air around seemed reverberant with the howling of wolves. The last sight that I remembered was a vague, white, moving mass, as if all the graves around me had sent out the phantoms of their sheeted dead, and that they were closing in on me through the white cloudiness of the driving hail.

Gradually there came a sort of vague beginning of consciousness, then a sense of weariness that was dreadful. For a time I remembered nothing, but slowly my senses returned. My feet seemed positively racked with pain, yet I could not move them.

They seemed to be numbed. There was an icy feeling at the back of my neck and all down my spine, and my ears, like my feet, were dead yet in torment; but there was in my breast a sense of warmth which was by comparison delicious. It was as a nightmare – a physical nightmare, if one may use such an expression; for some heavy weight on my chest made it difficult for me to breathe.

This period of semilethargy seemed to remain a long time, and as it faded away I must have slept or swooned. Then came a sort of loathing, like the first stage of seasickness, and a wild desire to be free of something – I knew not what. A vast stillness enveloped me, as though all the world were asleep or dead – only broken by the low panting as of some animal close to me. I felt a warm rasping at my throat, then came a consciousness of the awful truth which chilled me to the heart and sent the blood surging up through my brain. Some great animal was lying on me and now licking my throat. I feared to stir, for some instinct of prudence bade me lie still; but the brute seemed to realize that there was now some change in me, for it raised its head. Through my eyelashes I saw above me the two great flaming eyes of a gigantic wolf. Its sharp white teeth gleamed in the gaping red mouth, and I could feel its hot breath fierce and acrid upon me.

For another spell of time I remembered no more. Then I became conscious of a low growl, followed by a yelp, renewed again and again. Then seemingly very far away, I heard a "Holloa! Holloa!" as of many voices calling in unison. Cautiously I raised my head and looked in the direction whence the sound came, but the cemetery blocked my view. The wolf still continued to yelp in a strange way, and a red glare began to move round the grove of cypresses, as though following the sound. As the voices drew closer, the wolf yelped faster and louder. I feared to make either sound or motion. Nearer came the red glow over the white pall which stretched into the darkness around me. Then all at once from beyond the trees there came at a trot a troop of horsemen bearing torches. The wolf rose from my breast and made for the cemetery. I saw one of the horsemen (soldiers by their caps and their long military cloaks) raise his carbine and take aim. A companion knocked up his arm, and I heard the ball whiz over my head. He had evidently taken my body for that of the wolf. Another sighted the animal as it slunk away, and a shot followed. Then, at a gallop, the troop rode forward – some towards me, others following the wolf as it disappeared amongst the snow-clad cypresses.

As they drew nearer I tried to move but was powerless, although I could see and hear all that went on around me. Two or three of the soldiers jumped from their horses and knelt beside me. One of them raised my head and placed his hand over my heart.

"Good news, comrades!" he cried. "His heart still beats!"

Then some brandy was poured down my throat; it put vigor into me, and I was able to open my eyes fully and look around. Lights and shadows were moving among the trees, and I heard men call to one another. They drew together, uttering frightened exclamations; and the lights flashed as the others came pouring out of the cemetery pell-mell, like men possessed. When the further ones came close to us, those who were around me asked them eagerly, "Well, have you found him?"

The reply rang out hurriedly, "No! No! Come away quick – quick! This is no place to stay, and on this of all nights!"

"What was it?" was the question, asked in all manner of keys. The answer came variously and all indefinitely as though the men were moved by some common impulse to speak yet were restrained by some common fear from giving their thoughts.

"It – it – indeed!" gibbered one, whose wits had plainly given out for the moment.

"A wolf – and yet not a wolf!" another put in shudderingly.

"No use trying for him without the sacred bullet," a third remarked in a more ordinary manner.

"Serve us right for coming out on this night! Truly we have earned our thousand marks!" were the ejaculations of a fourth.

"There was blood on the broken marble," another said after a pause, "the lightning never brought that there. And for him – is he safe? Look at his throat! See comrades, the wolf has been lying on him and keeping his blood warm."

The officer looked at my throat and replied, "He is all right, the skin is not pierced. What does it all mean? We should never have found him but for the yelping of the wolf."

"What became of it?" asked the man who was holding up my head and who seemed the least panic-stricken of the party, for his hands were steady and without tremor. On his sleeve was the chevron of a petty officer.

"It went home," answered the man, whose long face was pallid and who actually shook with terror as he glanced around him fearfully. "There are graves enough there in which it may lie. Come, comrades – come quickly! Let us leave this cursed spot."

The officer raised me to a sitting posture, as he uttered a word of command; then several men placed me upon a horse. He sprang to the saddle behind me, took me in his arms, gave the word to advance; and, turning our faces away from the cypresses, we rode away in swift military order.

As yet my tongue refused its office, and I was perforce silent. I must have fallen asleep; for the next thing I remembered was finding myself standing up, supported by a soldier on each side of me. It was almost broad daylight, and to the north a red streak of sunlight was reflected like a path of blood over the waste of snow. The officer was telling the men to say nothing of what they had seen, except that they found an English stranger, guarded by a large dog.

"Dog! That was no dog," cut in the man who had exhibited such fear. "I think I know a wolf when I see one."

The young officer answered calmly, "I said a dog."

"Dog!" reiterated the other ironically. It was evident that his courage was rising with the sun; and, pointing to me, he said, "Look at his throat. Is that the work of a dog, master?"

Instinctively I raised my hand to my throat, and as I touched it I cried out in pain. The men crowded round to look, some stooping down from their saddles; and again there came the calm voice of the young officer, "A dog, as I said. If aught else were said we should only be laughed at."

I was then mounted behind a trooper, and we rode on into the suburbs of Munich. Here we came across a stray carriage into which I was lifted, and it was driven off to the Quatre Saisons – the young officer accompanying me, whilst a trooper followed with his horse, and the others rode off to their barracks.

When we arrived, Herr Delbruck rushed so quickly down the steps to meet me, that it was apparent he had been watching within. Taking me by both hands he solicitously led me in. The officer saluted me and was turning to withdraw, when I recognized his purpose and insisted that he should come to my rooms. Over a glass of wine I warmly thanked him and his brave comrades for saving me. He replied simply that he was more than glad, and that Herr Delbruck had at the first taken steps to make all the searching party pleased; at which ambiguous utterance the maitre d'hotel smiled, while the officer plead duty and withdrew.

"But Herr Delbruck," I enquired, "how and why was it that the soldiers searched for me?"

He shrugged his shoulders, as if in depreciation of his own deed, as he replied, "I was so fortunate as to obtain leave from the commander of the regiment in which I serve, to ask for volunteers."

"But how did you know I was lost?" I asked.

"The driver came hither with the remains of his carriage, which had been upset when the horses ran away."

"But surely you would not send a search party of soldiers merely on this account?"

"Oh, no!" he answered, "But even before the coachman arrived, I had this telegram from the Boyar whose guest you are," and he took from his pocket a telegram which he handed to me, and I read:

> *Bistritz.*
> *Be careful of my guest – his safety is most precious to me. Should aught happen to him, or if he be missed, spare nothing to find him and ensure his safety. He is English and therefore adventurous. There are often dangers from snow and wolves and night. Lose not a moment if you suspect harm to him. I answer your zeal with my fortune.*
> *Dracula.*

As I held the telegram in my hand, the room seemed to whirl around me, and if the attentive maitre d'hotel had not caught me, I think I should have fallen. There was something so strange in all this, something so weird and impossible to imagine, that there grew on me a sense of my being in some way the sport of opposite forces – the mere vague idea of which seemed in a way to paralyze me. I was certainly under some form of mysterious protection. From a distant country had come, in the very nick of time, a message that took me out of the danger of the snow sleep and the jaws of the wolf.

If you enjoyed this, you might also like...
Dracula (chapters I–IV), see page 81
'The Burial of the Rats, see page 347

Dracula
Chapters I–IV

Chapter I
Jonathan Harker's Journal
(Kept in shorthand.)

3 MAY. BISTRITZ. Left Munich at 8:35 p.m., on 1st May, arriving at Vienna early next morning; should have arrived at 6:46, but train was an hour late. Buda-Pesth seems a wonderful place, from the glimpse which I got of it from the train and the little I could walk through the streets. I feared to go very far from the station, as we had arrived late and would start as near the correct time as possible. The impression I had was that we were leaving the West and entering the East; the most western of splendid bridges over the Danube, which is here of noble width and depth, took us among the traditions of Turkish rule.

We left in pretty good time, and came after nightfall to Klausenburgh. Here I stopped for the night at the Hotel Royale. I had for dinner, or rather supper, a chicken done up some way with red pepper, which was very good but thirsty. (*Mem.*, get recipe for Mina.) I asked the waiter, and he said it was called 'paprika hendl,' and that, as it was a national dish, I should be able to get it anywhere along the Carpathians. I found my smattering of German very useful here; indeed, I don't know how I should be able to get on without it.

Having had some time at my disposal when in London, I had visited the British Museum, and made search among the books and maps in the library regarding Transylvania; it had struck me that some foreknowledge of the country could hardly fail to have some importance in dealing with a nobleman of that country. I find that the district he named is in the extreme east of the country, just on the borders of three states, Transylvania, Moldavia and Bukovina, in the midst of the Carpathian mountains; one of the wildest and least known portions of Europe. I was not able to light on any map or work giving the exact locality of the Castle Dracula, as there are no maps of this country as yet to compare with our own Ordnance Survey maps; but I found that Bistritz, the post town named by Count Dracula, is a fairly well-known place. I shall enter here some of my notes, as they may refresh my memory when I talk over my travels with Mina.

In the population of Transylvania there are four distinct nationalities: Saxons in the South, and mixed with them the Wallachs, who are the descendants of the Dacians; Magyars in the West, and Szekelys in the East and North. I am going among the latter, who claim to be descended from Attila and the Huns. This may be so, for when the Magyars conquered the country in the eleventh century they found the Huns settled in it. I read that every known superstition in the world is gathered into the horseshoe of the Carpathians, as if it were the centre of some sort of imaginative whirlpool; if so my stay may be very interesting. (*Mem.*, I must ask the Count all about them.)

I did not sleep well, though my bed was comfortable enough, for I had all sorts of queer dreams. There was a dog howling all night under my window, which may have had something to do with it; or it may have been the paprika, for I had to drink up all the water in my carafe, and was still thirsty. Towards morning I slept and was wakened by the continuous knocking at my door, so I guess I must have been sleeping soundly then. I had for breakfast more paprika, and a sort of porridge of maize flour which they said was 'mamaliga,' and egg-plant stuffed with forcemeat, a very excellent dish, which they call 'impletata.' (*Mem.*, get recipe for this also.) I had to hurry breakfast, for the train started a little before eight, or rather it ought to have done so, for after rushing to the station at 7:30 I had to sit in the carriage for more than an hour before we began to move. It seems to me that the further east you go the more unpunctual are the trains. What ought they to be in China?

All day long we seemed to dawdle through a country which was full of beauty of every kind. Sometimes we saw little towns or castles on the top of steep hills such as we see in old missals; sometimes we ran by rivers and streams which seemed from the wide stony margin on each side of them to be subject to great floods. It takes a lot of water, and running strong, to sweep the outside edge of a river clear. At every station there were groups of people, sometimes crowds, and in all sorts of attire. Some of them were just like the peasants at home or those I saw coming through France and Germany, with short jackets and round hats and home-made trousers; but others were very picturesque. The women looked pretty, except when you got near them, but they were very clumsy about the waist. They had all full white sleeves of some kind or other, and most of them had big belts with a lot of strips of something fluttering from them like the dresses in a ballet, but of course there were petticoats under them. The strangest figures we saw were the Slovaks, who were more barbarian than the rest, with their big cow-boy hats, great baggy dirty-white trousers, white linen shirts, and enormous heavy leather belts, nearly a foot wide, all studded over with brass nails. They wore high boots, with their trousers tucked into them, and had long black hair and heavy black moustaches. They are very picturesque, but do not look prepossessing. On the stage they would be set down at once as some old Oriental band of brigands. They are, however, I am told, very harmless and rather wanting in natural self-assertion.

It was on the dark side of twilight when we got to Bistritz, which is a very interesting old place. Being practically on the frontier – for the Borgo Pass leads from it into Bukovina – it has had a very stormy existence, and it certainly shows marks of it. Fifty years ago a series of great fires took place, which made terrible havoc on five separate occasions. At the very beginning of the seventeenth century it underwent a siege of three weeks and lost 13,000 people, the casualties of war proper being assisted by famine and disease.

Count Dracula had directed me to go to the Golden Krone Hotel, which I found, to my great delight, to be thoroughly old-fashioned, for of course I wanted to see all I could of the ways of the country. I was evidently expected, for when I got near the door I faced a cheery-looking elderly woman in the usual peasant dress – white undergarment with long double apron, front, and back, of coloured stuff fitting almost too tight for modesty. When I came close she bowed and said, "The Herr Englishman?" "Yes," I said, "Jonathan Harker." She smiled, and gave some message to an elderly man in white shirt-sleeves, who had followed her to the door. He went, but immediately returned with a letter:

> *My Friend.*
> *Welcome to the Carpathians. I am anxiously expecting you. Sleep well tonight. At three tomorrow the diligence will start for Bukovina; a place on it is kept for you. At the Borgo Pass my carriage will await you and will bring you to me. I trust that your journey from London has been a happy one, and that you will enjoy your stay in my beautiful land.*
> *Your friend,*
> *Dracula.*

* * *

4 May. I found that my landlord had got a letter from the Count, directing him to secure the best place on the coach for me; but on making inquiries as to details he seemed somewhat reticent, and pretended that he could not understand my German. This could not be true, because up to then he had understood it perfectly; at least, he answered my questions exactly as if he did. He and his wife, the old lady who had received me, looked at each other in a frightened sort of way. He mumbled out that the money had been sent in a letter, and that was all he knew. When I asked him if he knew Count Dracula, and could tell me anything of his castle, both he and his wife crossed themselves, and, saying that they knew nothing at all, simply refused to speak further. It was so near the time of starting that I had no time to ask any one else, for it was all very mysterious and not by any means comforting.

Just before I was leaving, the old lady came up to my room and said in a very hysterical way:

"Must you go? Oh! Young Herr, must you go?" She was in such an excited state that she seemed to have lost her grip of what German she knew, and mixed it all up with some other language which I did not know at all. I was just able to follow her by asking many questions. When I told her that I must go at once, and that I was engaged on important business, she asked again:

"Do you know what day it is?" I answered that it was the fourth of May. She shook her head as she said again:

"Oh, yes! I know that! I know that, but do you know what day it is?" On my saying that I did not understand, she went on:

"It is the eve of St. George's Day. Do you not know that tonight, when the clock strikes midnight, all the evil things in the world will have full sway? Do you know where you are going, and what you are going to?" She was in such evident distress that I tried to comfort her, but without effect. Finally she went down on her knees and implored me not to go; at least to wait a day or two before starting. It was all very ridiculous but I did not feel comfortable. However, there was business to be done, and I could allow nothing to interfere with it. I therefore tried to raise her up, and said, as gravely as I could, that I thanked her, but my duty was imperative, and that I must go. She then rose and dried her eyes, and taking a crucifix from her neck offered it to me. I did not know what to do, for, as an English Churchman, I have been taught to regard such things as in some measure idolatrous, and yet it seemed so ungracious to refuse an old lady meaning so well and in such a state of mind. She saw, I suppose, the doubt in my face, for she put the rosary round my neck, and said, "For your mother's sake," and went out of the room. I am writing up this part of the diary whilst I am waiting for the coach, which is, of course, late; and the crucifix is still round my neck. Whether it is the old lady's fear, or the many ghostly traditions of this place, or the crucifix itself, I do not know, but I am not feeling nearly as easy in my mind as usual. If this book should ever reach Mina before I do, let it bring my good-bye. Here comes the coach!

* * *

5 May. The Castle. The grey of the morning has passed, and the sun is high over the distant horizon, which seems jagged, whether with trees or hills I know not, for it is so far off that big things and little are mixed. I am not sleepy, and, as I am not to be called till I awake, naturally I write till sleep comes. There are many odd things to put down, and, lest who reads them may fancy that I dined too well before I left Bistritz, let me put down my dinner exactly. I dined on what they called 'robber steak' – bits of bacon, onion, and beef, seasoned with red pepper, and strung on sticks and roasted over the fire, in the simple style of the London cat's meat! The wine was Golden Mediasch, which produces a queer sting on the tongue, which is, however, not disagreeable. I had only a couple of glasses of this, and nothing else.

When I got on the coach the driver had not taken his seat, and I saw him talking with the landlady. They were evidently talking of me, for every now and then they looked at me, and some of the people who were sitting on the bench outside the door – which they call by a name meaning 'word-bearer' – came and listened, and then looked at me, most of them pityingly. I could hear a lot of words often repeated, queer words, for there were many nationalities in the crowd; so I quietly got my polyglot dictionary from my bag and looked them out. I must say they were not cheering to me, for amongst them were 'Ordog' – Satan, 'pokol' – hell, 'stregoica' – witch, 'vrolok' and 'vlkoslak' – both of which mean the same thing, one being Slovak and the other Serbian for something that is either were-wolf or vampire. (*Mem.*, I must ask the Count about these superstitions).

When we started, the crowd round the inn door, which had by this time swelled to a considerable size, all made the sign of the cross and pointed two fingers towards me. With some difficulty I got a fellow-passenger to tell me what they meant; he would not answer at first, but on learning that I was English, he explained that it was a charm or guard against the evil eye. This was not very pleasant for me, just starting for an unknown place to meet an unknown man; but every one seemed so kind-hearted, and so sorrowful, and so sympathetic that I could not but be touched. I shall never forget the last glimpse which I had of the inn-yard and its crowd of picturesque figures, all crossing themselves, as they stood round the wide archway, with its background of rich foliage of oleander and orange trees in green tubs clustered in the centre of the yard. Then our driver, whose wide linen drawers covered the whole front of the box-seat – 'gotza' they call them – cracked his big whip over his four small horses, which ran abreast, and we set off on our journey.

I soon lost sight and recollection of ghostly fears in the beauty of the scene as we drove along, although had I known the language, or rather languages, which my fellow-passengers were speaking, I might not have been able to throw them off so easily. Before us lay a green sloping land full of forests and woods, with here and there steep hills, crowned with clumps of trees or with farmhouses, the blank gable end to the road. There was everywhere a bewildering mass of fruit blossom – apple, plum, pear, cherry; and as we drove by I could see the green grass under the trees spangled with the fallen petals. In and out amongst these green hills of what they call here the 'Mittel Land' ran the road, losing itself as it swept round the grassy curve, or was shut out by the straggling ends of pine woods, which here and there ran down the hillsides like tongues of flame. The road was rugged, but still we seemed to fly over it with a feverish haste. I could not understand then what the haste meant, but the driver was evidently bent on losing no time in reaching Borgo Prund. I was told that this road is in summertime excellent, but that it had not yet been put in order after the winter snows. In this respect it is different from the general run of roads in the Carpathians, for it is an old tradition that they are not to be kept in too good order. Of old the Hospadars would not repair them, lest the Turk should think that they were preparing to bring in foreign troops, and so hasten the war which was always really at loading point.

Beyond the green swelling hills of the Mittel Land rose mighty slopes of forest up to the lofty steeps of the Carpathians themselves. Right and left of us they towered, with the afternoon sun falling full upon them and bringing out all the glorious colours of this beautiful range, deep blue and purple in the shadows of the peaks, green and brown where grass and rock mingled, and an endless perspective of jagged rock and pointed crags, till these were themselves lost in the distance, where the snowy peaks rose grandly. Here and there seemed mighty rifts in the mountains, through which, as the sun began to sink, we saw now and again the white gleam of falling water. One of my companions touched my arm as we swept round the base of a hill and opened up the lofty, snow-covered peak of a mountain, which seemed, as we wound on our serpentine way, to be right before us:

"Look! Isten szek!" – "God's seat!" – and he crossed himself reverently.

As we wound on our endless way, and the sun sank lower and lower behind us, the shadows of the evening began to creep round us. This was emphasised by the fact that the snowy mountain-top still held the sunset, and seemed to glow out with a delicate cool pink. Here and there we passed Cszeks and Slovaks, all in picturesque attire, but I noticed that goitre was painfully prevalent. By the roadside were many crosses, and as we swept by, my companions all crossed themselves. Here and there was a peasant man or woman kneeling before a shrine, who did not even turn round as we approached, but seemed in the self-surrender of devotion to have neither eyes nor ears for the outer world. There were many things new to me: for instance, hay-ricks in the trees, and here and there very beautiful masses of weeping birch, their white stems shining like silver through the delicate green of the leaves. Now and again we passed a leiter-wagon – the ordinary peasant's cart – with its long, snake-like vertebra, calculated to suit the inequalities of the road. On this were sure to be seated quite a group of home-coming peasants, the Cszeks with their white, and the Slovaks with their coloured, sheepskins, the latter carrying lance-fashion their long staves, with axe at end. As the evening fell it began to get very cold, and the growing twilight seemed to merge into one dark mistiness the gloom of the trees, oak, beech, and pine, though in the valleys which ran deep between the spurs of the hills, as we ascended through the Pass, the dark firs stood out here and there against the background of late-lying snow. Sometimes, as the road was cut through the pine woods that seemed in the darkness to be closing down upon us, great masses of greyness, which here and there bestrewed the trees, produced a peculiarly weird and solemn effect, which carried on the thoughts and grim fancies engendered earlier in the evening, when the falling sunset threw into strange relief the ghost-like clouds which amongst the Carpathians seem to wind ceaselessly through the valleys. Sometimes the hills were so steep that, despite our driver's haste, the horses could only go slowly. I wished to get down and walk up them, as we do at home, but the driver would not hear of it. "No, no," he said; "you must not walk here; the dogs are too fierce"; and then he added, with what he evidently meant for grim pleasantry – for he looked round to catch the approving smile of the rest – "and you may have enough of such matters before you go to sleep." The only stop he would make was a moment's pause to light his lamps.

When it grew dark there seemed to be some excitement amongst the passengers, and they kept speaking to him, one after the other, as though urging him to further speed. He lashed the horses unmercifully with his long whip, and with wild cries of encouragement urged them on to further exertions. Then through the darkness I could see a sort of patch of grey light ahead of us, as though there were a cleft in the hills. The excitement of the passengers grew greater; the crazy coach rocked on its great leather springs, and swayed like a boat tossed on a stormy sea. I had to hold on. The road grew more level, and we appeared to fly along. Then the mountains seemed to come nearer to us on each side and to frown down upon us; we were entering on the Borgo Pass. One by one several of the passengers offered me gifts, which they pressed upon me with an earnestness which would take no denial; these were certainly of an odd and varied kind, but each was given in simple good faith, with a kindly word, and a blessing, and that strange mixture of fear-meaning movements which I had seen outside the hotel at Bistritz – the sign of the cross and the guard against the evil eye. Then, as we flew along, the driver leaned forward, and on each side the passengers, craning over the edge of the coach, peered eagerly into the darkness. It was evident that something very exciting was either happening or expected, but though I asked each passenger, no one would give me the slightest explanation. This state of excitement kept on for some little time; and at last we saw before us the Pass opening out on the eastern side. There were dark, rolling clouds overhead, and in the air the heavy, oppressive sense of thunder. It seemed as though the mountain range had separated two atmospheres, and that now we had got into the thunderous one. I was now myself looking out for the conveyance which was to take me to the Count. Each moment I expected to see the glare of lamps through the blackness; but all was dark. The only light was the flickering rays of our own lamps, in which the steam from our hard-driven horses rose in a white cloud. We could see now the sandy road lying white before us, but there was on it no sign of a vehicle. The passengers drew back with a sigh of gladness, which seemed to mock my own disappointment. I was already thinking what I had best do, when the driver, looking at his watch, said to the others something which I could hardly hear, it was spoken so quietly and in so low a tone; I thought it was "An hour less than the time." Then turning to me, he said in German worse than my own:

"There is no carriage here. The Herr is not expected after all. He will now come on to Bukovina, and return tomorrow or the next day; better the next day." Whilst he was speaking the horses began to neigh and snort and plunge wildly, so that the driver had to hold them up. Then, amongst a chorus of screams from the peasants and a universal crossing of themselves, a calèche, with four horses, drove up behind us, overtook us, and drew up beside the coach. I could see from the flash of our lamps, as the rays fell on them, that the horses were coal-black and splendid animals. They were driven by a tall man, with a long brown beard and a great black hat, which seemed to hide his face from us. I could only see the gleam of a pair of very bright eyes, which seemed red in the lamplight, as he turned to us. He said to the driver:

"You are early tonight, my friend."

The man stammered in reply:

"The English Herr was in a hurry," to which the stranger replied:

"That is why, I suppose, you wished him to go on to Bukovina. You cannot deceive me, my friend; I know too much, and my horses are swift." As he spoke he smiled, and the lamplight fell on a hard-looking mouth, with very red lips and sharp-looking teeth, as white as ivory. One of my companions whispered to another the line from Burger's 'Lenore':

"Denn die Todten reiten schnell" –
("For the dead travel fast.")

The strange driver evidently heard the words, for he looked up with a gleaming smile. The passenger turned his face away, at the same time putting out his two fingers and crossing himself. "Give me the Herr's luggage," said the driver; and with exceeding alacrity my bags were handed out and put in the calèche. Then I descended from the side of the coach, as the calèche was close alongside, the driver helping me with a hand which caught my arm in a grip of steel; his strength must have been prodigious. Without a word he shook his reins, the horses turned, and we swept into the darkness of the Pass. As I looked back I saw the steam from the horses of the coach by the light of the lamps, and projected against it the figures of my late companions crossing themselves. Then the driver cracked his whip and called to his horses, and off they swept on their way to Bukovina. As they sank into the darkness I felt a strange chill, and a lonely feeling came over me; but a cloak was thrown over my shoulders, and a rug across my knees, and the driver said in excellent German:

"The night is chill, mein Herr, and my master the Count bade me take all care of you. There is a flask of slivovitz (the plum brandy of the country) underneath the seat, if you should require it." I did not take any, but it was a comfort to know it was there all the same. I felt a little strangely, and not a little frightened. I think had there been any alternative I should have taken it, instead of prosecuting that unknown night journey. The carriage went at a hard pace straight along, then we made a complete turn and went along another straight road. It seemed to me that we were simply going over and over the same ground again; and so I took note of some salient point, and found that this was so. I would have liked to have asked the driver what this all meant, but I really feared to do so, for I thought that, placed as

I was, any protest would have had no effect in case there had been an intention to delay. By-and-by, however, as I was curious to know how time was passing, I struck a match, and by its flame looked at my watch; it was within a few minutes of midnight. This gave me a sort of shock, for I suppose the general superstition about midnight was increased by my recent experiences. I waited with a sick feeling of suspense.

Then a dog began to howl somewhere in a farmhouse far down the road – a long, agonised wailing, as if from fear. The sound was taken up by another dog, and then another and another, till, borne on the wind which now sighed softly through the Pass, a wild howling began, which seemed to come from all over the country, as far as the imagination could grasp it through the gloom of the night. At the first howl the horses began to strain and rear, but the driver spoke to them soothingly, and they quieted down, but shivered and sweated as though after a runaway from sudden fright. Then, far off in the distance, from the mountains on each side of us began a louder and a sharper howling – that of wolves – which affected both the horses and myself in the same way – for I was minded to jump from the calèche and run, whilst they reared again and plunged madly, so that the driver had to use all his great strength to keep them from bolting. In a few minutes, however, my own ears got accustomed to the sound, and the horses so far became quiet that the driver was able to descend and to stand before them. He petted and soothed them, and whispered something in their ears, as I have heard of horse-tamers doing, and with extraordinary effect, for under his caresses they became quite manageable again, though they still trembled. The driver again took his seat, and shaking his reins, started off at a great pace. This time, after going to the far side of the Pass, he suddenly turned down a narrow roadway which ran sharply to the right.

Soon we were hemmed in with trees, which in places arched right over the roadway till we passed as through a tunnel; and again great frowning rocks guarded us boldly on either side. Though we were in shelter, we could hear the rising wind, for it moaned and whistled through the rocks, and the branches of the trees crashed together as we swept along. It grew colder and colder still, and fine, powdery snow began to fall, so that soon we and all around us were covered with a white blanket. The keen wind still carried the howling of the dogs, though this grew fainter as we went on our way. The baying of the wolves sounded nearer and nearer, as though they were closing round on us from every side. I grew dreadfully afraid, and the horses shared my fear. The driver, however, was not in the least disturbed; he kept turning his head to left and right, but I could not see anything through the darkness.

Suddenly, away on our left, I saw a faint flickering blue flame. The driver saw it at the same moment; he at once checked the horses, and, jumping to the ground, disappeared into the darkness. I did not know what to do, the less as the howling of the wolves grew closer; but while I wondered the driver suddenly appeared again, and without a word took his seat, and we resumed our journey. I think I must have fallen asleep and kept dreaming of the incident, for it seemed to be repeated endlessly, and now looking back, it is like a sort of awful nightmare. Once the flame appeared so near the road, that even in the darkness around us I could watch the driver's motions. He went rapidly to where the blue flame arose – it must have been very faint, for it did not seem to illumine the place around it at all – and gathering a few stones, formed them into some device. Once there appeared a strange optical effect: when he stood between me and the flame he did not obstruct it, for I could see its ghostly flicker all the same. This startled me, but as the effect was only momentary, I took it that my eyes deceived me straining through the darkness. Then for a time there were no blue flames, and we sped onwards through the gloom, with the howling of the wolves around us, as though they were following in a moving circle.

At last there came a time when the driver went further afield than he had yet gone, and during his absence, the horses began to tremble worse than ever and to snort and scream with fright. I could not see any cause for it, for the howling of the wolves had ceased altogether; but just then the moon, sailing through the black clouds, appeared behind the jagged crest of a beetling, pine-clad rock, and by its light I saw around us a ring of wolves, with white teeth and lolling red tongues, with long, sinewy limbs and shaggy hair. They were a hundred times more terrible in the grim silence which held them than even when they howled. For myself, I felt a sort of paralysis of fear. It is only when a man feels himself face to face with such horrors that he can understand their true import.

All at once the wolves began to howl as though the moonlight had had some peculiar effect on them. The horses jumped about and reared, and looked helplessly round with eyes that rolled in a way painful to see; but the living ring of terror encompassed them on every side; and they had perforce to remain within it. I called to the coachman to come, for it seemed to me that our only chance was to try to break out through the ring and to aid his approach. I shouted and beat the side of the calèche, hoping by the noise to scare the wolves from that side, so as to give him a chance of reaching the trap. How he came there, I know not, but I heard his voice raised in a tone of imperious command, and looking towards the sound, saw him stand in the roadway. As he swept his long arms, as though brushing aside some impalpable obstacle, the wolves fell back and back further still. Just then a heavy cloud passed across the face of the moon, so that we were again in darkness.

When I could see again the driver was climbing into the calèche, and the wolves had disappeared. This was all so strange and uncanny that a dreadful fear came upon me, and I was afraid to speak or move. The time seemed interminable as we swept on our way, now in almost complete darkness, for the rolling clouds obscured the moon. We kept on ascending, with occasional periods of quick descent, but in the main always ascending. Suddenly, I became conscious of the fact that the driver was in the act of pulling up the horses in the courtyard of a vast ruined castle, from whose tall black windows came no ray of light, and whose broken battlements showed a jagged line against the moonlit sky.

Chapter II
Jonathan Harker's Journal – Continued

5 MAY. I must have been asleep, for certainly if I had been fully awake I must have noticed the approach of such a remarkable place. In the gloom the courtyard looked of considerable size, and as several dark ways led from it under great round arches, it perhaps seemed bigger than it really is. I have not yet been able to see it by daylight.

When the calèche stopped, the driver jumped down and held out his hand to assist me to alight. Again I could not but notice his prodigious strength. His hand actually seemed like a steel vice that could have crushed mine if he had chosen.

Then he took out my traps, and placed them on the ground beside me as I stood close to a great door, old and studded with large iron nails, and set in a projecting doorway of massive stone. I could see even in the dim light that the stone was massively carved, but that the carving had been much worn by time and weather. As I stood, the driver jumped again into his seat and shook the reins; the horses started forward, and trap and all disappeared down one of the dark openings.

I stood in silence where I was, for I did not know what to do. Of bell or knocker there was no sign; through these frowning walls and dark window openings it was not likely that my voice could penetrate. The time I waited seemed endless, and I felt doubts and fears crowding upon me. What sort of place had I come to, and among what kind of people? What sort of grim adventure was it on which I had embarked? Was this a customary incident in the life of a solicitor's clerk sent out to explain the purchase of a London estate to a foreigner? Solicitor's clerk! Mina would not like that. Solicitor – for just before leaving London I got word that my examination was successful; and I am now a full-blown solicitor! I began to rub my eyes and pinch myself to see if I were awake. It all seemed like a horrible nightmare to me, and I expected that I should suddenly awake, and find myself at home, with the dawn struggling in through the windows, as I had now and again felt in the morning after a day of overwork. But my flesh answered the pinching test, and my eyes were not to be deceived. I was indeed awake and among the Carpathians. All I could do now was to be patient, and to wait the coming of the morning.

Just as I had come to this conclusion I heard a heavy step approaching behind the great door, and saw through the chinks the gleam of a coming light. Then there was the sound of rattling chains and the clanking of massive bolts drawn back. A key was turned with the loud grating noise of long disuse, and the great door swung back.

Within, stood a tall old man, clean shaven save for a long white moustache, and clad in black from head to foot, without a single speck of colour about him anywhere. He held in his hand an antique silver lamp, in which the flame burned without chimney or globe of any kind, throwing long quivering shadows as it flickered in the draught of the open door. The old man motioned me in with his right hand with a courtly gesture, saying in excellent English, but with a strange intonation:

"Welcome to my house! Enter freely and of your own will!" He made no motion of stepping to meet me, but stood like a statue, as though his gesture of welcome had fixed him into stone. The instant, however, that I had stepped over the threshold, he moved impulsively forward, and holding out his hand grasped mine with a strength which made me wince, an effect which was not lessened by the fact that it seemed as cold as ice – more like the hand of a dead than a living man. Again he said:

"Welcome to my house. Come freely. Go safely; and leave something of the happiness you bring!" The strength of the handshake was so much akin to that which I had noticed in the driver, whose face I had not seen, that for a moment I doubted if it were not the same person to whom I was speaking; so to make sure, I said interrogatively:

"Count Dracula?" He bowed in a courtly way as he replied:

"I am Dracula; and I bid you welcome, Mr. Harker, to my house. Come in; the night air is chill, and you must need to eat and rest." As he was speaking, he put the lamp on a bracket on the wall, and stepping out, took my luggage; he had carried it in before I could forestall him. I protested but he insisted:

"Nay, sir, you are my guest. It is late, and my people are not available. Let me see to your comfort myself." He insisted on carrying my traps along the passage, and then up a great winding stair, and along another great passage, on whose stone floor our steps rang heavily. At the end of this he threw open a heavy door, and I rejoiced to see within a well-lit room in which a table was spread for supper, and on whose mighty hearth a great fire of logs, freshly replenished, flamed and flared.

The Count halted, putting down my bags, closed the door, and crossing the room, opened another door, which led into a small octagonal room lit by a single lamp, and seemingly without a window of any sort. Passing through this, he opened another door, and motioned me to enter. It was a welcome sight; for here was a great bedroom well lighted and warmed with another log fire – also added to but lately, for the top logs were fresh – which sent a hollow roar up the wide chimney. The Count himself left my luggage inside and withdrew, saying, before he closed the door:

"You will need, after your journey, to refresh yourself by making your toilet. I trust you will find all you wish. When you are ready, come into the other room, where you will find your supper prepared."

The light and warmth and the Count's courteous welcome seemed to have dissipated all my doubts and fears. Having then reached my normal state, I discovered that I was half famished with hunger; so making a hasty toilet, I went into the other room.

I found supper already laid out. My host, who stood on one side of the great fireplace, leaning against the stonework, made a graceful wave of his hand to the table, and said:

"I pray you, be seated and sup how you please. You will, I trust, excuse me that I do not join you; but I have dined already, and I do not sup."

I handed to him the sealed letter which Mr. Hawkins had entrusted to me. He opened it and read it gravely; then, with a charming smile, he handed it to me to read. One passage of it, at least, gave me a thrill of pleasure.

"I must regret that an attack of gout, from which malady I am a constant sufferer, forbids absolutely any travelling on my part for some time to come; but I am happy to say I can send a sufficient substitute, one in whom I have every possible confidence. He is a young man, full of energy and talent in his own way, and of a very faithful disposition. He is discreet and silent, and has grown into manhood in my service. He shall be ready to attend on you when you will during his stay, and shall take your instructions in all matters."

The Count himself came forward and took off the cover of a dish, and I fell to at once on an excellent roast chicken. This, with some cheese and a salad and a bottle of old Tokay, of which I had two glasses, was my supper. During the time I was eating it the Count asked me many questions as to my journey, and I told him by degrees all I had experienced.

By this time I had finished my supper, and by my host's desire had drawn up a chair by the fire and begun to smoke a cigar which he offered me, at the same time excusing himself that he did not smoke. I had now an opportunity of observing him, and found him of a very marked physiognomy.

His face was a strong – a very strong – aquiline, with high bridge of the thin nose and peculiarly arched nostrils; with lofty domed forehead, and hair growing scantily round the temples but profusely elsewhere. His eyebrows were very massive, almost meeting over the nose, and with bushy hair that seemed to curl in its own profusion. The mouth, so far as I could see it under the heavy moustache, was fixed and rather cruel-looking, with peculiarly sharp white teeth; these protruded over the lips, whose remarkable ruddiness showed astonishing vitality in a man of his years. For the rest, his ears were pale, and at the tops extremely pointed; the chin was broad and strong, and the cheeks firm though thin. The general effect was one of extraordinary pallor.

Hitherto I had noticed the backs of his hands as they lay on his knees in the firelight, and they had seemed rather white and fine; but seeing them now close to me, I could not but notice that they were rather coarse – broad, with squat fingers. Strange to say, there were hairs in the centre of the palm. The nails were long and fine, and cut to a sharp point. As the Count leaned over me and his hands touched me, I could not repress a shudder. It may have been that his breath was rank, but a horrible feeling of nausea came over me, which, do what I would, I could not conceal. The Count, evidently noticing it, drew back; and with a grim sort of smile, which showed more than he had yet done his protuberant teeth, sat himself down again on his own side of the fireplace. We were both silent for a while; and as I looked towards the window I saw the first dim streak of the coming dawn. There seemed a strange stillness over everything; but as I listened I heard as if from down below in the valley the howling of many wolves. The Count's eyes gleamed, and he said:

"Listen to them – the children of the night. What music they make!" Seeing, I suppose, some expression in my face strange to him, he added:

"Ah, sir, you dwellers in the city cannot enter into the feelings of the hunter." Then he rose and said:

"But you must be tired. Your bedroom is all ready, and tomorrow you shall sleep as late as you will. I have to be away till the afternoon; so sleep well and dream well!" With a courteous bow, he opened for me himself the door to the octagonal room, and I entered my bedroom....

I am all in a sea of wonders. I doubt; I fear; I think strange things, which I dare not confess to my own soul. God keep me, if only for the sake of those dear to me!

* * *

7 May. It is again early morning, but I have rested and enjoyed the last twenty-four hours. I slept till late in the day, and awoke of my own accord. When I had dressed myself I went into the room where we had supped, and found a cold breakfast laid out, with coffee kept hot by the pot being placed on the hearth. There was a card on the table, on which was written:

"I have to be absent for a while. Do not wait for me. D." I set to and enjoyed a hearty meal. When I had done, I looked for a bell, so that I might let the servants know I had finished; but I could not find one. There are certainly odd deficiencies in the house, considering the extraordinary evidences of wealth which are round me. The table service is of gold, and so beautifully wrought that it must be of immense value. The curtains and upholstery of the chairs and sofas and the hangings of my bed are of the costliest and most beautiful fabrics, and must have been of fabulous value when they were made, for they are centuries old, though in excellent order.

I saw something like them in Hampton Court, but there they were worn and frayed and moth-eaten. But still in none of the rooms is there a mirror. There is not even a toilet glass on my table, and I had to get the little shaving glass from my bag before I could either shave or brush my hair. I have not yet seen a servant anywhere, or heard a sound near the castle except the howling of wolves. Some time after I had finished my meal – I do not know whether to call it breakfast or dinner, for it was between five and six o'clock when I had it – I looked about for something to read, for I did not like to go about the castle until I had asked the Count's permission. There was absolutely nothing in the room, book, newspaper, or even writing materials; so I opened another door in the room and found a sort of library. The door opposite mine I tried, but found it locked.

In the library I found, to my great delight, a vast number of English books, whole shelves full of them, and bound volumes of magazines and newspapers. A table in the centre was littered with English magazines and newspapers, though none of them were of very recent date. The books were of the most varied kind – history, geography, politics, political economy, botany, geology, law – all relating to England and English life and customs and manners. There were even such books of reference as the *London Directory*, the '*Red*' and '*Blue*' books, *Whitaker's Almanac*, the *Army and Navy Lists*, and – it somehow gladdened my heart to see it – the *Law List*.

Whilst I was looking at the books, the door opened, and the Count entered. He saluted me in a hearty way, and hoped that I had had a good night's rest. Then he went on:

"I am glad you found your way in here, for I am sure there is much that will interest you. These companions" – and he laid his hand on some of the books – "have been good friends to me, and for some years past, ever since I had the idea of going to London, have given me many, many hours of pleasure. Through them I have come to know your great England; and to know her is to love her. I long to go through the crowded streets of your mighty London, to be in the midst of the whirl and rush of humanity, to share its life, its change, its death, and all that makes it what it is. But alas! as yet I only know your tongue through books. To you, my friend, I look that I know it to speak."

"But, Count," I said, "you know and speak English thoroughly!" He bowed gravely.

"I thank you, my friend, for your all too-flattering estimate, but yet I fear that I am but a little way on the road I would travel. True, I know the grammar and the words, but yet I know not how to speak them."

"Indeed," I said, "you speak excellently."

"Not so," he answered. "Well, I know that, did I move and speak in your London, none there are who would not know me for a stranger. That is not enough for me. Here I am noble; I am *boyar*; the common people know me, and I am master. But a stranger in a strange land, he is no one; men know him not – and to know not is to care not for. I am content if I am like the rest, so that no man stops if he see me, or pause in his speaking if he hear my words, 'Ha, ha! A stranger!' I have been so long master that I would be master still – or at least that none other should be master of me. You come to me not alone as agent of my friend Peter Hawkins, of Exeter, to tell me all about my new estate in London. You shall, I trust, rest here with me awhile, so that by our talking I may learn the English intonation; and I would that you tell me when I make error, even of the smallest, in my speaking. I am sorry that I had to be away so long today; but you will, I know, forgive one who has so many important affairs in hand."

Of course I said all I could about being willing, and asked if I might come into that room when I chose. He answered: "Yes, certainly," and added:

"You may go anywhere you wish in the castle, except where the doors are locked, where of course you will not wish to go. There is reason that all things are as they are, and did you see with my eyes and know with my knowledge, you would perhaps better understand." I said I was sure of this, and then he went on:

"We are in Transylvania; and Transylvania is not England. Our ways are not your ways, and there shall be to you many strange things. Nay, from what you have told me of your experiences already, you know something of what strange things there may be."

This led to much conversation; and as it was evident that he wanted to talk, if only for talking's sake, I asked him many questions regarding things that had already happened to me or come within my notice. Sometimes he sheered off the subject, or turned the conversation by pretending not to understand; but generally he answered all I asked most frankly. Then as time went on, and I had got somewhat bolder, I asked him of some of the strange things of the preceding night, as, for instance, why the coachman went to the places where he had seen the blue flames. He then explained to me that it was commonly believed that on a certain night of the year – last night, in fact, when all evil spirits are supposed to have unchecked sway – a blue flame is seen over any place where treasure has been concealed. "That treasure has been hidden," he went on, "in the region through which you came last night, there can be but little doubt; for it was the ground fought over for centuries by the Wallachian, the Saxon, and the Turk. Why, there is hardly a foot of soil in all this region that has not been enriched by the blood of men, patriots or invaders. In old days there were stirring times, when the Austrian and the Hungarian came up in hordes, and the patriots went out to meet them – men and women, the aged and the children too – and waited their coming on the rocks above the passes, that they might sweep destruction on them with their artificial avalanches. When the invader was triumphant he found but little, for whatever there was had been sheltered in the friendly soil."

"But how," said I, "can it have remained so long undiscovered, when there is a sure index to it if men will but take the trouble to look?" The Count smiled, and as his lips ran back over his gums, the long, sharp, canine teeth showed out strangely; he answered:

"Because your peasant is at heart a coward and a fool! Those flames only appear on one night; and on that night no man of this land will, if he can help it, stir without his doors. And, dear sir, even if he did he would not know what to do. Why, even the peasant that you tell me of who marked the place of the flame would not know where to look in daylight even for his own work. Even you would not, I dare be sworn, be able to find these places again?"

"There you are right," I said. "I know no more than the dead where even to look for them." Then we drifted into other matters.

"Come," he said at last, "tell me of London and of the house which you have procured for me." With an apology for my remissness, I went into my own room to get the papers from my bag. Whilst I was placing them in order I heard a rattling of china and silver in the next room, and as I passed through, noticed that the table had been cleared and the lamp lit, for it was by this time deep into the dark. The lamps were also lit in the study or library, and I found the Count lying on the sofa, reading, of all things in the world, an English *Bradshaw's Guide*. When I came in he cleared the books and papers from the table; and with him I went into plans and deeds and figures of all sorts. He was interested in everything, and asked me a myriad questions about the place and its surroundings. He clearly had studied beforehand all he could get on the subject of the neighbourhood, for he evidently at the end knew very much more than I did. When I remarked this, he answered:

"Well, but, my friend, is it not needful that I should? When I go there I shall be all alone, and my friend Harker Jonathan – nay, pardon me, I fall into my country's habit of putting your patronymic first – my friend Jonathan Harker will not be by my side to correct and aid me. He will be in Exeter, miles away, probably working at papers of the law with my other friend, Peter Hawkins. So!"

We went thoroughly into the business of the purchase of the estate at Purfleet. When I had told him the facts and got his signature to the necessary papers, and had written a letter with them ready to post to Mr. Hawkins, he began to ask me how I had come across so suitable a place. I read to him the notes which I had made at the time, and which I inscribe here:

"At Purfleet, on a by-road, I came across just such a place as seemed to be required, and where was displayed a dilapidated notice that the place was for sale. It is surrounded by a high wall, of ancient structure, built of heavy stones, and has not been repaired for a large number of years. The closed gates are of heavy old oak and iron, all eaten with rust.

"The estate is called Carfax, no doubt a corruption of the old Quatre Face, as the house is four-sided, agreeing with the cardinal points of the compass. It contains in all some twenty acres, quite surrounded by the solid stone wall above mentioned. There are many trees on it, which make it in places gloomy, and there is a deep, dark-looking pond or small lake, evidently fed by some springs, as the water is clear and flows away in a fair-sized stream. The house is very large and of all periods back, I should say, to mediaeval times, for one part is of stone immensely thick, with only a few windows high up and heavily barred with iron. It looks like part of a keep, and is close to an old chapel or church. I could not enter it, as I had not the key of the door leading to it from the house, but I have taken with my kodak views of it from various points. The house has been added to, but in a very straggling way, and I can only guess at the amount of ground it covers, which must be very great. There are but few houses close at hand, one being a very large house only recently added to and formed into a private lunatic asylum. It is not, however, visible from the grounds."

When I had finished, he said:

"I am glad that it is old and big. I myself am of an old family, and to live in a new house would kill me. A house cannot be made habitable in a day; and, after all, how few days go to make up a century. I rejoice also that there is a chapel of old times. We Transylvanian nobles love not to think that our bones may lie amongst the common dead. I seek not gaiety nor mirth, not the bright voluptuousness of much sunshine and sparkling waters which please the young and gay. I am no longer young; and my heart, through weary years of mourning over the dead, is not attuned to mirth. Moreover, the walls of my castle are broken; the shadows are many, and the wind breathes cold through the broken battlements and casements. I love the shade and the shadow, and would be alone with my thoughts when I may." Somehow his words and his look did not seem to accord, or else it was that his cast of face made his smile look malignant and saturnine.

Presently, with an excuse, he left me, asking me to put all my papers together. He was some little time away, and I began to look at some of the books around me. One was an atlas, which I found opened naturally at England, as if that map had been much used. On looking at it I found in certain places little rings marked, and on examining these I noticed that one was near London on the east side, manifestly where his new estate was situated; the other two were Exeter, and Whitby on the Yorkshire coast.

It was the better part of an hour when the Count returned. "Aha!" he said; "Still at your books? Good! But you must not work always. Come; I am informed that your supper is ready." He took my arm, and we went into the next room, where I found an excellent supper ready on the table. The Count again excused himself as he had dined out on his being away from home. But he sat as on the previous night, and chatted whilst I ate. After supper I smoked, as on the last evening, and the Count stayed with me, chatting and asking questions on every conceivable subject, hour after hour. I felt that it was getting very late indeed, but I did not say anything, for I felt under obligation to meet my host's wishes in every way. I was not sleepy, as the long sleep yesterday had fortified me; but I could not help experiencing that chill which comes over one at the coming of the dawn, which is like, in its way, the turn of the tide. They say that people who are near death die generally at the change to the dawn or at the turn of the tide; any one who has when tired, and tied as it were to his post, experienced this change in the atmosphere can well believe it. All at once we heard the crow of a cock coming up with preternatural shrillness through the clear morning air; Count Dracula jumping to his feet, said:

"Why, there is the morning again! How remiss I am to let you stay up so long. You must make your conversation regarding my dear new country of England less interesting, so that I may not forget how time flies by us," and, with a courtly bow, he quickly left me.

I went into my own room and drew the curtains, but there was little to notice; my window opened into the courtyard, all I could see was the warm grey of quickening sky. So I pulled the curtains again, and have written of this day.

* * *

8 May. I began to fear as I wrote in this book that I was getting too diffuse; but now am glad that I went into detail from the first, for there is something so strange about this place and all in it that I cannot but feel uneasy. I wish I were safe out of it, or that I had never come. It may be that this strange night-existence is telling on me, but would that that were all! If there were any one to talk to I could bear it, but there is no one. I have only the Count to speak with, and he! – I fear I am myself the only living soul within the place. Let me be prosaic so far as facts can be; it will help me to bear up, and imagination must not run riot with me. If it does I am lost. Let me say at once how I stand – or seem to.

I only slept a few hours when I went to bed, and feeling that I could not sleep any more, got up. I had hung my shaving glass by the window, and was just beginning to shave. Suddenly I felt a hand on my shoulder, and heard the Count's voice saying to me, "Good-morning." I started, for it amazed me that I had not seen him, since the reflection of the glass covered the whole room behind me. In starting I had cut myself slightly, but did not notice it at the moment. Having answered the Count's salutation, I turned to the glass again to see how I had been mistaken. This time there could be no error, for the man was close to me, and I could see him over my shoulder. But there was no reflection of him in the mirror! The whole room behind me was displayed; but there was no sign of a man in it, except myself. This was startling, and, coming on the top of so many strange things, was beginning to increase that vague feeling of uneasiness which I always have when the Count is near; but at the instant I saw that the cut had bled a little, and the blood was trickling over my chin. I laid down the razor, turning as I did so half round to look for some sticking plaster. When the Count saw my face, his eyes blazed with a sort of demoniac fury, and he suddenly made a grab at my throat. I drew away, and his hand touched the string of beads which held the crucifix. It made an instant change in him, for the fury passed so quickly that I could hardly believe that it was ever there.

"Take care," he said, "take care how you cut yourself. It is more dangerous than you think in this country." Then seizing the shaving glass, he went on: "And this is the wretched thing that has done the mischief. It is a foul bauble of man's vanity. Away with it!" and opening the heavy window with one wrench of his terrible hand, he flung out the glass, which was shattered into a thousand pieces on the stones of the courtyard far below. Then he withdrew without a word. It is very annoying, for I do not see how I am to shave, unless in my watch-case or the bottom of the shaving-pot, which is fortunately of metal.

When I went into the dining-room, breakfast was prepared; but I could not find the Count anywhere. So I breakfasted alone. It is strange that as yet I have not seen the Count eat or drink. He must be a very peculiar man! After breakfast I did a little exploring in the castle. I went out on the stairs, and found a room looking towards the South. The view was magnificent, and from where I stood there was every opportunity of seeing it. The castle is on the very edge of a terrible precipice. A stone falling from the window would fall a thousand feet without touching anything! As far as the eye can reach is a sea of green tree tops, with occasionally a deep rift where there is a chasm. Here and there are silver threads where the rivers wind in deep gorges through the forests.

But I am not in heart to describe beauty, for when I had seen the view I explored further; doors, doors, doors everywhere, and all locked and bolted. In no place save from the windows in the castle walls is there an available exit.

The castle is a veritable prison, and I am a prisoner!

Chapter III
Jonathan Harker's Journal – Continued

WHEN I FOUND that I was a prisoner a sort of wild feeling came over me. I rushed up and down the stairs, trying every door and peering out of every window I could find; but after a little the conviction of my helplessness overpowered all other feelings. When I look back after a few hours I think I must have been mad for the time, for I behaved much as a rat does in a trap. When, however, the conviction had come to me that I was helpless I sat down quietly – as quietly as I have ever done anything in my life – and began to think over what was best to be done. I am thinking still, and as yet have come to no definite conclusion. Of one thing only am I certain; that it is no use making my ideas known to the Count. He knows well that I am imprisoned; and as he has done it himself, and has doubtless his own motives for it, he would only deceive me if I trusted him fully with the facts. So far as I can see, my only plan will be to keep my knowledge and my fears to myself, and my eyes open. I am, I know, either being deceived, like a baby, by my own fears, or else I am in desperate straits; and if the latter be so, I need, and shall need, all my brains to get through.

I had hardly come to this conclusion when I heard the great door below shut, and knew that the Count had returned. He did not come at once into the library, so I went cautiously to my own room and found him making the bed. This was odd, but only confirmed what I had all along thought – that there were no servants in the house. When later I saw him through the chink of the hinges of the door laying the table in the dining-room, I was assured of it; for if he does himself all these menial offices, surely it is proof that there is no one else to do them. This gave me a fright, for if there is no one else in the castle, it must have been the Count himself who was the driver of the coach that brought me here. This is a terrible thought; for if so, what does it mean that he could control the wolves, as he did, by only holding up his hand in silence. How was it that all the people at Bistritz and on the coach had some terrible fear for me? What meant the giving of the crucifix, of the garlic, of the wild rose, of the mountain ash? Bless that good, good woman who hung the crucifix round my neck! for it is a comfort and a strength to me whenever I touch it. It is odd that a thing which I have been taught to regard with disfavour and as idolatrous should in a time of loneliness and trouble be of help. Is it that there is something in the essence of the thing itself, or that it is a medium, a tangible help, in conveying memories of sympathy and comfort? Some time, if it may be, I must examine this matter and try to make up my mind about it. In the meantime I must find out all I can about Count Dracula, as it may help me to understand. Tonight he may talk of himself, if I turn the conversation that way. I must be very careful, however, not to awake his suspicion.

* * *

Midnight. I have had a long talk with the Count. I asked him a few questions on Transylvania history, and he warmed up to the subject wonderfully. In his speaking of things and people, and especially of battles, he spoke as if he had been present at them all. This he afterwards explained by saying that to a *boyar* the pride of his house and name is his own pride, that their glory is his glory, that their fate is his fate. Whenever he spoke of his house he always said 'we,' and spoke almost in the plural, like a king speaking. I wish I could put down all he said exactly as he said it, for to me it was most fascinating. It seemed to have in it a whole history of the country. He grew excited as he spoke, and walked about the room pulling his great white moustache and grasping anything on which he laid his hands as though he would crush it by main strength. One thing he said which I shall put down as nearly as I can; for it tells in its way the story of his race:

"We Szekelys have a right to be proud, for in our veins flows the blood of many brave races who fought as the lion fights, for lordship. Here, in the whirlpool of European races, the Ugric tribe bore down from Iceland the fighting spirit which Thor and Wodin gave them, which their Berserkers displayed to such fell intent on the seaboards of Europe, ay, and of Asia and Africa too, till the peoples thought that the were-wolves themselves had come. Here, too, when they came, they found the Huns, whose warlike fury had swept the earth like a living flame, till the dying peoples held that in their veins ran the blood of those old witches, who, expelled from Scythia had mated with the devils in the desert. Fools, fools! What devil or what witch was ever so great as Attila, whose blood is in these veins?" He held up his arms. "Is it a wonder that we were a conquering race; that we were proud; that when the Magyar, the Lombard, the Avar, the Bulgar, or the Turk poured his thousands on our frontiers, we drove them back? Is it strange that when Arpad and his legions swept through the Hungarian fatherland he found us here when he reached the frontier; that the Honfoglalas was completed there? And when the Hungarian flood swept eastward, the Szekelys were claimed as kindred by the victorious Magyars, and to us for centuries was trusted the guarding of the frontier of Turkey-land; ay, and more than that, endless duty of the frontier guard, for, as the Turks say, 'water sleeps, and enemy is sleepless.' Who more gladly than we throughout the Four Nations received the 'bloody sword,' or at its warlike call flocked quicker to the standard of the King? When was redeemed that great shame of my nation, the shame of Cassova, when the flags of the Wallach and the Magyar went down beneath the Crescent? Who was it but one of my own race who as Voivode crossed the Danube and beat the Turk on his own ground? This was a Dracula indeed! Woe was it that his own unworthy brother, when he had fallen, sold his people to the Turk and brought the shame of slavery on them! Was it not this Dracula, indeed, who inspired that other of his race who in a later age again and again brought his forces over the great river into Turkey-land; who, when he was beaten back, came again, and again, and again, though he had to come alone from the bloody field where his troops were being slaughtered, since he knew that he alone could ultimately triumph! They said that he thought only of himself. Bah! what good are peasants without a leader? Where ends the war without a brain and heart to conduct it? Again, when, after the battle of Mohács, we threw off the Hungarian yoke, we of the Dracula blood were amongst their leaders, for our spirit would not brook that we were not free. Ah, young sir, the Szekelys – and the Dracula as their heart's blood, their brains, and their swords – can boast a record that mushroom growths like the Hapsburgs and the Romanoffs can never reach. The warlike days are over. Blood is too precious a thing in these days of dishonourable peace; and the glories of the great races are as a tale that is told."

It was by this time close on morning, and we went to bed. (*Mem.*, this diary seems horribly like the beginning of the *Arabian Nights*, for everything has to break off at cockcrow – or like the ghost of Hamlet's father.)

* * *

12 May. Let me begin with facts – bare, meagre facts, verified by books and figures, and of which there can be no doubt. I must not confuse them with experiences which will have to rest on my own observation, or my memory of them. Last evening when the Count came from his room he began by asking me questions on legal matters and on the doing of certain kinds of business. I had spent the day wearily over books, and, simply to keep my mind occupied, went over some of the matters I had been examined in at Lincoln's Inn. There was a certain method in the Count's inquiries, so I shall try to put them down in sequence; the knowledge may somehow or some time be useful to me.

First, he asked if a man in England might have two solicitors or more. I told him he might have a dozen if he wished, but that it would not be wise to have more than one solicitor engaged in one transaction, as only one could act at a time, and that to change would be certain to militate against his interest. He seemed thoroughly to understand, and went on to ask if there would be any practical difficulty in having one man to attend, say, to banking, and another to look after shipping, in case local help were needed in a place far from the home of the banking solicitor. I asked him to explain more fully, so that I might not by any chance mislead him, so he said:

"I shall illustrate. Your friend and mine, Mr. Peter Hawkins, from under the shadow of your beautiful cathedral at Exeter, which is far from London, buys for me through your good self my place at London. Good! Now here let me say frankly, lest you should think it strange that I have sought the services of one so far off from London instead of some one resident there, that my motive was that no local interest might be served save my wish only; and as one of London residence might, perhaps, have some purpose of himself or friend to serve, I went thus afield to seek my agent, whose labours should be only to my interest. Now, suppose I, who have much of affairs, wish to ship goods, say, to Newcastle, or Durham, or Harwich, or Dover, might it not be that it could with more ease be done by consigning to one in these ports?" I answered that certainly it would be most easy, but that we solicitors had a system of agency one for the other, so that local work could be done locally on instruction from any solicitor, so that the client, simply placing himself in the hands of one man, could have his wishes carried out by him without further trouble.

"But," said he, "I could be at liberty to direct myself. Is it not so?"

"Of course," I replied; and "such is often done by men of business, who do not like the whole of their affairs to be known by any one person."

"Good!" he said, and then went on to ask about the means of making consignments and the forms to be gone through, and of all sorts of difficulties which might arise, but by forethought could be guarded against. I explained all these things to him to the best of my ability, and he certainly left me under the impression that he would have made a wonderful solicitor, for there was nothing that he did not think of or foresee. For a man who was never in the country, and who did not evidently do much in the way of business, his knowledge and acumen were wonderful. When he had satisfied himself on these points of which he had spoken, and I had verified all as well as I could by the books available, he suddenly stood up and said:

"Have you written since your first letter to our friend Mr. Peter Hawkins, or to any other?" It was with some bitterness in my heart that I answered that I had not, that as yet I had not seen any opportunity of sending letters to anybody.

"Then write now, my young friend," he said, laying a heavy hand on my shoulder: "write to our friend and to any other; and say, if it will please you, that you shall stay with me until a month from now."

"Do you wish me to stay so long?" I asked, for my heart grew cold at the thought.

"I desire it much; nay, I will take no refusal. When your master, employer, what you will, engaged that someone should come on his behalf, it was understood that my needs only were to be consulted. I have not stinted. Is it not so?"

What could I do but bow acceptance? It was Mr. Hawkins's interest, not mine, and I had to think of him, not myself; and besides, while Count Dracula was speaking, there was that in his eyes and in his bearing which made me remember that I was a prisoner, and that if I wished it I could have no choice. The Count saw his victory in my bow, and his mastery in the trouble of my face, for he began at once to use them, but in his own smooth, resistless way:

"I pray you, my good young friend, that you will not discourse of things other than business in your letters. It will doubtless please your friends to know that you are well, and that you look forward to getting home to them. Is it not so?" As he spoke he handed me three sheets of note-paper and three envelopes. They were all of the thinnest foreign post, and looking at them, then at him, and noticing his quiet smile, with the sharp, canine teeth lying over the red underlip, I understood as well as if he had spoken that I should be careful what I wrote, for he would be able to read it. So I determined to write only formal notes now, but to write fully to Mr. Hawkins in secret, and also to Mina, for to her I could write in shorthand, which would puzzle the Count, if he did see it. When I had written my two letters I sat quiet, reading a book whilst the Count wrote several notes, referring as he wrote them to some books on his table. Then he took up my two and placed them with his own, and put by his writing materials, after which, the instant the door had closed behind him, I leaned over and looked at the letters, which were face down on the table. I felt no compunction in doing so, for under the circumstances I felt that I should protect myself in every way I could.

One of the letters was directed to Samuel F. Billington, No. 7, The Crescent, Whitby, another to Herr Leutner, Varna; the third was to Coutts & Co., London, and the fourth to Herren Klopstock & Billreuth, bankers, Buda-Pesth. The second and fourth were unsealed. I was just about to look at them when I saw the door-handle move. I sank back in my seat, having just had time to replace the letters as they had been and to resume my book before the Count, holding still another letter in his hand, entered the room. He took up the letters on the table and stamped them carefully, and then turning to me, said:

"I trust you will forgive me, but I have much work to do in private this evening. You will, I hope, find all things as you wish." At the door he turned, and after a moment's pause said:

"Let me advise you, my dear young friend – nay, let me warn you with all seriousness, that should you leave these rooms you will not by any chance go to sleep in any other part of the castle. It is old, and has many memories, and there are bad dreams for those who sleep unwisely. Be warned! Should sleep now or ever overcome you, or be like to do, then haste to your own chamber or to these rooms, for your rest will then be safe. But if you be not careful in this respect, then" – He finished his speech in a gruesome way, for he motioned with his hands as if he were washing them. I quite understood; my only doubt was as to whether any dream could be more terrible than the unnatural, horrible net of gloom and mystery which seemed closing around me.

* * *

Later. I endorse the last words written, but this time there is no doubt in question. I shall not fear to sleep in any place where he is not. I have placed the crucifix over the head of my bed – I imagine that my rest is thus freer from dreams; and there it shall remain.

When he left me I went to my room. After a little while, not hearing any sound, I came out and went up the stone stair to where I could look out towards the South. There was some sense of freedom in the vast expanse, inaccessible though it was to me, as compared with the narrow darkness of the courtyard. Looking out on this, I felt that I was indeed in prison, and I seemed to want a breath of fresh air, though it were of the night. I am beginning to feel this nocturnal existence tell on me. It is destroying my nerve. I start at my own shadow, and am full of all sorts of horrible imaginings. God knows that there is ground for my terrible fear in this accursed place! I looked out over the beautiful expanse, bathed in soft yellow moonlight till it was almost as light as day. In the soft light the distant hills became melted, and the shadows in the valleys and gorges of velvety blackness. The mere beauty seemed to cheer me; there was peace and comfort in every breath I drew. As I leaned from the window my eye was caught by something moving a storey below me, and somewhat to my left, where I imagined, from the order of the rooms, that the windows of the Count's own room would look out. The window at which I stood was tall and deep, stone-mullioned, and though weatherworn, was still complete; but it was evidently many a day since the case had been there. I drew back behind the stonework, and looked carefully out.

What I saw was the Count's head coming out from the window. I did not see the face, but I knew the man by the neck and the movement of his back and arms. In any case I could not mistake the hands which I had had so many opportunities of studying. I was at first interested and somewhat amused, for it is wonderful how small a matter will interest and amuse a man when he is a prisoner. But my very feelings changed to repulsion and terror when I saw the whole man slowly emerge from the window and begin to crawl down the castle wall over that dreadful abyss, *face down* with his cloak spreading out around him like great wings. At first I could not believe my eyes. I thought it was some trick of the moonlight, some weird effect of shadow; but I kept looking, and it could be no delusion. I saw the fingers and toes grasp the corners of the stones, worn clear of the mortar by the stress of years, and by thus using every projection and inequality move downwards with considerable speed, just as a lizard moves along a wall.

What manner of man is this, or what manner of creature is it in the semblance of man? I feel the dread of this horrible place overpowering me; I am in fear – in awful fear – and there is no escape for me; I am encompassed about with terrors that I dare not think of....

* * *

15 May. Once more have I seen the Count go out in his lizard fashion. He moved downwards in a sidelong way, some hundred feet down, and a good deal to the left. He vanished into some hole or window. When his head had disappeared, I leaned out to try and see more, but without avail – the distance was too great to allow a proper angle of sight. I knew he had left the castle now, and thought to use the opportunity to explore more than I had dared to do as yet. I went back to the room, and taking a lamp, tried all the doors. They were all locked, as I had expected, and the locks were comparatively new; but I went down the stone stairs to the hall where I had entered originally. I found I could pull back the bolts easily enough and unhook the great chains; but the door was locked, and the key was gone! That key must be in the Count's room; I must watch should his door be unlocked, so that I may get it and escape.

I went on to make a thorough examination of the various stairs and passages, and to try the doors that opened from them. One or two small rooms near the hall were open, but there was nothing to see in them except old furniture, dusty with age and moth-eaten. At last, however, I found one door at the top of the stairway which, though it seemed to be locked, gave a little under pressure. I tried it harder, and found that it was not really locked, but that the resistance came from the fact that the hinges had fallen somewhat, and the heavy door rested on the floor. Here was an opportunity which I might not have again, so I exerted myself, and with many efforts forced it back so that I could enter.

I was now in a wing of the castle further to the right than the rooms I knew and a storey lower down. From the windows I could see that the suite of rooms lay along to the south of the castle, the windows of the end room looking out both west and south. On the latter side, as well as to the former, there was a great precipice. The castle was built on the corner of a great rock, so that on three sides it was quite impregnable, and great windows were placed here where sling, or bow, or culverin could not reach, and consequently light and comfort, impossible to a position which had to be guarded, were secured. To the west was a great valley, and then, rising far away, great jagged mountain fastnesses, rising peak on peak, the sheer rock studded with mountain ash and thorn, whose roots clung in cracks and crevices and crannies of the stone.

This was evidently the portion of the castle occupied by the ladies in bygone days, for the furniture had more air of comfort than any I had seen. The windows were curtainless, and the yellow moonlight, flooding in through the diamond panes, enabled one to see even colours, whilst it softened the wealth of dust which lay over all and disguised in some measure the ravages of time and the moth.

My lamp seemed to be of little effect in the brilliant moonlight, but I was glad to have it with me, for there was a dread loneliness in the place which chilled my heart and made my nerves tremble. Still, it was better than living alone in the rooms which I had come to hate from the presence of the Count, and after trying a little to school my nerves, I found a soft quietude come over me.

Here I am, sitting at a little oak table where in old times possibly some fair lady sat to pen, with much thought and many blushes, her ill-spelt love-letter, and writing in my diary in shorthand all that has happened since I closed it last. It is nineteenth century up-to-date with a vengeance. And yet, unless my senses deceive me, the old centuries had, and have, powers of their own which mere 'modernity' cannot kill.

* * *

Later: the Morning of 16 May. God preserve my sanity, for to this I am reduced. Safety and the assurance of safety are things of the past. Whilst I live on here there is but one thing to hope for, that I may not go mad, if, indeed, I be not mad already. If I be sane, then surely it is maddening to think that of all the foul things that lurk in this hateful place the Count is the least dreadful to me; that to him alone I can look for safety, even though this be only whilst I can serve his purpose. Great God! Merciful God! Let me be calm, for out of that way lies madness indeed. I begin to get new lights on certain things which have puzzled me. Up to now I never quite knew what Shakespeare meant when he made Hamlet say:

> *"My tablets! Quick, my tablets!*
> *'Tis meet that I put it down," etc.,*

For now, feeling as though my own brain were unhinged or as if the shock had come which must end in its undoing, I turn to my diary for repose. The habit of entering accurately must help to soothe me.

The Count's mysterious warning frightened me at the time; it frightens me more now when I think of it, for in future he has a fearful hold upon me. I shall fear to doubt what he may say!

When I had written in my diary and had fortunately replaced the book and pen in my pocket I felt sleepy. The Count's warning came into my mind, but I took a pleasure in disobeying it. The sense of sleep was upon me, and with it the obstinacy which sleep brings as outrider. The soft moonlight soothed, and the wide expanse without gave a sense of freedom which refreshed me. I determined not to return tonight to the gloom-haunted rooms, but to sleep here, where, of old, ladies had sat and sung and lived sweet lives whilst their gentle breasts were sad for their menfolk away in the midst of remorseless wars. I drew a great couch out of its place near the corner, so that as I lay, I could look at the lovely view to east and south, and unthinking of and uncaring for the dust, composed myself for sleep. I suppose I must have fallen asleep; I hope so, but I fear, for all that followed was startlingly real – so real that now sitting here in the broad, full sunlight of the morning, I cannot in the least believe that it was all sleep.

I was not alone. The room was the same, unchanged in any way since I came into it; I could see along the floor, in the brilliant moonlight, my own footsteps marked where I had disturbed the long accumulation of dust. In the moonlight opposite me were three young women, ladies by their dress and manner. I thought at the time that I must be dreaming when I saw them, for, though the moonlight was behind them, they threw no shadow on the floor. They came close to me, and looked at me for some time, and then whispered together. Two were dark, and had high aquiline noses, like the Count, and great dark, piercing eyes that seemed to be almost red when contrasted with the pale yellow moon. The other was fair, as fair as can be, with great wavy masses of golden hair and eyes like pale sapphires. I seemed somehow to know her face, and to know it in connection with some dreamy fear, but I could not recollect at the moment how or where. All three had brilliant white teeth that shone like pearls against the ruby of their voluptuous lips.

There was something about them that made me uneasy, some longing and at the same time some deadly fear. I felt in my heart a wicked, burning desire that they would kiss me with those red lips. It is not good to note this down, lest some day it should meet Mina's eyes and cause her pain; but it is the truth. They whispered together, and then they all three laughed – such a silvery, musical laugh, but as hard as though the sound never could have come through the softness of human lips. It was like the intolerable, tingling sweetness of water-glasses when played on by a cunning hand. The fair girl shook her head coquettishly, and the other two urged her on. One said:

"Go on! You are first, and we shall follow; yours is the right to begin." The other added:

"He is young and strong; there are kisses for us all." I lay quiet, looking out under my eyelashes in an agony of delightful anticipation. The fair girl advanced and bent over me till I could feel the movement of her breath upon me. Sweet it was in one sense, honey-sweet, and sent the same tingling through the nerves as her voice, but with a bitter underlying the sweet, a bitter offensiveness, as one smells in blood.

I was afraid to raise my eyelids, but looked out and saw perfectly under the lashes. The girl went on her knees, and bent over me, simply gloating. There was a deliberate voluptuousness which was both thrilling and repulsive, and as she arched her neck she actually licked her lips like an animal, till I could see in the moonlight the moisture shining on the scarlet lips and on the red tongue as it lapped the white sharp teeth. Lower and lower went her head as the lips went below the range of my mouth and chin and seemed about to fasten on my throat. Then she paused, and I could hear the churning sound of her tongue as it licked her teeth and lips, and could feel the hot breath on my neck. Then the skin of my throat began to tingle as one's flesh does when the hand that is to tickle it approaches nearer – nearer. I could feel the soft, shivering touch of the lips on the super-sensitive skin of my throat, and the hard dents of two sharp teeth, just touching and pausing there. I closed my eyes in a languorous ecstasy and waited – waited with beating heart.

But at that instant, another sensation swept through me as quick as lightning. I was conscious of the presence of the Count, and of his being as if lapped in a storm of fury. As my eyes opened involuntarily I saw his strong hand grasp the slender neck of the fair woman and with giant's power draw it back, the blue eyes transformed with fury, the white teeth champing with rage, and the fair cheeks blazing red with passion. But the Count! Never did I imagine such wrath and fury, even to the demons of the pit. His eyes were positively blazing. The red light in them was lurid, as if the flames of hell-fire blazed behind them. His face was deathly pale, and the lines of it were hard like drawn wires; the thick eyebrows that met over the nose now seemed like a heaving bar of white-hot metal. With a fierce sweep of his arm, he hurled the woman from him, and then motioned to the others, as though he were beating them back; it was the same imperious gesture that I had seen used to the wolves. In a voice which, though low and almost in a whisper seemed to cut through the air and then ring round the room he said:

"How dare you touch him, any of you? How dare you cast eyes on him when I had forbidden it? Back, I tell you all! This man belongs to me! Beware how you meddle with him, or you'll have to deal with me." The fair girl, with a laugh of ribald coquetry, turned to answer him:

"You yourself never loved; you never love!" On this the other women joined, and such a mirthless, hard, soulless laughter rang through the room that it almost made me faint to hear; it seemed like the pleasure of fiends. Then the Count turned, after looking at my face attentively, and said in a soft whisper:

"Yes, I too can love; you yourselves can tell it from the past. Is it not so? Well, now I promise you that when I am done with him you shall kiss him at your will. Now go! go! I must awaken him, for there is work to be done."

"Are we to have nothing tonight?" said one of them, with a low laugh, as she pointed to the bag which he had thrown upon the floor, and which moved as though there were some living thing within it. For answer he nodded his head. One of the women jumped forward and opened it. If my ears did not deceive me there was a gasp and a low wail, as of a half-smothered child. The women closed round, whilst I was aghast with horror; but as I looked they disappeared, and with them the dreadful bag. There was no door near them, and they could not have passed me without my noticing. They simply seemed to fade into the rays of the moonlight and pass out through the window, for I could see outside the dim, shadowy forms for a moment before they entirely faded away.

Then the horror overcame me, and I sank down unconscious.

Chapter IV
Jonathan Harker's Journal – Continued

I AWOKE in my own bed. If it be that I had not dreamt, the Count must have carried me here. I tried to satisfy myself on the subject, but could not arrive at any unquestionable result. To be sure, there were certain small evidences, such as that my clothes were folded and laid by in a manner which was not my habit. My watch was still unwound, and I am rigorously accustomed to wind it the last thing before going to bed, and many such details. But these things are no proof, for they may have been evidences that my mind was not as usual, and, from some cause or another, I had certainly been much upset. I must watch for proof. Of one thing I am glad: if it was that the Count carried me here and undressed me, he must have been hurried in his task, for my pockets are intact. I am sure this diary would have been a mystery to him which he would not have brooked. He would have taken or destroyed it. As I look round this room, although it has been to me so full of fear, it is now a sort of sanctuary, for nothing can be more dreadful than those awful women, who were – who *are* – waiting to suck my blood.

* * *

18 May. I have been down to look at that room again in daylight, for I *must* know the truth. When I got to the doorway at the top of the stairs I found it closed. It had been so forcibly driven against the jamb that part of the woodwork was splintered. I could see that the bolt of the lock had not been shot, but the door is fastened from the inside. I fear it was no dream, and must act on this surmise.

* * *

19 May. I am surely in the toils. Last night the Count asked me in the suavest tones to write three letters, one saying that my work here was nearly done, and that I should start for home within a few days, another that I was starting on the next morning from the time of the letter, and the third that I had left the castle and arrived at Bistritz. I would fain have rebelled, but felt that in the present state of things it would be madness to quarrel openly with the Count whilst I am so absolutely in his power; and to refuse would be to excite his suspicion and to arouse his anger. He knows that I know too much, and that I must not live, lest I be dangerous to him; my only chance is to prolong my opportunities. Something may occur which will give me a chance to escape. I saw in his eyes something of that gathering wrath which was manifest when he hurled that fair woman from him. He explained to me that posts were few and uncertain, and that my writing now would ensure ease of mind to my friends; and he assured me with so much impressiveness that he would countermand the later letters, which would be held over at Bistritz until due time in case chance would admit of my prolonging my stay, that to oppose him would have been to create new suspicion. I therefore pretended to fall in with his views, and asked him what dates I should put on the letters. He calculated a minute, and then said:

"The first should be June 12, the second June 19, and the third June 29."

I know now the span of my life. God help me!

* * *

28 May. There is a chance of escape, or at any rate of being able to send word home. A band of Szgany have come to the castle, and are encamped in the courtyard. These Szgany are gipsies; I have notes of them in my book. They are peculiar to this part of the world, though allied to the ordinary gipsies all the world over. There are thousands of them in Hungary and Transylvania, who are almost outside all law. They attach themselves as a rule to some great noble or *boyar*, and call themselves by his name. They are fearless and without religion, save superstition, and they talk only their own varieties of the Romany tongue.

I shall write some letters home, and shall try to get them to have them posted. I have already spoken them through my window to begin acquaintanceship. They took their hats off and made obeisance and many signs, which, however, I could not understand any more than I could their spoken language....

* * *

I have written the letters. Mina's is in shorthand, and I simply ask Mr. Hawkins to communicate with her. To her I have explained my situation, but without the horrors which I may only surmise. It would shock and frighten her to death were I to expose my heart to her. Should the letters not carry, then the Count shall not yet know my secret or the extent of my knowledge....

* * *

I have given the letters; I threw them through the bars of my window with a gold piece, and made what signs I could to have them posted. The man who took them pressed them to his heart and bowed, and then put them in his cap. I could do no more. I stole back to the study, and began to read. As the Count did not come in, I have written here....

* * *

The Count has come. He sat down beside me, and said in his smoothest voice as he opened two letters:

"The Szgany has given me these, of which, though I know not whence they come, I shall, of course, take care. See!" – he must have looked at it – "one is from you, and to my friend Peter Hawkins; the other" – here he caught sight of the strange symbols as he opened the envelope, and the dark look came into his face, and his eyes blazed wickedly – "the other is a vile thing, an outrage upon friendship and hospitality! It is not signed. Well! So it cannot matter to us." And he calmly held letter and envelope in the flame of the lamp till they were consumed. Then he went on:

"The letter to Hawkins – that I shall, of course, send on, since it is yours. Your letters are sacred to me. Your pardon, my friend, that unknowingly I did break the seal. Will you not cover it again?" He held out the letter to me, and with a courteous bow handed me a clean envelope. I could only redirect it and hand it to him in silence. When he went out of the room I could hear the key turn softly. A minute later I went over and tried it, and the door was locked.

When, an hour or two after, the Count came quietly into the room, his coming awakened me, for I had gone to sleep on the sofa. He was very courteous and very cheery in his manner, and seeing that I had been sleeping, he said:

"So, my friend, you are tired? Get to bed. There is the surest rest. I may not have the pleasure to talk tonight, since there are many labours to me; but you will sleep, I pray." I passed to my room and went to bed, and, strange to say, slept without dreaming. Despair has its own calms.

* * *

31 May. This morning when I woke I thought I would provide myself with some paper and envelopes from my bag and keep them in my pocket, so that I might write in case I should get an opportunity, but again a surprise, again a shock!

Every scrap of paper was gone, and with it all my notes, my memoranda, relating to railways and travel, my letter of credit, in fact all that might be useful to me were I once outside the castle. I sat and pondered awhile, and then some thought occurred to me, and I made search of my portmanteau and in the wardrobe where I had placed my clothes.

The suit in which I had travelled was gone, and also my overcoat and rug; I could find no trace of them anywhere. This looked like some new scheme of villainy....

* * *

17 June. This morning, as I was sitting on the edge of my bed cudgelling my brains, I heard without a cracking of whips and pounding and scraping of horses' feet up the rocky path beyond the courtyard. With joy I hurried to the window, and saw drive into the yard two great leiter-wagons, each drawn by eight sturdy horses, and at the head of each pair a Slovak, with his wide hat, great nail-studded belt, dirty sheepskin, and high boots. They had also their long staves in hand. I ran to the door, intending to descend and try and join them through the main hall, as I thought that way might be opened for them. Again a shock: my door was fastened on the outside.

Then I ran to the window and cried to them. They looked up at me stupidly and pointed, but just then the 'hetman' of the Szgany came out, and seeing them pointing to my window, said something, at which they laughed. Henceforth no effort of mine, no piteous cry or agonised entreaty, would make them even look at me. They resolutely turned away. The leiter-wagons contained great, square boxes, with handles of thick rope; these were evidently empty by the ease with which the Slovaks handled them, and by their resonance as they were roughly moved. When they were all unloaded and packed in a great heap in one corner of the yard, the Slovaks were given some money by the Szgany, and spitting on it for luck, lazily went each to his horse's head. Shortly afterwards, I heard the cracking of their whips die away in the distance.

* * *

24 June, Before Morning. Last night the Count left me early, and locked himself into his own room. As soon as I dared I ran up the winding stair, and looked out of the window, which opened south. I thought I would watch for the Count, for there is something going on. The Szgany are quartered somewhere in the castle and are doing work of some kind. I know it, for now and then I hear a far-away muffled sound as of mattock and spade, and, whatever it is, it must be the end of some ruthless villainy.

I had been at the window somewhat less than half an hour, when I saw something coming out of the Count's window. I drew back and watched carefully, and saw the whole man emerge. It was a new shock to me to find that he had on the suit of clothes which I had worn whilst travelling here, and slung over his shoulder the terrible bag which I had seen the women take away. There could be no doubt as to his quest, and in my garb, too! This, then, is his new scheme of evil: that he will allow others to see me, as they think, so that he may both leave evidence that I have been seen in the towns or villages posting my own letters, and that any wickedness which he may do shall by the local people be attributed to me.

It makes me rage to think that this can go on, and whilst I am shut up here, a veritable prisoner, but without that protection of the law which is even a criminal's right and consolation.

I thought I would watch for the Count's return, and for a long time sat doggedly at the window. Then I began to notice that there were some quaint little specks floating in the rays of the moonlight. They were like the tiniest grains of dust, and they whirled round and gathered in clusters in a nebulous sort of way. I watched them with a sense of soothing, and a sort of calm stole over me. I leaned back in the embrasure in a more comfortable position, so that I could enjoy more fully the aerial gambolling.

Something made me start up, a low, piteous howling of dogs somewhere far below in the valley, which was hidden from my sight. Louder it seemed to ring in my ears, and the floating motes of dust to take new shapes to the sound as they danced in the moonlight. I felt myself struggling to awake to some call of my instincts; nay, my very soul was struggling, and my half-remembered sensibilities were striving to answer the call. I was becoming hypnotised! Quicker and quicker danced the dust; the moonbeams seemed to quiver as they went by me into the mass of gloom beyond. More and more they gathered till they seemed to take dim phantom shapes. And then I started, broad awake and in full possession of my senses, and ran screaming from the place. The phantom shapes, which were becoming gradually materialised from the moonbeams, were those of the three ghostly women to whom I was doomed. I fled, and felt somewhat safer in my own room, where there was no moonlight and where the lamp was burning brightly.

When a couple of hours had passed I heard something stirring in the Count's room, something like a sharp wail quickly suppressed; and then there was silence, deep, awful silence, which chilled me. With a beating heart, I tried the door; but I was locked in my prison, and could do nothing. I sat down and simply cried.

As I sat I heard a sound in the courtyard without – the agonised cry of a woman. I rushed to the window, and throwing it up, peered out between the bars. There, indeed, was a woman with dishevelled hair, holding her hands over her heart as one distressed with running. She was leaning against a corner of the gateway. When she saw my face at the window she threw herself forward, and shouted in a voice laden with menace:

"Monster, give me my child!"

She threw herself on her knees, and raising up her hands, cried the same words in tones which wrung my heart. Then she tore her hair and beat her breast, and abandoned herself to all the violences of extravagant emotion. Finally, she threw herself forward, and, though I could not see her, I could hear the beating of her naked hands against the door.

Somewhere high overhead, probably on the tower, I heard the voice of the Count calling in his harsh, metallic whisper. His call seemed to be answered from far and wide by the howling of wolves. Before many minutes had passed a pack of them poured, like a pent-up dam when liberated, through the wide entrance into the courtyard.

There was no cry from the woman, and the howling of the wolves was but short. Before long they streamed away singly, licking their lips.

I could not pity her, for I knew now what had become of her child, and she was better dead.

What shall I do? what can I do? How can I escape from this dreadful thing of night and gloom and fear?

* * *

25 June, Morning. No man knows till he has suffered from the night how sweet and how dear to his heart and eye the morning can be. When the sun grew so high this morning that it struck the top of the great gateway opposite my window, the high spot which it touched seemed to me as if the dove from the ark had lighted there. My fear fell from me as if it had been a vaporous garment which dissolved in the warmth. I must take action of some sort whilst the courage of the day is upon me. Last night one of my post-dated letters went to post, the first of that fatal series which is to blot out the very traces of my existence from the earth.

Let me not think of it. Action!

It has always been at night-time that I have been molested or threatened, or in some way in danger or in fear. I have not yet seen the Count in the daylight. Can it be that he sleeps when others wake, that he may be awake whilst they sleep? If I could only get into his room! But there is no possible way. The door is always locked, no way for me.

Yes, there is a way, if one dares to take it. Where his body has gone why may not another body go? I have seen him myself crawl from his window. Why should not I imitate him, and go in by his window? The chances are desperate, but my need is more desperate still. I shall risk it. At the worst it can only be death; and a man's death is not a calf's, and the dreaded Hereafter may still be open to me. God help me in my task! Good-bye, Mina, if I fail; good-bye, my faithful friend and second father; good-bye, all, and last of all Mina!

* * *

Same Day, Later. I have made the effort, and God, helping me, have come safely back to this room. I must put down every detail in order. I went whilst my courage was fresh straight to the window on the south side, and at once got outside on the narrow ledge of stone which runs around the building on this side. The stones are big and roughly cut, and the mortar has by process of time been washed away between them. I took off my boots, and ventured out on the desperate way. I looked down once, so as to make sure that a sudden glimpse of the awful depth would not overcome me, but after that kept my eyes away from it.

I knew pretty well the direction and distance of the Count's window, and made for it as well as I could, having regard to the opportunities available. I did not feel dizzy – I suppose I was too excited – and the time seemed ridiculously short till I found myself standing on the window-sill and trying to raise up the sash. I was filled with agitation, however, when I bent down and slid feet foremost in through the window. Then I looked around for the Count, but, with surprise and gladness, made a discovery. The room was empty! It was barely furnished with odd things, which seemed to have never been used; the furniture was something the same style as that in the south rooms, and was covered with dust.

I looked for the key, but it was not in the lock, and I could not find it anywhere. The only thing I found was a great heap of gold in one corner – gold of all kinds, Roman, and British, and Austrian, and Hungarian, and Greek and Turkish money, covered with a film of dust, as though it had lain long in the ground. None of it that I noticed was less than three hundred years old. There were also chains and ornaments, some jewelled, but all of them old and stained.

At one corner of the room was a heavy door. I tried it, for, since I could not find the key of the room or the key of the outer door, which was the main object of my search, I must make further examination, or all my efforts would be in vain. It was open, and led through a stone passage to a circular stairway, which went steeply down. I descended, minding carefully where I went, for the stairs were dark, being only lit by loopholes in the heavy masonry. At the bottom there was a dark, tunnel-like passage, through which came a deathly, sickly odour, the odour of old earth newly turned. As I went through the passage the smell grew closer and heavier. At last I pulled open a heavy door which stood ajar, and found myself in an old, ruined chapel, which had evidently been used as a graveyard. The roof was broken, and in two places were steps leading to vaults, but the ground had recently been dug over, and the earth placed in great wooden boxes, manifestly those which had been brought by the Slovaks. There was nobody about, and I made search for any further outlet, but there was none. Then I went over every inch of the ground, so as not to lose a chance. I went down even into the vaults, where the dim light struggled, although to do so was a dread to my very soul. Into two of these I went, but saw nothing except fragments of old coffins and piles of dust; in the third, however, I made a discovery.

There, in one of the great boxes, of which there were fifty in all, on a pile of newly dug earth, lay the Count! He was either dead or asleep, I could not say which – for the eyes were open and stony, but without the glassiness of death – and the cheeks had the warmth of life through all their pallor; the lips were as red as ever. But there was no sign of movement, no pulse, no breath, no beating of the heart. I bent over him, and tried to find any sign of life, but in vain. He could not have lain there long, for the earthy smell would have passed away in a few hours. By the side of the box was its cover, pierced with holes here and there. I thought he might have the keys on him, but when I went to search I saw the dead eyes, and in them, dead though they were, such a look of hate, though unconscious of me or my presence, that I fled from the place, and leaving the Count's room by the window, crawled again up the castle wall. Regaining my room, I threw myself panting upon the bed and tried to think....

* * *

29 June. Today is the date of my last letter, and the Count has taken steps to prove that it was genuine, for again I saw him leave the castle by the same window, and in my clothes. As he went down the wall, lizard fashion, I wished I had a gun or some lethal weapon, that I might destroy him; but I fear that no weapon wrought alone by man's hand would have any effect on him. I dared not wait to see him return, for I feared to see those weird sisters. I came back to the library, and read there till I fell asleep.

I was awakened by the Count, who looked at me as grimly as a man can look as he said:

"Tomorrow, my friend, we must part. You return to your beautiful England, I to some work which may have such an end that we may never meet. Your letter home has been despatched; tomorrow I shall not be here, but all shall be ready for your journey. In the morning come the Szgany, who have some labours of their own here, and also come some Slovaks. When they have gone, my carriage shall come for you, and shall bear you to the Borgo Pass to meet the diligence from Bukovina to Bistritz. But I am in hopes that I shall see more of you at Castle Dracula." I suspected him, and determined to test his sincerity. Sincerity! It seems like a profanation of the word to write it in connection with such a monster, so asked him point-blank:

"Why may I not go tonight?"

"Because, dear sir, my coachman and horses are away on a mission."

"But I would walk with pleasure. I want to get away at once." He smiled, such a soft, smooth, diabolical smile that I knew there was some trick behind his smoothness. He said:

"And your baggage?"

"I do not care about it. I can send for it some other time."

The Count stood up, and said, with a sweet courtesy which made me rub my eyes, it seemed so real:

"You English have a saying which is close to my heart, for its spirit is that which rules our *boyars*: 'Welcome the coming; speed the parting guest.' Come with me, my dear young friend. Not an hour shall you wait in my house against your will, though sad am I at your going, and that you so suddenly desire it. Come!" With a stately gravity, he, with the lamp, preceded me down the stairs and along the hall. Suddenly he stopped.

"Hark!"

Close at hand came the howling of many wolves. It was almost as if the sound sprang up at the rising of his hand, just as the music of a great orchestra seems to leap under the bâton of the conductor. After a pause of a moment, he proceeded, in his stately way, to the door, drew back the ponderous bolts, unhooked the heavy chains, and began to draw it open.

To my intense astonishment I saw that it was unlocked. Suspiciously, I looked all round, but could see no key of any kind.

As the door began to open, the howling of the wolves without grew louder and angrier; their red jaws, with champing teeth, and their blunt-clawed feet as they leaped, came in through the opening door. I knew then that to struggle at the moment against the Count was useless. With such allies as these at his command, I could do nothing. But still the door continued slowly to open, and only the Count's body stood in the gap. Suddenly it struck me that this might be the moment and means of my doom; I was to be given to the wolves, and at my own instigation. There was a diabolical wickedness in the idea great enough for the Count, and as a last chance I cried out:

"Shut the door; I shall wait till morning!" and covered my face with my hands to hide my tears of bitter disappointment. With one sweep of his powerful arm, the Count threw the door shut, and the great bolts clanged and echoed through the hall as they shot back into their places.

In silence we returned to the library, and after a minute or two I went to my own room. The last I saw of Count Dracula was his kissing his hand to me; with a red light of triumph in his eyes, and with a smile that Judas in hell might be proud of.

When I was in my room and about to lie down, I thought I heard a whispering at my door. I went to it softly and listened. Unless my ears deceived me, I heard the voice of the Count:

"Back, back, to your own place! Your time is not yet come. Wait! Have patience! Tonight is mine. Tomorrow night is yours!" There was a low, sweet ripple of laughter, and in a rage I threw open the door, and saw without the three terrible women licking their lips. As I appeared they all joined in a horrible laugh, and ran away.

I came back to my room and threw myself on my knees. It is then so near the end? Tomorrow! Tomorrow! Lord, help me, and those to whom I am dear!

* * *

30 June, Morning. These may be the last words I ever write in this diary. I slept till just before the dawn, and when I woke threw myself on my knees, for I determined that if Death came he should find me ready.

At last I felt that subtle change in the air, and knew that the morning had come. Then came the welcome cock-crow, and I felt that I was safe. With a glad heart, I opened my door and ran down to the hall. I had seen that the door was unlocked, and now escape was before me. With hands that trembled with eagerness, I unhooked the chains and drew back the massive bolts.

But the door would not move. Despair seized me. I pulled, and pulled, at the door, and shook it till, massive as it was, it rattled in its casement. I could see the bolt shot. It had been locked after I left the Count.

Then a wild desire took me to obtain that key at any risk, and I determined then and there to scale the wall again and gain the Count's room. He might kill me, but death now seemed the happier choice of evils. Without a pause I rushed up to the east window, and scrambled down the wall, as before, into the Count's room. It was empty, but that was as I expected. I could not see a key anywhere, but the heap of gold remained. I went through the door in the corner and down the winding stair and along the dark passage to the old chapel. I knew now well enough where to find the monster I sought.

The great box was in the same place, close against the wall, but the lid was laid on it, not fastened down, but with the nails ready in their places to be hammered home. I knew I must reach the body for the key, so I raised the lid, and laid it back against the wall; and then I saw something which filled my very soul with horror. There lay the Count, but looking as if his youth had been half renewed, for the white hair and moustache were changed to dark iron-grey; the cheeks were fuller, and the white skin seemed ruby-red underneath; the mouth was redder than ever, for on the lips were gouts of fresh blood, which trickled from the corners of the mouth and ran over the chin and neck. Even the deep, burning eyes seemed set amongst swollen flesh, for the lids and pouches underneath were bloated. It seemed as if the whole awful creature were simply gorged with blood. He lay like a filthy leech, exhausted with his repletion. I shuddered as I bent over to touch him, and every sense in me revolted at the contact; but I had to search, or I was lost. The coming night might see my own body a banquet in a similar way to those horrid three.

I felt all over the body, but no sign could I find of the key. Then I stopped and looked at the Count. There was a mocking smile on the bloated face which seemed to drive me mad. This was the being I was helping to transfer to London, where, perhaps, for centuries to come he might, amongst its teeming millions, satiate his lust for blood, and create a new and ever-widening circle of semi-demons to batten on the helpless. The very thought drove me mad. A terrible desire came upon me to rid the world of such a monster. There was no lethal weapon at hand, but I seized a shovel which the workmen had been using to fill the cases, and lifting it high, struck, with the edge downward, at the hateful face. But as I did so the head turned, and the eyes fell full upon me, with all their blaze of basilisk horror. The sight seemed to paralyse me, and the shovel turned in my hand and glanced from the face, merely making a deep gash above the forehead. The shovel fell from my hand across the box, and as I pulled it away the flange of the blade caught the edge of the lid which fell over again, and hid the horrid thing from my sight. The last glimpse I had was of the bloated face, blood-stained and fixed with a grin of malice which would have held its own in the nethermost hell.

I thought and thought what should be my next move, but my brain seemed on fire, and I waited with a despairing feeling growing over me. As I waited I heard in the distance a gipsy song sung by merry voices coming closer, and through their song the rolling of heavy wheels and the cracking of whips; the Szgany and the Slovaks of whom the Count had spoken were coming. With a last look around and at the box which contained the vile body, I ran from the place and gained the Count's room, determined to rush out at the moment the door should be opened.

With strained ears, I listened, and heard downstairs the grinding of the key in the great lock and the falling back of the heavy door. There must have been some other means of entry, or some one had a key for one of the locked doors. Then there came the sound of many feet tramping and dying away in some passage which sent up a clanging echo. I turned to run down again towards the vault, where I might find the new entrance; but at the moment there seemed to come a violent puff of wind, and the door to the winding stair blew to with a shock that set the dust from the lintels flying. When I ran to push it open, I found that it was hopelessly fast. I was again a prisoner, and the net of doom was closing round me more closely.

As I write there is in the passage below a sound of many tramping feet and the crash of weights being set down heavily, doubtless the boxes, with their freight of earth. There is a sound of hammering; it is the box being nailed down. Now I can hear the heavy feet tramping again along the hall, with many other idle feet coming behind them.

The door is shut, and the chains rattle; there is a grinding of the key in the lock; I can hear the key withdraw: then another door opens and shuts; I hear the creaking of lock and bolt.

Hark! in the courtyard and down the rocky way the roll of heavy wheels, the crack of whips, and the chorus of the Szgany as they pass into the distance.

I am alone in the castle with those awful women. Faugh! Mina is a woman, and there is nought in common. They are devils of the Pit!

I shall not remain alone with them; I shall try to scale the castle wall farther than I have yet attempted. I shall take some of the gold with me, lest I want it later. I may find a way from this dreadful place.

And then away for home! away to the quickest and nearest train! away from this cursed spot, from this cursed land, where the devil and his children still walk with earthly feet!

At least God's mercy is better than that of these monsters, and the precipice is steep and high. At its foot a man may sleep – as a man. Good-bye, all! Mina!

The complete and unabridged text is available
online, *from flametreepublishing.com/extras*

If you enjoyed this, you might also like...
'Dracula's Guest,' see page 73
The Lady of the Shroud (chapters III–V), see page 420

The Jewel of Seven Stars

Chapter I
A Summons in the Night

IT ALL SEEMED SO REAL that I could hardly imagine that it had ever occurred before; and yet each episode came, not as a fresh step in the logic of things, but as something expected. It is in such a wise that memory plays its pranks for good or ill; for pleasure or pain; for weal or woe. It is thus that life is bittersweet, and that which has been done becomes eternal.

Again, the light skiff, ceasing to shoot through the lazy water as when the oars flashed and dripped, glided out of the fierce July sunlight into the cool shade of the great drooping willow branches – I standing up in the swaying boat, she sitting still and with deft fingers guarding herself from stray twigs or the freedom of the resilience of moving boughs. Again, the water looked golden-brown under the canopy of translucent green; and the grassy bank was of emerald hue. Again, we sat in the cool shade, with the myriad noises of nature both without and within our bower merging into that drowsy hum in whose sufficing environment the great world with its disturbing trouble, and its more disturbing joys, can be effectually forgotten. Again, in that blissful solitude the young girl lost the convention of her prim, narrow upbringing, and told me in a natural, dreamy way of the loneliness of her new life. With an undertone of sadness she made me feel how in that spacious home each one of the household was isolated by the personal magnificence of her father and herself; that there confidence had no altar, and sympathy no shrine; and that there even her father's face was as distant as the old country life seemed now. Once more, the wisdom of my manhood and the experience of my years laid themselves at the girl's feet. It was seemingly their own doing; for the individual 'I' had no say in the matter, but only just obeyed imperative orders. And once again the flying seconds multiplied themselves endlessly. For it is in the arcana of dreams that existences merge and renew themselves, change and yet keep the same – like the soul of a musician in a fugue. And so memory swooned, again and again, in sleep.

It seems that there is never to be any perfect rest. Even in Eden the snake rears its head among the laden boughs of the Tree of Knowledge. The silence of the dreamless night is broken by the roar of the avalanche; the hissing of sudden floods; the clanging of the engine bell marking its sweep through a sleeping American town; the clanking of distant paddles over the sea.... Whatever it is, it is breaking the charm of my Eden. The canopy of greenery above us, starred with diamond-points of light, seems to quiver in the ceaseless beat of paddles; and the restless bell seems as though it would never cease....

All at once the gates of Sleep were thrown wide open, and my waking ears took in the cause of the disturbing sounds. Waking existence is prosaic enough – there was somebody knocking and ringing at someone's street door.

I was pretty well accustomed in my Jermyn Street chambers to passing sounds; usually I did not concern myself, sleeping or waking, with the doings, however noisy, of my neighbours. But this noise was too continuous, too insistent, too imperative to be ignored. There was some active intelligence behind that ceaseless sound; and some stress or need behind the intelligence. I was not altogether selfish, and at the thought of someone's need I was, without premeditation, out of bed. Instinctively I looked at my watch. It was just three o'clock; there was a faint edging of grey round the green blind which darkened my room. It was evident that the knocking and ringing were at the door of our own house; and it was evident, too, that there was no one awake to answer the call. I slipped on my dressing-gown and slippers, and went down to the hall door. When I opened it there stood a dapper groom, with one hand pressed unflinchingly on the electric bell whilst with the other he raised a ceaseless clangour with the knocker. The instant he saw me the noise ceased; one hand went up instinctively to the brim of his hat, and the other produced a letter from his pocket. A neat brougham was opposite the door, the horses were breathing heavily as though they had come fast. A policeman, with his night lantern still alight at his belt, stood by, attracted to the spot by the noise.

"Beg pardon, sir, I'm sorry for disturbing you, but my orders was imperative; I was not to lose a moment, but to knock and ring till someone came. May I ask you, sir, if Mr. Malcolm Ross lives here?"

"I am Mr. Malcolm Ross."

"Then this letter is for you, sir, and the bro'am is for you too, sir!"

I took, with a strange curiosity, the letter which he handed to me. As a barrister I had had, of course, odd experiences now and then, including sudden demands upon my time; but never anything like this. I stepped back into the hall, closing the door to, but leaving it ajar; then I switched on the electric light. The letter was directed in a strange hand, a woman's. It began at once without 'dear sir' or any such address:

> You said you would like to help me if I needed it; and I believe you meant what you said. The time has come sooner than I expected. I am in dreadful trouble, and do not know where to turn, or to whom to apply. An attempt has, I fear, been made to murder my Father; though, thank God, he still lives. But he is quite unconscious. The doctors and police have been sent for; but there is no one here whom I can depend on. Come at once if you are able to; and forgive me if you can. I suppose I shall realise later what I have done in asking such a favour; but at present I cannot think. Come! Come at once!
> Margaret Trelawny.

Pain and exultation struggled in my mind as I read; but the mastering thought was that she was in trouble and had called on me – me! My dreaming of her, then, was not altogether without a cause. I called out to the groom:

"Wait! I shall be with you in a minute!" Then I flew upstairs.

A very few minutes sufficed to wash and dress; and we were soon driving through the streets as fast as the horses could go. It was market morning, and when we got out on Piccadilly there was an endless stream of carts coming from the west; but for the rest the roadway was clear, and we went quickly. I had told the groom to come into the brougham with me so that he could tell me what had happened as we went along. He sat awkwardly, with his hat on his knees as he spoke.

"Miss Trelawny, sir, sent a man to tell us to get out a carriage at once; and when we was ready she come herself and gave me the letter and told Morgan – the coachman, sir – to fly. She said as I was to lose not a second, but to keep knocking till someone come."

"Yes, I know, I know – you told me! What I want to know is, why she sent for me. What happened in the house?"

"I don't quite know myself, sir; except that master was found in his room senseless, with the sheets all bloody, and a wound on his head. He couldn't be waked nohow. 'Twas Miss Trelawny herself as found him."

"How did she come to find him at such an hour? It was late in the night, I suppose?"

"I don't know, sir; I didn't hear nothing at all of the details."

As he could tell me no more, I stopped the carriage for a moment to let him get out on the box; then I turned the matter over in my mind as I sat alone. There were many things which I could have asked the servant; and for a few moments after he had gone I was angry with myself for not having used my opportunity. On second thought, however, I was glad the temptation was gone. I felt that it would be more delicate to learn what I wanted to know of Miss Trelawny's surroundings from herself, rather than from her servants.

We bowled swiftly along Knightsbridge, the small noise of our well-appointed vehicle sounding hollowly in the morning air. We turned up the Kensington Palace Road and presently stopped opposite a great house on the left-hand side, nearer, so far as I could judge, the Notting Hill than the Kensington end of the avenue. It was a truly fine house, not only with regard to size but to architecture. Even in the dim grey light of the morning, which tends to diminish the size of things, it looked big.

Miss Trelawny met me in the hall. She was not in any way shy. She seemed to rule all around her with a sort of high-bred dominance, all the more remarkable as she was greatly agitated and as pale as snow. In the great hall were several servants, the men standing together near the hall door, and the women clinging together in the further corners and doorways. A police superintendent had been talking to Miss Trelawny; two men in uniform and one plain-clothes man stood near him. As she took my hand impulsively there was a look of relief in her eyes, and she gave a gentle sigh of relief. Her salutation was simple.

"I knew you would come!"

The clasp of the hand can mean a great deal, even when it is not intended to mean anything especially. Miss Trelawny's hand somehow became lost in my own. It was not that it was a small hand; it was fine and flexible, with long delicate fingers – a rare and beautiful hand; it was the unconscious self-surrender. And though at the moment I could not dwell on the cause of the thrill which swept me, it came back to me later.

She turned and said to the police superintendent:

"This is Mr. Malcolm Ross." The police officer saluted as he answered:

"I know Mr. Malcolm Ross, miss. Perhaps he will remember I had the honour of working with him in the Brixton Coining case." I had not at first glance noticed who it was, my whole attention having been taken with Miss Trelawny.

"Of course, Superintendent Dolan, I remember very well!" I said as we shook hands. I could not but note that the acquaintanceship seemed a relief to Miss Trelawny. There was a certain vague uneasiness in her manner which took my attention; instinctively I felt that it would be less embarrassing for her to speak with me alone. So I said to the Superintendent:

"Perhaps it will be better if Miss Trelawny will see me alone for a few minutes. You, of course, have already heard all she knows; and I shall understand better how things are if I may ask some questions. I will then talk the matter over with you if I may."

"I shall be glad to be of what service I can, sir," he answered heartily.

Following Miss Trelawny, I moved over to a dainty room which opened from the hall and looked out on the garden at the back of the house. When we had entered and I had closed the door she said:

"I will thank you later for your goodness in coming to me in my trouble; but at present you can best help me when you know the facts."

"Go on," I said. "Tell me all you know and spare no detail, however trivial it may at the present time seem to be." She went on at once:

"I was awakened by some sound; I do not know what. I only know that it came through my sleep; for all at once I found myself awake, with my heart beating wildly, listening anxiously for some sound from my Father's room. My room is next Father's, and I can often hear him moving about before I fall asleep. He works late at night, sometimes very late indeed; so that when I wake early, as I do occasionally, or in the grey of the dawn, I hear him still moving. I tried once to remonstrate with him about staying up so late, as it cannot be good for him; but I never ventured to repeat the experiment. You know how stern and cold he can be – at least you may remember what I told you about him; and when he is polite in this mood he is dreadful. When he is angry I can bear it much better; but when he is slow and deliberate, and the side of his mouth lifts up to show the sharp teeth, I think I feel – well, I don't know how! Last night I got up softly and stole to the door, for I really feared to disturb him. There was not any noise of moving, and no kind of cry at all; but there was a queer kind of dragging sound, and a slow, heavy breathing. Oh! It was dreadful, waiting there in the dark and the silence, and fearing – fearing I did not know what!

"At last I took my courage *a deux mains*, and turning the handle as softly as I could, I opened the door a tiny bit. It was quite dark within; I could just see the outline of the windows. But in the darkness the sound of breathing, becoming more distinct, was appalling. As I listened, this continued; but there was no other sound. I pushed the door open all at once. I was afraid to open it slowly; I felt as if there might be some dreadful thing behind it ready to pounce out on me! Then I switched on the electric light, and stepped into the room. I looked first at the bed. The sheets were all crumpled up, so that I knew Father had been in bed; but there was a great dark red patch in the centre of the bed, and spreading to the edge of it, that made my heart stand still. As I was gazing at it the sound of the breathing came across the room, and my eyes followed to it. There was Father on his right side with the other arm under him, just as if his dead body had been thrown there all in a heap. The track of blood went across the room up to the bed, and there was a pool all around him which looked terribly red and glittering as I bent over to examine him. The place where he lay was right in front of the big safe. He was in his pyjamas. The left sleeve was torn, showing his bare arm, and stretched out toward the safe. It looked – oh! so terrible, patched all with blood, and with the flesh torn or cut all around a gold chain bangle on his wrist. I did not know he wore such a thing, and it seemed to give me a new shock of surprise."

She paused a moment; and as I wished to relieve her by a moment's divergence of thought, I said:

"Oh, that need not surprise you. You will see the most unlikely men wearing bangles. I have seen a judge condemn a man to death, and the wrist of the hand he held up had a gold bangle." She did not seem to heed much the words or the idea; the pause, however, relieved her somewhat, and she went on in a steadier voice:

"I did not lose a moment in summoning aid, for I feared he might bleed to death. I rang the bell, and then went out and called for help as loudly as I could. In what must have been a very short time – though it seemed an incredibly long one to me – some of the servants came running up; and then others, till the room seemed full of staring eyes, and dishevelled hair, and night clothes of all sorts.

"We lifted Father on a sofa; and the housekeeper, Mrs. Grant, who seemed to have her wits about her more than any of us, began to look where the flow of blood came from. In a few seconds it became apparent that it came from the arm which was bare. There was a deep wound – not clean-cut as with a knife, but like a jagged rent or tear – close to the wrist, which seemed to have cut into the vein. Mrs. Grant tied a handkerchief round the cut, and screwed it up tight with a silver paper-cutter; and the flow of blood seemed to be checked at once. By this time I had come to my senses – or such of them as remained; and I sent off one man for the doctor and another for the police. When they had gone, I felt that, except for the servants, I was all alone in the house, and that I knew nothing – of my Father or anything else; and a great longing came to me to have someone with me who could help me. Then I thought of you and your kind offer in the boat under the willow-tree; and, without waiting to think, I told the men to get a carriage ready at once, and I scribbled a note and sent it on to you."

She paused. I did not like to say just then anything of how I felt. I looked at her; I think she understood, for her eyes were raised to mine for a moment and then fell, leaving her cheeks as red as peony roses. With a manifest effort she went on with her story:

"The Doctor was with us in an incredibly short time. The groom had met him letting himself into his house with his latchkey, and he came here running. He made a proper tourniquet for poor Father's arm, and then went home to get some appliances. I dare say he will be back almost immediately. Then a policeman came, and sent a message to the station; and very soon the Superintendent was here. Then you came."

There was a long pause, and I ventured to take her hand for an instant. Without a word more we opened the door, and joined the Superintendent in the hall. He hurried up to us, saying as he came:

"I have been examining everything myself, and have sent off a message to Scotland Yard. You see, Mr. Ross, there seemed so much that was odd about the case that I thought we had better have the best man of the Criminal Investigation Department that we could get. So I sent a note asking to have Sergeant Daw sent at once. You remember him, sir, in that American poisoning case at Hoxton."

"Oh yes," I said, "I remember him well; in that and other cases, for I have benefited several times by his skill and acumen. He has a mind that works as truly as any that I know. When I have been for the defence, and believed my man was innocent, I was glad to have him against us!"

"That is high praise, sir!" said the Superintendent gratified: "I am glad you approve of my choice; that I did well in sending for him."

I answered heartily:

"Could not be better. I do not doubt that between you we shall get at the facts – and what lies behind them!"

We ascended to Mr. Trelawny's room, where we found everything exactly as his daughter had described.

There came a ring at the house bell, and a minute later a man was shown into the room. A young man with aquiline features, keen grey eyes, and a forehead that stood out square and broad as that of a thinker. In his hand he had a black bag which he at once opened. Miss Trelawny introduced us: "Doctor Winchester, Mr. Ross, Superintendent Dolan." We bowed mutually, and he, without a moment's delay, began his work. We all waited, and eagerly watched him as he proceeded to dress the wound. As he went on he turned now and again to call the Superintendent's attention to some point about the wound, the latter proceeding to enter the fact at once in his notebook.

"See! Several parallel cuts or scratches beginning on the left side of the wrist and in some places endangering the radial artery.

"These small wounds here, deep and jagged, seem as if made with a blunt instrument. This in particular would seem as if made with some kind of sharp wedge; the flesh round it seems torn as if with lateral pressure."

Turning to Miss Trelawny he said presently:

"Do you think we might remove this bangle? It is not absolutely necessary, as it will fall lower on the wrist where it can hang loosely; but it might add to the patient's comfort later on." The poor girl flushed deeply as she answered in a low voice:

"I do not know. I – I have only recently come to live with my Father; and I know so little of his life or his ideas that I fear I can hardly judge in such a matter. The Doctor, after a keen glance at her, said in a very kindly way:

"Forgive me! I did not know. But in any case you need not be distressed. It is not required at present to move it. Were it so I should do so at once on my own responsibility. If it be necessary later on, we can easily remove it with a file. Your Father doubtless has some object in keeping it as it is. See! there is a tiny key attached to it...." As he was speaking he stopped and bent lower, taking from my hand the candle which I held and lowering it till its light fell on the bangle. Then motioning me to hold the candle in the same position, he took from his pocket a magnifying-glass which he adjusted. When he had made a careful examination he stood up and handed the magnifying-glass to Dolan, saying as he did so:

"You had better examine it yourself. That is no ordinary bangle. The gold is wrought over triple steel links; see where it is worn away. It is manifestly not meant to be removed lightly; and it would need more than an ordinary file to do it."

The Superintendent bent his great body; but not getting close enough that way knelt down by the sofa as the Doctor had done. He examined the bangle minutely, turning it slowly round so that no particle of it escaped observation. Then he stood up and handed the magnifying-glass to me. "When you have examined it yourself," he said, "let the lady look at it if she will," and he commenced to write at length in his notebook.

I made a simple alteration in his suggestion. I held out the glass toward Miss Trelawny, saying:

"Had you not better examine it first?" She drew back, slightly raising her hand in disclaimer, as she said impulsively:

"Oh no! Father would doubtless have shown it to me had he wished me to see it. I would not like to without his consent." Then she added, doubtless fearing lest her delicacy of view should give offence to the rest of us:

"Of course it is right that you should see it. You have to examine and consider everything; and indeed – indeed I am grateful to you..."

She turned away; I could see that she was crying quietly. It was evident to me that even in the midst of her trouble and anxiety there was a chagrin that she knew so little of her father; and that her ignorance had to be shown at such a time and amongst so many strangers. That they were all men did not make the shame more easy to bear, though there was a certain relief in it. Trying to interpret her feelings I could not but think that she must have been glad that no woman's eyes – of understanding greater than man's – were upon her in that hour.

When I stood up from my examination, which verified to me that of the Doctor, the latter resumed his place beside the couch and went on with his ministrations. Superintendent Dolan said to me in a whisper:

"I think we are fortunate in our doctor!" I nodded, and was about to add something in praise of his acumen, when there came a low tapping at the door.

Chapter II
Strange Instructions

SUPERINTENDENT DOLAN went quietly to the door; by a sort of natural understanding he had taken possession of affairs in the room. The rest of us waited. He opened the door a little way; and then with a gesture of manifest relief threw it wide, and a young man stepped in. A young man clean-shaven, tall and slight; with an eagle face and bright, quick eyes that seemed to take in everything around him at a glance. As he came in, the Superintendent held out his hand; the two men shook hands warmly.

"I came at once, sir, the moment I got your message. I am glad I still have your confidence."

"That you'll always have," said the Superintendent heartily. "I have not forgotten our old Bow Street days, and I never shall!" Then, without a word of preliminary, he began to tell everything he knew up to the moment of the newcomer's entry. Sergeant Daw asked a few questions – a very few – when it was necessary for his understanding of circumstances or the relative positions of persons; but as a rule Dolan, who knew his work thoroughly, forestalled every query, and explained all necessary matters as he went on. Sergeant Daw threw occasionally swift glances round him; now at one of us; now at the room or some part of it; now at the wounded man lying senseless on the sofa.

When the Superintendent had finished, the Sergeant turned to me and said:

"Perhaps you remember me, sir. I was with you in that Hoxton case."

"I remember you very well," I said as I held out my hand. The Superintendent spoke again:

"You understand, Sergeant Daw, that you are put in full charge of this case."

"Under you I hope, sir," he interrupted. The other shook his head and smiled as he said:

"It seems to me that this is a case that will take all a man's time and his brains. I have other work to do; but I shall be more than interested, and if I can help in any possible way I shall be glad to do so!"

"All right, sir," said the other, accepting his responsibility with a sort of modified salute; straightway he began his investigation.

First he came over to the Doctor and, having learned his name and address, asked him to write a full report which he could use, and which he could refer to headquarters if necessary. Doctor Winchester bowed gravely as he promised. Then the Sergeant approached me and said sotto voce:

"I like the look of your doctor. I think we can work together!" Turning to Miss Trelawny he asked:

"Please let me know what you can of your Father; his ways of life, his history – in fact of anything of whatsoever kind which interests him, or in which he may be concerned." I was about to interrupt to tell him what she had already said of her ignorance in all matters of her father and his ways, but her warning hand was raised to me pointedly and she spoke herself.

"Alas! I know little or nothing. Superintendent Dolan and Mr. Ross know already all I can say."

"Well, ma'am, we must be content to do what we can," said the officer genially. "I'll begin by making a minute examination. You say that you were outside the door when you heard the noise?"

"I was in my room when I heard the queer sound – indeed it must have been the early part of whatever it was which woke me. I came out of my room at once. Father's door was shut, and I could see the whole landing and the upper slopes of the staircase. No one could have left by the door unknown to me, if that is what you mean!"

"That is just what I do mean, miss. If every one who knows anything will tell me as well as that, we shall soon get to the bottom of this."

He then went over to the bed, looked at it carefully, and asked:

"Has the bed been touched?"

"Not to my knowledge," said Miss Trelawny, "but I shall ask Mrs. Grant – the housekeeper," she added as she rang the bell. Mrs. Grant answered it in person. "Come in," said Miss Trelawny. "These gentlemen want to know, Mrs. Grant, if the bed has been touched."

"Not by me, ma'am."

"Then," said Miss Trelawny, turning to Sergeant Daw, "it cannot have been touched by any one. Either Mrs. Grant or I myself was here all the time, and I do not think any of the servants who came when I gave the alarm were near the bed at all. You see, Father lay here just under the great safe, and every one crowded round him. We sent them all away in a very short time." Daw, with a motion of his hand, asked us all to stay at the other side of the room whilst with a magnifying-glass he examined the bed, taking care as he moved each fold of the bed-clothes to replace it in exact position. Then he examined with his magnifying-glass the floor beside it, taking especial pains where the blood had trickled over the side of the bed, which was of heavy red wood handsomely carved. Inch by inch, down on his knees, carefully avoiding any touch with the stains on the floor, he followed the blood-marks over to the spot, close under the great safe, where the body had lain. All around and about this spot he went for a radius of some yards; but seemingly did not meet with anything to arrest special attention. Then he examined the front of the safe; round the lock, and along the bottom and top of the double doors, more especially at the places of their touching in front.

Next he went to the windows, which were fastened down with the hasps.

"Were the shutters closed?" he asked Miss Trelawny in a casual way as though he expected the negative answer, which came.

All this time Doctor Winchester was attending to his patient; now dressing the wounds in the wrist or making minute examination all over the head and throat, and over the heart. More than once he put his nose to the mouth of the senseless man and sniffed. Each time he did so he finished up by unconsciously looking round the room, as though in search of something.

Then we heard the deep strong voice of the Detective:

"So far as I can see, the object was to bring that key to the lock of the safe. There seems to be some secret in the mechanism that I am unable to guess at, though I served a year in Chubb's before I joined the police. It is a combination lock of seven letters; but there seems to be a way of locking even the combination. It is one of Chatwood's; I shall call at their place and find out something about it." Then turning to the Doctor, as though his own work were for the present done, he said:

"Have you anything you can tell me at once, Doctor, which will not interfere with your full report? If there is any doubt I can wait, but the sooner I know something definite the better." Doctor Winchester answered at once:

"For my own part I see no reason in waiting. I shall make a full report of course. But in the meantime I shall tell you all I know – which is after all not very much, and all I think – which is less definite. There is no wound on the head which could account for the state of stupor in which the patient continues. I must, therefore, take it that either he has been drugged or is under some hypnotic influence. So far as I can judge, he has not been drugged – at least by means of any drug of whose qualities I am aware. Of course, there is ordinarily in this room so much of a mummy smell that it is difficult to be certain about anything having a delicate aroma. I dare say that you have noticed the peculiar Egyptians scents, bitumen, nard, aromatic gums and spices, and so forth. It is quite possible that somewhere in this room, amongst the curios and hidden by stronger scents, is some substance or liquid which may have the effect we see. It is possible that the patient has taken some drug, and that he may in some sleeping phase have injured himself. I do not think this is likely; and circumstances, other than those which I have myself been investigating, may prove that this surmise is not correct. But in the meantime it is possible; and must, till it be disproved, be kept within our purview." Here Sergeant Daw interrupted:

"That may be, but if so, we should be able to find the instrument with which the wrist was injured. There would be marks of blood somewhere."

"Exactly so!" said the Doctor, fixing his glasses as though preparing for an argument. "But if it be that the patient has used some strange drug, it may be one that does not take effect at once. As we are as yet ignorant of its potentialities – if indeed, the whole surmise is correct at all – we must be prepared at all points."

Here Miss Trelawny joined in the conversation:

"That would be quite right, so far as the action of the drug was concerned but according to the second part of your surmise the wound may have been self-inflicted, and this after the drug had taken effect."

"True!" said the Detective and the Doctor simultaneously. She went on:

"As however, Doctor, your guess does not exhaust the possibilities, we must bear in mind that some other variant of the same root-idea may be correct. I take it, therefore, that our first search, to be made on this assumption, must be for the weapon with which the injury was done to my Father's wrist."

"Perhaps he put the weapon in the safe before he became quite unconscious,' said I, giving voice foolishly to a half-formed thought.

"That could not be," said the Doctor quickly. "At least I think it could hardly be," he added cautiously, with a brief bow to me. "You see, the left hand is covered with blood; but there is no blood mark whatever on the safe."

"Quite right!" I said, and there was a long pause.

The first to break the silence was the Doctor.

"We shall want a nurse here as soon as possible; and I know the very one to suit. I shall go at once to get her if I can. I must ask that till I return some of you will remain constantly with the patient. It may be necessary to remove him to another room later on; but in the meantime he is best left here. Miss Trelawny, may I take it that either you or Mrs. Grant will remain here – not merely in the room, but close to the patient and watchful of him – till I return?"

She bowed in reply, and took a seat beside the sofa. The Doctor gave her some directions as to what she should do in case her father should become conscious before his return.

The next to move was Superintendent Dolan, who came close to Sergeant Daw as he said:

"I had better return now to the station – unless, of course, you should wish me to remain for a while."

He answered, "Is Johnny Wright still in your division?"

"Yes! Would you like him to be with you?" The other nodded reply. "Then I will send him on to you as soon as can be arranged. He shall then stay with you as long as you wish. I will tell him that he is to take his instructions entirely from you."

The Sergeant accompanied him to the door, saying as he went:

"Thank you, sir; you are always thoughtful for men who are working with you. It is a pleasure to me to be with you again. I shall go back to Scotland Yard and report to my chief. Then I shall call at Chatwood's; and I shall return here as soon as possible. I suppose I may take it, miss, that I may put up here for a day or two, if required. It may be some help, or possibly some comfort to you, if I am about, until we unravel this mystery."

"I shall be very grateful to you." He looked keenly at her for a few seconds before he spoke again.

"Before I go have I permission to look about your Father's table and desk? here might be something which would give us a clue – or a lead at all events." er answer was so unequivocal as almost to surprise him.

"You have the fullest possible permission to do anything which may help us a this dreadful trouble – to discover what it is that is wrong with my Father, or hich may shield him in the future!"

He began at once a systematic search of the dressing-table, and after that of the riting-table in the room. In one of the drawers he found a letter sealed; this he rought at once across the room and handed to Miss Trelawny.

"A letter – directed to me – and in my Father's hand!" she said as she eagerly pened it. I watched her face as she began to read; but seeing at once that ergeant Daw kept his keen eyes on her face, unflinchingly watching every flitting xpression, I kept my eyes henceforth fixed on his. When Miss Trelawny had read er letter through, I had in my mind a conviction, which, however, I kept locked a my own heart. Amongst the suspicions in the mind of the Detective was one, ather perhaps potential than definite, of Miss Trelawny herself.

For several minutes Miss Trelawny held the letter in her hand with her eyes owncast, thinking. Then she read it carefully again; this time the varying xpressions were intensified, and I thought I could easily follow them. When e had finished the second reading, she paused again. Then, though with some luctance, she handed the letter to the Detective. He read it eagerly but with nchanging face; read it a second time, and then handed it back with a bow. She aused a little again, and then handed it to me. As she did so she raised her eyes mine for a single moment appealingly; a swift blush spread over her pale cheeks nd forehead.

With mingled feelings I took it, but, all said, I was glad. She did not show any erturbation in giving the letter to the Detective – she might not have shown any anyone else. But to me... I feared to follow the thought further; but read on, onscious that the eyes of both Miss Trelawny and the Detective were fixed on me.

> *My Dear Daughter,*
>
> *I want you to take this letter as an instruction – absolute and imperative, and admitting of no deviation whatever – in case anything untoward or unexpected by you or by others should happen to me. If I should be suddenly and mysteriously stricken down – either by sickness, accident or attack – you must follow these directions implicitly. If I am not already in my bedroom when you are made cognisant of my state, I am to be brought there as quickly as possible. Even should I be dead, my body is to be brought there. Thenceforth, until I am either conscious and able to give instructions on my own account, or buried, I am never to be left alone – not for a single instant. From nightfall to sunrise at least two persons must remain in the room. It will be well that a trained nurse be in the room from time to time, and will note any symptoms, either permanent or changing, which may strike her. My solicitors, Marvin & Jewkes, of 27B Lincoln's Inn, have full instructions in case of my death; and Mr. Marvin has himself undertaken to see personally my wishes carried out. I should advise you, my dear Daughter, seeing that you have no relative to apply to, to get some friend whom you can trust to either remain within*

the house where instant communication can be made, or to come nightly to aid in the watching, or to be within call. Such friend may be either male or female; but, whichever it may be, there should be added one other watcher or attendant at hand of the opposite sex. Understand, that it is of the very essence of my wish that there should be, awake and exercising themselves to my purposes, both masculine and feminine intelligences. Once more, my dear Margaret, let me impress on you the need for observation and just reasoning to conclusions, howsoever strange. If I am taken ill or injured, this will be no ordinary occasion; and I wish to warn you, so that your guarding may be complete.

"Nothing in my room – I speak of the curios – must be removed or displaced in any way, or for any cause whatever. I have a special reason and a special purpose in the placing of each; so that any moving of them would thwart my plans.

Should you want money or counsel in anything, Mr. Marvin will carry out your wishes; to the which he has my full instructions."

Abel Trelawny.

I read the letter a second time before speaking, for I feared to betray myself. The choice of a friend might be a momentous occasion for me. I had already ground for hope, that she had asked me to help her in the first throe of her trouble; but love makes its own doubtings and I feared. My thoughts seemed to whirl with lightning rapidity, and in a few seconds a whole process of reasoning became formulated. I must not volunteer to be the friend that the father advised his daughter to have to aid her in her vigil; and yet that one glance had a lesson which I must not ignore. Also, did not she, when she wanted help, send to me – to me a stranger, except for one meeting at a dance and one brief afternoon of companionship on the river? Would it not humiliate her to make her ask me twice? Humiliate her! No! that pain I could at all events save her; it is not humiliation to refuse. So, as I handed her back the letter, I said:

"I know you will forgive me, Miss Trelawny, if I presume too much; but if you will permit me to aid in the watching I shall be proud. Though the occasion is a sad one I shall be so far happy to be allowed the privilege."

Despite her manifest and painful effort at self-control, the red tide swept her face and neck. Even her eyes seemed suffused, and in stern contrast with her pale cheeks when the tide had rolled back. She answered in a low voice:

"I shall be very grateful for your help!" Then in an afterthought she added:

"But you must not let me be selfish in my need! I know you have many duties to engage you; and though I shall value your help highly – most highly – it would not be fair to monopolise your time."

"As to that," I answered at once, "my time is yours. I can for today easily arrange my work so that I can come here in the afternoon and stay till morning. After that, if the occasion still demands it, I can so arrange my work that I shall have more time still at my disposal."

She was much moved. I could see the tears gather in her eyes, and she turned away her head. The Detective spoke:

"I am glad you will be here, Mr. Ross. I shall be in the house myself, as Miss Trelawny will allow me, if my people in Scotland Yard will permit. That letter seems to put a different complexion on everything; though the mystery remains greater than ever. If you can wait here an hour or two I shall go to headquarters, and then to the safe-makers. After that I shall return; and you can go away easier in your mind, for I shall be here."

When he had gone, we two, Miss Trelawny and I, remained in silence. At last she raised her eyes and looked at me for a moment; after that I would not have exchanged places with a king. For a while she busied herself round the extemporised bedside of her father. Then, asking me to be sure not to take my eyes off him till she returned, she hurried out.

In a few minutes she came back with Mrs. Grant and two maids and a couple of men, who bore the entire frame and furniture of a light iron bed. This they proceeded to put together and to make. When the work was completed, and the servants had withdrawn, she said to me:

"It will be well to be all ready when the Doctor returns. He will surely want to have Father put to bed; and a proper bed will be better for him than the sofa." She then got a chair close beside her father, and sat down watching him.

I went about the room, taking accurate note of all I saw. And truly there were enough things in the room to evoke the curiosity of any man – even though the attendant circumstances were less strange. The whole place, excepting those articles of furniture necessary to a well-furnished bedroom, was filled with magnificent curios, chiefly Egyptian. As the room was of immense size there was opportunity for the placing of a large number of them, even if, as with these, they were of huge proportions.

Whilst I was still investigating the room there came the sound of wheels on the gravel outside the house. There was a ring at the hall door, and a few minutes later, after a preliminary tap at the door and an answering "Come in!" Doctor Winchester entered, followed by a young woman in the dark dress of a nurse.

"I have been fortunate!" he said as he came in. "I found her at once and free. Miss Trelawny, this is Nurse Kennedy!"

Chapter III
The Watchers

I WAS STRUCK by the way the two young women looked at each other. I suppose I have been so much in the habit of weighing up in my own mind the personality of witnesses and of forming judgment by their unconscious action and mode of bearing themselves, that the habit extends to my life outside as well as within the court-house. At this moment of my life anything that interested Miss Trelawny interested me; and as she had been struck by the newcomer I instinctively weighed her up also. By comparison of the two I seemed somehow to gain a new knowledge of Miss Trelawny. Certainly, the two women made a good contrast. Miss Trelawny was of fine figure; dark, straight-featured. She had marvellous eyes; great, wide-open, and as black and soft as velvet, with a mysterious depth. To look in them was like gazing at a black mirror such as Doctor Dee used in his wizard rites. I heard an old gentleman at the picnic, a great oriental traveller, describe the effect of her eyes 'as looking at night at the great distant lamps of a mosque through the open door.' The eyebrows were typical. Finely arched and rich in long curling hair, they seemed like the proper architectural environment of the deep, splendid eyes.

Her hair was black also, but was as fine as silk. Generally black hair is a type of animal strength and seems as if some strong expression of the forces of a strong nature; but in this case there could be no such thought. There were refinement and high breeding; and though there was no suggestion of weakness, any sense of power there was, was rather spiritual than animal. The whole harmony of her being seemed complete. Carriage, figure, hair, eyes; the mobile, full mouth, whose scarlet lips and white teeth seemed to light up the lower part of the face – as the eyes did the upper; the wide sweep of the jaw from chin to ear; the long, fine fingers; the hand which seemed to move from the wrist as though it had a sentience of its own. All these perfections went to make up a personality that dominated either by its grace, its sweetness, its beauty, or its charm.

Nurse Kennedy, on the other hand, was rather under than over a woman's average height. She was firm and thickset, with full limbs and broad, strong, capable hands. Her colour was in the general effect that of an autumn leaf. The yellow-brown hair was thick and long, and the golden-brown eyes sparkled from the freckled, sunburnt skin. Her rosy cheeks gave a general idea of rich brown. The red lips and white teeth did not alter the colour scheme, but only emphasized it. She had a snub nose – there was no possible doubt about it; but like such noses in general it showed a nature generous, untiring, and full of good-nature. Her broad white forehead, which even the freckles had spared, was full of forceful thought and reason.

Doctor Winchester had on their journey from the hospital, coached her in the necessary particulars, and without a word she took charge of the patient and set to work. Having examined the new-made bed and shaken the pillows, she spoke to the Doctor, who gave instructions; presently we all four, stepping together, lifted the unconscious man from the sofa.

Early in the afternoon, when Sergeant Daw had returned, I called at my rooms in Jermyn Street, and sent out such clothes, books and papers as I should be likely to want within a few days. Then I went on to keep my legal engagements.

The Court sat late that day as an important case was ending; it was striking six as I drove in at the gate of the Kensington Palace Road. I found myself installed in a large room close to the sick chamber.

That night we were not yet regularly organised for watching, so that the early part of the evening showed an unevenly balanced guard. Nurse Kennedy, who had been on duty all day, was lying down, as she had arranged to come on again by twelve o'clock. Doctor Winchester, who was dining in the house, remained in the room until dinner was announced; and went back at once when it was over. During dinner Mrs. Grant remained in the room, and with her Sergeant Daw, who wished to complete a minute examination which he had undertaken of everything in the room and near it. At nine o'clock Miss Trelawny and I went in to relieve the Doctor. She had lain down for a few hours in the afternoon so as to be refreshed for her work at night. She told me that she had determined that for this night at least she would sit up and watch. I did not try to dissuade her, for I knew that her mind was made up. Then and there I made up my mind that I would watch with her – unless, of course, I should see that she really did not wish it. I said nothing of my intentions for the present. We came in on tiptoe, so silently that the Doctor, who was bending over the bed, did not hear us, and seemed a little startled when suddenly looking up he saw our eyes upon him. I felt that the mystery of the whole thing was getting on his nerves, as it had already got on the nerves of some others of us. He was, I fancied, a little annoyed with himself for having been so startled, and at once began to talk in a hurried manner as though to get over our idea of his embarrassment:

"I am really and absolutely at my wits' end to find any fit cause for this stupor. have made again as accurate an examination as I know how, and I am satisfied that there is no injury to the brain, that is, no external injury. Indeed, all his vital organs seem unimpaired. I have given him, as you know, food several times and it has manifestly done him good. His breathing is strong and regular, and his pulse is slower and stronger than it was this morning. I cannot find evidence of any known drug, and his unconsciousness does not resemble any of the many cases of hypnotic sleep which I saw in the Charcot Hospital in Paris. And as to these wounds" – he laid his finger gently on the bandaged wrist which lay outside the coverlet as he spoke, "I do not know what to make of them. They might have been made by a carding-machine; but that supposition is untenable. It is within the bounds of possibility that they might have been made by a wild animal if it had taken care to sharpen its claws. That too is, I take it, impossible. By the way, have you any strange pets here in the house; anything of an exceptional kind, such as a tiger-cat or anything out of the common?" Miss Trelawny smiled a sad smile which made my heart ache, as she made answer:

"Oh no! Father does not like animals about the house, unless they are dead and mummied." This was said with a touch of bitterness – or jealousy, I could hardly tell which. "Even my poor kitten was only allowed in the house on sufferance; and though he is the dearest and best-conducted cat in the world, he is now on a sort of parole, and is not allowed into this room."

As she was speaking a faint rattling of the door handle was heard. Instantly Miss Trelawny's face brightened. She sprang up and went over to the door, saying as she went:

"There he is! That is my Silvio. He stands on his hind legs and rattles the door handle when he wants to come into a room." She opened the door, speaking to the cat as though he were a baby: "Did him want his movver? Come then; but he must stay with her!" She lifted the cat, and came back with him in her arms. He was certainly a magnificent animal. A chinchilla grey Persian with long silky hair; a really lordly animal with a haughty bearing despite his gentleness; and with great paws which spread out as he placed them on the ground. Whilst she was fondling him, he suddenly gave a wriggle like an eel and slipped out of her arms. He ran across the room and stood opposite a low table on which stood the mummy of an animal, and began to mew and snarl. Miss Trelawny was after him in an instant and lifted him in her arms, kicking and struggling and wriggling to get away; but not biting or scratching, for evidently he loved his beautiful mistress. He ceased to make a noise the moment he was in her arms; in a whisper she admonished him:

"O you naughty Silvio! You have broken your parole that mother gave for you. Now, say goodnight to the gentlemen, and come away to mother's room!" As she was speaking she held out the cat's paw to me to shake. As I did so I could not but admire its size and beauty. "Why," said I, "his paw seems like a little boxing-glove full of claws." She smiled:

"So it ought to. Don't you notice that my Silvio has seven toes, see!" she opened the paw; and surely enough there were seven separate claws, each of them sheathed in a delicate, fine, shell-like case. As I gently stroked the foot the claws emerged and one of them accidentally – there was no anger now and the cat was purring – stuck into my hand. Instinctively I said as I drew back:

"Why, his claws are like razors!"

Doctor Winchester had come close to us and was bending over looking at the cat's claws; as I spoke he said in a quick, sharp way:

"Eh!" I could hear the quick intake of his breath. Whilst I was stroking the now quiescent cat, the Doctor went to the table and tore off a piece of blotting-paper from the writing-pad and came back. He laid the paper on his palm and, with a simple "pardon me!" to Miss Trelawny, placed the cat's paw on it and pressed it down with his other hand. The haughty cat seemed to resent somewhat the familiarity, and tried to draw its foot away. This was plainly what the Doctor wanted, for in the act the cat opened the sheaths of its claws and made several reefs in the soft paper. Then Miss Trelawny took her pet away. She returned in a couple of minutes; as she came in she said:

"It is most odd about that mummy! When Silvio came into the room first – indeed I took him in as a kitten to show to Father – he went on just the same way. He jumped up on the table, and tried to scratch and bite the mummy. That was what made Father so angry, and brought the decree of banishment on poor Silvio. Only his parole, given through me, kept him in the house."

Whilst she had been gone, Doctor Winchester had taken the bandage from her father's wrist. The wound was now quite clear, as the separate cuts showed out in fierce red lines. The Doctor folded the blotting-paper across the line of punctures made by the cat's claws, and held it down close to the wound. As he did so, he looked up triumphantly and beckoned us over to him.

The cuts in the paper corresponded with the wounds in the wrist! No explanation was needed, as he said:

"It would have been better if master Silvio had not broken his parole!"

We were all silent for a little while. Suddenly Miss Trelawny said:

"But Silvio was not in here last night!"

"Are you sure? Could you prove that if necessary?" She hesitated before replying:

"I am certain of it; but I fear it would be difficult to prove. Silvio sleeps in a basket in my room. I certainly put him to bed last night; I remember distinctly laying his little blanket over him, and tucking him in. This morning I took him out of the basket myself. I certainly never noticed him in here; though, of course, that would not mean much, for I was too concerned about poor father, and too much occupied with him, to notice even Silvio."

The Doctor shook his head as he said with a certain sadness:

"Well, at any rate it is no use trying to prove anything now. Any cat in the world would have cleaned blood-marks – did any exist – from his paws in a hundredth part of the time that has elapsed."

Again we were all silent; and again the silence was broken by Miss Trelawny:

"But now that I think of it, it could not have been poor Silvio that injured Father. My door was shut when I first heard the sound; and Father's was shut when I listened at it. When I went in, the injury had been done; so that it must have been before Silvio could possibly have got in." This reasoning commended itself, especially to me as a barrister, for it was proof to satisfy a jury. It gave me a distinct pleasure to have

Silvio acquitted of the crime – possibly because he was Miss Trelawny's cat and was loved by her. Happy cat! Silvio's mistress was manifestly pleased as I said:

"Verdict, 'not guilty!'" Doctor Winchester after a pause observed:

"My apologies to master Silvio on this occasion; but I am still puzzled to know why he is so keen against that mummy. Is he the same toward the other mummies in the house? There are, I suppose, a lot of them. I saw three in the hall as I came in."

"There are lots of them," she answered. "I sometimes don't know whether I am in a private house or the British Museum. But Silvio never concerns himself about any of them except that particular one. I suppose it must be because it is of an animal, not a man or a woman."

"Perhaps it is of a cat!" said the Doctor as he started up and went across the room to look at the mummy more closely. "Yes," he went on, "it is the mummy of a cat; and a very fine one, too. If it hadn't been a special favourite of some very special person it would never have received so much honour. See! A painted case and obsidian eyes – just like a human mummy. It is an extraordinary thing, that knowledge of kind to kind. Here is a dead cat – that is all; it is perhaps four or five thousand years old – and another cat of another breed, in what is practically another world, is ready to fly at it, just as it would if it were not dead. I should like to experiment a bit about that cat if you don't mind, Miss Trelawny." She hesitated before replying:

"Of course, do anything you may think necessary or wise; but I hope it will not be anything to hurt or worry my poor Silvio." The Doctor smiled as he answered:

"Oh, Silvio would be all right: it is the other one that my sympathies would be reserved for."

"How do you mean?"

"Master Silvio will do the attacking; the other one will do the suffering."

"Suffering?" There was a note of pain in her voice. The Doctor smiled more broadly:

"Oh, please make your mind easy as to that. The other won't suffer as we understand it; except perhaps in his structure and outfit."

"What on earth do you mean?"

"Simply this, my dear young lady, that the antagonist will be a mummy cat like this one. There are, I take it, plenty of them to be had in Museum Street. I shall get one and place it here instead of that one – you won't think that a temporary exchange will violate your Father's instructions, I hope. We shall then find out, to begin with, whether Silvio objects to all mummy cats, or only to this one in particular."

"I don't know," she said doubtfully. "Father's instructions seem very uncompromising." Then after a pause she went on: "But of course under the circumstances anything that is to be ultimately for his good must be done. I suppose there can't be anything very particular about the mummy of a cat."

Doctor Winchester said nothing. He sat rigid, with so grave a look on his face that his extra gravity passed on to me; and in its enlightening perturbation I began to realise more than I had yet done the strangeness of the case in which I was now so deeply concerned. When once this thought had begun there was no end to it. Indeed it grew, and blossomed, and reproduced itself in a thousand different ways. The room and all in it gave grounds for strange thoughts. There were so many ancient relics that unconsciously one was taken back to strange lands and strange times. There were so many mummies or mummy objects, round which there seemed to cling for ever the penetrating odours of bitumen, and spices and gums – "Nard and Circassia's balmy smells" – that one was unable to forget the past. Of course, there was but little light in the room, and that carefully shaded; so that there was no glare anywhere. None of that direct light which can manifest itself as a power or an entity, and so make for companionship. The room was a large one, and lofty in proportion to its size. In its vastness was place for a multitude of things not often found in a bedchamber. In far corners of the room were shadows of uncanny shape. More than once as I thought, the multitudinous presence of the dead and the past took such hold on me that I caught myself looking round fearfully as though some strange personality or influence was present. Even the manifest presence of Doctor Winchester and Miss Trelawny could not altogether comfort or satisfy me at such moments. It was with a distinct sense of relief that I saw a new personality in the room in the shape of Nurse Kennedy. There was no doubt that that business-like, self-reliant, capable young woman added an element of security to such wild imaginings as my own. She had a quality of common sense that seemed to pervade everything around her, as though it were some kind of emanation. Up to that moment I had been building fancies around the sick man; so that finally all about him, including myself, had become involved in them, or enmeshed, or saturated, or… But now that she had come, he relapsed into his proper perspective as a patient; the room was a sick-room, and the shadows lost their fearsome quality. The only thing which it could not altogether abrogate was the strange Egyptian smell. You may put a mummy in a glass case and hermetically seal it so that no corroding air can get within; but all the same it will exhale its odour. One might think that four or five thousand years would exhaust the olfactory qualities of anything; but experience teaches us that these smells remain, and that their secrets are unknown to us. Today they are as much mysteries as they were when the embalmers put the body in the bath of natron…

* * *

All at once I sat up. I had become lost in an absorbing reverie. The Egyptian smell had seemed to get on my nerves – on my memory – on my very will.

At that moment I had a thought which was like an inspiration. If I was influenced in such a manner by the smell, might it not be that the sick man, who lived half his life or more in the atmosphere, had gradually and by slow but sure process taken into his system something which had permeated him to such degree that it had a new power derived from quantity – or strength – or…

I was becoming lost again in a reverie. This would not do. I must take such precaution that I could remain awake, or free from such entrancing thought. I had had but half a night's sleep last night; and this night I must remain awake. Without stating my intention, for I feared that I might add to the trouble and uneasiness of Miss Trelawny, I went downstairs and out of the house. I soon found a chemist's shop, and came away with a respirator. When I got back, it was ten o'clock; the Doctor was going for the night. The Nurse came with him to the door of the sick-room, taking her last instructions. Miss Trelawny sat still beside the bed. Sergeant Daw, who had entered as the Doctor went out, was some little distance off.

When Nurse Kennedy joined us, we arranged that she should sit up till two o'clock, when Miss Trelawny would relieve her. Thus, in accordance with Mr. Trelawny's instructions, there would always be a man and a woman in the room; and each one of us would overlap, so that at no time would a new set of watchers come on duty without some one to tell of what – if anything – had occurred. I lay down on a sofa in my own room, having arranged that one of the servants should call me a little before twelve. In a few moments I was asleep.

When I was waked, it took me several seconds to get back my thoughts so as to recognise my own identity and surroundings. The short sleep had, however, done me good, and I could look on things around me in a more practical light than I had been able to do earlier in the evening. I bathed my face, and thus refreshed went into the sick-room. I moved very softly. The Nurse was sitting by the bed, quiet and alert; the Detective sat in an arm-chair across the room in deep shadow. He did not move when I crossed, until I got close to him, when he said in a dull whisper:

"It is all right; I have not been asleep!" An unnecessary thing to say, I thought – it always is, unless it be untrue in spirit. When I told him that his watch was over; that he might go to bed till I should call him at six o'clock, he seemed relieved and went with alacrity. At the door he turned and, coming back to me, said in a whisper:

"I sleep lightly and I shall have my pistols with me. I won't feel so heavy-headed when I get out of this mummy smell."

He too, then, had shared my experience of drowsiness!

I asked the Nurse if she wanted anything. I noticed that she had a vinaigrette in her lap. Doubtless she, too, had felt some of the influence which had so affected me. She said that she had all she required, but that if she should want anything she would at once let me know. I wished to keep her from noticing my respirator, so I went to the chair in the shadow where her back was toward me. Here I quietly put it on, and made myself comfortable.

For what seemed a long time, I sat and thought and thought. It was a wild medley of thoughts, as might have been expected from the experiences of the previous day and night. Again I found myself thinking of the Egyptian smell; and I remember that I felt a delicious satisfaction that I did not experience it as I had done. The respirator was doing its work.

It must have been that the passing of this disturbing thought made for repose of mind, which is the corollary of bodily rest, for, though I really cannot remember being asleep or waking from it, I saw a vision – I dreamed a dream, I scarcely know which.

I was still in the room, seated in the chair. I had on my respirator and knew that I breathed freely. The Nurse sat in her chair with her back toward me. She sat quite still. The sick man lay as still as the dead. It was rather like the picture of a scene than the reality; all were still and silent; and the stillness and silence were continuous. Outside, in the distance I could hear the sounds of a city, the occasional roll of wheels, the shout of a reveller, the far-away echo of whistles and the rumbling of trains. The light was very, very low; the reflection of it under the green-shaded lamp was a dim relief to the darkness, rather than light. The green silk fringe of the lamp had merely the colour of an emerald seen in the moonlight. The room, for all its darkness, was full of shadows. It seemed in my whirling thoughts as though all the real things had become shadows – shadows which moved, for they passed the dim outline of the high windows. Shadows which had sentience. I even thought there was sound, a faint sound as of the mew of a cat – the rustle of drapery and a metallic clink as of metal faintly touching metal. I sat as one entranced. At last I felt, as in nightmare, that this was sleep, and that in the passing of its portals all my will had gone.

All at once my senses were full awake. A shriek rang in my ears. The room was filled suddenly with a blaze of light. There was the sound of pistol shots – one, two, and a haze of white smoke in the room. When my waking eyes regained their power I could have shrieked with horror myself at what I saw before me.

Chapter IV
The Second Attempt

THE SIGHT WHICH met my eyes had the horror of a dream within a dream, with the certainty of reality added. The room was as I had seen it last; except that the shadowy look had gone in the glare of the many lights, and every article in it stood stark and solidly real.

By the empty bed sat Nurse Kennedy, as my eyes had last seen her, sitting bolt upright in the arm-chair beside the bed. She had placed a pillow behind her, so that her back might be erect; but her neck was fixed as that of one in a cataleptic trance. She was, to all intents and purposes, turned into stone. There was no special expression on her face – no fear, no horror; nothing such as might be expected of one in such a condition. Her open eyes showed neither wonder nor interest. She was simply a negative existence, warm, breathing, placid; but absolutely unconscious of the world around her. The bedclothes were disarranged, as though the patient had been drawn from under them without throwing them back. The corner of the upper sheet hung upon the floor; close by it lay one of the bandages with which the Doctor had dressed the wounded wrist. Another and another lay further along the floor, as though forming a clue to where the sick man now lay. This was almost exactly where he had been found on the previous night, under the great safe. Again, the left arm lay toward the safe. But there had been a new outrage, an attempt had been made to sever the arm close to the bangle which held the tiny key. A heavy 'kukri' knife – one of the leaf-shaped knives which the Gurkhas and others of the hill tribes of India use with such effect – had been taken from its place on the wall, and with it the attempt had been made. It was manifest that just at the moment of striking, the blow had been arrested, for only the point of the knife and not the edge of the blade had struck the flesh. As it was, the outer side of the arm had been cut to the bone and the blood was pouring out. In addition, the former wound in front of the arm had been cut or torn about terribly, one of the cuts seemed to jet out blood as if with each pulsation of the heart. By the side of her father knelt Miss Trelawny, her white nightdress stained with the blood in which she knelt. In the middle of the room Sergeant Daw, in his shirt and trousers and stocking feet, was putting fresh cartridges into his revolver in a dazed mechanical kind of way. His eyes were red and heavy, and he seemed only half awake, and less than half conscious of what was going on around him. Several servants, bearing lights of various kinds, were clustered round the doorway.

As I rose from my chair and came forward, Miss Trelawny raised her eyes toward me. When she saw me she shrieked and started to her feet, pointing towards me. Never shall I forget the strange picture she made, with her white drapery all smeared with blood which, as she rose from the pool, ran in streaks toward her bare feet. I believe that I had only been asleep; that whatever influence had worked on Mr. Trelawny and Nurse Kennedy – and in less degree on Sergeant Daw – had not touched me. The respirator had been of some service, though it had not kept off the tragedy whose dire evidences were before me. I can understand now – I could understand even then – the fright, added to that which had gone before, which my appearance must have evoked. I had still on the respirator, which covered mouth and nose; my hair had been tossed in my sleep. Coming suddenly forward, thus enwrapped and dishevelled, in that horrified crowd, I must have had, in the strange mixture of lights, an extraordinary and terrifying appearance. It was well that I recognised all this in time to avert another catastrophe; for the half-dazed, mechanically-acting Detective put in the cartridges and had raised his revolver to shoot at me when I succeeded in wrenching off the respirator and shouting to him to hold his hand. In this also he acted mechanically; the red, half-awake eyes had not in them even then the intention of conscious action. The danger, however, was averted. The relief of the situation, strangely enough, came in a simple fashion. Mrs. Grant, seeing that her young mistress had on only her nightdress, had gone to fetch a dressing-gown, which she now threw over her. This simple act brought us all back to the region of fact. With a long breath, one and all seemed to devote themselves to the most pressing matter before us, that of staunching the flow of blood from the arm of the wounded man. Even as the thought of action came, I rejoiced; for the bleeding was very proof that Mr. Trelawny still lived.

Last night's lesson was not thrown away. More than one of those present knew now what to do in such an emergency, and within a few seconds willing hands were at work on a tourniquet. A man was at once despatched for the doctor, and several of the servants disappeared to make themselves respectable. We lifted Mr. Trelawny on to the sofa where he had lain yesterday; and, having done what we could for him, turned our attention to the Nurse. In all the turmoil she had not stirred; she sat there as before, erect and rigid, breathing softly and naturally and with a placid smile. As it was manifestly of no use to attempt anything with her till the doctor had come, we began to think of the general situation.

Mrs. Grant had by this time taken her mistress away and changed her clothes; for she was back presently in a dressing-gown and slippers, and with the traces of blood removed from her hands. She was now much calmer, though she trembled sadly; and her face was ghastly white. When she had looked at her father's wrist, I holding the tourniquet, she turned her eyes round the room, resting them now and again on each one of us present in turn, but seeming to find no comfort. It was so apparent to me that she did not know where to begin or whom to trust that, to reassure her, I said:

"I am all right now; I was only asleep." Her voice had a gulp in it as she said in a low voice:

"Asleep! You! And my Father in danger! I thought you were on the watch!" I felt the sting of justice in the reproach; but I really wanted to help her, so I answered:

"Only asleep. It is bad enough, I know; but there is something more than an 'only' round us here. Had it not been that I took a definite precaution I might have been like the Nurse there." She turned her eyes swiftly on the weird figure, sitting grimly upright like a painted statue; and then her face softened. With the action of habitual courtesy she said:

"Forgive me! I did not mean to be rude. But I am in such distress and fear that I hardly know what I am saying. Oh, it is dreadful! I fear for fresh trouble and horror and mystery every moment." This cut me to the very heart, and out of the heart's fulness I spoke:

"Don't give me a thought! I don't deserve it. I was on guard, and yet I slept. All that I can say is that I didn't mean to, and I tried to avoid it; but it was over me before I knew it. Anyhow, it is done now; and can't be undone. Probably some day we may understand it all; but now let us try to get at some idea of what has happened. Tell me what you remember!" The effort to recollect seemed to stimulate her; she became calmer as she spoke:

"I was asleep, and woke suddenly with the same horrible feeling on me that Father was in great and immediate danger. I jumped up and ran, just as I was, into his room. It was nearly pitch dark, but as I opened the door there was light enough to see Father's nightdress as he lay on the floor under the safe, just as on that first awful night. Then I think I must have gone mad for a moment." She stopped and shuddered. My eyes lit on Sergeant Daw, still fiddling in an aimless way with the revolver. Mindful of my work with the tourniquet, I said calmly:

"Now tell us, Sergeant Daw, what did you fire at?" The policeman seemed to pull himself together with the habit of obedience. Looking around at the servants remaining in the room, he said with that air of importance which, I take it, is the regulation attitude of an official of the law before strangers:

"Don't you think, sir, that we can allow the servants to go away? We can then better go into the matter." I nodded approval; the servants took the hint and withdrew, though unwillingly, the last one closing the door behind him. Then the Detective went on:

"I think I had better tell you my impressions, sir, rather than recount my actions. That is, so far as I remember them." There was a mortified deference now in his manner, which probably arose from his consciousness of the awkward position in which he found himself. "I went to sleep half-dressed – as I am now, with a revolver under my pillow. It was the last thing I remember thinking of. I do not know how long I slept. I had turned off the electric light, and it was quite dark. I thought I heard a scream; but I can't be sure, for I felt thick-headed as a man does when he is called too soon after an extra long stretch of work. Not that such was the case this time. Anyhow my thoughts flew to the pistol. I took it out, and ran on to the landing. Then I heard a sort of scream, or rather a call for help, and ran into this room. The room was dark, for the lamp beside the Nurse was out, and the only light was that from the landing, coming through the open door. Miss Trelawny was kneeling on the floor beside her father, and was screaming. I thought I saw something move between me and the window; so, without thinking, and being half dazed and only half awake, I shot at it. It moved a little more to the right between the windows, and I shot again. Then you came up out of the big chair with all that muffling on your face. It seemed to me, being as I say half dazed and half awake – I know, sir, you will take this into account – as if it had been you, being in the same direction as the thing I had fired at. And so I was about to fire again when you pulled off the wrap." Here I asked him – I was cross-examining now and felt at home:

"You say you thought I was the thing you fired at. What thing?" The man scratched his head, but made no reply.

"Come, sir," I said, "what thing; what was it like?" The answer came in a low voice:

"I don't know, sir. I thought there was something; but what it was, or what it was like, I haven't the faintest notion. I suppose it was because I had been thinking of the pistol before I went to sleep, and because when I came in here I was half dazed and only half awake – which I hope you will in future, sir, always remember." He clung to that formula of excuse as though it were his sheet-anchor. I did not want to antagonise the man; on the contrary I wanted to have him with us. Besides, I had on me at that time myself the shadow of my own default; so I said as kindly as I knew how:

"Quite right! Sergeant. Your impulse was correct; though of course in the half-somnolent condition in which you were, and perhaps partly affected by the same influence – whatever it may be – which made me sleep and which has put the Nurse in that cataleptic trance, it could not be expected that you would paused to weigh matters. But now, whilst the matter is fresh, let me see exactly where you stood and where I sat. We shall be able to trace the course of your bullets." The prospect of action and the exercise of his habitual skill seemed to brace him at once; he seemed a different man as he set about his work. I asked Mrs. Grant to hold the tourniquet, and went and stood where he had stood and looked where, in the darkness, he had pointed. I could not but notice the mechanical exactness of his mind, as when he showed me where he had stood, or drew, as a matter of course, the revolver from his pistol pocket, and pointed with it. The chair from which I had risen still stood in its place. Then I asked him to point with his hand only, as I wished to move in the track of his shot.

Just behind my chair, and a little back of it, stood a high buhl cabinet. The glass door was shattered. I asked:

"Was this the direction of your first shot or your second?" The answer came promptly.

"The second; the first was over there!"

He turned a little to the left, more toward the wall where the great safe stood, and pointed. I followed the direction of his hand and came to the low table whereon rested, amongst other curios, the mummy of the cat which had raised Silvio's ire. I got a candle and easily found the mark of the bullet. It had broken a little glass vase and a tazza of black basalt, exquisitely engraved with hieroglyphics, the graven lines being filled with some faint green cement and the whole thing being polished to an equal surface. The bullet, flattened against the wall, lay on the table.

I then went to the broken cabinet. It was evidently a receptacle for valuable curios; for in it were some great scarabs of gold, agate, green jasper, amethyst, lapis lazuli, opal, granite, and blue-green china. None of these things happily were touched. The bullet had gone through the back of the cabinet; but no other damage, save the shattering of the glass, had been done. I could not but notice the strange arrangement of the curios on the shelf of the cabinet. All the scarabs, rings, amulets, etc. were arranged in an uneven oval round an exquisitely-carved golden miniature figure of a hawk-headed God crowned with a disk and plumes. I did not wait to look further at present, for my attention was demanded by more pressing things; but I determined to make a more minute examination when I should have time. It was evident that some of the strange Egyptian smell clung to these old curios; through the broken glass came an added whiff of spice and gum and bitumen, almost stronger than those I had already noticed as coming from others in the room.

All this had really taken but a few minutes. I was surprised when my eye met, through the chinks between the dark window blinds and the window cases, the brighter light of the coming dawn. When I went back to the sofa and took the tourniquet from Mrs. Grant, she went over and pulled up the blinds.

It would be hard to imagine anything more ghastly than the appearance of the room with the faint grey light of early morning coming in upon it. As the windows faced north, any light that came was a fixed grey light without any of the rosy possibility of dawn which comes in the eastern quarter of heaven. The electric lights seemed dull and yet glaring; and every shadow was of a hard intensity. There was nothing of morning freshness; nothing of the softness of night. All was hard and cold and inexpressibly dreary. The face of the senseless man on the sofa seemed of a ghastly yellow; and the Nurse's face had taken a suggestion of green from the shade of the lamp near her. Only Miss Trelawny's face looked white; and it was of a pallor which made my heart ache. It looked as if nothing on God's earth could ever again bring back to it the colour of life and happiness.

It was a relief to us all when Doctor Winchester came in, breathless with running. He only asked one question:

"Can anyone tell me anything of how this wound was gotten?" On seeing the headshake which went round us under his glance, he said no more, but applied himself to his surgical work. For an instant he looked up at the Nurse sitting so still; but then bent himself to his task, a grave frown contracting his brows. It was not till the arteries were tied and the wounds completely dressed that he spoke again, except, of course, when he had asked for anything to be handed to him or to be done for him. When Mr. Trelawny's wounds had been thoroughly cared for, he said to Miss Trelawny:

"What about Nurse Kennedy?" She answered at once:

"I really do not know. I found her when I came into the room at half-past two o'clock, sitting exactly as she does now. We have not moved her, or changed her position. She has not wakened since. Even Sergeant Daw's pistol-shots did not disturb her."

"Pistol-shots? Have you then discovered any cause for this new outrage?" The rest were silent, so I answered:

"We have discovered nothing. I was in the room watching with the Nurse. Earlier in the evening I fancied that the mummy smells were making me drowsy, so I went out and got a respirator. I had it on when I came on duty; but it did not keep me from going to sleep. I awoke to see the room full of people; that is, Miss Trelawny and Sergeant Daw, being only half awake and still stupefied by the same scent or influence which had affected us, fancied that he saw something moving through the shadowy darkness of the room, and fired twice. When I rose out of my chair, with my face swathed in the respirator, he took me for the cause of the trouble. Naturally enough, he was about to fire again, when I was fortunately in time to manifest my identity. Mr. Trelawny was lying beside the safe, just as he was found last night; and was bleeding profusely from the new wound in his wrist. We lifted him on the sofa, and made a tourniquet. That is, literally and absolutely, all that any of us know as yet. We have not touched the knife, which you see lies close by the pool of blood. Look!" I said, going over and lifting it. "The point is red with the blood which has dried."

Doctor Winchester stood quite still a few minutes before speaking:

"Then the doings of this night are quite as mysterious as those of last night?"

"Quite!" I answered. He said nothing in reply, but turning to Miss Trelawny said:

"We had better take Nurse Kennedy into another room. I suppose there is nothing to prevent it?"

"Nothing! Please, Mrs. Grant, see that Nurse Kennedy's room is ready; and ask two of the men to come and carry her in." Mrs. Grant went out immediately; and in a few minutes came back saying:

"The room is quite ready; and the men are here." By her direction two footmen came into the room and, lifting up the rigid body of Nurse Kennedy under the supervision of the Doctor, carried her out of the room. Miss Trelawny remained with me in the sick chamber, and Mrs. Grant went with the Doctor into the Nurse's room.

When we were alone Miss Trelawny came over to me, and taking both my hands in hers, said:

"I hope you won't remember what I said. I did not mean it, and I was distraught." I did not make reply; but I held her hands and kissed them. There are different ways of kissing a lady's hands. This way was intended as homage and respect; and it was accepted as such in the high-bred, dignified way which marked Miss Trelawny's bearing and every movement. I went over to the sofa and looked down at the senseless man. The dawn had come much nearer in the last few minutes, and there was something of the clearness of day in the light. As I looked at the stern, cold, set face, now as white as a marble monument in the pale grey light, I could not but feel that there was some deep mystery beyond all that had happened within the last twenty-six hours. Those beetling brows screened some massive purpose; that high, broad forehead held some finished train of reasoning, which the broad chin and massive jaw would help to carry into effect. As I looked and wondered, there began to steal over me again that phase of wandering thought which had last night heralded the approach of sleep. I resisted it, and held myself sternly to the present. This was easier to do when Miss Trelawny came close to me, and, leaning her forehead against my shoulder, began to cry silently. Then all the manhood in me woke, and to present purpose. It was of little use trying to speak; words were inadequate to thought. But we understood each other; she did not draw away when I put arm protectingly over her shoulder as I used to do with my little sister long ago when in her childish trouble she would come to her big brother to be comforted. That very act or attitude of protection made me more resolute in my purpose, and seemed to clear my brain of idle, dreamy wandering in thought. With an instinct of greater protection, however, I took away my arm as I heard the Doctor's footstep outside the door.

When Doctor Winchester came in he looked intently at the patient before speaking. His brows were set, and his mouth was a thin, hard line. Presently he said:

"There is much in common between the sleep of your Father and Nurse Kennedy. Whatever influence has brought it about has probably worked the same way in both cases. In Kennedy's case the coma is less marked. I cannot but feel, however, that with her we may be able to do more and more quickly than with this patient, as our hands are not tied. I have placed her in a draught; and already she shows some signs, though very faint ones, of ordinary unconsciousness. The rigidity of her limbs is less, and her skin seems more sensitive – or perhaps I should say less insensitive – to pain."

"How is it, then," I asked, "that Mr. Trelawny is still in this state of insensibility; and yet, so far as we know, his body has not had such rigidity at all?"

"That I cannot answer. The problem is one which we may solve in a few hours; or it may need a few days. But it will be a useful lesson in diagnosis to us all; and perhaps to many and many others after us, who knows!" he added, with the genuine fire of an enthusiast.

As the morning wore on, he flitted perpetually between the two rooms, watching anxiously over both patients. He made Mrs. Grant remain with the Nurse, but either Miss Trelawny or I, generally both of us, remained with the wounded man. We each managed, however, to get bathed and dressed; the Doctor and Mrs. Grant remained with Mr. Trelawny whilst we had breakfast.

Sergeant Daw went off to report at Scotland Yard the progress of the night; and then to the local station to arrange for the coming of his comrade, Wright, as fixed with Superintendent Dolan. When he returned I could not but think that he had been hauled over the coals for shooting in a sick-room; or perhaps for shooting at all without certain and proper cause. His remark to me enlightened me in the matter:

"A good character is worth something, sir, in spite of what some of them say. See! I've still got leave to carry my revolver."

That day was a long and anxious one. Toward nightfall Nurse Kennedy so far improved that the rigidity of her limbs entirely disappeared. She still breathed quietly and regularly; but the fixed expression of her face, though it was a calm enough expression, gave place to fallen eyelids and the negative look of sleep. Doctor Winchester had, towards evening, brought two more nurses, one of whom was to remain with Nurse Kennedy and the other to share in the watching with Miss Trelawny, who had insisted on remaining up herself. She had, in order to prepare for the duty, slept for several hours in the afternoon. We had all taken counsel together, and had arranged thus for the watching in Mr. Trelawny's room. Mrs. Grant was to remain beside the patient till twelve, when Miss Trelawny would relieve her. The new nurse was to sit in Miss Trelawny's room, and to visit the sick chamber each quarter of an hour. The Doctor would remain till twelve; when I was to relieve him. One or other of the detectives was to remain within hail of the room all night; and to pay periodical visits to see that all was well. Thus, the watchers would be watched; and the possibility of such events as last night, when the watchers were both overcome, would be avoided.

When the sun set, a strange and grave anxiety fell on all of us; and in our separate ways we prepared for the vigil. Doctor Winchester had evidently been thinking of my respirator, for he told me he would go out and get one. Indeed, he took to the idea so kindly that I persuaded Miss Trelawny also to have one which she could put on when her time for watching came.

And so the night drew on.

Chapter V
More Strange Instructions

WHEN I CAME FROM my room at half-past eleven o'clock I found all well in the sick-room. The new nurse, prim, neat, and watchful, sat in the chair by the bedside where Nurse Kennedy had sat last night. A little way off, between the bed and the safe, sat Dr. Winchester alert and wakeful, but looking strange and almost comic with the respirator over mouth and nose. As I stood in the doorway looking at them I heard a slight sound; turning round I saw the new detective, who nodded, held up the finger of silence and withdrew quietly. Hitherto no one of the watchers was overcome by sleep.

I took a chair outside the door. As yet there was no need for me to risk coming again under the subtle influence of last night. Naturally my thoughts went revolving round the main incidents of the last day and night, and I found myself arriving at strange conclusions, doubts, conjectures; but I did not lose myself, as on last night, in trains of thought. The sense of the present was ever with me, and I really felt as should a sentry on guard. Thinking is not a slow process; and when it is earnest the time can pass quickly. It seemed a very short time indeed till the door, usually left ajar, was pulled open and Dr. Winchester emerged, taking off his respirator as he came. His act, when he had it off, was demonstrative of his keenness. He turned up the outside of the wrap and smelled it carefully.

"I am going now," he said. "I shall come early in the morning; unless, of course, I am sent for before. But all seems well tonight."

The next to appear was Sergeant Daw, who went quietly into the room and took the seat vacated by the Doctor. I still remained outside; but every few minutes looked into the room. This was rather a form than a matter of utility, for the room was so dark that coming even from the dimly-lighted corridor it was hard to distinguish anything.

A little before twelve o'clock Miss Trelawny came from her room. Before coming to her father's she went into that occupied by Nurse Kennedy. After a couple of minutes she came out, looking, I thought, a trifle more cheerful. She had her respirator in her hand, but before putting it on, asked me if anything special had occurred since she had gone to lie down. I answered in a whisper – there was no loud talking in the house tonight – that all was safe, was well. She then put on her respirator, and I mine; and we entered the room. The Detective and the Nurse rose up, and we took their places. Sergeant Daw was the last to go out; he closed the door behind him as we had arranged.

For a while I sat quiet, my heart beating. The place was grimly dark. The only light was a faint one from the top of the lamp which threw a white circle on the high ceiling, except the emerald sheen of the shade as the light took its under edges. Even the light only seemed to emphasize the blackness of the shadows. These presently began to seem, as on last night, to have a sentience of their own. I did not myself feel in the least sleepy; and each time I went softly over to look at the patient, which I did about every ten minutes, I could see that Miss Trelawny was keenly alert. Every quarter of an hour one or other of the policemen looked in through the partly opened door. Each time both Miss Trelawny and I said through our mufflers, "all right," and the door was closed again.

As the time wore on, the silence and the darkness seemed to increase. The circle of light on the ceiling was still there, but it seemed less brilliant than at first. The green edging of the lamp-shade became like Maori greenstone rather than emerald. The sounds of the night without the house, and the starlight spreading pale lines along the edges of the window-cases, made the pall of black within more solemn and more mysterious.

We heard the clock in the corridor chiming the quarters with its silver bell till two o'clock; and then a strange feeling came over me. I could see from Miss Trelawny's movement as she looked round, that she also had some new sensation. The new detective had just looked in; we two were alone with the unconscious patient for another quarter of an hour.

My heart began to beat wildly. There was a sense of fear over me. Not for myself; my fear was impersonal. It seemed as though some new person had entered the room, and that a strong intelligence was awake close to me. Something brushed against my leg. I put my hand down hastily and touched the furry coat of Silvio. With a very faint far-away sound of a snarl he turned and scratched at me. I felt blood on my hand. I rose gently and came over to the bedside. Miss Trelawny, too, had stood up and was looking behind her, as though there was something close to her. Her eyes were wild, and her breast rose and fell as though she were fighting for air. When I touched her she did not seem to feel me; she worked her hands in front of her, as though she was fending off something.

There was not an instant to lose. I seized her in my arms and rushed over to the door, threw it open, and strode into the passage, calling loudly:

"Help! Help!"

In an instant the two Detectives, Mrs. Grant, and the Nurse appeared on the scene. Close on their heels came several of the servants, both men and women. Immediately Mrs. Grant came near enough, I placed Miss Trelawny in her arms, and rushed back into the room, turning up the electric light as soon as I could lay my hand on it. Sergeant Daw and the Nurse followed me.

We were just in time. Close under the great safe, where on the two successive nights he had been found, lay Mr. Trelawny with his left arm, bare save for the bandages, stretched out. Close by his side was a leaf-shaped Egyptian knife which had lain amongst the curios on the shelf of the broken cabinet. Its point was stuck in the parquet floor, whence had been removed the blood-stained rug.

But there was no sign of disturbance anywhere; nor any sign of any one or anything unusual. The Policemen and I searched the room accurately, whilst the Nurse and two of the servants lifted the wounded man back to bed; but no sign or clue could we get. Very soon Miss Trelawny returned to the room. She was pale but collected. When she came close to me she said in a low voice:

"I felt myself fainting. I did not know why; but I was afraid!"

The only other shock I had was when Miss Trelawny cried out to me, as I placed my hand on the bed to lean over and look carefully at her father:

"You are wounded. Look! Look! Your hand is bloody. There is blood on the sheets!" I had, in the excitement, quite forgotten Silvio's scratch. As I looked at it, the recollection came back to me; but before I could say a word Miss Trelawny had caught hold of my hand and lifted it up. When she saw the parallel lines of the cuts she cried out again:

"It is the same wound as Father's!" Then she laid my hand down gently but quickly, and said to me and to Sergeant Daw:

"Come to my room! Silvio is there in his basket." We followed her, and found Silvio sitting in his basket awake. He was licking his paws. The Detective said:

"He is there sure enough; but why licking his paws?"

Margaret – Miss Trelawny – gave a moan as she bent over and took one of the forepaws in her hand; but the cat seemed to resent it and snarled. At that Mrs. Grant came into the room. When she saw that we were looking at the cat she said:

"The Nurse tells me that Silvio was asleep on Nurse Kennedy's bed ever since you went to your Father's room until a while ago. He came there just after you had gone to master's room. Nurse says that Nurse Kennedy is moaning and muttering in her sleep as though she had a nightmare. I think we should send for Dr. Winchester."

"Do so at once, please!" said Miss Trelawny; and we went back to the room.

For a while Miss Trelawny stood looking at her father, with her brows wrinkled. Then, turning to me, as though her mind were made up, she said:

"Don't you think we should have a consultation on Father? Of course I have every confidence in Doctor Winchester; he seems an immensely clever young man. But he is a young man; and there must be men who have devoted themselves to this branch of science. Such a man would have more knowledge and more experience; and his knowledge and experience might help to throw light on poor Father's case. As it is, Doctor Winchester seems to be quite in the dark. Oh! I don't know what to do. It is all so terrible!" Here she broke down a little and cried; and I tried to comfort her.

Doctor Winchester arrived quickly. His first thought was for his patient; but when he found him without further harm, he visited Nurse Kennedy. When he saw her, a hopeful look came into his eyes. Taking a towel, he dipped a corner of it in cold water and flicked on the face. The skin coloured, and she stirred slightly. He said to the new nurse – Sister Doris he called her:

"She is all right. She will wake in a few hours at latest. She may be dizzy and distraught at first, or perhaps hysterical. If so, you know how to treat her."

"Yes, sir!" answered Sister Doris demurely; and we went back to Mr. Trelawny's room. As soon as we had entered, Mrs. Grant and the Nurse went out so that only Doctor Winchester, Miss Trelawny, and myself remained in the room. When the door had been closed Doctor Winchester asked me as to what had occurred. I told him fully, giving exactly every detail so far as I could remember. Throughout my narrative, which did not take long, however, he kept asking me questions as to who had been present and the order in which each one had come into the room. He asked other things, but nothing of any importance; these were all that took my attention, or remained in my memory. When our conversation was finished, he said in a very decided way indeed, to Miss Trelawny:

"I think, Miss Trelawny, that we had better have a consultation on this case." She answered at once, seemingly a little to his surprise:

"I am glad you have mentioned it. I quite agree. Who would you suggest?"

"Have you any choice yourself?" he asked. "Any one to whom your Father is known? Has he ever consulted any one?"

"Not to my knowledge. But I hope you will choose whoever you think would be best. My dear Father should have all the help that can be had; and I shall be deeply obliged by your choosing. Who is the best man in London – anywhere else – in such a case?"

"There are several good men; but they are scattered all over the world. Somehow, the brain specialist is born, not made; though a lot of hard work goes to the completing of him and fitting him for his work. He comes from no country. The most daring investigator up to the present is Chiuni, the Japanese; but he is rather a surgical experimentalist than a practitioner. Then there is Zammerfest of Uppsala, and Fenelon of the University of Paris, and Morfessi of Naples. These, of course, are in addition to our own men, Morrison of Aberdeen and Richardson of Birmingham. But before them all I would put Frere of King's College. Of all that I have named he best unites theory and practice. He has no hobbies – that have been discovered at all events; and his experience is immense. It is the regret of all of us who admire him that the nerve so firm and the hand so dexterous must yield to time. For my own part I would rather have Frere than any one living."

"Then," said Miss Trelawny decisively, "let us have Doctor Frere – by the way, is he 'Doctor' or 'Mister'? – as early as we can get him in the morning!"

A weight seemed removed from him, and he spoke with greater ease and geniality than he had yet shown:

"He is Sir James Frere. I shall go to him myself as early as it is possibly to see him, and shall ask him to come here at once." Then turning to me he said:

"You had better let me dress your hand."

"It is nothing," I said.

"Nevertheless it should be seen to. A scratch from any animal might turn out dangerous; there is nothing like being safe." I submitted; forthwith he began to dress my hand. He examined with a magnifying-glass the several parallel wounds, and compared them with the slip of blotting-paper, marked with Silvio's claws, which he took from his pocket-book. He put back the paper, simply remarking:

"It's a pity that Silvio slips in – and out – just when he shouldn't."

The morning wore slowly on. By ten o'clock Nurse Kennedy had so far recovered that she was able to sit up and talk intelligibly. But she was still hazy in her thoughts; and could not remember anything that had happened on the previous night, after her taking her place by the sick-bed. As yet she seemed neither to know nor care what had happened.

It was nearly eleven o'clock when Doctor Winchester returned with Sir James Frere. Somehow I felt my heart sink when from the landing I saw them in the hall below; I knew that Miss Trelawny was to have the pain of telling yet another stranger of her ignorance of her father's life.

Sir James Frere was a man who commanded attention followed by respect. He knew so thoroughly what he wanted himself, that he placed at once on one side all wishes and ideas of less definite persons. The mere flash of his piercing eyes, or the set of his resolute mouth, or the lowering of his great eyebrows, seemed to compel immediate and willing obedience to his wishes. Somehow, when we had all been introduced and he was well amongst us, all sense of mystery seemed to melt away. It was with a hopeful spirit that I saw him pass into the sick-room with Doctor Winchester.

They remained in the room a long time; once they sent for the Nurse, the new one, Sister Doris, but she did not remain long. Again they both went into Nurse Kennedy's room. He sent out the nurse attendant on her. Doctor Winchester told me afterward that Nurse Kennedy, though she was ignorant of later matters, gave full and satisfactory answers to all Doctor Frere's questions relating to her patient up to the time she became unconscious. Then they went to the study, where they remained so long, and their voices raised in heated discussion seemed in such determined opposition, that I began to feel uneasy. As for Miss Trelawny, she was almost in a state of collapse from nervousness before they joined us. Poor girl! she had had a sadly anxious time of it, and her nervous strength had almost broken down.

They came out at last, Sir James first, his grave face looking as unenlightening as that of the sphinx. Doctor Winchester followed him closely; his face was pale, but with that kind of pallor which looked like a reaction. It gave me the idea that it had been red not long before. Sir James asked that Miss Trelawny would come into the study. He suggested that I should come also. When we had entered, Sir James turned to me and said:

"I understand from Doctor Winchester that you are a friend of Miss Trelawny, and that you have already considerable knowledge of this case. Perhaps it will be well that you should be with us. I know you already as a keen lawyer, Mr. Ross, though I never had the pleasure of meeting you. As Doctor Winchester tells me that there are some strange matters outside this case which seem to puzzle him – and others – and in which he thinks you may yet be specially interested, it might be as well that you should know every phase of the case. For myself I do not take much account of mysteries – except those of science; and as there seems to be some idea of an attempt at assassination or robbery, all I can say is that if assassins were at work they ought to take some elementary lessons in anatomy before their next job, for they seem thoroughly ignorant. If robbery were their purpose, they seem to have worked with marvellous inefficiency. That, however, is not my business." Here he took a big pinch of snuff, and turning to to Miss Trelawny, went on: "Now as to the patient. Leaving out the cause of his illness, all we can say at present is that he appears to be suffering from a marked attack of catalepsy. At present nothing can be done, except to sustain his strength. The treatment of my friend Doctor Winchester is mainly such as I approve of; and I am confident that should any slight change arise he will be able to deal with it satisfactorily. It is an interesting case – most interesting; and should any new or abnormal development arise I shall be happy to come at any time. There is just one thing to which I wish to call your attention; and I put it to you, Miss Trelawny, directly, since it is your responsibility. Doctor Winchester informs me that you are not yourself free in the matter, but are bound by an instruction given by your Father in case just such a condition of things should arise. I would strongly advise that the patient be removed to another room; or, as an alternative, that those mummies and all such things should be removed from his chamber. Why, it's enough to put any man into an abnormal condition, to have such an assemblage of horrors round him, and to breathe the atmosphere which they exhale. You have evidence already of how such mephitic odour may act. That nurse – Kennedy, I think you said, Doctor – isn't yet out of her state of catalepsy; and you, Mr. Ross, have, I am told, experienced something of the same effects. I know this" – here his eyebrows came down more than ever, and his mouth hardened – "if I were in charge here I should insist on the patient having a different atmosphere; or I would throw up the case. Doctor Winchester already knows that I can only be again consulted on this condition being fulfilled. But I trust that you will see your way, as a good daughter to my mind should, to looking to your Father's health and sanity rather than to any whim of his – whether supported or not by a foregoing fear, or by any number of 'penny dreadful' mysteries. The day has hardly come yet, I am glad to say, when the British Museum and St. Thomas's Hospital have exchanged their normal functions. Good-day, Miss Trelawny. I earnestly hope that I may soon see your Father restored. Remember, that should you fulfil the elementary condition which I have laid down, I am at your service day or night. Good-morning, Mr. Ross. I hope you will be able to report to me soon, Doctor Winchester."

When he had gone we stood silent, till the rumble of his carriage wheels died away. The first to speak was Doctor Winchester:

"I think it well to say that to my mind, speaking purely as a physician, he is quite right. I feel as if I could have assaulted him when he made it a condition of not giving up the case; but all the same he is right as to treatment. He does not understand that there is something odd about this special case; and he will not realise the knot that we are all tied up in by Mr. Trelawny's instructions. Of course –" He was interrupted by Miss Trelawny:

"Doctor Winchester, do you, too, wish to give up the case; or are you willing to continue it under the conditions you know?"

"Give it up! Less now than ever. Miss Trelawny, I shall never give it up, so long as life is left to him or any of us!" She said nothing, but held out her hand, which he took warmly.

"Now," said she, "if Sir James Frere is a type of the cult of Specialists, I want no more of them. To start with, he does not seem to know any more than you do about my Father's condition; and if he were a hundredth part as much interested in it as you are, he would not stand on such punctilio. Of course, I am only too anxious about my poor Father; and if I can see a way to meet either of Sir James Frere's conditions, I shall do so. I shall ask Mr. Marvin to come here today, and advise me as to the limit of Father's wishes. If he thinks I am free to act in any way on my own responsibility, I shall not hesitate to do so." Then Doctor Winchester took his leave.

Miss Trelawny sat down and wrote a letter to Mr. Marvin, telling him of the state of affairs, and asking him to come and see her and to bring with him any papers which might throw any light on the subject. She sent the letter off with a carriage to bring back the solicitor; we waited with what patience we could for his coming.

It is not a very long journey for oneself from Kensington Palace Gardens to Lincoln's Inn Fields; but it seemed endlessly long when waiting for someone else to take it. All things, however, are amenable to Time; it was less than an hour all told when Mr. Marvin was with us.

He recognised Miss Trelawny's impatience, and when he had learned sufficient of her father's illness, he said to her:

"Whenever you are ready I can go with you into particulars regarding your Father's wishes."

"Whenever you like," she said, with an evident ignorance of his meaning. "Why not now?" He looked at me, as to a fellow man of business, and stammered out:

"We are not alone."

"I have brought Mr. Ross here on purpose," she answered. "He knows so much at present, that I want him to know more." The solicitor was a little disconcerted, a thing which those knowing him only in courts would hardly have believed. He answered, however, with some hesitation:

"But, my dear young lady – Your Father's wishes! – Confidence between father and child –"

Here she interrupted him; there was a tinge of red in her pale cheeks as she did so:

"Do you really think that applies to the present circumstances, Mr. Marvin? My Father never told me anything of his affairs; and I can now, in this sad extremity, only learn his wishes through a gentleman who is a stranger to me and of whom I never even heard till I got my Father's letter, written to be shown to me only in extremity. Mr. Ross is a new friend; but he has all my confidence, and I should like him to be present. Unless, of course," she added, "such a thing is forbidden by my Father. Oh! forgive me, Mr. Marvin, if I seem rude; but I have been in such dreadful trouble and anxiety lately, that I have hardly command of myself." She covered her eyes with her hand for a few seconds; we two men looked at each other and waited, trying to appear unmoved. She went on more firmly; she had recovered herself:

"Please! Please do not think I am ungrateful to you for your kindness in coming here and so quickly. I really am grateful; and I have every confidence in your judgment. If you wish, or think it best, we can be alone." I stood up; but Mr. Marvin made a dissentient gesture. He was evidently pleased with her attitude; there was geniality in his voice and manner as he spoke:

"Not at all! Not at all! There is no restriction on your Father's part; and on my own I am quite willing. Indeed, all told, it may be better. From what you have said of Mr. Trelawny's illness, and the other – incidental – matters, it will be well in case of any grave eventuality, that it was understood from the first, that circumstances were ruled by your Father's own imperative instructions. For, please understand me, his instructions are imperative – most imperative. They are so unyielding that he has given me a Power of Attorney, under which I have undertaken to act, authorising me to see his written wishes carried out. Please believe me once for all, that he intended fully everything mentioned in that letter to you! Whilst he is alive he is to remain in his own room; and none of his property is to be removed from it under any circumstances whatever. He has even given an inventory of the articles which are not to be displaced."

Miss Trelawny was silent. She looked somewhat distressed; so, thinking that I understood the immediate cause, I asked:

"May we see the list?" Miss Trelawny's face at once brightened; but it fell again as the lawyer answered promptly – he was evidently prepared for the question:

"Not unless I am compelled to take action on the Power of Attorney. I have brought that instrument with me. You will recognise, Mr. Ross" – he said this with a sort of business conviction which I had noticed in his professional work, as he handed me the deed – "how strongly it is worded, and how the grantor made his wishes apparent in such a way as to leave no loophole. It is his own wording, except for certain legal formalities; and I assure you I have seldom seen a more iron-clad document. Even I myself have no power to make the slightest relaxation of the instructions, without committing a distinct breach of faith. And that, I need not tell you, is impossible." He evidently added the last words in order to prevent an appeal to his personal consideration. He did not like the seeming harshness of his words, however, for he added:

"I do hope, Miss Trelawny, that you understand that I am willing – frankly and unequivocally willing – to do anything I can, within the limits of my power, to relieve your distress. But your Father had, in all his doings, some purpose of his own which he did not disclose to me. So far as I can see, there is not a word of his instructions that he had not thought over fully. Whatever idea he had in his mind was the idea of a lifetime; he had studied it in every possible phase, and was prepared to guard it at every point.

"Now I fear I have distressed you, and I am truly sorry for it; for I see you have much – too much – to bear already. But I have no alternative. If you want to consult me at any time about anything, I promise you I will come without a moment's delay, at any hour of the day or night. There is my private address," he scribbled in his pocket-book as he spoke, "and under it the address of my club, where I am generally to be found in the evening." He tore out the paper and handed it to her. She thanked him. He shook hands with her and with me and withdrew.

As soon as the hall door was shut on him, Mrs. Grant tapped at the door and came in. There was such a look of distress in her face that Miss Trelawny stood up, deadly white, and asked her:

"What is it, Mrs. Grant? What is it? Any new trouble?"

"I grieve to say, miss, that the servants, all but two, have given notice and want to leave the house today. They have talked the matter over among themselves; the butler has spoken for the rest. He says as how they are willing to forego their wages, and even to pay their legal obligations instead of notice; but that go today they must."

"What reason do they give?"

"None, miss. They say as how they're sorry, but that they've nothing to say. I asked Jane, the upper housemaid, miss, who is not with the rest but stops on; and she tells me confidential that they've got some notion in their silly heads that the house is haunted!"

We ought to have laughed, but we didn't. I could not look in Miss Trelawny's face and laugh. The pain and horror there showed no sudden paroxysm of fear; there was a fixed idea of which this was a confirmation. For myself, it seemed as if my brain had found a voice. But the voice was not complete; there was some other thought, darker and deeper, which lay behind it, whose voice had not sounded as yet.

Chapter VI
Suspicions

THE FIRST TO GET full self-command was Miss Trelawny. There was a haughty dignity in her bearing as she said:

"Very well, Mrs. Grant; let them go! Pay them up to today, and a month's wages. They have hitherto been very good servants; and the occasion of their leaving is not an ordinary one. We must not expect much faithfulness from any one who is beset with fears. Those who remain are to have in future double wages; and please send these to me presently when I send word." Mrs. Grant bristled with smothered indignation; all the housekeeper in her was outraged by such generous treatment of servants who had combined to give notice:

"They don't deserve it, miss; them to go on so, after the way they have been treated here. Never in my life have I seen servants so well treated or anyone so good to them and gracious to them as you have been. They might be in the household of a King for treatment. And now, just as there is trouble, to go and act like this. It's abominable, that's what it is!"

Miss Trelawny was very gentle with her, and smothered her ruffled dignity; so that presently she went away with, in her manner, a lesser measure of hostility to the undeserving. In quite a different frame of mind she returned presently to ask if her mistress would like her to engage a full staff of other servants, or at any rate try to do so. "For you know, ma'am," she went on, "when once a scare has been established in the servants' hall, it's wellnigh impossible to get rid of it. Servants may come; but they go away just as quick. There's no holding them. They simply won't stay; or even if they work out their month's notice, they lead you that life that you wish every hour of the day that you hadn't kept them. The women are bad enough, the huzzies; but the men are worse!" There was neither anxiety nor indignation in Miss Trelawny's voice or manner as she said:

"I think, Mrs. Grant, we had better try to do with those we have. Whilst my dear Father is ill we shall not be having any company, so that there will be only three now in the house to attend to. If those servants who are willing to stay are not enough, I should only get sufficient to help them to do the work. It will not, I should think, be difficult to get a few maids; perhaps some that you know already. And please bear in mind, that those whom you get, and who are suitable and will stay, are henceforth to have the same wages as those who are remaining. Of course, Mrs. Grant, you well enough understand that though I do not group you in any way with the servants, the rule of double salary applies to you too." As she spoke she extended her long, fine-shaped hand, which the other took and then, raising it to her lips, kissed it impressively with the freedom of an elder woman to a younger. I could not but admire the generosity of her treatment of her servants. In my mind I endorsed Mrs. Grant's sotto voce remark as she left the room:

"No wonder the house is like a King's house, when the mistress is a Princess!"

"A Princess!" That was it. The idea seemed to satisfy my mind, and to bring back in a wave of light the first moment when she swept across my vision at the ball in Belgrave Square. A queenly figure! Tall and slim, bending, swaying, undulating as the lily or the lotos. Clad in a flowing gown of some filmy black material shot with gold. For ornament in her hair she wore an old Egyptian jewel, a tiny crystal disk, set between rising plumes carved in lapis lazuli. On her wrist was a broad bangle or bracelet of antique work, in the shape of a pair of spreading wings wrought in gold, with the feathers made of coloured gems. For all her gracious bearing toward me, when our hostess introduced me, I was then afraid of her. It was only when later, at the picnic on the river, I had come to realise her sweet and gentle, that my awe changed to something else.

For a while she sat, making some notes or memoranda. Then putting them away, she sent for the faithful servants. I thought that she had better have this interview alone, and so left her. When I came back there were traces of tears in her eyes.

The next phase in which I had a part was even more disturbing, and infinitely more painful. Late in the afternoon Sergeant Daw came into the study where I was sitting. After closing the door carefully and looking all round the room to make certain that we were alone, he came close to me.

"What is it?" I asked him. "I see you wish to speak to me privately."

"Quite so, sir! May I speak in absolute confidence?"

"Of course you may. In anything that is for the good of Miss Trelawny – and of course Mr. Trelawny – you may be perfectly frank. I take it that we both want to serve them to the best of our powers." He hesitated before replying:

"Of course you know that I have my duty to do; and I think you know me well enough to know that I will do it. I am a policeman – a detective; and it is my duty to find out the facts of any case I am put on, without fear or favour to anyone. I would rather speak to you alone, in confidence if I may, without reference to any duty of anyone to anyone, except mine to Scotland Yard."

"Of course! of course!" I answered mechanically, my heart sinking, I did not know why. "Be quite frank with me. I assure you of my confidence."

"Thank you, sir. I take it that what I say is not to pass beyond you – not to anyone. Not to Miss Trelawny herself, or even to Mr. Trelawny when he becomes well again."

"Certainly, if you make it a condition!" I said a little more stiffly. The man recognised the change in my voice or manner, and said apologetically:

"Excuse me, sir, but I am going outside my duty in speaking to you at all on the subject. I know you, however, of old; and I feel that I can trust you. Not your word, sir, that is all right; but your discretion!"

I bowed. "Go on!" I said. He began at once:

"I have gone over this case, sir, till my brain begins to reel; but I can't find any ordinary solution of it. At the time of each attempt no one has seemingly come into the house; and certainly no one has got out. What does it strike you is the inference?"

"That the somebody – or the something – was in the house already," I answered, smiling in spite of myself.

"That's just what I think," he said, with a manifest sigh of relief. "Very well! Who can be that someone?"

"'Someone, or something,' was what I said," I answered.

"Let us make it 'someone,' Mr. Ross! That cat, though he might have scratched or bit, never pulled the old gentleman out of bed, and tried to get the bangle with the key off his arm. Such things are all very well in books where your amateur detectives, who know everything before it's done, can fit them into theories; but in Scotland Yard, where the men aren't all idiots either, we generally find that when crime is done, or attempted, it's people, not things, that are at the bottom of it."

"Then make it 'people' by all means, Sergeant."

"We were speaking of 'someone,' sir."

"Quite right. Someone, be it!"

"Did it ever strike you, sir, that on each of the three separate occasions where outrage was effected, or attempted, there was one person who was the first to be present and to give the alarm?"

"Let me see! Miss Trelawny, I believe, gave the alarm on the first occasion. I was present myself, if fast asleep, on the second; and so was Nurse Kennedy. When I woke there were several people in the room; you were one of them. I understand that on that occasion also Miss Trelawny was before you. At the last attempt I was Miss Trelawny fainted. I carried her out and went back. In returning, I was first; and I think you were close behind me."

Sergeant Daw thought for a moment before replying:

"She was present, or first, in the room on all the occasions; there was only damage done in the first and second!"

The inference was one which I, as a lawyer, could not mistake. I thought the best thing to do was to meet it half-way. I have always found that the best way to encounter an inference is to cause it to be turned into a statement.

"You mean," I said, "that as on the only occasions when actual harm was done, Miss Trelawny's being the first to discover it is a proof that she did it; or was in some way connected with the attempt, as well as the discovery?"

"I didn't venture to put it as clear as that; but that is where the doubt which I had leads." Sergeant Daw was a man of courage; he evidently did not shrink from any conclusion of his reasoning on facts.

We were both silent for a while. Fears began crowding in on my own mind. Not doubts of Miss Trelawny, or of any act of hers; but fears lest such acts should be misunderstood. There was evidently a mystery somewhere; and if no solution to it could be found, the doubt would be cast on someone. In such cases the guesses of the majority are bound to follow the line of least resistance; and if it could be proved that any personal gain to anyone could follow Mr. Trelawny's death, should such ensue, it might prove a difficult task for anyone to prove innocence in the face of suspicious facts. I found myself instinctively taking that deferential course which, until the plan of battle of the prosecution is unfolded, is so safe an attitude for the defence. It would never do for me, at this stage, to combat any theories which a detective might form. I could best help Miss Trelawny by listening and understanding. When the time should come for the dissipation and obliteration of the theories, I should be quite willing to use all my militant ardour, and all the weapons at my command.

"You will of course do your duty, I know," I said, "and without fear. What course do you intend to take?"

"I don't know as yet, sir. You see, up to now it isn't with me even a suspicion. If any one else told me that that sweet young lady had a hand in such a matter, I would think him a fool; but I am bound to follow my own conclusions. I know well that just as unlikely persons have been proved guilty, when a whole court – all except the prosecution who knew the facts, and the judge who had taught his mind to wait – would have sworn to innocence. I wouldn't, for all the world, wrong such a young lady; more especial when she has such a cruel weight to bear. And you will be sure that I won't say a word that'll prompt anyone else to make such a charge. That's why I speak to you in confidence, man to man. You are skilled in proofs; that is your profession. Mine only gets so far as suspicions, and what we call our own proofs – which are nothing but ex parte evidence after all. You know Miss Trelawny better than I do; and though I watch round the sick-room, and go where I like about the house and in and out of it, I haven't the same opportunities as you have of knowing the lady and what her life is, or her means are; or of anything else which might give me a clue to her actions. If I were to try to find out from her, it would at once arouse her suspicions. Then, if she were guilty, all possibility of ultimate proof would go; for she would easily find a way to baffle discovery. But if she be innocent, as I hope she is, it would be doing a cruel wrong to accuse her. I have thought the matter over according to my lights before I spoke to you; and if I have taken a liberty, sir, I am truly sorry."

"No liberty in the world, Daw," I said warmly, for the man's courage and honesty and consideration compelled respect. "I am glad you have spoken to me so frankly. We both want to find out the truth; and there is so much about this case that is strange – so strange as to go beyond all experiences – that to aim at truth is our only chance of making anything clear in the long-run – no matter what our views are, or what object we wish to achieve ultimately!" The Sergeant looked pleased as he went on:

"I thought, therefore, that if you had it once in your mind that somebody else held to such a possibility, you would by degrees get proof; or at any rate such ideas as would convince yourself, either for or against it. Then we would come to some conclusion; or at any rate we should so exhaust all other possibilities that the most likely one would remain as the nearest thing to proof, or strong suspicion, that we could get. After that we should have to –"

Just at this moment the door opened and Miss Trelawny entered the room. The moment she saw us she drew back quickly, saying:

"Oh, I beg pardon! I did not know you were here, and engaged." By the time I had stood up, she was about to go back.

"Do come in," I said; "Sergeant Daw and I were only talking matters over."

Whilst she was hesitating, Mrs. Grant appeared, saying as she entered the room: "Doctor Winchester is come, miss, and is asking for you."

I obeyed Miss Trelawny's look; together we left the room.

When the Doctor had made his examination, he told us that there was seemingly no change. He added that nevertheless he would like to stay in the house that night is he might. Miss Trelawny looked glad, and sent word to Mrs. Grant to get a room ready for him. Later in the day, when he and I happened to be alone together, he said suddenly:

"I have arranged to stay here tonight because I want to have a talk with you. And as I wish it to be quite private, I thought the least suspicious way would be to have a cigar together late in the evening when Miss Trelawny is watching her father." We still kept to our arrangement that either the sick man's daughter or I should be on watch all night. We were to share the duty at the early hours of the morning. I was anxious about this, for I knew from our conversation that the Detective would watch in secret himself, and would be particularly alert about that time.

The day passed uneventfully. Miss Trelawny slept in the afternoon; and after dinner went to relieve the Nurse. Mrs. Grant remained with her, Sergeant Daw being on duty in the corridor. Doctor Winchester and I took our coffee in the library. When we had lit our cigars he said quietly:

"Now that we are alone I want to have a confidential talk. We are 'tiled,' of course; for the present at all events?"

"Quite so!" I said, my heart sinking as I thought of my conversation with Sergeant Daw in the morning, and of the disturbing and harrowing fears which it had left in my mind. He went on:

"This case is enough to try the sanity of all of us concerned in it. The more I think of it, the madder I seem to get; and the two lines, each continually strengthened, seem to pull harder in opposite directions."

"What two lines?" He looked at me keenly for a moment before replying. Doctor Winchester's look at such moments was apt to be disconcerting. It would have been so to me had I had a personal part, other than my interest in Miss Trelawny, in the matter. As it was, however, I stood it unruffled. I was now an attorney in the case; an *amicus curiae* in one sense, in another retained for the defence. The mere thought that in this clever man's mind were two lines, equally strong and opposite, was in itself so consoling as to neutralise my anxiety as to a new attack. As he began to speak, the Doctor's face wore an inscrutable smile; this, however, gave place to a stern gravity as he proceeded:

"Two lines: Fact and – Fancy! In the first there is this whole thing; attacks, attempts at robbery and murder; stupefyings; organised catalepsy which points to either criminal hypnotism and thought suggestion, or some simple form of poisoning unclassified yet in our toxicology. In the other there is some influence at work which is not classified in any book that I know – outside the pages of romance. I never felt in my life so strongly the truth of Hamlet's words:

> "There are more things in Heaven and earth...
> Than are dreamt of in your philosophy."

"Let us take the 'Fact' side first. Here we have a man in his home; amidst his own household; plenty of servants of different classes in the house, which forbids the possibility of an organised attempt made from the servants' hall. He is wealthy, learned, clever. From his physiognomy there is no doubting that he is a man of iron will and determined purpose. His daughter – his only child, I take it, a young girl bright and clever – is sleeping in the very next room to his. There is seemingly no possible reason for expecting any attack or disturbance of any kind; and no reasonable opportunity for any outsider to effect it. And yet we have an attack made; a brutal and remorseless attack, made in the middle of the night. Discovery is made quickly; made with that rapidity which in criminal cases generally is found to be not accidental, but of premeditated intent. The attacker, or attackers, are manifestly disturbed before the completion of their work, whatever their ultimate intent may have been. And yet there is no possible sign of their escape; no clue, no disturbance of anything; no open door or window; no sound. Nothing whatever to show who had done the deed, or even that a deed has been done; except the victim, and his surroundings incidental to the deed!

"The next night a similar attempt is made, though the house is full of wakeful people; and though there are on watch in the room and around it a detective officer, a trained nurse, an earnest friend, and the man's own daughter. The nurse is thrown into a catalepsy, and the watching friend – though protected by a respirator – into a deep sleep. Even the detective is so far overcome with some phase of stupor that he fires off his pistol in the sick-room, and can't even tell what he thought he was firing at. That respirator of yours is the only thing that seems to have a bearing on the 'fact' side of the affair. That you did not lose your head as the others did – the effect in such case being in proportion to the amount of time each remained in the room – points to the probability that the stupefying medium was not hypnotic, whatever else it may have been. But again, there is a fact which is contradictory. Miss Trelawny, who was in the room more than any of you – for she was in and out all the time and did her share of permanent watching also – did not seem to be affected at all. This would show that the influence, whatever it is, does not affect generally – unless, of course, it was that she was in some way inured to it. If it should turn out that it be some strange exhalation from some of those Egyptian curios, that might account for it; only, we are then face to face with the fact that Mr. Trelawny, who was most of all in the room – who, in fact, lived more than half his life in it – was affected worst of all. What kind of influence could it be which would account for all these different and contradictory effects? No! the more I think of this form of the dilemma, the more I am bewildered! Why, even if it were that the attack, the physical attack, on Mr. Trelawny had been made by some one residing in the house and not within the sphere of suspicion, the oddness of the stupefyings would still remain a mystery.

It is not easy to put anyone into a catalepsy. Indeed, so far as is known yet in science, there is no way to achieve such an object at will. The crux of the whole matter is Miss Trelawny, who seems to be subject to none of the influences, or possibly of the variants of the same influence at work. Through all she goes unscathed, except for that one slight semi-faint. It is most strange!"

I listened with a sinking heart; for, though his manner was not illuminative of distrust, his argument was disturbing. Although it was not so direct as the suspicion of the Detective, it seemed to single out Miss Trelawny as different from all others concerned; and in a mystery to be alone is to be suspected, ultimately if not immediately. I thought it better not to say anything. In such a case silence is indeed golden; and if I said nothing now I might have less to defend, or explain, or take back later. I was, therefore, secretly glad that his form of putting his argument did not require any answer from me – for the present, at all events. Doctor Winchester did not seem to expect any answer – a fact which, when I recognised it, gave my pleasure, I hardly knew why. He paused for a while, sitting with his chin in his hand, his eyes staring at vacancy, whilst his brows were fixed. His cigar was held limp between his fingers; he had apparently forgotten it. In an even voice, as though commencing exactly where he had left off, he resumed his argument:

"The other horn of the dilemma is a different affair altogether; and if we once enter on it we must leave everything in the shape of science and experience behind us. I confess that it has its fascinations for me; though at every new thought I find myself romancing in a way that makes me pull up suddenly and look facts resolutely in the face. I sometimes wonder whether the influence or emanation from the sick-room at times affects me as it did the others – the Detective, for instance. Of course it may be that if it is anything chemical, any drug, for example, in vaporeal form, its effects may be cumulative. But then, what could there be that could produce such an effect? The room is, I know, full of mummy smell; and no wonder, with so many relics from the tomb, let alone the actual mummy of that animal which Silvio attacked. By the way, I am going to test him tomorrow; I have been on the trace of a mummy cat, and am to get possession of it in the morning. When I bring it here we shall find out if it be a fact that racial instinct can survive a few thousand years in the grave. However, to get back to the subject in hand. These very mummy smells arise from the presence of substances, and combinations of substances, which the Egyptian priests, who were the learned men and scientists of their time, found by the experience of centuries to be strong enough to arrest the natural forces of decay. There must be powerful agencies at work to effect such a purpose; and it is possible that we may have here some rare substance or combination whose qualities and powers are not understood in this later and more prosaic age. I wonder if Mr. Trelawny has any knowledge, or even suspicion, of such a kind? I only know this for certain, that a worse atmosphere for a sick chamber could not possibly be imagined; and I admire the courage of Sir James Frere in refusing to have anything to do with a case under such conditions. These instructions of Mr. Trelawny to his daughter, and from what you have told me, the care with which he has protected his wishes through his solicitor, show that he suspected something, at any rate. Indeed, it would almost seem as if he expected something to happen.... I wonder if it would be possible to learn anything about that! Surely his papers would show or suggest something.... It is a difficult matter to tackle; but it might have to be done. His present condition cannot go on for ever;

and if anything should happen there would have to be an inquest. In such case full examination would have to be made into everything.... As it stands, the police evidence would show a murderous attack more than once repeated. As no clue is apparent, it would be necessary to seek one in a motive."

He was silent. The last words seemed to come in a lower and lower tone as he went on. It had the effect of hopelessness. It came to me as a conviction that now was my time to find out if he had any definite suspicion; and as if in obedience to some command, I asked:

"Do you suspect anyone?" He seemed in a way startled rather than surprised as he turned his eyes on me:

"Suspect anyone? Any thing, you mean. I certainly suspect that there is some influence; but at present my suspicion is held within such limit. Later on, if there be any sufficiently definite conclusion to my reasoning, or my thinking – for there are not proper data for reasoning – I may suspect; at present however –"

He stopped suddenly and looked at the door. There was a faint sound as the handle turned. My own heart seemed to stand still. There was over me some grim, vague apprehension. The interruption in the morning, when I was talking with the Detective, came back upon me with a rush.

The door opened, and Miss Trelawny entered the room.

When she saw us, she started back; and a deep flush swept her face. For a few seconds she paused; at such a time a few succeeding seconds seem to lengthen in geometrical progression. The strain upon me, and, as I could easily see, on the Doctor also, relaxed as she spoke:

"Oh, forgive me, I did not know that you were engaged. I was looking for you, Doctor Winchester, to ask you if I might go to bed tonight with safety, as you will be here. I feel so tired and worn-out that I fear I may break down; and tonight I would certainly not be of any use." Doctor Winchester answered heartily:

"Do! Do go to bed by all means, and get a good night's sleep. God knows! you want it. I am more than glad you have made the suggestion, for I feared when I saw you tonight that I might have you on my hands a patient next."

She gave a sigh of relief, and the tired look seemed to melt from her face. Never shall I forget the deep, earnest look in her great, beautiful black eyes as she said to me:

"You will guard Father tonight, won't you, with Doctor Winchester? I am so anxious about him that every second brings new fears. But I am really worn-out; and if I don't get a good sleep, I think I shall go mad. I will change my room for tonight. I'm afraid that if I stay so close to Father's room I shall multiply every sound into a new terror. But, of course, you will have me waked if there be any cause. I shall be in the bedroom of the little suite next the boudoir off the hall. I had those rooms when first I came to live with Father, and I had no care then.... It will be easier to rest there; and perhaps for a few hours I may forget. I shall be all right in the morning. Good-night!"

When I had closed the door behind her and come back to the little table at which we had been sitting, Doctor Winchester said:

"That poor girl is overwrought to a terrible degree. I am delighted that she is to get a rest. It will be life to her; and in the morning she will be all right. Her nervous system is on the verge of a breakdown. Did you notice how fearfully disturbed she was, and how red she got when she came in and found us talking? An ordinary thing like that, in her own house with her own guests, wouldn't under normal circumstances disturb her!"

I was about to tell him, as an explanation in her defence, how her entrance was a repetition of her finding the Detective and myself alone together earlier in the day, when I remembered that that conversation was so private that even an allusion to it might be awkward in evoking curiosity. So I remained silent.

We stood up to go to the sick-room; but as we took our way through the dimly-lighted corridor I could not help thinking, again and again, and again – ay, and for many a day after – how strange it was that she had interrupted me on two such occasions when touching on such a theme.

There was certainly some strange web of accidents, in whose meshes we were all involved.

Chapter VII
The Traveller's Loss

THAT NIGHT everything went well. Knowing that Miss Trelawny herself was not on guard, Doctor Winchester and I doubled our vigilance. The Nurses and Mrs. Grant kept watch, and the Detectives made their visit each quarter of an hour. All night the patient remained in his trance. He looked healthy, and his chest rose and fell with the easy breathing of a child. But he never stirred; only for his breathing he might have been of marble. Doctor Winchester and I wore our respirators, and irksome they were on that intolerably hot night. Between midnight and three o'clock I felt anxious, and had once more that creepy feeling to which these last few nights had accustomed me; but the grey of the dawn, stealing round the edges of the blinds, came with inexpressible relief, followed by restfulness, went through the household. During the hot night my ears, strained to every sound, had been almost painfully troubled; as though my brain or sensoria were in anxious touch with them. Every breath of the Nurse or the rustle of her dress; every soft pat of slippered feet, as the Policeman went his rounds; every moment of watching life, seemed to be a new impetus to guardianship. Something of the same feeling must have been abroad in the house; now and again I could hear upstairs the sound of restless feet, and more than once downstairs the opening of a window. With the coming of the dawn, however, all this ceased, and the whole household seemed to rest. Doctor Winchester went home when Sister Doris came to relieve Mrs. Grant. He was, I think, a little disappointed or chagrined that nothing of an exceptional nature had happened during his long night vigil.

At eight o'clock Miss Trelawny joined us, and I was amazed as well as delighted to see how much good her night's sleep had done her. She was fairly radiant; just as I had seen her at our first meeting and at the picnic. There was even a suggestion of colour in her cheeks, which, however, looked startlingly white in contrast with her black brows and scarlet lips. With her restored strength, there seemed to have come a tenderness even exceeding that which she had at first shown to her sick father. I could not but be moved by the loving touches as she fixed his pillows and brushed the hair from his forehead.

I was wearied out myself with my long spell of watching; and now that she was on guard I started off to bed, blinking my tired eyes in the full light and feeling the weariness of a sleepless night on me all at once.

I had a good sleep, and after lunch I was about to start out to walk to Jermyn Street, when I noticed an importunate man at the hall door. The servant in charge was the one called Morris, formerly the 'odd man,' but since the exodus of the servants promoted to be butler pro tem. The stranger was speaking rather loudly, so that there was no difficulty in understanding his grievance. The servant man was respectful in both words and demeanour; but he stood squarely in front of the great double door, so that the other could not enter. The first words which I heard from the visitor sufficiently explained the situation:

"That's all very well, but I tell you I must see Mr. Trelawny! What is the use of your saying I can't, when I tell you I must. You put me off, and off, and off! I came here at nine; you said then that he was not up, and that as he was not well he could not be disturbed. I came at twelve; and you told me again he was not up. I asked then to see any of his household; you told me that Miss Trelawny was not up. Now I come again at three, and you tell me he is still in bed, and is not awake yet. Where is Miss Trelawny? 'She is occupied and must not be disturbed!' Well, she must be disturbed! Or some one must. I am here about Mr. Trelawny's special business; and I have come from a place where servants always begin by saying No. 'No' isn't good enough for me this time! I've had three years of it, waiting outside doors and tents when it took longer to get in than it did into the tombs; and then you would think, too, the men inside were as dead as the mummies. I've had about enough of it, I tell you. And when I come home, and find the door of the man I've been working for barred, in just the same way and with the same old answers, it stirs me up the wrong way. Did Mr. Trelawny leave orders that he would not see me when I should come?"

He paused and excitedly mopped his forehead. The servant answered very respectfully:

"I am very sorry, sir, if in doing my duty I have given any offence. But I have my orders, and must obey them. If you would like to leave any message, I will give it to Miss Trelawny; and if you will leave your address, she can communicate with you if she wishes." The answer came in such a way that it was easy to see that the speaker was a kind-hearted man, and a just one.

"My good fellow, I have no fault to find with you personally; and I am sorry if I have hurt your feelings. I must be just, even if I am angry. But it is enough to anger any man to find himself in the position I am. Time is pressing. There is not an hour – not a minute – to lose! And yet here I am, kicking my heels for six hours; knowing all the time that your master will be a hundred times angrier than I am, when he hears how the time has been fooled away. He would rather be waked out of a thousand sleeps than not see me just at present – and before it is too late. My God! it's simply dreadful, after all I've gone through, to have my work spoiled at the last and be foiled in the very doorway by a stupid flunkey! Is there no one with sense in the house; or with authority, even if he hasn't got sense? I could mighty soon convince him that your master must be awakened; even if he sleeps like the Seven Sleepers –"

There was no mistaking the man's sincerity, or the urgency and importance of his business; from his point of view at any rate. I stepped forward.

"Morris," I said, "you had better tell Miss Trelawny that this gentleman wants t
see her particularly. If she is busy, ask Mrs. Grant to tell her."

"Very good, sir!" he answered in a tone of relief, and hurried away.

I took the stranger into the little boudoir across the hall. As we went he asked me
"Are you the secretary?"

"No! I am a friend of Miss Trelawny's. My name is Ross."

"Thank you very much, Mr. Ross, for your kindness!" he said. "My name is Corbeck
I would give you my card, but they don't use cards where I've come from. And if I ha
had any, I suppose they, too, would have gone last night –"

He stopped suddenly, as though conscious that he had said too much. We bot
remained silent; as we waited I took stock of him. A short, sturdy man, brown as
coffee-berry; possibly inclined to be fat, but now lean exceedingly. The deep wrinkle
in his face and neck were not merely from time and exposure; there were thos
unmistakable signs where flesh or fat has fallen away, and the skin has become loose
The neck was simply an intricate surface of seams and wrinkles, and sun-scarred wit
the burning of the Desert. The Far East, the Tropic Seasons, and the Desert – eac
can have its colour mark. But all three are quite different; and an eye which has onc
known, can thenceforth easily distinguish them. The dusky pallor of one; the fierc
red-brown of the other; and of the third, the dark, ingrained burning, as thoug
it had become a permanent colour. Mr. Corbeck had a big head, massive and ful
with shaggy, dark red-brown hair, but bald on the temples. His forehead was a fin
one, high and broad; with, to use the terms of physiognomy, the frontal sinus boldl
marked. The squareness of it showed 'ratiocination'; and the fulness under the eye
'language'. He had the short, broad nose that marks energy; the square chin – marke
despite a thick, unkempt beard – and massive jaw that showed great resolution.

"No bad man for the Desert!" I thought as I looked.

Miss Trelawny came very quickly. When Mr. Corbeck saw her, he seemed somewha
surprised. But his annoyance and excitement had not disappeared; quite enoug
remained to cover up any such secondary and purely exoteric feeling as surprise. But a
she spoke he never took his eyes off her; and I made a mental note that I would fin
some early opportunity of investigating the cause of his surprise. She began with a
apology which quite smoothed down his ruffled feelings:

"Of course, had my Father been well you would not have been kept waiting
Indeed, had not I been on duty in the sick-room when you called the first time,
should have seen you at once. Now will you kindly tell me what is the matter whic
so presses?" He looked at me and hesitated. She spoke at once:

"You may say before Mr. Ross anything which you can tell me. He has my fulles
confidence, and is helping me in my trouble. I do not think you quite understan
how serious my Father's condition is. For three days he has not waked, or given an
sign of consciousness; and I am in terrible trouble about him. Unhappily I am i
great ignorance of my Father and his life. I only came to live with him a year ago; an
I know nothing whatever of his affairs. I do not even know who you are, or in wha
way your business is associated with him." She said this with a little deprecatin
smile, all conventional and altogether graceful; as though to express in the mos
genuine way her absurd ignorance.

He looked steadily at her for perhaps a quarter of a minute; then he spoke
beginning at once as though his mind were made up and his confidence establishec

"My name is Eugene Corbeck. I am a Master of Arts and Doctor of Laws and Master of Surgery of Cambridge; Doctor of Letters of Oxford; Doctor of Science and Doctor of Languages of London University; Doctor of Philosophy of Berlin; Doctor of Oriental Languages of Paris. I have some other degrees, honorary and otherwise, but I need not trouble you with them. Those I have name will show you that I am sufficiently feathered with diplomas to fly into even a sick-room. Early in life – fortunately for my interests and pleasures, but unfortunately for my pocket – I fell in with Egyptology. I must have been bitten by some powerful scarab, for I took it bad. I went out tomb-hunting; and managed to get a living of a sort, and to learn some things that you can't get out of books. I was in pretty low water when I met your Father, who was doing some explorations on his own account; and since then I haven't found that I have many unsatisfied wants. He is a real patron of the arts; no mad Egyptologist can ever hope for a better chief!"

He spoke with feeling; and I was glad to see that Miss Trelawny coloured up with pleasure at the praise of her father. I could not help noticing, however, that Mr. Corbeck was, in a measure, speaking as if against time. I took it that he wished, while speaking, to study his ground; to see how far he would be justified in taking into confidence the two strangers before him. As he went on, I could see that his confidence kept increasing. When I thought of it afterward, and remembered what he had said, I realised that the measure of the information which he gave us marked his growing trust.

"I have been several times out on expeditions in Egypt for your Father; and I have always found it a delight to work for him. Many of his treasures – and he has some rare ones, I tell you – he has procured through me, either by my exploration or by purchase – or – or – otherwise. Your Father, Miss Trelawny, has a rare knowledge. He sometimes makes up his mind that he wants to find a particular thing, of whose existence – if it still exists – he has become aware; and he will follow it all over the world till he gets it. I've been on just such a chase now."

He stopped suddenly, as suddenly as thought his mouth had been shut by the jerk of a string. We waited; when he went on he spoke with a caution that was new to him, as though he wished to forestall our asking any questions:

"I am not at liberty to mention anything of my mission; where it was to, what it was for, or anything at all about it. Such matters are in confidence between Mr. Trelawny and myself; I am pledged to absolute secrecy."

He paused, and an embarrassed look crept over his face. Suddenly he said:

"You are sure, Miss Trelawny, your Father is not well enough to see me today?"

A look of wonderment was on her face in turn. But it cleared at once; she stood up, saying in a tone in which dignity and graciousness were blended:

"Come and see for yourself!" She moved toward her father's room; he followed, and I brought up the rear.

Mr. Corbeck entered the sick-room as though he knew it. There is an unconscious attitude or bearing to persons in new surroundings which there is no mistaking. Even in his anxiety to see his powerful friend, he glanced for a moment round the room, as at a familiar place. Then all his attention became fixed on the bed. I watched him narrowly, for somehow I felt that on this man depended much of our enlightenment regarding the strange matter in which we were involved.

It was not that I doubted him. The man was of transparent honesty; it was this very quality which we had to dread. He was of that courageous, fixed trueness to his undertaking, that if he should deem it his duty to guard a secret he would do it to the last. The case before us was, at least, an unusual one; and it would, consequently, require more liberal recognition of bounds of the duty of secrecy than would hold under ordinary conditions. To us, ignorance was helplessness. If we could learn anything of the past we might at least form some idea of the conditions antecedent to the attack; and might, so, achieve some means of helping the patient to recovery. There were curios which might be removed.... My thoughts were beginning to whirl once again; I pulled myself up sharply and watched. There was a look of infinite pity on the sun-stained, rugged face as he gazed at his friend, lying so helpless. The sternness of Mr. Trelawny's face had not relaxed in sleep; but somehow it made the helplessness more marked. It would not have troubled one to see a weak or an ordinary face under such conditions; but this purposeful, masterful man, lying before us wrapped in impenetrable sleep, had all the pathos of a great ruin. The sight was not a new one to us; but I could see that Miss Trelawny, like myself, was moved afresh by it in the presence of the stranger. Mr. Corbeck's face grew stern. All the pity died away; and in its stead came a grim, hard look which boded ill for whoever had been the cause of this mighty downfall. This look in turn gave place to one of decision; the volcanic energy of the man was working to some definite purpose. He glanced around at us; and as his eyes lighted on Nurse Kennedy his eyebrows went up a trifle. She noted the look, and glanced interrogatively at Miss Trelawny, who flashed back a reply with a glance. She went quietly from the room, closing the door behind her. Mr. Corbeck looked first at me, with a strong man's natural impulse to learn from a man rather than a woman; then at Miss Trelawny, with a remembrance of the duty of courtesy, and said:

"Tell me all about it. How it began and when!" Miss Trelawny looked at me appealingly; and forthwith I told him all that I knew. He seemed to make no motion during the whole time; but insensibly the bronze face became steel. When, at the end, I told him of Mr. Marvin's visit and of the Power of Attorney, his look began to brighten. And when, seeing his interest in the matter, I went more into detail as to its terms, he spoke:

"Good! Now I know where my duty lies!"

With a sinking heart I heard him. Such a phrase, coming at such a time, seemed to close the door to my hopes of enlightenment.

"What do you mean?" I asked, feeling that my question was a feeble one.

His answer emphasized my fears:

"Trelawny knows what he is doing. He had some definite purpose in all that he did; and we must not thwart him. He evidently expected something to happen, and guarded himself at all points."

"Not at all points!" I said impulsively. "There must have been a weak spot somewhere, or he wouldn't be lying here like that!" Somehow his impassiveness surprised me. I had expected that he would find a valid argument in my phrase; but it did not move him, at least not in the way I thought. Something like a smile flickered over his swarthy face as he answered me:

"This is not the end! Trelawny did not guard himself to no purpose. Doubtless, he expected this too; or at any rate the possibility of it."

"Do you know what he expected, or from what source?" The questioner was Miss Trelawny.

The answer came at once: "No! I know nothing of either. I can guess..." He stopped suddenly.

"Guess what?" The suppressed excitement in the girl's voice was akin to anguish. The steely look came over the swarthy face again; but there was tenderness and courtesy in both voice and manner as he replied:

"Believe me, I would do anything I honestly could to relieve you anxiety. But in this I have a higher duty."

"What duty?"

"Silence!" As he spoke the word, the strong mouth closed like a steel trap.

We all remained silent for a few minutes. In the intensity of our thinking, the silence became a positive thing; the small sounds of life within and without the house seemed intrusive. The first to break it was Miss Trelawny. I had seen an idea – a hope – flash in her eyes; but she steadied herself before speaking:

"What was the urgent subject on which you wanted to see me, knowing that my father was – not available?" The pause showed her mastery of her thoughts.

The instantaneous change in Mr. Corbeck was almost ludicrous. His start of surprise, coming close upon his iron-clad impassiveness, was like a pantomimic change. But all idea of comedy was swept away by the tragic earnestness with which he remembered his original purpose.

"My God!" he said, as he raised his hand from the chair back on which it rested, and beat it down with a violence which would in itself have arrested attention. His brows corrugated as he went on: "I quite forgot! What a loss! Now of all times! Just at the moment of success! He lying there helpless, and my tongue tied! Not able to raise hand or foot in my ignorance of his wishes!"

"What is it? Oh, do tell us! I am so anxious about my dear Father! Is it any new trouble? I hope not! oh, I hope not! I have had such anxiety and trouble already! It alarms me afresh to hear you speak so! Won't you tell me something to allay this terrible anxiety and uncertainty?"

He drew his sturdy form up to his full height as he said:

"Alas! I cannot, may not, tell you anything. It is his secret." He pointed to the bed. "And yet – and yet I came here for his advice, his counsel, his assistance. And he lies here helpless.... And time is flying by us! It may soon be too late!"

"What is it? what is it?" broke in Miss Trelawny in a sort of passion of anxiety, her face drawn with pain. "Oh, speak! Say something! This anxiety, and horror, and mystery are killing me!" Mr. Corbeck calmed himself by a great effort.

"I may not tell you details; but I have had a great loss. My mission, in which I have spent three years, was successful. I discovered all that I sought – and more; and brought them home with me safely. Treasures, priceless in themselves, but doubly precious to him by whose wishes and instructions I sought them. I arrived in London only last night, and when I woke this morning my precious charge was stolen. Stolen in some mysterious way. Not a soul in London knew that I was arriving. No one but myself knew what was in the shabby portmanteau that I carried. My room had but one door, and that I locked and bolted. The room was high in the house, five stories up, so that no entrance could have been obtained by the window. Indeed, I had closed the window myself and shut the hasp, for I wished to be secure in every way. This morning the hasp was untouched.... And yet my portmanteau was empty. The lamps were gone!... There! It is out. I went to Egypt to search for a set of antique lamps which Mr. Trelawny wished to trace. With incredible labour, and through many dangers, I followed them. I brought them safe home.... And now!" He turned away much moved. Even his iron nature was breaking down under the sense of loss.

Miss Trelawny stepped over and laid her hand on his arm. I looked at her in amazement. All the passion and pain which had so moved her seemed to have taken the form of resolution. Her form was erect, her eyes blazed; energy was manifest in every nerve and fibre of her being. Even her voice was full of nervous power as she spoke. It was apparent that she was a marvellously strong woman, and that her strength could answer when called upon.

"We must act at once! My Father's wishes must be carried out if it is possible to us. Mr. Ross, you are a lawyer. We have actually in the house a man whom you consider one of the best detectives in London. Surely we can do something. We can begin at once!" Mr. Corbeck took new life from her enthusiasm.

"Good! You are your Father's daughter!" was all he said. But his admiration for her energy was manifested by the impulsive way in which he took her hand. I moved over to the door. I was going to bring Sergeant Daw; and from her look of approval, I knew that Margaret – Miss Trelawny – understood. I was at the door when Mr. Corbeck called me back.

"One moment," he said, "before we bring a stranger on the scene. It must be borne in mind that he is not to know what you know now, that the lamps were the objects of a prolonged and difficult and dangerous search. All I can tell him, all that he must know from any source, is that some of my property has been stolen. I must describe some of the lamps, especially one, for it is of gold; and my fear is lest the thief, ignorant of its historic worth, may, in order to cover up his crime, have it melted. I would willingly pay ten, twenty, a hundred, a thousand times its intrinsic value rather than have it destroyed. I shall tell him only what is necessary. So, please, let me answer any questions he may ask; unless, of course, I ask you or refer to either of you for the answer." We both nodded acquiescence. Then a thought struck me and I said:

"By the way, if it be necessary to keep this matter quiet it will be better to have it if possible a private job for the Detective. If once a thing gets to Scotland Yard it is out of our power to keep it quiet, and further secrecy may be impossible. I shall sound Sergeant Daw before he comes up. If I say nothing, it will mean that he accepts the task and will deal with it privately." Mr. Corbeck answered at once:

"Secrecy is everything. The one thing I dread is that the lamps, or some of them, may be destroyed at once." To my intense astonishment Miss Trelawny spoke out at once, but quietly, in a decided voice:

"They will not be destroyed; nor any of them!" Mr. Corbeck actually smiled in amazement.

"How on earth do you know?" he asked. Her answer was still more incomprehensible.

"I don't know how I know it; but know it I do. I feel it all through me; as though i were a conviction which has been with me all my life!"

Chapter VIII
The Finding of the Lamps

SERGEANT DAW at first made some demur; but finally agreed to advise privately on a matter which might be suggested to him. He added that I was to remember that he only undertook to advise; for if action were required he might have to refer the matter to headquarters. With this understanding I left him in the study, and brought Miss Trelawny and Mr. Corbeck to him. Nurse Kennedy resumed her place at the bedside before we left the room.

I could not but admire the cautious, cool-headed precision with which the traveller stated his case. He did not seem to conceal anything, and yet he gave the least possible description of the objects missing. He did not enlarge on the mystery of the case; he seemed to look on it as an ordinary hotel theft. Knowing, as I did, that his one object was to recover the articles before their identity could be obliterated, I could see the rare intellectual skill with which he gave the necessary matter and held back all else, though without seeming to do so. "Truly," thought I, "this man has learned the lesson of the Eastern bazaars; and with Western intellect has improved upon his masters!" He quite conveyed his idea to the Detective, who, after thinking the matter over for a few moments, said:

"Pot or scale? That is the question."

"What does that mean?" asked the other, keenly alert.

"An old thieves phrase from Birmingham. I thought that in these days of slang everyone knew that. In old times at Brum, which had a lot of small metal industries, the gold- and silver-smiths used to buy metal from almost anyone who came along. And as metal in small quantities could generally be had cheap when they didn't ask where it came from, it got to be a custom to ask only one thing – whether the customer wanted the goods melted, in which case the buyer made the price, and the melting-pot was always on the fire. If it was to be preserved in its present state at the buyer's option, it went into the scale and fetched standard price for old metal.

"There is a good deal of such work done still, and in other places than Brum. When we're looking for stolen watches we often come across the works, and it's not possible to identify wheels and springs out of a heap; but it's not often that we come across cases that are wanted. Now, in the present instance much will depend on whether the thief is a good man – that's what they call a man who knows his work. A first-class crook will know whether a thing is of more value than merely the metal in it; and in such case he would put it with someone who could place it later on – in America or France, perhaps. By the way, do you think anyone but yourself could identify your lamps?"

"No one but myself!"

"Are there others like them?"

"Not that I know of," answered Mr. Corbeck; "though there may be others that resemble them in many particulars." The Detective paused before asking again: "Would any other skilled person – at the British Museum, for instance, or a dealer, or a collector like Mr. Trelawny, know the value – the artistic value – of the lamps?"

"Certainly! Anyone with a head on his shoulders would see at a glance that the things were valuable."

The Detective's face brightened. "Then there is a chance. If your door was locked and the window shut, the goods were not stolen by the chance of a chambermaid or a boots coming along. Whoever did the job went after it special; and he ain't going to part with his swag without his price. This must be a case of notice to the pawnbrokers. There's one good thing about it, anyhow, that the hue and cry needn't be given. We needn't tell Scotland Yard unless you like; we can work the thing privately. If you wish to keep the thing dark, as you told me at the first, that is our chance." Mr. Corbeck, after a pause, said quietly:

"I suppose you couldn't hazard a suggestion as to how the robbery was effected?" The Policeman smiled the smile of knowledge and experience.

"In a very simple way, I have no doubt, sir. That is how all these mysterious crimes turn out in the long-run. The criminal knows his work and all the tricks of it; and he is always on the watch for chances. Moreover, he knows by experience what these chances are likely to be, and how they usually come. The other person is only careful; he doesn't know all the tricks and pits that may be made for him, and by some little oversight or other he falls into the trap. When we know all about this case, you will wonder that you did not see the method of it all along!" This seemed to annoy Mr. Corbeck a little; there was decided heat in his manner as he answered:

"Look here, my good friend, there is not anything simple about this case – except that the things were taken. The window was closed; the fireplace was bricked up. There is only one door to the room, and that I locked and bolted. There is no transom; I have heard all about hotel robberies through the transom. I never left my room in the night. I looked at the things before going to bed; and I went to look at them again when I woke up. If you can rig up any kind of simple robbery out of these facts you are a clever man. That's all I say; clever enough to go right away and get my things back." Miss Trelawny laid her hand upon his arm in a soothing way, and said quietly:

"Do not distress yourself unnecessarily. I am sure they will turn up." Sergeant Daw turned to her so quickly that I could not help remembering vividly his suspicions of her, already formed, as he said:

"May I ask, miss, on what you base that opinion?"

I dreaded to hear her answer, given to ears already awake to suspicion; but it came to me as a new pain or shock all the same:

"I cannot tell you how I know. But I am sure of it!" The Detective looked at her for some seconds in silence, and then threw a quick glance at me.

Presently he had a little more conversation with Mr. Corbeck as to his own movements, the details of the hotel and the room, and the means of identifying the goods. Then he went away to commence his inquiries, Mr. Corbeck impressing on him the necessity for secrecy lest the thief should get wind of his danger and destroy the lamps. Mr. Corbeck promised, when going away to attend to various matters of his own business, to return early in the evening, and to stay in the house.

All that day Miss Trelawny was in better spirits and looked in better strength than she had yet been, despite the new shock and annoyance of the theft which must ultimately bring so much disappointment to her father.

We spent most of the day looking over the curio treasures of Mr. Trelawny. From what I had heard from Mr. Corbeck I began to have some idea of the vastness of his enterprise in the world of Egyptian research; and with this light everything around me began to have a new interest. As I went on, the interest grew; any lingering doubts which I might have had changed to wonder and admiration. The house seemed to be a veritable storehouse of marvels of antique art. In addition to the curios, big and little, in Mr. Trelawny's own room – from the great sarcophagi down to the scarabs of all kinds in the cabinets – the great hall, the staircase landings, the study, and even the boudoir were full of antique pieces which would have made a collector's mouth water.

Miss Trelawny from the first came with me, and looked with growing interest at everything. After having examined some cabinets of exquisite amulets she said to me in quite a naive way:

"You will hardly believe that I have of late seldom even looked at any of these things. It is only since Father has been ill that I seem to have even any curiosity about them. But now, they grow and grow on me to quite an absorbing degree. I wonder if it is that the collector's blood which I have in my veins is beginning to manifest itself. If so, the strange thing is that I have not felt the call of it before. Of course I know most of the big things, and have examined them more or less; but really, in a sort of way I have always taken them for granted, as though they had always been there. I have noticed the same thing now and again with family pictures, and the way they are taken for granted by the family. If you will let me examine them with you it will be delightful!"

It was a joy to me to hear her talk in such a way; and her last suggestion quite thrilled me. Together we went round the various rooms and passages, examining and admiring the magnificent curios. There was such a bewildering amount and variety of objects that we could only glance at most of them; but as we went along we arranged that we should take them seriatim, day by day, and examine them more closely. In the hall was a sort of big frame of floriated steel work which Margaret said her father used for lifting the heavy stone lids of the sarcophagi. It was not heavy and could be moved about easily enough. By aid of this we raised the covers in turn and looked at the endless series of hieroglyphic pictures cut in most of them. In spite of her profession of ignorance Margaret knew a good deal about them; her year of life with her father had had unconsciously its daily and hourly lesson. She was a remarkably clever and acute-minded girl, and with a prodigious memory; so that her store of knowledge, gathered unthinkingly bit by bit, had grown to proportions that many a scholar might have envied.

And yet it was all so naive and unconscious; so girlish and simple. She was so fresh in her views and ideas, and had so little thought of self, that in her companionship I forgot for the time all the troubles and mysteries which enmeshed the house; and I felt like a boy again....

The most interesting of the sarcophagi were undoubtedly the three in Mr. Trelawny's room. Of these, two were of dark stone, one of porphyry and the other of a sort of ironstone. These were wrought with some hieroglyphs. But the third was strikingly different. It was of some yellow-brown substance of the dominating colour effect of Mexican onyx, which it resembled in many ways, excepting that the natural pattern of its convolutions was less marked. Here and there were patches almost transparent – certainly translucent. The whole chest, cover and all, was wrought with hundreds, perhaps thousands, of minute hieroglyphics, seemingly in an endless series. Back, front, sides, edges, bottom, all had their quota of the dainty pictures, the deep blue of their colouring showing up fresh and sharply edge in the yellow stone. It was very long, nearly nine feet; and perhaps a yard wide. The sides undulated, so that there was no hard line. Even the corners took such excellent curves that they pleased the eye. "Truly," I said, "this must have been made for a giant!"

"Or for a giantess!" said Margaret.

This sarcophagus stood near to one of the windows. It was in one respect different from all the other sarcophagi in the place. All the others in the house, of whatever material – granite, porphyry, ironstone, basalt, slate, or wood – were quite simple in form within. Some of them were plain of interior surface; others were engraved, in whole or part, with hieroglyphics. But each and all of them had no protuberances or uneven surface anywhere. They might have been used for baths; indeed, they resembled in many ways Roman baths of stone or marble which I had seen. Inside this, however, was a raised space, outlined like a human figure. I asked Margaret if she could explain it in any way. For answer she said:

"Father never wished to speak about this. It attracted my attention from the first; but when I asked him about it he said: 'I shall tell you all about it some day, little girl – if I live! But not yet! The story is not yet told, as I hope to tell it to you! Some day perhaps soon, I shall know all; and then we shall go over it together. And a mighty interesting story you will find it – from first to last!' Once afterward I said, rather lightly I am afraid: 'Is that story of the sarcophagus told yet, Father?' He shook his head, and looked at me gravely as he said: 'Not yet, little girl; but it will be – if I live – if I live!' His repeating that phrase about his living rather frightened me; I never ventured to ask him again."

Somehow this thrilled me. I could not exactly say how or why; but it seemed like a gleam of light at last. There are, I think, moments when the mind accepts something as true; though it can account for neither the course of the thought, nor, if there be more than one thought, the connection between them. Hitherto we had been in such outer darkness regarding Mr. Trelawny, and the strange visitation which had fallen on him, that anything which afforded a clue, even of the faintest and most shadowy kind, had at the outset the enlightening satisfaction of a certainty. Here were two lights of our puzzle. The first that Mr. Trelawny associated with this particular curio a doubt of his own living. The second that he had some purpose or expectation with regard to it, which he would not disclose, even to his daughter, till complete. Again it was to be borne in mind that this sarcophagus differed internally from all the others. What meant that odd raised place? I said nothing to Miss Trelawny, for I feared lest I should either frighten her or buoy her up with future hopes; but I made up my mind that I would take an early opportunity for further investigation.

Close beside the sarcophagus was a low table of green stone with red veins in it, like bloodstone. The feet were fashioned like the paws of a jackal, and round each leg was twined a full-throated snake wrought exquisitely in pure gold. On it rested a strange and very beautiful coffer or casket of stone of a peculiar shape. It was something like a small coffin, except that the longer sides, instead of being cut off square like the upper or level part were continued to a point. Thus it was an irregular septahedron, there being two planes on each of the two sides, one end and a top and bottom. The stone, of one piece of which it was wrought, was such as I had never seen before. At the base it was of a full green, the colour of emerald without, of course, its gleam. It was not by any means dull, however, either in colour or substance, and was of infinite hardness and fineness of texture. The surface was almost that of a jewel. The colour grew lighter as it rose, with gradation so fine as to be imperceptible, changing to a fine yellow almost of the colour of "mandarin" china. It was quite unlike anything I had ever seen, and did not resemble any stone or gem that I knew. I took t to be some unique mother-stone, or matrix of some gem. It was wrought all over, except in a few spots, with fine hieroglyphics, exquisitely done and coloured with the same blue-green cement or pigment that appeared on the sarcophagus. In length it was about two feet and a half; in breadth about half this, and was nearly a foot high. The vacant spaces were irregularly distributed about the top running to the pointed end. These places seemed less opaque than the rest of the stone. I tried to lift up the lid so that I might see if they were translucent; but it was securely fixed. It fitted so exactly that the whole coffer seemed like a single piece of stone mysteriously hollowed from within. On the sides and edges were some odd-looking protuberances wrought just as finely as any other portion of the coffer which had been sculptured by manifest design in the cutting of the stone. They had queer-shaped holes or hollows, different in each; and, like the rest, were covered with the hieroglyphic figures, cut finely and filled in with the same blue-green cement.

On the other side of the great sarcophagus stood another small table of alabaster, exquisitely chased with symbolic figures of gods and the signs of the zodiac. On this table stood a case of about a foot square composed of slabs of rock crystal set in a skeleton of bands of red gold, beautifully engraved with hieroglyphics, and coloured with a blue green, very much the tint of the figures on the sarcophagus and the coffer. The whole work was quite modern.

But if the case was modern what it held was not. Within, on a cushion of cloth of gold as fine as silk, and with the peculiar softness of old gold, rested a mummy hand, so perfect that it startled one to see it. A woman's hand, fine and long, with slim tapering fingers and nearly as perfect as when it was given to the embalmer thousands of years before. In the embalming it had lost nothing of its beautiful shape; even the wrist seemed to maintain its pliability as the gentle curve lay on the cushion. The skin was of a rich creamy or old ivory colour; a dusky fair skin which suggested heat, but heat in shadow. The great peculiarity of it, as a hand, was that it had in all seven fingers, there being two middle and two index fingers. The upper end of the wrist was jagged, as though it had been broken off, and was stained with a red-brown stain. On the cushion near the hand was a small scarab, exquisitely wrought of emerald.

"That is another of Father's mysteries. When I asked him about it he said that it was perhaps the most valuable thing he had, except one. When I asked him what that one was, he refused to tell me, and forbade me to ask him anything concerning it. 'I will tell you,' he said, 'all about it, too, in good time – if I live!'"

"If I live!" the phrase again. These three things grouped together, the Sarcophagus, the Coffer, and the Hand, seemed to make a trilogy of mystery indeed!

At this time Miss Trelawny was sent for on some domestic matter. I looked at the other curios in the room; but they did not seem to have anything like the same charm for me, now that she was away. Later on in the day I was sent for to the boudoir where she was consulting with Mrs. Grant as to the lodgment of Mr. Corbeck. They were in doubt as to whether he should have a room close to Mr. Trelawny's or quite away from it, and had thought it well to ask my advice on the subject. I came to the conclusion that he had better not be too near; for the first at all events, he could easily be moved closer if necessary. When Mrs. Grant had gone, I asked Miss Trelawny how it came that the furniture of this room, the boudoir in which we were, was so different from the other rooms of the house.

"Father's forethought!" she answered. "When I first came, he thought, and rightly enough, that I might get frightened with so many records of death and the tomb everywhere. So he had this room and the little suite off it – that door opens into the sitting-room – where I slept last night, furnished with pretty things. You see, they are all beautiful. That cabinet belonged to the great Napoleon."

"There is nothing Egyptian in these rooms at all then?" I asked, rather to show interest in what she had said than anything else, for the furnishing of the room was apparent. "What a lovely cabinet! May I look at it?"

"Of course! with the greatest pleasure!" she answered, with a smile. "Its finishing, within and without, Father says, is absolutely complete." I stepped over and looked at it closely. It was made of tulip wood, inlaid in patterns; and was mounted in ormolu. I pulled open one of the drawers, a deep one where I could see the work to great advantage. As I pulled it, something rattled inside as though rolling; there was a tinkle as of metal on metal.

"Hullo!" I said. "There is something in here. Perhaps I had better not open it."

"There is nothing that I know of," she answered. "Some of the housemaids may have used it to put something by for the time and forgotten it. Open it by all means!"

I pulled open the drawer; as I did so, both Miss Trelawny and I started back in amazement.

There before our eyes lay a number of ancient Egyptian lamps, of various sizes and of strangely varied shapes.

We leaned over them and looked closely. My own heart was beating like a trip-hammer; and I could see by the heaving of Margaret's bosom that she was strangely excited.

Whilst we looked, afraid to touch and almost afraid to think, there was a ring at the front door; immediately afterwards Mr. Corbeck, followed by Sergeant Daw, came into the hall. The door of the boudoir was open, and when they saw us Mr. Corbeck came running in, followed more slowly by the Detective. There was a sort of chastened joy in his face and manner as he said impulsively:

"Rejoice with me, my dear Miss Trelawny, my luggage has come and all my things are intact!" Then his face fell as he added, "Except the lamps. The lamps that were worth all the rest a thousand times...." He stopped, struck by the strange pallor of her face. Then his eyes, following her look and mine, lit on the cluster of lamps in the drawer. He gave a sort of cry of surprise and joy as he bent over and touched them:

"My lamps! My lamps! Then they are safe – safe – safe!... But how, in the name of God – of all the Gods – did they come here?"

We all stood silent. The Detective made a deep sound of in-taking breath. I looked at him, and as he caught my glance he turned his eyes on Miss Trelawny whose back was toward him.

There was in them the same look of suspicion which had been there when he had spoken to me of her being the first to find her father on the occasions of the attacks.

Chapter IX
The Need of Knowledge

MR. CORBECK seemed to go almost off his head at the recovery of the lamps. He took them up one by one and looked them all over tenderly, as though they were things that he loved. In his delight and excitement he breathed so hard that it seemed almost like a cat purring. Sergeant Daw said quietly, his voice breaking the silence like a discord in a melody:

"Are you quite sure those lamps are the ones you had, and that were stolen?"

His answer was in an indignant tone: "Sure! Of course I'm sure. There isn't another set of lamps like these in the world!"

"So far as you know!" The Detective's words were smooth enough, but his manner was so exasperating that I was sure he had some motive in it; so I waited in silence. He went on:

"Of course there may be some in the British Museum; or Mr. Trelawny may have had these already. There's nothing new under the sun, you know, Mr. Corbeck; not even in Egypt. These may be the originals, and yours may have been the copies. Are there any points by which you can identify these as yours?"

Mr. Corbeck was really angry by this time. He forgot his reserve; and in his indignation poured forth a torrent of almost incoherent, but enlightening, broken sentences:

"Identify! Copies of them! British Museum! Rot! Perhaps they keep a set in Scotland Yard for teaching idiot policemen Egyptology! Do I know them? When I have carried them about my body, in the desert, for three months; and lay awake night after night to watch them! When I have looked them over with a magnifying-glass, hour after hour, till my eyes ached; till every tiny blotch, and chip, and dinge became as familiar to me as his chart to a captain; as familiar as they doubtless have been all the time to every thick-headed area-prowler within the bounds of mortality. See here, young man, look at these!" He ranged the lamps in a row on the top of the cabinet. "Did you ever see a set of lamps of these shapes – of any one of these shapes? Look at these dominant figures on them! Did you ever see so complete a set – even in Scotland Yard; even in Bow Street? Look! one on each, the seven forms of Hathor. Look at that figure of the Ka of a Princess of the Two Egypts, standing between Ra and Osiris in the Boat of the Dead, with the Eye of Sleep, supported on legs, bending before her; and Harmochis rising in the north. Will you find that in the British Museum – or Bow Street? Or perhaps your studies in the Gizeh Museum, or the Fitzwilliam, or Paris, or Leyden, or Berlin, have shown you that the episode is common in hieroglyphics; and that this is only a copy. Perhaps you can tell me what that figure of Ptah-Seker-Ausar holding the Tet wrapped in the Sceptre of Papyrus means? Did you ever see it before; even in the British Museum, or Gizeh, or Scotland Yard?"

He broke off suddenly; and then went on in quite a different way:

"Look here! It seems to me that the thick-headed idiot is myself! I beg your pardon, old fellow, for my rudeness. I quite lost my temper at the suggestion that I do not know these lamps. You don't mind, do you?" The Detective answered heartily:

"Lord, sir, not I. I like to see folks angry when I am dealing with them, whether they are on my side or the other. It is when people are angry that you learn the truth from them. I keep cool; that is my trade! Do you know, you have told me more about those lamps in the past two minutes than when you filled me up with details of how to identify them."

Mr. Corbeck grunted; he was not pleased at having given himself away. All at once he turned to me and said in his natural way:

"Now tell me how you got them back?" I was so surprised that I said without thinking: "We didn't get them back!" The traveller laughed openly.

"What on earth do you mean?" he asked. "You didn't get them back! Why, there they are before your eyes! We found you looking at them when we came in." By this time I had recovered my surprise and had my wits about me.

"Why, that's just it," I said. "We had only come across them, by accident, that very moment!"

Mr. Corbeck drew back and looked hard at Miss Trelawny and myself; turning his eyes from one to the other as he asked:

"Do you mean to tell me that no one brought them here; that you found them in that drawer? That, so to speak, no one at all brought them back?"

"I suppose someone must have brought them here; they couldn't have come of their own accord. But who it was, or when, or how, neither of us knows. We shall have to make inquiry, and see if any of the servants know anything of it."

We all stood silent for several seconds. It seemed a long time. The first to speak was the Detective, who said in an unconscious way:

"Well, I'm damned! I beg your pardon, miss!" Then his mouth shut like a steel trap.

We called up the servants, one by one, and asked them if they knew anything of some articles placed in a drawer in the boudoir; but none of them could throw any light on the circumstance. We did not tell them what the articles were; or let them see them.

Mr. Corbeck packed the lamps in cotton wool, and placed them in a tin box. This, I may mention incidentally, was then brought up to the detectives' room, where one of the men stood guard over them with a revolver the whole night. Next day we got a small safe into the house, and placed them in it. There were two different keys. One of them I kept myself; the other I placed in my drawer in the Safe Deposit vault. We were all determined that the lamps should not be lost again.

About an hour after we had found the lamps, Doctor Winchester arrived. He had a large parcel with him, which, when unwrapped, proved to be the mummy of a cat. With Miss Trelawny's permission he placed this in the boudoir; and Silvio was brought close to it. To the surprise of us all, however, except perhaps Doctor Winchester, he did not manifest the least annoyance; he took no notice of it whatever. He stood on the table close beside it, purring loudly. Then, following out his plan, the Doctor brought him into Mr. Trelawny's room, we all following. Doctor Winchester was excited; Miss Trelawny anxious. I was more than interested myself, for I began to have a glimmering of the Doctor's idea. The Detective was calmly and coldly superior; but Mr. Corbeck, who was an enthusiast, was full of eager curiosity.

The moment Doctor Winchester got into the room, Silvio began to mew and wriggle; and jumping out of his arms, ran over to the cat mummy and began to scratch angrily at it. Miss Trelawny had some difficulty in taking him away; but so soon as he was out of the room he became quiet. When she came back there was a clamour of comments:

"I thought so!" from the Doctor.

"What can it mean?" from Miss Trelawny.

"That's a very strange thing!" from Mr. Corbeck.

"Odd! But it doesn't prove anything!" from the Detective.

"I suspend my judgment!" from myself, thinking it advisable to say something.

Then by common consent we dropped the theme – for the present.

In my room that evening I was making some notes of what had happened, when there came a low tap on the door. In obedience to my summons Sergeant Daw came n, carefully closing the door behind him.

"Well, Sergeant," said I, "sit down. What is it?"

"I wanted to speak to you, sir, about those lamps." I nodded and waited: he went on: "You know that that room where they were found opens directly into the room where Miss Trelawny slept last night?"

"Yes."

"During the night a window somewhere in that part of the house was opened, and shut again. I heard it, and took a look round; but I could see no sign of anything."

"Yes, I know that!" I said; "I heard a window moved myself."

"Does nothing strike you as strange about it, sir?"

"Strange!" I said; "Strange! Why it's all the most bewildering, maddening thing I have ever encountered. It is all so strange that one seems to wonder, and simply waits for what will happen next. But what do you mean by strange?"

The Detective paused, as if choosing his words to begin; and then said deliberately:

"You see, I am not one who believes in magic and such things. I am for facts all the time; and I always find in the long-run that there is a reason and a cause for everything. This new gentleman says these things were stolen out of his room in the hotel. The lamps, I take it from some things he has said, really belong to Mr. Trelawny. His daughter, the lady of the house, having left the room she usually occupies, sleeps that night on the ground floor. A window is heard to open and shut during the night. When we, who have been during the day trying to find a clue to the robbery, come to the house, we find the stolen goods in a room close to where she slept, and opening out of it!"

He stopped. I felt that same sense of pain and apprehension, which I had experienced when he had spoken to me before, creeping, or rather rushing, over me again. I had to face the matter out, however. My relations with her, and the feeling toward her which I now knew full well meant a very deep love and devotion, demanded so much. I said as calmly as I could, for I knew the keen eyes of the skilful investigator were on me:

"And the inference?"

He answered with the cool audacity of conviction:

"The inference to me is that there was no robbery at all. The goods were taken by someone to this house, where they were received through a window on the ground floor. They were placed in the cabinet, ready to be discovered when the proper time should come!"

Somehow I felt relieved; the assumption was too monstrous. I did not want, however, my relief to be apparent, so I answered as gravely as I could:

"And who do you suppose brought them to the house?"

"I keep my mind open as to that. Possibly Mr. Corbeck himself; the matter might be too risky to trust to a third party."

"Then the natural extension of your inference is that Mr. Corbeck is a liar and a fraud; and that he is in conspiracy with Miss Trelawny to deceive someone or other about those lamps."

"Those are harsh words, Mr. Ross. They're so plain-spoken that they bring a man up standing, and make new doubts for him. But I have to go where my reason points.

It may be that there is another party than Miss Trelawny in it. Indeed, if it hadn't been for the other matter that set me thinking and bred doubts of its own about her, I wouldn't dream of mixing her up in this. But I'm safe on Corbeck. Whoever else is in it, he is! The things couldn't have been taken without his connivance – if what he says is true. If it isn't – well! he is a liar anyhow. I would think it a bad job to have him stay in the house with so many valuables, only that it will give me and my mate a chance of watching him. We'll keep a pretty good look-out, too, I tell you. He's up in my room now, guarding those lamps; but Johnny Wright is there too. I go on before he comes off; so there won't be much chance of another house-breaking. Of course, Mr. Ross, all this, too, is between you and me."

"Quite so! You may depend on my silence!" I said; and he went away to keep a close eye on the Egyptologist.

It seemed as though all my painful experiences were to go in pairs, and that the sequence of the previous day was to be repeated; for before long I had another private visit from Doctor Winchester who had now paid his nightly visit to his patient and was on his way home. He took the seat which I proffered and began at once:

"This is a strange affair altogether. Miss Trelawny has just been telling me about the stolen lamps, and of the finding of them in the Napoleon cabinet. It would seem to be another complication of the mystery; and yet, do you know, it is a relief to me. I have exhausted all human and natural possibilities of the case, and am beginning to fall back on superhuman and supernatural possibilities. Here are such strange things that, if I am not going mad, I think we must have a solution before long. I wonder if I might ask some questions and some help from Mr. Corbeck, without making further complications and embarrassing us. He seems to know an amazing amount regarding Egypt and all relating to it. Perhaps he wouldn't mind translating a little bit of hieroglyphic. It is child's play to him. What do you think?"

When I had thought the matter over a few seconds I spoke. We wanted all the help we could get. For myself, I had perfect confidence in both men; and any comparing notes, or mutual assistance, might bring good results. Such could hardly bring evil.

"By all means I should ask him. He seems an extraordinarily learned man in Egyptology; and he seems to me a good fellow as well as an enthusiast. By the way, it will be necessary to be a little guarded as to whom you speak regarding any information which he may give you."

"Of course!" he answered. "Indeed I should not dream of saying anything to anybody, excepting yourself. We have to remember that when Mr. Trelawny recovers he may not like to think that we have been chattering unduly over his affairs."

"Look here!" I said, "Why not stay for a while: and I shall ask him to come and have a pipe with us. We can then talk over things."

He acquiesced: so I went to the room where Mr. Corbeck was, and brought him back with me. I thought the detectives were pleased at his going. On the way to my room he said:

"I don't half like leaving those things there, with only those men to guard them. They're a deal sight too precious to be left to the police!"

From which it would appear that suspicion was not confined to Sergeant Daw.

Mr. Corbeck and Doctor Winchester, after a quick glance at each other, became at once on most friendly terms. The traveller professed his willingness to be of any assistance which he could, provided, he added, that it was anything about which he was free to speak. This was not very promising; but Doctor Winchester began at once:

"I want you, if you will, to translate some hieroglyphic for me."

"Certainly, with the greatest pleasure, so far as I can. For I may tell you that hieroglyphic writing is not quite mastered yet; though we are getting at it! We are getting at it! What is the inscription?"

"There are two," he answered. "One of them I shall bring here."

He went out, and returned in a minute with the mummy cat which he had that evening introduced to Silvio. The scholar took it; and, after a short examination, said:

"There is nothing especial in this. It is an appeal to Bast, the Lady of Bubastis, to give her good bread and milk in the Elysian Fields. There may be more inside; and if you will care to unroll it, I will do my best. I do not think, however, that there is anything special. From the method of wrapping I should say it is from the Delta; and of a late period, when such mummy work was common and cheap. What is the other inscription you wish me to see?"

"The inscription on the mummy cat in Mr. Trelawny's room."

Mr. Corbeck's face fell. "No!" he said, "I cannot do that! I am, for the present at all events, practically bound to secrecy regarding any of the things in Mr. Trelawny's room."

Doctor Winchester's comment and my own were made at the same moment. I said only the one word "Checkmate!" from which I think he may have gathered that I guessed more of his idea and purpose than perhaps I had intentionally conveyed to him. He murmured:

"Practically bound to secrecy?"

Mr. Corbeck at once took up the challenge conveyed:

"Do not misunderstand me! I am not bound by any definite pledge of secrecy; but I am bound in honour to respect Mr. Trelawny's confidence, given to me, I may tell you, in a very large measure. Regarding many of the objects in his room he has a definite purpose in view; and it would not be either right or becoming for me, his trusted friend and confidant, to forestall that purpose. Mr. Trelawny, you may know – or rather you do not know or you would not have so construed my remark – is a scholar, a very great scholar. He has worked for years toward a certain end. For this he has spared no labour, no expense, no personal danger or self-denial. He is on the line of a result which will place him amongst the foremost discoverers or investigators of his age. And now, just at the time when any hour might bring him success, he is stricken down!"

He stopped, seemingly overcome with emotion. After a time he recovered himself and went on:

"Again, do not misunderstand me as to another point. I have said that Mr. Trelawny has made much confidence with me; but I do not mean to lead you to believe that I know all his plans, or his aims or objects. I know the period which he has been studying; and the definite historical individual whose life he has been investigating, and whose records he has been following up one by one with infinite patience. But beyond this I know nothing. That he has some aim or object in the completion of this knowledge I am convinced. What it is I may guess; but I must say nothing. Please to remember, gentlemen, that I have voluntarily accepted the position of recipient of a partial confidence. I have respected that; and I must ask any of my friends to do the same."

He spoke with great dignity; and he grew, moment by moment, in the respect and esteem of both Doctor Winchester and myself. We understood that he had not done speaking; so we waited in silence till he continued:

"I have spoken this much, although I know well that even such a hint as either of you might gather from my words might jeopardise the success of his work. But I am convinced that you both wish to help him – and his daughter," he said this looking me fairly between the eyes, "to the best of your power, honestly and unselfishly. He is so stricken down, and the manner of it is so mysterious that I cannot but think that it is in some way a result of his own work. That he calculated on some set-back is manifest to us all. God knows! I am willing to do what I can, and to use any knowledge I have in his behalf. I arrived in England full of exultation at the thought that I had fulfilled the mission with which he had trusted me. I had got what he said were the last objects of his search; and I felt assured that he would now be able to begin the experiment of which he had often hinted to me. It is too dreadful that at just such a time such a calamity should have fallen on him. Doctor Winchester, you are a physician; and, if your face does not belie you, you are a clever and a bold one. Is there no way which you can devise to wake this man from his unnatural stupor?"

There was a pause; then the answer came slowly and deliberately:

"There is no ordinary remedy that I know of. There might possibly be some extraordinary one. But there would be no use in trying to find it, except on one condition."

"And that?"

"Knowledge! I am completely ignorant of Egyptian matters, language, writing, history, secrets, medicines, poisons, occult powers – all that go to make up the mystery of that mysterious land. This disease, or condition, or whatever it may be called, from which Mr. Trelawny is suffering, is in some way connected with Egypt. I have had a suspicion of this from the first; and later it grew into a certainty, though without proof. What you have said tonight confirms my conjecture, and makes me believe that a proof is to be had. I do not think that you quite know all that has gone on in this house since the night of the attack – of the finding of Mr. Trelawny's body. Now I propose that we confide in you. If Mr. Ross agrees, I shall ask him to tell you. He is more skilled than I am in putting facts before other people. He can speak by his brief; and in this case he has the best of all briefs, the experience of his own eyes and ears, and the evidence that he has himself taken on the spot from participators in, or spectators of, what has happened. When you know all, you will, I hope, be in a position to judge as to whether you can best help Mr. Trelawny, and further his secret wishes, by your silence or your speech."

I nodded approval. Mr. Corbeck jumped up, and in his impulsive way held out a hand to each.

"Done!" he said. "I acknowledge the honour of your confidence; and on my part I pledge myself that if I find my duty to Mr. Trelawny's wishes will, in his own interest, allow my lips to open on his affairs, I shall speak so freely as I may."

Accordingly I began, and told him, as exactly as I could, everything that had happened from the moment of my waking at the knocking on the door in Jermyn Street. The only reservations I made were as to my own feeling toward Miss Trelawny and the matters of small import to the main subject which followed it; and my conversations with Sergeant Daw, which were in themselves private, and which would have demanded discretionary silence in any case. As I spoke, Mr. Corbeck followed with breathless interest. Sometimes he would stand up and pace about the room in uncontrollable excitement; and then recover himself suddenly, and sit down again. Sometimes he would be about to speak, but would, with an effort, restrain himself. I think the narration helped me to make up my own mind; for even as I talked, things seemed to appear in a clearer light. Things big and little, in relation of their importance to the case, fell into proper perspective. The story up to date became coherent, except as to its cause, which seemed a greater mystery than ever. This is the merit of entire, or collected, narrative. Isolated facts, doubts, suspicions, conjectures, give way to a homogeneity which is convincing.

That Mr. Corbeck was convinced was evident. He did not go through any process of explanation or limitation, but spoke right out at once to the point, and fearlessly like a man:

"That settles me! There is in activity some Force that needs special care. If we all go on working in the dark we shall get in one another's way, and by hampering each other, undo the good that any or each of us, working in different directions, might do. It seems to me that the first thing we have to accomplish is to get Mr. Trelawny waked out of that unnatural sleep. That he can be waked is apparent from the way the Nurse has recovered; though what additional harm may have been done to him in the time he has been lying in that room I suppose no one can tell. We must chance that, however. He has lain there, and whatever the effect might be, it is there now; and we have, and shall have, to deal with it as a fact. A day more or less won't hurt in the long-run. It is late now; and we shall probably have tomorrow a task before us that will require our energies afresh. You, Doctor, will want to get to your sleep; for I suppose you have other work as well as this to do tomorrow. As for you, Mr. Ross, I understand that you are to have a spell of watching in the sick-room tonight. I shall get you a book which will help to pass the time for you. I shall go and look for it in the library. I know where it was when I was here last; and I don't suppose Mr. Trelawny has used it since. He knew long ago all that was in it which was or might be of interest to him. But it will be necessary, or at least helpful, to understand other things which I shall tell you later. You will be able to tell Doctor Winchester all that would aid him. For I take it that our work will branch out pretty soon. We shall each have our own end to hold up; and it will take each of us all our time and understanding to get through his own tasks. It will not be necessary for you to read the whole book. All that will interest you – with regard to our matter I mean of course, for the whole book is interesting as a record of travel in a country then quite unknown – is the preface, and two or three chapters which I shall mark for you."

He shook hands warmly with Doctor Winchester who had stood up to go.

Whilst he was away I sat lonely, thinking. As I thought, the world around me seemed to be illimitably great. The only little spot in which I was interested seemed like a tiny speck in the midst of a wilderness. Without and around it were darkness and unknown danger, pressing in from every side. And the central figure in our little oasis was one of sweetness and beauty. A figure one could love; could work for; could die for...!

Mr. Corbeck came back in a very short time with the book; he had found it at once in the spot where he had seen it three years before. Having placed in it several slips of paper, marking the places where I was to read, he put it into my hands, saying:

"That is what started Mr. Trelawny; what started me when I read it; and which will, I have no doubt, be to you an interesting beginning to a special study – whatever the end may be. If, indeed, any of us here may ever see the end."

At the door he paused and said:

"I want to take back one thing. That Detective is a good fellow. What you have told me of him puts him in a new light. The best proof of it is that I can go quietly to sleep tonight, and leave the lamps in his care!"

When he had gone I took the book with me, put on my respirator, and went to my spell of duty in the sick-room!

Chapter X
The Valley of the Sorcerer

I PLACED THE BOOK on the little table on which the shaded lamp rested and moved the screen to one side. Thus I could have the light on my book; and by looking up, see the bed, and the Nurse, and the door. I cannot say that the conditions were enjoyable, or calculated to allow of that absorption in the subject which is advisable for effective study. However, I composed myself to the work as well as I could. The book was one which, on the very face of it, required special attention. It was a folio in Dutch, printed in Amsterdam in 1650. Some one had made a literal translation, writing generally the English word under the Dutch, so that the grammatical differences between the two tongues made even the reading of the translation a difficult matter. One had to dodge backward and forward among the words. This was in addition to the difficulty of deciphering a strange handwriting of two hundred years ago. I found, however, that after a short time I got into the habit of following in conventional English the Dutch construction; and, as I became more familiar with the writing, my task became easier.

At first the circumstances of the room, and the fear lest Miss Trelawny should return unexpectedly and find me reading the book, disturbed me somewhat. For we had arranged amongst us, before Doctor Winchester had gone home, that she was not to be brought into the range of the coming investigation. We considered that there might be some shock to a woman's mind in matters of apparent mystery; and further, that she, being Mr. Trelawny's daughter, might be placed in a difficult position with him afterward if she took part in, or even had a personal knowledge of, the disregarding of his expressed wishes. But when I remembered that she did not come on nursing duty till two o'clock, the fear of interruption passed away. I had still nearly three house before me. Nurse Kennedy sat in her chair by the bedside, patient and alert. A clock ticked on the landing; other clocks in the house ticked; the life of the city without manifested itself in the distant hum, now and again swelling into a roar as a breeze floating westward took the concourse of sounds with it. But still the dominant idea was of silence. The light on my book, and the soothing fringe of green silk round the shade intensified, whenever I looked up, the gloom of the sick-room. With every line I read, this seemed to grow deeper and deeper; so that when my eyes came back to the page the light seemed to dazzle me.

I stuck to my work, however, and presently began to get sufficiently into the subject to become interested in it.

The book was by one Nicholas van Huyn of Hoorn. In the preface he told how, attracted by the work of John Greaves of Merton College, Pyramidographia, he himself visited Egypt, where he became so interested in its wonders that he devoted some years of his life to visiting strange places, and exploring the ruins of many temples and tombs. He had come across many variants of the story of the building of the Pyramids as told by the Arabian historian, Ibn Abd Alhokin, some of which he set down. These I did not stop to read, but went on to the marked pages.

As soon as I began to read these, however, there grew on me some sense of a disturbing influence. Once or twice I looked to see if the Nurse had moved, for there was a feeling as though some one were near me. Nurse Kennedy sat in her place, as steady and alert as ever; and I came back to my book again.

The narrative went on to tell how, after passing for several days through the mountains to the east of Aswan, the explorer came to a certain place. Here I give his own words, simply putting the translation into modern English:

"Toward evening we came to the entrance of a narrow, deep valley, running east and west. I wished to proceed through this; for the sun, now nearly down on the horizon, showed a wide opening beyond the narrowing of the cliffs. But the fellaheen absolutely refused to enter the valley at such a time, alleging that they might be caught by the night before they could emerge from the other end. At first they would give no reason for their fear. They had hitherto gone anywhere I wished, and at any time, without demur. On being pressed, however, they said that the place was the Valley of the Sorcerer, where none might come in the night. On being asked to tell of the Sorcerer, they refused, saying that there was no name, and that they knew nothing. On the next morning, however, when the sun was up and shining down the valley, their fears had somewhat passed away. Then they told me that a great Sorcerer in ancient days – 'millions of millions of years' was the term they used – a King or a Queen, they could not say which, was buried there. They could not give the name, persisting to the last that there was no name; and that anyone who should name it would waste away in life so that at death nothing of him would remain to be raised again in the Other World. In passing through the valley they kept together in a cluster, hurrying on in front of me. None dared to remain behind. They gave, as their reason for so proceeding, that the arms of the Sorcerer were long, and that it was dangerous to be the last. The which was of little comfort to me who of this necessity took that honourable post. In the narrowest part of the valley, on the south side, was a great cliff of rock, rising sheer, of smooth and even surface. Hereon were graven certain cabalistic signs, and many figures of men and animals, fishes, reptiles and birds; suns and stars; and many quaint symbols. Some of these latter were disjointed limbs and features, such as arms and legs, fingers, eyes, noses, ears, and lips. Mysterious symbols which will puzzle the Recording Angel to interpret at the Judgment Day. The cliff faced exactly north. There was something about it so strange, and so different from the other carved rocks which I had visited, that I called a halt and spent the day in examining the rock front as well as I could with my telescope. The Egyptians of my company were terribly afraid, and used every kind of persuasion to induce me to pass on. I stayed till late in the afternoon, by which time I had failed to make out aright the entry of any tomb, for

I suspected that such was the purpose of the sculpture of the rock. By this time the men were rebellious; and I had to leave the valley if I did not wish my whole retinue to desert. But I secretly made up my mind to discover the tomb, and explore it. To this end I went further into the mountains, where I met with an Arab Sheik who was willing to take service with me. The Arabs were not bound by the same superstitious fears as the Egyptians; Sheik Abu Some and his following were willing to take a part in the explorations.

"When I returned to the valley with these Bedouins, I made effort to climb the face of the rock, but failed, it being of one impenetrable smoothness. The stone, generally flat and smooth by nature, had been chiselled to completeness. That there had been projecting steps was manifest, for there remained, untouched by the wondrous climate of that strange land, the marks of saw and chisel and mallet where the steps had been cut or broken away.

"Being thus baffled of winning the tomb from below, and being unprovided with ladders to scale, I found a way by much circuitous journeying to the top of the cliff. Thence I caused myself to be lowered by ropes, till I had investigated that portion of the rock face wherein I expected to find the opening. I found that there was an entrance, closed however by a great stone slab. This was cut in the rock more than a hundred feet up, being two-thirds the height of the cliff. The hieroglyphic and cabalistic symbols cut in the rock were so managed as to disguise it. The cutting was deep, and was continued through the rock and the portals of the doorway, and through the great slab which formed the door itself. This was fixed in place with such incredible exactness that no stone chisel or cutting implement which I had with me could find a lodgment in the interstices. I used much force, however; and by many heavy strokes won a way into the tomb, for such I found it to be. The stone door having fallen into the entrance I passed over it into the tomb, noting as I went a long iron chain which hung coiled on a bracket close to the doorway.

"The tomb I found to be complete, after the manner of the finest Egyptian tombs, with chamber and shaft leading down to the corridor, ending in the Mummy Pit. It had the table of pictures, which seems some kind of record – whose meaning is now for ever lost – graven in a wondrous colour on a wondrous stone.

"All the walls of the chamber and the passage were carved with strange writings in the uncanny form mentioned. The huge stone coffin or sarcophagus in the deep pit was marvellously graven throughout with signs. The Arab chief and two others who ventured into the tomb with me, and who were evidently used to such grim explorations, managed to take the cover from the sarcophagus without breaking it. At which they wondered; for such good fortune, they said, did not usually attend such efforts. Indeed they seemed not over careful; and did handle the various furniture of the tomb with such little concern that, only for its great strength and thickness, even the coffin itself might have been injured. Which gave me much concern, for it was very beautifully wrought of rare stone, such as I had no knowledge of. Much I grieved that it were not possible to carry it away. But time and desert journeyings forbade such; I could only take with me such small matters as could be carried on the person.

"Within the sarcophagus was a body, manifestly of a woman, swathed with many wrappings of linen, as is usual with all mummies. From certain embroiderings thereon, I gathered that she was of high rank. Across the breast was one hand, unwrapped. In the mummies which I had seen, the arms and hands are within the wrappings, and certain adornments of wood, shaped and painted to resemble arms and hands, lie outside the enwrapped body.

"But this hand was strange to see, for it was the real hand of her who lay enwrapped there; the arm projecting from the cerements being of flesh, seemingly made as like marble in the process of embalming. Arm and hand were of dusky white, being of the hue of ivory that hath lain long in air. The skin and the nails were complete and whole, as though the body had been placed for burial over night. I touched the hand and moved it, the arm being something flexible as a live arm; though stiff with long disuse, as are the arms of those faqueers which I have seen in the Indees. There was, too, an added wonder that on this ancient hand were no less than seven fingers, the same all being fine and long, and of great beauty. Sooth to say, it made me shudder and my flesh creep to touch that hand that had lain there undisturbed for so many thousands of years, and yet was like unto living flesh. Underneath the hand, as though guarded by it, lay a huge jewel of ruby; a great stone of wondrous bigness, for the ruby is in the main a small jewel. This one was of wondrous colour, being as of fine blood whereon the light shineth. But its wonder lay not in its size or colour, though these were, as I have said, of priceless rarity; but in that the light of it shone from seven stars, each of seven points, as clearly as though the stars were in reality there imprisoned. When that the hand was lifted, the sight of that wondrous stone lying there struck me with a shock almost to momentary paralysis. I stood gazing on it, as did those with me, as though it were that faded head of the Gorgon Medusa with the snakes in her hair, whose sight struck into stone those who beheld. So strong was the feeling that I wanted to hurry away from the place. So, too, those with me; therefore, taking this rare jewel, together with certain amulets of strangeness and richness being wrought of jewel-stones, I made haste to depart. I would have remained longer, and made further research in the wrappings of the mummy, but that I feared so to do. For it came to me all at once that I was in a desert place, with strange men who were with me because they were not over-scrupulous. That we were in a lone cavern of the dead, an hundred feet above the ground, where none could find me were ill done to me, nor would any ever seek. But in secret I determined that I would come again, though with more secure following. Moreover, was I tempted to seek further, as in examining the wrappings I saw many things of strange import in that wondrous tomb; including a casket of eccentric shape made of some strange stone, which methought might have contained other jewels, inasmuch as it had secure lodgment in the great sarcophagus itself. There was in the tomb also another coffer which, though of rare proportion and adornment, was more simply shaped. It was of ironstone of great thickness; but the cover was lightly cemented down with what seemed gum and Paris plaster, as though to insure that no air could penetrate. The Arabs with me so insisted in its opening, thinking that from its thickness much treasure was stored therein, that I consented thereto. But their hope was a false one, as it proved. Within, closely packed, stood four jars finely wrought and carved with various adornments. Of these one was the head of a man, another of a dog, another of a jackal, and another of a hawk. I had before known that such burial urns as these were used to contain the entrails and other organs of the mummied dead; but on opening these, for the fastening of wax, though complete, was thin, and yielded easily, we found that they held but oil. The Bedouins, spilling most of the oil in the process, groped with their hands in the jars lest treasure should have been there concealed. But their searching was of no avail; no treasure was there. I was warned of my danger by seeing in the eyes of the Arabs certain covetous glances. Whereon, in order to hasten their departure, I wrought upon those fears of superstition which even in these callous men were apparent. The chief of the Bedouins ascended from the Pit to give the signal to those above to raise us; and I, not caring to remain with the men whom I mistrusted, followed him immediately. The others did not come at once; from which I feared that they were rifling the tomb afresh on their own account. I refrained to speak of it, however, lest worse should befall. At last they came. One of them, who ascended first, in landing at the top of the cliff lost his foothold and fell below. He was instantly killed. The other followed, but in safety. The chief came next, and I came last. Before coming away I pulled into its place again, as well as I could, the slab of stone that covered the entrance to the tomb. I wished, if possible, to preserve it for my own examination should I come again.

"When we all stood on the hill above the cliff, the burning sun that was bright and full of glory was good to see after the darkness and strange mystery of the tomb. Even was I glad that the poor Arab who fell down the cliff and lay dead below, lay in the sunlight and not in that gloomy cavern. I would fain have gone with my companions to seek him and give him sepulture of some kind; but the Sheik made light of it, and sent two of his men to see to it whilst we went on our way.

"That night as we camped, one of the men only returned, saying that a lion of the desert had killed his companion after that they had buried the dead man in a deep sand without the valley, and had covered the spot where he lay with many great rocks, so that jackals or other preying beasts might not dig him up again as is their wont.

"Later, in the light of the fire round which the men sat or lay, I saw him exhibit to his fellows something white which they seemed to regard with special awe and reverence. So I drew near silently, and saw that it was none other than the white hand of the mummy which had lain protecting the Jewel in the great sarcophagus. I heard the Bedouin tell how he had found it on the body of him who had fallen from the cliff. There was no mistaking it, for there were the seven fingers which I had noted before. This man must have wrenched it off the dead body whilst his chief and I were otherwise engaged; and from the awe of the others I doubted not that he had hoped to use it as an Amulet, or charm. Whereas if powers it had, they were not for him who had taken it from the dead; since his death followed hard upon his theft. Already his Amulet had had an awesome baptism; for the wrist of the dead hand was stained with red as though it had been dipped in recent blood.

"That night I was in certain fear lest there should be some violence done to me; for if the poor dead hand was so valued as a charm, what must be the worth in such wise of the rare Jewel which it had guarded. Though only the chief knew of it, my doubt was perhaps even greater; for he could so order matters as to have me at his mercy when he would. I guarded myself, therefore, with wakefulness so well as I could, determined that at my earliest opportunity I should leave this party, and complete my journeying home, first to the Nile bank, and then down its course to Alexandria; with other guides who knew not what strange matters I had with me.

"At last there came over me a disposition of sleep, so potent that I felt it would be resistless. Fearing attack, or that being searched in my sleep the Bedouin might find the Star Jewel which he had seen me place with others in my dress, I took it out unobserved and held it in my hand. It seemed to give back the light of the flickering fire and the light of the stars – for there was no moon – with equal fidelity; and I could note that on its reverse it was graven deeply with certain signs such as I had seen in the tomb. As I sank into the unconsciousness of sleep, the graven Star Jewel was hidden in the hollow of my clenched hand.

"I waked out of sleep with the light of the morning sun on my face. I sat up and looked around me. The fire was out, and the camp was desolate; save for one figure which lay prone close to me. It was that of the Arab chief, who lay on his back, dead. His face was almost black; and his eyes were open, and staring horribly up at the sky, as though he saw there some dreadful vision. He had evidently been strangled; for on looking, I found on his throat the red marks where fingers had pressed. There seemed so many of these marks that I counted them. There were seven; and all parallel, except the thumb mark, as though made with one hand. This thrilled me as I thought of the mummy hand with the seven fingers.

"Even there, in the open desert, it seemed as if there could be enchantments!

"In my surprise, as I bent over him, I opened my right hand, which up to now I had held shut with the feeling, instinctive even in sleep, of keeping safe that which it held. As I did so, the Star Jewel held there fell out and struck the dead man on the mouth. *Mirabile dictu* there came forth at once from the dead mouth a great gush of blood, in which the red jewel was for the moment lost. I turned the dead man over to look for it, and found that he lay with his right hand bent under him as though he had fallen on it; and in it he held a great knife, keen of point and edge, such as Arabs carry at the belt. It may have been that he was about to murder me when vengeance came on him, whether from man or God, or the Gods of Old, I know not. Suffice it, that when I found my Ruby Jewel, which shone up as a living star from the mess of blood wherein it lay, I paused not, but fled from the place. I journeyed on alone through the hot desert, till, by God's grace, I came upon an Arab tribe camping by a well, who gave me salt. With them I rested till they had set me on my way.

"I know not what became of the mummy hand, or of those who had it. What strife, or suspicion, or disaster, or greed went with it I know not; but some such cause there must have been, since those who had it fled with it. It doubtless is used as a charm of potence by some desert tribe.

"At the earliest opportunity I made examination of the Star Ruby, as I wished to try to understand what was graven on it. The symbols – whose meaning, however, I could not understand – were as follows..."

Twice, whilst I had been reading this engrossing narrative, I had thought that I had seen across the page streaks of shade, which the weirdness of the subject had made to seem like the shadow of a hand. On the first of these occasions I found that the illusion came from the fringe of green silk around the lamp; but on the second I had looked up, and my eyes had lit on the mummy hand across the room on which the starlight was falling under the edge of the blind. It was of little wonder that I had connected it with such a narrative; for if my eyes told me truly, here, in this room with me, was the very hand of which the traveller Van Huyn had written. I looked over at the bed; and it comforted me to think that the Nurse still sat there, calm and wakeful. At such a time, with such surrounds, during such a narrative, it was well to have assurance of the presence of some living person.

I sat looking at the book on the table before me; and so many strange thoughts crowded on me that my mind began to whirl. It was almost as if the light on the white fingers in front of me was beginning to have some hypnotic effect. All at once, all thoughts seemed to stop; and for an instant the world and time stood still.

There lay a real hand across the book! What was there to so overcome me, as was the case? I knew the hand that I saw on the book – and loved it. Margaret Trelawny's hand was a joy to me to see – to touch; and yet at that moment, coming after other marvellous things, it had a strangely moving effect on me. It was but momentary, however, and had passed even before her voice had reached me.

"What disturbs you? What are you staring at the book for? I thought for an instant that you must have been overcome again!" I jumped up.

"I was reading," I said, "an old book from the library." As I spoke I closed it and put it under my arm. "I shall now put it back, as I understand that your Father wishes all things, especially books, kept in their proper places." My words were intentionally misleading; for I did not wish her to know what I was reading, and thought it best not to wake her curiosity by leaving the book about. I went away, but not to the library; I left the book in my room where I could get it when I had had my sleep in the day. When I returned Nurse Kennedy was ready to go to bed; so Miss Trelawny watched with me in the room. I did not want any book whilst she was present. We sat close together and talked in a whisper whilst the moments flew by. It was with surprise that I noted the edge of the curtains changing from grey to yellow light. What we talked of had nothing to do with the sick man, except in so far that all which concerned his daughter must ultimately concern him. But it had nothing to say to Egypt, or mummies, or the dead, or caves, or Bedouin chiefs. I could well take note in the growing light that Margaret's hand had not seven fingers, but five; for it lay in mine.

When Doctor Winchester arrived in the morning and had made his visit to his patient, he came to see me as I sat in the dining-room having a little meal – breakfast or supper, I hardly knew which it was – before I went to lie down. Mr. Corbeck came in at the same time; and we resumed out conversation where we had left it the night before. I told Mr. Corbeck that I had read the chapter about the finding of the tomb, and that I thought Doctor Winchester should read it, too. The latter said that, if he might, he would take it with him; he had that morning to make a railway journey to Ipswich, and would read it on the train. He said he would bring it back with him when he came again in the evening. I went up to my room to bring it down; but I could not find it anywhere. I had a distinct recollection of having left it on the little table beside my bed, when I had come up after Miss Trelawny's going on duty into the sick-room. It was very strange; for the book was not of a kind that any of the servants would be likely to take. I had to come back and explain to the others that I could not find it.

When Doctor Winchester had gone, Mr. Corbeck, who seemed to know the Dutchman's work by heart, talked the whole matter over with me. I told him that I was interrupted by a change of nurses, just as I had come to the description of the ring. He smiled as he said:

"So far as that is concerned, you need not be disappointed. Not in Van Huyn's time, nor for nearly two centuries later, could the meaning of that engraving have been understood. It was only when the work was taken up and followed by Young and Champollion, by Birch and Lepsius and Rosellini and Salvolini, by Mariette Bey and by Wallis Budge and Flinders Petrie and the other scholars of their times that great results ensued, and that the true meaning of hieroglyphic was known.

"Later, I shall explain to you, if Mr. Trelawny does not explain it himself, or if he does not forbid me to, what it means in that particular place. I think it will be better for you to know what followed Van Huyn's narrative; for with the description of the stone, and the account of his bringing it to Holland at the termination of his travels, the episode ends. Ends so far as his book is concerned. The chief thing about the book is that it sets others thinking – and acting. Amongst them were Mr. Trelawny and myself. Mr. Trelawny is a good linguist of the Orient, but he does not know Northern tongues. As for me I have a faculty for learning languages; and when I was pursuing my studies in Leyden I learned Dutch so that I might more easily make references in the library there. Thus it was, that at the very time when Mr. Trelawny, who, in making his great collection of works on Egypt, had, through a booksellers' catalogue, acquired this volume with the manuscript translation, was studying it, I was reading another copy, in original Dutch, in Leyden. We were both struck by the description of the lonely tomb in the rock; cut so high up as to be inaccessible to ordinary seekers: with all means of reaching it carefully obliterated; and yet with such an elaborate ornamentation of the smoothed surface of the cliff as Van Huyn has described. It also struck us both as an odd thing – for in the years between Van Huyn's time and our own the general knowledge of Egyptian curios and records has increased marvellously – that in the case of such a tomb, made in such a place, and which must have cost an immense sum of money, there was no seeming record or effigy to point out who lay within. Moreover, the very name of the place, 'the Valley of the Sorcerer', had, in a prosaic age, attractions of its own. When we met, which we did through his seeking the assistance of other Egyptologists in his work, we talked over this as we did over many other things; and we determined to make search for the mysterious valley. Whilst we were waiting to start on the travel, for many things were required which Mr. Trelawny undertook to see to himself, I went to Holland to try if I could by any traces verify Van Huyn's narrative. I went straight to Hoorn, and set patiently to work to find the house of the traveller and his descendants, if any. I need not trouble you with details of my seeking – and finding. Hoorn is a place that has not changed much since Van Huyn's time, except that it has lost the place which it held amongst commercial cities. Its externals are such as they had been then; in such a sleepy old place a century or two does not count for much. I found the house, and discovered that none of the descendants were alive. I searched records; but only to one end – death and extinction. Then I set me to work to find what had become of his treasures; for that such a traveller must have had great treasures was apparent. I traced a good many to museums in Leyden, Utrecht, and Amsterdam; and some few to the private houses of rich collectors. At last, in the shop of an old watchmaker and jeweller at Hoorn, I found what he considered his chiefest treasure; a great ruby, carven like a scarab, with seven stars, and engraven with hieroglyphics. The old man did not know hieroglyphic character, and in his old-world, sleepy life, the philological discoveries of recent years had not reached him. He did not know anything of Van Huyn, except that such a person had been, and that his name was, during two centuries, venerated in the town as a great traveller. He valued the jewel as only a rare stone, spoiled in part by the cutting; and though he was at first loth to part with such an unique gem he became amenable ultimately to commercial reason. I had a full purse, since I bought for Mr. Trelawny, who is, as I suppose you know, immensely wealthy. I was shortly on my way back to London, with the Star Ruby safe in my pocket-book; and in my heart a joy and exultation which knew no bounds.

"For here we were with proof of Van Huyn's wonderful story. The jewel was put in security in Mr. Trelawny's great safe; and we started out on our journey of exploration in full hope.

"Mr. Trelawny was, at the last, loth to leave his young wife whom he dearly loved; but she, who loved him equally, knew his longing to prosecute the search. So keeping to herself, as all good women do, all her anxieties – which in her case were special – she bade him follow out his bent."

Chapter XI
A Queen's Tomb

"MR. TRELAWNY'S HOPE was at least as great as my own. He is not so volatile a man as I am, prone to ups and downs of hope and despair; but he has a fixed purpose which crystallises hope into belief. At times I had feared that there might have been two such stones, or that the adventures of Van Huyn were traveller's fictions, based on some ordinary acquisition of the curio in Alexandria or Cairo, or London or Amsterdam. But Mr. Trelawny never faltered in his belief. We had many things to distract our minds from belief or disbelief. This was soon after Arabi Pasha, and Egypt was so safe place for travellers, especially if they were English. But Mr. Trelawny is a fearless man; and I almost come to think at times that I am not a coward myself. We got together a band of Arabs whom one or other of us had known in former trips to the desert, and whom we could trust; that is, we did not distrust them as much as others. We were numerous enough to protect ourselves from chance marauding bands, and we took with us large impedimenta. We had secured the consent and passive co-operation of the officials still friendly to Britain; in the acquiring of which consent I need hardly say that Mr. Trelawny's riches were of chief importance. We found our way in dhahabiyehs to Aswan; whence, having got some Arabs from the Sheik and having given our usual backsheesh, we set out on our journey through the desert.

"Well, after much wandering and trying every winding in the interminable jumble of hills, we came at last at nightfall on just such a valley as Van Huyn had described. A valley with high, steep cliffs; narrowing in the centre, and widening out to the eastern and western ends. At daylight we were opposite the cliff and could easily note the opening high up in the rock, and the hieroglyphic figures which were evidently intended originally to conceal it.

"But the signs which had baffled Van Huyn and those of his time – and later, were no secrets to us. The host of scholars who have given their brains and their lives to this work, had wrested open the mysterious prison-house of Egyptian language. On the hewn face of the rocky cliff we, who had learned the secrets, could read what the Theban priesthood had had there inscribed nearly fifty centuries before.

"For that the external inscription was the work of the priesthood – and a hostile priesthood at that – there could be no living doubt. The inscription on the rock, written in hieroglyphic, ran thus:

"'Hither the Gods come not at any summons. The 'Nameless One' has insulted them and is for ever alone. Go not nigh, lest their vengeance wither you away!'

"The warning must have been a terribly potent one at the time it was written and for thousands of years afterwards; even when the language in which it was given had become a dead mystery to the people of the land. The tradition of such a terror lasts longer than its cause. Even in the symbols used there was an added significance of alliteration. 'For ever' is given in the hieroglyphics as 'millions of years'. This symbol was repeated nine times, in three groups of three; and after each group a symbol of the Upper World, the Under World, and the Sky. So that for this Lonely One there could be, through the vengeance of all the Gods, resurrection in neither the World of Sunlight, in the World of the Dead, or for the soul in the region of the Gods.

"Neither Mr. Trelawny nor I dared to tell any of our people what the writing meant. For though they did not believe in the religion whence the curse came, or in the Gods whose vengeance was threatened, yet they were so superstitious that they would probably, had they known of it, have thrown up the whole task and run away.

"Their ignorance, however, and our discretion preserved us. We made an encampment close at hand, but behind a jutting rock a little further along the valley, so that they might not have the inscription always before them. For even that traditional name of the place: 'The Valley of the Sorcerer', had a fear for them; and for us through them. With the timber which we had brought, we made a ladder up the face of the rock. We hung a pulley on a beam fixed to project from the top of the cliff. We found the great slab of rock, which formed the door, placed clumsily in its place and secured by a few stones. Its own weight kept it in safe position. In order to enter, we had to push it in; and we passed over it. We found the great coil of chain which Van Huyn had described fastened into the rock. There were, however, abundant evidences amid the wreckage of the great stone door, which had revolved on iron hinges at top and bottom, that ample provision had been originally made for closing and fastening it from within.

"Mr. Trelawny and I went alone into the tomb. We had brought plenty of lights with us; and we fixed them as we went along. We wished to get a complete survey at first, and then make examination of all in detail. As we went on, we were filled with ever-increasing wonder and delight. The tomb was one of the most magnificent and beautiful which either of us had ever seen. From the elaborate nature of the sculpture and painting, and the perfection of the workmanship, it was evident that the tomb was prepared during the lifetime of her for whose resting-place it was intended. The drawing of the hieroglyphic pictures was fine, and the colouring superb; and in that high cavern, far away from even the damp of the Nile-flood, all was as fresh as when the artists had laid down their palettes. There was one thing which we could not avoid seeing. That although the cutting on the outside rock was the work of the priesthood, the smoothing of the cliff face was probably a part of the tomb-builder's original design. The symbolism of the painting and cutting within all gave the same idea. The outer cavern, partly natural and partly hewn, was regarded architecturally as only an ante-chamber. At the end of it, so that it would face the east, was a pillared portico, hewn out of the solid rock. The pillars were massive and were seven-sided, a thing which we had not come across in any other tomb. Sculptured on the architrave was the Boat of the Moon, containing Hathor, cow headed and bearing the disk and plumes, and the dog-headed Hapi, the God of the North. It was steered by Harpocrates towards the north, represented by the Pole Star surrounded by Draco and Ursa Major. In the latter the stars that form what we call the 'Plough' were cut larger than any of the other stars; and were filled with gold so that, in the light of torches, they seemed to flame with a special significance. Passing within the portico, we found two of the architectural features of a rock tomb, the Chamber, or Chapel, and the Pit, all complete as Van Huyn had noticed, though in his day the names given to these parts by the Egyptians of old were unknown.

"The Stele, or record, which had its place low down on the western wall, was so remarkable that we examined it minutely, even before going on our way to find the mummy which was the object of our search. This Stele was a great slab of lapis lazuli cut all over with hieroglyphic figures of small size and of much beauty. The cutting was filled in with some cement of exceeding fineness, and of the colour of pure vermilion. The inscription began:

"*'Tera, Queen of the Egypts, daughter of Antef, Monarch of the North and the South.' 'Daughter of the Sun,' 'Queen of the Diadems'.*

"It then set out, in full record, the history of her life and reign.

"The signs of sovereignty were given with a truly feminine profusion of adornment. The united Crowns of Upper and Lower Egypt were, in especial, cut with exquisite precision. It was new to us both to find the Hejet and the Desher – the White and the Red crowns of Upper and Lower Egypt – on the Stele of a queen; for it was a rule, without exception in the records, that in ancient Egypt either crown was worn only by a king; though they are to be found on goddesses. Later on we found an explanation, of which I shall say more presently.

"Such an inscription was in itself a matter so startling as to arrest attention from anyone anywhere at any time; but you can have no conception of the effect which it had upon us. Though our eyes were not the first which had seen it, they were the first which could see it with understanding since first the slab of rock was fixed in the cliff opening nearly five thousand years before. To us was given to read this message from the dead. This message of one who had warred against the Gods of Old, and claimed to have controlled them at a time when the hierarchy professed to be the only means of exciting their fears or gaining their good will.

"The walls of the upper chamber of the Pit and the sarcophagus Chamber were profusely inscribed; all the inscriptions, except that on the Stele, being coloured with bluish-green pigment. The effect when seen sideways as the eye caught the green facets, was that of an old, discoloured Indian turquoise.

"We descended the Pit by the aid of the tackle we had brought with us. Trelawny went first. It was a deep pit, more than seventy feet; but it had never been filled up. The passage at the bottom sloped up to the sarcophagus Chamber, and was longer than is usually found. It had not been walled up.

"Within, we found a great sarcophagus of yellow stone. But that I need not describe; you have seen it in Mr. Trelawny's chamber. The cover of it lay on the ground; it had not been cemented, and was just as Van Huyn had described it.

Needless to say, we were excited as we looked within. There must, however, be one sense of disappointment. I could not help feeling how different must have been the sight which met the Dutch traveller's eyes when he looked within and found that white hand lying lifelike above the shrouding mummy cloths. It is true that a part of the arm was there, white and ivory like.

"But there was a thrill to us which came not to Van Huyn!

"The end of the wrist was covered with dried blood! It was as though the body had bled after death! The jagged ends of the broken wrist were rough with the clotted blood; through this the white bone, sticking out, looked like the matrix of opal. The blood had streamed down and stained the brown wrappings as with rust. Here, then, was full confirmation of the narrative. With such evidence of the narrator's truth before us, we could not doubt the other matters which he had told, such as the blood on the mummy hand, or marks of the seven fingers on the throat of the strangled Sheik.

"I shall not trouble you with details of all we saw, or how we learned all we knew. Part of it was from knowledge common to scholars; part we read on the Stele in the tomb, and in the sculptures and hieroglyphic paintings on the walls.

"Queen Tera was of the Eleventh, or Theban Dynasty of Egyptian Kings which held sway between the twenty-ninth and twenty-fifth centuries before Christ. She succeeded as the only child of her father, Antef. She must have been a girl of extraordinary character as well as ability, for she was but a young girl when her father died. Her youth and sex encouraged the ambitious priesthood, which had then achieved immense power. By their wealth and numbers and learning they dominated all Egypt, more especially the Upper portion. They were then secretly ready to make an effort for the achievement of their bold and long-considered design, that of transferring the governing power from a Kingship to a Hierarchy. But King Antef had suspected some such movement, and had taken the precaution of securing to his daughter the allegiance of the army. He had also had her taught statecraft, and had even made her learned in the lore of the very priests themselves. He had used those of one cult against the other; each being hopeful of some present gain on its own part by the influence of the King, or of some ultimate gain from its own influence over his daughter. Thus, the Princess had been brought up amongst scribes, and was herself no mean artist. Many of these things were told on the walls in pictures or in hieroglyphic writing of great beauty; and we came to the conclusion that not a few of them had been done by the Princess herself. It was not without cause that she was inscribed on the Stele as 'Protector of the Arts'.

"But the King had gone to further lengths, and had had his daughter taught magic, by which she had power over Sleep and Will. This was real magic – 'black' magic; not the magic of the temples, which, I may explain, was of the harmless or 'white' order, and was intended to impress rather than to effect. She had been an apt pupil; and had gone further than her teachers. Her power and her resources had given her great opportunities, of which she had availed herself to the full. She had won secrets from nature in strange ways; and had even gone to the length of going down into the tomb herself, having been swathed and coffined and left as dead for a whole month. The priests had tried to make out that the real Princess Tera had died in the experiment, and that another girl had been substituted; but she had conclusively proved their error. All this was told in pictures of great merit. It was probably in her time that the impulse was given in the restoring the artistic greatness of the Fourth Dynasty which had found its perfection in the days of Chufu.

"In the Chamber of the sarcophagus were pictures and writings to show that she had achieved victory over Sleep. Indeed, there was everywhere a symbolism, wonderful even in a land and an age of symbolism. Prominence was given to the fact that she, though a Queen, claimed all the privileges of kingship and masculinity. In one place she was pictured in man's dress, and wearing the White and Red Crowns. In the following picture she was in female dress, but still wearing the Crowns of Upper and Lower Egypt, while the discarded male raiment lay at her feet. In every picture where hope, or aim, of resurrection was expressed there was the added symbol of the North; and in many places – always in representations of important events, past, present, or future – was a grouping of the stars of the Plough. She evidently regarded this constellation as in some way peculiarly associated with herself.

"Perhaps the most remarkable statement in the records, both on the Stele and in the mural writings, was that Queen Tera had power to compel the Gods. This, by the way, was not an isolated belief in Egyptian history; but was different in its cause. She had engraved on a ruby, carved like a scarab, and having seven stars of seven points, Master Words to compel all the Gods, both of the Upper and the Under Worlds.

"In the statement it was plainly set forth that the hatred of the priests was, she knew, stored up for her, and that they would after her death try to suppress her name. This was a terrible revenge, I may tell you, in Egyptian mythology; for without a name no one can after death be introduced to the Gods, or have prayers said for him. Therefore, she had intended her resurrection to be after a long time and in a more northern land, under the constellation whose seven stars had ruled her birth. To this end, her hand was to be in the air – 'unwrapped' – and in it the Jewel of Seven Stars, so that wherever there was air she might move even as her Ka could move! This, after thinking it over, Mr. Trelawny and I agreed meant that her body could become astral at command, and so move, particle by particle, and become whole again when and where required. Then there was a piece of writing in which allusion was made to a chest or casket in which were contained all the Gods, and Will, and Sleep, the two latter being personified by symbols. The box was mentioned as with seven sides. It was not much of a surprise to us when, underneath the feet of the mummy, we found the seven-sided casket, which you have also seen in Mr. Trelawny's room. On the underneath part of the wrapping – linen of the left foot was painted, in the same vermilion colour as that used in the Stele, the hieroglyphic symbol for much water, and underneath the right foot the symbol of the earth. We made out the symbolism to be that her body, immortal and transferable at will, ruled both the land and water, air and fire – the latter being exemplified by the light of the Jewel Stone, and further by the flint and iron which lay outside the mummy wrappings.

"As we lifted the casket from the sarcophagus, we noticed on its sides the strange protuberances which you have already seen; but we were unable at the time to account for them. There were a few amulets in the sarcophagus, but none of any special worth or significance. We took it that if there were such, they were within the wrappings; or more probably in the strange casket underneath the mummy's feet. This, however, we could not open. There were signs of there being a cover; certainly the upper portion and the lower were each in one piece. The fine line, a little way from the top, appeared to be where the cover was fixed; but it was made with such quisite fineness and finish that the joining could hardly be seen. Certainly the p could not be moved. We took it, that it was in some way fastened from within. ell you all this in order that you may understand things with which you may be in ntact later. You must suspend your judgment entirely. Such strange things have ppened regarding this mummy and all around it, that there is a necessity for new lief somewhere. It is absolutely impossible to reconcile certain things which have ppened with the ordinary currents of life or knowledge.

"We stayed around the Valley of the Sorcerer, till we had copied roughly all the drawings d writings on the walls, ceiling and floor. We took with us the Stele of lapis lazuli, whose aven record was coloured with vermilion pigment. We took the sarcophagus and the ummy; the stone chest with the alabaster jars; the tables of bloodstone and alabaster d onyx and carnelian; and the ivory pillow whose arch rested on 'buckles', round each which was twisted an uraeus wrought in gold. We took all the articles which lay in the hapel, and the Mummy Pit; the wooden boats with crews and the ushaptiu figures, and e symbolic amulets.

"When coming away we took down the ladders, and at a distance buried them in the nd under a cliff, which we noted so that if necessary we might find them again. Then ith our heavy baggage, we set out on our laborious journey back to the Nile. It was easy task, I tell you, to bring the case with that great sarcophagus over the desert. e had a rough cart and sufficient men to draw it; but the progress seemed terribly slow, for e were anxious to get our treasures into a place of safety. The night was an anxious me with us, for we feared attack from some marauding band. But more still we feared me of those with us. They were, after all, but predatory, unscrupulous men; and we ad with us a considerable bulk of precious things. They, or at least the dangerous nes amongst them, did not know why it was so precious; they took it for granted that was material treasure of some kind that we carried. We had taken the mummy from e sarcophagus, and packed it for safety of travel in a separate case. During the first ight two attempts were made to steal things from the cart; and two men were found ead in the morning.

"On the second night there came on a violent storm, one of those terrible simooms f the desert which makes one feel his helplessness. We were overwhelmed with rifting sand. Some of our Bedouins had fled before the storm, hoping to find helter; the rest of us, wrapped in our bournous, endured with what patience we ould. In the morning, when the storm had passed, we recovered from under the les of sand what we could of our impedimenta. We found the case in which the ummy had been packed all broken, but the mummy itself could nowhere be found. e searched everywhere around, and dug up the sand which had piled around us; ut in vain. We did not know what to do, for Trelawny had his heart set on taking ome that mummy. We waited a whole day in hopes that the Bedouins, who had ed, would return; we had a blind hope that they might have in some way removed e mummy from the cart, and would restore it. That night, just before dawn, Mr. relawny woke me up and whispered in my ear:

"'We must go back to the tomb in the Valley of the Sorcerer. Show no hesitation the morning when I give the orders! If you ask any questions as to where we are oing it will create suspicion, and will defeat our purpose.'

"'All right!' I answered. 'But why shall we go there?' His answer seemed to thrill hrough me as though it had struck some chord ready tuned within:

"'We shall find the mummy there! I am sure of it!' Then anticipating doubt or argument he added:

"'Wait, and you shall see!' and he sank back into his blanket again.

"The Arabs were surprised when we retraced our steps; and some of them were not satisfied. There was a good deal of friction, and there were several desertions; so that it was with a diminished following that we took our way eastward again. At first the Sheik did not manifest any curiosity as to our definite destination; but when it became apparent that we were again making for the Valley of the Sorcerer, he too showed concern. This grew as we drew near; till finally at the entrance of the valley he halted and refused to go further. He said he would await our return if we chose to go on alone. That he would wait three days; but if by that time we had not returned he would leave. No offer of money would tempt him to depart from this resolution. The only concession he would make was that he would find the ladders and bring them near the cliff. This he did; and then, with the rest of the troop, he went back to wait at the entrance of the valley.

"Mr. Trelawny and I took ropes and torches, and again ascended to the tomb. It was evident that someone had been there in our absence, for the stone slab which protected the entrance to the tomb was lying flat inside, and a rope was dangling from the cliff summit. Within, there was another rope hanging into the shaft of the Mummy Pit. We looked at each other; but neither said a word. We fixed our own rope, and as arranged Trelawny descended first, I following at once. It was not till we stood together at the foot of the shaft that the thought flashed across me that we might be in some sort of a trap, that someone might descend the rope from the cliff, and by cutting the rope by which we had lowered ourselves into the Pit, bury us there alive. The thought was horrifying, but it was too late to do anything. I remained silent. We both had torches, so that there was ample light as we passed through the passage and entered the Chamber where the sarcophagus had stood. The first thing noticeable was the emptiness of the place. Despite all its magnificent adornment, the tomb was made a desolation by the absence of the great sarcophagus, to hold which it was hewn in the rock; of the chest with the alabaster jars; of the tables which had held the implements and food for the use of the dead, and the ushaptiu figures.

"It was made more infinitely desolate still by the shrouded figure of the mummy of Queen Tera which lay on the floor where the great sarcophagus had stood! Beside it lay, in the strange contorted attitudes of violent death, three of the Arabs who had deserted from our party. Their faces were black, and their hands and necks were smeared with blood which had burst from mouth and nose and eyes.

"On the throat of each were the marks, now blackening, of a hand of seven fingers.

"Trelawny and I drew close, and clutched each other in awe and fear as we looked.

"For, most wonderful of all, across the breast of the mummied Queen lay a hand of seven fingers, ivory white, the wrist only showing a scar like a jagged red line from which seemed to depend drops of blood."

Chapter XII
The Magic Coffer

"**WHEN WE RECOVERED** our amazement, which seemed to last unduly long, we did not lose any time carrying the mummy through the passage, and hoisting it up the Pit shaft. I went first, to receive it at the top. As I looked down, I saw Mr. Trelawny lift the severed hand and put it in his breast, manifestly to save it from being injured or lost. We left the dead Arabs where they lay. With our ropes we lowered our precious burden to the ground; and then took it to the entrance of the valley where our escort was to wait. To our astonishment we found them on the move. When we remonstrated with the Sheik, he answered that he had fulfilled his contract to the letter; he had waited the three days as arranged. I thought that he was lying to cover up his base intention of deserting us; and I found when we compared notes that Trelawny had the same suspicion. It was not till we arrived at Cairo that we found he was correct. It was the 3rd of November 1884 when we entered the Mummy Pit for the second time; we had reason to remember the date.

"We had lost three whole days of our reckoning – out of our lives – whilst we had stood wondering in that chamber of the dead. Was it strange, then, that we had a superstitious feeling with regard to the dead Queen Tera and all belonging to her? Is it any wonder that it rests with us now, with a bewildering sense of some power outside ourselves or our comprehension? Will it be any wonder if it go down to the grave with us at the appointed time? If, indeed, there be any graves for us who have robbed the dead!" He was silent for quite a minute before he went on:

"We got to Cairo all right, and from there to Alexandria, where we were to take ship by the Messagerie service to Marseilles, and go thence by express to London. But 'The best-laid schemes o' mice and men Gang aft agley.' At Alexandria, Trelawny found waiting a cable stating that Mrs. Trelawny had died in giving birth to a daughter.

"Her stricken husband hurried off at once by the Orient Express; and I had to bring the treasure alone to the desolate house. I got to London all safe; there seemed to be some special good fortune to our journey. When I got to this house, the funeral had long been over. The child had been put out to nurse, and Mr. Trelawny had so far recovered from the shock of his loss that he had set himself to take up again the broken threads of his life and his work. That he had had a shock, and a bad one, was apparent. The sudden grey in his black hair was proof enough in itself; but in addition, the strong cast of his features had become set and stern. Since he received that cable in the shipping office at Alexandria I have never seen a happy smile on his face.

"Work is the best thing in such a case; and to his work he devoted himself heart and soul. The strange tragedy of his loss and gain – for the child was born after the mother's death – took place during the time that we stood in that trance in the Mummy Pit of Queen Tera. It seemed to have become in some way associated with his Egyptian studies, and more especially with the mysteries connected with the Queen. He told me very little about his daughter; but that two forces struggled in his mind regarding her was apparent. I could see that he loved, almost idolised her. Yet he could never forget that her birth had cost her mother's life. Also, there was something whose existence seemed to wring his father's heart, though he would never tell me what it was. Again, he once said in a moment of relaxation of his purpose of silence:

"'She is unlike her mother; but in both feature and colour she has a marvellous resemblance to the pictures of Queen Tera.'

"He said that he had sent her away to people who would care for her as he could not; and that till she became a woman she should have all the simple pleasures that a young girl might have, and that were best for her. I would often have talked with him about her; but he would never say much. Once he said to me: 'There are reasons why I should not speak more than is necessary. Some day you will know – and understand!' I respected his reticence; and beyond asking after her on my return after a journey, I have never spoken of her again. I had never seen her till I did so in your presence.

"Well, when the treasures which we had – ah! – taken from the tomb had been brought here, Mr. Trelawny arranged their disposition himself. The mummy, all except the severed hand, he placed in the great ironstone sarcophagus in the hall. This was wrought for the Theban High Priest Uni, and is, as you may have remarked, all inscribed with wonderful invocations to the old Gods of Egypt. The rest of the things from the tomb he disposed about his own room, as you have seen. Amongst them he placed, for special reasons of his own, the mummy hand. I think he regards this as the most sacred of his possessions, with perhaps one exception. That is the carven ruby which he calls the 'Jewel of Seven Stars', which he keeps in that great safe which is locked and guarded by various devices, as you know.

"I dare say you find this tedious; but I have had to explain it, so that you should understand all up to the present. It was a long time after my return with the mummy of Queen Tera when Mr. Trelawny re-opened the subject with me. He had been several times to Egypt, sometimes with me and sometimes alone; and I had been several trips, on my own account or for him. But in all that time, nearly sixteen years, he never mentioned the subject, unless when some pressing occasion suggested, if it did not necessitate, a reference.

"One morning early he sent for me in a hurry; I was then studying in the British Museum, and had rooms in Hart Street. When I came, he was all on fire with excitement. I had not seen him in such a glow since before the news of his wife's death. He took me at once into his room. The window blinds were down and the shutters closed; not a ray of daylight came in. The ordinary lights in the room were not lit, but there were a lot of powerful electric lamps, fifty candle-power at least, arranged on one side of the room. The little bloodstone table on which the heptagonal coffer stands was drawn to the centre of the room. The coffer looked exquisite in the glare of light which shone on it. It actually seemed to glow as if lit in some way from within.

"'What do you think of it?' he asked.

"'It is like a jewel,' I answered. 'You may well call it the "sorcerer's Magic Coffer", if it often looks like that. It almost seems to be alive.'

"'Do you know why it seems so?'

"'From the glare of the light, I suppose?'

"'Light of course,' he answered, 'but it is rather the disposition of light.' As he spoke he turned up the ordinary lights of the room and switched off the special ones. The effect on the stone box was surprising; in a second it lost all its glowing effect. It was still a very beautiful stone, as always; but it was stone and no more.

"'Do you notice anything about the arrangement of the lamps?' he asked.

"'No!'

"'They were in the shape of the stars in the Plough, as the stars are in the ruby! The statement came to me with a certain sense of conviction. I do not know why except that there had been so many mysterious associations with the mummy and all belonging to it that any new one seemed enlightening. I listened as Trelawny went on to explain:

"'For sixteen years I have never ceased to think of that adventure, or to try to find a clue to the mysteries which came before us; but never until last night did I seem to find a solution. I think I must have dreamed of it, for I woke all on fire about it. I jumped out of bed with a determination of doing something, before I quite knew what it was that I wished to do. Then, all at once, the purpose was clear before me. There were allusions in the writing on the walls of the tomb to the seven stars of the Great Bear that go to make up the Plough; and the North was again and again emphasized. The same symbols were repeated with regard to the "Magic Box", as we called it. We had already noticed those peculiar translucent spaces in the stone of the box. You remember the hieroglyphic writing had told that the jewel came from the heart of an aerolite, and that the coffer was cut from it also. It might be, I thought, that the light of the seven stars, shining in the right direction, might have some effect on the box, or something within it. I raised the blind and looked out. The Plough was high in the heavens, and both its stars and the Pole Star were straight opposite the window. I pulled the table with the coffer out into the light, and shifted it until the translucent patches were in the direction of the stars. Instantly the box began to glow, as you saw it under the lamps, though but slightly. I waited and waited; but the sky clouded over, and the light died away. So I got wires and lamps – you know how often I use them in experiments – and tried the effect of electric light. It took me some time to get the lamps properly placed, so that they would correspond to the parts of the stone, but the moment I got them right the whole thing began to glow as you have seen it.

"'I could get no further, however. There was evidently something wanting. All at once it came to me that if light could have some effect there should be in the tomb some means of producing light, for there could not be starlight in the Mummy Pit in the cavern. Then the whole thing seemed to become clear. On the bloodstone table, which has a hollow carved in its top, into which the bottom of the coffer fits, I laid the Magic Coffer; and I at once saw that the odd protuberances so carefully wrought in the substance of the stone corresponded in a way to the stars in the constellation. These, then, were to hold lights.

"'Eureka!' I cried. 'All we want now is the lamps.'" I tried placing the electric lights on, or close to, the protuberances. But the glow never came to the stone. So the conviction grew on me that there were special lamps made for the purpose. If we could find them, a step on the road to solving the mystery should be gained.

"'But what about the lamps?' I asked. 'Where are they? When are we to discover them? How are we to know them if we do find them? What –'

"He stopped me at once:

"'One thing at a time!' he said quietly. 'Your first question contains all the rest. Where are these lamps? I shall tell you: In the tomb!'

"'In the tomb!' I repeated in surprise. 'Why you and I searched the place ourselves from end to end; and there was not a sign of a lamp. Not a sign of anything remaining when we came away the first time; or on the second, except the bodies of the Arabs.'

"Whilst I was speaking, he had uncoiled some large sheets of paper which he had brought in his hand from his own room. These he spread out on the great table, keeping their edges down with books and weights. I knew them at a glance; they were the careful copies which he had made of our first transcripts from the writing in the tomb. When he had all ready, he turned to me and said slowly:

"'Do you remember wondering, when we examined the tomb, at the lack of one thing which is usually found in such a tomb?'

"'Yes! There was no serdab.'

"The serdab, I may perhaps explain," said Mr. Corbeck to me, "is a sort of niche built or hewn in the wall of a tomb. Those which have as yet been examined bear no inscriptions, and contain only effigies of the dead for whom the tomb was made." Then he went on with his narrative:

"Trelawny, when he saw that I had caught his meaning, went on speaking with something of his old enthusiasm:

"'I have come to the conclusion that there must be a serdab – a secret one. We were dull not to have thought of it before. We might have known that the maker of such a tomb – a woman, who had shown in other ways such a sense of beauty and completeness, and who had finished every detail with a feminine richness of elaboration – would not have neglected such an architectural feature. Even if it had not its own special significance in ritual, she would have had it as an adornment. Others had had it, and she liked her own work to be complete. Depend upon it, there was – there is – a serdab; and that in it, when it is discovered, we shall find the lamps. Of course, had we known then what we now know or at all events surmise, that there were lamps, we might have suspected some hidden spot, some cachet. I am going to ask you to go out to Egypt again; to seek the tomb; to find the serdab; and to bring back the lamps!'"

"'And if I find there is no serdab; or if discovering it I find no lamps in it, what then?' He smiled grimly with that saturnine smile of his, so rarely seen for years past, as he spoke slowly:

"'Then you will have to hustle till you find them!'

"'Good!' I said. He pointed to one of the sheets.

"'Here are the transcripts from the Chapel at the south and the east. I have been looking over the writings again; and I find that in seven places round this corner are the symbols of the constellation which we call the Plough, which Queen Tera held to rule her birth and her destiny. I have examined them carefully, and I notice that they are all representations of the grouping of the stars, as the constellation appears in different parts of the heavens. They are all astronomically correct; and as in the real sky the Pointers indicate the Pole Star, so these all point to one spot in the wall where usually the serdab is to be found!'

"'Bravo!' I shouted, for such a piece of reasoning demanded applause. He seemed pleased as he went on:

"'When you are in the tomb, examine this spot. There is probably some spring or mechanical contrivance for opening the receptacle. What it may be, there is no use guessing. You will know what best to do, when you are on the spot.'

"I started the next week for Egypt; and never rested till I stood again in the tomb. I had found some of our old following; and was fairly well provided with help. The country was now in a condition very different to that in which it had been sixteen years before; there was no need for troops or armed men.

"I climbed the rock face alone. There was no difficulty, for in that fine climate the woodwork of the ladder was still dependable. It was easy to see that in the years that had elapsed there had been other visitors to the tomb; and my heart sank within me when I thought that some of them might by chance have come across the secret place. It would be a bitter discovery indeed to find that they had forestalled me; and that my journey had been in vain.

"The bitterness was realised when I lit my torches, and passed between the seven-sided columns to the Chapel of the tomb.

"There, in the very spot where I had expected to find it, was the opening of a serdab. And the serdab was empty.

"But the Chapel was not empty; for the dried-up body of a man in Arab dress lay close under the opening, as though he had been stricken down. I examined all round the walls to see if Trelawny's surmise was correct; and I found that in all the positions of the stars as given, the Pointers of the Plough indicated a spot to the left hand, or south side, of the opening of the serdab, where was a single star in gold.

"I pressed this, and it gave way. The stone which had marked the front of the serdab, and which lay back against the wall within, moved slightly. On further examining the other side of the opening, I found a similar spot, indicated by other representations of the constellation; but this was itself a figure of the seven stars, and each was wrought in burnished gold. I pressed each star in turn; but without result. Then it struck me that if the opening spring was on the left, this on the right might have been intended for the simultaneous pressure of all the stars by one hand of seven fingers. By using both my hands, I managed to effect this.

"With a loud click, a metal figure seemed to dart from close to the opening of the serdab; the stone slowly swung back to its place, and shut with a click. The glimpse which I had of the descending figure appalled me for the moment. It was like that grim guardian which, according to the Arabian historian Ibn Abd Alhokin, the builder of the Pyramids, King Saurid Ibn Salhouk placed in the Western Pyramid to defend its treasure: 'A marble figure, upright, with lance in hand; with on his head a serpent wreathed. When any approached, the serpent would bite him on one side, and twining about his throat and killing him, would return again to his place.'

"I knew well that such a figure was not wrought to pleasantry; and that to brave it was no child's play. The dead Arab at my feet was proof of what could be done! So I examined again along the wall; and found here and there chippings as if someone had been tapping with a heavy hammer. This then had been what happened: The grave-robber, more expert at his work than we had been, and suspecting the presence of a hidden serdab, had made essay to find it. He had struck the spring by chance; had released the avenging 'Treasurer', as the Arabian writer designated him. The issue spoke for itself. I got a piece of wood, and, standing at a safe distance, pressed with the end of it upon the star.

"Instantly the stone flew back. The hidden figure within darted forward and thrust out its lance. Then it rose up and disappeared. I thought I might now safely press on the seven stars; and did so. Again the stone rolled back; and the 'Treasurer' flashed by to his hidden lair.

"I repeated both experiments several times; with always the same result. I should have liked to examine the mechanism of that figure of such malignant mobility; but it was not possible without such tools as could not easily be had. It might be necessary to cut into a whole section of the rock. Some day I hope to go back, properly equipped, and attempt it.

"Perhaps you do not know that the entrance to a serdab is almost always very narrow; sometimes a hand can hardly be inserted. Two things I learned from this serdab. The first was that the lamps, if lamps at all there had been, could not have been of large size; and secondly, that they would be in some way associated with Hathor, whose symbol, the hawk in a square with the right top corner forming a smaller square, was cut in relief on the wall within, and coloured the bright vermilion which we had found on the Stele. Hathor is the goddess who in Egyptian mythology answers to Venus of the Greeks, in as far as she is the presiding deity of beauty and pleasure. In the Egyptian mythology, however, each God has many forms; and in some aspects Hathor has to do with the idea of resurrection. There are seven forms or variants of the Goddess; why should not these correspond in some way to the seven lamps! That there had been such lamps, I was convinced. The first grave-robber had met his death; the second had found the contents of the serdab. The first attempt had been made years since; the state of the body proved this. I had no clue to the second attempt. It might have been long ago; or it might have been recently. If, however, others had been to the tomb, it was probable that the lamps had been taken long ago. Well! All the more difficult would be my search; for undertaken it must be!

"That was nearly three years ago; and for all that time I have been like the man in the *Arabian Nights*, seeking old lamps, not for new, but for cash. I dared not say what I was looking for, or attempt to give any description; for such would have defeated my purpose. But I had in my own mind at the start a vague idea of what I must find. In process of time this grew more and more clear; till at last I almost overshot my mark by searching for something which might have been wrong.

"The disappointments I suffered, and the wild-goose chases I made, would fill a volume; but I persevered. At last, not two months ago, I was shown by an old dealer in Mossul one lamp such as I had looked for. I had been tracing it for nearly a year, always suffering disappointment, but always buoyed up to further endeavour by a growing hope that I was on the track.

"I do not know how I restrained myself when I realised that, at last, I was at least close to success. I was skilled, however, in the finesse of Eastern trade; and the Jew-Arab-Portugee trader met his match. I wanted to see all his stock before buying; and one by one he produced, amongst masses of rubbish, seven different lamps. Each of them had a distinguishing mark; and each and all was some form of the symbol of Hathor. I think I shook the imperturbability of my swarthy friend by the magnitude of my purchases; for in order to prevent him guessing what form of goods I sought, I nearly cleared out his shop. At the end he nearly wept, and said I had ruined him; for now he had nothing to sell. He would have torn his hair had he known what price I should ultimately have given for some of his stock, that perhaps he valued least.

"I parted with most of my merchandise at normal price as I hurried home. I did not dare to give it away, or even lose it, lest I should incur suspicion. My burden was far too precious to be risked by any foolishness now. I got on as fast as it is possible to travel in such countries; and arrived in London with only the lamps and certain portable curios and papyri which I had picked up on my travels.

"Now, Mr. Ross, you know all I know; and I leave it to your discretion how much, if any of it, you will tell Miss Trelawny."

As he finished a clear young voice said behind us:

"What about Miss Trelawny? She is here!"

We turned, startled; and looked at each other inquiringly. Miss Trelawny stood n the doorway. We did not know how long she had been present, or how much she had heard.

Chapter XIII
Awaking from the Trance

THE FIRST UNEXPECTED WORDS may always startle a hearer; but when the shock is over, the listener's reason has asserted itself, and he can judge of the manner, as well as of the matter, of speech. Thus it was on this occasion. With intelligence now alert, I could not doubt of the simple sincerity of Margaret's next question.

"What have you two men been talking about all this time, Mr. Ross? I suppose, Mr. Corbeck has been telling you all his adventures in finding the lamps. I hope you will tell me too, some day, Mr. Corbeck; but that must not be till my poor Father is better. He would like, I am sure, to tell me all about these things himself; or to be present when I heard them." She glanced sharply from one to the other. "Oh, that was what you were saying as I came in? All right! I shall wait; but I hope it won't be long. The continuance of Father's condition is, I feel, breaking me down. A little while ago I felt that my nerves were giving out; so I determined to go out for a walk in the Park. I am sure it will do me good. I want you, if you will, Mr. Ross, to be with Father whilst I am away. I shall feel secure then."

I rose with alacrity, rejoicing that the poor girl was going out, even for half an hour. She was looking terribly wearied and haggard; and the sight of her pale cheeks made my heart ache. I went to the sick-room; and sat down in my usual place. Mrs. Grant was then on duty; we had not found it necessary to have more than one person in the room during the day. When I came in, she took occasion to go about some household duty. The blinds were up, but the north aspect of the room softened the hot glare of the sunlight without.

I sat for a long time thinking over all that Mr. Corbeck had told me; and weaving its wonders into the tissue of strange things which had come to pass since I had entered the house. At times I was inclined to doubt; to doubt everything and every one; to doubt even the evidences of my own five senses. The warnings of the skilled detective kept coming back to my mind. He had put down Mr. Corbeck as a clever liar, and a confederate of Miss Trelawny. Of Margaret! That settled it! Face to face with such a proposition as that, doubt vanished. Each time when her image, her name, the merest thought of her, came before my mind, each event stood out stark as a living fact. My life upon her faith!

I was recalled from my reverie, which was fast becoming a dream of love, in a startling manner. A voice came from the bed; a deep, strong, masterful voice. The first note of it called up like a clarion my eyes and my ears. The sick man was awake and speaking!

"Who are you? What are you doing here?"

Whatever ideas any of us had ever formed of his waking, I am quite sure that none of us expected to see him start up all awake and full master of himself. I was so surprised that I answered almost mechanically:

"Ross is my name. I have been watching by you!" He looked surprised for an instant, and then I could see that his habit of judging for himself came into play.

"Watching by me! How do you mean? Why watching by me?" His eye had now lit on his heavily bandaged wrist. He went on in a different tone; less aggressive, more genial, as of one accepting facts:

"Are you a doctor?" I felt myself almost smiling as I answered; the relief from the long pressure of anxiety regarding his life was beginning to tell:

"No, sir!"

"Then why are you here? If you are not a doctor, what are you?" His tone was again more dictatorial. Thought is quick; the whole train of reasoning on which my answer must be based flooded through my brain before the words could leave my lips. Margaret! I must think of Margaret! This was her father, who as yet knew nothing of me; even of my very existence. He would be naturally curious, if not anxious, to know why I amongst men had been chosen as his daughter's friend on the occasion of his illness. Fathers are naturally a little jealous in such matters as a daughter's choice, and in the undeclared state of my love for Margaret I must do nothing which could ultimately embarrass her.

"I am a Barrister. It is not, however, in that capacity I am here; but simply as a friend of your daughter. It was probably her knowledge of my being a lawyer which first determined her to ask me to come when she thought you had been murdered. Afterwards she was good enough to consider me to be a friend, and to allow me to remain in accordance with your expressed wish that someone should remain to watch."

Mr. Trelawny was manifestly a man of quick thought, and of few words. He gazed at me keenly as I spoke, and his piercing eyes seemed to read my thought. To my relief he said no more on the subject just then, seeming to accept my words in simple faith. There was evidently in his own mind some cause for the acceptance deeper than my own knowledge. His eyes flashed, and there was an unconscious movement of the mouth – it could hardly be called a twitch – which betokened satisfaction. He was following out some train of reasoning in his own mind. Suddenly he said:

"She thought I had been murdered! Was that last night?"

"No! four days ago." He seemed surprised. Whilst he had been speaking the first time he had sat up in bed; now he made a movement as though he would jump out. With an effort, however, he restrained himself; leaning back on his pillows he said quietly:

"Tell me all about it! All you know! Every detail! Omit nothing! But stay; first lock the door! I want to know, before I see anyone, exactly how things stand."

Somehow his last words made my heart leap. "Anyone!" He evidently accepted me, then, as an exception. In my present state of feeling for his daughter, this was a comforting thought. I felt exultant as I went over to the door and softly turned the key. When I came back I found him sitting up again. He said:

"Go on!"

Accordingly, I told him every detail, even of the slightest which I could remember, of what had happened from the moment of my arrival at the house. Of course I said nothing of my feeling towards Margaret, and spoke only concerning those things already within his own knowledge. With regard to Corbeck, I simply said that he had brought back some lamps of which he had been in quest. Then I proceeded to tell him fully of their loss, and of their re-discovery in the house.

He listened with a self-control which, under the circumstances, was to me little less than marvellous. It was impassiveness, for at times his eyes would flash or blaze, and the strong fingers of his uninjured hand would grip the sheet, pulling it into far-extending wrinkles. This was most noticeable when I told him of the return of Corbeck, and the finding of the lamps in the boudoir. At times he spoke, but only a few words, and as if unconsciously in emotional comment. The mysterious parts, those which had most puzzled us, seemed to have no special interest for him; he seemed to know them already. The utmost concern he showed was when I told him of Daw's shooting. His muttered comment: "stupid ass!" together with a quick glance across the room at the injured cabinet, marked the measure of his disgust. As I told him of his daughter's harrowing anxiety for him, of her unending care and devotion, of the tender love which she had shown, he seemed much moved. There was a sort of veiled surprise in his unconscious whisper:

"Margaret! Margaret!"

When I had finished my narration, bringing matters up to the moment when Miss Trelawny had gone out for her walk – I thought of her as "Miss Trelawny', not as 'Margaret' now, in the presence of her father – he remained silent for quite a long time. It was probably two or three minutes; but it seemed interminable. All at once he turned and said to me briskly:

"Now tell me all about yourself!" This was something of a floorer; I felt myself grow red-hot. Mr. Trelawny's eyes were upon me; they were now calm and inquiring, but never ceasing in their soul-searching scrutiny. There was just a suspicion of a smile on the mouth which, though it added to my embarrassment, gave me a certain measure of relief. I was, however, face to face with difficulty; and the habit of my life stood me in good stead. I looked him straight in the eyes as I spoke:

"My name, as I told you, is Ross, Malcolm Ross. I am by profession a Barrister. I was made a Q.C. in the last year of the Queen's reign. I have been fairly successful in my work." To my relief he said:

"Yes, I know. I have always heard well of you! Where and when did you meet Margaret?"

"First at the Hay's in Belgrave Square, ten days ago. Then at a picnic up the river with Lady Strathconnell. We went from Windsor to Cookham. Mar– Miss Trelawny was in my boat. I scull a little, and I had my own boat at Windsor. We had a good deal of conversation – naturally."

"Naturally!" there was just a suspicion of something sardonic in the tone of acquiescence; but there was no other intimation of his feeling. I began to think that as I was in the presence of a strong man, I should show something of my own strength. My friends, and sometimes my opponents, say that I am a strong man. In my present circumstances, not to be absolutely truthful would be to be weak. So I stood up to the difficulty before me; always bearing in mind, however, that my words might affect Margaret's happiness through her love for her father. I went on:

"In conversation at a place and time and amid surroundings so pleasing, and in solitude inviting to confidence, I got a glimpse of her inner life. Such a glimpse as a man of my years and experience may get from a young girl!" The father's face grew graver as I went on; but he said nothing. I was committed now to a definite line of speech, and went on with such mastery of my mind as I could exercise. The occasion might be fraught with serious consequences to me too.

"I could not but see that there was over her spirit a sense of loneliness which was habitual to her. I thought I understood it; I am myself an only child. I ventured to encourage her to speak to me freely; and was happy enough to succeed. A sort of confidence became established between us." There was something in the father's face which made me add hurriedly:

"Nothing was said by her, sir, as you can well imagine, which was not right and proper. She only told me in the impulsive way of one longing to give voice to thoughts long carefully concealed, of her yearning to be closer to the father whom she loved; more en rapport with him; more in his confidence; closer within the circle of his sympathies. Oh, believe me, sir, that it was all good! All that a father's heart could hope or wish for! It was all loyal! That she spoke it to me was perhaps because I was almost a stranger with whom there was no previous barrier to confidence."

Here I paused. It was hard to go on; and I feared lest I might, in my zeal, do Margaret a disservice. The relief of the strain came from her father.

"And you?"

"Sir, Miss Trelawny is very sweet and beautiful! She is young; and her mind is like crystal! Her sympathy is a joy! I am not an old man, and my affections were not engaged. They never had been till then. I hope I may say as much, even to a father!" My eyes involuntarily dropped. When I raised them again Mr. Trelawny was still gazing at me keenly. All the kindliness of his nature seemed to wreath itself in a smile as he held out his hand and said:

"Malcolm Ross, I have always heard of you as a fearless and honourable gentleman. I am glad my girl has such a friend! Go on!"

My heart leaped. The first step to the winning of Margaret's father was gained. I dare say I was somewhat more effusive in my words and my manner as I went on. I certainly felt that way.

"One thing we gain as we grow older: to use our age judiciously! I have had much experience. I have fought for it and worked for it all my life; and I felt that I was justified in using it. I ventured to ask Miss Trelawny to count on me as a friend; to let me serve her should occasion arise. She promised me that she would. I had little idea that my chance of serving her should come so soon or in such a way; but that very night you were stricken down. In her desolation and anxiety she sent for me!" I paused. He continued to look at me as I went on:

"When your letter of instructions was found, I offered my services. They were accepted, as you know."

"And these days, how did they pass for you?" The question startled me. There was in it something of Margaret's own voice and manner; something so greatly resembling her lighter moments that it brought out all the masculinity in me. I felt more sure of my ground now as I said:

"These days, sir, despite all their harrowing anxiety, despite all the pain they held for the girl whom I grew to love more and more with each passing hour, have been the happiest of my life!" He kept silence for a long time; so long that, as I waited for him to speak, with my heart beating, I began to wonder if my frankness had been too effusive. At last he said:

"I suppose it is hard to say so much vicariously. Her poor mother should have heard you; it would have made her heart glad!" Then a shadow swept across his face; and he went on more hurriedly.

"But are you quite sure of all this?"

"I know my own heart, sir; or, at least, I think I do!"

"No! no!" he answered, "I don't mean you. That is all right! But you spoke of my girl's affection for me ...and yet...! And yet she has been living here, in my house, a whole year.... Still, she spoke to you of her loneliness – her desolation. I never – it grieves me to say it, but it is true – I never saw sign of such affection towards myself in all the year!..." His voice trembled away into sad, reminiscent introspection.

"Then, sir," I said, "I have been privileged to see more in a few days than you in her whole lifetime!" My words seemed to call him up from himself; and I thought that it was with pleasure as well as surprise that he said:

"I had no idea of it. I thought that she was indifferent to me. That what seemed like the neglect of her youth was revenging itself on me. That she was cold of heart.... It is a joy unspeakable to me that her mother's daughter loves me too!" Unconsciously he sank back upon his pillow, lost in memories of the past.

How he must have loved her mother! It was the love of her mother's child, rather than the love of his own daughter, that appealed to him. My heart went out to him in a great wave of sympathy and kindliness. I began to understand. To understand the passion of these two great, silent, reserved natures, that successfully concealed the burning hunger for the other's love! It did not surprise me when presently he murmured to himself:

"Margaret, my child! Tender, and thoughtful, and strong, and true, and brave! Like her dear mother! like her dear mother!"

And then to the very depths of my heart I rejoiced that I had spoken so frankly. Presently Mr. Trelawny said:

"Four days! The sixteenth! Then this is the twentieth of July?" I nodded affirmation; he went on:

"So I have been lying in a trance for four days. It is not the first time. I was in a trance once under strange conditions for three days; and never even suspected it till I was told of the lapse of time. I shall tell you all about it some day, if you care to hear."

That made me thrill with pleasure. That he, Margaret's father, would so take me into his confidence made it possible.... The business-like, every-day alertness of his voice as he spoke next quite recalled me:

"I had better get up now. When Margaret comes in, tell her yourself that I am all right. It will avoid any shock! And will you tell Corbeck that I would like to see him as soon as I can. I want to see those lamps, and hear all about them!"

His attitude towards me filled me with delight. There was a possible father-in-law aspect that would have raised me from a death-bed. I was hurrying away to carry out his wishes; when, however, my hand was on the key of the door, his voice recalled me:

"Mr. Ross!"

I did not like to hear him say 'Mr.' After he knew of my friendship with his daughter he had called me Malcolm Ross; and this obvious return to formality not only pained, but filled me with apprehension. It must be something about Margaret. I thought of her as 'Margaret' and not as 'Miss Trelawny', now that there was danger of losing her. I know now what I felt then: that I was determined to fight for her rather than lose her. I came back, unconsciously holding myself erect. Mr. Trelawny, the keen observer of men, seemed to read my thought; his face, which was set in a new anxiety, relaxed as he said:

"Sit down a minute; it is better that we speak now than later. We are both men, and men of the world. All this about my daughter is very new to me, and very sudden; and I want to know exactly how and where I stand. Mind, I am making no objection; but as a father I have duties which are grave, and may prove to be painful. I – I" – he seemed slightly at a loss how to begin, and this gave me hope – "I suppose I am to take it, from what you have said to me of your feelings towards my girl, that it is in your mind to be a suitor for her hand, later on?" I answered at once:

"Absolutely! Firm and fixed; it was my intention the evening after I had been with her on the river, to seek you, of course after a proper and respectful interval, and to ask you if I might approach her on the subject. Events forced me into closer relationship more quickly than I had to hope would be possible; but that first purpose has remained fresh in my heart, and has grown in intensity, and multiplied itself with every hour which has passed since then." His face seemed to soften as he looked at me; the memory of his own youth was coming back to him instinctively. After a pause he said:

"I suppose I may take it, too, Malcolm Ross" – the return to the familiarity of address swept through me with a glorious thrill – "that as yet you have not made any protestation to my daughter?"

"Not in words, sir." The *arriere pensee* of my phrase struck me, not by its own humour, but through the grave, kindly smile on the father's face. There was a pleasant sarcasm in his comment:

"Not in words! That is dangerous! She might have doubted words, or even disbelieved them."

I felt myself blushing to the roots of my hair as I went on:

"The duty of delicacy in her defenceless position; my respect for her father – I did not know you then, sir, as yourself, but only as her father – restrained me. But even had not these barriers existed, I should not have dared in the presence of such grief and anxiety to have declared myself. Mr. Trelawny, I assure you on my word of honour that your daughter and I are as yet, on her part, but friends and nothing more!" Once again he held out his hands, and we clasped each other warmly. Then he said heartily:

"I am satisfied, Malcolm Ross. Of course, I take it that until I have seen her and have given you permission, you will not make any declaration to my daughter – in words," he added, with an indulgent smile. But his face became stern again as he went on:

"Time presses; and I have to think of some matters so urgent and so strange that I dare not lose an hour. Otherwise I should not have been prepared to enter, at so short a notice and to so new a friend, on the subject of my daughter's settlement in life, and of her future happiness." There was a dignity and a certain proudness in his manner which impressed me much.

"I shall respect your wishes, sir!" I said as I went back and opened the door. I heard him lock it behind me.

When I told Mr. Corbeck that Mr. Trelawny had quite recovered, he began to dance about like a wild man. But he suddenly stopped, and asked me to be careful not to draw any inferences, at all events at first, when in the future speaking of the finding of the lamps, or of the first visits to the tomb. This was in case Mr. Trelawny should speak to me on the subject; "as, of course, he will," he added, with a sidelong look at me which meant knowledge of the affairs of my heart. I agreed to this, feeling that it was quite right. I did not quite understand why; but I knew that Mr. Trelawny was a peculiar man. In no case could one make a mistake by being reticent. Reticence is a quality which a strong man always respects.

The manner in which the others of the house took the news of the recovery varied much. Mrs. Grant wept with emotion; then she hurried off to see if she could do anything personally, and to set the house in order for 'Master', as she always called him. The Nurse's face fell: she was deprived of an interesting case. But the disappointment was only momentary; and she rejoiced that the trouble was over. She was ready to come to the patient the moment she should be wanted; but in the meantime she occupied herself in packing her portmanteau.

I took Sergeant Daw into the study, so that we should be alone when I told him the news. It surprised even his iron self-control when I told him the method of the waking. I was myself surprised in turn by his first words:

"And how did he explain the first attack? He was unconscious when the second was made."

Up to that moment the nature of the attack, which was the cause of my coming to the house, had never even crossed my mind, except when I had simply narrated the various occurrences in sequence to Mr. Trelawny. The Detective did not seem to think much of my answer:

"Do you know, it never occurred to me to ask him!" The professional instinct was strong in the man, and seemed to supersede everything else.

"That is why so few cases are ever followed out," he said, "unless our people are in them. Your amateur detective neer hunts down to the death. As for ordinary people, the moment things begin to mend, and the strain of suspense is off them, they drop the matter in hand. It is like sea-sickness," he added philosophically after a pause; "the moment you touch the shore you never give it a thought, but run off to the buffet to feed! Well, Mr. Ross, I'm glad the case is over; for over it is, so far as I am concerned. I suppose that Mr. Trelawny knows his own business; and that now he is well again, he will take it up himself. Perhaps, however, he will not do anything. As he seemed to expect something to happen, but did not ask for protection from the police in any way, I take it that he don't want them to interfere with an eye to punishment. We'll be told officially, I suppose, that it was an accident, or sleep-walking, or something of the kind, to satisfy the conscience of our Record Department; and that will be the end. As for me, I tell you frankly, sir, that it will be the saving of me. I verily believe was beginning to get dotty over it all. There were too many mysteries, that aren't in my line, for me to be really satisfied as to either facts or the causes of them. Now I'll be able to wash my hands of it, and get back to clean, wholesome, criminal work. Of course, sir, I'll be glad to know if you ever do light on a cause of any kind. And I'll be grateful if you can ever tell me how the man was dragged out of bed when the cat bit him, and who used the knife the second time. For master Silvio could never have done it by himself. But there! I keep thinking of it still. I must look out and keep a check on myself, or I shall think of it when I have to keep my mind on other things!"

When Margaret returned from her walk, I met her in the hall. She was still pale and sad; somehow, I had expected to see her radiant after her walk. The moment she saw me her eyes brightened, and she looked at me keenly.

"You have some good news for me?" she said. "Is Father better?"

"He is! Why did you think so?"

"I saw it in your face. I must go to him at once." She was hurrying away when I stopped her.

"He said he would send for you the moment he was dressed."

"He said he would send for me!" she repeated in amazement. "Then he is awake again, and conscious? I had no idea he was so well as that! O Malcolm!"

She sat down on the nearest chair and began to cry. I felt overcome myself. The sight of her joy and emotion, the mention of my own name in such a way and at such a time, the rush of glorious possibilities all coming together, quite unmanned me. She saw my emotion, and seemed to understand. She put out her hand. I held it hard, and kissed it. Such moments as these, the opportunities of lovers, are gifts of the gods. Up to this instant, though I knew I loved her, and though I believed she returned my affection, I had had only hope. Now, however, the self-surrender manifest in her willingness to let me squeeze her hand, the ardour of her pressure in return, and the glorious flush of love in her beautiful, deep, dark eyes as she lifted them to mine were all the eloquences which the most impatient or exacting lover could expect or demand.

No word was spoken; none was needed. Even had I not been pledged to verbal silence, words would have been poor and dull to express what we felt. Hand in hand like two little children, we went up the staircase and waited on the landing, till the summons from Mr. Trelawny should come.

I whispered in her ear – it was nicer than speaking aloud and at a greater distance – how her father had awakened, and what he had said; and all that had passed between us, except when she herself had been the subject of conversation.

Presently a bell rang from the room. Margaret slipped from me, and looked back with warning finger on lip. She went over to her father's door and knocked softly.

"Come in!" said the strong voice.

"It is I, Father!" The voice was tremulous with love and hope.

There was a quick step inside the room; the door was hurriedly thrown open, and in an instant Margaret, who had sprung forward, was clasped in her father's arms. There was little speech; only a few broken phrases.

"Father! Dear, dear Father!"

"My child! Margaret! My dear, dear child!"

"O Father, Father! At last! At last!"

Here the father and daughter went into the room together, and the door closed.

Chapter XIV
The Birth-Mark

DURING MY WAITING for the summons to Mr. Trelawny's room, which I knew would come, the time was long and lonely. After the first few moments of emotional happiness at Margaret's joy, I somehow felt apart and alone; and for a little time the selfishness of a lover possessed me. But it was not for long. Margaret's happiness was all to me; and in the conscious sense of it I lost my baser self. Margaret's last words as the door closed on them gave the key to the whole situation, as it had been and as it was. These two proud, strong people, though father and daughter, had only come to know each other when the girl was grown up. Margaret's nature was of that kind which matures early.

The pride and strength of each, and the reticence which was their corollary, made a barrier at the beginning. Each had respected the other's reticence too much hereafter; and the misunderstanding grew to habit. And so these two loving hearts, each of which yearned for sympathy from the other, were kept apart. But now all was well, and in my heart of hearts I rejoiced that at last Margaret was happy. Whilst I was still musing on the subject, and dreaming dreams of a personal nature, the door was opened, and Mr. Trelawny beckoned to me.

"Come in, Mr. Ross!" he said cordially, but with a certain formality which I dreaded. I entered the room, and he closed the door again. He held out his hand, and I put mine in it. He did not let it go, but still held it as he drew me over toward his daughter. Margaret looked from me to him, and back again; and her eyes fell. When I was close to her, Mr. Trelawny let go my hand, and, looking his daughter straight in the face, said:

"If things are as I fancy, we shall not have any secrets between us. Malcolm Ross knows so much of my affairs already, that I take it he must either let matters stop where they are and go away in silence, or else he must know more. Margaret! Are you willing to let Mr. Ross see your wrist?"

She threw one swift look of appeal in his eyes; but even as she did so she seemed to make up her mind. Without a word she raised her right hand, so that the bracelet of spreading wings which covered the wrist fell back, leaving the flesh bare. Then an icy chill shot through me.

On her wrist was a thin red jagged line, from which seemed to hang red stains like drops of blood!

She stood there, a veritable figure of patient pride.

Oh! but she looked proud! Through all her sweetness, all her dignity, all her high-souled negation of self which I had known, and which never seemed more marked than now – through all the fire that seemed to shine from the dark depths of her eyes into my very soul, pride shone conspicuously. The pride that has faith; the pride that is born of conscious purity; the pride of a veritable queen of Old Time, when to be royal was to be the first and greatest and bravest in all high things. As we stood thus for some seconds, the deep, grave voice of her father seemed to sound a challenge in my ears:

"What do you say now?"

My answer was not in words. I caught Margaret's right hand in mine as it fell, and, holding it tight, whilst with the other I pushed back the golden cincture, stooped and kissed the wrist. As I looked up at her, but never letting go her hand, there was a look of joy on her face such as I dream of when I think of heaven. Then I faced her father.

"You have my answer, sir!" His strong face looked gravely sweet. He only said one word as he laid his hand on our clasped ones, whilst he bent over and kissed his daughter:

"Good!"

We were interrupted by a knock at the door. In answer to an impatient "Come in!" from Mr. Trelawny, Mr. Corbeck entered. When he saw us grouped he would have drawn back; but in an instant Mr. Trelawny had sprung forth and dragged him forward As he shook him by both hands, he seemed a transformed man. All the enthusiasm of his youth, of which Mr. Corbeck had told us, seemed to have come back to him in an instant.

"So you have got the lamps!" he almost shouted. "My reasoning was right after all Come to the library, where we will be alone, and tell me all about it! And while he does it, Ross," said he, turning to me, "do you, like a good fellow, get the key from the safe deposit, so that I may have a look at the lamps!"

Then the three of them, the daughter lovingly holding her father's arm, went into the library, whilst I hurried off to Chancery Lane.

When I returned with the key, I found them still engaged in the narrative; but Doctor Winchester, who had arrived soon after I left, was with them. Mr. Trelawny on hearing from Margaret of his great attention and kindness, and how he had, under much pressure to the contrary, steadfastly obeyed his written wishes, had asked him to remain and listen. "It will interest you, perhaps," he said, "to learn the end of the story!"

We all had an early dinner together. We sat after it a good while, and then Mr Trelawny said:

"Now, I think we had all better separate and go quietly to bed early. We may have much to talk about tomorrow; and tonight I want to think."

Doctor Winchester went away, taking, with a courteous forethought, Mr. Corbeck with him, and leaving me behind. When the others had gone Mr. Trelawny said:

"I think it will be well if you, too, will go home for tonight. I want to be quite alone with my daughter; there are many things I wish to speak of to her, and to her alone. Perhaps, even tomorrow, I will be able to tell you also of them; but in the meantime there will be less distraction to us both if we are alone in the house." I quite understood and sympathised with his feelings; but the experiences of the last few days were strong on me, and with some hesitation I said:

"But may it not be dangerous? If you knew as we do –" To my surprise Margaret interrupted me:

"There will be no danger, Malcolm. I shall be with Father!" As she spoke she clung to him in a protective way. I said no more, but stood up to go at once. Mr. Trelawny said heartily:

"Come as early as you please, Ross. Come to breakfast. After it, you and will want to have a word together." He went out of the room quietly, leaving us together. I clasped and kissed Margaret's hands, which she held out to me, and then drew her close to me, and our lips met for the first time.

I did not sleep much that night. Happiness on the one side of my bed and Anxiety on the other kept sleep away. But if I had anxious care, I had also happiness which had not equal in my life – or ever can have. The night went by so quickly that the dawn seemed to rush on me, not stealing as is its wont.

Before nine o'clock I was at Kensington. All anxiety seemed to float away like a cloud as I met Margaret, and saw that already the pallor of her face had given to the rich bloom which I knew. She told me that her father had slept well, and that he would be with us soon.

"I do believe," she whispered, "that my dear and thoughtful Father has kept back on purpose, so that I might meet you first, and alone!"

After breakfast Mr. Trelawny took us into the study, saying as he passed in: "I have asked Margaret to come too." When we were seated, he said gravely:

"I told you last night that we might have something to say to each other. I dare say that you may have thought that it was about Margaret and yourself. Isn't that so?"

"I thought so."

"Well, my boy, that is all right. Margaret and I have been talking, and I know her wishes." He held out his hand. When I wrung it, and had kissed Margaret, who drew her chair close to mine, so that we could hold hands as we listened, he went on, but with a certain hesitation – it could hardly be called nervousness – which was new to me.

"You know a good deal of my hunt after this mummy and her belongings; and I dare say you have guessed a good deal of my theories. But these at any rate I shall explain later, concisely and categorically, if it be necessary. What I want to consult you about now is this: Margaret and I disagree on one point. I am about to make an experiment; the experiment which is to crown all that I have devoted twenty years of research, and danger, and labour to prepare for. Through it we may learn things that have been hidden from the eyes and the knowledge of men for centuries; for scores of centuries. I do not want my daughter to be present; for I cannot blind myself to the fact that there may be danger in it – great danger, and of an unknown kind. I have, however, already faced very great dangers, and of an unknown kind; and so has that brave scholar who has helped me in the work. As to myself, I am willing to run any risk. For science, and history, and philosophy may benefit; and we may turn one old page of a wisdom unknown in this prosaic age. But for my daughter to run such a risk I am loth. Her young bright life is too precious to throw lightly away; now especially when she is on the very threshold of new happiness. I do not wish to see her life given, as her dear mother's was –"

He broke down for a moment, and covered his eyes with his hands. In an instant Margaret was beside him, clasping him close, and kissing him, and comforting him with loving words. Then, standing erect, with one hand on his head, she said:

"Father! Mother did not bid you stay beside her, even when you wanted to go on that journey of unknown danger to Egypt; though that country was then upset from end to end with war and the dangers that follow war. You have told me how she left you free to go as you wished; though that she thought of danger for you and and feared it for you, is proved by this!" She held up her wrist with the scar that seemed to run blood. "Now, mother's daughter does as mother would have done herself!" Then she turned to me:

"Malcolm, you know I love you! But love is trust; and you must trust me in danger as well as in joy. You and I must stand beside Father in this unknown peril. Together we shall come through it; or together we shall fail; together we shall die. That is my wish; my first wish to my husband that is to be! Do you not think that, as a daughter, I am right? Tell my Father what you think!"

She looked like a Queen stooping to plead. My love for her grew and grew. I stood up beside her; and took her hand and said:

"Mr. Trelawny! In this Margaret and I are one!"

He took both our hands and held them hard. Presently he said with deep emotion: "It is as her mother would have done!"

Mr. Corbeck and Doctor Winchester came exactly at the time appointed, and joined us in the library. Despite my great happiness I felt our meeting to be a very solemn function. For I could never forget the strange things that had been; and the idea of the strange things which might be, was with me like a cloud, pressing down on us all. From the gravity of my companions I gathered that each of them also was ruled by some such dominating thought.

Instinctively we gathered our chairs into a circle round Mr. Trelawny, who had taken the great armchair near the window. Margaret sat by him on his right, and I was next to her. Mr. Corbeck was on his left, with Doctor Winchester on the other side. After a few seconds of silence Mr. Trelawny said to Mr. Corbeck:

"You have told Doctor Winchester all up to the present, as we arranged?"

"Yes," he answered; so Mr. Trelawny said:

"And I have told Margaret, so we all know!" Then, turning to the Doctor, he asked:

"And am I to take it that you, knowing all as we know it who have followed the matter for years, wish to share in the experiment which we hope to make?" His answer was direct and uncompromising:

"Certainly! Why, when this matter was fresh to me, I offered to go on with it to the end. Now that it is of such strange interest, I would not miss it for anything which you could name. Be quite easy in your mind, Mr. Trelawny. I am a scientist and an investigator of phenomena. I have no one belonging to me or dependent on me. I am quite alone, and free to do what I like with my own – including my life!" Mr. Trelawny bowed gravely, and turning to Mr. Corbeck said:

"I have known your ideas for many years past, old friend; so I need ask you nothing. As to Margaret and Malcolm Ross, they have already told me their wishes in no uncertain way." He paused a few seconds, as though to put his thoughts or his words in order; then he began to explain his views and intentions. He spoke very carefully, seeming always to bear in mind that some of us who listened were ignorant of the very root and nature of some things touched upon, and explaining them to us as he went on:

"The experiment which is before us is to try whether or no there is any force, any reality, in the old Magic. There could not possibly be more favourable conditions for the test; and it is my own desire to do all that is possible to make the original design effective. That there is some such existing power I firmly believe. It might not be possible to create, or arrange, or organise such a power in our own time; but I take it that if in Old Time such a power existed, it may have some exceptional survival. After all, the Bible is not a myth; and we read there that the sun stood still at a man's command, and that an ass – not a human one – spoke. And if the Witch at Endor could call up to Saul the spirit of Samuel, why may not there have been others with equal powers; and why may not one among them survive? Indeed, we are told in the Book of Samuel that the Witch of Endor was only one of many, and her being consulted by Saul was a matter of chance. He only sought one among the many whom he had driven out of Israel; 'all those that had Familiar Spirits, and the Wizards.' This Egyptian Queen, Tera, who reigned nearly two thousand years before Saul, had a Familiar, and was a Wizard too. See how the priests of her time, and those after it tried to wipe out her name from the face of the earth, and put a curse over the very door of her tomb so that none might ever discover the lost name. Ay, and they succeeded so well that even Manetho, the historian of the Egyptian Kings, writing in the tenth century before Christ, with all the lore of the priesthood for forty centuries behind him, and with possibility of access to every existing record, could not even find her name. Did it strike any of you, in thinking of the late events, who or what her Familiar was?" There was an interruption, for Doctor Winchester struck one hand loudly on the other as he ejaculated:

"The cat! The mummy cat! I knew it!" Mr. Trelawny smiled over at him.

"You are right! There is every indication that the Familiar of the Wizard Queen was that cat which was mummied when she was, and was not only placed in her tomb, but was laid in the sarcophagus with her. That was what bit into my wrist, what cut me with sharp claws." He paused. Margaret's comment was a purely girlish one:

"Then my poor Silvio is acquitted! I am glad!" Her father stroked her hair and went on:

"This woman seems to have had an extraordinary foresight. Foresight far, far beyond her age and the philosophy of her time. She seems to have seen through the weakness of her own religion, and even prepared for emergence into a different world. All her aspirations were for the North, the point of the compass whence blew the cool invigorating breezes that make life a joy. From the first, her eyes seem to have been attracted to the seven stars of the Plough from the fact, as recorded in the hieroglyphics in her tomb, that at her birth a great aerolite fell, from whose heart was finally extracted that Jewel of Seven Stars which she regarded as the talisman of her life. It seems to have so far ruled her destiny that all her thought and care circled round it. The Magic Coffer, so wondrously wrought with seven sides, we learn from the same source, came from the aerolite. Seven was to her a magic number; and no wonder. With seven fingers on one hand, and seven toes on one foot. With a talisman of a rare ruby with seven stars in the same position as in that constellation which ruled her birth, each star of the seven having seven points – in itself a geological wonder – it would have been odd if she had not been attracted by it. Again, she was born, we learn in the Stele of her tomb, in the seventh month of the year – the month beginning with the Inundation of the Nile. Of which month the presiding Goddess was Hathor, the Goddess of her own house, of the Antefs of the Theban line – the Goddess who in various forms symbolises beauty, and pleasure, and resurrection. Again, in this seventh month – which, by later Egyptian astronomy began on October 28th, and ran to the 27th of our November – on the seventh day the Pointer of the Plough just rises above the horizon of the sky at Thebes.

"In a marvellously strange way, therefore, are grouped into this woman's life these various things. The number seven; the Pole Star, with the constellation of seven stars; the God of the month, Hathor, who was her own particular God, the God of her family, the Antefs of the Theban Dynasty, whose Kings' symbol it was, and whose seven forms ruled love and the delights of life and resurrection. If ever there was ground for magic; for the power of symbolism carried into mystic use; for a belief in finites spirits in an age which knew not the Living God, it is here.

"Remember, too, that this woman was skilled in all the science of her time. Her wise and cautious father took care of that, knowing that by her own wisdom she must ultimately combat the intrigues of the Hierarchy. Bear in mind that in old Egypt the science of Astronomy began and was developed to an extraordinary height; and that Astrology followed Astronomy in its progress. And it is possible that in the later developments of science with regard to light rays, we may yet find that Astrology is on a scientific basis. Our next wave of scientific thought may deal with this. I shall have something special to call your minds to on this point presently. Bear in mind also that the Egyptians knew sciences, of which today, despite all our advantages, we are profoundly ignorant. Acoustics, for instance, an exact science with the builders of the temples of Karnak, of Luxor, of the Pyramids, is today a mystery to Bell, and Kelvin, and Edison, and Marconi. Again, these old miracle-workers probably understood some practical way of using other forces, and amongst them the forces of light that at present we do not dream of. But of this matter I shall speak later. That Magic Coffer of Queen Tera is probably a magic box in more ways than one. It may – possibly it does – contain forces that we wot not of. We cannot open it; it must be closed from within. How then was it closed? It is a coffer of solid stone, of amazing hardness, more like a jewel than an ordinary marble, with a lid equally solid; and yet all is so finely wrought that the finest tool made today cannot be inserted under the flange. How was it wrought to such perfection? How was the stone so chosen that those translucent patches match the relations of the seven stars of the constellation? How is it, or from what cause, that when the starlight shines on it, it glows from within – that when I fix the lamps in similar form the glow grows greater still; and yet the box is irresponsive to ordinary light however great? I tell you that that box hides some great mystery of science. We shall find that the light will open it in some way: either by striking on some substance, sensitive in a peculiar way to its effect, or in releasing some greater power. I only trust that in our ignorance we may not so bungle things as to do harm to its mechanism; and so deprive the knowledge of our time of a lesson handed down, as by a miracle, through nearly five thousand years.

"In another way, too, there may be hidden in that box secrets which, for good or ill, may enlighten the world. We know from their records, and inferentially also, that the Egyptians studied the properties of herbs and minerals for magic purposes – white magic as well as black. We know that some of the wizards of old could induce from sleep dreams of any given kind. That this purpose was mainly effected by hypnotism, which was another art or science of Old Nile, I have little doubt. But still, they must have had a mastery of drugs that is far beyond anything we know. With our own pharmacopoeia we can, to a certain extent, induce dreams. We may even differentiate between good and bad – dreams of pleasure, or disturbing and harrowing dreams. But these old practitioners seemed to have been able to command at will any form or colour of dreaming; could work round any given subject or thought in almost any was required. In that coffer, which you have seen, may rest a very armoury of dreams. Indeed, some of the forces that lie within it may have been already used in my household." Again there was an interruption from Doctor Winchester.

"But if in your case some of these imprisoned forces were used, what set them free at the opportune time, or how? Besides, you and Mr. Corbeck were once before put into a trance for three whole days, when you were in the Queen's tomb for the second time. And then, as I gathered from Mr. Corbeck's story, the coffer was not back in the tomb, though the mummy was. Surely in both these cases there must have been some active intelligence awake, and with some other power to wield." Mr. Trelawny's answer was equally to the point:

"There was some active intelligence awake. I am convinced of it. And it wielded power which it never lacks. I believe that on both those occasions hypnotism was the power wielded."

"And wherein is that power contained? What view do you hold on the subject?" Doctor Winchester's voice vibrated with the intensity of his excitement as he leaned forward, breathing hard, and with eyes staring. Mr. Trelawny said solemnly:

"In the mummy of the Queen Tera! I was coming to that presently. Perhaps we had better wait till I clear the ground a little. What I hold is, that the preparation of that box was made for a special occasion; as indeed were all the preparations of the tomb and all belonging to it. Queen Tera did not trouble herself to guard against snakes and scorpions, in that rocky tomb cut in the sheer cliff face a hundred feet above the level of the valley, and fifty down from the summit. Her precautions were against the disturbances of human hands; against the jealousy and hatred of the priests, who, had they known of her real aims, would have tried to baffle them. From her point of view, she made all ready for the time of resurrection, whenever that might be. I gather from the symbolic pictures in the tomb that she so far differed from the belief of her time that she looked for a resurrection in the flesh. It was doubtless this that intensified the hatred of the priesthood, and gave them an acceptable cause for obliterating the very existence, present and future, of one who had outrage their theories and blasphemed their gods. All that she might require, either in the accomplishment of the resurrection or after it, were contained in that almost hermetically sealed suite of chambers in the rock. In the great sarcophagus, which as you know is of a size quite unusual even for kings, was the mummy of her familiar, the cat, which from its great size I take to be a sort of tiger-cat. In the tomb, also in a strong receptacle, were the canopic jars usually containing those internal organs which are separately embalmed, but which in this case had no such contents. So that, I take it, there was in her case a departure in embalming; and that the organs were restored to the body, each in its proper place – if, indeed, they had ever been removed. If this surmise be true, we shall find that the brain of the Queen either was never extracted in the usual way, or, if so taken out, that it was duly replaced, instead of being enclosed within the mummy wrappings. Finally, in the sarcophagus there was the Magic Coffer on which her feet rested. Mark you also, the care taken in the preservance of her power to control the elements. According to her belief, the open hand outside the wrappings controlled the Air, and the strange Jewel Stone with the shining stars controlled Fire. The symbolism inscribed on the soles of her feet gave sway over Land and Water. About the Star Stone I shall tell you later; but whilst we are speaking of the sarcophagus, mark how she guarded her secret in case of grave-wrecking or intrusion. None could open her Magic Coffer without the lamps, for we know now that ordinary light will not be effective. The great lid of the sarcophagus was not sealed down as usual, because she wished to control the air. But she hid the lamps, which in structure belong to the Magic Coffer, in a place where none could find them, except by following the secret guidance which she had prepared for only the eyes of wisdom. And even there she had guarded against chance discovery, by preparing a bolt of death for the unwary discoverer. To do this she had applied the lesson of the tradition of the avenging guard of the treasures of the pyramid, built by her great predecessor of the Fourth Dynasty of the throne of Egypt.

"You have noted, I suppose, how there were, in the case of her tomb, certain deviations from the usual rules. For instance, the shaft of the Mummy Pit, which is usually filled up solid with stones and rubbish, was left open. Why was this? I take it that she had made arrangements for leaving the tomb when, after her resurrection, she should be a new woman, with a different personality, and less inured to the hardships that in her first existence she had suffered. So far as we can judge of her intent, all things needful for her exit into the world had been thought of, even to the iron chain, described by Van Huyn, close to the door in the rock, by which she might be able to lower herself to the ground. That she expected a long period to elapse was shown in the choice of material. An ordinary rope would be rendered weaker or unsafe in process of time, but she imagined, and rightly, that the iron would endure.

"What her intentions were when once she trod the open earth afresh we do not know, and we never shall, unless her own dead lips can soften and speak."

Chapter XV
The Purpose of Queen Tera

"NOW, AS TO THE Star Jewel! This she manifestly regarded as the greatest of her treasures. On it she had engraven words which none of her time dared to speak.

"In the old Egyptian belief it was held that there were words, which, if used properly – for the method of speaking them was as important as the words themselves – could command the Lords of the Upper and the Lower Worlds. The 'hekau', or word of power, was all-important in certain ritual. On the Jewel of Seven Stars, which, as you know, is carved into the image of a scarab, are graven in hieroglyphic two such hekau, one above, the other underneath. But you will understand better when you see it! Wait here! Do not stir!"

As he spoke, he rose and left the room. A great fear for him came over me; but I was in some strange way relieved when I looked at Margaret. Whenever there had been any possibility of danger to her father, she had shown great fear for him; now she was calm and placid. I said nothing, but waited.

In two or three minutes, Mr. Trelawny returned. He held in his hand a little golden box. This, as he resumed his seat, he placed before him on the table. We all leaned forward as he opened it.

On a lining of white satin lay a wondrous ruby of immense size, almost as big as the top joint of Margaret's little finger. It was carven – it could not possibly have been its natural shape, but jewels do not show the working of the tool – into the shape of a scarab, with its wings folded, and its legs and feelers pressed back to its sides. Shining through its wondrous 'pigeon's blood' colour were seven different stars, each of seven points, in such position that they reproduced exactly the figure of the Plough. There could be no possible mistake as to this in the mind of anyone who had ever noted the constellation. On it were some hieroglyphic figures, cut with the most exquisite precision, as I could see when it came to my turn to use the magnifying-glass, which Mr. Trelawny took from his pocket and handed to us.

When we all had seen it fully, Mr. Trelawny turned it over so that it rested on its back in a cavity made to hold it in the upper half of the box. The reverse was no less wonderful than the upper, being carved to resemble the under side of the beetle. It, too, had some hieroglyphic figures cut on it. Mr. Trelawny resumed his lecture as we all sat with our heads close to this wonderful jewel:

"As you see, there are two words, one on the top, the other underneath. The symbols on the top represent a single word, composed of one syllable prolonged, with its determinatives. You know, all of you, I suppose, that the Egyptian language was phonetic, and that the hieroglyphic symbol represented the sound. The first symbol here, the hoe, means 'mer', and the two pointed ellipses the prolongation of the final r: mer-r-r. The sitting figure with the hand to its face is what we call the 'determinative' of 'thought'; and the roll of papyrus that of 'abstraction'. Thus we get the word 'mer', love, in its abstract, general, and fullest sense. This is the hekau which can command the Upper World."

Margaret's face was a glory as she said in a deep, low, ringing tone:

"Oh, but it is true. How the old wonder-workers guessed at almighty Truth!" Then a hot blush swept her face, and her eyes fell. Her father smiled at her lovingly as he resumed:

"The symbolisation of the word on the reverse is simpler, though the meaning is more abstruse. The first symbol means 'men', 'abiding', and the second, 'ab', 'the heart'. So that we get 'abiding of heart', or in our own language 'patience'. And this is the hekau to control the Lower World!"

He closed the box, and motioning us to remain as we were, he went back to his room to replace the Jewel in the safe. When he had returned and resumed his seat, he went on:

"That Jewel, with its mystic words, and which Queen Tera held under her hand in the sarcophagus, was to be an important factor – probably the most important – in the working out of the act of her resurrection. From the first I seemed by a sort of instinct to realise this. I kept the Jewel within my great safe, whence none could extract it; not even Queen Tera herself with her astral body."

"Her 'astral body'? What is that, Father? What does that mean?" There was a keenness in Margaret's voice as she asked the question which surprised me a little; but Trelawny smiled a sort of indulgent parental smile, which came through his grim solemnity like sunshine through a rifted cloud, as he spoke:

"The astral body, which is a part of Buddhist belief, long subsequent to the time I speak of, and which is an accepted fact of modern mysticism, had its rise in Ancient Egypt; at least, so far as we know. It is that the gifted individual can at will, quick as thought itself, transfer his body whithersoever he chooses, by the dissolution and reincarnation of particles. In the ancient belief there were several parts of a human being. You may as well know them; so that you will understand matters relative to them or dependent on them as they occur.

"First there is the 'Ka', or 'Double', which, as Doctor Budge explains, may be defined as 'an abstract individuality of personality' which was imbued with all the characteristic attributes of the individual it represented, and possessed an absolutely independent existence. It was free to move from place to place on earth at will; and it could enter into heaven and hold converse with the gods. Then there was the Ba', or 'soul', which dwelt in the 'Ka', and had the power of becoming corporeal or incorporeal at will; 'it had both substance and form.... It had power to leave the tomb.... It could revisit the body in the tomb ... and could reincarnate it and hold converse with it.' Again there was the 'Khu', the 'spiritual intelligence', or spirit.

It took the form of 'a shining, luminous, intangible shape of the body.'... Then, again there was the 'Sekhem', or 'power' of a man, his strength or vital force personified These were the 'Khaibit', or 'shadow', the 'Ren', or 'name', the 'Khat', or 'physica body', and 'Ab', the 'heart', in which life was seated, went to the full making up o a man.

"Thus you will see, that if this division of functions, spiritual and bodily, etherea and corporeal, ideal and actual, be accepted as exact, there are all the possibilitie and capabilities of corporeal transference, guided always by an unimprisonable will or intelligence." As he paused I murmured the lines from Shelley's *Prometheus Unbound*

"The Magnus Zoroaster...
Met his own image walking in the garden."

Mr. Trelawny was not displeased. "Quite so!" he said, in his quiet way. "Shelley had a better conception of ancient beliefs than any of our poets." With a voice changed again he resumed his lecture, for so it was to some of us:

"There is another belief of the ancient Egyptian which you must bear in mind; that regarding the ushaptiu figures of Osiris, which were placed with the dead to its work in the Under World. The enlargement of this idea came to a belief that it was possible to transmit, by magical formulae, the soul and qualities of any living creature to a figure made in its image. This would give a terrible extension of power to one who held the gift of magic.

"It is from a union of these various beliefs, and their natural corollaries, that I have come to the conclusion that Queen Tera expected to be able to effect her own resurrection, when, and where, and how, she would. That she may have held before her a definite time for making her effort is not only possible but likely. I shall not stop now to explain it, but shall enter upon the subject later on. With a soul with the Gods, a spirit which could wander the earth at will, and a power of corporeal transference, or an astral body, there need be no bounds or limits to her ambition. The belief is forced upon us that for these forty or fifty centuries she lay dormant in her tomb – waiting. Waiting with that 'patience' which could rule the Gods of the Under World, for that 'love' which could command those of the Upper World. What she may have dreamt we know not; but her dream must have been broken when the Dutch explorer entered her sculptured cavern, and his follower violated the sacred privacy of her tomb by his rude outrage in the theft of her hand.

"That theft, with all that followed, proved to us one thing, however: that each part of her body, though separated from the rest, can be a central point or rallying place for the items or particles of her astral body. That hand in my room could ensure her instantaneous presence in the flesh, and its equally rapid dissolution.

"Now comes the crown of my argument. The purpose of the attack on me was to get the safe open, so that the sacred Jewel of Seven Stars could be extracted. That immense door of the safe could not keep out her astral body, which, or any part of it, could gather itself as well within as without the safe. And I doubt not that in the darkness of the night that mummied hand sought often the Talisman Jewel, and drew new inspiration from its touch. But despite all its power, the astral body could not remove the Jewel through the chinks of the safe. The Ruby is not astral; and it could only be moved in the ordinary way by the opening of the doors. To this end, the Queen used her astral body and the fierce force of her Familiar, to bring to the keyhole of the safe the master key which debarred her wish. For years I have suspected, nay, have believed as much; and I, too, guarded myself against powers of the Nether World. I, too, waited in patience till I should have gathered together all the factors required for the opening of the Magic Coffer and the resurrection of the mummied Queen!" He paused, and his daughter's voice came out sweet and clear, and full of intense feeling:

"Father, in the Egyptian belief, was the power of resurrection of a mummied body a general one, or was it limited? That is: could it achieve resurrection many times in the course of ages; or only once, and that one final?"

"There was but one resurrection," he answered. "There were some who believed that this was to be a definite resurrection of the body into the real world. But in the common belief, the Spirit found joy in the Elysian Fields, where there was plenty of food and no fear of famine. Where there was moisture and deep-rooted reeds, and all the joys that are to be expected by the people of an arid land and burning clime."

Then Margaret spoke with an earnestness which showed the conviction of her inmost soul:

"To me, then, it is given to understand what was the dream of this great and far-thinking and high-souled lady of old; the dream that held her soul in patient waiting for its realisation through the passing of all those tens of centuries. The dream of a love that might be; a love that she felt she might, even under new conditions, herself evoke. The love that is the dream of every woman's life; of the Old and of the New; Pagan or Christian; under whatever sun; in whatever rank or calling; however may have been the joy or pain of her life in other ways. Oh! I know it! I know it! I am a woman, and I know a woman's heart. What were the lack of food or the plenitude of it; what were feast or famine to this woman, born in a palace, with the shadow of the Crown of the Two Egypts on her brows! What were reedy morasses or the tinkle of running water to her whose barges could sweep the great Nile from the mountains to the sea. What were petty joys and absence of petty fears to her, the raising of whose hand could hurl armies, or draw to the water-stairs of her palaces the commerce of the world! At whose word rose temples filled with all the artistic beauty of the Times of Old which it was her aim and pleasure to restore! Under whose guidance the solid rock yawned into the sepulchre that she designed!

"Surely, surely, such a one had nobler dreams! I can feel them in my heart; I can see them with my sleeping eyes!"

As she spoke she seemed to be inspired; and her eyes had a far-away look as though they saw something beyond mortal sight. And then the deep eyes filled up with unshed tears of great emotion. The very soul of the woman seemed to speak in her voice; whilst we who listened sat entranced.

"I can see her in her loneliness and in the silence of her mighty pride, dreaming her own dream of things far different from those around her. Of some other land, far, far away under the canopy of the silent night, lit by the cool, beautiful light of the stars. A land under that Northern star, whence blew the sweet winds that cooled the feverish desert air. A land of wholesome greenery, far, far away. Where were no scheming and malignant priesthood; whose ideas were to lead to power through gloomy temples and more gloomy caverns of the dead, through an endless ritual of death! A land where love was not base, but a divine possession of the soul! Where there might be some one kindred spirit which could speak to hers through mortal lips like her own; whose being could merge with hers in a sweet communion of soul to soul, even as their breath could mingle in the ambient air! I know the feeling, for I have shared it myself. I may speak of it now, since the blessing has come into my own life. I may speak of it since it enables me to interpret the feelings, the very longing soul, of that sweet and lovely Queen, so different from her surroundings, so high above her time! Whose nature put into a word, could control the forces of the Under World; and the name of whose aspiration, though but graven on a star-lit jewel, could command all the powers in the Pantheon of the High Gods.

"And in the realisation of that dream she will surely be content to rest!"

We men sat silent, as the young girl gave her powerful interpretation of the design or purpose of the woman of old. Her every word and tone carried with it the conviction of her own belief. The loftiness of her thoughts seemed to uplift us all as we listened. Her noble words, flowing in musical cadence and vibrant with internal force, seemed to issue from some great instrument of elemental power. Even her tone was new to us all; so that we listened as to some new and strange being from a new and strange world. Her father's face was full of delight. I knew now its cause. I understood the happiness that had come into his life, on his return to the world that he knew, from that prolonged sojourn in the world of dreams. To find in his daughter, whose nature he had never till now known, such a wealth of affection, such a splendour of spiritual insight, such a scholarly imagination, such... The rest of his feeling was of hope!

The two other men were silent unconsciously. One man had had his dreaming; for the other, his dreams were to come.

For myself, I was like one in a trance. Who was this new, radiant being who had won to existence out of the mist and darkness of our fears? Love has divine possibilities for the lover's heart! The wings of the soul may expand at any time from the shoulders of the loved one, who then may sweep into angel form. I knew that in my Margaret's nature were divine possibilities of many kinds. When under the shade of the overhanging willow-tree on the river, I had gazed into the depths of her beautiful eyes, I had thenceforth a strict belief in the manifold beauties and excellences of her nature; but this soaring and understanding spirit was, indeed, a revelation. My pride, like her father's, was outside myself; my joy and rapture were complete and supreme!

When we had all got back to earth again in our various ways, Mr. Trelawny, holding his daughter's hand in his, went on with his discourse:

"Now, as to the time at which Queen Tera intended her resurrection to take place! We are in contact with some of the higher astronomical calculations in connection with true orientation. As you know, the stars shift their relative positions in the heavens; but though the real distances traversed are beyond all ordinary comprehension, the effects as we see them are small. Nevertheless, they are susceptible of measurement, not by years, indeed, but by centuries. It was by this means that Sir John Herschel arrived at the date of the building of the Great Pyramid – a date fixed by the time necessary to change the star of the true north from Draconis to the Pole Star, and since then verified by later discoveries. From the above there can be no doubt whatever that astronomy was an exact science with the Egyptians at least a thousand years before the time of Queen Tera. Now e stars that go to make up a constellation change in process of time their relative ositions, and the Plough is a notable example. The changes in the position of stars even forty centuries is so small as to be hardly noticeable by an eye not trained minute observances, but they can be measured and verified. Did you, or any of ou, notice how exactly the stars in the Ruby correspond to the position of the stars the Plough; or how the same holds with regard to the translucent places in the agic Coffer?"

We all assented. He went on:

"You are quite correct. They correspond exactly. And yet when Queen Tera was id in her tomb, neither the stars in the Jewel nor the translucent places in the Coffer orresponded to the position of the stars in the Constellation as they then were!"

We looked at each other as he paused: a new light was breaking upon us. With a ng of mastery in his voice he went on:

"Do you not see the meaning of this? Does it not throw a light on the intention of e Queen? She, who was guided by augury, and magic, and superstition, naturally ose a time for her resurrection which seemed to have been pointed out by the igh Gods themselves, who had sent their message on a thunderbolt from other orlds. When such a time was fixed by supernal wisdom, would it not be the height human wisdom to avail itself of it? Thus it is" – here his voice deepened and embled with the intensity of his feeling – "that to us and our time is given the pportunity of this wondrous peep into the old world, such as has been the privilege none other of our time; which may never be again.

"From first to last the cryptic writing and symbolism of that wondrous tomb of at wondrous woman is full of guiding light; and the key of the many mysteries lies that most wondrous Jewel which she held in her dead hand over the dead heart, hich she hoped and believed would beat again in a newer and nobler world!

"There are only loose ends now to consider. Margaret has given us the true inwardness the feeling of the other Queen!" He looked at her fondly, and stroked her hand as he id it. "For my own part I sincerely hope she is right; for in such case it will be a joy, I n sure, to all of us to assist at such a realisation of hope. But we must not go too fast, believe too much in our present state of knowledge. The voice that we hearken for omes out of times strangely other than our own; when human life counted for little, d when the morality of the time made little account of the removing of obstacles in e way to achievement of desire. We must keep our eyes fixed on the scientific side, d wait for the developments on the psychic side.

"Now, as to this stone box, which we call the Magic Coffer. As I have said, I n convinced that it opens only in obedience to some principle of light, or the xercise of some of its forces at present unknown to us. There is here much ground r conjecture and for experiment; for as yet the scientists have not thoroughly ifferentiated the kinds, and powers, and degrees of light. Without analysing rious rays we may, I think, take it for granted that there are different qualities and owers of light; and this great field of scientific investigation is almost virgin soil. e know as yet so little of natural forces, that imagination need set no bounds to its ights in considering the possibilities of the future. Within but a few years we have ade such discoveries as two centuries ago would have sent the discoverer's to the ames. The liquefaction of oxygen; the existence of radium, of helium, of polonium, argon; the different powers of Roentgen and Cathode and Bequerel rays. And as we may finally prove that there are different kinds and qualities of light, so we may find that combustion may have its own powers of differentiation; that there are qualities in some flames non-existent in others. It may be that some of the essential conditions of substance are continuous, even in the destruction of their bases. Last night I was thinking of this, and reasoning that as there are certain qualities in some oils which are not in others, so there may be certain similar or corresponding qualities or powers in the combinations of each. I suppose we have all noticed some time or other that the light of colza oil is not quite the same as that of paraffin, or that the flames of coal gas and whale oil are different. The find it so in the light-houses! All at once it occurred to me that there might be some special virtue in the oil which had been found in the jars when Queen Tera's tomb was opened. These had not been used to preserve the intestines as usual so they must have been placed there for some other purpose. I remembered that in Van Huyn's narrative he had commented on the way the jars were sealed. This was lightly, though effectually; they could be opened without force. The jars were themselves preserved in a sarcophagus which, though of immense strength and hermetically sealed, could be opened easily. Accordingly, I went at once to examine the jars. A little – a very little of the oil still remained, but it had grown thick in the two and a half centuries in which the jars had been open. Still, it was not rancid and on examining it I found it was cedar oil, and that it still exhaled something of its original aroma. This gave me the idea that it was to be used to fill the lamps Whoever had placed the oil in the jars, and the jars in the sarcophagus, knew that there might be shrinkage in process of time, even in vases of alabaster, and full allowed for it; for each of the jars would have filled the lamps half a dozen times With part of the oil remaining I made some experiments, therefore, which may give useful results. You know, Doctor, that cedar oil, which was much used in the preparation and ceremonials of the Egyptian dead, has a certain refractive power which we do not find in other oils. For instance, we use it on the lenses of our microscopes to give additional clearness of vision. Last night I put some in one of the lamps, and placed it near a translucent part of the Magic Coffer. The effect was very great; the glow of light within was fuller and more intense than I could have imagined, where an electric light similarly placed had little, if any, effect. I should have tried others of the seven lamps, but that my supply of oil ran out. This, however, is on the road to rectification. I have sent for more cedar oil, and expect to have before long an ample supply. Whatever may happen from other causes, our experiment shall not, at all events, fail from this. We shall see! We shall see!"

Doctor Winchester had evidently been following the logical process of the other's mind, for his comment was:

"I do hope that when the light is effective in opening the box, the mechanism will not be impaired or destroyed."

His doubt as to this gave anxious thought to some of us.

Chapter XVI
The Cavern

IN THE EVENING Mr. Trelawny took again the whole party into the study. When we were all attention he began to unfold his plans:

"I have come to the conclusion that for the proper carrying out of what we will call our Great Experiment we must have absolute and complete isolation. Isolation not merely for a day or two, but for as long as we may require. Here such a thing would be impossible; the needs and habits of a great city with its ingrained possibilities of interruption, would, or might, quite upset us. Telegrams, registered letters, or express messengers would alone be sufficient; but the great army of those who want to get something would make disaster certain. In addition, the occurrences of the last week have drawn police attention to this house. Even if special instructions to keep an eye on it have not been issued from Scotland Yard or the District Station, you may be sure that the individual policeman on his rounds will keep it well under observation. Besides, the servants who have discharged themselves will before long begin to talk. They must; for they have, for the sake of their own characters, to give some reason for the termination of a service which has I should say a position in the neighbourhood. The servants of the neighbours will begin to talk, and, perhaps the neighbours themselves. Then the active and intelligent Press will, with its usual zeal for the enlightenment of the public and its eye to increase of circulation, get hold of the matter. When the reporter is after us we shall not have much chance of privacy. Even if we were to bar ourselves in, we should not be free from interruption, possibly from intrusion. Either would ruin our plans, and so we must take measures to effect a retreat, carrying all our impedimenta with us. For this I am prepared. For a long time past I have foreseen such a possibility, and have made preparation for it. Of course, I had no foreknowledge of what has happened; but I knew something would, or might, happen. For more than two years past my house in Cornwall has been made ready to receive all the curios which are preserved here. When Corbeck went off on his search for the lamps I had the old house at Kyllion made ready; it is fitted with electric light all over, and all the appliances for manufacture of the light are complete. I had perhaps better tell you, for none of you, not even Margaret, knows anything of it, that the house is absolutely shut out from public access or even from view. It stands on a little rocky promontory behind a steep hill, and except from the sea cannot be seen. Of old it was fenced in by a high stone wall, for the house which it succeeded was built by an ancestor of mine in the days when a great house far away from a centre had to be prepared to defend itself. Here, then, is a place so well adapted to our needs that it might have been prepared on purpose. I shall explain it to you when we are all there. This will not be long, for already our movement is in train. I have sent word to Marvin to have all preparation for our transport ready. He is to have a special train, which is to run at night so as to avoid notice. Also a number of carts and stone-wagons, with sufficient men and appliances to take all our packing-cases to Paddington. We shall be away before the Argus-eyed Pressman is on the watch. We shall today begin our packing up; and I dare say that by tomorrow night we shall be ready. In the outhouses I have all the packing-cases which were used for bringing the things from Egypt, and I am satisfied that as they were sufficient for the journey across the desert and down the Nile to Alexandria and thence on to London, they will serve without fail between here and Kyllion. We four men, with Margaret to hand us such things as we may require, will be able to get the things packed safely; and the carrier's men will take them to the trucks.

"Today the servants go to Kyllion, and Mrs. Grant will make such arrangements as may be required. She will take a stock of necessaries with her, so that we will not attract local attention by our daily needs; and will keep us supplied with perishable food from London. Thanks to Margaret's wise and generous treatment of the servants who decided to remain, we have got a staff on which we can depend. They have been already cautioned to secrecy, so that we need not fear gossip from within. Indeed, as the servants will be in London after their preparations at Kyllion are complete, there will not be much subject for gossip, in detail at any rate.

"As, however, we should commence the immediate work of packing at once, we will leave over the after proceedings till later when we have leisure."

Accordingly we set about our work. Under Mr. Trelawny's guidance, and aided by the servants, we took from the outhouses great packing-cases. Some of these were of enormous strength, fortified by many thicknesses of wood, and by iron bands and rods with screw-ends and nuts. We placed them throughout the house, each close to the object which it was to contain. When this preliminary work had been effected, and there had been placed in each room and in the hall great masses of new hay, cotton-waste and paper, the servants were sent away. Then we set about packing.

No one, not accustomed to packing, could have the slightest idea of the amount of the amount of work involved in such a task as that in which in we were engaged. For my own part I had had a vague idea that there were a large number of Egyptian objects in Mr. Trelawny's house; but until I came to deal with them seriatim I had little idea of either their importance, the size of some of them, or of their endless number. Far into the night we worked. At times we used all the strength which we could muster on a single object; again we worked separately, but always under Mr. Trelawny's immediate direction. He himself, assisted by Margaret, kept an exact tall of each piece.

It was only when we sat down, utterly wearied, to a long-delayed supper that we began to realised that a large part of the work was done. Only a few of the packing-cases, however, were closed; for a vast amount of work still remained. We had finished some of the cases, each of which held only one of the great sarcophagi. The cases which held many objects could not be closed till all had been differentiated and packed.

I slept that night without movement or without dreams; and on our comparing notes in the morning, I found that each of the others had had the same experience.

By dinner-time next evening the whole work was complete, and all was ready for the carriers who were to come at midnight. A little before the appointed time we heard the rumble of carts; then we were shortly invaded by an army of workmen, who seemed by sheer force of numbers to move without effort, in an endless procession, all our prepared packages. A little over an hour sufficed them, and when the carts had rumbled away, we all got ready to follow them to Paddington. Silvio was of course to be taken as one of our party.

Before leaving we went in a body over the house, which looked desolate indeed. As the servants had all gone to Cornwall there had been no attempt at tidying-up; every room and passage in which we had worked, and all the stairways, were strewn with paper and waste, and marked with dirty feet.

The last thing which Mr. Trelawny did before coming away was to take from the great safe the Ruby with the Seven Stars. As he put it safely into his pocket-book Margaret, who had all at once seemed to grow deadly tired and stood beside her

ther pale and rigid, suddenly became all aglow, as though the sight of the Jewel
ad inspired her. She smiled at her father approvingly as she said:

"You are right, Father. There will not be any more trouble tonight. She will not
wreck your arrangements for any cause. I would stake my life upon it."

"She – or something – wrecked us in the desert when we had come from the
tomb in the Valley of the Sorcerer!" was the grim comment of Corbeck, who was
standing by. Margaret answered him like a flash:

"Ah! she was then near her tomb from which for thousands of years her body had
not been moved. She must know that things are different now."

"How must she know?" asked Corbeck keenly.

"If she has that astral body that Father spoke of, surely she must know! How can
she fail to, with an invisible presence and an intellect that can roam abroad even
to the stars and the worlds beyond us!" She paused, and her father said solemnly:

"It is on that supposition that we are proceeding. We must have the courage of
our convictions, and act on them – to the last!"

Margaret took his hand and held it in a dreamy kind of way as we filed out of the
house. She was holding it still when he locked the hall door, and when we moved
to the road to the gateway, whence we took a cab to Paddington.

When all the goods were loaded at the station, the whole of the workmen went
on to the train; this took also some of the stone-wagons used for carrying the
cases with the great sarcophagi. Ordinary carts and plenty of horses were to be
found at Westerton, which was our station for Kyllion. Mr. Trelawny had ordered a
sleeping-carriage for our party; as soon as the train had started we all turned into
our cubicles.

That night I slept sound. There was over me a conviction of security which was
absolute and supreme. Margaret's definite announcement: "There will not be any trouble
tonight!" seemed to carry assurance with it. I did not question it; nor did anyone else.
It was only afterwards that I began to think as to how she was so sure. The train was a
slow one, stopping many times and for considerable intervals. As Mr. Trelawny did not
wish to arrive at Westerton before dark, there was no need to hurry; and arrangements
had been made to feed the workmen at certain places on the journey. We had our own
hamper with us in the private car.

All that afternoon we talked over the Great Experiment, which seemed to have
become a definite entity in our thoughts. Mr. Trelawny became more and more
enthusiastic as the time wore on; hope was with him becoming certainty. Doctor
Winchester seemed to become imbued with some of his spirit, though at times he
would throw out some scientific fact which would either make an impasse to the
other's line of argument, or would come as an arresting shock. Mr. Corbeck, on
the other hand, seemed slightly antagonistic to the theory. It may have been that
whilst the opinions of the others advanced, his own stood still; but the effect was
an attitude which appeared negative, if not wholly one of negation.

As for Margaret, she seemed to be in some way overcome. Either it was some new
phase of feeling with her, or else she was taking the issue more seriously than she
had yet done. She was generally more or less distraite, as though sunk in a brown
study; from this she would recover herself with a start. This was usually when there
occurred some marked episode in the journey, such as stopping at a station, or
when the thunderous rumble of crossing a viaduct woke the echoes of the hills or

cliffs around us. On each such occasion she would plunge into the conversation, taking such a part in it as to show that, whatever had been her abstracted thought, her senses had taken in fully all that had gone on around her. Towards myself her manner was strange. Sometimes it was marked by a distance, half shy, half haughty, which was new to me. At other times there were moments of passion in look and gesture which almost made me dizzy with delight. Little, however, of a marked nature transpired during the journey. There was but one episode which had in it any element of alarm, but as we were all asleep at the time it did not disturb us. We only learned it from a communicative guard in the morning. Whilst running between Dawlish and Teignmouth the train was stopped by a warning given by someone who moved a torch to and fro right on the very track. The driver had found on pulling up that just ahead of the train a small landslip had taken place, some of the red earth from the high bank having fallen away. It did not however reach to the metals; and the driver had resumed his way, none too well pleased at the delay. To use his own words, the guard thought "there was too much bally caution on this 'ere line!'"

We arrived at Westerton about nine o'clock in the evening. Carts and horses were in waiting, and the work of unloading the train began at once. Our own party did not wait to see the work done, as it was in the hands of competent people. We took the carriage which was in waiting, and through the darkness of the night sped on to Kyllion.

We were all impressed by the house as it appeared in the bright moonlight. A great grey stone mansion of the Jacobean period; vast and spacious, standing high over the sea on the very verge of a high cliff. When we had swept round the curve of the avenue cut through the rock, and come out on the high plateau on which the house stood, the crash and murmur of waves breaking against rock far below us came with an invigorating breath of moist sea air. We understood then in an instant how well we were shut out from the world on that rocky shelf above the sea.

Within the house we found all ready. Mrs. Grant and her staff had worked well and all was bright and fresh and clean. We took a brief survey of the chief rooms and then separated to have a wash and to change our clothes after our long journey of more than four-and-twenty hours.

We had supper in the great dining-room on the south side, the walls of which actually hung over the sea. The murmur came up muffled, but it never ceased. As the little promontory stood well out into the sea, the northern side of the house was open and the due north was in no way shut out by the great mass of rock, which, reared high above us, shut out the rest of the world. Far off across the bay we could see the trembling lights of the castle, and here and there along the shore the faint light of a fisher's window. For the rest the sea was a dark blue plain with an occasional flicker of light as the gleam of starlight fell on the slope of a swelling wave.

When supper was over we all adjourned to the room which Mr. Trelawny had set aside as his study, his bedroom being close to it. As we entered, the first thing I noticed was a great safe, somewhat similar to that which stood in his room in London. When we were in the room Mr. Trelawny went over to the table, and, taking out his pocket-book, laid it on the table. As he did so he pressed down on it with the palm of his hand. A strange pallor came over his face. With fingers that trembled he opened the book, saying as he did so:

"Its bulk does not seem the same; I hope nothing has happened!"

All three of us men crowded round close. Margaret alone remained calm; she stood erect and silent, and still as a statue. She had a far-away look in her eyes, as though she did not either know or care what was going on around her.

With a despairing gesture Trelawny threw open the pouch of the pocket-book wherein he had placed the Jewel of Seven Stars. As he sank down on the chair which stood close to him, he said in a hoarse voice:

"My God! It is gone. Without it the Great Experiment can come to nothing!"

His words seemed to wake Margaret from her introspective mood. An agonised spasm swept her face; but almost on the instant she was calm. She almost smiled as she said:

"You may have left it in your room, Father. Perhaps it has fallen out of the pocket-book whilst you were changing." Without a word we all hurried into the next room through the open door between the study and the bedroom. And then a sudden calm fell on us like a cloud of fear.

There! on the table, lay the Jewel of Seven Stars, shining and sparkling with lurid light, as though each of the seven points of each the seven stars gleamed through blood!

Timidly we each looked behind us, and then at each other. Margaret was now like the rest of us. She had lost her statuesque calm. All the introspective rigidity had gone from her; and she clasped her hands together till the knuckles were white.

Without a word Mr. Trelawny raised the Jewel, and hurried with it into the next room. As quietly as he could he opened the door of the safe with the key fastened to his wrist and placed the Jewel within. When the heavy doors were closed and locked he seemed to breathe more freely.

Somehow this episode, though a disturbing one in many ways, seemed to bring us back to our old selves. Since we had left London we had all been overstrained; and this was a sort of relief. Another step in our strange enterprise had been effected.

The change back was more marked in Margaret than in any of us. Perhaps it was that she was a woman, whilst we were men; perhaps it was that she was younger than the rest; perhaps both reasons were effective, each in its own way. At any rate the change was there, and I was happier than I had been through the long journey. All her buoyancy, her tenderness, her deep feeling seemed to shine forth once more; now and again as her father's eyes rested on her, his face seemed to light up.

Whilst we waited for the carts to arrive, Mr. Trelawny took us through the house, pointing out and explaining where the objects which we had brought with us were to be placed. In one respect only did he withhold confidence. The positions of all those things which had connection with the Great Experiment were not indicated. The cases containing them were to be left in the outer hall, for the present.

By the time we had made the survey, the carts began to arrive; and the stir and bustle of the previous night were renewed. Mr. Trelawny stood in the hall beside the massive ironbound door, and gave directions as to the placing of each of the great packing-cases. Those containing many items were placed in the inner hall where they were to be unpacked.

In an incredibly short time the whole consignment was delivered; and the men departed with a douceur for each, given through their foreman, which made them effusive in their thanks. Then we all went to our own rooms. There was a strange confidence over us all. I do not think that any one of us had a doubt as to the quiet passing of the remainder of the night.

The faith was justified, for on our re-assembling in the morning we found that all had slept well and peaceably.

During that day all the curios, except those required for the Great Experiment were put into the places designed for them. Then it was arranged that all the servants should go back with Mrs. Grant to London on the next morning.

When they had all gone Mr. Trelawny, having seen the doors locked, took us into the study.

"Now," said he when we were seated, "I have a secret to impart; but, according to an old promise which does not leave me free, I must ask you each to give me a solemn promise not to reveal it. For three hundred years at least such a promise has been exacted from everyone to whom it was told, and more than once life and safety were secured through loyal observance of the promise. Even as it is, I am breaking the letter, if not the spirit of the tradition; for I should only tell it to the immediate members of my family."

We all gave the promise required. Then he went on:

"There is a secret place in this house, a cave, natural originally but finished by labour, underneath this house. I will not undertake to say that it has always been used according to the law. During the Bloody Assize more than a few Cornishmen found refuge in it; and later, and earlier, it formed, I have no doubt whatever, a useful place for storing contraband goods. 'Tre Pol and Pen', I suppose you know have always been smugglers; and their relations and friends and neighbours have not held back from the enterprise. For all such reasons a safe hiding-place was always considered a valuable possession; and as the heads of our House have always insisted on preserving the secret, I am in honour bound to it. Later on, if all be well I shall of course tell you, Margaret, and you too, Ross, under the conditions that am bound to make."

He rose up, and we all followed him. Leaving us in the outer hall, he went away alone for a few minutes; and returning, beckoned us to follow him.

In the inside hall we found a whole section of an outstanding angle moved away and from the cavity saw a great hole dimly dark, and the beginning of a rough staircase cut in the rock. As it was not pitch dark there was manifestly some means of lighting it naturally, so without pause we followed our host as he descended After some forty or fifty steps cut in a winding passage, we came to a great cave whose further end tapered away into blackness. It was a huge place, dimly lit by a few irregular slits of eccentric shape. Manifestly these were faults in the rock which would readily allow the windows be disguised. Close to each of them was a hanging shutter which could be easily swung across by means of a dangling rope. The sound of the ceaseless beat of the waves came up muffled from far below. Mr. Trelawny at once began to speak:

"This is the spot which I have chosen, as the best I know, for the scene of our Great Experiment. In a hundred different ways it fulfils the conditions which I am led to believe are primary with regard to success. Here, we are, and shall be, as isolated as Queen Tera herself would have been in her rocky tomb in the Valley of the Sorcerer, and still in a rocky cavern. For good or ill we must here stand by our chances, and abide by results. If we are successful we shall be able to let in on the

orld of modern science such a flood of light from the Old World as will change
very condition of thought and experiment and practice. If we fail, then even the
nowledge of our attempt will die with us. For this, and all else which may come,
believe we are prepared!" He paused. No one spoke, but we all bowed our heads
ravely in acquiescence. He resumed, but with a certain hesitancy:

"It is not yet too late! If any of you have a doubt or misgiving, for God's sake
peak it now! Whoever it may be, can go hence without let or hindrance. The rest
f us can go on our way alone!"

Again he paused, and looked keenly at us in turn. We looked at each other; but
o one quailed. For my own part, if I had had any doubt as to going on, the look on
largaret's face would have reassured me. It was fearless; it was intense; it was full
f a divine calm.

Mr. Trelawny took a long breath, and in a more cheerful, as well as in a more
ecided tone, went on:

"As we are all of one mind, the sooner we get the necessary matters in train the
etter. Let me tell you that this place, like all the rest of the house, can be lit with
lectricity. We could not join the wires to the mains lest our secret should become
nown, but I have a cable here which we can attach in the hall and complete the
ircuit!" As he was speaking, he began to ascend the steps. From close to the
ntrance he took the end of a cable; this he drew forward and attached to a switch
1 the wall. Then, turning on a tap, he flooded the whole vault and staircase below
vith light. I could now see from the volume of light streaming up into the hallway
hat the hole beside the staircase went direct into the cave. Above it was a pulley and
mass of strong tackle with multiplying blocks of the Smeaton order. Mr. Trelawny,
eeing me looking at this, said, correctly interpreting my thoughts:

"Yes! it is new. I hung it there myself on purpose. I knew we should have to lower
reat weights; and as I did not wish to take too many into my confidence, I arranged
tackle which I could work alone if necessary."

We set to work at once; and before nightfall had lowered, unhooked, and placed
1 the positions designated for each by Trelawny, all the great sarcophagi and all the
urios and other matters which we had taken with us.

It was a strange and weird proceeding, the placing of those wonderful monuments
f a bygone age in that green cavern, which represented in its cutting and purpose
nd up-to-date mechanism and electric lights both the old world and the new. But
s time went on I grew more and more to recognise the wisdom and correctness
f Mr. Trelawny's choice. I was much disturbed when Silvio, who had been brought
nto the cave in the arms of his mistress, and who was lying asleep on my coat
vhich I had taken off, sprang up when the cat mummy had been unpacked, and
lew at it with the same ferocity which he had previously exhibited. The incident
howed Margaret in a new phase, and one which gave my heart a pang. She had
een standing quite still at one side of the cave leaning on a sarcophagus, in one
f those fits of abstraction which had of late come upon her; but on hearing the
ound, and seeing Silvio's violent onslaught, she seemed to fall into a positive fury
f passion. Her eyes blazed, and her mouth took a hard, cruel tension which was
ew to me. Instinctively she stepped towards Silvio as if to interfere in the attack.
3ut I too had stepped forward; and as she caught my eye a strange spasm came
pon her, and she stopped. Its intensity made me hold my breath; and I put up

my hand to clear my eyes. When I had done this, she had on the instant recovered her calm, and there was a look of brief wonder on her face. With all her old grace and sweetness she swept over and lifted Silvio, just as she had done on former occasions, and held him in her arms, petting him and treating him as though he were a little child who had erred.

As I looked a strange fear came over me. The Margaret that I knew seemed to be changing; and in my inmost heart I prayed that the disturbing cause might soon come to an end. More than ever I longed at that moment that our terrible Experiment should come to a prosperous termination.

When all had been arranged in the room as Mr. Trelawny wished he turned to us, one after another, till he had concentrated the intelligence of us all upon him. Then he said:

"All is now ready in this place. We must only await the proper time to begin."

We were silent for a while. Doctor Winchester was the first to speak:

"What is the proper time? Have you any approximation, even if you are not satisfied as to the exact day?" He answered at once:

"After the most anxious thought I have fixed on July 31!"

"May I ask why that date?" He spoke his answer slowly:

"Queen Tera was ruled in great degree by mysticism, and there are so many evidences that she looked for resurrection that naturally she would choose a period ruled over by a God specialised to such a purpose. Now, the fourth month of the season of Inundation was ruled by Harmachis, this being the name for 'Ra', the Sun-God, at his rising in the morning, and therefore typifying the awakening or arising. This arising is manifestly to physical life, since it is of the mid-world of human daily life. Now as this month begins on our 25th July, the seventh day would be July 31st, for you may be sure that the mystic Queen would not have chosen any day but the seventh or some power of seven.

"I dare say that some of you have wondered why our preparations have been so deliberately undertaken. This is why! We must be ready in every possible way when the time comes; but there was no use in having to wait round for a needless number of days."

And so we waited only for the 31st of July, the next day but one, when the Great Experiment would be made.

Chapter XVII
Doubts and Fears

WE LEARN OF great things by little experiences. The history of ages is but an indefinite repetition of the history of hours. The record of a soul is but a multiple of the story of a moment. The Recording Angel writes in the Great Book in no rainbow tints; his pen is dipped in no colours but light and darkness. For the eye of infinite wisdom there is no need of shading. All things, all thoughts, all emotions, all experiences, all doubts and hopes and fears, all intentions, all wishes, seen down to the lower strata of their concrete and multitudinous elements, are finally resolved into direct opposites.

Did any human being wish for the epitome of a life wherein were gathered and grouped all the experiences that a child of Adam could have, the history, fully and frankly written, of my own mind during the next forty-eight hours would afford him all that could be wanted. And the Recorder could have wrought as usual in sunlight and shadow, which may be taken to represent the final expressions of Heaven and Hell. For in the highest Heaven is Faith; and Doubt hangs over the yawning blackness of Hell.

There were of course times of sunshine in those two days; moments when, in the realisation of Margaret's sweetness and her love for me, all doubts were dissipated like morning mist before the sun. But the balance of the time – and an overwhelming balance it was – gloom hung over me like a pall. The hour, in whose coming I had acquiesced, was approaching so quickly and was already so near that the sense of finality was bearing upon me! The issue was perhaps life or death to any of us; but for this we were all prepared. Margaret and I were one as to the risk. The question of the moral aspect of the case, which involved the religious belief in which I had been reared, was not one to trouble me; for the issues, and the causes that lay behind them, were not within my power even to comprehend. The doubt of the success of the Great Experiment was such a doubt as exists in all enterprises which have great possibilities. To me, whose life was passed in a series of intellectual struggles, this form of doubt was a stimulus, rather than deterrent. What then was it that made for me a trouble, which became an anguish when my thoughts dwelt long on it?

I was beginning to doubt Margaret!

What it was that I doubted I knew not. It was not her love, or her honour, or her truth, or her kindness, or her zeal. What then was it?

It was herself!

Margaret was changing! At times during the past few days I had hardly known her as the same girl whom I had met at the picnic, and whose vigils I had shared in the sick-room of her father. Then, even in her moments of greatest sorrow or fright or anxiety, she was all life and thought and keenness. Now she was generally distraite, and at times in a sort of negative condition as though her mind – her very being – was not present. At such moments she would have full possession of observation and memory. She would know and remember all that was going on, and had gone on around her; but her coming back to her old self had to me something the sensation of a new person coming into the room. Up to the time of leaving London I had been content whenever she was present. I had over me that delicious sense of security which comes with the consciousness that love is mutual. But now doubt had taken its place. I never knew whether the personality present was my Margaret – the old Margaret whom I had loved at the first glance – or the other new Margaret, whom I hardly understood, and whose intellectual aloofness made an impalpable barrier between us. Sometimes she would become, as it were, awake all at once. At such times, though she would say to me sweet and pleasant things which she had often said before, she would seem most unlike herself. It was almost as if she was speaking parrot-like or at dictation of one who could read words or acts, but not thoughts. After one or two experiences of this kind, my own doubting began to make a barrier; for I could not speak with the ease and freedom which were usual to me. And so hour by hour we drifted apart. Were it not for the few odd moments when the old Margaret was back with me full of her charm I do not know what would have happened. As it was, each such moment gave me a fresh start and kept my love from changing.

I would have given the world for a confidant; but this was impossible. How could I speak a doubt of Margaret to anyone, even her father! How could I speak a doubt to Margaret, when Margaret herself was the theme! I could only endure – and hope. And of the two the endurance was the lesser pain.

I think that Margaret must have at times felt that there was some cloud between us, for towards the end of the first day she began to shun me a little; or perhaps it was that she had become more diffident that usual about me. Hitherto she had sought every opportunity of being with me, just as I had tried to be with her; so that now any avoidance, one of the other, made a new pain to us both.

On this day the household seemed very still. Each one of us was about his own work, or occupied with his own thoughts. We only met at meal times; and then, though we talked, all seemed more or less preoccupied. There was not in the house even the stir of the routine of service. The precaution of Mr. Trelawny in having three rooms prepared for each of us had rendered servants unnecessary. The dining-room was solidly prepared with cooked provisions for several days. Towards evening I went out by myself for a stroll. I had looked for Margaret to ask her to come with me; but when I found her, she was in one of her apathetic moods, and the charm of her presence seemed lost to me. Angry with myself, but unable to quell my own spirit of discontent, I went out alone over the rocky headland.

On the cliff, with the wide expanse of wonderful sea before me, and no sound but the dash of waves below and the harsh screams of the seagulls above, my thoughts ran free. Do what I would, they returned continuously to one subject, the solving of the doubt that was upon me. Here in the solitude, amid the wide circle of Nature's force and strife, my mind began to work truly. Unconsciously I found myself asking a question which I would not allow myself to answer. At last the persistence of a mind working truly prevailed; I found myself face to face with my doubt. The habit of my life began to assert itself, and I analysed the evidence before me.

It was so startling that I had to force myself into obedience to logical effort. My starting-place was this: Margaret was changed – in what way, and by what means? Was it her character, or her mind, or her nature? for her physical appearance remained the same. I began to group all that I had ever heard of her, beginning at her birth.

It was strange at the very first. She had been, according to Corbeck's statement, born of a dead mother during the time that her father and his friend were in a trance in the tomb at Aswan. That trance was presumably effected by a woman; a woman mummied, yet preserving as we had every reason to believe from after experience, an astral body subject to a free will and an active intelligence. With that astral body, space ceased to exist. The vast distance between London and Aswan became as naught; and whatever power of necromancy the Sorceress had might have been exercised over the dead mother, and possibly the dead child.

The dead child! Was it possible that the child was dead and was made alive again? Whence then came the animating spirit – the soul? Logic was pointing the way to me now with a vengeance!

If the Egyptian belief was true for Egyptians, then the 'Ka' of the dead Queen and her 'Khu' could animate what she might choose. In such case Margaret would not be an individual at all, but simply a phase of Queen Tera herself; an astral body obedient to her will!

Here I revolted against logic. Every fibre of my being resented such a conclusion. How could I believe that there was no Margaret at all; but just an animated image, used by the Double of a woman of forty centuries ago to its own ends...! Somehow, the outlook was brighter to me now, despite the new doubts.

At least I had Margaret!

Back swung the logical pendulum again. The child then was not dead. If so, had the Sorceress had anything to do with her birth at all? It was evident – so I took it again from Corbeck – that there was a strange likeness between Margaret and the pictures of Queen Tera. How could this be? It could not be any birth-mark reproducing what had been in the mother's mind; for Mrs. Trelawny had never seen the pictures. Nay, even her father had not seen them till he had found his way into the tomb only a few days before her birth. This phase I could not get rid of so easily as the last; the fibres of my being remained quiet. There remained to me the horror of doubt. And even then, so strange is the mind of man, Doubt itself took a concrete image; a vast and impenetrable gloom, through which flickered irregularly and spasmodically tiny points of evanescent light, which seemed to quicken the darkness into a positive existence.

The remaining possibility of relations between Margaret and the mummied Queen was, that in some occult way the Sorceress had power to change places with the other. This view of things could not be so lightly thrown aside. There were too many suspicious circumstances to warrant this, now that my attention was fixed on it and my intelligence recognised the possibility. Hereupon there began to come into my mind all the strange incomprehensible matters which had whirled through our lives in the last few days. At first they all crowded in upon me in a jumbled mass; but again the habit of mind of my working life prevailed, and they took order. I found it now easier to control myself; for there was something to grasp, some work to be done; though it was of a sorry kind, for it was or might be antagonistic to Margaret. But Margaret was herself at stake! I was thinking of her and fighting for her; and yet if I were to work in the dark, I might be even harmful to her. My first weapon in her defence was truth. I must know and understand; I might then be able to act. Certainly, I could not act beneficently without a just conception and recognition of the facts. Arranged in order these were as follows:

Firstly: the strange likeness of Queen Tera to Margaret who had been born in another country a thousand miles away, where her mother could not possibly have had even a passing knowledge of her appearance.

Secondly: the disappearance of Van Huyn's book when I had read up to the description of the Star Ruby.

Thirdly: the finding of the lamps in the boudoir. Tera with her astral body could have unlocked the door of Corbeck's room in the hotel, and have locked it again after her exit with the lamps. She could in the same way have opened the window, and put the lamps in the boudoir. It need not have been that Margaret in her own person should have had any hand in this; but – but it was at least strange.

Fourthly: here the suspicions of the Detective and the Doctor came back to me with renewed force, and with a larger understanding.

Fifthly: there were the occasions on which Margaret foretold with accuracy the coming occasions of quietude, as though she had some conviction or knowledge of the intentions of the astral-bodied Queen.

Sixthly: there was her suggestion of the finding of the Ruby which her father had lost. As I thought now afresh over this episode in the light of suspicion in which her own powers were involved, the only conclusion I could come to was – always supposing that the theory of the Queen's astral power was correct – that Queen Tera being anxious that all should go well in the movement from London to Kyllion had in her own way taken the Jewel from Mr. Trelawny's pocket-book, finding it of some use in her supernatural guardianship of the journey. Then in some mysterious way she had, through Margaret, made the suggestion of its loss and finding.

Seventhly, and lastly, was the strange dual existence which Margaret seemed of late to be leading; and which in some way seemed a consequence or corollary of all that had gone before.

The dual existence! This was indeed the conclusion which overcame all difficulties and reconciled opposites. If indeed Margaret were not in all ways a free agent, but could be compelled to speak or act as she might be instructed; or if her whole being could be changed for another without the possibility of any one noticing the doing of it, then all things were possible. All would depend on the spirit of the individuality by which she could be so compelled. If this individuality were just and kind and clean, all might be well. But if not! ... The thought was too awful for words. I ground my teeth with futile rage, as the ideas of horrible possibilities swept through me.

Up to this morning Margaret's lapses into her new self had been few and hardly noticeable, save when once or twice her attitude towards myself had been marked by a bearing strange to me. But today the contrary was the case; and the change presaged badly. It might be that that other individuality was of the lower, not of the better sort! Now that I thought of it I had reason to fear. In the history of the mummy, from the time of Van Huyn's breaking into the tomb, the record of deaths that we knew of, presumably effected by her will and agency, was a startling one. The Arab who had stolen the hand from the mummy; and the one who had taken it from his body. The Arab chief who had tried to steal the Jewel from Van Huyn, and whose throat bore the marks of seven fingers. The two men found dead on the first night of Trelawny's taking away the sarcophagus; and the three on the return to the tomb. The Arab who had opened the secret serdab. Nine dead men, one of them slain manifestly by the Queen's own hand! And beyond this again the several savage attacks on Mr. Trelawny in his own room, in which, aided by her Familiar, she had tried to open the safe and to extract the Talisman jewel. His device of fastening the key to his wrist by a steel bangle, though successful in the end, had wellnigh cost him his life.

If then the Queen, intent on her resurrection under her own conditions had, so to speak, waded to it through blood, what might she not do were her purpose thwarted? What terrible step might she not take to effect her wishes? Nay, what were her wishes; what was her ultimate purpose? As yet we had had only Margaret's statement of them, given in all the glorious enthusiasm of her lofty soul. In her record there was no expression of love to be sought or found. All we knew for certain was that she had set before her the object of resurrection, and that in it the North which she had manifestly loved was to have a special part. But that the resurrection was to be accomplished in the lonely tomb in the Valley of the Sorcerer was apparent. All preparations had been carefully made for accomplishment from within, and for her ultimate exit in her new and living form. The sarcophagus was unlidded. The oil jars, though hermetically sealed, were to be easily opened by hand; and in them provision was made for shrinkage through a vast period of time. Even flint and steel were provided for the production of flame. The Mummy Pit was left open in violation of usage; and beside the stone door on the cliff side was fixed an imperishable chain by which she might in safety descend to earth. But as to what her after intentions were we had no clue. If it was that she meant to begin life again as a humble individual, there was something so noble in the thought that it even warmed my heart to her and turned my wishes to her success.

The very idea seemed to endorse Margaret's magnificent tribute to her purpose, and helped to calm my troubled spirit.

Then and there, with this feeling strong upon me, I determined to warn Margaret and her father of dire possibilities; and to await, as well content as I could in my ignorance, the development of things over which I had no power.

I returned to the house in a different frame of mind to that in which I had left it; and was enchanted to find Margaret – the old Margaret – waiting for me.

After dinner, when I was alone for a time with the father and daughter, I opened the subject, though with considerable hesitation:

"Would it not be well to take every possible precaution, in case the Queen may not wish what we are doing, with regard to what may occur before the Experiment; and at or after her waking, if it comes off?" Margaret's answer came back quickly; so quickly that I was convinced she must have had it ready for some one:

"But she does approve! Surely it cannot be otherwise. Father is doing, with all his brains and all his energy and all his great courage, just exactly what the great Queen had arranged!"

"But," I answered, "that can hardly be. All that she arranged was in a tomb high up in a rock, in a desert solitude, shut away from the world by every conceivable means. She seems to have depended on this isolation to insure against accident. Surely, here in another country and age, with quite different conditions, she may in her anxiety make mistakes and treat any of you – of us – as she did those others in times gone past. Nine men that we know of have been slain by her own hand or by her instigation. She can be remorseless if she will." It did not strike me till afterwards when I was thinking over this conversation, how thoroughly I had accepted the living and conscious condition of Queen Tera as a fact. Before I spoke, I had feared I might offend Mr. Trelawny; but to my pleasant surprise he smiled quite genially as he answered me:

"My dear fellow, in a way you are quite right. The Queen did undoubtedly intend isolation; and, all told, it would be best that her experiment should be made as she arranged it. But just think, that became impossible when once the Dutch explorer had broken into her tomb. That was not my doing. I am innocent of it, though it was the cause of my setting out to rediscover the sepulchre. Mind, I do not say for a moment that I would not have done just the same as Van Huyn. I went into the tomb from curiosity; and I took away what I did, being fired with the zeal of acquisitiveness which animates the collector. But, remember also, that at this time I did not know of the Queen's intention of resurrection; I had no idea of the completeness of her preparations. All that came long afterwards. But when it did come, I have done all that I could to carry out her wishes to the full.

My only fear is that I may have misinterpreted some of her cryptic instructions, or have omitted or overlooked something. But of this I am certain; I have left undone nothing that I can imagine right to be done; and I have done nothing that I know of to clash with Queen Tera's arrangement. I want her Great Experiment to succeed. To this end I have not spared labour or time or money – or myself. I have endured hardship, and braved danger. All my brains; all my knowledge and learning, such as they are; all my endeavours such as they can be, have been, are, and shall be devoted to this end, till we either win or lose the great stake that we play for."

"The great stake?" I repeated; "The resurrection of the woman, and the woman's life? The proof that resurrection can be accomplished; by magical powers; by scientific knowledge; or by use of some force which at present the world does not know?"

Then Mr. Trelawny spoke out the hopes of his heart which up to now he had indicated rather than expressed. Once or twice I had heard Corbeck speak of the fiery energy of his youth; but, save for the noble words of Margaret when she had spoken of Queen Tera's hope – which coming from his daughter made possible a belief that her power was in some sense due to heredity – I had seen no marked sign of it. But now his words, sweeping before them like a torrent all antagonistic thought, gave me a new idea of the man.

"'A woman's life!' What is a woman's life in the scale with what we hope for! Why, we are risking already a woman's life; the dearest life to me in all the world, and that grows more dear with every hour that passes. We are risking as well the lives of four men; yours and my own, as well as those two others who have been won to our confidence. 'The proof that resurrection can be accomplished!' That is much. A marvellous thing in this age of science, and the scepticism that knowledge makes. But life and resurrection are themselves but items in what may be won by the accomplishment of this Great Experiment. Imagine what it will be for the world of thought – the true world of human progress – the veritable road to the Stars, the *itur ad astra* of the Ancients – if there can come back to us out of the unknown past one who can yield to us the lore stored in the great Library of Alexandria, and lost in its consuming flames. Not only history can be set right, and the teachings of science made veritable from their beginnings; but we can be placed on the road to the knowledge of lost arts, lost learning, lost sciences, so that our feet may tread on the indicated path to their ultimate and complete restoration. Why, this woman can tell us what the world was like before what is called 'the Flood'; can give us the origin of that vast astounding myth; can set the mind back to the consideration of things which to us now seem primeval, but which were old stories before the days of the Patriarchs. But this is not the end! No, not even the beginning! If the story of this woman be all that we think – which some of us most firmly believe; if her powers and the restoration of them prove to be what we expect, why, then we may yet achieve a knowledge beyond what our age has ever known – beyond what is believed today possible for the children of men. If indeed this resurrection can be accomplished, how can we doubt the old knowledge, the old magic, the old belief! And if this be so, we must take it that the 'Ka' of this great and learned Queen has won secrets of more than mortal worth from her surroundings amongst the stars. This woman in her life voluntarily went down living to the grave, and came back again, as we learn from the records in her tomb; she chose to die her mortal death whilst young, so that at her resurrection in another age, beyond a trance of countless magnitude, she might emerge from her tomb in all the fulness and splendour of her youth and power. Already we have evidence that though her body slept in patience through those many centuries, her intelligence never passed away, that her resolution never flagged, that her will remained supreme; and, most important of all, that her memory was unimpaired. Oh, what possibilities are there in the coming of such a being into our midst! One whose history began before the concrete teaching of our Bible; whose experiences were antecedent to the formulation of the Gods of Greece; who can link together the Old and the New, Earth and Heaven, and yield to the known worlds of thought and physical existence the mystery of the Unknown – of the Old World in its youth, and of Worlds beyond our ken!"

He paused, almost overcome. Margaret had taken his hand when he spoke of her being so dear to him, and held it hard. As he spoke she continued to hold it. But there came over her face that change which I had so often seen of late; that mysterious veiling of her own personality which gave me the subtle sense of separation from her. In his impassioned vehemence her father did not notice; but when he stopped she seemed all at once to be herself again. In her glorious eyes came the added brightness of unshed tears; and with a gesture of passionate love and admiration, she stooped and kissed her father's hand. Then, turning to me, she too spoke:

"Malcolm, you have spoken of the deaths that came from the poor Queen; or rather that justly came from meddling with her arrangements and thwarting her purpose. Do you not think that, in putting it as you have done, you have been unjust? Who would not have done just as she did? Remember she was fighting for her life! Ay, and for more than her life! For life, and love, and all the glorious possibilities of that dim future in the unknown world of the North which had such enchanting hopes for her! Do you not think that she, with all the learning of her time, and with all the great and resistless force of her mighty nature, had hopes of spreading in a wider way the lofty aspirations of her soul! That she hoped to bring to the conquering of unknown worlds, and using to the advantage of her people, all that she had won from sleep and death and time; all of which might and could have been frustrated by the ruthless hand of an assassin or a thief. Were it you, in such case would you not struggle by all means to achieve the object of your life and hope; whose possibilities grew and grew in the passing of those endless years? Can you think that that active brain was at rest during all those weary centuries, whilst her free soul was flitting from world to world amongst the boundless regions of the stars? Had these stars in their myriad and varied life no lessons for her; as they have had for us since we followed the glorious path which she and her people marked for us, when they sent their winged imaginations circling amongst the lamps of the night!"

Here she paused. She too was overcome, and the welling tears ran down her cheeks. I was myself more moved than I can say. This was indeed my Margaret; and in the consciousness of her presence my heart leapt. Out of my happiness came boldness, and I dared to say now what I had feared would be impossible: something which would call the attention of Mr. Trelawny to what I imagined was the dual existence of his daughter. As I took Margaret's hand in mine and kissed it, I said to her father:

"Why, sir! she couldn't speak more eloquently if the very spirit of Queen Tera was with her to animate her and suggest thoughts!"

Mr. Trelawny's answer simply overwhelmed me with surprise. It manifested to me that he too had gone through just such a process of thought as my own.

"And what if it was; if it is! I know well that the spirit of her mother is within her. If in addition there be the spirit of that great and wondrous Queen, then she would be no less dear to me, but doubly dear! Do not have fear for her, Malcolm Ross; at least have no more fear than you may have for the rest of us!" Margaret took up the theme, speaking so quickly that her words seemed a continuation of her father's, rather than an interruption of them.

"Have no special fear for me, Malcolm. Queen Tera knows, and will offer us no harm. I know it! I know it, as surely as I am lost in the depth of my own love for you!"

There was something in her voice so strange to me that I looked quickly into her eyes. They were bright as ever, but veiled to my seeing the inward thought behind them as are the eyes of a caged lion.

Then the two other men came in, and the subject changed.

Chapter XVIII
The Lesson of the 'Ka'

THAT NIGHT we all went to bed early. The next night would be an anxious one, and Mr. Trelawny thought that we should all be fortified with what sleep we could get. The day, too, would be full of work. Everything in connection with the Great Experiment would have to be gone over, so that at the last we might not fail from any unthought-of flaw in our working. We made, of course, arrangements for summoning aid in case such should be needed; but I do not think that any of us had any real apprehension of danger. Certainly we had no fear of such danger from violence as we had had to guard against in London during Mr. Trelawny's long trance.

For my own part I felt a strange sense of relief in the matter. I had accepted Mr. Trelawny's reasoning that if the Queen were indeed such as we surmised – such as indeed we now took for granted – there would not be any opposition on her part; for we were carrying out her own wishes to the very last. So far I was at ease – far more at ease than earlier in the day I should have thought possible; but there were other sources of trouble which I could not blot out from my mind. Chief amongst them was Margaret's strange condition. If it was indeed that she had in her own person a dual existence, what might happen when the two existences became one? Again, and again, and again I turned this matter over in my mind, till I could have shrieked out in nervous anxiety. It was no consolation to me to remember that Margaret was herself satisfied, and her father acquiescent. Love is, after all, a selfish thing; and it throws a black shadow on anything between which and the light it stands. I seemed to hear the hands go round the dial of the clock; I saw darkness turn to gloom, and gloom to grey, and grey to light without pause or hindrance to the succession of my miserable feelings. At last, when it was decently possible without the fear of disturbing others, I got up. I crept along the passage to find if all was well with the others; for we had arranged that the door of each of our rooms should be left slightly open so that any sound of disturbance would be easily and distinctly heard.

One and all slept; I could hear the regular breathing of each, and my heart rejoiced that this miserable night of anxiety was safely passed. As I knelt in my own room in a burst of thankful prayer, I knew in the depths of my own heart the measure of my fear. I found my way out of the house, and went down to the water by the long stairway cut in the rock. A swim in the cool bright sea braced my nerves and made me my old self again.

As I came back to the top of the steps I could see the bright sunlight, rising from behind me, turning the rocks across the bay to glittering gold. And yet I felt somehow disturbed. It was all too bright; as it sometimes is before the coming of a storm. As I paused to watch it, I felt a soft hand on my shoulder; and, turning, found Margaret close to me; Margaret as bright and radiant as the morning glory of the sun! It was my own Margaret this time! My old Margaret, without alloy of any other; and I felt that, at least, this last and fatal day was well begun.

But alas! the joy did not last. When we got back to the house from a stroll around the cliffs, the same old routine of yesterday was resumed: gloom and anxiety, hope, high spirits, deep depression, and apathetic aloofness.

But it was to be a day of work; and we all braced ourselves to it with an energy which wrought its own salvation.

After breakfast we all adjourned to the cave, where Mr. Trelawny went over, point by point, the position of each item of our paraphernalia. He explained as he went on why each piece was so placed. He had with him the great rolls of paper with the measured plans and the signs and drawings which he had had made from his own and Corbeck's rough notes. As he had told us, these contained the whole of the hieroglyphics on walls and ceilings and floor of the tomb in the Valley of the Sorcerer. Even had not the measurements, made to scale, recorded the position of each piece of furniture, we could have eventually placed them by a study of the cryptic writings and symbols.

Mr. Trelawny explained to us certain other things, not laid down on the chart. Such as, for instance, that the hollowed part of the table was exactly fitted to the bottom of the Magic Coffer, which was therefore intended to be placed on it. The respective legs of this table were indicated by differently shaped uraei outlined on the floor, the head of each being extended in the direction of the similar uraeus twined round the leg. Also that the mummy, when laid on the raised portion in the bottom of the sarcophagus, seemingly made to fit the form, would lie head to the West and feet to the East, thus receiving the natural earth currents. "If this be intended," he said, "as I presume it is, I gather that the force to be used has something to do with magnetism or electricity, or both. It may be, of course, that some other force, such, for instance, as that emanating from radium, is to be employed. I have experimented with the latter, but only in such small quantity as I could obtain; but so far as I can ascertain the stone of the Coffer is absolutely impervious to its influence. There must be some such unsusceptible substances in nature. Radium does not seemingly manifest itself when distributed through pitchblende; and there are doubtless other such substances in which it can be imprisoned. Possibly these may belong to that class of 'inert' elements discovered or isolated by Sir William Ramsay. It is therefore possible that in this Coffer, made from an aerolite and therefore perhaps containing some element unknown in our world, may be imprisoned some mighty power which is to be released on its opening."

This appeared to be an end of this branch of the subject; but as he still kept the fixed look of one who is engaged in a theme we all waited in silence. After a pause he went on:

"There is one thing which has up to now, I confess, puzzled me. It may not be of prime importance; but in a matter like this, where all is unknown, we must take it that everything is important. I cannot think that in a matter worked out with such extraordinary scrupulosity such a thing should be overlooked. As you may see by the ground-plan of the tomb the sarcophagus stands near the north wall, with the Magic Coffer to the south of it. The space covered by the former is left quite bare of symbol or ornamentation of any kind. At the first glance this would seem to imply that the drawings had been made after the sarcophagus had been put into its place. But a more minute examination will show that the symbolisation on the floor is so arranged that a definite effect is produced. See, here the writings run in correct order as though they had jumped across the gap. It is only from certain effects that it becomes clear that there is a meaning of some kind. What that meaning may be is what we want to know. Look at the top and bottom of the vacant space, which lies West and East corresponding to the head and foot of the sarcophagus. In both are duplications of the same symbolisation, but so arranged that the parts of each one of them are integral portions of some other writing running crosswise. It is only when we get a coup d'oeil from either the head or the foot that you recognise that there are symbolisations. See! they are in triplicate at the corners and the centre of both top and bottom. In every case there is a sun cut in half by the line of the sarcophagus, as by the horizon. Close behind each of these and faced away from it, as though in some way dependent on it, is the vase which in hieroglyphic writing symbolises the heart – 'Ab' the Egyptians called it. Beyond each of these again is the figure of a pair of widespread arms turned upwards from the elbow; this is the determinative of the 'Ka' or 'Double'. But its relative position is different at top and bottom. At the head of the sarcophagus the top of the 'Ka' is turned towards the mouth of the vase, but at the foot the extended arms point away from it.

"The symbolisation seems to mean that during the passing of the Sun from West to East – from sunset to sunrise, or through the Under World, otherwise night – the Heart, which is material even in the tomb and cannot leave it, simply revolves, so that it can always rest on 'Ra' the Sun-God, the origin of all good; but that the Double, which represents the active principle, goes whither it will, the same by night as by day. If this be correct it is a warning – a caution – a reminder that the consciousness of the mummy does not rest but is to be reckoned with.

"Or it may be intended to convey that after the particular night of the resurrection, the 'Ka' would leave the heart altogether, thus typifying that in her resurrection the Queen would be restored to a lower and purely physical existence. In such case what would become of her memory and the experiences of her wide-wandering soul? The chiefest value of her resurrection would be lost to the world! This, however, does not alarm me. It is only guess-work after all, and is contradictory to the intellectual belief of the Egyptian theology, that the 'Ka' is an essential portion of humanity." He paused and we all waited. The silence was broken by Doctor Winchester:

"But would not all this imply that the Queen feared intrusion of her tomb?" Mr. Trelawny smiled as he answered:

"My dear sir, she was prepared for it. The grave robber is no modern application of endeavour; he was probably known in the Queen's own dynasty. Not only was she prepared for intrusion, but, as shown in several ways, she expected it. The hiding of the lamps in the serdab, and the institution of the avenging 'treasurer' shows that there was defence, positive as well as negative. Indeed, from the many indications afforded in the clues laid out with the most consummated thought, we may almost gather that she entertained it as a possibility that others – like ourselves, for instance – might in all seriousness undertake the work which she had made ready for her own hands when the time should have come. This very matter that I have been speaking of is an instance. The clue is intended for seeing eyes!"

Again we were silent. It was Margaret who spoke:

"Father, may I have that chart? I should like to study it during the day!"

"Certainly, my dear!" answered Mr. Trelawny heartily, as he handed it to her. He resumed his instructions in a different tone, a more matter-of-fact one suitable to a practical theme which had no mystery about it:

"I think you had better all understand the working of the electric light in case any sudden contingency should arise. I dare say you have noticed that we have a complete supply in every part of the house, so that there need not be a dark corner anywhere. This I had specially arranged. It is worked by a set of turbines moved by the flowing and ebbing tide, after the manner of the turbines at Niagara. I hope by this means to nullify accident and to have without fail a full supply ready at any time. Come with me and I will explain the system of circuits, and point out to you the taps and the fuses." I could not but notice, as we went with him all over the house, how absolutely complete the system was, and how he had guarded himself against any disaster that human thought could foresee.

But out of the very completeness came a fear! In such an enterprise as ours the bounds of human thought were but narrow. Beyond it lay the vast of Divine wisdom, and Divine power!

When we came back to the cave, Mr. Trelawny took up another theme:

"We have now to settle definitely the exact hour at which the Great Experiment is to be made. So far as science and mechanism go, if the preparations are complete, all hours are the same. But as we have to deal with preparations made by a woman of extraordinarily subtle mind, and who had full belief in magic and had a cryptic meaning in everything, we should place ourselves in her position before deciding. It is now manifest that the sunset has an important place in the arrangements. As those suns, cut so mathematically by the edge of the sarcophagus, were arranged of full design, we must take our cue from this. Again, we find all along that the number seven has had an important bearing on every phase of the Queen's thought and reasoning and action. The logical result is that the seventh hour after sunset was the time fixed on. This is borne out by the fact that on each of the occasions when action was taken in my house, this was the time chosen. As the sun sets tonight in Cornwall at eight, our hour is to be three in the morning!" He spoke in a matter-of-fact way, though with great gravity; but there was nothing of mystery in his word or manner. Still, we were all impressed to a remarkable degree. I could see this in the other men by the pallor that came on some of their faces, and by the stillness and unquestioning silence with which the decision was received. The only one who remained in any way at ease was Margaret, who had lapsed into one of her moods of abstraction, but who seemed to wake up to a note of gladness. Her father, who was watching her intently, smiled; her mood was to him a direct confirmation of his theory.

For myself I was almost overcome. The definite fixing of the hour seemed like the voice of Doom. When I think of it now, I can realise how a condemned man feels at his sentence, or at the sounding of the last hour he is to hear.

There could be no going back now! We were in the hands of God!

The hands of God...! And yet...! What other forces were arrayed? ... What would become of us all, poor atoms of earthly dust whirled in the wind which cometh whence and goeth whither no man may know. It was not for myself... Margaret...!

I was recalled by Mr. Trelawny's firm voice:

"Now we shall see to the lamps and finish our preparations." Accordingly we set to work, and under his supervision made ready the Egyptian lamps, seeing that they were well filled with the cedar oil, and that the wicks were adjusted and in good order. We lighted and tested them one by one, and left them ready so that they would light at once and evenly. When this was done we had a general look round; and fixed all in readiness for our work at night.

All this had taken time, and we were I think all surprised when as we emerged from the cave we heard the great clock in the hall chime four.

We had a late lunch, a thing possible without trouble in the present state of our commissariat arrangements. After it, by Mr. Trelawny's advice, we separated; each to prepare in our own way for the strain of the coming night. Margaret looked pale and somewhat overwrought, so I advised her to lie down and try to sleep. She promised that she would. The abstraction which had been upon her fitfully all day lifted for the time; with all her old sweetness and loving delicacy she kissed me good-bye for the present! With the sense of happiness which this gave me I went out for a walk on the cliffs. I did not want to think; and I had an instinctive feeling that fresh air and God's sunlight, and the myriad beauties of the works of His hand would be the best preparation of fortitude for what was to come.

When I got back, all the party were assembling for a late tea. Coming fresh from the exhilaration of nature, it struck me as almost comic that we, who were nearing the end of so strange – almost monstrous – an undertaking, should be yet bound by the needs and habits of our lives.

All the men of the party were grave; the time of seclusion, even if it had given them rest, had also given opportunity for thought. Margaret was bright, almost buoyant; but I missed about her something of her usual spontaneity. Towards myself there was a shadowy air of reserve, which brought back something of my suspicion. When tea was over, she went out of the room; but returned in a minute with the roll of drawing which she had taken with her earlier in the day. Coming close to Mr. Trelawny, she said:

"Father, I have been carefully considering what you said today about the hidden meaning of those suns and hearts and 'Ka's', and I have been examining the drawings again."

"And with what result, my child?" asked Mr. Trelawny eagerly.

"There is another reading possible!"

"And that?" His voice was now tremulous with anxiety. Margaret spoke with a strange ring in her voice; a ring that cannot be, unless there is the consciousness of truth behind it:

"It means that at the sunset the 'Ka' is to enter the 'Ab'; and it is only at the sunrise that it will leave it!"

"Go on!" said her father hoarsely.

"It means that for this night the Queen's Double, which is otherwise free, will remain in her heart, which is mortal and cannot leave its prison-place in the mummy-shrouding. It means that when the sun has dropped into the sea, Queen Tera will cease to exist as a conscious power, till sunrise; unless the Great Experiment can recall her to waking life. It means that there will be nothing whatever for you or others to fear from her in such way as we have all cause to remember. Whatever change may come from the working of the Great Experiment, there can come none from the poor, helpless, dead woman who has waited all those centuries for this night; who has given up to the coming hour all the freedom of eternity, won in the old way, in hope of a new life in a new world such as she longed for...!" She stopped suddenly. As she had gone on speaking there had come with her words a strange pathetic, almost pleading, tone which touched me to the quick. As she stopped, I could see, before she turned away her head, that her eyes were full of tears.

For once the heart of her father did not respond to her feeling. He looked exultant, but with a grim masterfulness which reminded me of the set look of his stern face as he had lain in the trance. He did not offer any consolation to his daughter in her sympathetic pain. He only said:

"We may test the accuracy of your surmise, and of her feeling, when the time comes!" Having said so, he went up the stone stairway and into his own room. Margaret's face had a troubled look as she gazed after him.

Strangely enough her trouble did not as usual touch me to the quick.

When Mr. Trelawny had gone, silence reigned. I do not think that any of us wanted to talk. Presently Margaret went to her room, and I went out on the terrace over the sea. The fresh air and the beauty of all before helped to restore the good spirits which I had known earlier in the day. Presently I felt myself actually rejoicing in the belief that the danger which I had feared from the Queen's violence on the coming night was obviated. I believed in Margaret's belief so thoroughly that it did not occur to me to dispute her reasoning. In a lofty frame of mind, and with less anxiety than I had felt for days, I went to my room and lay down on the sofa.

I was awaked by Corbeck calling to me, hurriedly:

"Come down to the cave as quickly as you can. Mr. Trelawny wants to see us all there at once. Hurry!"

I jumped up and ran down to the cave. All were there except Margaret, who came immediately after me carrying Silvio in her arms. When the cat saw his old enemy he struggled to get down; but Margaret held him fast and soothed him. I looked at my watch. It was close to eight.

When Margaret was with us her father said directly, with a quiet insistence which was new to me:

"You believe, Margaret, that Queen Tera has voluntarily undertaken to give up her freedom for this night? To become a mummy and nothing more, till the

Experiment has been completed? To be content that she shall be powerless under all and any circumstances until after all is over and the act of resurrection has been accomplished, or the effort has failed?" After a pause Margaret answered in a low voice:

"Yes!"

In the pause her whole being, appearance, expression, voice, manner had changed. Even Silvio noticed it, and with a violent effort wriggled away from her arms; she did not seem to notice the act. I expected that the cat, when he had achieved his freedom, would have attacked the mummy; but on this occasion he did not. He seemed too cowed to approach it. He shrunk away, and with a piteous 'miaou' came over and rubbed himself against my ankles. I took him up in my arms, and he nestled there content. Mr. Trelawny spoke again:

"You are sure of what you say! You believe it with all your soul?" Margaret's face had lost the abstracted look; it now seemed illuminated with the devotion of one to whom is given to speak of great things. She answered in a voice which, though quiet, vibrated with conviction:

"I know it! My knowledge is beyond belief!" Mr. Trelawny spoke again:

"Then you are so sure, that were you Queen Tera herself, you would be willing to prove it in any way that I might suggest?"

"Yes, any way!" the answer rang out fearlessly. He spoke again, in a voice in which was no note of doubt:

"Even in the abandonment of your Familiar to death – to annihilation."

She paused, and I could see that she suffered – suffered horribly. There was in her eyes a hunted look, which no man can, unmoved, see in the eyes of his beloved. I was about to interrupt, when her father's eyes, glancing round with a fierce determination, met mine. I stood silent, almost spellbound; so also the other men. Something was going on before us which we did not understand!

With a few long strides Mr. Trelawny went to the west side of the cave and tore back the shutter which obscured the window. The cool air blew in, and the sunlight streamed over them both, for Margaret was now by his side. He pointed to where the sun was sinking into the sea in a halo of golden fire, and his face was as set as flint. In a voice whose absolute uncompromising hardness I shall hear in my ears at times till my dying day, he said:

"Choose! Speak! When the sun has dipped below the sea, it will be too late!" The glory of the dying sun seemed to light up Margaret's face, till it shone as if lit from within by a noble light, as she answered:

"Even that!"

Then stepping over to where the mummy cat stood on the little table, she placed her hand on it. She had now left the sunlight, and the shadows looked dark and deep over her. In a clear voice she said:

"Were I Tera, I would say 'Take all I have! This night is for the Gods alone!'"

As she spoke the sun dipped, and the cold shadow suddenly fell on us. We all stood still for a while. Silvio jumped from my arms and ran over to his mistress, rearing himself up against her dress as if asking to be lifted. He took no notice whatever of the mummy now.

Margaret was glorious with all her wonted sweetness as she said sadly:

"The sun is down, Father! Shall any of us see it again? The night of nights is come!"

Chapter XIX
The Great Experiment

IF ANY EVIDENCE had been wanted of how absolutely one and all of us had come to believe in the spiritual existence of the Egyptian Queen, it would have been found in the change which in a few minutes had been effected in us by the statement of voluntary negation made, we all believed, through Margaret. Despite the coming of the fearful ordeal, the sense of which it was impossible to forget, we looked and acted as though a great relief had come to us. We had indeed lived in such a state of terrorism during the days when Mr. Trelawny was lying in a trance that the feeling had bitten deeply into us. No one knows till he has experienced it, what it is to be in constant dread of some unknown danger which may come at any time and in any form.

The change was manifested in different ways, according to each nature. Margaret was sad. Doctor Winchester was in high spirits, and keenly observant; the process of thought which had served as an antidote to fear, being now relieved from this duty, added to his intellectual enthusiasm. Mr. Corbeck seemed to be in a retrospective rather than a speculative mood. I was myself rather inclined to be gay; the relief from certain anxiety regarding Margaret was sufficient for me for the time.

As to Mr. Trelawny he seemed less changed than any. Perhaps this was only natural, as he had had in his mind the intention for so many years of doing that in which we were tonight engaged, that any event connected with it could only seem to him as an episode, a step to the end. His was that commanding nature which looks so to the end of an undertaking that all else is of secondary importance. Even now, though his terrible sternness relaxed under the relief from the strain, he never flagged nor faltered for a moment in his purpose. He asked us men to come with him; and going to the hall we presently managed to lower into the cave an oak table, fairly long and not too wide, which stood against the wall in the hall. This we placed under the strong cluster of electric lights in the middle of the cave. Margaret looked on for a while; then all at once her face blanched, and in an agitated voice she said:

"What are you going to do, Father?"

"To unroll the mummy of the cat! Queen Tera will not need her Familiar tonight. If she should want him, it might be dangerous to us; so we shall make him safe. You are not alarmed, dear?"

"Oh no!" she answered quickly. "But I was thinking of my Silvio, and how I should feel if he had been the mummy that was to be unswathed!"

Mr. Trelawny got knives and scissors ready, and placed the cat on the table. It was a grim beginning to our work; and it made my heart sink when I thought of what might happen in that lonely house in the mid-gloom of the night. The sense of loneliness and isolation from the world was increased by the moaning of the wind which had now risen ominously, and by the beating of waves on the rocks below. But we had too grave a task before us to be swayed by external manifestations: the unrolling of the mummy began.

There was an incredible number of bandages; and the tearing sound – they being stuck fast to each other by bitumen and gums and spices – and the little cloud of red pungent dust that arose, pressed on the senses of all of us. As the last wrappings came away, we saw the animal seated before us. He was all hunkered up; his hair and teeth and claws were complete. The eyes were closed, but the eyelids had not the fierce look which I expected. The whiskers had been pressed down on the side of the face by the bandaging; but when the pressure was taken away they stood out, just as they would have done in life. He was a magnificent creature, a tiger-cat of great size. But as we looked at him, our first glance of admiration changed to one of fear, and a shudder ran through each one of us; for here was a confirmation of the fears which we had endured.

His mouth and his claws were smeared with the dry, red stains of recent blood!

Doctor Winchester was the first to recover; blood in itself had small disturbing quality for him. He had taken out his magnifying-glass and was examining the stains on the cat's mouth. Mr. Trelawny breathed loudly, as though a strain had been taken from him.

"It is as I expected," he said. "This promises well for what is to follow."

By this time Doctor Winchester was looking at the red stained paws. "As I expected!" he said. "He has seven claws, too!" Opening his pocket-book, he took out the piece of blotting-paper marked by Silvio's claws, on which was also marked in pencil a diagram of the cuts made on Mr. Trelawny's wrist. He placed the paper under the mummy cat's paw. The marks fitted exactly.

When we had carefully examined the cat, finding, however, nothing strange about it but its wonderful preservation, Mr. Trelawny lifted it from the table. Margaret started forward, crying out:

"Take care, Father! Take care! He may injure you!"

"Not now, my dear!" he answered as he moved towards the stairway. Her face fell. "Where are you going?" she asked in a faint voice.

"To the kitchen," he answered. "Fire will take away all danger for the future; even an astral body cannot materialise from ashes!" He signed to us to follow him. Margaret turned away with a sob. I went to her; but she motioned me back and whispered:

"No, no! Go with the others. Father may want you. Oh! it seems like murder! The poor Queen's pet...!" The tears were dropping from under the fingers that covered her eyes.

In the kitchen was a fire of wood ready laid. To this Mr. Trelawny applied a match; in a few seconds the kindling had caught and the flames leaped. When the fire was solidly ablaze, he threw the body of the cat into it. For a few seconds it lay a dark mass amidst the flames, and the room was rank with the smell of burning hair. Then the dry body caught fire too. The inflammable substances used in embalming became new fuel, and the flames roared. A few minutes of fierce conflagration; and then we breathed freely. Queen Tera's Familiar was no more!

When we went back to the cave we found Margaret sitting in the dark. She had switched off the electric light, and only a faint glow of the evening light came through the narrow openings. Her father went quickly over to her and put his arms round her in a loving protective way. She laid her head on his shoulder for a minute and seemed comforted. Presently she called to me:

"Malcolm, turn up the light!" I carried out her orders, and could see that, though she had been crying, her eyes were now dry. Her father saw it too and looked glad. He said to us in a grave tone:

"Now we had better prepare for our great work. It will not do to leave anything to the last!" Margaret must have had a suspicion of what was coming, for it was with a sinking voice that she asked:

"What are you going to do now?" Mr. Trelawny too must have had a suspicion of her feelings, for he answered in a low tone:

"To unroll the mummy of Queen Tera!" She came close to him and said pleadingly in a whisper:

"Father, you are not going to unswathe her! All you men...! And in the glare of light!"

"But why not, my dear?"

"Just think, Father, a woman! All alone! In such a way! In such a place! Oh! It's cruel, cruel!" She was manifestly much overcome. Her cheeks were flaming red, and her eyes were full of indignant tears. Her father saw her distress; and, sympathising with it, began to comfort her. I was moving off; but he signed to me to stay. I took it that after the usual manner of men he wanted help on such an occasion, and man-like wished to throw on someone else the task of dealing with a woman in indignant distress. However, he began to appeal first to her reason:

"Not a woman, dear; a mummy! She has been dead nearly five thousand years!"

"What does that matter? Sex is not a matter of years! A woman is a woman, if she had been dead five thousand centuries! And you expect her to arise out of that long sleep! It could not be real death, if she is to rise out of it! You have led me to believe that she will come alive when the Coffer is opened!"

"I did, my dear; and I believe it! But if it isn't death that has been the matter with her all these years, it is something uncommonly like it. Then again, just think; it was men who embalmed her. They didn't have women's rights or lady doctors in ancient Egypt, my dear! And besides," he went on more freely, seeing that she was accepting his argument, if not yielding to it, "we men are accustomed to such things. Corbeck and I have unrolled a hundred mummies; and there were as many women as men amongst them. Doctor Winchester in his work has had to deal with women as well of men, till custom has made him think nothing of sex. Even Ross has in his work as a barrister..." He stopped suddenly.

"You were going to help too!" she said to me, with an indignant look.

I said nothing; I thought silence was best. Mr. Trelawny went on hurriedly; I could see that he was glad of interruption, for the part of his argument concerning a barrister's work was becoming decidedly weak:

"My child, you will be with us yourself. Would we do anything which would hurt or offend you? Come now! be reasonable! We are not at a pleasure party. We are all grave men, entering gravely on an experiment which may unfold the wisdom of old times, and enlarge human knowledge indefinitely; which may put the minds of men on new tracks of thought and research. An experiment," as he went on his voice deepened, "which may be fraught with death to any one of us – to us all! We know from what has been, that there are, or may be, vast and unknown dangers ahead of us, of which none in the house today may ever see the end. Take it, my child, that we are not acting lightly; but with all the gravity of deeply earnest men! Besides, my dear, whatever feelings you or any of us may have on the subject, it is necessary for the success of the experiment to unswathe her. I think that under any circumstances it would be necessary to remove the wrappings before she became again a live human being instead of a spiritualised corpse with an astral body. Were her original intention carried out, and did she come to new life within her mummy wrappings, it might be to exchange a coffin for a grave! She would die the death of the buried alive! But now, when she has voluntarily abandoned for the time her astral power, there can be no doubt on the subject."

Margaret's face cleared. "All right, Father!" she said as she kissed him. "But oh! It seems a horrible indignity to a Queen, and a woman."

I was moving away to the staircase when she called me:

"Where are you going?" I came back and took her hand and stroked it as I answered:

"I shall come back when the unrolling is over!" She looked at me long, and a faint suggestion of a smile came over her face as she said:

"Perhaps you had better stay, too! It may be useful to you in your work as a barrister!" She smiled out as she met my eyes: but in an instant she changed. Her face grew grave, and deadly white. In a far away voice she said:

"Father is right! It is a terrible occasion; we need all to be serious over it. But all the same – nay, for that very reason you had better stay, Malcolm! You may be glad, later on, that you were present tonight!"

My heart sank down, down, at her words; but I thought it better to say nothing. Fear was stalking openly enough amongst us already!

By this time Mr. Trelawny, assisted by Mr. Corbeck and Doctor Winchester, had raised the lid of the ironstone sarcophagus which contained the mummy of the Queen. It was a large one; but it was none too big. The mummy was both long and broad and high; and was of such weight that it was no easy task, even for the four of us, to lift it out. Under Mr. Trelawny's direction we laid it out on the table prepared for it.

Then, and then only, did the full horror of the whole thing burst upon me! There, in the full glare of the light, the whole material and sordid side of death seemed staringly real. The outer wrappings, torn and loosened by rude touch, and with the colour either darkened by dust or worn light by friction, seemed creased as by rough treatment; the jagged edges of the wrapping-cloths looked fringed; the painting was patchy, and the varnish chipped. The coverings were evidently many, for the bulk was great. But through all, showed that unhidable human figure, which seems to look more horrible when partially concealed than at any other time. What was before us was Death, and nothing else. All the romance and sentiment of fancy had disappeared. The two elder men, enthusiasts who had often done such work, were not disconcerted; and Doctor Winchester seemed to hold himself in a business-like attitude, as if before the operating-table. But I felt low-spirited, and miserable, and ashamed; and besides I was pained and alarmed by Margaret's ghastly pallor.

Then the work began. The unrolling of the mummy cat had prepared me somewhat for it; but this was so much larger, and so infinitely more elaborate, that it seemed a different thing. Moreover, in addition to the ever present sense of death and humanity, there was a feeling of something finer in all this. The cat had been embalmed with coarser materials; here, all, when once the outer coverings were removed, was more delicately done. It seemed as if only the finest gums and spices had been used in this embalming. But there were the same surroundings,

he same attendant red dust and pungent presence of bitumen; there was the
ame sound of rending which marked the tearing away of the bandages. There
vere an enormous number of these, and their bulk when opened was great. As
he men unrolled them, I grew more and more excited. I did not take a part in it
nyself; Margaret had looked at me gratefully as I drew back. We clasped hands,
nd held each other hard. As the unrolling went on, the wrappings became finer,
nd the smell less laden with bitumen, but more pungent. We all, I think, began
o feel it as though it caught or touched us in some special way. This, however,
lid not interfere with the work; it went on uninterruptedly. Some of the inner
vrappings bore symbols or pictures. These were done sometimes wholly in pale
green colour, sometimes in many colours; but always with a prevalence of green.
Now and again Mr. Trelawny or Mr. Corbeck would point out some special drawing
before laying the bandage on the pile behind them, which kept growing to a
monstrous height.

At last we knew that the wrappings were coming to an end. Already the
proportions were reduced to those of a normal figure of the manifest height of
he Queen, who was more than average height. And as the end drew nearer, so
Margaret's pallor grew; and her heart beat more and more wildly, till her breast
heaved in a way that frightened me.

Just as her father was taking away the last of the bandages, he happened to
ook up and caught the pained and anxious look of her pale face. He paused, and
aking her concern to be as to the outrage on modesty, said in a comforting way:

"Do not be uneasy, dear! See! there is nothing to harm you. The Queen has on
a robe. – Ay, and a royal robe, too!"

The wrapping was a wide piece the whole length of the body. It being removed,
a profusely full robe of white linen had appeared, covering the body from the
hroat to the feet.

And such linen! We all bent over to look at it.

Margaret lost her concern, in her woman's interest in fine stuff. Then the rest
of us looked with admiration; for surely such linen was never seen by the eyes of
our age. It was as fine as the finest silk. But never was spun or woven silk which
ay in such gracious folds, constrict though they were by the close wrappings of
he mummy cloth, and fixed into hardness by the passing of thousands of years.

Round the neck it was delicately embroidered in pure gold with tiny sprays of
sycamore; and round the feet, similarly worked, was an endless line of lotus plants
of unequal height, and with all the graceful abandon of natural growth.

Across the body, but manifestly not surrounding it, was a girdle of jewels.
A wondrous girdle, which shone and glowed with all the forms and phases and
colours of the sky!

The buckle was a great yellow stone, round of outline, deep and curved, as if a
yielding globe had been pressed down. It shone and glowed, as though a veritable
sun lay within; the rays of its light seemed to strike out and illumine all round.
Flanking it were two great moonstones of lesser size, whose glowing, beside the
glory of the sunstone, was like the silvery sheen of moonlight.

And then on either side, linked by golden clasps of exquisite shape, was a line
of flaming jewels, of which the colours seemed to glow. Each of these stones
seemed to hold a living star, which twinkled in every phase of changing light.

Margaret raised her hands in ecstasy. She bent over to examine more closely but suddenly drew back and stood fully erect at her grand height. She seemed to speak with the conviction of absolute knowledge as she said:

"That is no cerement! It was not meant for the clothing of death! It is a marriage robe!"

Mr. Trelawny leaned over and touched the linen robe. He lifted a fold at the neck, and I knew from the quick intake of his breath that something had surprised him. He lifted yet a little more; and then he, too, stood back and pointed, saying

"Margaret is right! That dress is not intended to be worn by the dead! See! Her figure is not robed in it. It is but laid upon her." He lifted the zone of jewels and handed it to Margaret. Then with both hands he raised the ample robe, and laid it across the arms which she extended in a natural impulse. Things of such beauty were too precious to be handled with any but the greatest care.

We all stood awed at the beauty of the figure which, save for the face cloth now lay completely nude before us. Mr. Trelawny bent over, and with hands that trembled slightly, raised this linen cloth which was of the same fineness as the robe. As he stood back and the whole glorious beauty of the Queen was revealed I felt a rush of shame sweep over me. It was not right that we should be there gazing with irreverent eyes on such unclad beauty: it was indecent; it was almost sacrilegious! And yet the white wonder of that beautiful form was something to dream of. It was not like death at all; it was like a statue carven in ivory by the hand of a Praxiteles. There was nothing of that horrible shrinkage which death seems to effect in a moment. There was none of the wrinkled toughness which seems to be a leading characteristic of most mummies. There was not the shrunken attenuation of a body dried in the sand, as I had seen before in museums. All the pores of the body seemed to have been preserved in some wonderful way. The flesh was full and round, as in a living person; and the skin was as smooth as satin. The colour seemed extraordinary. It was like ivory, new ivory; except where the right arm, with shattered, bloodstained wrist and missing hand had lain bare to exposure in the sarcophagus for so many tens of centuries.

With a womanly impulse; with a mouth that drooped with pity, with eyes that flashed with anger, and cheeks that flamed, Margaret threw over the body the beautiful robe which lay across her arm. Only the face was then to be seen. This was more startling even than the body, for it seemed not dead, but alive. The eyelids were closed; but the long, black, curling lashes lay over on the cheeks. The nostrils, set in grave pride, seemed to have the repose which, when it is seen in life, is greater than the repose of death. The full, red lips, though the mouth was not open, showed the tiniest white line of pearly teeth within. Her hair, glorious in quantity and glossy black as the raven's wing, was piled in great masses over the white forehead, on which a few curling tresses strayed like tendrils. I was amazed at the likeness to Margaret, though I had had my mind prepared for this by Mr. Corbeck's quotation of her father's statement. This woman – I could not think of her as a mummy or a corpse – was the image of Margaret as my eyes had first lit on her. The likeness was increased by the jewelled ornament which she wore in her hair, the "Disk and Plumes", such as Margaret, too, had worn. It, too, was a glorious jewel; one noble pearl of moonlight lustre, flanked by carven pieces of moonstone.

Mr. Trelawny was overcome as he looked. He quite broke down; and when Margaret flew to him and held him close in her arms and comforted him, I heard him murmur brokenly:

"It looks as if you were dead, my child!"

There was a long silence. I could hear without the roar of the wind, which was now risen to a tempest, and the furious dashing of the waves far below. Mr. Trelawny's voice broke the spell:

"Later on we must try and find out the process of embalming. It is not like any that I know. There does not seem to have been any opening cut for the withdrawing of the viscera and organs, which apparently remain intact within the body. Then, again, there is no moisture in the flesh; but its place is supplied with something else, as though wax or stearine had been conveyed into the veins by some subtle process. I wonder could it be possible that at that time they could have used paraffin. It might have been, by some process that we know not, pumped into the veins, where it hardened!"

Margaret, having thrown a white sheet over the Queen's body, asked us to bring it to her own room, where we laid it on her bed. Then she sent us away, saying:

"Leave her alone with me. There are still many hours to pass, and I do not like to leave her lying there, all stark in the glare of light. This may be the Bridal she prepared for – the Bridal of Death; and at least she shall wear her pretty robes."

When presently she brought me back to her room, the dead Queen was dressed in the robe of fine linen with the embroidery of gold; and all her beautiful jewels were in place. Candles were lit around her, and white flowers lay upon her breast.

Hand in hand we stood looking at her for a while. Then with a sigh, Margaret covered her with one of her own snowy sheets. She turned away; and after softly closing the door of the room, went back with me to the others who had now come into the dining room. Here we all began to talk over the things that had been, and that were to be.

Now and again I could feel that one or other of us was forcing conversation, as if we were not sure of ourselves. The long wait was beginning to tell on our nerves. It was apparent to me that Mr. Trelawny had suffered in that strange trance more than we suspected, or than he cared to show. True, his will and his determination were as strong as ever; but the purely physical side of him had been weakened somewhat. It was indeed only natural that it should be. No man can go through a period of four days of absolute negation of life without being weakened by it somehow.

As the hours crept by, the time passed more and more slowly. The other men seemed to get unconsciously a little drowsy. I wondered if in the case of Mr. Trelawny and Mr. Corbeck, who had already been under the hypnotic influence of the Queen, the same dormance was manifesting itself. Doctor Winchester had periods of distraction which grew longer and more frequent as the time wore on.

As to Margaret, the suspense told on her exceedingly, as might have been expected in the case of a woman. She grew paler and paler still; till at last about midnight, I began to be seriously alarmed about her. I got her to come into the library with me, and tried to make her lie down on a sofa for a little while. As Mr. Trelawny had decided that the experiment was to be made exactly at the seventh hour after sunset, it would be as nearly as possible three o'clock in the morning when the great trial should be made. Even allowing a whole hour for the fina preparations, we had still two hours of waiting to go through, and I promised faithfully to watch her and to awake her at any time she might name. She would not hear of it, however. She thanked me sweetly and smiled at me as she did so but she assured me that she was not sleepy, and that she was quite able to bea up. That it was only the suspense and excitement of waiting that made her pale I agreed perforce; but I kept her talking of many things in the library for more than an hour; so that at last, when she insisted on going back to her father's room I fel that I had at least done something to help her pass the time.

We found the three men sitting patiently in silence. With manlike fortitude the were content to be still when they felt they had done all in their power. And so we waited.

The striking of two o'clock seemed to freshen us all up. Whatever shadows had been settling over us during the long hours preceding seemed to lift at once; and we went about our separate duties alert and with alacrity. We looked first to the windows to see that they were closed, and we got ready our respirators to pu them on when the time should be close at hand. We had from the first arranged to use them for we did not know whether some noxious fume might not come from the magic coffer when it should be opened. Somehow, it never seemed to occur to any of us that there was any doubt as to its opening.

Then, under Margaret's guidance, we carried the mummied body of Queen Tera from her room into her father's, and laid it on a couch. We put the sheet lightly ove it, so that if she should wake she could at once slip from under it. The severed hand was placed in its true position on her breast, and under it the Jewel of Seven Star: which Mr. Trelawny had taken from the great safe. It seemed to flash and blaze a he put it in its place.

It was a strange sight, and a strange experience. The group of grave silent men carried the white still figure, which looked like an ivory statue when through ou moving the sheet fell back, away from the lighted candles and the white flowers We placed it on the couch in that other room, where the blaze of the electric light shone on the great sarcophagus fixed in the middle of the room ready for the fina experiment, the great experiment consequent on the researches during a lifetim of these two travelled scholars. Again, the startling likeness between Margare and the mummy, intensified by her own extraordinary pallor, heightened th strangeness of it all. When all was finally fixed three-quarters of an hour hac gone, for we were deliberate in all our doings. Margaret beckoned me, and I wen out with her to bring in Silvio. He came to her purring. She took him up anc handed him to me; and then did a thing which moved me strangely and brough home to me keenly the desperate nature of the enterprise on which we wer embarked. One by one, she blew out the candles carefully and placed them bacl in their usual places. When she had finished she said to me:

"They are done with now. Whatever comes – life or death – there will be no purpose in their using now." Then taking Silvio into her arms, and pressing him close to her bosom where he purred loudly, we went back to the room. I closec the door carefully behind me, feeling as I did so a strange thrill as of finality There was to be no going back now. Then we put on our respirators, and took ou places as had been arranged. I was to stand by the taps of the electric lights besid

ιe door, ready to turn them off or on as Mr. Trelawny should direct. Doctor
/inchester was to stand behind the couch so that he should not be between the
ιummy and the sarcophagus; he was to watch carefully what should take place
·ith regard to the Queen. Margaret was to be beside him; she held Silvio ready to
lace him upon the couch or beside it when she might think right. Mr. Trelawny
nd Mr. Corbeck were to attend to the lighting of the lamps. When the hands of
ιe clock were close to the hour, they stood ready with their linstocks.

The striking of the silver bell of the clock seemed to smite on our hearts like a
nell of doom. One! Two! Three!

Before the third stroke the wicks of the lamps had caught, and I had turned out
ιe electric light. In the dimness of the struggling lamps, and after the bright glow
f the electric light, the room and all within it took weird shapes, and all seemed
ι an instant to change. We waited with our hearts beating. I know mine did, and
fancied I could hear the pulsation of the others.

The seconds seemed to pass with leaden wings. It were as though all the world
·ere standing still. The figures of the others stood out dimly, Margaret's white
·ress alone showing clearly in the gloom. The thick respirators which we all
·ore added to the strange appearance. The thin light of the lamps showed Mr.
·relawny's square jaw and strong mouth and the brown shaven face of Mr. Corbeck.
·heir eyes seemed to glare in the light. Across the room Doctor Winchester's
·yes twinkled like stars, and Margaret's blazed like black suns. Silvio's eyes were
·ke emeralds.

Would the lamps never burn up!

It was only a few seconds in all till they did blaze up. A slow, steady light, growing
ιore and more bright, and changing in colour from blue to crystal white. So they
·ayed for a couple of minutes without change in the coffer; till at last there began
> appear all over it a delicate glow. This grew and grew, till it became like a blazing
·wel, and then like a living thing whose essence of life was light. We waited and
·aited, our hearts seeming to stand still.

All at once there was a sound like a tiny muffled explosion and the cover lifted
·ght up on a level plane a few inches; there was no mistaking anything now, for
ιe whole room was full of a blaze of light. Then the cover, staying fast at one
·de rose slowly up on the other, as though yielding to some pressure of balance.
·he coffer still continued to glow; from it began to steal a faint greenish smoke.
·could not smell it fully on account of the respirator; but, even through that, I was
·onscious of a strange pungent odour. Then this smoke began to grow thicker,
·nd to roll out in volumes of ever increasing density till the whole room began to
·et obscure. I had a terrible desire to rush over to Margaret, whom I saw through
ιe smoke still standing erect behind the couch. Then, as I looked, I saw Doctor
/inchester sink down. He was not unconscious; for he waved his hand back and
·rward, as though to forbid any one to come to him. At this time the figures
·f Mr. Trelawny and Mr. Corbeck were becoming indistinct in the smoke which
·olled round them in thick billowy clouds. Finally I lost sight of them altogether.
·he coffer still continued to glow; but the lamps began to grow dim. At first I
ιought that their light was being overpowered by the thick black smoke; but
·resently I saw that they were, one by one, burning out. They must have burned
·uickly to produce such fierce and vivid flames.

I waited and waited, expecting every instant to hear the command to turn up the light; but none came. I waited still, and looked with harrowing intensity at the rolling billows of smoke still pouring out of the glowing casket, whilst the lamps sank down and went out one by one.

Finally there was but one lamp alight, and that was dimly blue and flickering. The only effective light in the room was from the glowing casket. I kept my eyes fixed toward Margaret; it was for her now that all my anxiety was claimed. I could just see her white frock beyond the still white shrouded figure on the couch. Silvio was troubled; his piteous mewing was the only sound in the room. Deeper and denser grew the black mist and its pungency began to assail my nostrils as well as my eyes. Now the volume of smoke coming from the coffer seemed to lessen, and the smoke itself to be less dense. Across the room I saw something white move where the couch was. There were several movements. I could just catch the quick glint of white through the dense smoke in the fading light; for now the glow of the coffer began quickly to subside. I could still hear Silvio, but his mewing came from close under; a moment later I could feel him piteously crouching on my foot.

Then the last spark of light disappeared, and through the Egyptian darkness I could see the faint line of white around the window blinds. I felt that the time had come to speak; so I pulled off my respirator and called out:

"Shall I turn up the light?" There was no answer; so before the thick smoke choked me, I called again but more loudly:

"Mr. Trelawny, shall I turn up the light?" He did not answer; but from across the room I heard Margaret's voice, sounding as sweet and clear as a bell:

"Yes, Malcolm!" I turned the tap and the lamps flashed out. But they were only dim points of light in the midst of that murky ball of smoke. In that thick atmosphere there was little possibility of illumination. I ran across to Margaret, guided by her white dress, and caught hold of her and held her hand. She recognised my anxiety and said at once:

"I am all right."

"Thank God!" I said. "How are the others? Quick, let us open all the windows and get rid of this smoke!" To my surprise, she answered in a sleepy way:

"They will be all right. They won't get any harm." I did not stop to inquire how or on what ground she formed such an opinion, but threw up the lower sashes of all the windows, and pulled down the upper. Then I threw open the door.

A few seconds made a perceptible change as the thick, black smoke began to roll out of the windows. Then the lights began to grow into strength and I could see the room. All the men were overcome. Beside the couch Doctor Winchester lay on his back as though he had sunk down and rolled over; and on the farther side of the sarcophagus, where they had stood, lay Mr. Trelawny and Mr. Corbeck. It was a relief to me to see that, though they were unconscious, all three were breathing heavily as though in a stupor. Margaret still stood behind the couch. She seemed at first to be in a partially dazed condition; but every instant appeared to get more command of herself. She stepped forward and helped me to raise her father and drag him close to a window. Together we placed the others similarly, and she flew down to the dining-room and returned with a decanter of brandy. This we proceeded to administer to them all in turn. It was not many minutes after we had pened the windows when all three were struggling back to consciousness. During this time my entire thoughts and efforts had been concentrated on their restoration; but now that this strain was off, I looked round the room to see what had been the effect of the experiment. The thick smoke had nearly cleared away; but the room was still misty and was full of a strange pungent acrid odour.

The great sarcophagus was just as it had been. The coffer was open, and in it, scattered through certain divisions or partitions wrought in its own substance, was scattering of black ashes. Over all, sarcophagus, coffer and, indeed, all in the room, was a sort of black film of greasy soot. I went over to the couch. The white sheet still lay over part of it; but it had been thrown back, as might be when one is stepping out of bed.

But there was no sign of Queen Tera! I took Margaret by the hand and led her over. She reluctantly left her father to whom she was administering, but she came docilely enough. I whispered to her as I held her hand:

"What has become of the Queen? Tell me! You were close at hand, and must have seen if anything happened!" She answered me very softly:

"There was nothing that I could see. Until the smoke grew too dense I kept my eyes on the couch, but there was no change. Then, when all grew so dark that I could not see, I thought I heard a movement close to me. It might have been Doctor Winchester who had sunk down overcome; but I could not be sure. I thought that it might be the Queen waking, so I put down poor Silvio. I did not see what became of him; but I felt as if he had deserted me when I heard him mewing over by the door. I hope he is not offended with me!" As if in answer, Silvio came running into the room and reared himself against her dress, pulling it as though clamouring to be taken up. She stooped down and took him up and began to pet and comfort him.

I went over and examined the couch and all around it most carefully. When Mr. Trelawny and Mr. Corbeck recovered sufficiently, which they did quickly, though Doctor Winchester took longer to come round, we went over it afresh. But all we could find was a sort of ridge of impalpable dust, which gave out a strange dead odour. On the couch lay the jewel of the disk and plumes which the Queen had worn in her hair, and the Star Jewel which had words to command the Gods.

Other than this we never got clue to what had happened. There was just one thing which confirmed our idea of the physical annihilation of the mummy. In the sarcophagus in the hall, where we had placed the mummy of the cat, was a small patch of similar dust.

In the autumn Margaret and I were married. On the occasion she wore the mummy robe and zone and the jewel which Queen Tera had worn in her hair. On her breast, set in a ring of gold make like a twisted lotus stalk, she wore the strange Jewel of Seven Stars which held words to command the God of all the worlds. At the marriage the sunlight streaming through the chancel windows fell on it, and it seemed to glow like a living thing.

The graven words may have been of efficacy; for Margaret holds to them, and here is no other life in all the world so happy as my own.

We often think of the great Queen, and we talk of her freely. Once, when I said with a sigh that I was sorry she could not have waked into a new life in a new world, my wife, putting both her hands in mine and looking into my eyes with that far-away eloquent dreamy look which sometimes comes into her own said lovingly:

"Do not grieve for her! Who knows, but she may have found the joy she sought Love and patience are all that make for happiness in this world; or in the world of the past or of the future; of the living or the dead. She dreamed her dream; and that is all that any of us can ask!"

If you enjoyed this, you might also like...
'The Secret of the Growing Gold,' see page 303
'The Red Stockade,' see page 336

The Lair of the White Worm
Chapter V; Chapters XIX–XXVIII

Publisher's Note: The protagonist of this story is the Australian Adam Salton, who is contacted by his great-uncle Richard in England, who wants to make Adam his heir. In the following chapter, Adam – who has come to England to stay with his uncle – is told of a local legend by Richard's friend Sir Nathaniel: that of the terrifying white worm.]

Chapter V
The White Worm

MR. SALTON INTRODUCED ADAM to Mr. Watford and his grand-daughters, and they all moved on together. Of course neighbours in the position of the Watfords knew all about Adam Salton, his relationship, circumstances, and prospects. So it would have been strange indeed if both girls did not dream of possibilities of the future. In agricultural England, eligible men of any class are rare. This particular man was specially eligible, for he did not belong to a class in which barriers of caste were strong. So when it began to be noticed that he walked beside Mimi Watford and seemed to desire her society, all their friends endeavoured to give the promising affair a helping hand. When the gongs sounded for the banquet, he went with her into the tent where her grandfather had seats. Mr. Salton and Sir Nathaniel noticed that the young man did not come to claim his appointed place at the dais table; but they understood and made no remark, or indeed did not seem to notice his absence.

Lady Arabella sat as before at Edgar Caswall's right hand. She was certainly a striking and unusual woman, and to all it seemed fitting from her rank and personal qualities that she should be the chosen partner of the heir on his first appearance. Of course nothing was said openly by those of her own class who were present; but words were not necessary when so much could be expressed by nods and smiles. It seemed to be an accepted thing that at last there was to be a mistress of Castra Regis, and that she was present amongst them. There were not lacking some who, whilst admitting all her charm and beauty, placed her in the second rank, Lilla Watford being marked as first. There was sufficient divergence of type, as well as of individual beauty, to allow of fair comment; Lady Arabella represented the aristocratic type, and Lilla that of the commonalty.

When the dusk began to thicken, Mr. Salton and Sir Nathaniel walked home – the trap had been sent away early in the day – leaving Adam to follow in his own time. He came in earlier than was expected, and seemed upset about something. Neither of the elders made any comment. They all lit cigarettes, and, as dinner-time was close at hand, went to their rooms to get ready.

Adam had evidently been thinking in the interval. He joined the others in th
drawing-room, looking ruffled and impatient – a condition of things seen for the fir
time. The others, with the patience – or the experience – of age, trusted to time t
unfold and explain things. They had not long to wait. After sitting down and standin
up several times, Adam suddenly burst out.

"That fellow seems to think he owns the earth. Can't he let people alone! He seem
to think that he has only to throw his handkerchief to any woman, and be her master

This outburst was in itself enlightening. Only thwarted affection in some guis
could produce this feeling in an amiable young man. Sir Nathaniel, as an ol
diplomatist, had a way of understanding, as if by foreknowledge, the true inwardnes
of things, and asked suddenly, but in a matter-of-fact, indifferent voice:

"Was he after Lilla?"

"Yes, and the fellow didn't lose any time either. Almost as soon as they met, h
began to butter her up, and tell her how beautiful she was. Why, before he left h
side, he had asked himself to tea tomorrow at Mercy Farm. Stupid ass! He might se
that the girl isn't his sort! I never saw anything like it. It was just like a hawk an
a pigeon."

As he spoke, Sir Nathaniel turned and looked at Mr. Salton – a keen look whic
implied a full understanding.

"Tell us all about it, Adam. There are still a few minutes before dinner, and we sha
all have better appetites when we have come to some conclusion on this matter."

"There is nothing to tell, sir; that is the worst of it. I am bound to say that ther
was not a word said that a human being could object to. He was very civil, and all tha
was proper – just what a landlord might be to a tenant's daughter.... Yet – yet – wel
I don't know how it was, but it made my blood boil."

"How did the hawk and the pigeon come in?" Sir Nathaniel's voice was soft an
soothing, nothing of contradiction or overdone curiosity in it – a tone eminent
suited to win confidence.

"I can hardly explain. I can only say that he looked like a hawk and she like a dov
– and, now that I think of it, that is what they each did look like; and do look like i
their normal condition."

"That is so!" came the soft voice of Sir Nathaniel.

Adam went on:

"Perhaps that early Roman look of his set me off. But I wanted to protect her; sh
seemed in danger."

"She seems in danger, in a way, from all you young men. I couldn't help noticin
the way that even you looked – as if you wished to absorb her!"

"I hope both you young men will keep your heads cool," put in Mr. Salton. "Yo
know, Adam, it won't do to have any quarrel between you, especially so soon after h
home-coming and your arrival here. We must think of the feelings and happiness o
our neighbours; mustn't we?"

"I hope so, sir. I assure you that, whatever may happen, or even threaten, I sha
obey your wishes in this as in all things."

"Hush!" whispered Sir Nathaniel, who heard the servants in the passag
bringing dinner.

After dinner, over the walnuts and the wine, Sir Nathaniel returned to the subje
of the local legends.

"It will perhaps be a less dangerous topic for us to discuss than more recent ones."
"All right, sir," said Adam heartily. "I think you may depend on me now with regard to any topic. I can even discuss Mr. Caswall. Indeed, I may meet him tomorrow. He is going, as I said, to call at Mercy Farm at three o'clock – but I have an appointment at two."

"I notice," said Mr. Salton, "that you do not lose any time."

The two old men once more looked at each other steadily. Then, lest the mood of his listener should change with delay, Sir Nathaniel began at once:

"I don't propose to tell you all the legends of Mercia, or even to make a selection of them. It will be better, I think, for our purpose if we consider a few facts – recorded or unrecorded – about this neighbourhood. I think we might begin with Diana's Grove. It has roots in the different epochs of our history, and each has its special crop of legend. The Druid and the Roman are too far off for matters of detail; but it seems to me the Saxon and the Angles are near enough to yield material for legendary lore. We find that this particular place had another name besides Diana's Grove. This was manifestly of Roman origin, or of Grecian accepted as Roman. The other is more pregnant of adventure and romance than the Roman name. In Mercian tongue it was 'The Lair of the White Worm.' This needs a word of explanation at the beginning.

"In the dawn of the language, the word 'worm' had a somewhat different meaning from that in use today. It was an adaptation of the Anglo-Saxon 'wyrm,' meaning a dragon or snake; or from the Gothic 'waurms,' a serpent; or the Icelandic 'ormur,' or the German 'wurm.' We gather that it conveyed originally an idea of size and power, not as now in the diminutive of both these meanings. Here legendary history helps us. We have the well-known legend of the 'Worm Well' of Lambton Castle, and that of the 'Laidly Worm of Spindleston Heugh' near Bamborough. In both these legends the 'worm' was a monster of vast size and power – a veritable dragon or serpent, such as legend attributes to vast fens or quags where there was illimitable room for expansion. A glance at a geological map will show that whatever truth there may have been of the actuality of such monsters in the early geologic periods, at least there was plenty of possibility. In England there were originally vast plains where the plentiful supply of water could gather. The streams were deep and slow, and there were holes of abysmal depth, where any kind and size of antediluvian monster could find a habitat. In places, which now we can see from our windows, were mud-holes a hundred or more feet deep. Who can tell us when the age of the monsters which flourished in slime came to an end? There must have been places and conditions which made for greater longevity, greater size, greater strength than was usual. Such over-lappings may have come down even to our earlier centuries. Nay, are there not now creatures of a vastness of bulk regarded by the generality of men as impossible? Even in our own day there are seen the traces of animals, if not the animals themselves, of stupendous size – veritable survivals from earlier ages, preserved by some special qualities in their habitats. I remember meeting a distinguished man in India, who had the reputation of being a great shikaree, who told me that the greatest temptation he had ever had in his life was to shoot a giant snake which he had come across in the Terai of Upper India. He was on a tiger-shooting expedition, and as his elephant was crossing a nullah, it squealed. He looked down from his howdah and saw that the elephant had stepped across the body of a snake which was dragging itself through

the jungle. 'So far as I could see,' he said, 'it must have been eighty or one hundred fee
in length. Fully forty or fifty feet was on each side of the track, and though the weigh
which it dragged had thinned it, it was as thick round as a man's body. I suppose yo
know that when you are after tiger, it is a point of honour not to shoot at anything else
as life may depend on it. I could easily have spined this monster, but I felt that I mus
not – so, with regret, I had to let it go.'

"Just imagine such a monster anywhere in this country, and at once we could ge
a sort of idea of the 'worms,' which possibly did frequent the great morasses whic
spread round the mouths of many of the great European rivers."

"I haven't the least doubt, sir, that there may have been such monsters as you hav
spoken of still existing at a much later period than is generally accepted," replied Adam
"Also, if there were such things, that this was the very place for them. I have tried t
think over the matter since you pointed out the configuration of the ground. But i
seems to me that there is a hiatus somewhere. Are there not mechanical difficulties?

"In what way?"

"Well, our antique monster must have been mighty heavy, and the distances h
had to travel were long and the ways difficult. From where we are now sitting dow
to the level of the mud-holes is a distance of several hundred feet – I am leavin
out of consideration altogether any lateral distance. Is it possible that there was
way by which a monster could travel up and down, and yet no chance recorder hav
ever seen him? Of course we have the legends; but is not some more exact evidenc
necessary in a scientific investigation?"

"My dear Adam, all you say is perfectly right, and, were we starting on such a
investigation, we could not do better than follow your reasoning. But, my dea
boy, you must remember that all this took place thousands of years ago. You mus
remember, too, that all records of the kind that would help us are lacking. Also, tha
the places to be considered were desert, so far as human habitation or populatio
are considered. In the vast desolation of such a place as complied with the necessar
conditions, there must have been such profusion of natural growth as would bar th
progress of men formed as we are. The lair of such a monster would not have bee
disturbed for hundreds – or thousands – of years. Moreover, these creatures mus
have occupied places quite inaccessible to man. A snake who could make himsel
comfortable in a quagmire, a hundred feet deep, would be protected on the outskirt
by such stupendous morasses as now no longer exist, or which, if they exist anywher
at all, can be on very few places on the earth's surface. Far be it from me to say that i
more elemental times such things could not have been. The condition belongs to th
geologic age – the great birth and growth of the world, when natural forces ran riot
when the struggle for existence was so savage that no vitality which was not founde
in a gigantic form could have even a possibility of survival. That such a time existed
we have evidences in geology, but there only; we can never expect proofs such as thi
age demands. We can only imagine or surmise such things – or such conditions an
such forces as overcame them."

* * *

*[Publisher's Note: The following extract comes from much later in the book. Adam ha
just witnessed the murder of Oolanga – a servant of the mysterious Lady Arabella Marsh*

by Arabella herself. He begins to suspect Arabella of having a hand in previous crimes, where children seemed to have been attacked by animals.]

Chapter XIX
An Enemy in the Dark

ADAM SALTON went for a walk before returning to Lesser Hill; he felt that it might be well, not only to steady his nerves, shaken by the horrible scene, but to get his thoughts into some sort of order, so as to be ready to enter on the matter with Sir Nathaniel. He was a little embarrassed as to telling his uncle, for affairs had so vastly progressed beyond his original view that he felt a little doubtful as to what would be the old gentleman's attitude when he should hear of the strange events for the first time. Mr. Salton would certainly not be satisfied at being treated as an outsider with regard to such things, most of which had points of contact with the inmates of his own house. It was with an immense sense of relief that Adam heard that his uncle had telegraphed to the housekeeper that he was detained by business at Walsall, where he would remain for the night; and that he would be back in the morning in time for lunch.

When Adam got home after his walk, he found Sir Nathaniel just going to bed. He did not say anything to him then of what had happened, but contented himself with arranging that they would walk together in the early morning, as he had much to say that would require serious attention.

Strangely enough he slept well, and awoke at dawn with his mind clear and his nerves in their usual unshaken condition. The maid brought up, with his early morning cup of tea, a note which had been found in the letter-box. It was from Lady Arabella, and was evidently intended to put him on his guard as to what he should say about the previous evening.

He read it over carefully several times, before he was satisfied that he had taken in its full import.

Dear Mr. Salton,

I cannot go to bed until I have written to you, so you must forgive me if I disturb you, and at an unseemly time. Indeed, you must also forgive me if, in trying to do what is right, I err in saying too much or too little. The fact is that I am quite upset and unnerved by all that has happened in this terrible night. I find it difficult even to write; my hands shake so that they are not under control, and I am trembling all over with memory of the horrors we saw enacted before our eyes. I am grieved beyond measure that I should be, however remotely, a cause of this horror coming on you. Forgive me if you can, and do not think too hardly of me. This I ask with confidence, for since we shared together the danger – the very pangs – of death, I feel that we should be to one another something more than mere friends, that I may lean on you and trust you, assured that your sympathy and pity are for me. You really must let me thank you for the friendliness, the help, the confidence, the real aid at a time of deadly danger and deadly fear which you showed me. That awful man – I shall see him for ever in my dreams. His black, malignant face will shut out all memory of sunshine and happiness. I shall eternally see his evil eyes as he threw himself into that well-hole in a vain effort to escape from the consequences of his own misdoing. The more I think of it, the more apparent it seems to me that he had premeditated the whole thing – of course, except his own horrible death.

Perhaps you have noticed a fur collar I occasionally wear. It is one of my most valued treasures – an ermine collar studded with emeralds. I had often seen the nigger's eyes gleam covetously when he looked at it. Unhappily, I wore it yesterday. That may have been the cause that lured the poor man to his doom. On the very brink of the abyss he tore the collar from my neck – that was the last I saw of him. When he sank into the hole, I was rushing to the iron door, which I pulled behind me. When I heard that soul-sickening yell, which marked his disappearance in the chasm, I was more glad than I can say that my eyes were spared the pain and horror which my ears had to endure.

When I tore myself out of the negro's grasp as he sank into the well-hole; I realised what freedom meant. Freedom! Freedom! Not only from that noisome prison-house, which has now such a memory, but from the more noisome embrace of that hideous monster. Whilst I live, I shall always thank you for my freedom. A woman must sometimes express her gratitude; otherwise it becomes too great to bear. I am not a sentimental girl, who merely likes to thank a man; I am a woman who knows all, of bad as well as good, that life can give. I have known what it is to love and to lose. But you must not let me bring any unhappiness into your life. I must live on – as I have lived – alone, and, in addition, bear with other woes the memory of this latest insult and horror. In the meantime, I must get away as quickly as possible from Diana's Grove. In the morning I shall go up to town, where I shall remain for a week – I cannot stay longer, as business affairs demand my presence here. I think, however, that a week in the rush of busy London, surrounded with multitudes of commonplace people, will help to soften – I cannot expect total obliteration – the terrible images of the bygone night. When I can sleep easily – which will be, I hope, after a day or two – I shall be fit to return home and take up again the burden which will, I suppose, always be with me.

I shall be most happy to see you on my return – or earlier, if my good fortune sends you on any errand to London. I shall stay at the Mayfair Hotel. In that busy spot we may forget some of the dangers and horrors we have shared together. Adieu, and thank you, again and again, for all your kindness and consideration to me.
Arabella Marsh.

Adam was surprised by this effusive epistle, but he determined to say nothing of it to Sir Nathaniel until he should have thought it well over. When Adam met Sir Nathaniel at breakfast, he was glad that he had taken time to turn things over in his mind. The result had been that not only was he familiar with the facts in all their bearings, but he had already so far differentiated them that he was able to arrange them in his own mind according to their values. Breakfast had been a silent function, so it did not interfere in any way with the process of thought.

So soon as the door was closed, Sir Nathaniel began:

"I see, Adam, that something has occurred, and that you have much to tell me."

"That is so, sir. I suppose I had better begin by telling you all I know – all that has happened since I left you yesterday?"

Accordingly Adam gave him details of all that had happened during the previous evening. He confined himself rigidly to the narration of circumstances, taking care not to colour events by any comment of his own, or any opinion of the meaning of things which he did not fully understand. At first, Sir Nathaniel seemed disposed to ask questions, but shortly gave this up when he recognised that the narration was concise and self-explanatory. Thenceforth, he contented himself with quick looks and glances, easily interpreted, or by some acquiescent motions of his hands, when such could be convenient, to emphasise his idea of the correctness of any inference. Until Adam ceased speaking, having evidently come to an end of what he had to say with regard to this section of his story, the elder man made no comment whatever. Even when Adam took from his pocket Lady Arabella's letter, with the manifest intention of reading it, he did not make any comment. Finally, when Adam folded up the letter and put it, in its envelope, back in his pocket, as an intimation that he had now quite finished, the old diplomatist carefully made a few notes in his pocket-book.

"Your narrative, my dear Adam, is altogether admirable. I think I may now take it that we are both well versed in the actual facts, and that our conference had better take the shape of a mutual exchange of ideas. Let us both ask questions as they may arise; and I do not doubt that we shall arrive at some enlightening conclusions."

"Will you kindly begin, sir? I do not doubt that, with your longer experience, you will be able to dissipate some of the fog which envelops certain of the things which we have to consider."

"I hope so, my dear boy. For a beginning, then, let me say that Lady Arabella's letter makes clear some things which she intended – and also some things which she did not intend. But, before I begin to draw deductions, let me ask you a few questions. Adam, are you heart-whole, quite heart-whole, in the matter of Lady Arabella?"

His companion answered at once, each looking the other straight in the eyes during question and answer.

"Lady Arabella, sir, is a charming woman, and I should have deemed it a privilege to meet her – to talk to her – even – since I am in the confessional – to flirt a little with her. But if you mean to ask if my affections are in any way engaged, I can emphatically answer 'No!' – as indeed you will understand when presently I give you the reason. Apart from that, there are the unpleasant details we discussed the other day."

"Could you – would you mind giving me the reason now? It will help us to understand what is before us, in the way of difficulty."

"Certainly, sir. My reason, on which I can fully depend, is that I love another woman!"

"That clinches it. May I offer my good wishes, and, I hope, my congratulations?"

"I am proud of your good wishes, sir, and I thank you for them. But it is too soon for congratulations – the lady does not even know my hopes yet. Indeed, I hardly knew them myself, as definite, till this moment."

"I take it then, Adam, that at the right time I may be allowed to know who the lady is?"

Adam laughed a low, sweet laugh, such as ripples from a happy heart.

"There need not be an hour's, a minute's delay. I shall be glad to share my secret with you, sir. The lady, sir, whom I am so happy as to love, and in whom my dreams of life-long happiness are centred, is Mimi Watford!"

"Then, my dear Adam, I need not wait to offer congratulations. She is indeed a very charming young lady. I do not think I ever saw a girl who united in such perfection the qualities of strength of character and sweetness of disposition. With all my heart,

I congratulate you. Then I may take it that my question as to your heart-wholeness answered in the affirmative?"

"Yes; and now, sir, may I ask in turn why the question?"

"Certainly! I asked because it seems to me that we are coming to a point where m questions might be painful to you."

"It is not merely that I love Mimi, but I have reason to look on Lady Arabella as he enemy," Adam continued.

"Her enemy?"

"Yes. A rank and unscrupulous enemy who is bent on her destruction."

Sir Nathaniel went to the door, looked outside it and returned, locking it carefull behind him.

Chapter XX
Metabolism

"AM I LOOKING GRAVE?" asked Sir Nathaniel inconsequently when he re-entere the room.

"You certainly are, sir."

"We little thought when first we met that we should be drawn into such a vortex Already we are mixed up in robbery, and probably murder, but – a thousand time worse than all the crimes in the calendar – in an affair of ghastly mystery whicl has no bottom and no end – with forces of the most unnerving kind, which ha their origin in an age when the world was different from the world which we know We are going back to the origin of superstition – to an age when dragons tore eacl other in their slime. We must fear nothing – no conclusion, however improbable almost impossible it may be. Life and death is hanging on our judgment, not onl for ourselves, but for others whom we love. Remember, I count on you as I hop you count on me."

"I do, with all confidence."

"Then," said Sir Nathaniel, "let us think justly and boldly and fear nothing, howeve terrifying it may seem. I suppose I am to take as exact in every detail your account o all the strange things which happened whilst you were in Diana's Grove?"

"So far as I know, yes. Of course I may be mistaken in recollection of some detai or another, but I am certain that in the main what I have said is correct."

"You feel sure that you saw Lady Arabella seize the negro round the neck, and dra him down with her into the hole?"

"Absolutely certain, sir, otherwise I should have gone to her assistance."

"We have, then, an account of what happened from an eye-witness whom we trus – that is yourself. We have also another account, written by Lady Arabella under he own hand. These two accounts do not agree. Therefore we must take it that one o the two is lying."

"Apparently, sir."

"And that Lady Arabella is the liar!"

"Apparently – as I am not."

"We must, therefore, try to find a reason for her lying. She has nothing to fear from Oolanga, who is dead. Therefore the only reason which could actuate her would b to convince someone else that she was blameless. This 'someone' could not be you r you had the evidence of your own eyes. There was no one else present; therefore must have been an absent person."

"That seems beyond dispute, sir."

"There is only one other person whose good opinion she could wish to keep – dgar Caswall. He is the only one who fills the bill. Her lies point to other things esides the death of the African. She evidently wanted it to be accepted that his lling into the well was his own act. I cannot suppose that she expected to convince ou, the eye-witness; but if she wished later on to spread the story, it was wise of her o try to get your acceptance of it."

"That is so!"

"Then there were other matters of untruth. That, for instance, of the ermine ollar embroidered with emeralds. If an understandable reason be required for nis, it would be to draw attention away from the green lights which were seen in ne room, and especially in the well-hole. Any unprejudiced person would accept ne green lights to be the eyes of a great snake, such as tradition pointed to living n the well-hole. In fine, therefore, Lady Arabella wanted the general belief to be nat there was no snake of the kind in Diana's Grove. For my own part, I don't elieve in a partial liar – this art does not deal in veneer; a liar is a liar right nrough. Self-interest may prompt falsity of the tongue; but if one prove to be a ar, nothing that he says can ever be believed. This leads us to the conclusion that ecause she said or inferred that there was no snake, we should look for one – and xpect to find it, too.

"Now let me digress. I live, and have for many years lived, in Derbyshire, a ounty more celebrated for its caves than any other county in England. I have een through them all, and am familiar with every turn of them; as also with ther great caves in Kentucky, in France, in Germany, and a host of other places in many of these are tremendously deep caves of narrow aperture, which are alued by intrepid explorers, who descend narrow gullets of abysmal depth – and ometimes never return. In many of the caverns in the Peak I am convinced that ome of the smaller passages were used in primeval times as the lairs of some of he great serpents of legend and tradition. It may have been that such caverns vere formed in the usual geologic way – bubbles or flaws in the earth's crust – vhich were later used by the monsters of the period of the young world. It may ave been, of course, that some of them were worn originally by water; but in time hey all found a use when suitable for living monsters.

"This brings us to another point, more difficult to accept and understand han any other requiring belief in a base not usually accepted, or indeed entered n – whether such abnormal growths could have ever changed in their nature. ome day the study of metabolism may progress so far as to enable us to accept tructural changes proceeding from an intellectual or moral base. We may lean owards a belief that great animal strength may be a sound base for changes of all orts. If this be so, what could be a more fitting subject than primeval monsters vhose strength was such as to allow a survival of thousands of years? We do not now yet if brain can increase and develop independently of other parts of the iving structure.

"After all, the mediaeval belief in the Philosopher's Stone which could transmute netals, has its counterpart in the accepted theory of metabolism which changes living tissue. In an age of investigation like our own, when we are returning to scienc as the base of wonders – almost of miracles – we should be slow to refuse to accep facts, however impossible they may seem to be.

"Let us suppose a monster of the early days of the world – a dragon of the prim – of vast age running into thousands of years, to whom had been conveyed i some way – it matters not – a brain just sufficient for the beginning of growth Suppose the monster to be of incalculable size and of a strength quite abnormal – veritable incarnation of animal strength. Suppose this animal is allowed to remai in one place, thus being removed from accidents of interrupted development; migh not, would not this creature, in process of time – ages, if necessary – have tha rudimentary intelligence developed? There is no impossibility in this; it is only th natural process of evolution. In the beginning, the instincts of animals are confine to alimentation, self-protection, and the multiplication of their species. As tim goes on and the needs of life become more complex, power follows need. We hav been long accustomed to consider growth as applied almost exclusively to size i its various aspects. But Nature, who has no doctrinaire ideas, may equally apply to concentration. A developing thing may expand in any given way or form. Now, i is a scientific law that increase implies gain and loss of various kinds; what a thin gains in one direction it may lose in another. May it not be that Mother Natur may deliberately encourage decrease as well as increase – that it may be an axio that what is gained in concentration is lost in size? Take, for instance, monster that tradition has accepted and localised, such as the Worm of Lambton or tha of Spindleston Heugh. If such a creature were, by its own process of metabolism to change much of its bulk for intellectual growth, we should at once arrive at new class of creature – more dangerous, perhaps, than the world has ever had an experience of – a force which can think, which has no soul and no morals, an therefore no acceptance of responsibility. A snake would be a good illustration o this, for it is cold-blooded, and therefore removed from the temptations which ofte weaken or restrict warm-blooded creatures. If, for instance, the Worm of Lambto – if such ever existed – were guided to its own ends by an organised intelligenc capable of expansion, what form of creature could we imagine which would equal i in potentialities of evil? Why, such a being would devastate a whole country. Now, al these things require much thought, and we want to apply the knowledge usefully and we should therefore be exact. Would it not be well to resume the subject late in the day?"

"I quite agree, sir. I am in a whirl already; and want to attend carefully to what you say; so that I may try to digest it."

Both men seemed fresher and better for the 'easy,' and when they met in the afternoon each of them had something to contribute to the general stock o information. Adam, who was by nature of a more militant disposition than his elderly friend, was glad to see that the conference at once assumed a practical trend. Si Nathaniel recognised this, and, like an old diplomatist, turned it to present use.

"Tell me now, Adam, what is the outcome, in your own mind, of our conversation?"

"That the whole difficulty already assumes practical shape; but with added dangers, that at first I did not imagine."

"What is the practical shape, and what are the added dangers? I am not disputing, but only trying to clear my own ideas by the consideration of yours –"

So Adam went on:

"In the past, in the early days of the world, there were monsters who were so vast that they could exist for thousands of years. Some of them must have overlapped the Christian era. They may have progressed intellectually in process of time. If they had in any way so progressed, or even got the most rudimentary form of brain, they would be the most dangerous things that ever were in the world. Tradition says that one of these monsters lived in the Marsh of the East, and came up to a cave in Diana's Grove, which was also called the Lair of the White Worm. Such creatures may have grown down as well as up. They may have grown into, or something like, human beings. Lady Arabella March is of snake nature. She has committed crimes to our knowledge. She retains something of the vast strength of her primal being – can see in the dark – has the eyes of a snake. She used the nigger, and then dragged him through the snake's hole down to the swamp; she is intent on evil, and hates some one we love. Result..."

"Yes, the result?"

"First, that Mimi Watford should be taken away at once – then –"

"Yes?"

"The monster must be destroyed."

"Bravo! That is a true and fearless conclusion. At whatever cost, it must be carried out."

"At once?"

"Soon, at all events. That creature's very existence is a danger. Her presence in his neighbourhood makes the danger immediate."

As he spoke, Sir Nathaniel's mouth hardened and his eyebrows came down till they met. There was no doubting his concurrence in the resolution, or his readiness to help in carrying it out. But he was an elderly man with much experience and knowledge of law and diplomacy. It seemed to him to be a stern duty to prevent anything irrevocable taking place till it had been thought out and all was ready. There were all sorts of legal cruxes to be thought out, not only regarding the taking of life, even of a monstrosity in human form, but also of property. Lady Arabella, be she woman or snake or devil, owned the ground she moved in, according to British law, and the law is jealous and swift to avenge wrongs done within its ken. All such difficulties should be – must be – avoided for Mr. Salton's sake, for Adam's own sake, and, most of all, for Mimi Watford's sake.

Before he spoke again, Sir Nathaniel had made up his mind that he must try to postpone decisive action until the circumstances on which they depended – which, after all, were only problematical – should have been tested satisfactorily, one way or another. When he did speak, Adam at first thought that his friend was wavering in his intention, or 'funking' the responsibility. However, his respect for Sir Nathaniel was so great that he would not act, or even come to a conclusion on a vital point, without his sanction.

He came close and whispered in his ear:

"We will prepare our plans to combat and destroy this horrible menace, after we have cleared up some of the more baffling points. Meanwhile, we must wait for the night – I hear my uncle's footsteps echoing down the hall."

Sir Nathaniel nodded his approval.

Chapter XXI
Green Light

WHEN OLD MR. SALTON had retired for the night, Adam and Sir Nathaniel returned to the study. Things went with great regularity at Lesser Hill, so they knew that there would be no interruption to their talk.

When their cigars were lighted, Sir Nathaniel began.

"I hope, Adam, that you do not think me either slack or changeable of purpose. I mean to go through this business to the bitter end – whatever it may be. Be satisfied that my first care is, and shall be, the protection of Mimi Watford. To that I am pledged; my dear boy, we who are interested are all in the same danger. That semi-human monster out of the pit hates and means to destroy us all – you and me certainly, and probably your uncle. I wanted especially to talk with you tonight, for I cannot help thinking that the time is fast coming – if it has not come already – when we must take your uncle into our confidence. It was one thing when fancied evils threatened, but now he is probably marked for death, and it is only right that he should know all."

"I am with you, sir. Things have changed since we agreed to keep him out of the trouble. Now we dare not; consideration for his feelings might cost his life. It is a duty – and no light or pleasant one, either. I have not a shadow of doubt that he will want to be one with us in this. But remember, we are his guests; his name, his honour, have to be thought of as well as his safety."

"All shall be as you wish, Adam. And now as to what we are to do? We cannot murder Lady Arabella off-hand. Therefore we shall have to put things in order for the killing, and in such a way that we cannot be taxed with a crime."

"It seems to me, sir, that we are in an exceedingly tight place. Our first difficulty is to know where to begin. I never thought this fighting an antediluvian monster would be such a complicated job. This one is a woman, with all a woman's wit, combined with the heartlessness of a cocotte. She has the strength and impregnability of a diplodocus. We may be sure that in the fight that is before us there will be no semblance of fair-play. Also that our unscrupulous opponent will not betray herself!"

"That is so – but being feminine, she will probably over-reach herself. Now, Adam, it strikes me that, as we have to protect ourselves and others against feminine nature, our strong game will be to play our masculine against her feminine. Perhaps we had better sleep on it. She is a thing of the night; and the night may give us some ideas."

So they both turned in.

Adam knocked at Sir Nathaniel's door in the grey of the morning, and, on being bidden, came into the room. He had several letters in his hand. Sir Nathaniel sat up in bed.

"Well!"

"I should like to read you a few letters, but, of course, I shall not send them unless you approve. In fact" – with a smile and a blush – "there are several things which I want to do; but I hold my hand and my tongue till I have your approval."

"Go on!" said the other kindly. "Tell me all, and count at any rate on my sympathy, and on my approval and help if I can see my way."

Accordingly Adam proceeded:

"When I told you the conclusions at which I had arrived, I put in the foreground that Mimi Watford should, for the sake of her own safety, be removed – and that the monster which had wrought all the harm should be destroyed."

"Yes, that is so."

"To carry this into practice, sir, one preliminary is required – unless harm of another kind is to be faced. Mimi should have some protector whom all the world would recognise. The only form recognised by convention is marriage!"

Sir Nathaniel smiled in a fatherly way.

"To marry, a husband is required. And that husband should be you."

"Yes, yes."

"And the marriage should be immediate and secret – or, at least, not spoken of outside ourselves. Would the young lady be agreeable to that proceeding?"

"I do not know, sir!"

"Then how are we to proceed?"

"I suppose that we – or one of us – must ask her."

"Is this a sudden idea, Adam, a sudden resolution?"

"A sudden resolution, sir, but not a sudden idea. If she agrees, all is well and good. The sequence is obvious."

"And it is to be kept a secret amongst ourselves?"

"I want no secret, sir, except for Mimi's good. For myself, I should like to shout it from the house-tops! But we must be discreet; untimely knowledge to our enemy might work incalculable harm."

"And how would you suggest, Adam, that we could combine the momentous question with secrecy?"

Adam grew red and moved uneasily.

"Someone must ask her – as soon as possible!"

"And that someone?"

"I thought that you, sir, would be so good!"

"God bless my soul! This is a new kind of duty to take on – at my time of life. Adam, I hope you know that you can count on me to help in any way I can!"

"I have already counted on you, sir, when I ventured to make such a suggestion. I can only ask," he added, "that you will be more than ever kind to me – to us – and look on the painful duty as a voluntary act of grace, prompted by kindness and affection."

"Painful duty!"

"Yes," said Adam boldly. "Painful to you, though to me it would be all joyful."

"It is a strange job for an early morning! Well, we all live and learn. I suppose the sooner I go the better. You had better write a line for me to take with me. For, you see, this is to be a somewhat unusual transaction, and it may be embarrassing to the lady, even to myself. So we ought to have some sort of warrant, something to show that we have been mindful of her feelings. It will not do to take acquiescence for granted – although we act for her good."

"Sir Nathaniel, you are a true friend; I am sure that both Mimi and I shall be grateful to you for all our lives – however long they may be!"

So the two talked it over and agreed as to points to be borne in mind by the ambassador. It was striking ten when Sir Nathaniel left the house, Adam seeing him quietly off.

As the young man followed him with wistful eyes – almost jealous of the privileg
which his kind deed was about to bring him – he felt that his own heart was in hi
friend's breast.

The memory of that morning was like a dream to all those concerned in it. Si
Nathaniel had a confused recollection of detail and sequence, though the main fact
stood out in his memory boldly and clearly. Adam Salton's recollection was of a
illimitable wait, filled with anxiety, hope, and chagrin, all dominated by a sense c
the slow passage of time and accompanied by vague fears. Mimi could not for a lon;
time think at all, or recollect anything, except that Adam loved her and was savin;
her from a terrible danger. When she had time to think, later on, she wondered whei
she had any ignorance of the fact that Adam loved her, and that she loved him with al
her heart. Everything, every recollection however small, every feeling, seemed to fi
into those elemental facts as though they had all been moulded together. The mai
and crowning recollection was her saying goodbye to Sir Nathaniel, and entrustin;
to him loving messages, straight from her heart, to Adam Salton, and of his bearin;
when – with an impulse which she could not check – she put her lips to his anc
kissed him. Later, when she was alone and had time to think, it was a passing grief tc
her that she would have to be silent, for a time, to Lilla on the happy events of tha
strange mission.

She had, of course, agreed to keep all secret until Adam should give her leave
to speak.

The advice and assistance of Sir Nathaniel was a great help to Adam in carrying ou
his idea of marrying Mimi Watford without publicity. He went with him to London
and, with his influence, the young man obtained the license of the Archbishop o
Canterbury for a private marriage. Sir Nathaniel then persuaded old Mr. Salton tc
allow his nephew to spend a few weeks with him at Doom Tower, and it was here that
Mimi became Adam's wife. But that was only the first step in their plans; before going
further, however, Adam took his bride off to the Isle of Man. He wished to place a
stretch of sea between Mimi and the White Worm, while things matured. On their
return, Sir Nathaniel met them and drove them at once to Doom, taking care to avoid
any one that he knew on the journey.

Sir Nathaniel had taken care to have the doors and windows shut and locked –
all but the door used for their entry. The shutters were up and the blinds down.
Moreover, heavy curtains were drawn across the windows. When Adam commented
on this, Sir Nathaniel said in a whisper:

"Wait till we are alone, and I'll tell you why this is done; in the meantime not a
word or a sign. You will approve when we have had a talk together."

They said no more on the subject till after dinner, when they were ensconced in
Sir Nathaniel's study, which was on the top storey. Doom Tower was a lofty structure,
situated on an eminence high up in the Peak. The top commanded a wide prospect,
ranging from the hills above the Ribble to the near side of the Brow, which marked
the northern bound of ancient Mercia. It was of the early Norman period, less than
a century younger than Castra Regis. The windows of the study were barred and
locked, and heavy dark curtains closed them in. When this was done not a gleam of
light from the tower could be seen from outside.

When they were alone, Sir Nathaniel explained that he had taken his old friend,
Mr. Salton, into full confidence, and that in future all would work together.

"It is important for you to be extremely careful. In spite of the fact that our marriage was kept secret, as also your temporary absence, both are known."

"How? To whom?"

"How, I know not; but I am beginning to have an idea."

"To her?" asked Adam, in momentary consternation.

Sir Nathaniel shivered perceptibly.

"The White Worm – yes!"

Adam noticed that from now on, his friend never spoke of Lady Arabella otherwise, except when he wished to divert the suspicion of others.

Sir Nathaniel switched off the electric light, and when the room was pitch dark, he came to Adam, took him by the hand, and led him to a seat set in the southern window. Then he softly drew back a piece of the curtain and motioned his companion to look out.

Adam did so, and immediately shrank back as though his eyes had opened on pressing danger. His companion set his mind at rest by saying in a low voice:

"It is all right; you may speak, but speak low. There is no danger here – at present!"

Adam leaned forward, taking care, however, not to press his face against the glass. What he saw would not under ordinary circumstances have caused concern to anybody. With his special knowledge, it was appalling – though the night was now so dark that in reality there was little to be seen.

On the western side of the tower stood a grove of old trees, of forest dimensions. They were not grouped closely, but stood a little apart from each other, producing the effect of a row widely planted. Over the tops of them was seen a green light, something like the danger signal at a railway-crossing. It seemed at first quite still; but presently, when Adam's eye became accustomed to it, he could see that it moved as if trembling. This at once recalled to Adam's mind the light quivering above the well-hole in the darkness of that inner room at Diana's Grove, Oolanga's awful shriek, and the hideous black face, now grown grey with terror, disappearing into the impenetrable gloom of the mysterious orifice. Instinctively he laid his hand on his revolver, and stood up ready to protect his wife. Then, seeing that nothing happened, and that the light and all outside the tower remained the same, he softly pulled the curtain over the window.

Sir Nathaniel switched on the light again, and in its comforting glow they began to talk freely.

Chapter XXII
At Close Quarters

"SHE HAS DIABOLICAL CUNNING," said Sir Nathaniel. "Ever since you left, she has ranged along the Brow and wherever you were accustomed to frequent. I have not heard whence the knowledge of your movements came to her, nor have I been able to learn any data whereon to found an opinion. She seems to have heard both of your marriage and your absence; but I gather, by inference, that she does not actually know where you and Mimi are, or of your return. So soon as the dusk fails, she goes out on her rounds, and before dawn covers the whole ground round the Brow, and away up into the heart of the Peak. The White Worm, in her own proper shape, certainly has great facilities for the business on which she is now engaged. She can look into windows of any ordinary kind. Happily, this house is beyond her reach, if she wishes – as she manifestly does – to remain unrecognised. But, even at this height, it is wise to show no lights, lest she might learn something of our presence or absence."

"Would it not be well, sir, if one of us could see this monster in her real shape at close quarters? I am willing to run the risk – for I take it there would be no slight risk in the doing. I don't suppose anyone of our time has seen her close and lived to tell the tale."

Sir Nathaniel held up an expostulatory hand.

"Good God, lad, what are you suggesting? Think of your wife, and all that is at stake."

"It is of Mimi that I think – for her sake that I am willing to risk whatever is to be risked."

Adam's young bride was proud of her man, but she blanched at the thought of the ghastly White Worm. Adam saw this and at once reassured her.

"So long as her ladyship does not know whereabout I am, I shall have as much safety as remains to us; bear in mind, my darling, that we cannot be too careful."

Sir Nathaniel realised that Adam was right; the White Worm had no supernatural powers and could not harm them until she discovered their hiding place. It was agreed, therefore, that the two men should go together.

When the two men slipped out by the back door of the house, they walked cautiously along the avenue which trended towards the west. Everything was pitch dark – so dark that at times they had to feel their way by the palings and tree-trunks. They could still see, seemingly far in front of them and high up, the baleful light which at the height and distance seemed like a faint line. As they were now on the level of the ground, the light seemed infinitely higher than it had from the top of the tower. At the sight Adam's heart fell; the danger of the desperate enterprise which he had undertaken burst upon him. But this feeling was shortly followed by another which restored him to himself – a fierce loathing, and a desire to kill, such as he had never experienced before.

They went on for some distance on a level road, fairly wide, from which the green light was visible. Here Sir Nathaniel spoke softly, placing his lips to Adam's ear for safety.

"We know nothing whatever of this creature's power of hearing or smelling, though I presume that both are of no great strength. As to seeing, we may presume the opposite, but in any case we must try to keep in the shade behind the tree-trunks. The slightest error would be fatal to us."

Adam only nodded, in case there should be any chance of the monster seeing the movement.

After a time that seemed interminable, they emerged from the circling wood. It was like coming out into sunlight by comparison with the misty blackness which had been around them. There was light enough to see by, though not sufficient to distinguish things at a distance. Adam's eyes sought the green light in the sky. It was still in about the same place, but its surroundings were more visible. It was now at the summit of what seemed to be a long white pole, near the top of which were two pendant white masses, like rudimentary arms or fins. The green light, strangely enough, did not seem lessened by the surrounding starlight, but had a clearer effect and a deeper green. Whilst they were carefully regarding this – Adam with the aid of an opera-glass – their nostrils were assailed by a horrid stench, something like that which rose from the well-hole in Diana's Grove.

By degrees, as their eyes got the right focus, they saw an immense towering mass that seemed snowy white. It was tall and thin. The lower part was hidden by the trees which lay between, but they could follow the tall white shaft and the duplicate green lights which topped it. As they looked there was a movement – the shaft seemed to bend, and the line of green light descended amongst the trees. They could see the green light twinkle as it passed between the obstructing branches.

Seeing where the head of the monster was, the two men ventured a little further forward, and saw that the hidden mass at the base of the shaft was composed of vast coils of the great serpent's body, forming a base from which the upright mass rose. As they looked, this lower mass moved, the glistening folds catching the moonlight, and they could see that the monster's progress was along the ground. It was coming towards them at a swift pace, so they turned and ran, taking care to make as little noise as possible, either by their footfalls or by disturbing the undergrowth close to them. They did not stop or pause till they saw before them the high dark tower of Doom.

Chapter XXIII
In the Enemy's House

SIR NATHANIEL WAS in the library next morning, after breakfast, when Adam came to him carrying a letter.

"Her ladyship doesn't lose any time. She has begun work already!"

Sir Nathaniel, who was writing at a table near the window, looked up.

"What is it?" said he.

Adam held out the letter he was carrying. It was in a blazoned envelope.

"Ha!" said Sir Nathaniel, "From the White Worm! I expected something of the kind."

"But," said Adam, "how could she have known we were here? She didn't know last night."

"I don't think we need trouble about that, Adam. There is so much we do not understand. This is only another mystery. Suffice it that she does know – perhaps it is all the better and safer for us."

"How is that?" asked Adam with a puzzled look.

"General process of reasoning, my boy; and the experience of some years in the diplomatic world. This creature is a monster without heart or consideration for anything or anyone. She is not nearly so dangerous in the open as when she has the dark to protect her. Besides, we know, by our own experience of her movements, that for some reason she shuns publicity. In spite of her vast bulk and abnormal strength, she is afraid to attack openly. After all, she is only a snake and with a snake's nature, which is to keep low and squirm, and proceed by stealth and cunning. She will never attack when she can run away, although she knows well that running away would probably be fatal to her. What is the letter about?"

Sir Nathaniel's voice was calm and self-possessed. When he was engaged in any struggle of wits he was all diplomatist.

"She asks Mimi and me to tea this afternoon at Diana's Grove, and hopes that you also will favour her."

Sir Nathaniel smiled.

"Please ask Mrs. Salton to accept for us all."

"She means some deadly mischief. Surely – surely it would be wiser not."

"It is an old trick that we learn early in diplomacy, Adam – to fight on ground of your own choice. It is true that she suggested the place on this occasion; but by accepting it we make it ours. Moreover, she will not be able to understand our reason for doing so, and her own bad conscience – if she has any, bad or good – and her own fears and doubts will play our game for us. No, my dear boy, let us accept, by all means."

Adam said nothing, but silently held out his hand, which his companion shook: no words were necessary.

When it was getting near tea-time, Mimi asked Sir Nathaniel how they were going.

"We must make a point of going in state. We want all possible publicity." Mimi looked at him inquiringly. "Certainly, my dear, in the present circumstances publicity is a part of safety. Do not be surprised if, whilst we are at Diana's Grove, occasional messages come for you – for all or any of us."

"I see!" said Mrs. Salton. "You are taking no chances."

"None, my dear. All I have learned at foreign courts, and amongst civilised and uncivilised people, is going to be utilised within the next couple of hours."

Sir Nathaniel's voice was full of seriousness, and it brought to Mimi in a convincing way the awful gravity of the occasion.

In due course, they set out in a carriage drawn by a fine pair of horses, who soon devoured the few miles of their journey. Before they came to the gate, Sir Nathaniel turned to Mimi.

"I have arranged with Adam certain signals which may be necessary if certain eventualities occur. These need be nothing to do with you directly. But bear in mind that if I ask you or Adam to do anything, do not lose a second in the doing of it. We must try to pass off such moments with an appearance of unconcern. In all probability, nothing requiring such care will occur. The White Worm will not try force, though she has so much of it to spare. Whatever she may attempt today, of harm to any of us, will be in the way of secret plot. Some other time she may try force, but – if I am able to judge such a thing – not today. The messengers who may ask for any of us will not be witnesses only, they may help to stave off danger." Seeing query in her face, he went on: "Of what kind the danger may be, I know not, and cannot guess. It will doubtless be some ordinary circumstance; but none the less dangerous on that account. Here we are at the gate. Now, be careful in all matters, however small. To keep your head is half the battle."

There were a number of men in livery in the hall when they arrived. The doors of the drawing-room were thrown open, and Lady Arabella came forth and offered them cordial welcome. This having been got over, Lady Arabella led them into another room where tea was served.

Adam was acutely watchful and suspicious of everything, and saw on the far side of this room a panelled iron door of the same colour and configuration as the outer door of the room where was the well-hole wherein Oolanga had disappeared. Something in the sight alarmed him, and he quietly stood near the door. He made no movement, even of his eyes, but he could see that Sir Nathaniel was watching him intently, and, he fancied, with approval.

They all sat near the table spread for tea, Adam still near the door. Lady Arabella fanned herself, complaining of heat, and told one of the footmen to throw all the outer doors open.

Tea was in progress when Mimi suddenly started up with a look of fright on her face; at the same moment, the men became cognisant of a thick smoke which began to spread through the room – a smoke which made those who experienced it gasp and choke. The footmen began to edge uneasily towards the inner door. Denser and denser grew the smoke, and more acrid its smell. Mimi, towards whom the draught from the open door wafted the smoke, rose up choking, and ran to the inner door, which she threw open to its fullest extent, disclosing on the outside a curtain of thin silk, fixed to the doorposts. The draught from the open door swayed the thin silk towards her, and in her fright, she tore down the curtain, which enveloped her from head to foot. Then she ran through the still open door, heedless of the fact that she could not see where she was going. Adam, followed by Sir Nathaniel, rushed forward and joined her – Adam catching his wife by the arm and holding her tight. It was well that he did so, for just before her lay the black orifice of the well-hole, which, of course, she could not see with the silk curtain round her head. The floor was extremely slippery; something like thick oil had been spilled where she had to pass; and close to the edge of the hole her feet shot from under her, and she stumbled forward towards the well-hole.

When Adam saw Mimi slip, he flung himself backward, still holding her. His weight told, and he dragged her up from the hole and they fell together on the floor outside the zone of slipperiness. In a moment he had raised her up, and together they rushed out through the open door into the sunlight, Sir Nathaniel close behind them. They were all pale except the old diplomatist, who looked both calm and cool. It sustained and cheered Adam and his wife to see him thus master of himself. Both managed to follow his example, to the wonderment of the footmen, who saw the three who had just escaped a terrible danger walking together gaily, as, under the guiding pressure of Sir Nathaniel's hand, they turned to re-enter the house.

Lady Arabella, whose face had blanched to a deadly white, now resumed her ministrations at the tea-board as though nothing unusual had happened. The slop-basin was full of half-burned brown paper, over which tea had been poured.

Sir Nathaniel had been narrowly observing his hostess, and took the first opportunity afforded him of whispering to Adam:

"The real attack is to come – she is too quiet. When I give my hand to your wife to lead her out, come with us – and caution her to hurry. Don't lose a second, even if you have to make a scene. Hs-s-s-h!"

Then they resumed their places close to the table, and the servants, in obedience to Lady Arabella's order, brought in fresh tea.

Thence on, that tea-party seemed to Adam, whose faculties were at their utmost intensity, like a terrible dream. As for poor Mimi, she was so overwrought both with present and future fear, and with horror at the danger she had escaped, that her faculties were numb. However, she was braced up for a trial, and she felt assured that whatever might come she would be able to go through with it. Sir Nathaniel seemed just as usual – suave, dignified, and thoughtful – perfect master of himself.

To her husband, it was evident that Mimi was ill at ease. The way she kept turning her head to look around her, the quick coming and going of the colour of her face, her hurried breathing, alternating with periods of suspicious calm, were evidence of mental perturbation. To her, the attitude of Lady Arabella seemed compounded of social sweetness and personal consideration. It would be hard to imagine more thoughtful and tender kindness towards an honoured guest.

When tea was over and the servants had come to clear away the cups, Lady Arabella putting her arm round Mimi's waist, strolled with her into an adjoining room, where she collected a number of photographs which were scattered about, and, sitting down beside her guest, began to show them to her. While she was doing this, the servant closed all the doors of the suite of rooms, as well as that which opened from the room outside – that of the well-hole into the avenue. Suddenly, without any seeming cause the light in the room began to grow dim. Sir Nathaniel, who was sitting close to Mimi rose to his feet, and, crying, "Quick!" caught hold of her hand and began to drag her from the room. Adam caught her other hand, and between them they drew her through the outer door which the servants were beginning to close. It was difficult at first to find the way, the darkness was so great; but to their relief when Adam whistled shrilly, the carriage and horses, which had been waiting in the angle of the avenue dashed up. Her husband and Sir Nathaniel lifted – almost threw – Mimi into the carriage. The postillion plied whip and spur, and the vehicle, rocking with its speed swept through the gate and tore up the road. Behind them was a hubbub – servants rushing about, orders being shouted out, doors shutting, and somewhere, seemingly far back in the house, a strange noise. Every nerve of the horses was strained as they dashed recklessly along the road. The two men held Mimi between them, the arms of both of them round her as though protectingly. As they went, there was a sudden rise in the ground; but the horses, breathing heavily, dashed up it at racing speed not slackening their pace when the hill fell away again, leaving them to hurry along the downgrade.

It would be foolish to say that neither Adam nor Mimi had any fear in returning to Doom Tower. Mimi felt it more keenly than her husband, whose nerves were harder and who was more inured to danger. Still she bore up bravely, and as usual the effort was helpful to her. When once she was in the study in the top of the turret, she almost forgot the terrors which lay outside in the dark. She did not attempt to peep out of the window; but Adam did – and saw nothing. The moonlight showed all the surrounding country, but nowhere was to be observed that tremulous line of green light.

The peaceful night had a good effect on them all; danger, being unseen, seemed far off. At times it was hard to realise that it had ever been. With courage restored, Adam rose early and walked along the Brow, seeing no change in the signs of life in Castra Regis. What he did see, to his wonder and concern, on his returning homeward was Lady Arabella, in her tight-fitting white dress and ermine collar, but without her emeralds; she was emerging from the gate of Diana's Grove and walking toward the Castle. Pondering on this, and trying to find some meaning in it, occupied his thoughts till he joined Mimi and Sir Nathaniel at breakfast. They began the meal in silence. What had been had been, and was known to them all. Moreover, it was not pleasant topic.

A fillip was given to the conversation when Adam told of his seeing Lady Arabella on her way to Castra Regis. They each had something to say of her, and of what her wishes or intentions were towards Edgar Caswall. Mimi spoke bitterly of her in every aspect. She had not forgotten – and never would – never could – the occasion when o harm Lilla, the woman had consorted even with the nigger. As a social matter, she was disgusted with her for following up the rich landowner – "throwing herself at his head so shamelessly," was how she expressed it. She was interested to know that the great kite still flew from Caswall's tower. But beyond such matters she did not try to go. The only comment she made was of strongly expressed surprise at her ladyship's 'cheek' in ignoring her own criminal acts, and her impudence in taking it for granted that others had overlooked them also.

Chapter XXIV
A Startling Proposition

THE MORE MIMI thought over the late events, the more puzzled she was. What did all mean – what could it mean, except that there was an error of fact somewhere. Could it be possible that some of them – all of them had been mistaken, that there had been no White Worm at all? On either side of her was a belief impossible of reception. Not to believe in what seemed apparent was to destroy the very foundations of belief... Yet in old days there had been monsters on the earth, and certainly some people had believed in just such mysterious changes of identity. It was all very strange. Just fancy how any stranger – say a doctor – would regard her, if she were to tell him that she had been to a tea-party with an antediluvian monster, and that they had been waited on by up-to-date men-servants.

Adam had returned, exhilarated by his walk, and more settled in his mind than he had been for some time. Like Mimi, he had gone through the phase of doubt and inability to believe in the reality of things, though it had not affected him to the same extent. The idea, however, that his wife was suffering ill-effects from her terrible ordeal, braced him up. He remained with her for a time, then he sought Sir Nathaniel in order to talk over the matter with him. He knew that the calm common sense and self-reliance of the old man, as well as his experience, would be helpful to them all.

Sir Nathaniel had come to the conclusion that, for some reason which he did not understand, Lady Arabella had changed her plans, and, for the present at all events, was pacific. He was inclined to attribute her changed demeanour to the fact that her influence over Edgar Caswall was so far increased, as to justify a more fixed belief in his submission to her charms.

As a matter of fact, she had seen Caswall that morning when she visited Castra Regis, and they had had a long talk together, during which the possibility of their union had been discussed. Caswall, without being enthusiastic on the subject, had been courteous and attentive; as she had walked back to Diana's Grove, she almost congratulated herself on her new settlement in life. That the idea was becoming fixed in her mind, was shown by a letter which she wrote later in the day to Adam Salton, and sent to him by hand. It ran as follows:

Dear Mr. Salton,

I wonder if you would kindly advise, and, if possible, help me in a matter of business. I have been for some time trying to make up my mind to sell Diana's Grove, I have put off and put off the doing of it till now. The place is my own property, and no one has to be consulted with regard to what I may wish to do about it. It was bought by my late husband, Captain Adolphus Ranger

March, who had another residence, The Crest, Appleby. He acquired all rights of all kinds, including mining and sporting. When he died, he left his whole property to me. I shall feel leaving this place, which has become endeared to me by many sacred memories and affections – the recollection of many happy days of my young married life, and the more than happy memories of the man I loved and who loved me so much. I should be willing to sell the place for any fair price – so long, of course, as the purchaser was one I liked and of whom I approved. May I say that you yourself would be the ideal person. But I dare not hope for so much. It strikes me, however, that among your Australian friends may be someone who wishes to make a settlement in the Old Country, and would care to fix the spot in one of the most historic regions in England, full of romance and legend, and with a never-ending vista of historical interest – an estate which, though small, is in perfect condition and with illimitable possibilities of development, and many doubtful – or unsettled – rights which have existed before the time of the Romans or even Celts, who were the original possessors. In addition, the house has been kept up to the dernier cri. Immediate possession can be arranged. My lawyers can provide you, or whoever you may suggest, with all business and historical details. A word from you of acceptance or refusal is all that is necessary, and we can leave details to be thrashed out by our agents. Forgive me, won't you, for troubling you in the matter, and believe me, yours very sincerely.
Arabella March.

Adam read this over several times, and then, his mind being made up, he went to Mimi and asked if she had any objection. She answered – after a shudder – that she was, in this, as in all things, willing to do whatever he might wish.

"Dearest, I am willing that you should judge what is best for us. Be quite free to act as you see your duty, and as your inclination calls. We are in the hands of God, and He has hitherto guided us, and will do so to His own end."

From his wife's room Adam Salton went straight to the study in the tower, where he knew Sir Nathaniel would be at that hour. The old man was alone, so, when he had entered in obedience to the "Come in," which answered his query, he closed the door and sat down beside him.

"Do you think, sir, that it would be well for me to buy Diana's Grove?"

"God bless my soul!" said the old man, startled, "why on earth would you want to do that?"

"Well, I have vowed to destroy that White Worm, and my being able to do whatever I may choose with the Lair would facilitate matters and avoid complications."

Sir Nathaniel hesitated longer than usual before speaking. He was thinking deeply.

"Yes, Adam, there is much common sense in your suggestion, though it startled me at first. I think that, for all reasons, you would do well to buy the property and to have the conveyance settled at once. If you want more money than is immediately convenient, let me know, so that I may be your banker."

"Thank you, sir, most heartily; but I have more money at immediate call than I shall want. I am glad you approve."

"The property is historic, and as time goes on it will increase in value. Moreover, I may tell you something, which indeed is only a surmise, but which, if I am right, will add great value to the place." Adam listened. "Has it ever struck you why the old name, 'The Lair of the White Worm,' was given? We know that there was a snake which in early days was called a worm; but why white?"

"I really don't know, sir; I never thought of it. I simply took it for granted."

"So did I at first – long ago. But later I puzzled my brain for a reason."

"And what was the reason, sir?"

"Simply and solely because the snake or worm was white. We are near the county of Stafford, where the great industry of china-burning was originated and grew. Stafford owes much of its wealth to the large deposits of the rare china clay found in it from time to time. These deposits become in time pretty well exhausted; but for centuries Stafford adventurers looked for the special clay, as Ohio and Pennsylvania farmers and explorers looked for oil. Anyone owning real estate on which china clay can be discovered strikes a sort of gold mine."

"Yes, and then –" The young man looked puzzled.

"The original 'Worm' so-called, from which the name of the place came, had to find a direct way down to the marshes and the mud-holes. Now, the clay is easily penetrable, and the original hole probably pierced a bed of china clay. When once the way was made it would become a sort of highway for the Worm. But as much movement was necessary to ascend such a great height, some of the clay would become attached to its rough skin by attrition. The downway must have been easy work, but the ascent was different, and when the monster came to view in the upper world, it would be fresh from contact with the white clay. Hence the name, which has no cryptic significance, but only fact. Now, if that surmise be true – and I do not see why not – there must be a deposit of valuable clay – possibly of immense depth."

Adam's comment pleased the old gentleman.

"I have it in my bones, sir, that you have struck – or rather reasoned out – a great truth."

Sir Nathaniel went on cheerfully. "When the world of commerce wakes up to the value of your find, it will be as well that your title to ownership has been perfectly secured. If anyone ever deserved such a gain, it is you."

With his friend's aid, Adam secured the property without loss of time. Then he went to see his uncle, and told him about it. Mr. Salton was delighted to find his young relative already constructively the owner of so fine an estate – one which gave him an important status in the county. He made many anxious enquiries about Mimi, and the doings of the White Worm, but Adam reassured him.

The next morning, when Adam went to his host in the smoking-room, Sir Nathaniel asked him how he purposed to proceed with regard to keeping his vow.

"It is a difficult matter which you have undertaken. To destroy such a monster is something like one of the labours of Hercules, in that not only its size and weight and power of using them in little-known ways are against you, but the occult side is alone an unsurpassable difficulty. The Worm is already master of all the elements except fire – and I do not see how fire can be used for the attack. It has only to sink into the earth in its usual way, and you could not overtake it if you had the resources of the biggest coal-mine in existence. But I daresay you have mapped out some plan in your mind," he added courteously.

"I have, sir. But, of course, it may not stand the test of practice."

"May I know the idea?"

"Well, sir, this was my argument: At the time of the Chartist trouble, an idea spread amongst financial circles that an attack was going to be made on the Bank of England. Accordingly, the directors of that institution consulted many persons who were supposed to know what steps should be taken, and it was finally decided that the best protection against fire – which is what was feared – was not water but sand. To carry the scheme into practice great store of fine sea-sand – the kind that blows about and is used to fill hour-glasses – was provided throughout the building, especially at the points liable to attack, from which it could be brought into use.

"I propose to provide at Diana's Grove, as soon as it comes into my possession, an enormous amount of such sand, and shall take an early occasion of pouring it into the well-hole, which it will in time choke. Thus Lady Arabella, in her guise of the White Worm, will find herself cut off from her refuge. The hole is a narrow one, and is some hundreds of feet deep. The weight of the sand this can contain would not in itself be sufficient to obstruct; but the friction of such a body working up against it would be tremendous."

"One moment. What use would the sand be for destruction?"

"None, directly; but it would hold the struggling body in place till the rest of my scheme came into practice."

"And what is the rest?"

"As the sand is being poured into the well-hole, quantities of dynamite can also be thrown in!"

"Good. But how would the dynamite explode – for, of course, that is what you intend. Would not some sort of wire or fuse he required for each parcel of dynamite?"

Adam smiled.

"Not in these days, sir. That was proved in New York. A thousand pounds of dynamite, in sealed canisters, was placed about some workings. At the last a charge of gunpowder was fired, and the concussion exploded the dynamite. It was most successful. Those who were non-experts in high explosives expected that every pane of glass in New York would be shattered. But, in reality, the explosive did no harm outside the area intended, although sixteen acres of rock had been mined and only the supporting walls and pillars had been left intact. The whole of the rocks were shattered."

Sir Nathaniel nodded approval.

"That seems a good plan – a very excellent one. But if it has to tear down so many feet of precipice, it may wreck the whole neighbourhood."

"And free it for ever from a monster," added Adam, as he left the room to find his wife.

Chapter XXV
The Last Battle

LADY ARABELLA had instructed her solicitors to hurry on with the conveyance of Diana's Grove, so no time was lost in letting Adam Salton have formal possession of the estate. After his interview with Sir Nathaniel, he had taken steps to begin putting his plan into action. In order to accumulate the necessary amount of fine sea-sand he ordered the steward to prepare for an elaborate system of top-dressing all the grounds. A great heap of the sand, brought from bays on the Welsh coast, began to grow at the back of the Grove. No one seemed to suspect that it was there for any purpose other than what had been given out.

Lady Arabella, who alone could have guessed, was now so absorbed in her matrimonial pursuit of Edgar Caswall, that she had neither time nor inclination for thought extraneous to this. She had not yet moved from the house, though she had formally handed over the estate.

Adam put up a rough corrugated-iron shed behind the Grove, in which he stored his explosives. All being ready for his great attempt whenever the time should come, he was now content to wait, and, in order to pass the time, interested himself in other things – even in Caswall's great kite, which still flew from the high tower of Castra Regis.

The mound of fine sand grew to proportions so vast as to puzzle the bailiffs and farmers round the Brow. The hour of the intended cataclysm was approaching apace. Adam wished – but in vain – for an opportunity, which would appear to be natural, of visiting Caswall in the turret of Castra Regis. At last, one morning, he met Lady Arabella moving towards the Castle, so he took his courage à deux mains and asked to be allowed to accompany her. She was glad, for her own purposes, to comply with his wishes. So together they entered, and found their way to the turret-room. Caswall was much surprised to see Adam come to his house, but lent himself to the task of seeming to be pleased. He played the host so well as to deceive even Adam. They all went out on the turret roof, where he explained to his guests the mechanism for raising and lowering the kite, taking also the opportunity of testing the movements of the multitudes of birds, how they answered almost instantaneously to the lowering or raising of the kite.

As Lady Arabella walked home with Adam from Castra Regis, she asked him if she might make a request. Permission having been accorded, she explained that before she finally left Diana's Grove, where she had lived so long, she had a desire to know the depth of the well-hole. Adam was really happy to meet her wishes, not from any sentiment, but because he wished to give some valid and ostensible reason for examining the passage of the Worm, which would obviate any suspicion resulting from his being on the premises. He brought from London a Kelvin sounding apparatus, with a sufficient length of piano-wire for testing any probable depth. The wire passed easily over the running wheel, and when this was once fixed over the hole, he was satisfied to wait till the most advantageous time for his final experiment.

* * *

In the meantime, affairs had been going quietly at Mercy Farm. Lilla, of course, felt lonely in the absence of her cousin, but the even tenor of life went on for her as for others. After the first shock of parting was over, things went back to their accustomed routine. In one respect, however, there was a marked difference. So long as home conditions had remained unchanged, Lilla was content to put ambition far from her, and to settle down to the life which had been hers as long as she could remember. But Mimi's marriage set her thinking; naturally, she came to the conclusion that she too might have a mate. There was not for her much choice – there was little movement in the matrimonial direction at the farmhouse. She did not approve of the personality of Edgar Caswall, and his struggle with Mimi had frightened her; but he was unmistakably an excellent parti, much better than she could have any right to expect. This weighs much with a woman, and more particularly one of her class. So, on the whole, she was content to let things take their course, and to abide by the issue.

As time went on, she had reason to believe that things did not point to happiness. She could not shut her eyes to certain disturbing facts, amongst which were the existence of Lady Arabella and her growing intimacy with Edgar Caswall; as well as his own cold and haughty nature, so little in accord with the ardour which is the foundation of a young maid's dreams of happiness. How things would, of necessity, alter if she were to marry, she was afraid to think. All told, the prospect was not happy for her, and she had a secret longing that something might occur to upset the order of things as at present arranged.

When Lilla received a note from Edgar Caswall asking if he might come to tea on the following afternoon, her heart sank within her. If it was only for her father's sake, she must not refuse him or show any disinclination which he might construe into incivility. She missed Mimi more than she could say or even dared to think. Hitherto, she had always looked to her cousin for sympathy, for understanding, for loyal support. Now she and all these things, and a thousand others – gentle, assuring, supporting – were gone. And instead there was a horrible aching void.

For the whole afternoon and evening, and for the following forenoon, poor Lilla's loneliness grew to be a positive agony. For the first time she began to realise the sense of her loss, as though all the previous suffering had been merely a preparation. Everything she looked at, everything she remembered or thought of, became laden with poignant memory. Then on the top of all was a new sense of dread. The reaction from the sense of security, which had surrounded her all her life, to a never-quieted apprehension, was at times almost more than she could bear. It so filled her with fear that she had a haunting feeling that she would as soon die as live. However, whatever might be her own feelings, duty had to be done, and as she had been brought up to consider duty first, she braced herself to go through, to the very best of her ability, what was before her.

Still, the severe and prolonged struggle for self-control told upon Lilla. She looked as she felt, ill and weak. She was really in a nerveless and prostrate condition, with black circles round her eyes, pale even to her lips, and with an instinctive trembling which she was quite unable to repress. It was for her a sad mischance that Mimi was away, for her love would have seen through all obscuring causes, and have brought to light the girl's unhappy condition of health. Lilla was utterly unable to do anything to escape from the ordeal before her; but her cousin, with the experience of her former struggles with Mr. Caswall and of the condition in which these left her, would have taken steps – even peremptory ones, if necessary – to prevent a repetition.

Edgar arrived punctually to the time appointed by herself. When Lilla, through the great window, saw him approaching the house, her condition of nervous upset was pitiable. She braced herself up, however, and managed to get through the interview in its preliminary stages without any perceptible change in her normal appearance and bearing. It had been to her an added terror that the black shadow of Oolanga, whom she dreaded, would follow hard on his master. A load was lifted from her mind when he did not make his usual stealthy approach. She had also feared, though in lesser degree, lest Lady Arabella should be present to make trouble for her as before.

With a woman's natural forethought in a difficult position, she had provided the furnishing of the tea-table as a subtle indication of the social difference between her and her guest. She had chosen the implements of service, as well as all the provender set forth, of the humblest kind. Instead of arranging the silver teapot and china cups, she had set out an earthen teapot, such as was in common use in the farm kitchen. The same idea was carried out in the cups and saucers of thick homely delft, and in the cream-jug of similar kind. The bread was of simple whole-meal, home-baked. The butter was good, since she had made it herself, while the preserves and honey came from her own garden. Her face beamed with satisfaction when the guest eyed the appointments with a supercilious glance. It was a shock to the poor girl herself, for she enjoyed offering to a guest the little hospitalities possible to her; but that had to be sacrificed with other pleasures.

Caswall's face was more set and iron-clad than ever – his piercing eyes seemed from the very beginning to look her through and through. Her heart quailed when she thought of what would follow – of what would be the end, when this was only the beginning. As some protection, though it could be only of a sentimental kind, she brought from her own room the photographs of Mimi, of her grandfather, and of Adam Salton, whom by now she had grown to look on with reliance, as a brother whom she could trust. She kept the pictures near her heart, to which her hand naturally strayed when her feelings of constraint, distrust, or fear became so poignant as to interfere with the calm which she felt was necessary to help her through her ordeal.

At first Edgar Caswall was courteous and polite, even thoughtful; but after a little while, when he found her resistance to his domination grow, he abandoned all forms of self-control and appeared in the same dominance as he had previously shown. She was prepared, however, for this, both by her former experience and the natural fighting instinct within her. By this means, as the minutes went on, both developed the power and preserved the equality in which they had begun.

Without warning, the psychic battle between the two individualities began afresh. This time both the positive and negative causes were all in favour of the man. The woman was alone and in bad spirits, unsupported; nothing at all was in her favour except the memory of the two victorious contests; whereas the man, though unaided, as before, by either Lady Arabella or Oolanga, was in full strength, well rested, and in flourishing circumstances. It was not, therefore, to be wondered at that his native dominance of character had full opportunity of asserting itself. He began his preliminary stare with a conscious sense of power, and, as it appeared to have immediate effect on the girl, he felt an ever-growing conviction of ultimate victory.

After a little Lilla's resolution began to flag. She felt that the contest was unequal – that she was unable to put forth her best efforts. As she was an unselfish person, she could not fight so well in her own battle as in that of someone whom she loved and to whom she was devoted. Edgar saw the relaxing of the muscles of face and brow, and the almost collapse of the heavy eyelids which seemed tumbling downward in sleep. Lilla made gallant efforts to brace her dwindling powers, but for a time unsuccessfully. At length there came an interruption, which seemed like a powerful stimulant. Through the wide window she saw Lady Arabella enter the plain gateway of the farm, and advance towards the hall door. She was clad as usual in tight-fitting white, which accentuated her thin, sinuous figure.

The sight did for Lilla what no voluntary effort could have done. Her eyes flashed and in an instant she felt as though a new life had suddenly developed within her. Lady Arabella's entry, in her usual unconcerned, haughty, supercilious way, heightened the effect, so that when the two stood close to each other battle was joined. Mr. Caswall too, took new courage from her coming, and all his masterfulness and power came back to him. His looks, intensified, had more obvious effect than had been noticeable that day. Lilla seemed at last overcome by his dominance. Her face became red and pale – violently red and ghastly pale – by rapid turns. Her strength seemed gone. Her knees collapsed, and she was actually sinking on the floor, when to her surprise and joy Mimi came into the room, running hurriedly and breathing heavily.

Lilla rushed to her, and the two clasped hands. With that, a new sense of power greater than Lilla had ever seen in her, seemed to quicken her cousin. Her hand swept the air in front of Edgar Caswall, seeming to drive him backward more and more by each movement, till at last he seemed to be actually hurled through the door which Mimi's entrance had left open, and fell at full length on the gravel path without.

Then came the final and complete collapse of Lilla, who, without a sound, sank down on the floor.

Chapter XXVI
Face to Face

MIMI WAS GREATLY DISTRESSED when she saw her cousin lying prone. She had a few times in her life seen Lilla on the verge of fainting, but never senseless; and now she was frightened. She threw herself on her knees beside Lilla, and tried, by rubbing her hands and other measures commonly known, to restore her. But all her efforts were unavailing. Lilla still lay white and senseless. In fact, each moment she looked worse; her breast, that had been heaving with the stress, became still, and the pallor of her face grew like marble.

At these succeeding changes Mimi's fright grew, till it altogether mastered her. She succeeded in controlling herself only to the extent that she did not scream.

Lady Arabella had followed Caswall, when he had recovered sufficiently to get up and walk – though stumblingly – in the direction of Castra Regis. When Mimi was quite alone with Lilla and the need for effort had ceased, she felt weak and trembled. In her own mind, she attributed it to a sudden change in the weather – it was momentarily becoming apparent that a storm was coming on.

She raised Lilla's head and laid it on her warm young breast, but all in vain. The cold of the white features thrilled through her, and she utterly collapsed when it was borne in on her that Lilla had passed away.

The dusk gradually deepened and the shades of evening closed in, but Mimi did not seem to notice or to care. She sat on the floor with her arms round the body of the girl whom she loved. Darker and blacker grew the sky as the coming storm and the closing night joined forces. Still she sat on – alone – tearless – unable to think. Mimi did not know how long she sat there. Though it seemed to her that ages had passed, it could not have been more than half-an-hour. She suddenly came to herself and was surprised to find that her grandfather had not returned. For a while she lay quiet, thinking of the immediate past. Lilla's hand was still in hers, and to her surprise it was still warm. Somehow this helped her consciousness, and without any special act of will she stood up. She lit a lamp and looked at her cousin. There was no doubt that Lilla was dead; but when the lamp-light fell on her eyes, they seemed to look at Mimi with intent – with meaning. In this state of dark isolation a new resolution came to her, and grew and grew until it became a fixed definite purpose. She would face Caswall and call him to account for his murder of Lilla – that was what she called it to herself. She would also take steps – she knew not what or how – to avenge the part taken by Lady Arabella.

In this frame of mind she lit all the lamps in the room, got water and linen from her room, and set about the decent ordering of Lilla's body. This took some time; but when it was finished, she put on her hat and cloak, put out the lights, and set out quietly for Castra Regis.

As Mimi drew near the Castle, she saw no lights except those in and around the tower room. The lights showed her that Mr. Caswall was there, so she entered by the hall door, which as usual was open, and felt her way in the darkness up the staircase to the lobby of the room. The door was ajar, and the light from within showed brilliantly through the opening. She saw Edgar Caswall walking restlessly to and fro in the room, with his hands clasped behind his back. She opened the door without knocking, and walked right into the room. As she entered, he ceased walking, and stared at her in surprise. She made no remark, no comment, but continued the fixed look which he had seen on her entrance.

For a time silence reigned, and the two stood looking fixedly at each other. Mimi was the first to speak.

"You murderer! Lilla is dead!"

"Dead! Good God! When did she die?"

"She died this afternoon, just after you left her."

"Are you sure?"

"Yes – and so are you – or you ought to be. You killed her!"

"I killed her! Be careful what you say!"

"As God sees us, it is true; and you know it. You came to Mercy Farm on purpose to break her – if you could. And the accomplice of your guilt, Lady Arabella March, came for the same purpose."

"Be careful, woman," he said hotly. "Do not use such names in that way, or you shall suffer for it."

"I am suffering for it – have suffered for it – shall suffer for it. Not for speaking the truth as I have done, but because you two, with devilish malignity, did my darling to death. It is you and your accomplice who have to dread punishment, not I."

"Take care!" he said again.

"Oh, I am not afraid of you or your accomplice," she answered spiritedly. "I am content to stand by every word I have said, every act I have done. Moreover, I believe in God's justice. I fear not the grinding of His mills; if necessary I shall set the wheels in motion myself. But you don't care for God, or believe in Him. Your god is your great kite, which cows the birds of a whole district. But be sure that His hand, when it rises, always falls at the appointed time. It may be that your name is being called even at this very moment at the Great Assize. Repent while there is still time. Happy you, if you may be allowed to enter those mighty halls in the company of the pure-souled angel whose voice has only to whisper one word of justice, and you disappear for ever into everlasting torment."

The sudden death of Lilla caused consternation among Mimi's friends and well-wishers. Such a tragedy was totally unexpected, as Adam and Sir Nathaniel had been expecting the White Worm's vengeance to fall upon themselves.

Adam, leaving his wife free to follow her own desires with regard to Lilla and her grandfather, busied himself with filling the well-hole with the fine sand prepared for the purpose, taking care to have lowered at stated intervals quantities of the store of dynamite, so as to be ready for the final explosion. He had under his immediate supervision a corps of workmen, and was assisted by Sir Nathaniel, who had come over for the purpose, and all were now staying at Lesser Hill.

Mr. Salton, too, showed much interest in the job, and was constantly coming in and out, nothing escaping his observation.

Since her marriage to Adam and their coming to stay at Doom Tower, Mimi had been fettered by fear of the horrible monster at Diana's Grove. But now she dreaded it no longer. She accepted the fact of its assuming at will the form of Lady Arabella. She had still to tax and upbraid her for her part in the unhappiness which had been wrought on Lilla, and for her share in causing her death.

One evening, when Mimi entered her own room, she went to the window and threw an eager look round the whole circle of sight. A single glance satisfied her that the White Worm in propriâ personâ was not visible. So she sat down in the window-seat and enjoyed the pleasure of a full view, from which she had been so long cut off. The maid who waited on her had told her that Mr. Salton had not yet returned home, so she felt free to enjoy the luxury of peace and quiet.

As she looked out of the window, she saw something thin and white move along the avenue. She thought she recognised the figure of Lady Arabella, and instinctively drew back behind the curtain. When she had ascertained, by peeping out several times, that the lady had not seen her, she watched more carefully, all her instinctive hatred flooding back at the sight of her. Lady Arabella was moving swiftly and stealthily, looking back and around her at intervals, as if she feared to be followed. This gave Mimi an idea that she was up to no good, so she determined to seize the occasion for watching her in more detail.

Hastily putting on a dark cloak and hat, she ran downstairs and out into the avenue. Lady Arabella had moved, but the sheen of her white dress was still to be seen among the young oaks around the gateway. Keeping in shadow, Mimi followed, taking care not to come so close as to awake the other's suspicion, and watched her quarry pass along the road in the direction of Castra Regis.

She followed on steadily through the gloom of the trees, depending on the glint of the white dress to keep her right. The wood began to thicken, and presently, when the road widened and the trees grew farther back, she lost sight of any indication of her whereabouts. Under the present conditions it was impossible for her to do any more, so, after waiting for a while, still hidden in the shadow to see if she could catch another glimpse of the white frock, she determined to go on slowly towards Castra Regis, and trust to the chapter of accidents to pick up the trail again. She went on slowly, taking advantage of every obstacle and shadow to keep herself concealed.

At last she entered on the grounds of the Castle, at a spot from which the windows of the turret were dimly visible, without having seen again any sign of Lady Arabella.

Meanwhile, during most of the time that Mimi Salton had been moving warily along in the gloom, she was in reality being followed by Lady Arabella, who had caught sight of her leaving the house and had never again lost touch with her. It was a case of the hunter being hunted. For a time Mimi's many turnings, with the natural obstacles that were perpetually intervening, caused Lady Arabella some trouble; but when she was close to Castra Regis, there was no more possibility of concealment, and the strange double following went swiftly on.

When she saw Mimi close to the hall door of Castra Regis and ascending the steps, she followed. When Mimi entered the dark hall and felt her way up the staircase, still, as she believed, following Lady Arabella, the latter kept on her way. When they reached the lobby of the turret-rooms, Mimi believed that the object of her search was ahead of her.

Edgar Caswall sat in the gloom of the great room, occasionally stirred to curiosity when the drifting clouds allowed a little light to fall from the storm-swept sky. But nothing really interested him now. Since he had heard of Lilla's death, the gloom of his remorse, emphasised by Mimi's upbraiding, had made more hopeless his cruel, selfish, saturnine nature. He heard no sound, for his normal faculties seemed benumbed.

Mimi, when she came to the door, which stood ajar, gave a light tap. So light was it that it did not reach Caswall's ears. Then, taking her courage in both hands, she boldly pushed the door and entered. As she did so, her heart sank, for now she was face to face with a difficulty which had not, in her state of mental perturbation, occurred to her.

Chapter XXVII
On the Turret Roof

THE STORM which was coming was already making itself manifest, not only in the wide scope of nature, but in the hearts and natures of human beings. Electrical disturbance in the sky and the air is reproduced in animals of all kinds, and particularly in the highest type of them all – the most receptive – the most electrical. So it was with Edgar Caswall, despite his selfish nature and coldness of blood. So it was with Mimi Salton, despite her unselfish, unchanging devotion for those she loved. So it was even with Lady Arabella, who, under the instincts of a primeval serpent, carried the ever-varying wishes and customs of womanhood, which is always old – and always new.

Edgar, after he had turned his eyes on Mimi, resumed his apathetic position and sullen silence. Mimi quietly took a seat a little way apart, whence she could look on the progress of the coming storm and study its appearance throughout the whole visible circle of the neighbourhood. She was in brighter and better spirits than she had been for many days past. Lady Arabella tried to efface herself behind the now open door.

Without, the clouds grew thicker and blacker as the storm-centre came closer. As yet the forces, from whose linking the lightning springs, were held apart, and the silence of nature proclaimed the calm before the storm. Caswall felt the effect of the gathering electric force. A sort of wild exultation grew upon him, such as he had sometimes felt just before the breaking of a tropical storm. As he became conscious of this, he raised his head and caught sight of Mimi. He was in the grip of an emotion greater than himself; in the mood in which he was he felt the need upon him of doing some desperate deed. He was now absolutely reckless, and as Mimi was associated with him in the memory which drove him on, he wished that she too should be engaged in this enterprise. He had no knowledge of the proximity of Lady Arabella and thought that he was far removed from all he knew and whose interests he share – alone with the wild elements, which were being lashed to fury, and with the woma who had struggled with him and vanquished him, and on whom he would shower th full measure of his hate.

The fact was that Edgar Caswall was, if not mad, close to the border-line. Madness in its first stage – monomania – is a lack of proportion. So long as this is general, it i not always noticeable, for the uninspired onlooker is without the necessary means c comparison. But in monomania the errant faculty protrudes itself in a way that ma not be denied. It puts aside, obscures, or takes the place of something else – just a the head of a pin placed before the centre of the iris will block out the whole scope c vision. The most usual form of monomania has commonly the same beginning as tha from which Edgar Caswall suffered – an over-large idea of self-importance. Alienist who study the matter exactly, probably know more of human vanity and its effect than do ordinary men. Caswall's mental disturbance was not hard to identify. Ever asylum is full of such cases – men and women, who, naturally selfish and egotistica so appraise to themselves their own importance that every other circumstance i life becomes subservient to it. The disease supplies in itself the material for sel magnification. When the decadence attacks a nature naturally proud and selfish an vain, and lacking both the aptitude and habit of self-restraint, the development of th disease is more swift, and ranges to farther limits. It is such persons who becom imbued with the idea that they have the attributes of the Almighty – even that the themselves are the Almighty.

Mimi had a suspicion – or rather, perhaps, an intuition – of the true state of thing when she heard him speak, and at the same time noticed the abnormal flush on hi face, and his rolling eyes. There was a certain want of fixedness of purpose which sh had certainly not noticed before – a quick, spasmodic utterance which belongs rathe to the insane than to those of intellectual equilibrium. She was a little frightened, nc only by his thoughts, but by his staccato way of expressing them.

Caswall moved to the door leading to the turret stair by which the roof wa reached, and spoke in a peremptory way, whose tone alone made her feel defiant.

"Come! I want you."

She instinctively drew back – she was not accustomed to such words, mor especially to such a tone. Her answer was indicative of a new contest.

"Why should I go? What for?"

He did not at once reply – another indication of his overwhelming egotism. Sh repeated her questions; habit reasserted itself, and he spoke without thinking th words which were in his heart.

"I want you, if you will be so good, to come with me to the turret roof. I am muc interested in certain experiments with the kite, which would be, if not a pleasure, a least a novel experience to you. You would see something not easily seen otherwise

"I will come," she answered simply; Edgar moved in the direction of the stair, sh following close behind him.

She did not like to be left alone at such a height, in such a place, in the darknes with a storm about to break. Of himself she had no fear; all that had been seemed t have passed away with her two victories over him in the struggle of wills. Moreove, the more recent apprehension – that of his madness – had also ceased. In th conversation of the last few minutes he seemed so rational, so clear, so unaggressive, that she no longer saw reason for doubt. So satisfied was she that even when he put out a hand to guide her to the steep, narrow stairway, she took it without thought in the most conventional way.

Lady Arabella, crouching in the lobby behind the door, heard every word that had been said, and formed her own opinion of it. It seemed evident to her that there had been some rapprochement between the two who had so lately been hostile to each other, and that made her furiously angry. Mimi was interfering with her plans! She had made certain of her capture of Edgar Caswall, and she could not tolerate even the slightest and most contemptuous fancy on his part which might divert him from the main issue. When she became aware that he wished Mimi to come with him to the roof and that she had acquiesced, her rage got beyond bounds. She became oblivious to any danger there might be in a visit to such an exposed place at such a time, and to all lesser considerations, and made up her mind to forestall them. She stealthily and noiselessly crept through the wicket, and, ascending the stair, stepped out on the roof. It was bitterly cold, for the fierce gusts of the storm which swept round the turret drove in through every unimpeded way, whistling at the sharp corners and singing round the trembling flagstaff. The kite-string and the wire which controlled the runners made a concourse of weird sounds which somehow, perhaps from the violence which surrounded them, acting on their length, resolved themselves into some kind of harmony – a fitting accompaniment to the tragedy which seemed about to begin.

Mimi's heart beat heavily. Just before leaving the turret-chamber she had a shock which she could not shake off. The lights of the room had momentarily revealed to her, as they passed out, Edgar's face, concentrated as it was whenever he intended to use his mesmeric power. Now the black eyebrows made a thick line across his face, under which his eyes shone and glittered ominously. Mimi recognised the danger, and assumed the defiant attitude that had twice already served her so well. She had fear that the circumstances and the place were against her, and she wanted to be forearmed.

The sky was now somewhat lighter than it had been. Either there was lightning afar off, whose reflections were carried by the rolling clouds, or else the gathered force, though not yet breaking into lightning, had an incipient power of light. It seemed to affect both the man and the woman. Edgar seemed altogether under its influence. His spirits were boisterous, his mind exalted. He was now at his worst; madder than he had been earlier in the night.

Mimi, trying to keep as far from him as possible, moved across the stone floor of the turret roof, and found a niche which concealed her. It was not far from Lady Arabella's place of hiding.

Edgar, left thus alone on the centre of the turret roof, found himself altogether his own master in a way which tended to increase his madness. He knew that Mimi was close at hand, though he had lost sight of her. He spoke loudly, and the sound of his own voice, though it was carried from him on the sweeping wind as fast as the words were spoken, seemed to exalt him still more. Even the raging of the elements round him appeared to add to his exaltation. To him it seemed that these manifestations were obedient to his own will. He had reached the sublime of his madness; he was now in his own mind actually the Almighty, and whatever might happen would be

the direct carrying out of his own commands. As he could not see Mimi, nor fi
whereabout she was, he shouted loudly:

"Come to me! You shall see now what you are despising, what you are warrin,
against. All that you see is mine – the darkness as well as the light. I tell you that I ar
greater than any other who is, or was, or shall be. When the Master of Evil took Chris
up on a high place and showed Him all the kingdoms of the earth, he was doing wha
he thought no other could do. He was wrong – he forgot Me. I shall send you ligh
up to the very ramparts of heaven. A light so great that it shall dissipate those blac
clouds that are rushing up and piling around us. Look! Look! At the very touch of m
hand that light springs into being and mounts up – and up – and up!"

He made his way whilst he was speaking to the corner of the turret whence fle
the giant kite, and from which the runners ascended. Mimi looked on, appalled an
afraid to speak lest she should precipitate some calamity. Within the niche Lad
Arabella cowered in a paroxysm of fear.

Edgar took up a small wooden box, through a hole in which the wire of the runne
ran. This evidently set some machinery in motion, for a sound as of whirring came
From one side of the box floated what looked like a piece of stiff ribbon, whicl
snapped and crackled as the wind took it. For a few seconds Mimi saw it as it rushe
along the sagging line to the kite. When close to it, there was a loud crack, and
sudden light appeared to issue from every chink in the box. Then a quick flam
flashed along the snapping ribbon, which glowed with an intense light – a light s
great that the whole of the countryside around stood out against the background c
black driving clouds. For a few seconds the light remained, then suddenly disappeare
in the blackness around. It was simply a magnesium light, which had been fired b
the mechanism within the box and carried up to the kite. Edgar was in a state c
tumultuous excitement, shouting and yelling at the top of his voice and dancing abou
like a lunatic.

This was more than Lady Arabella's curious dual nature could stand – the ghoulis
element in her rose triumphant, and she abandoned all idea of marriage with Edga
Caswall, gloating fiendishly over the thought of revenge.

She must lure him to the White Worm's hole – but how? She glanced around an
quickly made up her mind. The man's whole thoughts were absorbed by his wonderfu
kite, which he was showing off, in order to fascinate her imaginary rival, Mimi.

On the instant she glided through the darkness to the wheel whereon the strin
of the kite was wound. With deft fingers she unshipped this, took it with her, reelin
out the wire as she went, thus keeping, in a way, in touch with the kite. Then sh
glided swiftly to the wicket, through which she passed, locking the gate behind he
as she went.

Down the turret stair she ran quickly, letting the wire run from the wheel whic
she carried carefully, and, passing out of the hall door, hurried down the avenue wit
all her speed. She soon reached her own gate, ran down the avenue, and with her ke
opened the iron door leading to the well-hole.

She felt well satisfied with herself. All her plans were maturing, or had already mature
The Master of Castra Regis was within her grasp. The woman whose interference she ha
feared, Lilla Watford, was dead. Truly, all was well, and she felt that she might pause
while and rest. She tore off her clothes, with feverish fingers, and in full enjoyment c
her natural freedom, stretched her slim figure in animal delight. Then she lay down o

the sofa – to await her victim! Edgar Caswall's life blood would more than satisfy her for some time to come.

Chapter XXVIII
The Breaking of the Storm

WHEN LADY ARABELLA had crept away in her usual noiseless fashion, the two others remained for a while in their places on the turret roof: Caswall because he had nothing to say, Mimi because she had much to say and wished to put her thoughts in order. For quite a while – which seemed interminable – silence reigned between them. At last Mimi made a beginning – she had made up her mind how to act.

"Mr. Caswall," she said loudly, so as to make sure of being heard through the blustering of the wind and the perpetual cracking of the electricity.

Caswall said something in reply, but his words were carried away on the storm. However, one of her objects was effected: she knew now exactly whereabout on the roof he was. So she moved close to the spot before she spoke again, raising her voice almost to a shout.

"The wicket is shut. Please to open it. I can't get out."

As she spoke, she was quietly fingering a revolver which Adam had given to her in case of emergency and which now lay in her breast. She felt that she was caged like a rat in a trap, but did not mean to be taken at a disadvantage, whatever happened. Caswall also felt trapped, and all the brute in him rose to the emergency. In a voice which was raucous and brutal – much like that which is heard when a wife is being beaten by her husband in a slum – he hissed out, his syllables cutting through the roaring of the storm:

"You came of your own accord – without permission, or even asking it. Now you can stay or go as you choose. But you must manage it for yourself; I'll have nothing to do with it."

Her answer was spoken with dangerous suavity

"I am going. Blame yourself if you do not like the time and manner of it. I daresay Adam – my husband – will have a word to say to you about it!"

"Let him say, and be damned to him, and to you too! I'll show you a light. You shan't be able to say that you could not see what you were doing."

As he spoke, he was lighting another piece of the magnesium ribbon, which made a blinding glare in which everything was plainly discernible, down to the smallest detail. This exactly suited Mimi. She took accurate note of the wicket and its fastening before the glare had died away. She took her revolver out and fired into the lock, which was shivered on the instant, the pieces flying round in all directions, but happily without causing hurt to anyone. Then she pushed the wicket open and ran down the narrow stair, and so to the hall door. Opening this also, she ran down the avenue, never lessening her speed till she stood outside the door of Lesser Hill. The door was opened at once on her ringing.

"Is Mr. Adam Salton in?" she asked.

"He has just come in, a few minutes ago. He has gone up to the study," replied a servant.

She ran upstairs at once and joined him. He seemed relieved when he saw her, but scrutinised her face keenly. He saw that she had been in some concern, so led her over to the sofa in the window and sat down beside her.

"Now, dear, tell me all about it!" he said.

She rushed breathlessly through all the details of her adventure on the turret roof. Adam listened attentively, helping her all he could, and not embarrassing her by any questioning. His thoughtful silence was a great help to her, for it allowed her to collect and organise her thoughts.

"I must go and see Caswall tomorrow, to hear what he has to say on the subject."

"But, dear, for my sake, don't have any quarrel with Mr. Caswall. I have had too much trial and pain lately to wish it increased by any anxiety regarding you."

"You shall not, dear – if I can help it – please God," he said solemnly, and he kissed her.

Then, in order to keep her interested so that she might forget the fears and anxieties that had disturbed her, he began to talk over the details of her adventure, making shrewd comments which attracted and held her attention. Presently, inter alia, he said:

"That's a dangerous game Caswall is up to. It seems to me that that young man – though he doesn't appear to know it – is riding for a fall!"

"How, dear? I don't understand."

"Kite flying on a night like this from a place like the tower of Castra Regis is, to say the least of it, dangerous. It is not merely courting death or other accident from lightning, but it is bringing the lightning into where he lives. Every cloud that is blowing up here – and they all make for the highest point – is bound to develop into a flash of lightning. That kite is up in the air and is bound to attract the lightning. Its cord makes a road for it on which to travel to earth. When it does come, it will strike the top of the tower with a weight a hundred times greater than a whole park of artillery, and will knock Castra Regis into pieces. Where it will go after that, no one can tell. If there should be any metal by which it can travel, such will not only point the road, but be the road itself."

"Would it be dangerous to be out in the open air when such a thing is taking place?" she asked.

"No, little woman. It would be the safest possible place – so long as one was not in the line of the electric current."

"Then, do let us go outside. I don't want to run into any foolish danger – or, far more, to ask you to do so. But surely if the open is safest, that is the place for us."

Without another word, she put on again the cloak she had thrown off, and a small, tight-fitting cap. Adam too put on his cap, and, after seeing that his revolver was all right, gave her his hand, and they left the house together.

"I think the best thing we can do will be to go round all the places which are mixed up in this affair."

"All right, dear, I am ready. But, if you don't mind, we might go first to Mercy. I am anxious about grandfather, and we might see that – as yet, at all events – nothing has happened there."

So they went on the high-hung road along the top of the Brow. The wind here was of great force, and made a strange booming noise as it swept high overhead; though not the sound of cracking and tearing as it passed through the woods of high slender trees which grew on either side of the road. Mimi could hardly keep her feet. She was not afraid; but the force to which she was opposed gave her a good excuse to hold on to her husband extra tight.

At Mercy there was no one up – at least, all the lights were out. But to Mimi, accustomed to the nightly routine of the house, there were manifest signs that all was well, except in the little room on the first floor, where the blinds were down. Mimi could not bear to look at that, to think of it. Adam understood her pain, for he had been keenly interested in poor Lilla. He bent over and kissed her, and then took her hand and held it hard. Thus they passed on together, returning to the high road towards Castra Regis.

At the gate of Castra Regis they were extra careful. When drawing near, Adam stumbled upon the wire that Lady Arabella had left trailing on the ground.

Adam drew his breath at this, and spoke in a low, earnest whisper:

"I don't want to frighten you, Mimi dear, but wherever that wire is there is danger."

"Danger! How?"

"That is the track where the lightning will go; at any moment, even now whilst we are speaking and searching, a fearful force may be loosed upon us. Run on, dear; you know the way to where the avenue joins the highroad. If you see any sign of the wire, keep away from it, for God's sake. I shall join you at the gateway."

"Are you going to follow that wire alone?"

"Yes, dear. One is sufficient for that work. I shall not lose a moment till I am with you."

"Adam, when I came with you into the open, my main wish was that we should be together if anything serious happened. You wouldn't deny me that right, would you, dear?"

"No, dear, not that or any right. Thank God that my wife has such a wish. Come; we will go together. We are in the hands of God. If He wishes, we shall be together at the end, whenever or wherever that may be."

They picked up the trail of the wire on the steps and followed it down the avenue, taking care not to touch it with their feet. It was easy enough to follow, for the wire, if not bright, was self-coloured, and showed clearly. They followed it out of the gateway and into the avenue of Diana's Grove.

Here a new gravity clouded Adam's face, though Mimi saw no cause for fresh concern. This was easily enough explained. Adam knew of the explosive works in progress regarding the well-hole, but the matter had been kept from his wife. As they stood near the house, Adam asked Mimi to return to the road, ostensibly to watch the course of the wire, telling her that there might be a branch wire leading somewhere else. She was to search the undergrowth, and if she found it, was to warn him by the Australian native "Coo-ee!"

Whilst they were standing together, there came a blinding flash of lightning, which lit up for several seconds the whole area of earth and sky. It was only the first note of the celestial prelude, for it was followed in quick succession by numerous flashes, whilst the crash and roll of thunder seemed continuous.

Adam, appalled, drew his wife to him and held her close. As far as he could estimate by the interval between lightning and thunder-clap, the heart of the storm was still some distance off, so he felt no present concern for their safety. Still, it was apparent that the course of the storm was moving swiftly in their direction. The lightning flashes came faster and faster and closer together; the thunder-roll was almost continuous, not stopping for a moment – a new crash beginning before the old one had ceased. Adam kept looking up in the direction where the kite strained and struggled at its detaining cord, but, of course, the dull evening light prevented any distinct scrutiny.

At length there came a flash so appallingly bright that in its glare Nature seemed to be standing still. So long did it last, that there was time to distinguish its configuration. It seemed like a mighty tree inverted, pendent from the sky. The whole country around within the angle of vision was lit up till it seemed to glow. Then a broad ribbon of fire seemed to drop on to the tower of Castra Regis just as the thunder crashed. By the glare, Adam could see the tower shake and tremble, and finally fall to pieces like a house of cards. The passing of the lightning left the sky again dark, but a blue flame fell downward from the tower, and, with inconceivable rapidity, running along the ground in the direction of Diana's Grove, reached the dark silent house which in the instant burst into flame at a hundred different points.

At the same moment there rose from the house a rending, crashing sound of woodwork, broken or thrown about, mixed with a quick scream so appalling that Adam, stout of heart as he undoubtedly was, felt his blood turn into ice. Instinctively, despite the danger and their consciousness of it, husband and wife took hands and listened, trembling. Something was going on close to them, mysterious, terrible, deadly! The shrieks continued, though less sharp in sound, as though muffled. In the midst of them was a terrific explosion, seemingly from deep in the earth.

The flames from Castra Regis and from Diana's Grove made all around almost as light as day, and now that the lightning had ceased to flash, their eyes, unblinded, were able to judge both perspective and detail. The heat of the burning house caused the iron doors to warp and collapse. Seemingly of their own accord, they fell open and exposed the interior. The Saltons could now look through to the room beyond where the well-hole yawned, a deep narrow circular chasm. From this the agonised shrieks were rising, growing ever more terrible with each second that passed.

But it was not only the heart-rending sound that almost paralysed poor Mimi with terror. What she saw was sufficient to fill her with evil dreams for the remainder of her life. The whole place looked as if a sea of blood had been beating against it. Each of the explosions from below had thrown out from the well-hole, as if it had been the mouth of a cannon, a mass of fine sand mixed with blood, and a horrible repulsive slime in which were great red masses of rent and torn flesh and fat. As the explosions kept on, more and more of this repulsive mass was shot up, the great bulk of it falling back again. Many of the awful fragments were of something which had lately been alive. They quivered and trembled and writhed as though they were still in torment, a supposition to which the unending scream gave a horrible credence. At moments some mountainous mass of flesh surged up through the narrow orifice, as though forced by a measureless power through an opening infinitely smaller than itself. Some of these fragments were partially covered with white skin as of a human being, and others – the largest and most numerous – with scaled skin as of a gigantic lizard or serpent. Once, in a sort of lull or pause, the seething contents of the hole rose, after the manner of a bubbling spring, and Adam saw part of the thin form of Lady Arabella, forced up to the top amid a mass of blood and slime, and what looked as if it had been the entrails of a monster torn into shreds. Several times some masses of enormous bulk were forced up through the well-hole with inconceivable violence, and, suddenly expanding as they came into larger space, disclosed sections of the White Worm which Adam and Sir Nathaniel had seen looking over the trees with its enormous eyes of emerald-green flickering like great lamps in a gale.

At last the explosive power, which was not yet exhausted, evidently reached the main store of dynamite which had been lowered into the worm hole. The result was appalling. The ground for far around quivered and opened in long deep chasms, whose edges shook and fell in, throwing up clouds of sand which fell back and hissed amongst the rising water. The heavily built house shook to its foundations. Great stones were thrown up as from a volcano, some of them, great masses of hard stone, squared and grooved with implements wrought by human hands, breaking up and splitting in mid air as though riven by some infernal power. Trees near the house — and therefore presumably in some way above the hole, which sent up clouds of dust and steam and fine sand mingled, and which carried an appalling stench which sickened the spectators – were torn up by the roots and hurled into the air. By now, flames were bursting violently from all over the ruins, so dangerously that Adam caught up his wife in his arms, and ran with her from the proximity of the flames.

Then almost as quickly as it had begun, the whole cataclysm ceased, though a deep-down rumbling continued intermittently for some time. Then silence brooded over all – silence so complete that it seemed in itself a sentient thing – silence which seemed like incarnate darkness, and conveyed the same idea to all who came within its radius. To the young people who had suffered the long horror of that awful night, it brought relief – relief from the presence or the fear of all that was horrible – relief which seemed perfected when the red rays of sunrise shot up over the far eastern sea, bringing a promise of a new order of things with the coming day.

* * *

His bed saw little of Adam Salton for the remainder of that night. He and Mimi walked hand in hand in the brightening dawn round by the Brow to Castra Regis and on to Lesser Hill. They did so deliberately, in an attempt to think as little as possible of the terrible experiences of the night. The morning was bright and cheerful, as a morning sometimes is after a devastating storm. The clouds, of which there were plenty in evidence, brought no lingering idea of gloom. All nature was bright and joyous, being in striking contrast to the scenes of wreck and devastation, the effects of obliterating fire and lasting ruin.

The only evidence of the once stately pile of Castra Regis and its inhabitants was a shapeless huddle of shattered architecture, dimly seen as the keen breeze swept aside the cloud of acrid smoke which marked the site of the once lordly castle. As for Diana's Grove, they looked in vain for a sign which had a suggestion of permanence. The oak trees of the Grove were still to be seen – some of them – emerging from a haze of smoke, the great trunks solid and erect as ever, but the larger branches broken and twisted and rent, with bark stripped and chipped, and the smaller branches broken and dishevelled looking from the constant stress and threshing of the storm.

Of the house as such, there was, even at the short distance from which they looked, no trace. Adam resolutely turned his back on the devastation and hurried on. Mimi was not only upset and shocked in many ways, but she was physically 'dog tired,' and falling asleep on her feet. Adam took her to her room and made her undress and get into bed, taking care that the room was well lighted both by sunshine and lamps. The only obstruction was from a silk curtain, drawn across the window to keep out the glare. He sat beside her, holding her hand, well knowing that the comfort of his presence was the best restorative for her. He stayed with her till sleep had overmastered her wearied body. Then he went softly away. He found his uncle and Sir Nathaniel in the study, having an early cup of tea, amplified to the dimensions of a possible breakfast. Adam explained that he had not told his wife that he was going over the horrible places again, lest it should frighten her, for the rest and sleep in ignorance would help her and make a gap of peacefulness between the horrors.

Sir Nathaniel agreed.

"We know, my boy," he said, "that the unfortunate Lady Arabella is dead, and that the foul carcase of the Worm has been torn to pieces – pray God that its evil soul will never more escape from the nethermost hell."

They visited Diana's Grove first, not only because it was nearer, but also because it was the place where most description was required, and Adam felt that he could tell his story best on the spot. The absolute destruction of the place and everything in it seen in the broad daylight was almost inconceivable. To Sir Nathaniel, it was as a story of horror full and complete. But to Adam it was, as it were, only on the fringes. He knew what was still to be seen when his friends had got over the knowledge of externals. As yet, they had only seen the outside of the house – or rather, where the outside of the house once had been. The great horror lay within. However, age – and the experience of age – counts.

A strange, almost elemental, change in the aspect had taken place in the time which had elapsed since the dawn. It would almost seem as if Nature herself had tried to obliterate the evil signs of what had occurred. True, the utter ruin of the house was made even more manifest in the searching daylight; but the more appalling destruction which lay beneath was not visible. The rent, torn, and dislocated stonework looked worse than before; the upheaved foundations, the piled-up fragments of masonry, the fissures in the torn earth – all were at the worst. The Worm's hole was still evident, a round fissure seemingly leading down into the very bowels of the earth. But all the horrid mass of blood and slime, of torn, evil-smelling flesh and the sickening remnants of violent death, were gone. Either some of the later explosions had thrown up from the deep quantities of water which, though foul and corrupt itself, had still some cleansing power left, or else the writhing mass which stirred from far below had helped to drag down and obliterate the items of horror. A grey dust, partly of fine sand, partly of the waste of the falling ruin, covered everything, and, though ghastly itself, helped to mask something still worse.

After a few minutes of watching, it became apparent to the three men that the turmoil far below had not yet ceased. At short irregular intervals the hell-broth in the hole seemed as if boiling up. It rose and fell again and turned over, showing in fresh form much of the nauseous detail which had been visible earlier. The worst parts were the great masses of the flesh of the monstrous Worm, in all its red and sickening aspect. Such fragments had been bad enough before, but now they were infinitely worse. Corruption comes with startling rapidity to beings whose destruction has been due wholly or in part to lightning – the whole mass seemed to have become all at once corrupt! The whole surface of the fragments, once alive, was covered with insects, worms, and vermin of all kinds. The sight was horrible enough, but, with the awful smell added, was simply unbearable. The Worm's hole appeared to breathe forth death in its most repulsive forms. The friends, with one impulse, moved to the top of the Brow, where a fresh breeze from the sea was blowing up.

At the top of the Brow, beneath them as they looked down, they saw a shining mass of white, which looked strangely out of place amongst such wreckage as they had been viewing. It appeared so strange that Adam suggested trying to find a way down, so that they might see it more closely.

"We need not go down; I know what it is," Sir Nathaniel said. "The explosions of last night have blown off the outside of the cliffs – that which we see is the vast bed of china clay through which the Worm originally found its way down to its lair. I can catch the glint of the water of the deep quags far down below. Well, her ladyship didn't deserve such a funeral – or such a monument."

* * *

The horrors of the last few hours had played such havoc with Mimi's nerves, that a change of scene was imperative – if a permanent breakdown was to be avoided.

"I think," said old Mr. Salton, "it is quite time you young people departed for that honeymoon of yours!" There was a twinkle in his eye as he spoke.

Mimi's soft shy glance at her stalwart husband, was sufficient answer.

The complete and unabridged text is available online, *from flametreepublishing.com/extras*

If you enjoyed this, you might also like...
The Judge's House,' see page 47
The Squaw,' see page 312

The Gipsy Prophecy

"I REALLY THINK," said the Doctor, "that, at any rate, one of us should go and try whether or not the thing is an imposture.'

"Good!" said Considine. "After dinner we will take our cigars and stroll over to the camp."

Accordingly, when the dinner was over, and the *La Tour* finished, Joshua Considine and his friend, Dr. Burleigh, went over to the east side of the moor where the gipsy encampment lay. As they were leaving, Mary Considine, who had walked as far as the end of the garden where it opened into the laneway, called after her husband:

"Mind, Joshua, you are to give them a fair chance, but don't give them any clue to a fortune – and don't you get flirting with any of the gipsy maidens – and take care to keep Gerald out of harm."

For answer Considine held up his hand, as if taking a stage oath, and whistled the air of the old song, 'The Gipsy Countess.' Gerald joined in the strain, and then, breaking into merry laughter, the two men passed along the laneway to the common, turning now and then to wave their hands to Mary, who leaned over the gate, in the twilight, looking after them.

It was a lovely evening in the summer; the very air was full of rest and quiet happiness, as though an outward type of the peacefulness and joy which made a heaven of the home of the young married folk. Considine's life had not been an eventful one. The only disturbing element which he had ever known was in his wooing of Mary Winston, and the long-continued objection of her ambitious parents, who expected a brilliant match for their only daughter. When Mr. and Mrs. Winston had discovered the attachment of the young barrister, they had tried to keep the young people apart by sending their daughter away for a long round of visits, having made her promise not to correspond with her lover during her absence. Love, however, had stood the test. Neither absence nor neglect seemed to cool the passion of the young man, and jealousy seemed a thing unknown to his sanguine nature; so, after a long period of waiting, the parents had given in, and the young folk were married.

They had been living in the cottage a few months, and were just beginning to feel at home. Gerald Burleigh, Joshua's old college chum, and himself a sometime victim of Mary's beauty, had arrived a week before, to stay with them for as long a time as he could tear himself away from his work in London.

When her husband had quite disappeared Mary went into the house, and, sitting down at the piano, gave an hour to Mendelssohn.

It was but a short walk across the common, and before the cigars required renewing the two men had reached the gipsy camp. The place was as picturesque as gipsy camps – when in villages and when business is good – usually are. There were some few persons round the fire, investing their money in prophecy, and a large number of others, poorer or more parsimonious, who stayed just outside the bounds but near enough to see all that went on.

As the two gentlemen approached, the villagers, who knew Joshua, made way a little, and a pretty, keen-eyed gipsy girl tripped up and asked to tell their fortunes. Joshua held out his hand, but the girl, without seeming to see it, stared at his face in a very odd manner. Gerald nudged him:

"You must cross her hand with silver," he said. "It is one of the most important parts of the mystery." Joshua took from his pocket a half-crown and held it out to her, but, without looking at it, she answered:

"You have to cross the gipsy's hand with gold."

Gerald laughed. "You are at a premium as a subject," he said. Joshua was of the kind of man – the universal kind – who can tolerate being stared at by a pretty girl; so, with some little deliberation, he answered:

"All right; here you are, my pretty girl; but you must give me a real good fortune for it," and he handed her a half sovereign, which she took, saying:

"It is not for me to give good fortune or bad, but only to read what the Stars have said." She took his right hand and turned it palm upward; but the instant her eyes met it she dropped it as though it had been red hot, and, with a startled look, glided swiftly away. Lifting the curtain of the large tent, which occupied the centre of the camp, she disappeared within.

"Sold again!" said the cynical Gerald. Joshua stood a little amazed, and not altogether satisfied. They both watched the large tent. In a few moments there emerged from the opening not the young girl, but a stately looking woman of middle age and commanding presence.

The instant she appeared the whole camp seemed to stand still. The clamour of tongues, the laughter and noise of the work were, for a second or two, arrested, and every man or woman who sat, or crouched, or lay, stood up and faced the imperial looking gipsy.

"The Queen, of course," murmured Gerald. "We are in luck tonight." The gipsy Queen threw a searching glance around the camp, and then, without hesitating an instant, came straight over and stood before Joshua.

"Hold out your hand," she said in a commanding tone.

Again Gerald spoke, *sotto voce*: "I have not been spoken to in that way since I was at school."

"Your hand must be crossed with gold."

"A hundred per cent at this game," whispered Gerald, as Joshua laid another half sovereign on his upturned palm.

The gipsy looked at the hand with knitted brows; then suddenly looking up into his face, said:

"Have you a strong will – have you a true heart that can be brave for one you love?"

"I hope so; but I am afraid I have not vanity enough to say 'yes.'"

"Then I will answer for you; for I read resolution in your face – resolution desperate and determined if need be. You have a wife you love?"

"Yes," emphatically.

"Then leave her at once – never see her face again. Go from her now, while love is fresh and your heart is free from wicked intent. Go quick – go far, and never see her face again!"

Joshua drew away his hand quickly, and said, "Thank you!" stiffly but sarcastically, a he began to move away.

"I say!" said Gerald, "You're not going like that, old man; no use in being indignant with the Stars or their prophet – and, moreover, your sovereign – what of it? At least hear the matter out."

"Silence, ribald!" commanded the Queen, "You know not what you do. Let him go and go ignorant, if he will not be warned."

Joshua immediately turned back. "At all events, we will see this thing out," he said "Now, madam, you have given me advice, but I paid for a fortune."

"Be warned!" said the gipsy. "The Stars have been silent for long; let the mystery still wrap them round."

"My dear madam, I do not get within touch of a mystery every day, and I prefer for my money knowledge rather than ignorance. I can get the latter commodity for nothing when I want any of it."

Gerald echoed the sentiment. "As for me I have a large and unsaleable stock on hand."

The gipsy Queen eyed the two men sternly, and then said: "As you wish. You have chosen for yourself, and have met warning with scorn, and appeal with levity. On your own heads be the doom!"

"Amen!" said Gerald.

With an imperious gesture the Queen took Joshua's hand again, and began to tell his fortune.

"I see here the flowing of blood; it will flow before long; it is running in my sight It flows through the broken circle of a severed ring."

"Go on!" said Joshua, smiling. Gerald was silent.

"Must I speak plainer?"

"Certainly; we commonplace mortals want something definite. The Stars are a long way off, and their words get somewhat dulled in the message."

The gipsy shuddered, and then spoke impressively. "This is the hand of a murderer – the murderer of his wife!" She dropped the hand and turned away.

Joshua laughed. "Do you know," said he, "I think if I were you I should prophesy some jurisprudence into my system. For instance, you say 'this hand is the hand of a murderer.' Well, whatever it may be in the future – or potentially – it is at present not one. You ought to give your prophecy in such terms as 'the hand which will be a murderer's', or, rather, 'the hand of one who will be the murderer of his wife'. The Stars are really not good on technical questions."

The gipsy made no reply of any kind, but, with drooping head and despondent mien walked slowly to her tent, and, lifting the curtain, disappeared.

Without speaking the two men turned homewards, and walked across the moor Presently, after some little hesitation, Gerald spoke.

"Of course, old man, this is all a joke; a ghastly one, but still a joke. But would it not be well to keep it to ourselves?"

"How do you mean?"

"Well, not tell your wife. It might alarm her."

"Alarm her! My dear Gerald, what are you thinking of? Why, she would not be alarmed or afraid of me if all the gipsies that ever didn't come from Bohemia agreed that I was to murder her, or even to have a hard thought of her, whilst so long as she was saying 'Jack Robinson.'"

Gerald remonstrated. "Old fellow, women are superstitious – far more than we men are; and, also they are blessed – or cursed – with a nervous system to which we are strangers. I see too much of it in my work not to realise it. Take my advice and do not let her know, or you will frighten her."

Joshua's lips unconsciously hardened as he answered: "My dear fellow, I would not have a secret from my wife. Why, it would be the beginning of a new order of things between us. We have no secrets from each other. If we ever have, then you may begin to look out for something odd between us."

"Still," said Gerald, "at the risk of unwelcome interference, I say again be warned in time."

"The gipsy's very words," said Joshua. "You and she seem quite of one accord. Tell me, old man, is this a put-up thing? You told me of the gipsy camp – did you arrange it all with Her Majesty?" This was said with an air of bantering earnestness. Gerald assured him that he only heard of the camp that morning; but he made fun of every answer of his friend, and, in the process of this raillery, the time passed, and they entered the cottage.

Mary was sitting at the piano but not playing. The dim twilight had waked some very tender feelings in her breast, and her eyes were full of gentle tears. When the men came in she stole over to her husband's side and kissed him. Joshua struck a tragic attitude.

"Mary," he said in a deep voice, "before you approach me, listen to the words of Fate. The Stars have spoken and the doom is sealed."

"What is it, dear? Tell me the fortune, but do not frighten me."

"Not at all, my dear; but there is a truth which it is well that you should know. Nay, it is necessary so that all your arrangements can be made beforehand, and everything be decently done and in order."

"Go on, dear; I am listening."

"Mary Considine, your effigy may yet be seen at Madame Tussaud's. The juris-imprudent Stars have announced their fell tidings that this hand is red with blood – your blood. Mary! Mary! My God!" He sprang forward, but too late to catch her as she fell fainting on the floor.

"I told you," said Gerald. "You don't know them as well as I do."

After a little while Mary recovered from her swoon, but only to fall into strong hysterics, in which she laughed and wept and raved and cried, "Keep him from me – from me, Joshua, my husband," and many other words of entreaty and of fear.

Joshua Considine was in a state of mind bordering on agony, and when at last Mary became calm he knelt by her and kissed her feet and hands and hair and called her all the sweet names and said all the tender things his lips could frame. All that night he sat by her bedside and held her hand. Far through the night and up to the early morning she kept waking from sleep and crying out as if in fear, till she was comforted by the consciousness that her husband was watching beside her.

Breakfast was late the next morning, but during it Joshua received a telegram which required him to drive over to Withering, nearly twenty miles. He was loth to go; but Mary would not hear of his remaining, and so before noon he drove off in his dog-cart alone.

When he was gone Mary retired to her room. She did not appear at lunch, but when afternoon tea was served on the lawn under the great weeping willow, she came to join her guest. She was looking quite recovered from her illness of the evening before. After some casual remarks, she said to Gerald: "Of course it was very silly about last night, but I could not help feeling frightened. Indeed I would feel so still if I let myself think of it. But, after all these people may only imagine things, and I have got a test that can hardly fail to show that the prediction is false – if indeed it be false,' she added sadly.

"What is your plan?" asked Gerald.

"I shall go myself to the gipsy camp, and have my fortune told by the Queen."

"Capital. May I go with you?"

"Oh, no! That would spoil it. She might know you and guess at me, and suit her utterance accordingly. I shall go alone this afternoon."

When the afternoon was gone Mary Considine took her way to the gipsy encampment. Gerald went with her as far as the near edge of the common, and returned alone.

Half-an-hour had hardly elapsed when Mary entered the drawing-room, where he lay on a sofa reading. She was ghastly pale and was in a state of extreme excitement. Hardly had she passed over the threshold when she collapsed and sank moaning on the carpet. Gerald rushed to aid her, but by a great effort she controlled herself and motioned him to be silent. He waited, and his ready attention to her wish seemed to be her best help, for, in a few minutes, she had somewhat recovered, and was able to tell him what had passed.

"When I got to the camp," she said, "there did not seem to be a soul about, I went into the centre and stood there. Suddenly a tall woman stood beside me. 'Something told me I was wanted!' she said. I held out my hand and laid a piece of silver on it. She took from her neck a small golden trinket and laid it there also; and then, seizing the two, threw them into the stream that ran by. Then she took my hand in hers and spoke: 'Naught but blood in this guilty place,' and turned away. I caught hold of her and asked her to tell me more. After some hesitation, she said: "Alas! Alas! I see you lying at your husband's feet, and his hands are red with blood."'

Gerald did not feel at all at ease, and tried to laugh it off. "Surely," he said, "this woman has a craze about murder."

"Do not laugh," said Mary, "I cannot bear it," and then, as if with a sudden impulse, she left the room.

Not long after Joshua returned, bright and cheery, and as hungry as a hunter after his long drive. His presence cheered his wife, who seemed much brighter, but she did not mention the episode of the visit to the gipsy camp, so Gerald did not mention it either. As if by tacit consent the subject was not alluded to during the evening. But there was a strange, settled look on Mary's face, which Gerald could not but observe.

In the morning Joshua came down to breakfast later than usual. Mary had been up and about the house from an early hour; but as the time drew on she seemed to get a little nervous and now and again threw around an anxious look.

Gerald could not help noticing that none of those at breakfast could get on satisfactorily with their food. It was not altogether that the chops were tough, but that the knives were all so blunt. Being a guest, he, of course, made no sign; but presently saw Joshua draw his thumb across the edge of his knife in an unconscious sort of way. At the action Mary turned pale and almost fainted.

After breakfast they all went out on the lawn. Mary was making up a bouquet, and said to her husband, "Get me a few of the tea-roses, dear."

Joshua pulled down a cluster from the front of the house. The stem bent, but was too tough to break. He put his hand in his pocket to get his knife; but in vain. "Lend me your knife, Gerald," he said. But Gerald had not got one, so he went into the breakfast room and took one from the table. He came out feeling its edge and grumbling. "What on earth has happened to all the knives – the edges seem all round off?" Mary turned away hurriedly and entered the house.

Joshua tried to sever the stalk with the blunt knife as country cooks sever the necks of fowl – as schoolboys cut twine. With a little effort he finished the task. The cluster of roses grew thick, so he determined to gather a great bunch.

He could not find a single sharp knife in the sideboard where the cutlery was kept, so he called Mary, and when she came, told her the state of things. She looked so agitated and so miserable that he could not help knowing the truth, and, as if astounded and hurt, asked her:

"Do you mean to say that *you* have done it?"

She broke in, "Oh, Joshua, I was so afraid."

He paused, and a set, white look came over his face. "Mary!' said he, "Is this all the trust you have in me? I would not have believed it."

"Oh, Joshua! Joshua!' she cried entreatingly, "Forgive me," and wept bitterly.

Joshua thought a moment and then said: "I see how it is. We shall better end this or we shall all go mad."

He ran into the drawing-room.

"Where are you going?" almost screamed Mary.

Gerald saw what he meant – that he would not be tied to blunt instruments by the force of a superstition, and was not surprised when he saw him come out through the French window, bearing in his hand a large Ghourka knife, which usually lay on the centre table, and which his brother had sent him from Northern India. It was one of those great hunting-knives which worked such havoc, at close quarters with the enemies of the loyal Ghourkas during the mutiny, of great weight but so evenly balanced in the hand as to seem light, and with an edge like a razor. With one of these knives a Ghourka can cut a sheep in two.

When Mary saw him come out of the room with the weapon in his hand she screamed in an agony of fright, and the hysterics of last night were promptly renewed.

Joshua ran toward her, and, seeing her falling, threw down the knife and tried to catch her.

However, he was just a second too late, and the two men cried out in horror simultaneously as they saw her fall upon the naked blade.

When Gerald rushed over he found that in falling her left hand had struck the blade, which lay partly upwards on the grass. Some of the small veins were cut through, and the blood gushed freely from the wound. As he was tying it up he pointed out to Joshua that the wedding ring was severed by the steel.

They carried her fainting to the house. When, after a while, she came out, with her arm in a sling, she was peaceful in her mind and happy. She said to her husband:

"The gipsy was wonderfully near the truth; too near for the real thing ever to occur now, dear."

Joshua bent over and kissed the wounded hand.

If you enjoyed this, you might also like...
'A Dream of Red Hands,' see page 329
'A Star Trap,' see page 400

The Secret of the Growing Gold

WHEN MARGARET DELANDRE went to live at Brent's Rock the whole neighbourhood awoke to the pleasure of an entirely new scandal. Scandals in connection with either the Delandre family or the Brents of Brent's Rock, were not few; and if the secret history of the county had been written in full both names would have been found well represented. It is true that the status of each was so different that they might have belonged to different continents – or to different worlds for the matter of that – for hitherto their orbits had never crossed. The Brents were accorded by the whole section of the country a unique social dominance, and had ever held themselves as high above the yeoman class to which Margaret Delandre belonged, as a blue-blooded Spanish hidalgo out-tops his peasant tenantry.

The Delandres had an ancient record and were proud of it in their way as the Brents were of theirs. But the family had never risen above yeomanry; and although they had been once well-to-do in the good old times of foreign wars and protection, their fortunes had withered under the scorching of the free trade sun and the 'piping times of peace.' They had, as the elder members used to assert, 'stuck to the land', with the result that they had taken root in it, body and soul. In fact, they, having chosen the life of vegetables, had flourished as vegetation does – blossomed and thrived in the good season and suffered in the bad.

Their holding, Dander's Croft, seemed to have been worked out, and to be typical of the family which had inhabited it. The latter had declined generation after generation, sending out now and again some abortive shoot of unsatisfied energy in the shape of a soldier or sailor, who had worked his way to the minor grades of the services and had there stopped, cut short either from unheeding gallantry in action or from that destroying cause to men without breeding or youthful care – the recognition of a position above them which they feel unfitted to fill. So, little by little, the family dropped lower and lower, the men brooding and dissatisfied, and drinking themselves into the grave, the women drudging at home, or marrying beneath them – or worse. In process of time all disappeared, leaving only two in the Croft, Wykham Delandre and his sister Margaret. The man and woman seemed to have inherited in masculine and feminine form respectively the evil tendency of their race, sharing in common the principles, though manifesting them in different ways, of sullen passion, voluptuousness and recklessness.

The history of the Brents had been something similar, but showing the causes of decadence in their aristocratic and not their plebeian forms. They, too, had sent their shoots to the wars; but their positions had been different and they had often attained honour – for without flaw they were gallant, and brave deeds were done by them before the selfish dissipation which marked them had sapped their vigour.

The present head of the family – if family it could now be called when one remained of the direct line – was Geoffrey Brent. He was almost a type of worn out race, manifesting in some ways its most brilliant qualities, and in others its utter degradation. He might be fairly compared with some of those antique Italian nobles whom the painters have preserved to us with their courage, their unscrupulousness, their refinement of lust and cruelty – the voluptuary actual with the fiend potential. He was certainly handsome, with that dark, aquiline, commanding beauty which women so generally recognise as dominant. With men he was distant and cold; but such a bearing never deters womankind. The inscrutable laws of sex have so arranged that even a timid woman is not afraid of a fierce and haughty man. And so it was that there was hardly a woman of any kind or degree, who lived within view of Brent's Rock, who did not cherish some form of secret admiration for the handsome wastrel. The category was a wide one, for Brent's Rock rose up steeply from the midst of a level region and for a circuit of a hundred miles it lay on the horizon, with its high old towers and steep roofs cutting the level edge of wood and hamlet, and far-scattered mansions.

So long as Geoffrey Brent confined his dissipations to London and Paris and Vienna – anywhere out of sight and sound of his home – opinion was silent. It is easy to listen to far off echoes unmoved, and we can treat them with disbelief, or scorn, or disdain, or whatever attitude of coldness may suit our purpose. But when the scandal came close home it was another matter; and the feelings of independence and integrity which is in people of every community which is not utterly spoiled, asserted itself and demanded that condemnation should be expressed. Still there was a certain reticence in all, and no more notice was taken of the existing facts than was absolutely necessary. Margaret Delandre bore herself so fearlessly and so openly – she accepted her position as the justified companion of Geoffrey Brent so naturally that people came to believe that she was secretly married to him, and therefore thought it wiser to hold their tongues lest time should justify her and also make her an active enemy.

The one person who, by his interference, could have settled all doubts was debarred by circumstances from interfering in the matter. Wykham Delandre had quarrelled with his sister – or perhaps it was that she had quarrelled with him – and they were on terms not merely of armed neutrality but of bitter hatred. The quarrel had been antecedent to Margaret going to Brent's Rock. She and Wykham had almost come to blows. There had certainly been threats on one side and on the other; and in the end Wykham, overcome with passion, had ordered his sister to leave his house. She had risen straightway, and, without waiting to pack up even her own personal belongings, had walked out of the house. On the threshold she had paused for a moment to hurl a bitter threat at Wykham that he would rue in shame and despair to the last hour of his life his act of that day.

Some weeks had since passed; and it was understood in the neighbourhood that Margaret had gone to London, when she suddenly appeared driving out with Geoffrey Brent, and the entire neighbourhood knew before nightfall that she had taken up her abode at the Rock. It was no subject of surprise that Brent had come back unexpectedly, for such was his usual custom. Even his own servants never knew when to expect him, for there was a private door, of which he alone had the key, by which he sometimes entered without anyone in the house being aware of his coming. This was his usual method of appearing after a long absence.

Wykham Delandre was furious at the news. He vowed vengeance – and to keep his mind level with his passion drank deeper than ever. He tried several times to see his sister, but she contemptuously refused to meet him. He tried to have an interview with Brent and was refused by him also. Then he tried to stop him in the road, but without avail, for Geoffrey was not a man to be stopped against his will. Several actual encounters took place between the two men, and many more were threatened and avoided. At last Wykham Delandre settled down to a morose, vengeful acceptance of the situation.

Neither Margaret nor Geoffrey was of a pacific temperament, and it was not long before there began to be quarrels between them. One thing would lead to another, and wine flowed freely at Brent's Rock. Now and again the quarrels would assume a bitter aspect, and threats would be exchanged in uncompromising language that fairly awed the listening servants. But such quarrels generally ended where domestic altercations do, in reconciliation, and in a mutual respect for the fighting qualities proportionate to their manifestation. Fighting for its own sake is found by a certain class of persons, all the world over, to be a matter of absorbing interest, and there is no reason to believe that domestic conditions minimise its potency. Geoffrey and Margaret made occasional absences from Brent's Rock, and on each of these occasions Wykham Delandre also absented himself; but as he generally heard of the absence too late to be of any service, he returned home each time in a more bitter and discontented frame of mind than before.

At last there came a time when the absence from Brent's Rock became longer than before. Only a few days earlier there had been a quarrel, exceeding in bitterness anything which had gone before; but this, too, had been made up, and a trip on the Continent had been mentioned before the servants. After a few days Wykham Delandre also went away, and it was some weeks before he returned. It was noticed that he was full of some new importance – satisfaction, exaltation – they hardly knew how to call it. He went straightway to Brent's Rock, and demanded to see Geoffrey Brent, and on being told that he had not yet returned, said, with a grim decision which the servants noted:

"I shall come again. My news is solid – it can wait!" and turned away. Week after week went by, and month after month; and then there came a rumour, certified later on, that an accident had occurred in the Zermatt valley. Whilst crossing a dangerous pass the carriage containing an English lady and the driver had fallen over a precipice, the gentleman of the party, Mr. Geoffrey Brent, having been fortunately saved as he had been walking up the hill to ease the horses. He gave information, and search was made. The broken rail, the excoriated roadway, the marks where the horses had struggled on the decline before finally pitching over into the torrent – all told the sad tale. It was a wet season, and there had been much snow in the winter, so that the river was swollen beyond its usual volume, and the eddies of the stream were packed with ice. All search was made, and finally the wreck of the carriage and the body of one horse were found in an eddy of the river. Later on the body of the driver was found on the sandy, torrent-swept waste near Täsch; but the body of the lady, like that of the other horse, had quite disappeared, and was – what was left of it by that time – whirling amongst the eddies of the Rhone on its way down to the Lake of Geneva.

Wykham Delandre made all the enquiries possible, but could not find any trace of the missing woman. He found, however, in the books of the various hotels the name of 'Mr. and Mrs. Geoffrey Brent'. And he had a stone erected at Zermatt to his sister's memory, under her married name, and a tablet put up in the church at Bretten, the parish in which both Brent's Rock and Dander's Croft were situated.

There was a lapse of nearly a year, after the excitement of the matter had worn away, and the whole neighbourhood had gone on its accustomed way. Brent was still absent, and Delandre more drunken, more morose, and more revengeful than before.

Then there was a new excitement. Brent's Rock was being made ready for a new mistress. It was officially announced by Geoffrey himself in a letter to the Vicar, that he had been married some months before to an Italian lady, and that they were then on their way home. Then a small army of workmen invaded the house; and hammer and plane sounded, and a general air of size and paint pervaded the atmosphere. One wing of the old house, the south, was entirely re-done; and then the great body of the workmen departed, leaving only materials for the doing of the old hall when Geoffrey Brent should have returned, for he had directed that the decoration was only to be done under his own eyes. He had brought with him accurate drawings of a hall in the house of his bride's father, for he wished to reproduce for her the place to which she had been accustomed. As the moulding had all to be re-done, some scaffolding poles and boards were brought in and laid on one side of the great hall, and also a great wooden tank or box for mixing the lime, which was laid in bags beside it.

When the new mistress of Brent's Rock arrived the bells of the church rang out, and there was a general jubilation. She was a beautiful creature, full of the poetry and fire and passion of the South; and the few English words which she had learned were spoken in such a sweet and pretty broken way that she won the hearts of the people almost as much by the music of her voice as by the melting beauty of her dark eyes.

Geoffrey Brent seemed more happy than he had ever before appeared; but there was a dark, anxious look on his face that was new to those who knew him of old, and he started at times as though at some noise that was unheard by others.

And so months passed and the whisper grew that at last Brent's Rock was to have an heir. Geoffrey was very tender to his wife, and the new bond between them seemed to soften him. He took more interest in his tenants and their needs than he had ever done; and works of charity on his part as well as on his sweet young wife's were not lacking. He seemed to have set all his hopes on the child that was coming, and as he looked deeper into the future the dark shadow that had come over his face seemed to die gradually away.

All the time Wykham Delandre nursed his revenge. Deep in his heart had grown up a purpose of vengeance which only waited an opportunity to crystallise and take a definite shape. His vague idea was somehow centred in the wife of Brent, for he knew that he could strike him best through those he loved, and the coming time seemed to hold in its womb the opportunity for which he longed.

One night he sat alone in the living-room of his house. It had once been a handsome room in its way, but time and neglect had done their work and it was now little better than a ruin, without dignity or picturesqueness of any kind. He had been drinking heavily for some time and was more than half stupefied. He thought he heard a noise as of someone at the door and looked up. Then he called half savagely to come in; but there was no response. With a muttered blasphemy he renewed his potations.

Presently he forgot all around him, sank into a daze, but suddenly awoke to see standing before him someone or something like a battered, ghostly edition of his sister. For a few moments there came upon him a sort of fear. The woman before him, with distorted features and burning eyes seemed hardly human, and the only thing that seemed a reality of his sister, as she had been, was her wealth of golden hair, and this was now streaked with grey. She eyed her brother with a long, cold stare; and he, too, as he looked and began to realise the actuality of her presence, found the hatred of her which he had had, once again surging up in his heart. All the brooding passion of the past year seemed to find a voice at once as he asked her:

"Why are you here? You're dead and buried."

"I am here, Wykham Delandre, for no love of you, but because I hate another even more than I do you!" A great passion blazed in her eyes.

"Him?" he asked, in so fierce a whisper that even the woman was for an instant startled till she regained her calm.

"Yes, him!" she answered. "But make no mistake, my revenge is my own; and I merely use you to help me to it." Wykham asked suddenly:

"Did he marry you?"

The woman's distorted face broadened out in a ghastly attempt at a smile. It was a hideous mockery, for the broken features and seamed scars took strange shapes and strange colours, and queer lines of white showed out as the straining muscles pressed on the old cicatrices.

"So you would like to know! It would please your pride to feel that your sister was truly married! Well, you shall not know. That was my revenge on you, and I do not mean to change it by a hair's breadth. I have come here tonight simply to let you know that I am alive, so that if any violence be done me where I am going there may be a witness."

"Where are you going?" demanded her brother.

"That is my affair! and I have not the least intention of letting you know!" Wykham stood up, but the drink was on him and he reeled and fell. As he lay on the floor he announced his intention of following his sister; and with an outburst of splenetic humour told her that he would follow her through the darkness by the light of her hair, and of her beauty. At this she turned on him, and said that there were others beside him that would rue her hair and her beauty too. "As he will," she hissed; "for the hair remains though the beauty be gone. When he withdrew the lynch-pin and sent us over the precipice into the torrent, he had little thought of my beauty. Perhaps his beauty would be scarred like mine were he whirled, as I was, among the rocks of the Visp, and frozen on the ice pack in the drift of the river. But let him beware! His time is coming!" and with a fierce gesture she flung open the door and passed out into the night.

* * *

Later on that night, Mrs. Brent, who was but half-asleep, became suddenly awake and spoke to her husband:

"Geoffrey, was not that the click of a lock somewhere below our window?"

But Geoffrey – though she thought that he, too, had started at the noise – seemed sound asleep, and breathed heavily. Again Mrs. Brent dozed; but this time awoke to the fact that her husband had arisen and was partially dressed. He was deadly pale, and when the light of the lamp which he had in his hand fell on his face, she was frightened at the look in his eyes.

"What is it, Geoffrey? What dost thou?" she asked.

"Hush! little one," he answered, in a strange, hoarse voice. "Go to sleep. I am restless, and wish to finish some work I left undone."

"Bring it here, my husband,' she said; "I am lonely and I fear when thou art away."

For reply he merely kissed her and went out, closing the door behind him. She lay awake for awhile, and then nature asserted itself, and she slept.

Suddenly she started broad awake with the memory in her ears of a smothered cry from somewhere not far off. She jumped up and ran to the door and listened, but there was no sound. She grew alarmed for her husband, and called out: "Geoffrey! Geoffrey!"

After a few moments the door of the great hall opened, and Geoffrey appeared at it, but without his lamp.

"Hush!" he said, in a sort of whisper, and his voice was harsh and stern. "Hush! Get to bed! I am working, and must not be disturbed. Go to sleep, and do not wake the house!"

With a chill in her heart – for the harshness of her husband's voice was new to her – she crept back to bed and lay there trembling, too frightened to cry, and listened to every sound. There was a long pause of silence, and then the sound of some iron implement striking muffled blows! Then there came a clang of a heavy stone falling, followed by a muffled curse. Then a dragging sound, and then more noise of stone on stone. She lay all the while in an agony of fear, and her heart beat dreadfully. She heard a curious sort of scraping sound; and then there was silence. Presently the door opened gently, and Geoffrey appeared. His wife pretended to be asleep; but through her eyelashes she saw him wash from his hands something white that looked like lime.

In the morning he made no allusion to the previous night, and she was afraid to ask any question.

From that day there seemed some shadow over Geoffrey Brent. He neither ate nor slept as he had been accustomed, and his former habit of turning suddenly as though someone were speaking from behind him revived. The old hall seemed to have some kind of fascination for him. He used to go there many times in the day, but grew impatient if anyone, even his wife, entered it. When the builder's foreman came to inquire about continuing his work Geoffrey was out driving; the man went into the hall, and when Geoffrey returned the servant told him of his arrival and where he was. With a frightful oath he pushed the servant aside and hurried up to the old hall. The workman met him almost at the door; and as Geoffrey burst into the room he ran against him. The man apologised:

"Beg pardon, sir, but I was just going out to make some enquiries. I directed twelve sacks of lime to be sent here, but I see there are only ten."

"Damn the ten sacks and the twelve too!" was the ungracious and incomprehensible rejoinder.

The workman looked surprised, and tried to turn the conversation.

"I see, sir, there is a little matter which our people must have done; but the governor will of course see it set right at his own cost."

"What do you mean?"

"That 'ere 'arth-stone, sir: Some idiot must have put a scaffold pole on it and cracked it right down the middle, and it's thick enough you'd think to stand

1anythink." Geoffrey was silent for quite a minute, and then said in a constrained
voice and with much gentler manner:

"Tell your people that I am not going on with the work in the hall at present. I want
o leave it as it is for a while longer."

"All right sir. I'll send up a few of our chaps to take away these poles and lime
bags and tidy the place up a bit."

"No! No!" said Geoffrey, "Leave them where they are. I shall send and tell
you when you are to get on with the work." So the foreman went away, and his
comment to his master was:

"I'd send in the bill, sir, for the work already done. 'Pears to me that money's a
ittle shaky in that quarter."

Once or twice Delandre tried to stop Brent on the road, and, at last, finding
that he could not attain his object rode after the carriage, calling out:

"What has become of my sister, your wife?" Geoffrey lashed his horses into
a gallop, and the other, seeing from his white face and from his wife's collapse
almost into a faint that his object was attained, rode away with a scowl and a laugh.

That night when Geoffrey went into the hall he passed over to the great
fireplace, and all at once started back with a smothered cry. Then with an effort
he pulled himself together and went away, returning with a light. He bent down
over the broken hearth-stone to see if the moonlight falling through the storied
window had in any way deceived him. Then with a groan of anguish he sank to
his knees.

There, sure enough, through the crack in the broken stone were protruding a
multitude of threads of golden hair just tinged with grey!

He was disturbed by a noise at the door, and looking round, saw his wife standing
in the doorway. In the desperation of the moment he took action to prevent
discovery, and lighting a match at the lamp, stooped down and burned away the
hair that rose through the broken stone. Then rising nonchalantly as he could, he
pretended surprise at seeing his wife beside him.

For the next week he lived in an agony; for, whether by accident or design, he
could not find himself alone in the hall for any length of time. At each visit the
hair had grown afresh through the crack, and he had to watch it carefully lest his
terrible secret should be discovered. He tried to find a receptacle for the body
of the murdered woman outside the house, but someone always interrupted him;
and once, when he was coming out of the private doorway, he was met by his wife,
who began to question him about it, and manifested surprise that she should not
have before noticed the key which he now reluctantly showed her. Geoffrey dearly
and passionately loved his wife, so that any possibility of her discovering his dread
secrets, or even of doubting him, filled him with anguish; and after a couple of
days had passed, he could not help coming to the conclusion that, at least, she
suspected something.

That very evening she came into the hall after her drive and found him there
sitting moodily by the deserted fireplace. She spoke to him directly.

"Geoffrey, I have been spoken to by that fellow Delandre, and he says horrible
things. He tells to me that a week ago his sister returned to his house, the wreck
and ruin of her former self, with only her golden hair as of old, and announced
some fell intention. He asked me where she is – and oh, Geoffrey, she is dead, she

is dead! So how can she have returned? Oh! I am in dread, and I know not where to turn!"

For answer, Geoffrey burst into a torrent of blasphemy which made her shudder. He cursed Delandre and his sister and all their kind, and in especial he hurled curse after curse on her golden hair.

"Oh, hush! Hush!" she said, and was then silent, for she feared her husband when she saw the evil effect of his humour. Geoffrey in the torrent of his anger stood up and moved away from the hearth; but suddenly stopped as he saw a new look of terror in his wife's eyes. He followed their glance, and then he too, shuddered – for there on the broken hearth-stone lay a golden streak as the point of the hair rose though the crack.

"Look, look!" she shrieked. "Is it some ghost of the dead! Come away – come away!" and seizing her husband by the wrist with the frenzy of madness, she pulled him from the room.

That night she was in a raging fever. The doctor of the district attended her at once, and special aid was telegraphed for to London. Geoffrey was in despair, and in his anguish at the danger of his young wife almost forgot his own crime and its consequences. In the evening the doctor had to leave to attend to others; but he left Geoffrey in charge of his wife. His last words were:

"Remember, you must humour her till I come in the morning, or till some other doctor has her case in hand. What you have to dread is another attack of emotion. See that she is kept warm. Nothing more can be done."

Late in the evening, when the rest of the household had retired, Geoffrey's wife got up from her bed and called to her husband.

"Come!" she said. "Come to the old hall! I know where the gold comes from! I want to see it grow!"

Geoffrey would fain have stopped her, but he feared for her life or reason on the one hand, and lest in a paroxysm she should shriek out her terrible suspicion, and seeing that it was useless to try to prevent her, wrapped a warm rug around her and went with her to the old hall. When they entered, she turned and shut the door and locked it.

"We want no strangers amongst us three tonight!" she whispered with a wan smile.

"We three! Nay we are but two," said Geoffrey with a shudder; he feared to say more.

"Sit here," said his wife as she put out the light. "Sit here by the hearth and watch the gold growing. The silver moonlight is jealous! See, it steals along the floor towards the gold – our gold!" Geoffrey looked with growing horror, and saw that during the hours that had passed the golden hair had protruded further through the broken hearth-stone. He tried to hide it by placing his feet over the broken place; and his wife, drawing her chair beside him, leant over and laid her head on his shoulder.

"Now do not stir, dear," she said; "let us sit still and watch. We shall find the secret of the growing gold!' He passed his arm round her and sat silent; and as the moonlight stole along the floor she sank to sleep.

He feared to wake her; and so sat silent and miserable as the hours stole away.

Before his horror-struck eyes the golden-hair from the broken stone grew and grew; and as it increased, so his heart got colder and colder, till at last he had not power to stir, and sat with eyes full of terror watching his doom.

* * *

n the morning when the London doctor came, neither Geoffrey nor his wife could
e found. Search was made in all the rooms, but without avail. As a last resource the
great door of the old hall was broken open, and those who entered saw a grim and
orry sight.

There by the deserted hearth Geoffrey Brent and his young wife sat cold and white
nd dead. Her face was peaceful, and her eyes were closed in sleep; but his face was a
ight that made all who saw it shudder, for there was on it a look of unutterable horror.
The eyes were open and stared glassily at his feet, which were twined with tresses of
golden hair, streaked with grey, which came through the broken hearth-stone.

f you enjoyed this, you might also like...

The Chain of Destiny,' see page 10
The Dualitists,' see page 363

The Squaw

NURNBERG AT THE TIME was not so much exploited as it has been since then Irving had not been playing *Faust*, and the very name of the old town was hardly known to the great bulk of the travelling public. My wife and I being in the second week of our honeymoon, naturally wanted someone else to join our party, so that when the cheery stranger, Elias P. Hutcheson, hailing from Isthmian City, Bleeding Gulch, Maple Tree County, Neb. turned up at the station at Frankfort, and casually remarked that he was going on to see the most all-fired old Methuselah of a town in Yurrup, and that he guessed that so much travelling alone was enough to send an intelligent, active citizen into the melancholy ward of a daft house, we took the pretty broad hint and suggested that we should join forces. We found, on comparing notes afterwards, that we had each intended to speak with some diffidence or hesitation so as not to appear too eager, such not being a good compliment to the success of our married life; but the effect was entirely marred by our both beginning to speak at the same instant – stopping simultaneously and then going on together again.

Anyhow, no matter how, it was done; and Elias P. Hutcheson became one of our party. Straightway Amelia and I found the pleasant benefit; instead of quarrelling, as we had been doing, we found that the restraining influence of a third party was such that we now took every opportunity of spooning in odd corners. Amelia declares that ever since she has, as the result of that experience, advised all her friends to take a friend on the honeymoon. Well, we 'did' Nurnberg together, and much enjoyed the racy remarks of our Transatlantic friend, who, from his quaint speech and his wonderful stock of adventures, might have stepped out of a novel. We kept for the last object of interest in the city to be visited the Burg, and on the day appointed for the visit strolled round the outer wall of the city by the eastern side.

The Burg is seated on a rock dominating the town and an immensely deep fosse guards it on the northern side. Nurnberg has been happy in that it was never sacked, had it been it would certainly not be so spick and span perfect as it is at present. The ditch has not been used for centuries, and now its base is spread with tea-gardens and orchards, of which some of the trees are of quite respectable growth. As we wandered round the wall, dawdling in the hot July sunshine, we often paused to admire the views spread before us, and in especial the great plain covered with towns and villages and bounded with a blue line of hills, like a landscape of Claude Lorraine.

From this we always turned with new delight to the city itself, with its myriad of quaint old gables and acre-wide red roofs dotted with dormer windows, tier upon tier. A little to our right rose the towers of the Burg, and nearer still, standing grim, the Torture Tower, which was, and is, perhaps, the most interesting place in the city. For centuries the tradition of the Iron Virgin of Nurnberg has been handed down as an instance of the horrors of cruelty of which man is capable; we had long looked forward to seeing it; and here at last was its home.

In one of our pauses we leaned over the wall of the moat and looked down. The garden seemed quite fifty or sixty feet below us, and the sun pouring into it with an intense, moveless heat like that of an oven. Beyond rose the grey, grim wall seemingly of endless height, and losing itself right and left in the angles of bastion and counterscarp. Trees and bushes crowned the wall, and above again towered the lofty houses on whose massive beauty Time has only set the hand of approval.

The sun was hot and we were lazy; time was our own, and we lingered, leaning on the wall. Just below us was a pretty sight – a great black cat lying stretched in the sun, whilst round her gambolled prettily a tiny black kitten. The mother would wave her tail for the kitten to play with, or would raise her feet and push away the little one as an encouragement to further play. They were just at the foot of the wall, and Elias P. Hutcheson, in order to help the play, stooped and took from the walk a moderate sized pebble.

"See!" he said, "I will drop it near the kitten, and they will both wonder where it came from."

"Oh, be careful," said my wife; "you might hit the dear little thing!"

"Not me, ma'am," said Elias P. "Why, I'm as tender as a Maine cherry-tree. Lor, bless ye. I wouldn't hurt the poor pooty little critter more'n I'd scalp a baby. An' you may bet your variegated socks on that! See, I'll drop it fur away on the outside so's not to go near her!" Thus saying, he leaned over and held his arm out at full length and dropped the stone. It may be that there is some attractive force which draws lesser matters to greater; or more probably that the wall was not plump but sloped to its base – we not noticing the inclination from above; but the stone fell with a sickening thud that came up to us through the hot air, right on the kitten's head, and shattered out its little brains then and there. The black cat cast a swift upward glance, and we saw her eyes like green fire fixed an instant on Elias P. Hutcheson; and then her attention was given to the kitten, which lay still with just a quiver of her tiny limbs, whilst a thin red stream trickled from a gaping wound. With a muffled cry, such as a human being might give, she bent over the kitten licking its wounds and moaning. Suddenly she seemed to realise that it was dead, and again threw her eyes up at us. I shall never forget the sight, for she looked the perfect incarnation of hate. Her green eyes blazed with lurid fire, and the white, sharp teeth seemed to almost shine through the blood which dabbled her mouth and whiskers. She gnashed her teeth, and her claws stood out stark and at full length on every paw. Then she made a wild rush up the wall as if to reach us, but when the momentum ended fell back, and further added to her horrible appearance for she fell on the kitten, and rose with her black fur smeared with its brains and blood. Amelia turned quite faint, and I had to lift her back from the wall. There was a seat close by in shade of a spreading plane-tree, and here I placed her whilst she composed herself. Then I went back to Hutcheson, who stood without moving, looking down on the angry cat below.

As I joined him, he said:

"Wall, I guess that air the savagest beast I ever see – 'cept once when an Apache squaw had an edge on a half-breed what they nicknamed 'Splinters' 'cos of the way he fixed up her papoose which he stole on a raid just to show that he appreciated the way they had given his mother the fire torture. She got that kinder look so set on her face that it jest seemed to grow there. She followed Splinters mor'n three year till at last the braves got him and handed him over to her. They did say that no man, white or Injun, had ever been so long a-dying under the tortures of the Apaches. The only time I ever see her smile was when I wiped her out. I kem on the camp just in time to see Splinters pass in his checks, and he wasn't sorry to go either. He was a hard citizen, and though I never could shake with him after that papoose business – for it was bitter bad, and he should have been a white man, for he looked like one – I see he had got paid out in full. Durn me, but I took a piece of his hide from one of his skinnin' posts an' had it made into a pocket-book. It's here now!" and he slapped the breast pocket of his coat.

Whilst he was speaking the cat was continuing her frantic efforts to get up the wall. She would take a run back and then charge up, sometimes reaching an incredible height. She did not seem to mind the heavy fall which she got each time but started with renewed vigour; and at every tumble her appearance became more horrible. Hutcheson was a kind-hearted man – my wife and I had both noticed little acts of kindness to animals as well as to persons – and he seemed concerned at the state of fury to which the cat had wrought herself.

"Wall, now!" he said, "I du declare that that poor critter seems quite desperate. There! There! Poor thing, it was all an accident – though that won't bring back your little one to you. Say! I wouldn't have had such a thing happen for a thousand! Just shows what a clumsy fool of a man can do when he tries to play! Seems I'm too darned slipperhanded to even play with a cat. Say Colonel!" – it was a pleasant way he had to bestow titles freely – "I hope your wife don't hold no grudge against me on account of this unpleasantness? Why, I wouldn't have had it occur on no account."

He came over to Amelia and apologised profusely, and she with her usual kindness of heart hastened to assure him that she quite understood that it was an accident. Then we all went again to the wall and looked over.

The cat missing Hutcheson's face had drawn back across the moat, and was sitting on her haunches as though ready to spring. Indeed, the very instant she saw him she did spring, and with a blind unreasoning fury, which would have been grotesque, only that it was so frightfully real. She did not try to run up the wall, but simply launched herself at him as though hate and fury could lend her wings to pass straight through the great distance between them. Amelia, womanlike, got quite concerned, and said to Elias P. in a warning voice:

"Oh! You must be very careful. That animal would try to kill you if she were here; her eyes look like positive murder."

He laughed out jovially. "Excuse me, ma'am," he said, "but I can't help laughin'. Fancy a man that has fought grizzlies an' Injuns bein' careful of bein' murdered by a cat!"

When the cat heard him laugh, her whole demeanour seemed to change. She no longer tried to jump or run up the wall, but went quietly over, and sitting again beside the dead kitten began to lick and fondle it as though it were alive.

"See!" said I, "the effect of a really strong man. Even that animal in the midst of her fury recognises the voice of a master, and bows to him!"

"Like a squaw!" was the only comment of Elias P. Hutcheson, as we moved on our way round the city fosse. Every now and then we looked over the wall and each time saw the cat following us. At first she had kept going back to the dead kitten, and then as the distance grew greater took it in her mouth and so followed. After a while, however, she abandoned this, for we saw her following all alone; she had evidently hidden the body somewhere. Amelia's alarm grew at the cat's persistence, and more than once she repeated her warning; but the American always laughed with amusement, till finally, seeing that she was beginning to be worried, he said:

"I say, ma'am, you needn't be skeered over that cat. I go heeled, I du!" Here he lapped his pistol pocket at the back of his lumbar region. "Why sooner'n have you worried, I'll shoot the critter, right here, an' risk the police interferin' with a citizen of the United States for carryin' arms contrairy to reg'lations!" As he spoke he looked over the wall, but the cat on seeing him, retreated, with a growl, into a bed of tall flowers, and was hidden. He went on: "Blest if that ar critter ain't got more sense of what's good for her than most Christians. I guess we've seen the last of her! You bet, she'll go back now to that busted kitten and have a private funeral of it, all to herself!"

Amelia did not like to say more, lest he might, in mistaken kindness to her, fulfil his threat of shooting the cat: and so we went on and crossed the little wooden bridge leading to the gateway whence ran the steep paved roadway between the Burg and the pentagonal Torture Tower. As we crossed the bridge we saw the cat again down below us. When she saw us her fury seemed to return, and she made frantic efforts to get up the steep wall. Hutcheson laughed as he looked down at her, and said:

"Goodbye, old girl. Sorry I injured your feelin's, but you'll get over it in time! So long!" And then we passed through the long, dim archway and came to the gate of the Burg.

When we came out again after our survey of this most beautiful old place which not even the well-intentioned efforts of the Gothic restorers of forty years ago have been able to spoil – though their restoration was then glaring white – we seemed to have quite forgotten the unpleasant episode of the morning. The old lime tree with its great trunk gnarled with the passing of nearly nine centuries, the deep well cut through the heart of the rock by those captives of old, and the lovely view from the city wall whence we heard, spread over almost a full quarter of an hour, the multitudinous chimes of the city, had all helped to wipe out from our minds the incident of the slain kitten.

We were the only visitors who had entered the Torture Tower that morning – so at least said the old custodian – and as we had the place all to ourselves were able to make a minute and more satisfactory survey than would have otherwise been possible. The custodian, looking to us as the sole source of his gains for the day, was willing to meet our wishes in any way. The Torture Tower is truly a grim place, even now when many thousands of visitors have sent a stream of life, and the joy that follows life, into the place; but at the time I mention it wore its grimmest and most gruesome aspect. The dust of ages seemed to have settled on it, and the darkness and the horror of its memories seem to have become sentient in a way that would have satisfied the Pantheistic souls of Philo or Spinoza.

The lower chamber where we entered was seemingly, in its normal state, filled with incarnate darkness; even the hot sunlight streaming in through the door seemed to be lost in the vast thickness of the walls, and only showed the masonry rough as when the builder's scaffolding had come down, but coated with dust and marked here and there with patches of dark stain which, if walls could speak, could have given their own dread memories of fear and pain.

We were glad to pass up the dusty wooden staircase, the custodian leaving the outer door open to light us somewhat on our way; for to our eyes the one long-wick'd, evil-smelling candle stuck in a sconce on the wall gave an inadequate light. When we came up through the open trap in the corner of the chamber overhead, Amelia held on to me so tightly that I could actually feel her heart beat. I must say for my own part that I was not surprised at her fear, for this room was even more gruesome than that below. Here there was certainly more light, but only just sufficient to realise the horrible surroundings of the place. The builders of the tower had evidently intended that only they who should gain the top should have any of the joys of light and prospect. There as we had noticed from below, were ranges of windows, albeit of mediaeval smallness but elsewhere in the tower were only a very few narrow slits such as were habitual in places of mediaeval defence. A few of these only lit the chamber, and these so high up in the wall that from no part could the sky be seen through the thickness of the walls.

In racks, and leaning in disorder against the walls, were a number of headsmen' swords, great double-handed weapons with broad blade and keen edge. Hard by were several blocks whereon the necks of the victims had lain, with here and there deep notches where the steel had bitten through the guard of flesh and shored into the wood. Round the chamber, placed in all sorts of irregular ways, were many implements of torture which made one's heart ache to see – chairs full of spike which gave instant and excruciating pain; chairs and couches with dull knobs whose torture was seemingly less, but which, though slower, were equally efficacious; racks belts, boots, gloves, collars, all made for compressing at will; steel baskets in which the head could be slowly crushed into a pulp if necessary; watchmen's hooks with long handle and knife that cut at resistance – this a speciality of the old Nurnberg police system; and many, many other devices for man's injury to man.

Amelia grew quite pale with the horror of the things, but fortunately did not faint for being a little overcome she sat down on a torture chair, but jumped up again with a shriek, all tendency to faint gone. We both pretended that it was the injury done to her dress by the dust of the chair, and the rusty spikes which had upset her, and Mr Hutcheson acquiesced in accepting the explanation with a kind-hearted laugh.

But the central object in the whole of this chamber of horrors was the engine known as the Iron Virgin, which stood near the centre of the room. It was a rudely-shaped figure of a woman, something of the bell order, or, to make a closer comparison, or the figure of Mrs. Noah in the children's Ark, but without that slimness of waist and perfect *rondeur* of hip which marks the aesthetic type of the Noah family. One would hardly have recognised it as intended for a human figure at all had not the founder shaped on the forehead a rude semblance of a woman's face.

This machine was coated with rust without, and covered with dust; a rope was fastened to a ring in the front of the figure, about where the waist should have been and was drawn through a pulley, fastened on the wooden pillar which sustained the flooring above. The custodian pulling this rope showed that a section of the front was hinged like a door at one side; we then saw that the engine was of considerable thickness, leaving just room enough inside for a man to be placed. The door was of equal thickness and of great weight, for it took the custodian all his strength, aided though he was by the contrivance of the pulley, to open it. This weight was partly due to the fact that the door was of manifest purpose hung so as to throw its weight downwards, so that it might shut of its own accord when the strain was released.

The inside was honeycombed with rust – nay more, the rust alone that come through time would hardly have eaten so deep into the iron walls; the rust of the cruel

ains was deep indeed! It was only, however, when we came to look at the inside of
the door that the diabolical intention was manifest to the full. Here were several long
pikes, square and massive, broad at the base and sharp at the points, placed in such a
position that when the door should close the upper ones would pierce the eyes of the
victim, and the lower ones his heart and vitals. The sight was too much for poor Amelia,
and this time she fainted dead off, and I had to carry her down the stairs, and place her
on a bench outside till she recovered. That she felt it to the quick was afterwards shown
by the fact that my eldest son bears to this day a rude birthmark on his breast, which
has, by family consent, been accepted as representing the Nurnberg Virgin.

When we got back to the chamber we found Hutcheson still opposite the Iron
Virgin; he had been evidently philosophising, and now gave us the benefit of his
thought in the shape of a sort of exordium.

"Wall, I guess I've been learnin' somethin' here while madam has been gettin' over
her faint. "Pears to me that we're a long way behind the times on our side of the big
drink. We uster think out on the plains that the Injun could give us points in tryin'
to make a man uncomfortable; but I guess your old mediaeval law-and-order party
could raise him every time. Splinters was pretty good in his bluff on the squaw, but
this here young miss held a straight flush all high on him. The points of them spikes
air sharp enough still, though even the edges air eaten out by what uster be on them.
It'd be a good thing for our Indian section to get some specimens of this here play-
toy to send round to the Reservations jest to knock the stuffin' out of the bucks, and
the squaws too, by showing them as how old civilisation lays over them at their best.
Guess but I'll get in that box a minute jest to see how it feels!"

"Oh no! No!' said Amelia. "It is too terrible!"

"Guess, ma'am, nothin's too terrible to the explorin' mind. I've been in some queer
places in my time. Spent a night inside a dead horse while a prairie fire swept over
me in Montana Territory – an' another time slept inside a dead buffler when the
'Omanches was on the war path an' I didn't keer to leave my kyard on them. I've been
two days in a caved-in tunnel in the Billy Broncho gold mine in New Mexico, an' was
one of the four shut up for three parts of a day in the caisson what slid over on her
side when we was settin' the foundations of the Buffalo Bridge. I've not funked an
odd experience yet, an' I don't propose to begin now!"

We saw that he was set on the experiment, so I said: "Well, hurry up, old man, and
get through it quick!"

"All right, General," said he, "but I calculate we ain't quite ready yet. The gentlemen,
my predecessors, what stood in that thar canister, didn't volunteer for the office –
not much! And I guess there was some ornamental tyin' up before the big stroke was
made. I want to go into this thing fair and square, so I must get fixed up proper first.
I dare say this old galoot can rise some string and tie me up accordin' to sample?"

This was said interrogatively to the old custodian, but the latter, who understood
the drift of his speech, though perhaps not appreciating to the full the niceties of
dialect and imagery, shook his head. His protest was, however, only formal and
made to be overcome. The American thrust a gold piece into his hand, saying: "Take
it, pard! It's your pot; and don't be skeer'd. This ain't no necktie party that you're
asked to assist in!' He produced some thin frayed rope and proceeded to bind our
companion with sufficient strictness for the purpose. When the upper part of his
body was bound, Hutcheson said:

"Hold on a moment, Judge. Guess I'm too heavy for you to tote into the canister. You jest let me walk in, and then you can wash up regardin' my legs!"

Whilst speaking he had backed himself into the opening which was just enough to hold him. It was a close fit and no mistake. Amelia looked on with fear in her eyes, but she evidently did not like to say anything. Then the custodian completed his task by tying the American's feet together so that he was now absolutely helpless and fixed in his voluntary prison. He seemed to really enjoy it, and the incipient smile which was habitual to his face blossomed into actuality as he said:

"Guess this here Eve was made out of the rib of a dwarf! There ain't much room for a full-grown citizen of the United States to hustle. We uster make our coffins more roomier in Idaho territory. Now, Judge, you jest begin to let this door down, slow, or to me. I want to feel the same pleasure as the other jays had when those spikes began to move toward their eyes!"

"Oh no! No! No!" broke in Amelia hysterically. "It is too terrible! I can't bear to see it! – I can't! I can't!" But the American was obdurate. "Say, Colonel," said he, "why not take Madame for a little promenade? I wouldn't hurt her feelin's for the world; but now that I am here, havin' kem eight thousand miles, wouldn't it be too hard to give up the very experience I've been pinin' an' pantin' fur? A man can't get to feel like canned goods every time! Me and the Judge here'll fix up this thing in no time, an' then you'll come back, an' we'll all laugh together!"

Once more the resolution that is born of curiosity triumphed, and Amelia stayed holding tight to my arm and shivering whilst the custodian began to slacken slowly inch by inch the rope that held back the iron door. Hutcheson's face was positively radiant as his eyes followed the first movement of the spikes.

"Wall!" he said, "I guess I've not had enjoyment like this since I left Noo York. Bar scrap with a French sailor at Wapping – an' that warn't much of a picnic neither – I've not had a show fur real pleasure in this dod-rotted Continent, where there ain't no b'ars nor no Injuns, an' wheer nary man goes heeled. Slow there, Judge! Don't yo rush this business! I want a show for my money this game – I du!"

The custodian must have had in him some of the blood of his predecessors in that ghastly tower, for he worked the engine with a deliberate and excruciating slowness which after five minutes, in which the outer edge of the door had not moved half as many inches, began to overcome Amelia. I saw her lips whiten, and felt her hold upon my arm relax. I looked around an instant for a place whereon to lay her, and when I looked at her again found that her eye had become fixed on the side of the Virgin Following its direction I saw the black cat crouching out of sight. Her green eyes shone like danger lamps in the gloom of the place, and their colour was heightened by the blood which still smeared her coat and reddened her mouth. I cried out:

"The cat! Look out for the cat!" for even then she sprang out before the engine. At this moment she looked like a triumphant demon. Her eyes blazed with ferocity, her hair bristled out till she seemed twice her normal size, and her tail lashed about as does a tiger's when the quarry is before it. Elias P. Hutcheson when he saw her was amused, and his eyes positively sparkled with fun as he said:

"Darned if the squaw hain't got on all her war paint! Jest give her a shove off if she comes any of her tricks on me, for I'm so fixed everlastingly by the boss, that durn my skin if I can keep my eyes from her if she wants them! Easy there, Judge! Don't yo slack that ar rope or I'm euchered!"

At this moment Amelia completed her faint, and I had to clutch hold of her round e waist or she would have fallen to the floor. Whilst attending to her I saw the black t crouching for a spring, and jumped up to turn the creature out.

But at that instant, with a sort of hellish scream, she hurled herself, not as we pected at Hutcheson, but straight at the face of the custodian. Her claws seemed be tearing wildly as one sees in the Chinese drawings of the dragon rampant, and I looked I saw one of them light on the poor man's eye, and actually tear through and down his cheek, leaving a wide band of red where the blood seemed to spurt om every vein.

With a yell of sheer terror which came quicker than even his sense of pain, the man aped back, dropping as he did so the rope which held back the iron door. I jumped r it, but was too late, for the cord ran like lightning through the pulley-block, and e heavy mass fell forward from its own weight.

As the door closed I caught a glimpse of our poor companion's face. He seemed zen with terror. His eyes stared with a horrible anguish as if dazed, and no sound me from his lips.

And then the spikes did their work. Happily the end was quick, for when I wrenched en the door they had pierced so deep that they had locked in the bones of the skull rough which they had crushed, and actually tore him – it – out of his iron prison l, bound as he was, he fell at full length with a sickly thud upon the floor, the face rning upward as he fell.

I rushed to my wife, lifted her up and carried her out, for I feared for her very reason she should wake from her faint to such a scene. I laid her on the bench outside and n back. Leaning against the wooden column was the custodian moaning in pain ilst he held his reddening handkerchief to his eyes. And sitting on the head of e poor American was the cat, purring loudly as she licked the blood which trickled rough the gashed socket of his eyes.

I think no one will call me cruel because I seized one of the old executioner's ords and shore her in two as she sat.

you enjoyed this, you might also like...

rooken Sands,' see page 59
he Burial of the Rats,' see page 347

The Man from Shorrox

THROTH, YER 'ANN'RS, I'll tell ye wid pleasure; though, trooth to tell, it's only poor wurrk telling the same shtory over an' over agin. But I niver object to tell it to rale gintlemin, like yer 'ann'rs, what don't forget that a poor man has a mouth on to him as much as Creeshus himself has.

The place was a market town in Kilkenny – or maybe King's County or Queen's County. At all evints, it was wan of them counties what Cromwell – bad cess to him – gev his name to. An' the house was called after him that was the Lord Liftinin an' invinted the polis – God forgive him! It was kep' be a man iv the name iv Misther Mickey Byrne an' his good lady – at laste it was till wan dark night whin the bhoys mistuk him for another gindeman, an unknown man, what had bought a contagious property – mind ye the impidence iv him. Mickey was comin' back from the Curragh Races wid his skin that tight wid the full of the whiskey inside of him that he couldn't open his eyes to see what was goin' on, or his mouth to set the bhoys right afther he had got the first tap on the head wid wan of the blackthorn what they done such jobs wid. The poor bhoys was that full of sorra for their mishap whin they brung him home to his widdy that the crather hadn't the hearrt to be too sevare on thim. At the first iv course she was wroth, bein' only a woman afther all an' weemun not bein' gave to rayson like nun is. Millia murdher! But for a bit sh was like a madwoman, and was nigh to have cut the heads from affav thim wid th mate chopper, till, seein' thim so white and quite, she all at wance flung down th chopper an' knelt down be the corp.

"Lave me to me dead," she sez. "Oh mm! It's no use more people nor is needfu bein' made unhappy over this night's terrible wurrk. Mick Byrne would have no ma worse for him whin he was living, and he'll have harm to none for his death! No go; an', oh bhoys, be dacent and quite, an' don't thry a poor widdied sowl too hard'

Well, afther that she made no change in things ginerally, but kep' on the hotel ji the same; an' whin some iv her friends wanted her to get help, she only sez: "Mic an' me run this house well enough; an' whin I'm thinkin' of takun' help I'll tell ye I'll go on be meself, as I mane to, till Mick an' me comes together agun."

An', sure enough, the ould place wint on jist the same, though, more betoke there wasn't Mick wid his shillelagh to kape the pace whin things got pretty hot c fair nights, an' in the gran' ould election times, when heads was bruk like eggs glory be to God!

My! But she was the fine woman, was the Widdy Byrne! A gran' crathur intirel a fine upshtandin' woman, nigh as tall as a modheratesized man, wid a forrm c her that'd warrm yer hearrt to look at, it sthood out that way in the right place She had shkin like satin, wid a warrm flush in it, like the sun shinun' on a cro iv yestherday's crame; an' her cheeks an' her neck was that firrm that ye couldr take a pinch iv thim – though sorra wan iver dar'd to thry, the worse luck! But h hair! Begor, that was the finishing touch that set all the min crazy. It was jist wa

nass iv red, like the heart iv a burnun' furze-bush whin the smoke goes from aff iv
it. Musha! but it'd make the blood come up in yer eyes to see the glint iv that hair
wid the light shunun' on it. There was niver a man, what was a man at all at all, iver
kem in be the door that he didn't want to put his two arrms round the widdy an' giv'
her a hug immadiate. They was fine min too, some iv thim – and warrm men – big
graziers from Kildare, and the like, that counted their cattle be scores, an' used to
come ridin' in to market on huntin' horses what they'd refuse hundlireds iv pounds
or from officers in the Curragh an' the quality. Begor, but some iv thim an' the
dhrovers was rare miii in a fight. More nor wance I seen them, forty, maybe half a
hundred, strong, clear the market-place at Banagher or Athy. Well do I remimber
the way the big, red, hairy wrists iv thim'd go up in the air, an' down'd come the
springy ground-ash saplins what they carried for switches. The whole lot iv thim
wanted to come coortun' the widdy; but sorra wan iv her'd look at thim. She'd flirt
an' be coy an' taze thim and make thim mad for love iv her, as weemin likes to do.
Thank God for the same! For mayhap we min wouldn't love thim as we do only for
their thricky ways; an' thin what'd become iv the counthry wid nothin' in it at all
except single min an' ould maids jist dyin', and growin' crabbed for want iv chuidher
to kiss an' tache an' shpank an' make love to? Shure, yer 'ann'rs, 'tis childher as
makes the hearrt iv man green, jist as it is fresh wather that makes the grass grow.
Divil a shtep nearer would the widdy iver let mortial man come. "No," she'd say;
"whin I see a man fit to fill Mick's place, I'll let yez know iv it; thank ye kindly"; an'
wid that she'd shake her head till the beautiful red hair iv it'd be like shparks iv fire
– an' the mm more mad for her nor iver.

But, mind ye, she wasn't no shpoil-shport; Mick's wife knew more nor that, an'
his widdy didn't forgit the thrick iv it. She'd lade the laugh herself if 'twas anything a
dacent woman could shmile at; an' if it wasn't, she'd send the girrls aff to their beds,
an' tell the min they might go on talkin' that way, for there was only herself to be
insulted; an' that'd shut thim up pretty quick I'm tellin' yez. But av any iv thim'd thry
to git affectionate, as min do whin they've had all they can carry, well, thin she had
a playful way iv dalin' wid thim what'd always turn the laugh agin' thim. She used
to say that she lamed the beginnun' iv it at the school an' the rest iv it from Mick.
She always kep by her on the counther iv the bar wan iv thim rattan canes wid the curly
ends, what the soldiers carries whin they can't barry a whip, an' are goin' out wid
their cap on three hairs, an' thim new oiled, to scorch the girrls. An' thin whin any
v the shuitors'd get too affectionate she'd lift the cane an' swish them wid it, her
laughin' out iv her like mad all the time. At first wan or two iv the min'd say that a
kiss at the widdy was worth a clip iv a cane; an' wan iv thim, a warrm horse-fanner
from Poul-a-Phoka, said he'd complate the job av she was to cut him into ribbons.
But she was a handy woman wid the cane – which was shtrange enough, for she
had no childer to be practisin' on – an' whin she threw what was left iv him back
over the bar, wid his face like a gridiron, the other min what was laughin' along wid
her tuk the lesson to hearrt. Whiniver afther that she laid her hand on the cane, no
matther how quietly, there'd be no more talk iv thryin' for kissin' in that quarther.

Well, at the time I'm comm' to there was great divarshuns intirely goin' on in the town.
The fair was on the morra, an' there was a power iv people in the town; an' cattle, an'
geese, an' turkeys, an' butther, an' pigs, an' vegetables, an' all kinds iv divilment, includin'
a berryin' – the same bein' an ould attorney-man, savin' yer prisince; a lone man widout

friends, lyin' out there in the gran' room iv the hotel what they call the 'Queen's Room.' Well, I needn't tell yer 'ann'rs that the place was pretty full that night. Musha but it's the fleas thimselves what had the bad time iv it, wid thim crowded out on the outside, an' shakin', an' thrimblin' wid the cowld. The widdy, av coorse, was in the bar passin' the time iv the day wid all that kem in, an' keepin' her eyes afore an' ahin' her to hould the girrls up to their wurrk an' not to be thriflin' wid the mm. My! but there was a power iv min at the bar that night; warrm farmers from four counties, an' graziers wid their ground-ash plants an' big frieze coats, an' plinty iv commercials too. In the middle iv it all, up the shtreet at a hand gallop comes an Athy carriage wid two horses, an' pulls up at the door wid the horses shmokin'. An' begor, the man in it was smokin' too, a big cygar nigh as long as yer arrm. He jumps out an' walks up as bould as brass to the bar, jist as if there was niver a livin' sowl but himself in the place. He chucks the widdy undher the chin at wanst, an', taking aff his hat, sez: "I want the best room in the house. I travel for Shorrox", the greatest long-cotton firrm in the whole worrld, an' I want to open up a new line here! The best is what I want an' that's not good enough for me!"

Well, gintlemun, ivery wan in the place was spacheless at his impidence; an', begor that was the only time in her life I'm tould whin the widdy was tuk back. But, glory be it didn't take long for her to recover herself, an' sez she quitely: "I don't doubt ye, sur The best can't be too good for a gintleman what makes himself so aisy at home!" an she shmiled at him till her teeth shone like jools.

God knows, gintlemin, what does be in weemin's minds whin they're dalin' wid a man! Maybe it was that Widdy Byrne only wanted to kape the pace wid all thim min crowdin' roun' her, an' thim clutchin' on tight to their shticks an' aiger for a fight wid any man on her account. Or maybe it was that she forgive him his impidence; for well I know that it's not the most modest man, nor him what kapes his distance, that the girrls, much less the widdies, like the best. But anyhow she spake out iv her to the man from Manchesther: "I'm sorry, sur, that I can't give ye the best room – what we call the best – for it is engaged already."

"Then turn him out!" sez he.

"I can't," she says – "at laste not till tomorra; an' ye can have the room thin iv ye like."

There was a kind iv a sort iv a shnicker among some iv the min, thim knowin' iv the corp, an' the Manchesther man tuk it that they was laughin' at him; so he sez: "I'll shleep in that room tonight; the other gintleman can put up wid me iv I can wid him. Unless," sez he, oglin' the widdy, "I can have the place iv the masther of the house, if there's a priest or a parson handy in this town – an' sober," sez he.

Well, tho" the widdy got as red as a Claddagh cloak, she jist laughed an' turned aside, sayin": "Throth, sur, but it's poor Mick's place ye might have, an' welkim, this night."

"An' where might that be now, ma'am?" sez he, lanin' over the bar; an' him would have chucked her under the chin agun, only that she moved her head away that quick.

"In the churchyard!" she sez. "Ye might take Mick's place there, av ye like, an' I'll not be wan to say ye no."

At that the min round all laughed, an' the man from Manchesther got mad, an' shpoke out, rough enough too it seemed: "Oh, he's all right where he is. I daresay he's

uiter times where he is than whin he had my luk out. Him an' the Devil can toss for
hoice in bein' lonely or bein' quite."

Wid that the widdy blazes up all iv a suddunt, like a live sod shtuck in the thatch,
n' sez she: "Who are ye that dares to shpake ill iv the dead, an' to couple his name
id the Divil, an' to his widdy's very face? It's aisy seen that poor Mick is gone!" an'
id that she threw her apron over her head an' sot down an' rocked herself to and
o, as widdies do whin the fit is on thim iv missin' the dead.

There was more nor wan man there what'd like to have shtud opposite the
Manchesther man wid a bit iv a blackthorn in his hand; but they knew the widdy too
ell to dar to intherfere till they were let. At length wan iv thim – Mr Hogan, from
igh Portarlington, a warrm man, that'd put down a thousand pounds iv dhry money
ny day in the week – kem over to the bar an' tuk aff his hat, an' sez he: "Mrs Byrne,
ma'am, as a friend of poor dear ould Mick, I'd be glad to take his quarrel on meself on
is account, an' more than proud to take it on his widdy's, if, ma'am, ye'll only honour
ne be saying the wurrd."

Wid that she tuk down the apron from aff iv her head an' wiped away the tears in
er jools iv eyes wid the corner iv it.

"Thank ye kindly," sez she; "but, guntlemin, Mick an' me run this hotel long
ogether, an' I've run it alone since thin, an' I mane to go on running it be meself,
ven if new min from Manchesther itself does be bringin' us new ways. As to you,
ur," sez she, turnin' to him, "it's powerful afraid I am that there isn't accommodation
ere for a guntlemin what's so requireful. An' so I think I'll be askin' ye to find
onvanience in some other hotel in the town."

Wid that he turned on her an' sez, "I'm here now, an' I offer to pay me charges.
e the law ye can't refuse to resave me or refuse me lodgmint, especially whin I'm on
ne primises."

So the Widdy Byrne drewed herself up, an' sez she, "Sur, ye ask yer legal rights; ye
hall have them. Tell me what it is ye require."

Sez he sthraight out: "I want the best room."

"I've tould you already," sez she, "there's a gintleman in it."

"Well," sez he, "what other room have ye vacant?"

"Sorra wan at all," sez she. "Every room in the house is tuk. Perhaps, sur, ye don't
hink or remimber that there's a fair on tomorra."

She shpoke so polite that ivery man in the place knew there was somethin' comin'
later on. The Manchesther man felt that the laugh was on him; but he didn't want
or impidence, so he up, an' sez he: "Thin, if I have to share wid another, I'll share wid
ne best! It's the Queen's Room I'll be shleepin' in this night."

Well, the min shtandin' by wasn't too well plazed wid what was going on; for the
nan from Manchesther he was plumin' himself for all the world like a cock on a
unghill. He laned agin over the bar an' began makin' love to the widdy hot an' fast.
He was a fine, shtout-made man, wid a bull neck on to him an' short hair, like wan iv
nim 'two-to-wan-bar-wans' what I've seen at Punchestown an' Fairy House an' the
Galway races. But he seemed to have no manners at all in his coortin', but done it as
uick an' business-like as takun' his commercial ordhers. It was like this: "I want to
nake love; you want to be made love to, bein' a woman. Hould up yer head!"

We all could see the widdy was boilin' mad; but, to do him fair, the man from
Manchesther didn't seem to care what any wan thought. But we all seen what he

didn't see at first, that the widdy began widout thinkin' to handle the rattan cane on the bar. Well, prisintly he began agun to ask about his room, an' what kind iv a man it was that was to share it wid him.

So sez the widdy, "A man wid less wickedness in him nor you have, an' less impidence."

"I hope he's a quite man," sez he.

So the widdy began to laugh, an' sez she: "I'll warrant he's quite enough."

"Does he shnore? I hate a man – or a woman ayther – what shnores."

"Throth," sez she, "there's no shnore in him"; an' she laughed agin.

Some iv the min round what knew iv the ould attorney-man – saving yer prisince – began to laugh too; and this made the Manchesther man suspicious. When the likes iv him gets suspicious he gets rale nasty; so he sez, wid a shneer: "You seem to be pretty well up in his habits, ma'am!"

The widdy looked round at the graziers, what was clutchin' their ash plants hard, an' there was a laughin' divil in her eye that kep' thim quite; an' thin she turned round to the man, and sez she: "Oh, I know that much, anyhow, wid wan thing an' another, begor!" But she looked more enticin' nor iver at that moment. For sure the man from Manchesther thought so, for he laned nigh his whole body over the counther, an' whispered somethin' at her, puttin' out his hand as he did so, an' layin' it on her neck to dhraw her to him. The widdy seemed to know what was comm', an' had her hand on the rattan; so whin he was draggin' her to him an' puttin' out his lips to kiss her – an' her first as red as a turkey-cock an' thin as pale as a sheet – she ups wid the cane and gev him wan skelp across the face wid it, shpringin' back as she done so. Oh jool! But that was a skelp! A big wale iv blood riz up as quick as the blow was shtruck, jist as I've seen on the pigs' backs whin they do be prayin' aloud not to be tuk where they're wanted.

"Hands off, Misther Impidence!" sez she. The man from Manchesther was that mad that he ups wid the tumbler formnst him an' was goin' to throw it at her, whin there kem an odd sound from the graziers – a sort of "Ach!" as whin a man is workin' a sledge, an' I seen the ground-ash plants an' the big fists what held thim, and the big hairy wrists go up in the air. Begor, but polis thimselves wid bayonets wouldn't care to face thim like that! In the half of two twos the man from Manchesther would have been cut in ribbons, but there came a cry from the widdy what made the glasses ring: "Shtop! I'm not goin' to have any fightin' here; an' besides, there's bounds to the bad manners iv even a man from Shorrox". He wouldn't dar to shtrike me – though I have no head! Maybe I hit a thought too hard; but I had rayson to remimber that somethin' was due on Mick's account too. I'm sorry, sur," sez she to the man, quite polite, "that I had to defind meself; but whin a gintleman claims the law to come into a house, an' thin assaults th' owner iv it, though she has no head, it's more restrainful he should be intirely!"

"Hear, hear!" cried some iv the mm, an' wan iv thim sez "Amen," sez he, an' they al begin to laugh. The Manchesther man he didn't know what to do; for begor he didn' like the look of thim ash plants up in the air, an' yit he was not wan to like the laugh agin' him or to take it aisy. So he turns to the widdy an' he lifts his hat an' sez he wic mock politeness: "I must complimint ye, ma'am, upon the shtrength iv yer arrm, a upon the mildness iv yer disposition. Throth, an' I'm thinkin' that it's misther Mick that has the best iv it, wid his body lyin' paceful in the churchyard, anyhow; thougl

the poor sowi doesn't seem to have much good in changin' wan devil for another!"
An' he looked at her rale spiteful.

Well, for a minit her eyes blazed, but thin she shmiled at him, an' made a low
curtsey, an' sez she – oh! mind ye, she was a gran' woman at givin' back as good as she
got – "Thank ye kindly, sur, for yer polite remarks about me arrm. Sure me poor dear
Mick often said the same; only he said more an' wid shuparior knowledge! "Molly",
sez he – "I'd mislike the shtrength iv yer arrm whin ye shtrike, only that I forgive ye
for it whin it comes to the huggin'!" But as to poor Mick's prisint condition I'm not
goin' to argue wid ye, though I can't say that I forgive ye for the way you've shpoke iv
him that's gone. Bedad, it's fond iv the dead y'are, for ye seem onable to kape thim
out iv yer mouth. Maybe ye'll be more respectful to thim before ye die!"

"I don't want no sarmons!" sez he, wery savage. "Am I to have me room tonight, or
am I not?"

"Did I undherstand ye to say," sez she, "that ye wanted a share iv the Queen's Room?"

"I did! An' I demand it."

"Very well, sur," sez she very quitely, "ye shall have it!" Jist thin the supper war
ready, and most iv the mm at the bar thronged into the coffee-room, an' among thim
the man from Manchesther, what wint bang up to the top iv the table an sot down as
though he owned the place, an' him niver in the house before.

A few iv the bhoys shtayed a minit to say another word to the widdy, an' as soon as
they was alone Misther Hogan up, an' sez he: "Oh, darlint! But it's a jool iv a woman
y' are! Do ye raly mane to put him in the room wid the corp?"

"He said he insisted on being in that room!" she says, quite sarious; an' thin givin'
a look undher her lashes at the bhoys as made thim lep, sez she: "Oh! min, an ye love
me give him his shkin that full that he'll tumble into his bed this night wid his sinses
obscurifled. Dhrink toasts till he misremimbers where he is! Whist! Go, quick, so that
he won't suspect nothin'!"

That was a warrm night, I'm telling ye! The man from Shorrox had wine galore wid
his mate; an' afther, whin the plates an' dishes was tuk away an' the nuts was brought
in, Hogan got up an' proposed his health, an' wished him prosperity in his new line.
Iv coorse he had to dhrink that; an' thin others got up, an' there was more toasts
dhrunk than there was min in the room, till the man, him not bein' used to whiskey-
punch, began to git onsartin in his shpache. So they gev him more toasts – "Ireland
as a nation," an' "Home Rule," an' "The ruimory iv Dan O'Connell," an' "Bad luck to
Boney," an' "God save the Queen," an' "More power to Manchesther," an' other things
what they thought would plaze him, him bein' English. Long hours before it was time
for the house to shut, he was as dhrunk as a whole row of fiddlers, an' kep shakin'
hands wid ivery man an' promisin' thim to open a new line in Home Rule, an' sich
nonsinse. So they tuk him up to the door iv the Queen's Room an' left him there.

He managed to undhress himself all except his hat, and got into bed wid the corp
v th' ould attorney-man, an' thin an' there fell asleep widout noticin' him.

Well, prisintly he woke wid a cowld feelin' all over him. He had lit no candle, an'
here was only the light from the passage comm' in through the glass over the door.
He felt himself nigh fallin' out iv the bed wid him almost on the edge, an' the cowld
shtrange gindeman lyin' shlap on the broad iv his back in the middle. He had enough
v the dhrink in him to be quarrelsome.

"I'll throuble ye," sez he, "to kape over yer own side iv the bed – or I'll soon let ye know the rayson why." An' wid that he give him a shove. But iv coorse the ould attorney-man tuk no notice whatsumiver.

"Y'are not that warrm that one'd like to lie contagious to ye," sez he. "Move over I say, to yer own side!" But divil a shtir iv the corp.

Well, thin he began to get fightin' angry, an' to kick an' shove the corp; but not gittin' any answer at all, he turned round an' hit him a clip on the side iv the head.

"Gitup," he sez, "iv ye're a man at all, an' put up yer dooks."

Then he got more madder shrill, for the dhrink was shtirrin' in him, an' he kicked an' shoved an' grabbed him be the leg an' the arrm to move him.

"Begor!" sez he, "but ye're the cowldest chap I iver kem anigh iv. Musha! but yer hairs is like icicles."

Thin he tuk him be the head, an' shuk him an' brung him to the bedside, an kicked him clane out on to the flure on the far side iv the bed.

"Lie there," he sez, "ye ould blast furnace! Ye can warrm yerself up on the flure till tomorra."

Be this time the power iv the dhrink he had tuk got ahoult iv him agin, an' he fell back in the middle iv the bed, wid his head on the pilla an' his toes up, an' wint aff ashleep, like a cat in the frost.

By-an'-by, whin the house was about shuttin' up, the watcher from th' undhertaker's kem to sit be the corp till the mornin', an' th' attorney him bein' a Protestan' there was no candles. Whin the house was quite, wan iv the girris, what was coortin' wid the watcher, shtole into the room.

"Are ye there, Michael?" sez she.

"Yis, me darlint!" he sez, comm' to her; an' there they shtood be the door, wid the lamp in the passage shinin' on the red heads iv the two iv thim.

"I've come," sez Katty, "to kape ye company for a bit, Michael; for it's crool lonesome worrk sittin' there alone all night. But I mustn't shtay long, for they're all goin' to bed soon, when the dishes is washed up."

"Give us a kiss," sez Michael.

"Oh, Michael!" sez she: "Kissin' in the prisince iv a corp! It's ashamed iv ye I am."

"Sorra cause, Katty. Sure, it's more respectful than any other way. Isn't it next to kissin' in the chapel? – An' ye do that whin ye're bein' married. If ye kiss me now, begor but I don't know as it's mortial nigh a weddin' it is! Anyhow, give us a kiss, an' we'll talk iv the rights an' wrongs iv it aftherwards."

Well, somehow, yer 'ann'rs, that kiss was bein' gave – an' a kiss in the prisince iv a corp is a sarious thing an' takes a long time. Thim two was payin' such attintion to what was going on betune thim that they didn't heed nothin', whin suddint Katty stops, and sez: "Whist! What is that?"

Michael felt creepy too, for there was a quare sound comm' from the bed. So they grabbed one another as they shtud in the doorway an looked at the bed almost afraid to breathe till the hair on both iv thim began to shtand up in horror; for the corp rose up in the bed, an' they seen it pointin' at thim, an' heard a hoarse voice say, "It's in hell I am – Divils around me! Don't I see thim burnin' wid their heads like flames? an' it's burnin' lam too – burnin', burnin', burnin'! Me throat is on fire, an' me face is burnin'! Wather! Wather! Give me wather, if only a dhrop on me tongue's tip!"

Well, thin Katty let one screetch out iv her, like to wake the dead, an' tore down the passage till she kem to the shtairs, and tuk a flyin' lep down an' fell in a dead faint on the mat below; and Michael yelled 'murdher' wid all his might.

It wasn't long till there was a crowd in that room, I tell ye; an' a mighty shtrange thing it was that sorra wan iv the graziers had even tuk his coat from aff iv him to go to bed, or laid by his shtick. An' the widdy too, she was as nate an' tidy as iver, though seemin' surprised out iv a sound shleep, an' her clothes onto her, all savin' a white bedgown, an' a candle in her hand. There was some others what had been in bed, min an' wimin wid their bare feet an' slippers on to some iv thim, wid their bracers down their backs, an' their petticoats flung on anyhow. An' some iv thim in big nightcaps, an' some wid their hair all screwed up in knots wid little wisps iv paper, like farden screws iv Limerick twist or Lundy Foot snuff. Musha! but it was the ould weemin what was afraid iv things what didn't alarrm the young wans at all. Divil resave me! but the sole thing they seemed to dhread was the min – dead or alive it was all wan to thim – an' 'twas ghosts an' corpses an' mayhap divils that the rest was afeard iv.

Well, whin the Manchesther man seen thim all come tumblin' into the room he began to git his wits about him; for the dhrink was wearin' aff, an' he was thryin' to remimber where he was. So whin he seen the widdy he put his hand up to his face where the red welt was, an' at wance seemed to undhershtand, for he got mad agin an' roared out: "What does this mane? Why this invasion iv me chamber? Clear out the whole kit, or I'll let yez know!"

Wid that he was goin' to jump out of bed, but the moment they seen his toes the ould weemin let a screech out iv thim, an' clung to the mm an' implored thim to save thim from murdher – an' worse. An' there was the Widdy Byrne laughin' like mad; an' Misther Hogan shtepped out, an' sez he: "Do jump out, Misther Shorrox! The boys has their switches, an' it's a mighty handy costume ye're in for a leatherin'!"

So wid that he jumped back into bed an' covered the clothes over him.

"In the name of God," sez he, "what does it all mane?"

"It manes this," sez Hogan, goin' round the bed an' draggin' up the corp an' layin' it on the bed beside him. "Begorra! but it's cantankerous kind iv a scut y'are. First nothin' will do ye but sharin' a room wid a corp; an' thin ye want the whole place to yerself."

"Take it away! Take it away," he yells out.

"Begorra," sez Mister Hogan, "I'll do no such thing. The gintleman ordhered the room first, an' it's he has the right to ordher you to be brung out!"

"Did he shnore much, sur?" says the widdy; an' wid that she burst out laughin' an' cryin' all at wanst. "That'll tache ye to shpake ill iv the dead agin!" An' she flung her petticoat over her head an' run out iv the room.

Well, we turned the min all back to their own rooms; for the most part iv thim had plenty iv dhrink on board, an' we feared for a row. Now that the fun was over, we didn't want any unplisintness to follow. So two iv the graziers wint into wan bed, an' we put the man from Manchesther in th' other room, an' gev him a screechin' tumbler iv punch to put the heartt in him agin.

I thought the widdy had gone to her bed; but whin I wint to put out the lights I seen one in the little room behind the bar, an' I shtepped quite, not to dishturb her, and peeped in. There she was on a low shtool rockin' herself to an' fro, an' goin' on wid her laughin' an' cryin' both together, while she tapped wid her fut on the flume. She was talkin' to herselfin a kind iv a whisper, an' I heerd her say: "Oh, but it's the crool woman I am to have such a thing done in me house – an' that poor sowl, wid none to weep for him, knocked about that a way for shport iv dhrunken min while me poor dear darlin himself is in the cowid clay! – But oh! Mick, Mick, if ye were only here! Wouldn't it be you – you wid the fun iv ye an' yer merry hearrt – that'd be plazed wid the doin's iv this night

If you enjoyed this, you might also like...
The Jewel of the Seven Stars, see page 117
'The Secret of the Growing Gold,' see page 303

A Dream of Red Hands

THE FIRST OPINION given to me regarding Jacob Settle was a simple descriptive statement, "He's a down-in-the-mouth chap": but I found that it embodied the thoughts and ideas of all his fellow-workmen. There was in the phrase a certain easy tolerance, an absence of positive feeling of any kind, rather than any complete opinion, which marked pretty accurately the man's place in public esteem. Still, there was some dissimilarity between this and his appearance which unconsciously set me thinking, and by degrees, as I saw more of the place and the workmen, I came to have a special interest in him. He was, I found, for ever doing kindnesses, not involving money expenses beyond his humble means, but in the manifold ways of forethought and forbearance and self-repression which are of the truer charities of life. Women and children trusted him implicitly, though, strangely enough, he rather shunned them, except when anyone was sick, and then he made his appearance to help if he could, timidly and awkwardly. He led a very solitary life, keeping house by himself in a tiny cottage, or rather hut, of one room, far on the edge of the moorland. His existence seemed so sad and solitary that I wished to cheer it up, and for the purpose took the occasion when we had both been sitting up with a child, injured by me through accident, to offer to lend him books. He gladly accepted, and as we parted in the grey of the dawn I felt that something of mutual confidence had been established between us.

The books were always most carefully and punctually returned, and in time Jacob Settle and I became quite friends. Once or twice as I crossed the moorland on Sundays I looked in on him; but on such occasions he was shy and ill at ease so that I felt diffident about calling to see him. He would never under any circumstances come into my own lodgings.

One Sunday afternoon, I was coming back from a long walk beyond the moor, and as I passed Settle's cottage stopped at the door to say "How do you do?" to him. As the door was shut, I thought that he was out, and merely knocked for form's sake, or through habit, not expecting to get any answer. To my surprise, I heard a feeble voice from within, though what was said I could not hear. I entered at once, and found Jacob lying half-dressed upon his bed. He was as pale as death, and the sweat was simply rolling off his face. His hands were unconsciously gripping the bedclothes as a drowning man holds on to whatever he may grasp. As I came in he half arose, with a wild, hunted look in his eyes, which were wide open and staring, as though something of horror had come before him; but when he recognised me he sank back on the couch with a smothered sob of relief and closed his eyes. I stood by him for a while, quite a minute or two, while he gasped. Then he opened his eyes and looked at me, but with such a despairing, woeful expression that, as I am a living man, I would have rather seen that frozen look of horror. I sat down beside him and asked after his health. For a while he would not answer me except to say that he was not ill; but then, after scrutinising me closely, he half arose on his elbow and said:

"I thank you kindly, sir, but I'm simply telling you the truth. I am not ill, as men call it, though God knows whether there be not worse sicknesses than doctors know of. I'll tell you, as you are so kind, but I trust that you won't even mention such a thing to a living soul, for it might work me more and greater woe. I am suffering from a bad dream."

"A bad dream!" I said, hoping to cheer him; "But dreams pass away with the light – even with waking." There I stopped, for before he spoke I saw the answer in his desolate look round the little place.

"No! No! That's all well for people that live in comfort and with those they love around them. It is a thousand times worse for those who live alone and have to do so. What cheer is there for me, waking here in the silence of the night, with the wide moor around me full of voices and full of faces that make my waking a worse dream than my sleep? Ah, young sir, you have no past that can send its legions to people the darkness and the empty space, and I pray the good God that you may never have!" As he spoke, there was such an almost irresistible gravity of conviction in his manner that I abandoned my remonstrance about his solitary life. I felt that I was in the presence of some secret influence which I could not fathom. To my relief, for I knew not what to say, he went on:

"Two nights past have I dreamed it. It was hard enough the first night, but I came through it. Last night the expectation was in itself almost worse than the dream – until the dream came, and then it swept away every remembrance of lesser pain. I stayed awake till just before the dawn, and then it came again, and ever since I have been in such an agony as I am sure the dying feel, and with it all the dread of tonight." Before he had got to the end of the sentence my mind was made up, and I felt that I could speak to him more cheerfully.

"Try and get to sleep early tonight – in fact, before the evening has passed away. The sleep will refresh you, and I promise you there will not be any bad dreams after tonight." He shook his head hopelessly, so I sat a little longer and then left him.

When I got home I made my arrangements for the night, for I had made up my mind to share Jacob Settle's lonely vigil in his cottage on the moor. I judged that if he got to sleep before sunset he would wake well before midnight, and so, just as the bells of the city were striking eleven, I stood opposite his door armed with a bag, in which were my supper, an extra large flask, a couple of candles, and a book. The moonlight was bright, and flooded the whole moor, till it was almost as light as day; but ever and anon black clouds drove across the sky, and made a darkness which by comparison seemed almost tangible. I opened the door softly, and entered without waking Jacob, who lay asleep with his white face upward. He was still, and again bathed in sweat. I tried to imagine what visions were passing before those closed eyes which could bring with them the misery and woe which were stamped on the face, but fancy failed me, and I waited for the awakening. It came suddenly, and in a fashion which touched me to the quick, for the hollow groan that broke from the man's white lips as he half arose and sank back was manifestly the realisation or completion of some train of thought which had gone before.

"If this be dreaming," said I to myself, "then it must be based on some very terrible reality. What can have been that unhappy fact that he spoke of?"

While I thus spoke, he realised that I was with him. It struck me as strange that he had no period of that doubt as to whether dream or reality surrounded him which commonly marks an expected environment of waking men. With a positive cry of joy, he seized my hand and held it in his two wet, trembling hands, as a frightened child clings on to someone whom it loves. I tried to soothe him:

"There, there! It is all right. I have come to stay with you tonight, and together we will try to fight this evil dream." He let go my hand suddenly, and sank back on his bed and covered his eyes with his hands.

"Fight it? – The evil dream! Ah! No, sir, no! No mortal power can fight that dream, for it comes from God – and is burned in here;" and he beat upon his forehead. Then he went on:

"It is the same dream, ever the same, and yet it grows in its power to torture me every time it comes."

"What is the dream?" I asked, thinking that the speaking of it might give him some relief, but he shrank away from me, and after a long pause said:

"No, I had better not tell it. It may not come again."

There was manifestly something to conceal from me – something that lay behind the dream, so I answered:

"All right. I hope you have seen the last of it. But if it should come again, you will tell me, will you not? I ask, not out of curiosity, but because I think it may relieve you to speak." He answered with what I thought was almost an undue amount of solemnity:

"If it comes again, I shall tell you all."

Then I tried to get his mind away from the subject to more mundane things, so I produced supper, and made him share it with me, including the contents of the flask. After a little he braced up, and when I lit my cigar, having given him another, we smoked a full hour, and talked of many things. Little by little the comfort of his body stole over his mind, and I could see sleep laying her gentle hands on his eyelids. He felt it, too, and told me that now he felt all right, and I might safely leave him; but I told him that, right or wrong, I was going to see in the daylight. So I lit my other candle, and began to read as he fell asleep.

By degrees I got interested in my book, so interested that presently I was startled by its dropping out of my hands. I looked and saw that Jacob was still asleep, and I was rejoiced to see that there was on his face a look of unwonted happiness, while his lips seemed to move with unspoken words. Then I turned to my work again, and again woke, but this time to feel chilled to my very marrow by hearing the voice from the bed beside me:

"Not with those red hands! Never! Never!" On looking at him, I found that he was still asleep. He woke, however, in an instant, and did not seem surprised to see me; there was again that strange apathy as to his surroundings. Then I said:

"Settle, tell me your dream. You may speak freely, for I shall hold your confidence sacred. While we both live I shall never mention what you may choose to tell me."

He replied:

"I said I would; but I had better tell you first what goes before the dream, that you may understand. I was a schoolmaster when I was a very young man; it was only a parish school in a little village in the West Country. No need to mention any names. Better not. I was engaged to be married to a young girl whom I loved and almost reverenced.

It was the old story. While we were waiting for the time when we could afford to set up house together, another man came along. He was nearly as young as I was, and handsome, and a gentleman, with all a gentleman's attractive ways for a woman of our class. He would go fishing, and she would meet him while I was at my work in school. I reasoned with her and implored her to give him up. I offered to get married at once and go away and begin the world in a strange country; but she would not listen to anything I could say, and I could see that she was infatuated with him. Then I took it on myself to meet the man and ask him to deal well with the girl, for I thought he might mean honestly by her, so that there might be no talk or chance of talk on the part of others. I went where I should meet him with none by, and we met!" Here Jacob Settle had to pause, for something seemed to rise in his throat, and he almost gasped for breath. Then he went on:

"Sir, as God is above us, there was no selfish thought in my heart that day, I loved my pretty Mabel too well to be content with a part of her love, and I had thought of my own unhappiness too often not to have come to realise that, whatever might come to her, my hope was gone. He was insolent to me – you, sir, who are a gentleman, cannot know, perhaps, how galling can be the insolence of one who is above you in station – but I bore with that. I implored him to deal well with the girl, for what might be only a pastime of an idle hour with him might be the breaking of her heart. For I never had a thought of her truth, or that the worst of harm could come to her – it was only the unhappiness to her heart I feared. But when I asked him when he intended to marry her his laughter galled me so that I lost my temper and told him that I would not stand by and see her life made unhappy. Then he grew angry too, and in his anger said such cruel things of her that then and there I swore he should not live to do her harm. God knows how it came about, for in such moments of passion it is hard to remember the steps from a word to a blow, but I found myself standing over his dead body, with my hands crimson with the blood that welled from his torn throat. We were alone and he was a stranger, with none of his kin to seek for him and murder does not always out – not all at once. His bones may be whitening still, for all I know, in the pool of the river where I left him. No one suspected his absence, or why it was, except my poor Mabel, and she dared not speak. But it was all in vain, for when I came back again after an absence of months – for I could not live in the place – I learned that her shame had come and that she had died in it. Hitherto I had been borne up by the thought that my ill deed had saved her future, but now, when I learned that I had been too late, and that my poor love was smirched with that man's sin, I fled away with the sense of my useless guilt upon me more heavily than I could bear. Ah! Sir, you that have not done such a sin don't know what it is to carry it with you. You may think that custom makes it easy to you, but it is not so. It grows and grows with every hour, till it becomes intolerable, and with it growing, too, the feeling that you must for ever stand outside Heaven. You don't know what that means, and I pray God that you never may. Ordinary men, to whom all things are possible, don't often, if ever, think of Heaven. It is a name, and nothing more, and they are content to wait and let things be, but to those who are doomed to be shut out for ever you cannot think what it means, you cannot guess or measure the terrible endless longing to see the gates opened, and to be able to join the white figures within.

"And this brings me to my dream. It seemed that the portal was before me, with great gates of massive steel with bars of the thickness of a mast, rising to the very clouds, and so close that between them was just a glimpse of a crystal grotto, on whose shining walls were figured many white-clad forms with faces radiant with joy. When I stood before the gate my heart and my soul were so full of rapture and longing that I forgot. And there stood at the gate two mighty angels with sweeping wings, and, oh! so stern of countenance. They held each in one hand a flaming sword, and in the other the latchet, which moved to and fro at their lightest touch. Nearer were figures all draped in black, with heads covered so that only the eyes were seen, and they handed to each who came white garments such as the angels wear. A low murmur came that told that all should put on their own robes, and without soil, or the angels would not pass them in, but would smite them down with the flaming swords. I was eager to don my own garment, and hurriedly threw it over me and stepped swiftly to the gate; but it moved not, and the angels, loosing the latchet, pointed to my dress, I looked down, and was aghast, for the whole robe was smeared with blood. My hands were red; they glittered with the blood that dripped from them as on that day by the river bank. And then the angels raised their flaming swords to smite me down, and the horror was complete – I awoke. Again, and again, and again, that awful dream comes to me. I never learn from the experience, I never remember, but at the beginning the hope is ever there to make the end more appalling; and I know that the dream does not come out of the common darkness where the dreams abide, but that it is sent from God as a punishment! Never, never shall I be able to pass the gate, for the soil on the angel garments must ever come from these bloody hands!"

I listened as in a spell as Jacob Settle spoke. There was something so far away in the tone of his voice – something so dreamy and mystic in the eyes that looked as if through me at some spirit beyond – something so lofty in his very diction and in such marked contrast to his workworn clothes and his poor surroundings that I wondered if the whole thing were not a dream.

We were both silent for a long time. I kept looking at the man before me in growing wonderment. Now that his confession had been made, his soul, which had been crushed to the very earth, seemed to leap back again to uprightness with some resilient force. I suppose I ought to have been horrified with his story, but, strange to say, I was not. It certainly is not pleasant to be made the recipient of the confidence of a murderer, but this poor fellow seemed to have had, not only so much provocation, but so much self-denying purpose in his deed of blood that I did not feel called upon to pass judgment upon him. My purpose was to comfort, so I spoke out with what calmness I could, for my heart was beating fast and heavily:

"You need not despair, Jacob Settle. God is very good, and His mercy is great. Live on and work on in the hope that some day you may feel that you have atoned for the past." Here I paused, for I could see that deep, natural sleep this time, was creeping upon him. "Go to sleep," I said; "I shall watch with you here and we shall have no more evil dreams tonight."

He made an effort to pull himself together, and answered:

"I don't know how to thank you for your goodness to me this night, but I think you had best leave me now. I'll try and sleep this out; I feel a weight off my mind since I have told you all. If there's anything of the man left in me, I must try and fight out life alone."

"I'll go tonight, as you wish it," I said; "but take my advice, and do not live in such a solitary way. Go among men and women; live among them. Share their joys and sorrows, and it will help you to forget. This solitude will make you melancholy mad."

"I will!" he answered, half unconsciously, for sleep was overmastering him.

I turned to go, and he looked after me. When I had touched the latch I dropped it, and, coming back to the bed, held out my hand. He grasped it with both his as he rose to a sitting posture, and I said my goodnight, trying to cheer him:

"Heart, man, heart! There is work in the world for you to do, Jacob Settle. You can wear those white robes yet and pass through that gate of steel!"

Then I left him.

A week after I found his cottage deserted, and on asking at the works was told that he had 'gone north', no one exactly knew whither.

Two years afterwards, I was staying for a few days with my friend Dr. Munro in Glasgow. He was a busy man, and could not spare much time for going about with me, so I spent my days in excursions to the Trossachs and Loch Katrine and down the Clyde. On the second last evening of my stay I came back somewhat later than I had arranged, but found that my host was late too. The maid told me that he had been sent for to the hospital – a case of accident at the gas-works, and the dinner was postponed an hour; so telling her I would stroll down to find her master and walk back with him, I went out. At the hospital I found him washing his hands preparatory to starting for home. Casually, I asked him what his case was.

"Oh, the usual thing! A rotten rope and men's lives of no account. Two men were working in a gasometer, when the rope that held their scaffolding broke. It must have occurred just before the dinner hour, for no one noticed their absence till the men had returned. There was about seven feet of water in the gasometer, so they had a hard fight for it, poor fellows. However, one of them was alive, just alive, but we have had a hard job to pull him through. It seems that he owes his life to his mate, for I have never heard of greater heroism. They swam together while their strength lasted, but at the end they were so done up that even the lights above, and the men slung with ropes, coming down to help them, could not keep them up. But one of them stood on the bottom and held up his comrade over his head, and those few breaths made all the difference between life and death. They were a shocking sight when they were taken out, for that water is like a purple dye with the gas and the tar. The man upstairs looked as if he had been washed in blood. Ugh!"

"And the other?"

"Oh, he's worse still. But he must have been a very noble fellow. That struggle under the water must have been fearful; one can see that by the way the blood has been drawn from the extremities. It makes the idea of the *Stigmata* possible to look at him. Resolution like this could, you would think, do anything in the world. Ay! It might almost unbar the gates of Heaven. Look here, old man, it is not a very pleasant sight, especially just before dinner, but you are a writer, and this is an odd case. Here is something you would not like to miss, for in all human probability you will never see anything like it again." While he was speaking he had brought me into the mortuary of the hospital.

On the bier lay a body covered with a white sheet, which was wrapped close round it.

"Looks like a chrysalis, don't it? I say, Jack, if there be anything in the old myth that a soul is typified by a butterfly, well, then the one that this chrysalis sent forth was a very noble specimen and took all the sunlight on its wings. See here!" He uncovered the face. Horrible, indeed, it looked, as though stained with blood. But I knew him at once, Jacob Settle! My friend pulled the winding sheet further down.

The hands were crossed on the purple breast as they had been reverently placed by some tender-hearted person. As I saw them my heart throbbed with a great exultation, for the memory of his harrowing dream rushed across my mind. There was no stain now on those poor, brave hands, for they were blanched white as snow.

And somehow as I looked I felt that the evil dream was all over. That noble soul had won a way through the gate at last. The white robe had now no stain from the hands that had put it on.

If you enjoyed this, you might also like...
'Dracula's Guest,' see page 73
'A Star Trap,' see page 400

The Red Stockade

WE WAS ON THE southern part of the China station, when the *George Ranger* was ordered to the Straits of Malacca, to put down the pirates that had been showing themselves of late. It was in the forties, when ships was ships, not iron-kettles full of wheels, and other devilments, and there was a chance of hand-to-hand fighting – not being blown up in an iron cellar by you don't know who. Ships was ships in them days!

There had been a lot of throat-cutting and scuttling, for them devils stopped at nothing. Some of us had been through the straits before, when we was in the *Polly Phemus*, seventy-four, going to the China station, and although we had never come to quarters with the Malays, we had seen some of their work, and knew what kind they was. So, when we had left Singapore in the *George Ranger*, for that was our saucy, little thirty-eight-gun frigate – the place wasn't in them days what it is now – many and many 's the yarn was told in the fo'c'sle, and on the watches, of what the yellow devils could do, and had done. Some of us took it one way, and some another, but all, save a few, wanted to get into hand-grips with the pirates, for all their kreeses, and their stinkpots, and the devil's engines what they used. There was some that didn't mind cold steel of an ordinary kind, and would have faced cutlasses and boarding-pikes, any day, for a holiday, but that didn't like the idea of those knives like crooked flames, and that sliced a man in two, and hacked through the bowels of him. Naturally, we didn't take much stock of this kind; and many's the joke we had on them, and some of them cruel enough jokes, too.

You may be sure there was good stories, with plenty of cutting, and blood, and tortures in them, told in their watches, and nigh the whole ship's crew was busy, day and night, remembering and inventing things that'd make them gasp and grow white. I think that, somehow, the captain and the officers must have known what was goin' on, for there came tales from the ward-room that was worse nor any of ours. The midshipmen used to delight in them, like the ship's boys did, and one of them, that had a kreese, used to bring it out when he could, and show how the pirates used it when they cut the hearts out of men and women, and ripped them up to the chins. It was a bit cruel, at times, on them poor, white-livered chaps – a man can't help his liver, I suppose – but, anyhow, there's no place for them in a warship, for they're apt to do more harm by living where there's men of all sorts, than they can do by dying. So there wasn't any mercy for them, and the captain was worse on them than any.

Captain Wynyard was him that commanded the corvette *Sentinel* on the China station, and was promoted to the *George Ranger* for cutting up a fleet of junks that was hammering at the *Rajah*, from Canton, racing for Southampton with the first of the season's tea. He was a man, if you like, a bulldog full of hellfire, when he was on for fighting; he wouldn't have a white liver at any price. "God hates a coward," he aid once, "and under Her Britannic Majesty I'm here to carry out God's will. Trice im up, and give him a dozen!" At least, that's the story they tell of him when he was ound Shanghai, and one of his men had held back when the time came for boarding fire-junk that was coming down the tide. And with that he went in, and steered her ff with his own hands.

Well, the captain knew what work there was before us, and that it weren't no time or kid gloves and hair-oil, much less a bokey in your buttonhole and a top-hat, and e didn't mean that there should be any funk on his ship. So you take your davy that wasn't his fault if things was made too pleasant aboard for men what feared fallin' nto the clutches of the Malays.

Now and then he went out of his way to be nasty over such folk, and, boy or man, e never checked his tongue on a hard word when any one's face was pale before im. There was one old chap on board that we called 'Old Land's End,' for he came rom that part, and that had a boy of his on the *Billy Ruffian*, when he sailed on er, and after got lost, one night, in cutting out a Greek sloop at Navarino, in 1827. Ve used to chaff him when there was trouble with any of the boys, for he used to say hat his boy might have been in that trouble, too. And now, when the chaff was on bout bein' afeered of the Malay's, we used to rub it into the old man; but he would lame up, and answer us that his boy died in his duty, and that he couldn't be afeered f nought.

One night there was a row on among the midshipmen, for they said that one of hem, Tempest by name, owned up to being afraid of being kreesed. He was a rare right little chap of about thirteen, that was always in fun and trouble of some kind; ut he was soft-hearted, and sometimes the other lads would tease him. He would wn up truthfully to anything he thought, or felt, and now they had drawn him to wn something that none of them would – no matter how true it might be. Well, hey had a rare fight, for the boy was never backward with his fists, and by accident t came to the notice of the captain. He insisted on being told what it was all about, nd when young Tempest spoke out, and told him, he stamped on the deck, and alled out:

"I'll have no cowards in this ship," and was going on, when the boy cut in:

"I'm no coward, sir; I'm a gentleman!"

"Did you say you were afraid? Answer me – yes, or no?"

"Yes, sir, I did, and it was true! I said I feared the Malay kreeses; but I did not mean o shirk them, for all that. Henry of Navarre was afraid, but, all the same, he –"

"Henry of Navarre be damned," shouted the captain, "and you, too! You said you vere afraid, and that, let me tell you, is what we call a coward in the Queen's navy. And if you are one, you can, at least, have the grace to keep it to yourself! No answer o me! To the masthead for the remainder of the day! I want my crew to know what o avoid, and to know it when they see it!" and he walked away, while the lad, without word, ran up the maintop.

Some way, the men didn't say much about this. The only one that said anything to he point was Old Land's End, and says he:

"That may be a coward, but I'd chance it that he was a boy of mine."

As we went up the straits and got the sun on us, and the damp heat of that kettle f a place – Lor' bless ye! Ye steam there, all day and all night like a copper at the galley – we began to look around for the pirates, and there wasn't a man that got drowsy on the watch. We coasted along as we went up north, and took a look into the creeks and rivers as we went. It was up these that the Malays hid themselves; for the fevers and such that swept off their betters like flies, didn't seem to have any effect on them. There was pretty bad bits, I tell you, up some of them rivers through the mango groves, where the marshes spread away, mile after mile, as far as you could see, and where every thing that is noxious, both beast, and bird, and fish, and crawling thing, and insect, and tree, and bush, and flower, and creeper, is most at home.

But the pirate ships kept ahead of us; or, if they came south again, passed us by in the night, and so we ran up till about the middle of the peninsula, where the worst of the piracies had happened. There we got up as well as we could to look like a ship in distress; and, sure enough, we deceived the beggars, for two of them came out one early dawn and began to attack us. They was ugly looking craft, too – long, low hull and lateen – sails, and a double crew twice told in every one of them.

But if the crafts was ugly the men was worse, for uglier devils I never saw. Swarthy, yellow chaps, some of them, and some with shaven crowns and white eyeballs, and others as black as your shoe, with one or two white men, more shame, among them, but all carrying kreeses as long as your arm, and pistols in their belts.

They didn't get much change from us, I tell you. We let them get close, and then gave them a broadside that swept their decks like a hail-storm; but we was unlucky that we didn't grapple them, for they managed to shift off and ran for it. Our boats was out quick, but we daren't follow them where they ran into a wide creek, with mango swamps on each side as far as the eye could reach. The boat came back after a bit and reported that they had run up the river which was deep enough but with a winding channel between great mud-banks, where alligators lay in hundreds. There seemed some sort of fort where the river narrowed, and the pirates ran in behind it and disappeared up the bend of the river.

Then the preparations began. We knew that we had got two craft, at any rate, caged in the river, and there was every chance that we had found their lair. Our captain wasn't one that let things go asleep, and by daylight the next morning we was ready for an attack. The pinnace and four other boats started out under the first lieutenant to prospect, and the rest that was left on board waited, as well as they could, till we came back.

That was an awful day. I was in the second boat, and we all kept well together when we began to get into the narrows of the mouth of the river. When we started, we went in a couple of hours after the flood-tide, and so all we saw when the light came seemed fresh and watery. But as the tide ran out, and the big black mud-banks began to show their heads above everywhere, it wasn't nice, I can tell you. It was hardly possible for us to tell the channels, for everywhere the tide raced quick, and it was only when the boat began to touch the black slime that you knew that you was on a bank. Twice our boat was almost caught this way, but by good luck we pulled and pushed off in time into the ebbing tide; and hardly a boat but touched somewhere. One that was a bit out from the rest of us got stuck at last in a nasty cut between two mud-banks, and as the water ran away the boat turned over on the slope, despite all her crew could do, and we saw the poor fellows thrown out into the slime. More than one of them began to swim toward us, but behind each came a rush of something dark, and though we shouted and made what noise we could, and fired many shots, the alligators was too close, and with shriek after shriek they went down to the bottom of the filth and slime.

Oh, man! it was a dreadful sight, and none the better that it was new to nigh all of us. How it would have taken us if we had time to think about it, I hardly know, but I doubt that more than a few would have grown cold over it; but just then there flew amongst us a hail of small shot from a fleet of boats that had stolen down on us. They drove out from behind a big mud-bank that rose steeper than the others and that seemed solider, too, for the gravel of it showed, as the scour of the tide washed the mud away. We was not sorry, I tell you, to have men to fight with, instead of alligators and mud-banks, in an ebbing tide, in a strange tropical river.

We gave chase at once, and the pinnace fired the twelve-pounder which she carried in the bows, in among the huddle of the boats, and the yells arose as the rush of the alligators turned to where the Malay heads bobbed up and down in the drift of the tide. Then the pirates turned and ran, and we after them as hard as we could pull, till round a sharp bend of the river we came to a narrow place, where one side was steep for a bit and then tailed away to a wilderness of marsh, worse than we had seen. The other side was crowned by a sort of fort, built on the top of a high bank, but guarded by a stockade and a mud-bank which lay at its base. From this there came a rain of bullets, and we saw some guns turned toward us. We was hardly strong enough to attack such a position without reconnoitring, and so we drew away; but not quite quick enough, for before we could get out of range of their guns a round shot carried away the whole of the starboard oars of one of our boats.

It was a dreary pull to the ship, and the tide was agin us, for we all got thinking of what we had to tell – one boat and crew lost entirely, and a set of oars shot away – and no work done.

The captain was furious; and, in the ward-room, and in the fo'c'sle that night, there was nothing that wasn't flavored with anger and curses. Even the boys, of all sorts, from the cabin-boys to the midshipmen, was wanting to get at the Malays. However, sharp was the order; and by daylight three boats was up at the stockaded fort, making an accurate survey. I was again in one of the boats; and, in spite of what the captain had said to make us all so angry – and he had a tongue like vitriol, I tell you – we all felt pretty down and cold when we got again amongst those terrible mud-banks and saw the slime that shone on them bubble up, when the gray of the morning let us see anything

We found that the fort was one that we would have to take if we wanted to follow the pirates up the river, for it barred the way without a chance. There was a gut of the river between the two great ridges of gravel, and this was the only channel where there was a chance of passing. But it had been staked on both sides, so that only the center was left free. Why, from the fort they could have stoned any one in the boats passing there, only that there wasn't any stone, that we could see, in their whole blasted country!

When we got back, with two cases of sunstroke among us, and reported, the captain ordered preparations for an attack on the fort, and the next morning the ball began. It was ugly work. We got close up to the fort, but, as the tide ran out, we had to sheer away somewhat so as not to get stranded. The whole place swarmed with those grinning devils. They evidently had some way of getting to and from their boats behind the stockade. They did not fire a shot at us – not at first – and that was the most aggravating thing that you can imagine. They seemed to know something that we did not, and they only just waited. As the tide sank lower and lower, and the mud-banks grew steeper, and the sun on them began to fizzle, a steam arose that nigh turned our stomachs. Why, the sight of them alone would make your heart sink

The slime shimmered in all kinds of colors, like the water when there's tarring work on hand, and the whole place seemed alive with all that was horrible. The alligators kept off the boats and the banks close to us, but the thick water was full of eels and water-snakes, and the mud was alive with water-worms and leeches, and horrible, gaudy-colored crabs. The very air was filled with pests – flies of all kinds and a sort of big-striped insect that they call the 'tiger mosquito,' which comes out in the daytime and bites you like red-hot pincers. It was bad enough, I tell you, for us men with hair on our faces, but some of the boys got very white and pale, and they was all pretty silent for a while. All at once the crowd of Malays behind the stockade began to roll their eyes and wave their kreeses and to shout. We knew that there was some cause for it, but couldn't make it out, and this exasperated us more than ever. Then the captain sings out to us to attack the stockade; so out we all jumped into the mud. We knew it couldn't be very deep just there, on account of the gravel beneath. We was knee-deep in a moment, but we struggled, and slipped, and fell over each other; and, when we got to the top of that bank, we was the queerest, filthiest-looking crowd you ever see. But the mud hadn't took the heart out of us, and the Malays, with their necks craned over the stockade, and with the nearest thing to a laugh or a smile that the devil lets them have, drew back and fell, one on another, when they heard our cheer.

Between them and us there was a bit of a dip where the water had been running in the ebb-tide, but which seemed now as dry as the rest, and the foremost of our men charged down the slope, and then we knew why they had kept silent and waited! We was in a regular trap. The first ranks disappeared at once in the mud and ooze in the hollow, and those next were up to their armpits before they could stop. Then those Malay devils opened on us, and while we tried to pull our chaps out, they mowed us down with every kind of small arm they had – and they had a queer assortment, I tell you.

It was all we could do to get back over the slope and to the boats again – what was left of us – and, as we hadn't hands enough left even to row with full strength, we had to make for the ship as fast as we could, for their boats began to pass out in a cloud through the narrow by the stockade. But before we went we saw them dragging the live and dead out of the mud with hooks on the end of long bamboos; and there was terrible shrieks from some poor fellows when the kreeses gashed through them. We daren't wait; but we saw enough to make us swear revenge. When we saw them devils stick the bleeding heads of our comrades on the spikes of the stockade, there was nigh a mutiny because the captain wouldn't let us go back and have another try for it. He was cool enough now; and those of us that knew him and understood what was in his mind, when the smile on him showed the white teeth in the corners of his mouth, felt that it was no good day's work that the pirates had done for themselves.

When we got back to the ship and told our tale, it wasn't long till the men was all on fire; and nigh every man took a turn with the grindstone at his cutlass, till they was all like razors. The captain mustered every one on board, and detailed very man to his work in the boats, ready for the next time; and we knew that, by daylight, we were to have another slap at the pirates. We got six-pounders and twelve-pounders in most of the boats, for we was to give them a dose of big shot before we came to close quarters.

When we got up near the stockade, the tide had turned, and we thought it better to wait till dawn, for it was bad work among the mud-banks at the ebb in the dark. So we hung on a while, and then when the sky began to lighten, we made for the fort. When we got nigh enough to see it, there wasn't a man of us who didn't want to have some bloody revenge, for there, on the spikes of the stockade, were the heads of all the poor fellows that we had lost the day before, with a cloud of mosquitoes and flies already beginning to buzz around them in the dawn. But beyond that again, they had painted the outside of the stockade with blood, so that the whole place was a crimson mass. You could smell it as the sun came up!

Well, that day was a hard one. We opened fire with our guns, and the Malays returned it, with all they had got. A fleet of boats came out from beyond the fort, and for a while we had to turn our attention to these. The small guns served us well, and we made a rare havoc among the boats, for our shot went crashing through them, and quite a half of them were sunk. The water was full of bobbing heads; but the tide carried them away from us, and their cries and shrieks came from beyond the fort and then died away. The other boats recognized their danger, and turned and ran in through the narrow, and let us alone for hours after.

Then we went at the fort again. We turned our guns at the piles of the stockade, and, of course, every shot told – but their fire was at too close quarters, and with their rifles and matchlocks, and the rest, they picked us off too fast, and we had to sheer off where our heavy metal could tell without our being within their range. Before we sheered off, we could see that the hole we had knocked in the stockade was only in the outer work, and that the real fort was within. We had to go down the river, as we couldn't go far enough across without danger from the banks, and this only gave us a side view, and, do what we would, we couldn't make an impression – at least any that we could see.

That was a long and awful day! The sun was blazing on us like a furnace, and we was nigh mad with heat, and flies, and drouth, and anger. It was that hot that if you touched metal it fairly burned you. When the tide was near the flood, the captain ordered up the boats in the wide water now opposite the fort; and there, for a while, we got a fair chance, till, when the ebb began, we should have to sheer off again. By this time our shot was nearly run out, and we thought that we should have to give over; but all at once came order to prepare for attack, and in a few minutes we was working for dear life across the river, straight for the stockade. The men set up a cheer, and the pirates showed over the top of the stockade and waved their kreeses, and more than one of them sliced off pieces of the heads on the spikes, and jeered at us, as much as to say that they would do the same for us in our turn!

When we got close up, every one of them had disappeared, and there was a silence of the grave. We knew that there was something up, but what the move was we could not tell, till from behind the fort came rushing again a fleet of boats. We turned on them, and, like we did before, we made mincemeat of them. This time the tide made for us, and the bobbing heads went by us in dozens. Now and then there was a wild yell, as an alligator pulled some one down into the mud. This went on for a little,

and we had beaten them off enough to be able to get our grappling – irons read
for climbing the stockade, when the second lieutenant, who was in the outer boa
called out:

"Back with the boats! Back, quick, the tide is falling!" and with one impulse w
began to shove off. Then, in an instant, the place became alive again with the Malay
and they began firing on us so quickly that before we could get out into the whirl o
tide there was many a dead man in our boats.

There was no use trying to do any more that day, and after we had done wha
could be done for the wounded, and patched up our boats, for there was plenty o
shot-holes to plug, we pulled back to the ship. The alligators had had a good da
and as we went along, and the mud-banks grew higher and higher with the falling o
the tide, we could see them lie out lazily, as if they had been gorged. Aye! And ther
was enough left for the ground-sharks out in the offing; for the men on board tol
us that every while on the ebb something would go along, bobbing up and down i
the swell, till presently there would be a swift ripple of a fin, and then there was n
more pirate.

Well! When we got aboard, the rest was mighty anxious to know what had bee
done; and when we began, with the heads on spikes of the red stockade, the me
ground their teeth, and Old Land's End up, and says he:

"The Red Stockade! We'll not forget the name! It'll be our turn next, and then we'
paint it inside this time." And so it was that we came to know the place by that name
That night the captain was like a man that would do murder. His face was like stee
and his eyes was as red as flames. He didn't seem to have a thought for any one; an
everything he did was as hard as though his heart were brass. He ordered all tha
was needful to be done for the wounded, but he added to the doctor: "And, min
you, get them well as soon as you can. We're too shorthanded already!"

Up to now, we all had known him treat men as men, but now he only thought o
us as machines for fighting! True enough, he thought the same of himself. Twic
that very night he cut up rough in a new way. Of course, the men was talking of th
attack, and there was lots of brag and chaff, for all they was so grim earnest, an
some of the old fooling went on about blood and tortures. The captain came o
deck, and as he walked along, he saw one of the men that didn't like the kreeses, an
he didn't evidently like the looks of him, for he turned on his heel and said savagely

"Send the doctor here!" So the doctor came, and the captain he says to him, col
as ice, and as polite as you please:

"Dr. Fairbrother, there is a sick man here! look at his pale face. Something wron
with his liver, I suppose. It's the only thing that makes a seaman's face white whe
there's fighting ahead. Take him down to sick bay, and do something for him. I'd lik
to cut the accursed white liver out of him altogether!" and with that he went dow
to his cabin.

Well if we was hot for fighting before, we was boiling after that, and we all cam
to know that the next attack on the Red Stockade would be the last, one way o
the other! We had to wait two more days before that could come off, for the boat
and tackle had to be made ready, and there wasn't going to be any mistakes mad
this time.

It was just after midnight when we began to get ready. Every man was to his post
The moon was up, and it was lighter nor a London day, and the captain stood by an

aw every man to his place, and nothing escaped him. By and by, as No. 6 boat was
lling, and before the officer in charge of it got in, came the midshipman, young
empest, and when the captain saw him he called him up and hissed out before all
ie crew:

"Why are you so white? What's wrong with you, anyway? Is your liver out of
rder, too?"

True enough, the boy was white, but at the flaming insult the blood rushed to
is face and we could see it red in the starlight. Then in another moment it passed
way and left him paler than ever, and he said with a gentle voice, though standing
s straight as a ramrod:

"I can't help the blood in my face, sir. If I'm a coward because I'm pale, perhaps
ou are right. But I shall do my duty all the same!" and with that he pulled himself
p, touched his cap, and went down into the boat.

Old Land's End was behind me in the boat with him, number five to my six, and
e whispered to me through his shut teeth:

"Too rough that! He might have thought a bit that he's only a child. And he came
ll the same, even if he was afeer'd!"

We stole away with muffled oars, and dropped silently into the river on the
loodtide. If any man had had any doubts as to whether we was in earnest at other
imes, he had none then, anyhow. It was a pretty grim time, I tell you, for the most of
s felt that whether we won or not this time, there would be many empty hammocks
hat night in the *George Ranger*; but we meant to win even if we went into the maws
f the sharks and crocodiles for it. When we came up close on the flood we lost no
ime but went slap at the fort.

At first, of course, we had crawled up the river in silence, and I think that we
ook the beggars by surprise, for we was there before the time they expected us.
Iowsomever, they turned out quick enough and there was soon music on both sides
f the stockade. We didn't want to take any chance on the mud-banks this time, so
ve ran in close under the stockade at once and hooked on. We found that they had
epaired the breach we had made the last time. They fought like devils, for they
new that we could beat them hand to hand, if we could once get in, and they sent
ound the boats to take us on the flank, as they had done each time before. But this
ime we wasn't to be drawn away from our attack, and we let our boats outside tackle
hem, while we minded our own business closer home.

It was a long fight and a bloody one. They was sheltered inside, and they knew
hat time was with them, for when the tide should have fallen, if we hadn't got in
ve should have our old trouble with the mud-banks all over again. But we knew it,
oo, and we didn't lose no time. Still, men is only men, after all, and we couldn't fly
p over a stockade out of a boat, and them as did get up was sliced about dreadful –
hey are handy workmen with their kreeses, and no doubt! We was so hot on the job
ve had on hand that we never took no note of time at all, and all at once we found
he boat fixed tight under us.

The tide had fallen and left us on the bank under the Red Stockade, and the best
alf of the boats was cut off from us. We had some thirty men left, and we knew we
ad to fight whether we liked it or not. It didn't much matter, anyhow, for we was
ame to go through with it. The captain, when he seen the state of things, gave his
rders to take the boats out into mid-stream, and shell and shot the fort, whilst we

was to do what we could to get in. It was no use trying to bridge over the slobs, for the masts of an old seventy-four wouldn't have done it.

We was in a tight place, then, I can tell you, between two fires, for the guns in the boats couldn't fire high enough to clear us every time, without going over the for altogether, and more than one of our own shots did some of us a harm. The cutter came into the game, and began sending the war-rockets from the tubes. The pirates didn't like that, I tell you, and more betoken, no more did we, for we got as much of them as they did, till the captain saw the harm to us, and bade them cease. But he knew his business, and he kept all the fire of the guns on the one side of the stockade till he knocked a hole that we could get in by. When this was done, the Malays left the outer wall and went within the fort proper. This gave us some protection, since they couldn't fire right down on us, and our guns kept the boats away that would have taken us from the riverside. But it was hot work, and we began dropping away with stray shots, and with the stinkpots and hand-grenades that they kept hurling over the stockade on to us.

So the time came when we found that we must make a dash for the fort, or get picked out, one by one, where we stood. By this time some of our boats was making for the opening, and there seemed less life behind the stockade; some of them was up to some move, and was sheering off to make up some other devilment. Still, they had their guns in the fort, and there was danger to our boats if they tried to cross the opening between the piles. One did, and went down with a hole in her within a minute. So we made a burst inside the stockade, and found ourselves in a narrow place between the two walls of piles. Anyhow, the place was drier, and we felt a relief in getting out of up to our knees in steaming mud. There was no time to lose and the second lieutenant, Webster by name, told us to try to scale the stockade in front.

It wasn't high, but it was slimy below and greasy above, and do what we would we couldn't get no nigher. A shot from a pistol wiped out the lieutenant, and for a moment we thought we was without a leader. Young Tempest was with us, silent all the time, with his face as white as a ghost, though he done his best, like the rest of us. Suddenly he called out:

"Here, lads! Take and throw me in. I'm light enough to do it, and I know that when I'm in you'll all follow."

Ne'er a man stirred. Then the lad stamped his foot and called again, and remember his young, high voice now:

"Seamen to your duty! I command here!"

At the word we all stood at attention, just as if we was at quarters. Then Jack Pring, that we called the Giant, for he was six feet four and as strong as a bullock spoke out:

"It's no duty, sir, to fling an officer into hell!" The lad looked at him and nodded

"Volunteers for dangerous duty!" he called, and every man of the crowd stepped out.

"All right, boys!" says he. "Now take me up and throw me in. We'll get down that flag, anyhow," and he pointed to the black flag that the pirates flew on the flagstaff in the fort. Then he took the small flag of the float and put it on his breast, and says he: "This'll suit better."

"Won't I do, sir?" said Jack, and the lad laughed a laugh that rang again.

"Oh, my eye!" says he, has any one got a crane to hoist in the Giant?" The lad told s to catch hold of him, and when Jack hesitated, says he:

"We've always been friends, Jack, and I want you to be one of the last to touch 1e!" So Jack laid hold of him by one side, and Old Land's End stepped out and took im by the other. The rest of us was, by this time, kicking off our shoes and pulling ff our shirts, and getting our knives open in our teeth. The two men gave a great eave together and they sent the boy clean over the top of the stockade. We heard cross the river a cheer from our boats, as we began to scramble. There was a pause ithin the fort for a few seconds, and then we saw the lad swarm up the bamboo agstaff that swayed under him, and tear down the black flag. He pulled our own ag from his breast and hung it over the top of the post. And he waved his hand nd cheered, and the cheer was echoed in thunder across the river. And then a shot ²tched him down, and with a wild yell they all went for him, while the cheering from 1e boats came like a storm.

We never knew quite how we got over that stockade. To this day I can't even nagine how we done it! But when we leaped down, we saw something lying at the oot of the flagstaff all red – and the kreeses was red, too! The devils had done their ork! But it was their last, for we came at them with our cutlasses – there was never sound from the lips of any of us – and we drove them like a hail-storm beats down tanding corn! We didn't leave a living thing within the Red Stockade that day, and e wouldn't if there had been a million there!

It was a while before we heard the shouting again, for the boats was coming up 1e river, now that the fort was ours, and the men had other work for their breath 1an cheering.

Between us, we made a rare clearance of the pirates' nest that day. We destroyed very boat on the river, and the two ships that we was looking for, and one other 1at was careened. We tore down and burned every house, and jetty, and stockade in 1e place, and there was no quarter for them we caught. Some of them got away by path they knew through the swamp where we couldn't follow them. The sun was etting low when we pulled back to the ship. It would have been a merry enough ome-coming, despite our losses – all but for one thing, and that was covered up rith a Union Jack in the captain's own boat. Poor lad! when they lifted him on deck, nd the men came round to look at him, his face was pale enough now, and, one and ll, we felt that it was to make amends, as the captain stooped over and kissed him n the forehead.

"We'll bury him tomorrow," he said, "but in blue water, as becomes a gallant seaman."

At the dawn, next day, he lay on a grating, sewn in his hammock, with the shot t his feet, and the whole crew was mustered, and the chaplain read the service for 1e dead. Then he spoke a bit about him – how he had done his duty, and was an xample to all – and he said how all loved and honored him. Then the men told off or the duty stood ready to slip the grating and let the gallant boy go plunging down ɔ join the other heroes under the sea; but Old Land's End stepped out and touched is cap to the captain, and asked if he might say a word.

"Say on, my man!" said the captain, and he stood, with his cocked hat in his hand, rhilst Old Land's End spoke:

"Mates! Ye've heerd what the chaplain said. The boy done his duty, and died like 1e brave gentleman he was! And we wish he was here now. But, for all that, we can't be sorry for him, or for what he done, though it cost him his life. I had a lad once of my own, and I hoped for him what I never wanted for myself – that he would win fame and honor, and become an admiral of the fleet, as others have done before. But, so help me God! I'd rather see him lying under the flag as we see that brave boy lie now, and know why he was there, than I'd see him in his epaulettes on the quarter-deck of the flagship! He died for his Queen and country, and for the honor of the flag! And what more would you have him do!"

If you enjoyed this, you might also like...
The Lair of the White Worm (chapter V; chapters XIX–XXVIII), see page 255
'The Burial of the Rats,' see page 347

The Burial of the Rats

LEAVING PARIS by the Orleans road, cross the Enceinte, and, turning to the right, you find yourself in a somewhat wild and not at all savoury district. Right and left, before and behind, on every side rise great heaps of dust and waste accumulated by the process of time.

Paris has its night as well as its day life, and the sojourner who enters his hotel in the Rue de Rivoli or the Rue St. Honore late at night or leaves it early in the morning, can guess, in coming near Montrouge – if he has not done so already – the purpose of those great waggons that look like boilers on wheels which he finds halting everywhere as he passes.

Every city has its peculiar institutions created out of its own needs; and one of the most notable institutions of Paris is its rag-picking population. In the early morning – and Parisian life commences at an early hour – may be seen in most streets standing on the pathway opposite every court and alley and between every few houses, as still in some American cities, even in parts of New York, large wooden boxes into which the domestics or tenement-holders empty the accumulated dust of the past day. Round these boxes gather and pass on, when the work is done, to fresh fields of labour and pastures new, squalid, hungry-looking men and women, the implements of whose craft consist of a coarse bag or basket slung over the shoulder and a little rake with which they turn over and probe and examine in the minutest manner the dustbins. They pick up and deposit in their baskets, by aid of their rakes, whatever they may find, with the same facility as a Chinaman uses his chopsticks.

Paris is a city of centralisation – and centralisation and classification are closely allied. In the early times, when centralisation is becoming a fact, its forerunner is classification. All things which are similar or analogous become grouped together, and from the grouping of groups rises one whole or central point. We see radiating many long arms with innumerable tentaculae, and in the centre rises a gigantic head with a comprehensive brain and keen eyes to look on every side and ears sensitive to hear – and a voracious mouth to swallow.

Other cities resemble all the birds and beasts and fishes whose appetites and digestions are normal. Paris alone is the analogical apotheosis of the octopus. Product of centralisation carried to an ad absurdum, it fairly represents the devil fish; and in no respects is the resemblance more curious than in the similarity of the digestive apparatus.

Those intelligent tourists who, having surrendered their individuality into the hands of Messrs. Cook or Gaze, 'do' Paris in three days, are often puzzled to know how it is that the dinner which in London would cost about six shillings, can be had for three francs in a cafe in the Palais Royal. They need have no more wonder if they will but consider the classification which is a theoretic speciality of Parisian life, and adopt all round the fact from which the chiffonier has his genesis.

The Paris of 1850 was not like the Paris of today, and those who see the Paris of Napoleon and Baron Haussmann can hardly realise the existence of the state of things forty-five years ago.

Amongst other things, however, which have not changed are those districts where the waste is gathered. Dust is dust all the world over, in every age, and the family likeness of dust-heaps is perfect. The traveller, therefore, who visits the environs of Montrouge can go back in fancy without difficulty to the year 1850.

In this year I was making a prolonged stay in Paris. I was very much in love with a young lady who, though she returned my passion, so far yielded to the wishes of her parents that she had promised not to see me or to correspond with me for a year. I, too, had been compelled to accede to these conditions under a vague hope of parental approval. During the term of probation I had promised to remain out of the country and not to write to my dear one until the expiration of the year.

Naturally the time went heavily with me. There was no one of my own family or circle who could tell me of Alice, and none of her own folk had, I am sorry to say, sufficient generosity to send me even an occasional word of comfort regarding her health and well-being. I spent six months wandering about Europe, but as I could find no satisfactory distraction in travel, I determined to come to Paris, where, at least, I would be within easy hail of London in case any good fortune should call me thither before the appointed time. That 'hope deferred maketh the heart sick' was never better exemplified than in my case, for in addition to the perpetual longing to see the face I loved there was always with me a harrowing anxiety lest some accident should prevent me showing Alice in due time that I had, throughout the long period of probation, been faithful to her trust and my own love. Thus, every adventure which I undertook had a fierce pleasure of its own, for it was fraught with possible consequences greater than it would have ordinarily borne.

Like all travellers I exhausted the places of most interest in the first month of my stay, and was driven in the second month to look for amusement whithersoever I might. Having made sundry journeys to the better-known suburbs, I began to see that there was a terra incognita, in so far as the guide book was concerned, in the social wilderness lying between these attractive points. Accordingly I began to systematise my researches, and each day took up the thread of my exploration at the place where I had on the previous day dropped it.

In process of time my wanderings led me near Montrouge, and I saw that hereabouts lay the Ultima Thule of social exploration – a country as little known as that round the source of the White Nile. And so I determined to investigate philosophically the chiffonier-his habitat, his life, and his means of life.

The job was an unsavoury one, difficult of accomplishment, and with little hope of adequate reward. However, despite reason, obstinacy prevailed, and I entered into my new investigation with a keener energy than I could have summoned to aid me in any investigation leading to any end, valuable or worthy.

One day, late in a fine afternoon, toward the end of September, I entered the holy of holies of the city of dust. The place was evidently the recognised abode of a number of chiffoniers, for some sort of arrangement was manifested in the formation of the dust heaps near the road. I passed amongst these heaps, which stood like orderly sentries, determined to penetrate further and trace dust to its ultimate location.

As I passed along I saw behind the dust heaps a few forms that flitted to and fro, evidently watching with interest the advent of any stranger to such a place. The district

as like a small Switzerland, and as I went forward my tortuous course shut out the
ath behind me.

Presently I got into what seemed a small city or community of chiffoniers. There
ere a number of shanties or huts, such as may be met with in the remote parts of
ne Bog of Allan – rude places with wattled walls, plastered with mud and roofs of
ude thatch made from stable refuse – such places as one would not like to enter for
ny consideration, and which even in water-colour could only look picturesque if
idiciously treated. In the midst of these huts was one of the strangest adaptations
I cannot say habitations – I had ever seen. An immense old wardrobe, the colossal
emnant of some boudoir of Charles VII or Henry II, had been converted into a
welling-house. The double doors lay open, so that the entire menage was open
o public view. In the open half of the wardrobe was a common sitting-room of
ome four feet by six, in which sat, smoking their pipes round a charcoal brazier, no
ewer than six old soldiers of the First Republic, with their uniforms torn and worn
areadbare. Evidently they were of the mauvais sujet class; their blear eyes and limp
aws told plainly of a common love of absinthe; and their eyes had that haggard, worn
ook which stamps the drunkard at his worst, and that look of slumbering ferocity
which follows hard in the wake of drink. The other side stood as of old, with its
helves intact, save that they were cut to half their depth, and in each shelf of which
here were six, was a bed made with rags and straw. The half-dozen of worthies who
nhabited this structure looked at me curiously as I passed; and when I looked back
fter going a little way I saw their heads together in a whispered conference. I did not
ke the look of this at all, for the place was very lonely, and the men looked very, very
illainous. However, I did not see any cause for fear, and went on my way, penetrating
urther and further into the Sahara. The way was tortuous to a degree, and from
oing round in a series of semi-circles, as one goes in skating with the Dutch roll, I
ot rather confused with regard to the points of the compass.

When I had penetrated a little way I saw, as I turned the corner of a half-made
eap, sitting on a heap of straw an old soldier with threadbare coat.

"Hallo!" said I to myself; "The First Republic is well represented here in its soldiery."

As I passed him the old man never even looked up at me, but gazed on the ground
vith stolid persistency. Again I remarked to myself: "See what a life of rude warfare
an do! This old man's curiosity is a thing of the past."

When I had gone a few steps, however, I looked back suddenly, and saw that
uriosity was not dead, for the veteran had raised his head and was regarding me with
very queer expression. He seemed to me to look very like one of the six worthies
n the press. When he saw me looking he dropped his head; and without thinking
urther of him I went on my way, satisfied that there was a strange likeness between
hese old warriors.

Presently I met another old soldier in a similar manner. He, too, did not notice me
vhilst I was passing.

By this time it was getting late in the afternoon, and I began to think of retracing
ny steps. Accordingly I turned to go back, but could see a number of tracks leading
etween different mounds and could not ascertain which of them I should take.
n my perplexity I wanted to see someone of whom to ask the way, but could see no
ne. I determined to go on a few mounds further and so try to see someone – not
veteran.

I gained my object, for after going a couple of hundred yards I saw before m a single shanty such as I had seen before – with, however, the difference that th was not one for living in, but merely a roof with three walls open in front. From th evidences which the neighbourhood exhibited I took it to be a place for sortin, Within it was an old woman wrinkled and bent with age; I approached her to as the way.

She rose as I came close and I asked her my way. She immediately commenced conversation; and it occurred to me that here in the very centre of the Kingdom (Dust was the place to gather details of the history of Parisian rag-picking – particular as I could do so from the lips of one who looked like the oldest inhabitant.

I began my inquiries, and the old woman gave me most interesting answers – sh had been one of the ceteuces who sat daily before the guillotine and had taken a active part among the women who signalised themselves by their violence in th revolution. While we were talking she said suddenly: "But m'sieur must be tire standing," and dusted a rickety old stool for me to sit down. I hardly liked to do so fc many reasons; but the poor old woman was so civil that I did not like to run the ris of hurting her by refusing, and moreover the conversation of one who had been a the taking of the Bastille was so interesting that I sat down and so our conversatio went on.

While we were talking an old man – older and more bent and wrinkled even tha the woman – appeared from behind the shanty. "Here is Pierre," said she. "M'sieu can hear stories now if he wishes, for Pierre was in everything, from the Bastille t Waterloo." The old man took another stool at my request and we plunged into a se of revolutionary reminiscences. This old man, albeit clothed like a scare-crow, wa like any one of the six veterans.

I was now sitting in the centre of the low hut with the woman on my left hand an the man on my right, each of them being somewhat in front of me. The place was fu of all sorts of curious objects of lumber, and of many things that I wished far awa In one corner was a heap of rags which seemed to move from the number of vermin contained, and in the other a heap of bones whose odour was something shockin; Every now and then, glancing at the heaps, I could see the gleaming eyes of some c the rats which infested the place. These loathsome objects were bad enough, but wha looked even more dreadful was an old butcher's axe with an iron handle stained wit clots of blood leaning up against the wall on the right hand side. Still these things di not give me much concern. The talk of the two old people was so fascinating that stayed on and on, till the evening came and the dust heaps threw dark shadows ove the vales between them.

After a time I began to grow uneasy, I could not tell how or why, but somehow I di not feel satisfied. Uneasiness is an instinct and means warning. The psychic facultie are often the sentries of the intellect; and when they sound alarm the reason begin to act, although perhaps not consciously.

This was so with me. I began to bethink me where I was and by what surrounded and to wonder how I should fare in case I should be attacked; and then the though suddenly burst upon me, although without any overt cause, that I was in dange Prudence whispered: "Be still and make no sign," and so I was still and made no sign for I knew that four cunning eyes were on me. "Four eyes – if not more." My God, wha a horrible thought! The whole shanty might be surrounded on three sides with villains might be in the midst of a band of such desperadoes as only half a century of periodic revolution can produce.

With a sense of danger my intellect and observation quickened, and I grew more watchful than was my wont. I noticed that the old woman's eyes were constantly wandering toward my hands. I looked at them too, and saw the cause – my rings. On my left little finger I had a large signet and on the right a good diamond.

I thought that if there was any danger my first care was to avert suspicion. Accordingly I began to work the conversation round to rag-picking – to the drains – of the things found there; and so by easy stages to jewels. Then, seizing a favourable opportunity, I asked the old woman if she knew anything of such things. She answered that she did, a little. I held out my right hand, and, showing her the diamond, asked her what she thought of that. She answered that her eyes were bad, and stooped over my hand. I said as nonchalantly as I could: "Pardon me! You will see better thus!" and taking it off handed it to her. An unholy light came into her withered old face, as she touched it. She stole one glance at me swift and keen as a flash of lightning.

She bent over the ring for a moment, her face quite concealed as though examining it. The old man looked straight out of the front of the shanty before him, at the same time fumbling in his pockets and producing a screw of tobacco in a paper and a pipe, which he proceeded to fill. I took advantage of the pause and the momentary rest from the searching eyes on my face to look carefully round the place, now dim and shadowy in the gloaming. There still lay all the heaps of varied reeking foulness; there the terrible blood-stained axe leaning against the wall in the right hand corner, and everywhere, despite the gloom, the baleful glitter of the eyes of the rats. I could see them even through some of the chinks of the boards at the back low down close to the ground. But stay! These latter eyes seemed more than usually large and bright and baleful!

For an instant my heart stood still, and I felt in that whirling condition of mind in which one feels a sort of spiritual drunkenness, and as though the body is only maintained erect in that there is no time for it to fall before recovery. Then, in another second, I was calm – coldly calm, with all my energies in full vigour, with a self-control which I felt to be perfect and with all my feeling and instincts alert.

Now I knew the full extent of my danger: I was watched and surrounded by desperate people! I could not even guess at how many of them were lying there on the ground behind the shanty, waiting for the moment to strike. I knew that I was big and strong, and they knew it, too. They knew also, as I did, that I was an Englishman and would make a fight for it; and so we waited. I had, I felt, gained an advantage in the last few seconds, for I knew my danger and understood the situation. Now, I thought, is the test of my courage-the enduring test: the fighting test may come later!

The old woman raised her head and said to me in a satisfied kind of way:

"A very fine ring, indeed – a beautiful ring! Oh, me! I once had such rings, plenty of them, and bracelets and earrings! Oh! For in those fine days I led the town a dance! But they've forgotten me now! They've forgotten me! They? Why they never heard me! Perhaps their grandfathers remember me, some of them!" and she laughed a harsh, croaking laugh. And then I am bound to say that she astonished me, for she handed me back the ring with a certain suggestion of old-fashioned grace which was not without its pathos.

The old man eyed her with a sort of sudden ferocity, half rising from his stool, and said to me suddenly and hoarsely:

"Let me see!"

I was about to hand the ring when the old woman said:

"No! No, do not give it to Pierre! Pierre is eccentric. He loses things; and such a pretty ring!"

"Cat!" said the old man, savagely. Suddenly the old woman said, rather more loudly than was necessary:

"Wait! I shall tell you something about a ring." There was something in the sound of her voice that jarred upon me. Perhaps it was my hyper-sensitiveness, wrought up as I was to such a pitch of nervous excitement, but I seemed to think that she was not addressing me. As I stole a glance round the place I saw the eyes of the rats in the bone heaps, but missed the eyes along the back. But even as I looked I saw them again appear. The old woman's "Wait!" had given me a respite from attack, and the men had sunk back to their reclining posture.

"I once lost a ring – a beautiful diamond hoop that had belonged to a queen, and which was given to me by a farmer of the taxes, who afterwards cut his throat because I sent him away. I thought it must have been stolen, and taxed my people; but I could get no trace. The police came and suggested that it had found its way to the drain. We descended – in my fine clothes, for I would not trust them with my beautiful ring! I know more of the drains since then, and of rats, too! But I shall never forget the horror of that place – alive with blazing eyes, a wall of them just outside the light of our torches. Well, we got beneath my house. We searched the outlet of the drain, and there in the filth found my ring, and we came out.

"But we found something else also before we came! As we were coming toward the opening a lot of sewer rats – human ones this time – came toward us. They told the police that one of their number had gone into the drain, but had not returned. He had gone in only shortly before we had, and, if lost, could hardly be far off. They asked help to seek him, so we turned back. They tried to prevent me going, but I insisted. It was a new excitement, and had I not recovered my ring? Not far did we go till we came on something. There was but little water, and the bottom of the drain was raised with brick, rubbish, and much matter of the kind. He had made a fight for it, even when his torch had gone out. But they were too many for him! They had not been long about it. The bones were still warm; but they were picked clean. They had even eaten their own dead ones and there were bones of rats as well as of the man. They took it cool enough those other – the human ones – and joked of their comrade when they found him dead, though they would have helped him living. Bah! What matters it – life or death?"

"And had you no fear?" I asked her.

"Fear!" she said with a laugh. "Me have fear? Ask Pierre! But I was younger then, and as I came through that horrible drain with its wall of greedy eyes, always moving with the circle of the light from the torches, I did not feel easy. I kept on before the men though! It is a way I have! I never let the men get it before me. All I want is a chance and a means! And they ate him up – took every trace away except the bones; and no one knew it, nor no sound of him was ever heard!" Here she broke into a chuckling of the ghastliest merriment which it was ever my lot to hear and see. A great poetess describes her heroine singing: "Oh! To see or hear her singing! Scarce I know which were the divinest."

And I can apply the same idea to the old crone – in all save the divinity, for I scarce could tell which was the most hellish – the harsh, malicious, satisfied, cruel laugh r the leering grin, and the horrible square opening of the mouth like a tragic mask, nd the yellow gleam of the few discoloured teeth in the shapeless gums. In that ugh and with that grin and the chuckling satisfaction I knew as well as if it had been poken to me in words of thunder that my murder was settled, and the murderers nly bided the proper time for its accomplishment. I could read between the lines f her gruesome story the commands to her accomplices. "Wait," she seemed to say, bide your time. I shall strike the first blow. Find the weapon for me, and I shall make he opportunity! He shall not escape! Keep him quiet, and then no one will be wiser. here will be no outcry, and the rats will do their work!"

It was growing darker and darker; the night was coming. I stole a glance round the hanty, still all the same! The bloody axe in the corner, the heaps of filth, and the eyes n the bone heaps and in the crannies of the floor.

Pierre had been still ostensibly filling his pipe; he now struck a light and began to uff away at it. The old woman said:

"Dear heart, how dark it is! Pierre, like a good lad, light the lamp!"

Pierre got up and with the lighted match in his hand touched the wick of a lamp hich hung at one side of the entrance to the shanty, and which had a reflector hat threw the light all over the place. It was evidently that which was used for their orting at night.

"Not that, stupid! Not that! The lantern!" she called out to him.

He immediately blew it out, saying: "All right, mother, I'll find it," and he hustled bout the left corner of the room – the old woman saying through the darkness:

"The lantern! The lantern! Oh! That is the light that is most useful to us poor folks. he lantern was the friend of the revolution! It is the friend of the chiffonier! It helps s when all else fails."

Hardly had she said the word when there was a kind of creaking of the whole lace, and something was steadily dragged over the roof.

Again I seemed to read between the lines of her words. I knew the lesson of he lantern.

"One of you get on the roof with a noose and strangle him as he passes out if we il within."

As I looked out of the opening I saw the loop of a rope outlined black against the rid sky. I was now, indeed, beset!

Pierre was not long in finding the lantern. I kept my eyes fixed through the darkness n the old woman. Pierre struck his light, and by its flash I saw the old woman raise om the ground beside her where it had mysteriously appeared, and then hide in he folds of her gown, a long sharp knife or dagger. It seemed to be like a butcher's harpening iron fined to a keen point.

The lantern was lit.

"Bring it here, Pierre," she said. "Place it in the doorway where we can see it. See ow nice it is! It shuts out the darkness from us; it is just right!"

Just right for her and her purposes! It threw all its light on my face, leaving in loom the faces of both Pierre and the woman, who sat outside of me on each side.

I felt that the time of action was approaching; but I knew now that the first signal nd movement would come from the woman, and so watched her.

I was all unarmed, but I had made up my mind what to do. At the first movement I ould seize the butcher's axe in the right-hand corner and fight my way out. At least,

I would die hard. I stole a glance round to fix its exact locality so that I could not fail to seize it at the first effort, for then, if ever, time and accuracy would be precious.

Good God! It was gone! All the horror of the situation burst upon me; but the bitterest thought of all was that if the issue of the terrible position should be against me Alice would infallibly suffer. Either she would believe me false – and any lover, or any one who has ever been one, can imagine the bitterness of the thought – or else she would go on loving long after I had been lost to her and to the world, so that her life would be broken and embittered, shattered with disappointment and despair. The very magnitude of the pain braced me up and nerved me to bear the dread scrutiny of the plotters.

I think I did not betray myself. The old woman was watching me as a cat does a mouse; she had her right hand hidden in the folds of her gown, clutching, I knew, that long, cruel-looking dagger. Had she seen any disappointment in my face she would, I felt, have known that the moment had come, and would have sprung on me like a tigress, certain of taking me unprepared.

I looked out into the night, and there I saw new cause for danger. Before and around the hut were at a little distance some shadowy forms; they were quite still, but I knew that they were all alert and on guard. Small chance for me now in that direction.

Again I stole a glance round the place. In moments of great excitement and of great danger, which is excitement, the mind works very quickly, and the keenness of the faculties which depend on the mind grows in proportion. I now felt this. In an instant I took in the whole situation. I saw that the axe had been taken through a small hole made in one of the rotten boards. How rotten they must be to allow of such a thing being done without a particle of noise.

The hut was a regular murder-trap, and was guarded all around. A garroter lay on the roof ready to entangle me with his noose if I should escape the dagger of the old hag. In front the way was guarded by I know not how many watchers. And at the back was a row of desperate men – I had seen their eyes still through the crack in the boards of the floor, when last I looked – as they lay prone waiting for the signal to start erect. If it was to be ever, now for it!

As nonchalantly as I could I turned slightly on my stool so as to get my right leg well under me. Then with a sudden jump, turning my head, and guarding it with my hands, and with the fighting instinct of the knights of old, I breathed my lady's name and hurled myself against the back wall of the hut.

Watchful as they were, the suddenness of my movement surprised both Pierre and the old woman. As I crashed through the rotten timbers I saw the old woman rise with a leap like a tiger and heard her low gasp of baffled rage. My feet lit on something that moved, and as I jumped away I knew that I had stepped on the back of one of the row of men lying on their faces outside the hut. I was torn with nails and splinters, but otherwise unhurt. Breathless I rushed up the mound in front of me hearing as I went the dull crash of the shanty as it collapsed into a mass.

It was a nightmare climb. The mound, though but low, was awfully steep, and with each step I took the mass of dust and cinders tore down with me and gave way under my feet. The dust rose and choked me; it was sickening, foetid, awful; but my climb was, I felt, for life or death, and I struggled on. The seconds seemed hours; but the few moments I had in starting, combined with my youth and strength, gave me a great advantage, and, though several forms struggled after me in deadly silence which was more dreadful than any sound, I easily reached the top. Since then I have climbed the cone of Vesuvius, and as I struggled up that dreary steep amid the sulphurous fumes the memory of that awful night at Montrouge came back to me so vividly that I almost grew faint.

The mound was one of the tallest in the region of dust, and as I struggled to the top, panting for breath and with my heart beating like a sledge-hammer, I saw away to my left the dull red gleam of the sky, and nearer still the flashing of lights. Thank God! I knew where I was now and where lay the road to Paris!

For two or three seconds I paused and looked back. My pursuers were still well behind me, but struggling up resolutely, and in deadly silence. Beyond, the shanty was a wreck – a mass of timber and moving forms. I could see it well, for flames were already bursting out; the rags and straw had evidently caught fire from the lantern. Still silence there! Not a sound! These old wretches could die game, anyhow.

I had no time for more than a passing glance, for as I cast an eye round the mound preparatory to making my descent I saw several dark forms rushing round on either side to cut me off on my way. It was now a race for life. They were trying to head me on my way to Paris, and with the instinct of the moment I dashed down to the right-hand side. I was just in time, for, though I came as it seemed to me down the steep in a few steps, the wary old men who were watching me turned back, and one, as I rushed by into the opening between the two mounds in front, almost struck me a blow with that terrible butcher's axe. There could surely not be two such weapons about!

Then began a really horrible chase. I easily ran ahead of the old men, and even when some younger ones and a few women joined in the hunt I easily distanced them. But I did not know the way, and I could not even guide myself by the light in the sky, for I was running away from it. I had heard that, unless of conscious purpose, hunted men turn always to the left, and so I found it now; and so, I suppose, knew also my pursuers, who were more animals than men, and with cunning or instinct had found out such secrets for themselves: for on finishing a quick spurt, after which I intended to take a moment's breathing space, I suddenly saw ahead of me two or three forms swiftly passing behind a mound to the right.

I was in the spider's web now indeed! But with the thought of this new danger came the resource of the hunted, and so I darted down the next turning to the right. I continued in this direction for some hundred yards, and then, making a turn to the left again, felt certain that I had, at any rate, avoided the danger of being surrounded.

But not of pursuit, for on came the rabble after me, steady, dogged, relentless, and still in grim silence.

In the greater darkness the mounds seemed now to be somewhat smaller than before, although – for the night was closing – they looked bigger in proportion. I was now well ahead of my pursuers, so I made a dart up the mound in front.

Oh joy of joys! I was close to the edge of this inferno of dustheaps. Away behind me the red light of Paris in the sky, and towering up behind rose the heights of Montmartre – a dim light, with here and there brilliant points like stars.

Restored to vigour in a moment, I ran over the few remaining mounds of decreasing size, and found myself on the level land beyond. Even then, however, the prospect was not inviting. All before me was dark and dismal, and I had evidently come on one of those dank, low-lying waste places which are found here and there in the neighbourhood of great cities. Places of waste and desolation, where the space is required for the ultimate agglomeration of all that is noxious, and the ground is so poor as to create no desire of occupancy even in the lowest squatter. With eyes accustomed to the gloom of the evening, and away now from the shadows of those dreadful dust heaps, I could see much more easily than I could a little while ago. It might have been of course, that the glare in the sky of the lights of Paris, though the city was some miles away, was reflected here. Howsoever it was, I saw well enough to take bearings for certainly some little distance around me.

In front was a bleak, flat waste that seemed almost dead level, with here and there the dark shimmering of stagnant pools. Seemingly far off on the right, amid a small cluster of scattered lights, rose a dark mass of Fort Montrouge, and away to the left in the dim distance, pointed with stray gleams from cottage windows, the lights in the sky showed the locality of Bicetre. A moment's thought decided me to take to the right and try to reach Montrouge. There at least would be some sort of safety, and I might possibly long before come on some of the cross roads which I knew. Somewhere, not far off, must lie the strategic road made to connect the outlying chain of forts circling the city.

Then I looked back. Coming over the mounds, and outlined black against the glare of the Parisian horizon, I saw several moving figures, and still a way to the right several more deploying out between me and my destination. They evidently meant to cut me off in this direction, and so my choice became constricted; it lay now between going straight ahead or turning to the left. Stooping to the ground, so as to get the advantage of the horizon as a line of sight, I looked carefully in this direction, but could detect no sign of my enemies. I argued that as they had not guarded or were not trying to guard that point, there was evidently danger to me there already. So made up my mind to go straight on before me.

It was not an inviting prospect, and as I went on the reality grew worse. The ground became soft and oozy, and now and again gave way beneath me in a sickening kind of way. I seemed somehow to be going down, for I saw round me places seemingly more elevated than where I was, and this in a place which from a little way back seemed dead level. I looked around, but could see none of my pursuers. This was strange, for all along these birds of the night had followed me through the darkness as well as though it was broad daylight. How I blamed myself for coming out in my light-coloured tourist suit of tweed. The silence, and my not being able to see my enemies, whilst I felt that they were watching me, grew appalling, and in the hope of some one not of this ghastly crew hearing me I raised my voice and shouted several times. There was not the slightest response; not even an echo rewarded my efforts. For a while I stood stock still and kept my eyes in one direction. On one of the rising places around me I saw something dark move along, then another, and another. This was to my left, and seemingly moving to head me off.

I thought that again I might with my skill as a runner elude my enemies at this game, and so with all my speed darted forward.

Splash!

My feet had given way in a mass of slimy rubbish, and I had fallen headlong into a reeking, stagnant pool. The water and the mud in which my arms sank up to the elbows was filthy and nauseous beyond description, and in the suddenness of my fall I had actually swallowed some of the filthy stuff, which nearly choked me, and made me gasp for breath. Never shall I forget the moments during which I stood trying to recover myself almost fainting from the foetid odour of the filthy pool, whose white mist rose ghostlike around. Worst of all, with the acute despair of the hunted animal when he sees the pursuing pack closing on him, I saw before my eyes whilst I stood helpless the dark forms of my pursuers moving swiftly to surround me.

It is curious how our minds work on odd matters even when the energies of thought are seemingly concentrated on some terrible and pressing need. I was in momentary peril of my life: my safety depended on my action, and my choice of alternatives coming now with almost every step I took, and yet I could not but think of the strange dogged persistency of these old men. Their silent resolution, their steadfast, grim, persistency even in such a cause commanded, as well as fear, even a measure of respect. What must they have been in the vigour of their youth. I could understand now that whirlwind rush on the bridge of Arcola, that scornful exclamation of the Old Guard at Waterloo! Unconscious cerebration has its own pleasures, even at such moments; but fortunately it does not in any way clash with the thought from which action springs.

I realised at a glance that so far I was defeated in my object, my enemies as yet had won. They had succeeded in surrounding me on three sides, and were bent on driving me off to the left-hand, where there was already some danger for me, for they had left no guard. I accepted the alternative-it was a case of Hobson's choice and run. I had to keep the lower ground, for my pursuers were on the higher places. However, though the ooze and broken ground impeded me my youth and training made me able to hold my ground, and by keeping a diagonal line I not only kept them from gaining on me but even began to distance them. This gave me new heart and strength, and by this time habitual training was beginning to tell and my second wind had come. Before me the ground rose slightly. I rushed up the slope and found before me a waste of watery slime, with a low dyke or bank looking black and grim beyond. I felt that if I could but reach that dyke in safety I could there, with solid ground under my feet and some kind of path to guide me, find with comparative ease a way out of my troubles. After a glance right and left and seeing no one near, I kept my eyes for a few minutes to their rightful work of aiding my feet whilst I crossed the swamp. It was rough, hard work, but there was little danger, merely toil; and a short time took me to the dyke. I rushed up the slope exulting; but here again I met a new shock. On either side of me rose a number of crouching figures. From right and left they rushed at me. Each body held a rope.

The cordon was nearly complete. I could pass on neither side, and the end was near.

There was only one chance, and I took it. I hurled myself across the dyke, and escaping out of the very clutches of my foes threw myself into the stream.

At any other time I should have thought that water foul and filthy, but now it was as welcome as the most crystal stream to the parched traveller. It was a highway of safety!

My pursuers rushed after me. Had only one of them held the rope it would have been all up with me, for he could have entangled me before I had time to swim a stroke; but the many hands holding it embarrassed and delayed them, and when the rope struck the water I heard the splash well behind me. A few minutes' hard swimming took me across the stream. Refreshed with the immersion and encouraged by the escape, I climbed the dyke in comparative gaiety of spirits.

From the top I looked back. Through the darkness I saw my assailants scattering up and down along the dyke. The pursuit was evidently not ended, and again I had to choose my course. Beyond the dyke where I stood was a wild, swampy space very similar to that which I had crossed. I determined to shun such a place, and thought for a moment whether I would take up or down the dyke. I thought I heard a sound – the muffled sound of oars, so I listened, and then shouted.

No response; but the sound ceased. My enemies had evidently got a boat of some kind. As they were on the up side of me I took the down path and began to run. As I passed to the left of where I had entered the water I heard several splashes, soft and stealthy, like the sound a rat makes as he plunges into the stream, but vastly greater and as I looked I saw the dark sheen of the water broken by the ripples of several advancing heads. Some of my enemies were swimming the stream also.

And now behind me, up the stream, the silence was broken by the quick rattle and creak of oars; my enemies were in hot pursuit. I put my best leg foremost and ran on. After a break of a couple of minutes I looked back, and by a gleam of light through the ragged clouds I saw several dark forms climbing the bank behind me. The wind had now begun to rise, and the water beside me was ruffled and beginning to break in tiny waves on the bank. I had to keep my eyes pretty well on the ground before me, lest I should stumble, for I knew that to stumble was death. After a few minutes I looked back behind me. On the dyke were only a few dark figures, but crossing the waste, swampy ground were many more. What new danger this portended I did not know – could only guess. Then as I ran it seemed to me that my track kept ever sloping away to the right. I looked up ahead and saw that the river was much wider than before, and that the dyke on which I stood fell quite away, and beyond it was another stream on whose near bank I saw some of the dark forms now across the marsh. I was on an island of some kind.

My situation was now indeed terrible, for my enemies had hemmed me in on every side. Behind came the quickening roll of the oars, as though my pursuers knew that the end was close. Around me on every side was desolation; there was not a roof or light, as far as I could see. Far off to the right rose some dark mass, but what it was I knew not. For a moment I paused to think what I should do, not for more, for my pursuers were drawing closer. Then my mind was made up. I slipped down the bank and took to the water. I struck out straight ahead, so as to gain the current by clearing the backwater of the island for such I presume it was, when I had passed into the stream. I waited till a cloud came driving across the moon and leaving all in darkness. Then I took off my hat and laid it softly on the water floating with the stream, and a second after dived to the right and struck out under water with all my might. I was I suppose, half a minute under water, and when I rose came up as softly as I could and turning, looked back. There went my light brown hat floating merrily away. Close behind it came a rickety old boat, driven furiously by a pair of oars. The moon was still partly obscured by the drifting clouds, but in the partial light I could see a man in the bows holding aloft ready to strike what appeared to me to be that same dreadful pole-axe which I had before escaped. As I looked the boat drew closer, closer, and the man struck savagely. The hat disappeared. The man fell forward, almost out of the boat. His comrades dragged him in but without the axe, and then as I turned with all my energies bent on reaching the further bank, I heard the fierce whirr of the muttered "Sacre!" which marked the anger of my baffled pursuers.

That was the first sound I had heard from human lips during all this dreadful chase, and full as it was of menace and danger to me it was a welcome sound for t broke that awful silence which shrouded and appalled me. It was as though an overt sign that my opponents were men and not ghosts, and that with them I had, at least, the chance of a man, though but one against many.

But now that the spell of silence was broken the sounds came thick and fast. From boat to shore and back from shore to boat came quick question and answer, all in the fiercest whispers. I looked back – a fatal thing to do – for in the instant someone caught sight of my face, which showed white on the dark water, and shouted. Hands pointed to me, and in a moment or two the boat was under weigh, and following hard after me. I had but a little way to go, but quicker and quicker came the boat after me. A few more strokes and I would be on the shore, but I felt the oncoming of the boat, and expected each second to feel the crash of an oar or other weapon on my head. Had I not seen that dreadful axe disappear in the water I do not think that I could have won the shore. I heard the muttered curses of those not rowing and the laboured breath of the rowers. With one supreme effort for life or liberty I touched the bank and sprang up it. There was not a single second to spare, for hard behind me the boat grounded and several dark forms sprang after me. I gained the top of the dyke, and keeping to the left ran on again. The boat put off and followed down the stream. Seeing this I feared danger in this direction, and quickly turning, ran down the dyke on the other side, and after passing a short stretch of marshy ground gained a wild, open flat country and sped on.

Still behind me came on my relentless pursuers. Far away, below me, I saw the same dark mass as before, but now grown closer and greater. My heart gave a great thrill of delight, for I knew that it must be the fortress of Bicetre, and with new courage I ran on. I had heard that between each and all of the protecting forts of Paris there are strategic ways, deep sunk roads, where soldiers marching should be sheltered from an enemy. I knew that if I could gain this road I would be safe, but in the darkness I could not see any sign of it, so, in blind hope of striking it, I ran on.

Presently I came to the edge of a deep cut, and found that down below me ran a road guarded on each side by a ditch of water fenced on either side by a straight, high wall.

Getting fainter and dizzier, I ran on; the ground got more broken – more and more still, till I staggered and fell, and rose again, and ran on in the blind anguish of the hunted. Again the thought of Alice nerved me. I would not be lost and wreck her life: I would fight and struggle for life to the bitter end. With a great effort I caught the top of the wall. As, scrambling like a catamount, I drew myself up, I actually felt a hand touch the sole of my foot. I was now on a sort of causeway, and before me I saw a dim light. Blind and dizzy, I ran on, staggered, and fell, rising, covered with dust and blood.

"Halt la!"

The words sounded like a voice from heaven. A blaze of light seemed to enwrap me, and I shouted with joy.

"Qui va la?" The rattle of musketry, the flash of steel before my eyes. Instinctively I stopped, though close behind me came a rush of my pursuers.

Another word or two, and out from a gateway poured, as it seemed to me, a tide of red and blue, as the guard turned out. All around seemed blazing with light, and the flash of steel, the clink and rattle of arms, and the loud, harsh voices of command. As I fell forward, utterly exhausted, a soldier caught me. I looked back in dreadful expectation, and saw the mass of dark forms disappearing into the night. Then I must have fainted. When I recovered my senses I was in the guard room. They gave me brandy, and after awhile I was able to tell them something of what had passed. Then a commissary of police appeared, apparently out of the empty air, as is the way of the Parisian police officer. He listened attentively, and then had a moment's consultation with the officer in command. Apparently they were agreed, for they asked me if I were ready now to come with them.

"Where to?" I asked, rising to go.

"Back to the dust heaps. We shall, perhaps, catch them yet!"

"I shall try!" said I.

He eyed me for a moment keenly, and said suddenly:

"Would you like to wait awhile or till tomorrow, young Englishman?" This touched me to the quick, as, perhaps, he intended, and I jumped to my feet.

"Come now!" I said; "now! Now! An Englishman is always ready for his duty!"

The commissary was a good fellow, as well as a shrewd one; he slapped my shoulder kindly. "Brave garcon!" he said. "Forgive me, but I knew what would do you most good. The guard is ready. Come!"

And so, passing right through the guard room, and through a long vaulted passage, we were out into the night. A few of the men in front had powerful lanterns. Through courtyards and down a sloping way we passed out through a low archway to a sunken road, the same that I had seen in my flight. The order was given to get at the double, and with a quick, springing stride, half run, half walk, the soldiers went swiftly along. I felt my strength renewed again – such is the difference between hunter and hunted. A very short distance took us to a low-lying pontoon bridge across the stream, and evidently very little higher up than I had struck it. Some effort had evidently been made to damage it, for the ropes had all been cut, and one of the chains had been broken. I heard the officer say to the commissary:

"We are just in time! A few more minutes, and they would have destroyed the bridge. Forward, quicker still!" And on we went. Again we reached a pontoon on the winding stream; as we came up we heard the hollow boom of the metal drums as the efforts to destroy the bridge was again renewed. A word of command was given, and several men raised their rifles.

"Fire!" A volley rang out. There was a muffled cry, and the dark forms dispersed. But the evil was done, and we saw the far end of the pontoon swing into the stream. This was a serious delay, and it was nearly an hour before we had renewed ropes and restored the bridge sufficiently to allow us to cross.

We renewed the chase. Quicker, quicker we went towards the dust heaps.

After a time we came to a place that I knew. There were the remains of a fire – a few smouldering wood ashes still cast a red glow, but the bulk of the ashes were cold. I knew the site of the hut and the hill behind it up which I had rushed, and in the flickering glow the eyes of the rats still shone with a sort of phosphorescence. The commissary spoke a word to the officer, and he cried:

"Halt!"

The soldiers were ordered to spread around and watch, and then we commenced to examine the ruins. The commissary himself began to lift away the charred boards and rubbish. These the soldiers took and piled together. Presently he started back, then bent down and rising beckoned me.

"See!" he said.

It was a gruesome sight. There lay a skeleton face downwards, a woman by the lines – an old woman by the coarse fibre of the bone. Between the ribs rose a long spike-like dagger made from a butcher's sharpening knife, its keen point buried in the spine.

"You will observe," said the commissary to the officer and to me as he took out his note book, "that the woman must have fallen on her dagger. The rats are many here – see their eyes glistening among that heap of bones – and you will also notice" – I shuddered as he placed his hand on the skeleton – "that but little time was lost by them, for the bones are scarcely cold!"

There was no other sign of any one near, living or dead; and so deploying again into line the soldiers passed on. Presently we came to the hut made of the old wardrobe. We approached. In five of the six compartments was an old man sleeping – sleeping so soundly that even the glare of the lanterns did not wake them. Old and grim and grizzled they looked, with their gaunt, wrinkled, bronzed faces and their white moustaches.

The officer called out harshly and loudly a word of command, and in an instant each one of them was on his feet before us and standing at "attention!"

"What do you here?"

"We sleep," was the answer.

"Where are the other chiffoniers?" asked the commissary.

"Gone to work."

"And you?"

"We are on guard!"

"Peste!" laughed the officer grimly, as he looked at the old men one after the other in the face and added with cool deliberate cruelty, "Asleep on duty! Is this the manner of the Old Guard? No wonder, then, a Waterloo!"

By the gleam of the lantern I saw the grim old faces grow deadly pale, and almost shuddered at the look in the eyes of the old men as the laugh of the soldiers echoed the grim pleasantry of the officer.

I felt in that moment that I was in some measure avenged.

For a moment they looked as if they would throw themselves on the taunter, but years of their life had schooled them and they remained still.

"You are but five," said the commissary; "where is the sixth?" The answer came with a grim chuckle.

"He is there!" and the speaker pointed to the bottom of the wardrobe. "He died last night. You won't find much of him. The burial of the rats is quick!"

The commissary stooped and looked in. Then he turned to the officer and said calmly:

"We may as well go back. No trace here now; nothing to prove that man was the one wounded by your soldiers' bullets! Probably they murdered him to cover up the trace. See!" Again he stooped and placed his hands on the skeleton. "The rats work quickly and they are many. These bones are warm!"

I shuddered, and so did many more of those around me.

"Form!" said the officer, and so in marching order, with the lanterns swinging in front and the manacled veterans in the midst, with steady tramp we took ourselves out of the dust-heaps and turned backward to the fortress of Bicetre.

* * *

My year of probation has long since ended, and Alice is my wife. But when I look back upon that trying twelvemonth one of the most vivid incidents that memory recalls is that associated with my visit to the City of Dust.

If you enjoyed this, you might also like...
'The Judge's House,' see page 47
'The Red Stockade,' see page 336

The Dualitists

Chapter I
Bis Dat Qui Non Cito Dat

HERE WAS JOY in the house of Bubb.

For ten long years had Ephraim and Sophonisba Bubb mourned in vain the loneliness of their life. Unavailingly had they gazed into the emporia of baby-linen, and fixed their searching glances on the basket-makers' warehouses where the cradles hung in tempting rows. In vain had they prayed, and sighed, and groaned, and wished, and waited, and wept, but never had even a ray of hope been held out by the family physician.

* * *

But now at last the wished-for moment had arrived. Month after month had flown by on leaden wings, and the destined days had slowly measured their course. The months had become weeks; the weeks had dwindled down to days; the days had been attenuated to hours; the hours had lapsed into minutes, the minutes had slowly died away, and but seconds remained.

Ephraim Bubb sat cowering on the stairs, and tried with high-strung ears to catch the strain of blissful music from the lips of his first-born. There was silence in the house – silence as of the deadly calm before the cyclone. Ah! Ephra Bubb, little thinkest thou that another moment may for ever destroy the peaceful, happy course of thy life, and open to thy too craving eyes the portals of that wondrous land where Childhood reigns supreme, and where the tyrant infant with the wave of his tiny hand and the imperious treble of his tiny voice sentences his parent to the deadly vault beneath the castle moat. As the thought strikes thee thou becomest pale. How thou tremblest as thou findest thyself upon the brink of the abyss! Wouldst that thou could recall the past!

But hark! The die is cast for good or ill. The long years of praying and hoping have found an end at last. From the chamber within comes a sharp cry, which shortly after is repeated. Ah! Ephraim, that cry is the feeble effort of childish lips as yet unused to the rough, worldly form of speech to frame the word Father. In the glow of thy transport all doubts are forgotten; and when the doctor cometh forth as the harbinger of joy he findeth thee radiant with new found delight.

"My dear sir, allow me to congratulate you – to offer two fold felicitations. Mr. Bubb, sir, you are the father of Twins!"

Chapter II
Halcyon Days

THE TWINS were the finest children that ever were seen – so at least said the cognoscenti, and the parents were not slow to believe. The nurse's opinion was in itself a proof.

It was not, ma'am, that they was fine for twins, but they was fine for singles, and she had ought to know, for she had nussed a many in her time, both twins and singles. All they wanted was to have their dear little legs cut off and little wings on their dear little shoulders, for to be put one on each side of a white marble tombstone cut beautiful, sacred to the relic of Ephraim Bubb, that they might, sir, if so be that missus was to survive the father of two such lovely twins – although she would make bold to say, and no offence intended, that a handsome gentleman, though a trifle of two older than his good lady, though for the matter of that she heerd that gentlemen was never too old at all, and for her own part she liked them the better for it: not like bits of boys that didn't know their own minds – that a gentleman what was the father of two such 'eavenly twins (God bless them!) couldn't be called anything but a boy; though for the matter of that she never knowed in her experience – which it was much – of a boy as had such twins, or any twins at all so much for the matter of that.

The twins were the idols of their parents, and at the same time their pleasure and their pain. Did Zerubbabel cough, Ephraim would start from his balmy slumbers with an agonised cry of consternation, for visions of innumerable twins black in the face from croup haunted his nightly pillow. Did Zacariah rail at aetherea expansion, Sophonisba with pallid hue and dishevelled locks would fly to the cradle of her offspring. Did pins torture or strings afflict, or flannel or flies tickle, or light dazzle, or darkness affright, or hunger or thirst assail the synchronous productions, the household of Bubb would be roused from quiet slumbers or the current of its manifold workings changed.

The twins grew apace; were weaned; teethed; and at length arrived at the stage of three years!

"They grew in beauty side by side. They filled one home," etc.

Chapter III
Rumours of Wars

HARRY MERFORD and Tommy Santon lived in the same range of villas as Ephraim Bubb. Harry's parents had taken up their abode in No. 25, No. 27 was happy in the perpetual sunshine of Tommy's smiles, and between these two residences Ephraim Bubb reared his blossoms, the number of his mansion being 26. Harry and Tommy had been accustomed from the earliest times to meet each other daily. Their prima method of communication had been by the housetops, till their respective sires had been obliged to pay compensation to Bubb for damages to his roof and dormer windows; and from that time they had been forbidden by the home authorities to meet, whilst their mutual neighbour had taken the precaution of having his garden walls pebble-dashed and topped with broken glass to prevent their incursions. Harry and Tommy, however, being gifted with daring souls, lofty ambitions, impetuous natures, and strong seats to their trousers, defied the rugged walls of Bubb and continued to meet in secret.

Compared with these two youths, Castor and Pollux, Damon and Pythias, Eloisa and Abelard are but tame examples of duality or constancy and friendship. All the poets from Hyginus to Schiller might sing of noble deeds done and desperate dangers held as naught for friendship's sake, but they would have been mute had they but known of the mutual affection of Harry and Tommy. Day by day, and often night by ight, would these two brave the perils of nurse, and father, and mother, of whip and mprisonment, and hunger and thirst, and solitude and darkness to meet together. What they discussed in secret none other knew. What deeds of darkness were perpetrated in their symposia none could tell. Alone they met, alone they remained, nd alone they departed to their several abodes. There was in the garden of Bubb . summer house overgrown with trailing plants, and surrounded by young poplars which the fond father had planted on his children's natal day, and whose rapid growth he had proudly watched. These trees quite obscured the summerhouse, and ere Harry and Tommy, knowing after a careful observation that none ever entered he place, held their conclaves. Time after time they met in full security and followed heir customary pursuit of pleasure. Let us raise the mysterious veil and see what was he great Unknown at whose shrine they bent the knee.

Harry and Tommy had each been given as a Christmas box a new knife; and for a ong time – nearly a year – these knives, similar in size and pattern, were their chief delights. With them they cut and hacked in their respective homes all things which vould not be likely to be noticed; for the young gentlemen were wary and had no wish hat their moments of pleasure should be atoned for by moments of pain. The insides of drawers, and desks, and boxes, and underparts of tables and chairs, the backs of picture frames, even the floors, where corners of the carpets could surreptitiously be turned up, all bore marks of their craftsmanship; and to compare notes on these artistic triumphs was a source of joy. At length, however, a critical time came, some new field of action should be opened up, for the old appetites were sated, and the old joys had begun to pall. It was absolutely necessary that the existing schemes of destruction should be enlarged; and yet this could hardly be done without a terrible risk of discovery, for the limits of safety had long since been reached and passed. But, be the risk great or small, some new ground should be broken – some new joy found, or the old earth was barren, and the craving for pleasure was growing fiercer with each successive day.

The crisis had come: who could tell the issue?

Chapter IV
The Tucket Sounds

THEY MET IN THE ARBOUR, determined to discuss this grave question. The heart of each was big with revolution, the head of each was full of scheme and strategy, and the pocket of each was full of sweet-stuff, the sweeter for being stolen. After having despatched the sweets, the conspirators proceeded to explain their respective views with regard to the enlargement of their artistic operations. Tommy unfolded with much pride a scheme which he had in contemplation of cutting a series of holes in the sounding board of the piano, so as to destroy its musical properties. Harry was in no wise behindhand in his ideas of reform. He had conceived the project of cutting the canvas at the back of his great grandfather's portrait, which his father held in high regard among his lares and penates, so that in time when the picture should be moved the skin of paint would be broken, the head fall bodily out from the frame.

At this point of the council a brilliant thought occurred to Tommy. "Why should not the enjoyment be doubled, and the musical instruments and family pictures of both establishments be sacrificed on the altar of pleasure?" This was agreed to *nem. con.*;

and then the meeting adjourned for dinner. When they next met it was evident that there was a screw loose somewhere – that there was 'something rotten in the state of Denmark.' After a little fencing on both sides, it came out that all the schemes of domestic reform had been foiled by maternal vigilance, and that so sharp had been the reprimand consequent on a partial discovery of the schemes that they would have to be abandoned – till such time, at least, as increased physical strength would allow the reformers to laugh to scorn parental threats and injunctions.

Sadly the two forlorn youths took out their knives and regarded them; sadly, sadly they thought, as erst did Othello, of all the fair chances of honour and triumph and glory gone for ever. They compared knives with almost the fondness of doting parents. There they were – so equal in size and strength and beauty – dimmed by no corrosive rust, tarnished by no stain, and with unbroken edges of the keenness of Saladin's sword.

So like were the knives that but for the initials scratched in the handles neither boy could have been sure which was his own. After a little while they began mutually to brag of the superior excellence of their respective weapons. Tommy insisted that his was the sharper, Harry asserted that his was the stronger of the two. Hotter and hotter grew the war of words. The tempers of Harry and Tommy got inflamed, and their boyish bosoms glowed with manly thoughts of daring and of hate. But there was abroad in that hour a spirit of a bygone age – one that penetrated even to that dim arbour in the grove of Bubb. The world-old scheme of ordeal was whispered by the spirit in the ear of each, and suddenly the tumult was allayed. With one impulse the boys suggested that they should test the quality of their knives by the ordeal of the Hack.

No sooner said than done. Harry held out his knife edge uppermost; and Tommy, grasping his firmly by the handle, brought down the edge of the blade crosswise on Harry's. The process was then reversed, and Harry became in turn the aggressor. Then they paused and eagerly looked for the result. It was not hard to see; in each knife were two great dents of equal depth; and so it was necessary to renew the contest, and seek a further proof.

What needs it to relate seriatim the details of that direful strife? The sun had long since gone down, and the moon with fair, smiling face had long risen over the roof of Bubb, when, wearied and jaded, Harry and Tommy sought their respective homes. Alas! The splendour of the knives was gone for ever. Ichabod! – Ichabod! The glory had departed and naught remained but two useless wrecks, with keen edges destroyed, and now like unto nothing save the serried hills of Spain.

But though they mourned for their fondly cherished weapons, the hearts of the boys were glad; for the bygone day had opened to their gaze a prospect of pleasure as boundless as the limits of the world.

Chapter V
The First Crusade

FROM THAT DAY a new era dawned in the lives of Harry and Tommy. So long as the resources of the parental establishments could hold out so long would their new amusement continue. Subtly they obtained surreptitious possession of articles of family cutlery not in general use, and brought them one by one to their rendezvous.

These came fair and spotless from the sanctity of the butlers' pantry. Alas! They returned not as they came.

But in course of time the stock of available cutlery became exhausted, and again the inventive faculties of the youths were called into requisition. They reasoned thus: "The knife game, it is true, is played out, but the excitement of the Hack is not to be dispensed with. Let us carry, then, this Great Idea into new worlds; let us still live in the sunshine of pleasure; let us continue to hack, but with objects other than knives."

It was done. Not knives now engaged the attention of the ambitious youths. Spoons and forks were daily flattened and beaten out of shape; pepper castor met pepper castor in combat, and both were borne dying from the field; candlesticks met in fray to part no more on this side of the grave; even epergnes were used as weapons in the crusade of Hack.

At last all the resources of the butler's pantry became exhausted, and then began a system of miscellaneous destruction that proved in a little time ruinous to the furniture of the respective homes of Harry and Tommy. Mrs. Santon and Mrs. Merford began to notice that the wear and tear in their households became excessive. Day after day some new domestic calamity seemed to have occurred. Today a valuable edition of some book whose luxurious binding made it an object for public display would appear to have suffered some dire misfortune, for the edges were frayed and broken and the back loose if not altogether displaced; tomorrow the same awful fate would seem to have followed some miniature frame; the day following the legs of some chair or spider-table would show signs of extraordinary hardship. Even in the nursery the sounds of lamentation were heard. It was a thing of daily occurrence for the little girls to state that when going to bed at night they had laid their dear dollies in their beds with tender care, but that when again seeking them in the period of recess they had found them with all their beauty gone, with legs and arms amputated and faces beaten from all semblance of human form.

Then articles of crockery began to be missed. The thief could in no case be discovered, and the wages of the servants, from constant stoppages, began to be nominal rather than real. Mrs. Merford and Mrs. Santon mourned their losses, but Harry and Tommy gloated day after day over their spoils, which lay in an ever-increasing heap in the hidden grove of Bubb. To such an extent had the fondness of the Hack now grown that with both youths it was an infatuation – a madness – a frenzy.

At length one awful day arrived. The butlers of the houses of Merford and Santon, harassed by constant losses and complaints, and finding that their breakage account was in excess of their wages, determined to seek some sphere of occupation where, if they did not meet with a suitable reward or recognition of their services, they would, at least, not lose whatever fortune and reputation they had already acquired. Accordingly, before rendering up their keys and the goods entrusted to their charge, they proceeded to take a preliminary stock of their own accounts, to make sure of their accredited accuracy. Dire indeed was their distress when they knew to the full the havoc which had been wrought; terrible their anguish of the present, bitter their thoughts of the future. Their hearts, bowed down with weight of woe, failed them quite; reeled the strong brains that had erst overcome foes of deadlier spirit than grief; and fell their stalwart forms prone on the floors of their respective sancta sanctorum.

Late in the day when their services were required they were sought for in bower and hall, and at length discovered where they lay.

But alas for justice! They were accused of being drunk and for having, whilst in that degraded condition, deliberately injured all the property on which they could lay hands. Were not the evidences of their guilt patent to all in the hecatombs of the destroyed? Then they were charged with all the evils wrought in the houses, and on their indignant denial Harry and Tommy, each in his own home, according to their concerted scheme of action, stepped forward and relieved their minds of the deadly weight that had for long in secret borne them down. The story of each ran that time after time he had seen the butler, when he thought that nobody was looking, knocking knives together in the pantry, chairs and books and pictures in the drawing-room and study, dolls in the nursery, and plates in the kitchen. Then, indeed, was the master of each household stern and uncompromising in his demands for justice. Each butler was committed to the charge of myrmidons of the law under the double charge of drunkenness and wilful destruction of property.

* * *

Softly and sweetly slept Harry and Tommy in their little beds that night. Angels seemed to whisper to them, for they smiled as though lost in pleasant dreams. The rewards given by proud and grateful parents lay in their pockets, and in their hearts the happy consciousness of having done their duty.

Truly sweet should be the slumbers of the just.

Chapter VI
'Let the Dead Past Bury its Dead.'

IT MIGHT BE SUPPOSED that now the operations of Harry and Tommy would be obliged to be abandoned.

Not so, however. The minds of these youths were of no common order, nor were their souls of such weak nature as to yield at the first summons of necessity. Like Nelson, they knew not fear; like Napoleon, they held 'impossible' to be the adjective of fools; and they revelled in the glorious truth that in the lexicon of youth is no such word as 'fail.' Therefore on the day following the éclaircissement of the butlers' misdeeds, they met in the arbour to plan a new campaign.

In the hour when all seemed blackest to them, and when the narrowing walls of possibility hedged them in on every side, thus ran the deliberations of these dauntless youths:

"We have played out the meaner things that are inanimate and inert; why not then trench on the domains of life? The dead have lapsed into the regions of the forgotten past – let the living look to themselves."

That night they met when all households had retired to balmy sleep, and naught but the amorous wailings of nocturnal cats told of the existence of life and sentience. Each bore into the arbour in his arms a pet rabbit and a piece of sticking-plaster. Then, in the peaceful, quiet moonlight, commenced a work of mystery, blood, and gloom. The proceedings began by the fixing of a piece of sticking-plaster over the mouth of each rabbit to prevent it making a noise, if so inclined. Then Tommy held up his rabbit by its scutty tail, and it hung wriggling, a white mass in the moonlight. Slowly Harry raised his rabbit holding it in the same manner, and when level with his head brought it down on Tommy's client.

But the chances had been miscalculated. The boys held firmly to the tails, but the chief portions of the rabbits fell to earth. Ere the doomed beasts could escape, however, the operators had pounced upon them, and this time holding them by the hind legs renewed the trial.

Deep into the night the game was kept up, and the Eastern sky began to show signs of approaching day as each boy bore triumphantly the dead corse of his favourite bunny and placed it within its sometime hutch.

Next night the same game was renewed with a new rabbit on each side, and for more than a week – so long as the hutches supplied the wherewithal – the battle was sustained. True that there were sad hearts and red eyes in the juveniles of Santon and Merford as one by one the beloved pets were found dead, but Harry and Tommy, with the hearts of heroes steeled to suffering and deaf to the pitiful cries of childhood, still fought the good fight on to the bitter end.

When the supply of rabbits was exhausted, other munition was not wanting, and for some days the war was continued with white mice, dormice, hedgehogs, guinea pigs, pigeons, lambs, canaries, parroqueets, linnets, squirrels, parrots, marmots, poodles, ravens, tortoises, terriers, and cats. Of these, as might be expected, the most difficult to manipulate were the terriers and the cats, and of these two classes the proportion of the difficulties in the way of terrier-hacking was, when compared with those of cat-hacking, about that which the simple Lac of the British Pharmacopoeia bears to water in the compound which dairymen palm off upon a too confiding public as milk. More than once when engaged in the rapturous delights of cat-hacking had Harry and Tommy wished that the silent tomb could open its ponderous and massy jaws and engulf them, for the feline victims were not patient in their death agonies, and often broke the bonds in which the security of the artists rested, and turned fiercely on their executioners.

At last, however, all the animals available were sacrificed; but the passion for hacking still remained. How was it all to end?

Chapter VII
A Cloud with Golden Lining

TOMMY AND HARRY sat in the arbour dejected and disconsolate. They wept like two Alexanders because there were no more worlds to conquer. At last the conviction had been forced upon them that the resources available for hacking were exhausted. That very morning they had had a desperate battle, and their attire showed the ravages of direful war. Their hats were battered into shapeless masses, their shoes were soleless and heelless and had the uppers broken, the ends of their braces, their sleeves, and their trousers were frayed, and had they indulged in the manly luxury of coat tails these too would have gone.

Truly, hacking had become an absorbing passion with them. Long and fiercely had they been swept onward on the wings of the demon of strife, and powerless at the best of times had been the promptings of good; but now, heated with combat, maddened by the equal success of arms, and with the lust for victory still unsated, they longed more fiercely than ever for some new pleasure: like tigers that have tasted blood they thirsted for a larger and more potent libation.

As they sat, with their souls in a tumult of desire and despair, some evil genius guided into the garden the twin blossoms of the tree of Bubb. Hand in hand Zacariah and Zerubbabel advanced from the back door; they had escaped from their nurses, and with the exploring instinct of humanity, advanced boldly into the great world – the terra incognita, the Ultima Thule of the paternal domain.

In the course of time they approached the hedge of poplars, from behind which the anxious eyes of Harry and Tommy looked for their approach, for the boys knew that where the twins were the nurses were accustomed to be gathered together, and they feared discovery if their retreat should be cut off.

It was a touching sight, these lovely babes, alike in form, feature, size, expression, and dress; in fact, so like each other that one 'might not have told either from which.' When the startling similarity was recognised by Harry and Tommy, each suddenly turned, and, grasping the other by the shoulder, spoke in a keen whisper:

"Hack! They are exactly equal! This is the very apotheosis of our art!"

With excited faces and trembling hands they laid their plans to lure the unsuspecting babes within the precincts of their charnel house, and they were so successful in their efforts that in a little time the twins had toddled behind the hedge and were lost to the sight of the parental mansion.

Harry and Tommy were not famed for gentleness within the immediate precincts of their respective homes, but it would have delighted the heart of any philanthropist to see the kindly manner in which they arranged for the pleasures of the helpless babes. With smiling faces and playful words and gentle wiles they led them within the arbour, and then, under pretence of giving them some of those sudden jumps in which infants rejoice, they raised them from the ground. Tommy held Zacariah across his arm with his baby moon-face smiling up at the cobwebs on the arbour roof, and Harry, with a mighty effort, raised the cherubic Zerubbabel aloft.

Each nerved himself for a great endeavour, Harry to give, Tommy to endure a shock, and then the form of Zerubbabel was seen whirling through the air round Harry's glowing and determined face. There was a sickening crash and the arm of Tommy yielded visibly.

The pasty face of Zerubbabel had fallen fair on that of Zacariah, for Tommy and Harry were by this time artists of too great experience to miss so simple a mark. The putty-like noses collapsed, the putty-like cheeks became for a moment flattened, and when in an instant more they parted, the faces of both were dabbled in gore. Immediately the firmament was rent with a series of such yells as might have awakened the dead. Forthwith from the house of Bubb came the echoes in parental cries and footsteps. As the sounds of scurrying feet rang through the mansion, Harry cried to Tommy:

"They will be on us soon. Let us cut to the roof of the stable and draw up the ladder."

Tommy answered by a nod, and the two boys, regardless of consequences, and bearing each a twin, ascended to the roof of the stable by means of a ladder which usually stood against the wall, and which they pulled up after them.

As Ephraim Bubb issued from his house in pursuit of his lost darlings, the sight which met his gaze froze his very soul. There, on the coping of the stable roof, stood Harry and Tommy renewing their game. They seemed like two young demons forging ome diabolical implement, for each in turn the twins were lifted high in air and let fall with stunning force on the supine form of its fellow. How Ephraim felt none but a tender and imaginative father can conceive. It would be enough to wring the heart of even a callous parent to see his children, the darlings of his old age – his own beloved twins – being sacrificed to the brutal pleasure of unregenerate youths, without being made unconsciously and helplessly guilty of the crime of fratricide.

Loudly did Ephraim and also Sophonisba, who, with dishevelled locks, had now appeared upon the scene, bewail their unhappy lot and shriek in vain for aid; but by rare ill chance no eyes save their own saw the work of butchery or heard the shrieks of anguish and despair. Wildly did Ephraim, mounting on the shoulders of his spouse, strive, but in vain, to scale the stable wall.

Baffled in every effort, he rushed into the house and appeared in a moment bearing in his hands a double-barrelled gun, into which he poured the contents of a shot pouch as he ran. He came anigh the stable and hailed the murderous youths: "Drop them twins and come down here or I'll shoot you like a brace of dogs."

"Never!" exclaimed the heroic two with one impulse, and continued their awful pastime with a zest tenfold as they knew that the agonised eyes of parents wept at the cause of their joy.

"Then die!" shrieked Ephraim, as he fired both barrels, right-left, at the hackers.

But, alas! Love for his darlings shook the hand that never shook before. As the smoke cleared off and Ephraim recovered from the kick of his gun, he heard a loud twofold laugh of triumph and saw Harry and Tommy, all unhurt, waving in the air the trunks of the twins – the fond father had blown the heads completely off his own offspring.

Tommy and Harry shrieked aloud in glee, and after playing catch with the bodies for some time, seen only by the agonised eyes of the infanticide and his wife, flung them high in the air. Ephraim leaped forward to catch what had once been Zacariah, and Sophonisba grabbed wildly for the loved remains of her Zerubbabel.

But the weight of the bodies and the height from which they fell were not reckoned by either parent, and from being ignorant of a simple dynamical formula each tried to effect an object which calm, common sense, united with scientific knowledge, would have told them was impossible. The masses fell, and Ephraim and Sophonisba were stricken dead by the falling twins, who were thus posthumously guilty of the crime of parricide.

An intelligent coroner's jury found the parents guilty of the crimes of infanticide and suicide, on the evidence of Harry and Tommy, who swore, reluctantly, that the inhuman monsters, maddened by drink, had killed their offspring by shooting them into the air out of a cannon – since stolen – whence like curses they had fallen on their own heads; and that then they had slain themselves suis manibus with their own hands.

Accordingly Ephraim and Sophonisba were denied the solace of Christian burial, and were committed to the earth with 'maimed rites,' and had stakes driven through their middles to pin them down in their unhallowed graves till the Crack of Doom.

Harry and Tommy were each rewarded with National honours and were knighted, even at their tender years.

Fortune seemed to smile upon them all the long after years, and they lived to a ripe old age, hale of body, and respected and beloved of all.

Often in the golden summer eves, when all nature seemed at rest, when the oldest cask was opened and the largest lamp was lit, when the chestnuts glowed in the embers and the kid turned on the spit, when their great-grandchildren pretended to mend fictional armour and to trim an imaginary helmet's plume, when the shuttles of the good wives of their grandchildren went flashing each through its proper loom, with shouting and with laughter they were accustomed to tell the tale of The Dualists; or, the Death-doom of the Double-born.

If you enjoyed this, you might also like...
The Lair of the White Worm (chapter V; chapters XIX–XXVIII), see page 255
'The Squaw,' see page 312

The Crystal Cup

Chapter I
The Dream-Birth

THE BLUE WATERS touch the walls of the palace; I can hear their soft, lapping wash against the marble whenever I listen. Far out at sea I can see the waves glancing in the sunlight, ever-smiling, ever-glancing, ever-sunny. Happy waves! Happy in your gladness, thrice happy that ye are free!

I rise from my work and spring up the wall till I reach the embrasure. I grasp the corner of the stonework and draw myself up till I crouch in the wide window. Sea, sea, out away as far as my vision extends. There I gaze till my eyes grow dim; and in the dimness of my eyes my spirit finds its sight. My soul flies on the wings of memory away beyond the blue, smiling sea – away beyond the glancing waves and the gleaming sails, to the land I call my home. As the minutes roll by, my actual eyesight seems to be restored, and I look round me in my old birth-house. The rude simplicity of the dwelling comes back to me as something new. There I see my old books and manuscripts and pictures, and there, away on their old shelves, high up above the door, I see my first rude efforts in art.

How poor they seem to me now! And yet, were I free, I would not give the smallest of them for all I now possess. Possess? How I dream.

The dream calls me back to waking life. I spring down from my window-seat and work away frantically, for every line I draw on paper, every new form that springs on the plaster, brings me nearer freedom. I will make a vase whose beauty will put to shame the glorious works of Greece in her golden prime! Surely a love like mine and a hope like mine must in time make some form of beauty spring to life! When He beholds it, he will exclaim with rapture, and will order my instant freedom. I can forget my hate, and the deep debt of revenge which I owe him when I think of liberty – even from his hands. Ah! Then on the wings of the morning shall I fly beyond the sea to my home – her home – and clasp her to my arms, never more to be separated!

But, oh Spirit of Day! If she should be – No, no, I cannot think of it, or I shall go mad. Oh Time, Time! Maker and destroyer of men's fortunes, why hasten so fast for others whilst thou laggest so slowly for me? Even now my home may have become desolate, and she – my bride of an hour – may sleep calmly in the cold earth. Oh this suspense will drive me mad! Work, work! Freedom is before me; Aurora is the reward of my labour!

So I rush to my work; but to my brain and hand, heated alike, no fire or no strength descends. Half mad with despair, I beat myself against the walls of my prison, and then climb into the embrasure, and once more gaze upon the ocean, but find there no hope. And so I stay till night, casting its pall of blackness over nature, puts the possibility of effort away from me for yet another day.

So my days go on, and grow to weeks and months. So will they grow to years, should life so long remain an unwelcome guest within me; for what is man without hope? and is not hope nigh dead within this weary breast?

* * *

Last night, in my dreams, there came, like an inspiration from the Day-Spirit, a design for my vase.

All day my yearning for freedom – for Aurora, or news of her – had increased tenfold, and my heart and brain were on fire. Madly I beat myself, like a caged bird, against my prison-bars. Madly I leaped to my window-seat, and gazed with bursting eyeballs out on the free, open sea. And there I sat till my passion had worn itself out; and then I slept, and dreamed of thee, Aurora – of thee and freedom. In my ears I heard again the old song we used to sing together, when as children we wandered on the beach; when, as lovers, we saw the sun sink in the ocean, and I would see its glory doubled as it shone in thine eyes, and was mellowed against thy cheek; and when, as my bride, you clung to me as my arms went round you on that desert tongue of land whence rushed that band of sea-robbers that tore me away. Oh! How my heart curses those men – not men, but fiends! But one solitary gleam of joy remains from that dread encounter, that my struggle stayed those hell-hounds, and that, ere I was stricken down, this right hand sent one of them to his home. My spirit rises as I think of that blow that saved thee from a life worse than death. With the thought I feel my cheeks burning, and my forehead swelling with mighty veins. My eyes burn, and I rush wildly round my prison-house, "Oh! For one of my enemies, that I might dash out his brains against these marble walls, and trample his heart out as he lay before me!" These walls would spare him not. They are pitiless, alas! I know too well. "Oh, cruel mockery of kindness, to make a palace a prison, and to taunt a captive's aching heart with forms of beauty and sculptured marble!" Wondrous, indeed, are these sculptured walls! Men call them passing fair; but oh, Aurora! with thy beauty ever before my eyes, what form that men call lovely can be fair to me? Like him who gazes sun-wards, and then sees no light on earth, from the glory that dyes his iris, so thy beauty or its memory has turned the fairest things of earth to blackness and deformity.

In my dream last night, when in my ears came softly, like music stealing across the waters from afar, the old song we used to sing together, then to my brain, like a ray of light, came an idea whose grandeur for a moment struck me dumb. Before my eyes grew a vase of such beauty that I knew my hope was born to life, and that the Great Spirit had placed my foot on the ladder that leads from this my palace-dungeon to freedom and to thee. Today I have got a block of crystal – for only in such pellucid substance can I body forth my dream – and have commenced my work.

I found at first that my hand had lost its cunning, and I was beginning to despair, when, like the memory of a dream, there came back in my ears the strains of the old song. I sang it softly to myself, and as I did so I grew calmer; but oh! how differently the song sounded to me when thy voice, Aurora, rose not in unison with my own! But what avails pining? To work! To work! Every touch of my chisel will bring me nearer thee.

* * *

My vase is daily growing nearer to completion. I sing as I work, and my constant song is the one I love so well. I can hear the echo of my voice in the vase; and as I end, the wailing song note is prolonged in sweet, sad music in the crystal cup. I listen, ear down, and sometimes I weep as I listen, so sadly comes the echo to my song. Imperfect though it be, my voice makes sweet music, and its echo in the cup guides my hand towards perfection as I work. Would that thy voice rose and fell with mine, Aurora, and then the world would behold a vase of such beauty as never before woke up the slumbering fires of mans love for what is fair; for if I do such work in sadness, imperfect as I am in my solitude and sorrow, what would I do in joy, perfect when with thee? I know that my work is good as an artist, and I feel that it is as a man; and the cup itself, as it daily grows in beauty, gives back a clearer echo. Oh! If I worked in joy how gladly would it give back our voices! Then would we hear an echo and music such as mortals seldom hear; but now the echo, like my song, seems imperfect. I grow daily weaker; but still I work on – work with my whole soul – for am I not working for freedom and for thee?

* * *

My work is nearly done. Day by day, hour by hour, the vase grows more finished. Ever clearer comes the echo whilst I sing; ever softer, ever more sad and heart-rending comes the echo of the wail at the end of the song. Day by day I grow weaker and weaker; still I work on with all my soul. At night the thought comes to me, whilst I think of thee, that I will never see thee more – that I breathe out my life into the crystal cup, and that it will last there when I am gone.

So beautiful has it become, so much do I love it, that I could gladly die to be maker of such a work, were it not for thee – for my love for thee, and my hope of thee, and my fear for thee, and my anguish for thy grief when thou knowest I am gone.

* * *

My work requires but few more touches. My life is slowly ebbing away, and I feel that with my last touch my life will pass out for ever into the cup. Till that touch is given I must not die – I will not die. My hate has passed away. So great are my wrongs that revenge of mine would be too small a compensation for my woe. I leave revenge to a juster and a mightier than I. Thee, oh Aurora, I will await in the land of flowers, where thou and I will wander, never more to part, never more! Ah, never more! Farewell, Aurora – Aurora – Aurora!

Chapter II
The Feast of Beauty

THE FEAST OF BEAUTY approaches rapidly, yet hardly so fast as my royal master wishes. He seems to have no other thought than to have this feast greater and better than any ever held before. Five summers ago his Feast of Beauty was nobler than all held in his sires reign together; yet scarcely was it over, and the rewards given to the victors, when he conceived the giant project whose success is to be tested when the moon reaches her full. It was boldly chosen and boldly done; chosen and done as boldly as the project of a monarch should be. But still I cannot think that it will end well. This yearning after completeness must be unsatisfied in the end – this desire that makes a monarch fling his kingly justice to the winds, and strive to reach his Mecca over a desert of blighted hopes and lost lives. But hush! I must not dare to think ill of my master or his deeds; and besides, walls have ears. I must leave alone these dangerous topics, and confine my thoughts within proper bounds.

The moon is waxing quickly, and with its fulness comes the Feast of Beauty, whose success as a whole rests almost solely on my watchfulness and care; for if the ruler of the feast should fail in his duty, who could fill the void? Let me see what arts are represented, and what works compete. All the arts will have trophies: poetry in its various forms, and prose-writing; sculpture with carving in various metals, and glass, and wood, and ivory, and engraving gems, and setting jewels; painting on canvas, and glass, and wood, and stone and metal; music, vocal and instrumental; and dancing. If that woman will but sing, we will have a real triumph of music; but she appears sickly too. All our best artists either get ill or die, although we promise them freedom or rewards or both if they succeed.

Surely never yet was a Feast of Beauty so fair or so richly dowered as this which the full moon shall behold and hear; but ah! the crowning glory of the feast will be the crystal cup. Never yet have these eyes beheld such a form of beauty, such a wondrous mingling of substance and light. Surely some magic power must have helped to draw such loveliness from a cold block of crystal. I must be careful that no harm happens the vase. Today when I touched it, it gave forth such a ringing sound that my heart jumped with fear lest it should sustain any injury. Henceforth, till I deliver it up to my master, no hand but my own shall touch it lest any harm should happen to it.

Strange story has that cup. Born to life in the cell of a captive torn from his artist home beyond the sea, to enhance the splendour of a feast by his labour – seen at work by spies, and traced and followed till a chance – cruel chance for him – gave him into the hands of the emissaries of my master. He too, poor moth, fluttered about the flame: the name of freedom spurred him on to exertion till he wore away his life. The beauty of that cup was dearly bought for him. Many a man would forget his captivity whilst he worked at such a piece of loveliness; but he appeared to have some sorrow at his heart, some sorrow so great that it quenched his pride.

How he used to rave at first! How he used to rush about his chamber, and then climb into the embrasure of his window, and gaze out away over the sea! Poor captive! Perhaps over the sea some one waited for his coming who was dearer to him than many cups, even many cups as beautiful as this, if such could be on earth.... Well, well, we must all die soon or late, and who dies first escapes the more sorrow, perhaps, who knows? How, when he had commenced the cup, he used to sing all day long, from the moment the sun shot its first fiery arrow into the retreating hosts of night-clouds, till the shades of evening advancing drove the lingering sunbeams into the west – and always the same song!

How he used to sing, all alone! Yet sometimes I could almost imagine I heard not one voice from his chamber, but two.... No more will it echo again from the wall of a dungeon, or from a hillside in free air. No more will his eyes behold the beauty of his crystal cup.

It was well he lived to finish it. Often and often have I trembled to think of his death, as I saw him day by day grow weaker as he worked at the unfinished vase. Must his eyes never more behold the beauty that was born of his soul? Oh, never more! Oh Death, grim King of Terrors, how mighty is thy sceptre! All-powerful is the wave of thy hand that summons us in turn to thy kingdom away beyond the poles!

Would that thou, poor captive, hadst lived to behold thy triumph, for victory will be thine at the Feast of Beauty such as man never before achieved. Then thou mightst have heard the shout that hails the victor in the contest, and the plaudits that greet him as he passes out, a free man, through the palace gates. But now thy cup will come to light amid the smiles of beauty and rank and power, whilst thou liest there in thy lonely chamber, cold as the marble of its walls.

And, after all, the feast will be imperfect, since the victors cannot all be crowned. I must ask my master's direction as to how a blank place of a competitor, should he prove a victor, is to be filled up. So late? I must see him ere the noontide hour of rest be past.

* * *

Great Spirit! How I trembled as my master answered my question!

I found him in his chamber, as usual in the noontide. He was lying on his couch disrobed, half-sleeping; and the drowsy zephyr, scented with rich odours from the garden, wafted through the windows at either side by the fans, lulled him to complete repose. The darkened chamber was cool and silent. From the vestibule came the murmuring of many fountains, and the pleasant splash of falling waters. "Oh, happy," said I, in my heart, "oh, happy great King, that has such pleasures to enjoy!" The breeze from the fans swept over the strings of the Aeolian harps, and a sweet, confused, happy melody arose like the murmuring of children's voices singing afar off in the valleys, and floating on the wind.

As I entered the chamber softly, with muffled foot-fall and pent-in breath, I felt a kind of awe stealing over me. To me who was born and have dwelt all my life within the precincts of the court – to me who talk daily with my royal master, and take his minutest directions as to the coming feast – to me who had all my life looked up to my king as to a spirit, and had venerated him as more than mortal – came a feeling of almost horror; for my master looked then, in his quiet chamber, half-sleeping amid the drowsy music of the harps and fountains, more like a common man than a God. As the thought came to me I shuddered in affright, for it seemed to me that I had been guilty of sacrilege. So much had my veneration for my royal master become a part of my nature, that but to think of him as another man seemed like the anarchy of my own soul.

I came beside the couch, and watched him in silence. He seemed to be half-listening to the fitful music; and as the melody swelled and died away his chest rose and fell as he breathed in unison with the sound.

After a moment or two he appeared to become conscious of the presence of some one in the room, although by no motion of his face could I see that he heard any sound, and his eyes were shut. He opened his eyes, and, seeing me, asked, "Was all right about the Feast of Beauty?" for that is the subject ever nearest to his thoughts. I answered that all was well, but that I had come to ask his royal pleasure as to how a vacant place amongst the competitors was to be filled up. He asked, "How vacant?" and on my telling him, "From death," he asked again, quickly, "Was the work finished?" When I told him that it was, he lay back again on his couch with a sigh of relief, for he had half arisen in his anxiety as he asked the question. Then he said, after a minute, "All the competitors must be present at the feast." "All?" said I. "All," he answered again, "alive or dead; for the old custom must be preserved, and the victors crowned." He stayed still for a minute more, and then said, slowly, "Victors or martyrs." And I could see that the kingly spirit was coming back to him.

Again he went on. "This will be my last Feast of Beauty; and all the captives shall be set free. Too much sorrow has sprung already from my ambition. Too much injustice has soiled the name of king."

He said no more, but lay still and closed his eyes. I could see by the working of his hands and the heaving of his chest that some violent emotion troubled him, and the thought arose, "He is a man, but he is yet a king; and, though a king as he is, still happiness is not for him. Great Spirit of Justice! thou metest out his pleasures and his woes to man, to king and slave alike! Thou lovest best to whom thou givest peace!"

Gradually my master grew more calm, and at length sunk into a gentle slumber; but even in his sleep he breathed in unison with the swelling murmur of the harps.

"To each is given," said I gently, "something in common with the world of actual things. Thy life, oh King, is bound by chains of sympathy to the voice of Truth, which is Music! Tremble, lest in the presence of a master-strain thou shouldst feel thy littleness, and die!" and I softly left the room.

Chapter III
The Story of the Moonbeam

SLOWLY I CREEP along the bosom of the waters.

Sometimes I look back as I rise upon a billow, and see behind me many of my kin sitting each upon a wave-summit as upon a throne. So I go on for long, a power that I wist not forcing me onward, without will or purpose of mine.

At length, as I rise upon a mimic wave, I see afar a hazy light that springs from a vast palace, through whose countless windows flame lamps and torches. But at the first view, as if my coming had been the signal, the lights disappear in an instant.

Impatiently I await what may happen; and as I rise with each heart-beat of the sea I look forward to where the torches had gleamed. Can it be a deed of darkness that shuns the light?

* * *

The time has come when I can behold the palace without waiting to mount upon the waves. It is built of white marble, and rises steep from the brine. Its sea-front

s glorious with columns and statues; and from the portals the marble steps sweep
own, broad and wide to the waters, and below them, down as deep as I can see.

No sound is heard, no light is seen. A solemn silence abounds, a perfect calm.

Slowly I climb the palace walls, my brethren following as soldiers up a breach.
slide along the roofs, and as I look behind me walls and roofs are glistening as
vith silver. At length I meet with something smooth and hard and translucent;
ut through it I pass and enter a vast hall, where for an instant I hang in mid-air
nd wonder.

My coming has been the signal for such a burst of harmony as brings back to my
memory the music of the spheres as they rush through space; and in the full-swelling
nthem of welcome I feel that I am indeed a sun-spirit, a child of light, and that this
s homage to my master.

I look upon the face of a great monarch, who sits at the head of a banquet-table.
Ie has turned his head upwards and backwards, and looks as if he had been awaiting
ny approach. He rises and fronts me with the ringing out of the welcome-song, and
ll the others in the great hall turn towards me as well. I can see their eyes gleaming.
Down along the immense table, laden with plate and glass and flowers, they stand
olding each a cup of ruby wine, with which they pledge the monarch when the song
s ended, as they drink success to him and to the 'Feast of Beauty.'

I survey the hall. An immense chamber, with marble walls covered with bas-reliefs
nd frescoes and sculptured figures, and panelled by great columns that rise along
he surface and support a dome-ceiling painted wondrously; in its centre the glass
antern by which I entered.

On the walls are hung pictures of various forms and sizes, and down the centre of
he table stretches a raised platform on which are placed works of art of various kinds.

At one side of the hall is a dais on which sit persons of both sexes with noble faces
nd lordly brows, but all wearing the same expression – care tempered by hope. All these
old scrolls in their hands.

At the other side of the hall is a similar dais, on which sit others fairer to earthly view,
ess spiritual and more marked by surface-passion. They hold music-scores. All these
ook more joyous than those on the other platform, all save one, a woman, who sits with
owncast face and dejected mien, as of one without hope. As my light falls at her feet she
ooks up, and I feel happy. The sympathy between us has called a faint gleam of hope to
heer that poor pale face.

Many are the forms of art that rise above the banquet-table, and all are lovely to
ehold. I look on all with pleasure one by one, till I see the last of them at the end
f the table away from the monarch, and then all the others seem as nothing to me.
What is this that makes other forms of beauty seem as nought when compared with
, when brought within the radius of its lustre? A crystal cup, wrought with such
vondrous skill that light seems to lose its individual glory as it shines upon it and is
merged in its beauty. "Oh Universal Mother, let me enter there. Let my life be merged
n its beauty, and no more will I regret my sun-strength hidden deep in the chasms
f my moon-mother. Let me live there and perish there, and I will be joyous whilst it
asts, and content to pass into the great vortex of nothingness to be born again when
he glory of the cup has fled."

Can it be that my wish is granted, that I have entered the cup and become a part
f its beauty? "Great Mother, I thank thee."

Has the cup life? or is it merely its wondrous perfectness that makes it tremble like a beating heart, in unison with the ebb and flow, the great wave-pulse of nature To me it feels as if it had life.

I look through the crystal walls and see at the end of the table, isolated from all others, the figure of a man seated. Are those cords that bind his limbs? How suits that crown of laurel those wide, dim eyes, and that pallid hue? It is passing strange This Feast of Beauty holds some dread secrets, and sees some wondrous sights.

I hear a voice of strange, rich sweetness, yet wavering – the voice of one almost a king by nature. He is standing up; I see him through my palace-wall. He calls a name and sits down again.

Again I hear a voice from the platform of scrolls, the Throne of Brows; and again I look and behold a man who stands trembling yet flushed, as though the morning light shone bright upon his soul. He reads in cadenced measure a song in praise of my moon-mother, the Feast of Beauty, and the king. As he speaks, he trembles no more, but seems inspired, and his voice rises to a tone of power and grandeur, and rings back from walls and dome. I hear his words distinctly, though saddened in tone, in the echo from my crystal home. He concludes and sits down, half-fainting amid a whirlwind of applause, every note, every beat of which is echoed as the words had been.

Again the monarch rises and calls "Aurora," that she may sing for freedom. The name echoes in the cup with a sweet, sad sound. So sad, so despairing seems the echo, that the hall seems to darken and the scene to grow dim.

"Can a sun-spirit mourn, or a crystal vessel weep?"

She, the dejected one, rises from her seat on the Throne of Sound, and all eyes turn upon her save those of the pale one, laurel-crowned. Thrice she essays to begin and thrice nought comes from her lips but a dry, husky sigh, till an old man who has been moving round the hall settling all things, cries out, in fear lest she should fail, "Freedom!"

The word is re-echoed from the cup. She hears the sound, turns towards it and begins.

Oh, the melody of that voice! And yet it is not perfect alone; for after the first note comes an echo from the cup that swells in unison with the voice, and the two sounds together, seem as if one strain came ringing sweet from the lips of the All-Father himself. So sweet it is, that all throughout the hall sit spell-bound, and scarcely dare to breathe.

In the pause after the first verses of the song, I hear the voice of the old man speaking to a comrade, but his words are unheard by any other, "Look at the king His spirit seems lost in a trance of melody. Ah! I fear me some evil: the nearer the music approaches to perfection the more rapt he becomes. I dread lest a perfect note shall prove his death-call." His voice dies away as the singer commences the last verse.

Sad and plaintive is the song; full of feeling and tender love, but love overshadowed by grief and despair. As it goes on the voice of the singer grows sweeter and more thrilling, more real; and the cup, my crystal time-home, vibrates more and more as it gives back the echo. The monarch looks like one entranced and no movement is within the hall.... The song dies away in a wild wail that seems to tear the heart of the singer in twain; and the cup vibrates still more as it ives back the echo. As the note, long-swelling, reaches its highest, the cup, the Crystal Cup, my wondrous home, the gift of the All-Father, shivers into millions of atoms, and passes away.

Ere I am lost in the great vortex I see the singer throw up her arms and fall, freed at last, and the King sitting, glory-faced, but pallid with the hue of Death.

f you enjoyed this, you might also like...

The Invisible Giant,' see page 38

'he Lady of the Shroud (chapters III–V), see page 420

The Shadow Builder

THE LONELY Shadow Builder watches ever in his lonely abode.

The walls are of cloud, and round and through them, changing ever as they come pass the dim shades of all the things that have been.

This endless, shadowy, wheeling, moving circle is called The *Procession of the Dead Past*. In it everything is just as it has been in the great world. There is no change in any part; for each moment, as it passes, sends its shade into this dim Procession. Here there are moving people and events – cares – thoughts – follies – crimes – joy, – sorrows – places – scenes – hopes and fears, and all that make the sum of life with all its lights and shadows. Every picture in nature where shadow dwells – and that i every one – has here its dim phantom.

Here are all pictures that are most fair and most sad to see – the passing gloom over a sunny cornfield when with the breeze comes the dark sway of the full ear as they bend and rise; the ripple on the glassy surface of a summer sea; the dark expanse that lies beyond and without the broad track of moonlight on the water the lacework of glare and gloom that flickers over the road as one passes in autumn when the moonlight is falling through the naked branches of overhanging trees; the cool, restful shade under the thick trees in summer time when the sun is flaming down on the haymaker at work; the dark clouds that flit across the moon, hiding her light, which leaps out again hollowly and coldly; the gloom of violet and black that rises on the horizon when rain is near in summer time; the dark recesses and gloomy caverns where the waterfall hurls itself shrieking into the pool below – all these shadow pictures, and a thousand others that come by night and day, circle in the Procession among the things that have been.

Here, too, every act that any human being does, every thought – good and bad – every wish, every hope – everything that is secret – is pictured, and becomes a lasting record which cannot be blotted out; for at any time the Shadow Builder may summon with his special hand any one – sleeping or waking – to behold what is pictured of the Dead Past, in the dim, mysterious distance which encompasses his lonely abode.

In this ever-moving Procession of the Dead Past there is but one place where the circling phantoms are not, and where the cloudy walls are lost. There is here a grea blackness, dense and deep, and full of gloom, and behind which lies the great rea world without.

This blackness is called *The Gate of Dread*.

The Procession afar off takes from it its course, and when passing on its way it circles again towards the darkness, the shadowy phantoms melt again into the mysterious gloom.

Sometimes the Shadow Builder passes through the vapoury walls of his abode and mingles in the ranks of the Procession; and sometimes a figure summoned by the wave of his spectral hand, with silent footfall stalks out of the mist and pauses beside him. Sometimes from a sleeping body the Shadow Builder summons a dreaming soul

hen for a time the quick and the dead stand face to face, and men call it a dream
f the Past. When this happens, friend meets friend or foe meets foe; and over the
oul of the dreamer comes a happy memory long vanished, or the troubled agony of
emorse. But no spectre passes through the misty wall, save to the Shadow Builder
lone; and no human being – even in a dream – can enter the dimness where the
rocession moves along.

So lives the lonely Shadow Builder amid his gloom; and his habitation is peopled
by a spectral past.

His only people are of the past; for though he creates shadows they dwell not with
im. His children go out at once to their homes in the big world, and he knows them
o more till, in the fulness of time, they join the Precession of the Dead Past, and
each, in turn, the misty walls of his home.

For the Shadow Builder there is not night nor day, nor season of the year; but for
ver round his lonely dwelling passes the silent Procession of the Dead Past.

Sometimes he sits and muses with eyes fixed and staring, and seeing nothing; and
hen out at sea there is a cloudless calm or the black gloom of night. Towards the far
orth or south for long months together he never looks, and then the stillness of the
rctic night reigns alone. When the dreamy eyes again become conscious, the hard
ilence softens into the sounds of life and light.

Sometimes, with set frown on his face and a hard look in the eyes, which flash
nd gleam dark lightnings, the Shadow Builder sways resolute to his task, and round
he world the shadows troop thick and fast. Over the sea sweeps the blackness of
he tempest; the dim lights flicker in the cots away upon the lonely moors; and even
n the palaces of kings dark shadows pass and fly and glide over all things – yea,
hrough the hearts of the kings themselves – for the Shadow Builder is then dread
o look upon.

Now and again, with long whiles between, the Shadow Builder as he completes his
ask lingers over the work as though he loves it. His heart yearns to the children of
is will; and he fain would keep even one shadow to be a companion to him in his
oneliness. But the voice of the Great Present is ever ringing in his ears at such times,
njoining him to haste. The giant voice booms out:

"Onwards, onwards."

Whilst the words ring in the ears of the Shadow Builder the completed shadow
ades from beneath his hands, and passing unseen through the Gate of Dread,
ningles in the great world without, in which it is to play its part. When, in the fulness
of time, this shadow comes into the ranks of the Procession of the Dead Past, the
Shadow Builder knows it and remembers it; but in his dead heart there is no gleam of
oving remembrance, for he can only love the Present, that slips ever from his grasp.

And oh! it is a lonely life which the Shadow Builder lives; and in the weird, sad,
solemn, mysterious, silent gloom which encompasses him, he toils on ever at his
onely task.

But sometimes too the Shadow Builder has his joys. Baby shadows spring up,
nd sunny pictures, alight with sweetness and love, glide from under his touch, and
re gone.

Before the Shadow Builder at his task lies a space wherein is neither light nor
darkness, neither joy nor gloom. Whatsoever touches it fades away as sand heaps
nelt before the incoming tide, or like words writ on water. In it all things lose their

being and become part of the great Is-Not; and this terrible line of mystery is called *The Threshold*. Whatsoever passes into it disappears; and whatsoever emerges from it is complete as it comes and passes into the great world as a thing to run its course. Before the Threshold the Shadow Builder himself is as naught; and in its absorbing might there is that which he cannot sway or rule.

When at his task he summons; and out of the impalpable nothingness of the Threshold there comes the object of his will. Sometimes the shadow bursts full and freshly and is suddenly lost in the gloom of the Gate of Dread; and sometimes it grows softly and faintly, getting fuller as it comes, and so melts away into the gloom.

The lonely Shadow Builder is working in his lonely abode; around him, beyond the vapoury walls, pressing onward as ever, is the circling Procession of the Dead Past. Storm and calm have each been summoned from the Threshold, and have gone; and now in this calm, wistful moment the Shadow Builder pauses at his task, and wishes and wishes till, to his lonely longing wistfulness, the nothingness of *The Threshold* sends an answer.

Forth from it grows the shadow of a Baby's foot, stepping with tottering gait out towards the world; then follows the little round body and the big head, and the Baby shadow moves onwards, swaying and balancing with uncertain step. Swift behind it come the Mother's hands stretched out in loving helpfulness, lest it should fall. One step – two – it totters, and is falling; but the Mother's arms are swift, and the gentle hands bear it firmly up. The Child turns and toddles again into its Mother's arms.

Again it strives to walk; and again the Mother's watchful hands are ready. This time it needs not the help; but when the race is over, the shadow Child turns again lovingly to its Mother's breast.

Once again it strives, and it walks boldly and firmly; but the Mother's hands quiver as they hang by her side, whilst a tear sweeps down the cheek, although that cheek is gladdened by a smile.

The Baby shadow turns, and goes a little way off. Then over the misty Nothing on which the shadows fall, flits the flickering shadow of a tiny hand waving; and onward with firm tread, the shadow of the little feet moves out into the misty gloom of the Gate of Dread, and passes away.

But the Mother's shadow moves not. The hands are pressed to the heart, the loving face is upturned in prayer, and down the cheeks roll great tears. Then her head bows lower as the little feet pass beyond her ken; and lower and lower bends the weeping Mother till she lies prone. Even as he looks, the Shadow Builder sees the shadows fade away, away, and the terrible nothingness of the Threshold only is there.

Then presently in the Procession of the Dead Past circle round the misty walls the shadows that had been – the Mother and the Child.

Now from out the Threshold steps a Youth with brave and buoyant tread; and as on the misty veil his shadow falls, the dress and bearing proclaim him a sailor lad. Close to this shadow comes another – the Mother's. Older and thinner she is, as if with watching, but still the same. The old loving hands array prettily the knotted kerchief hanging loosely on the open throat; and the Boy's hands reach out, take the Mother's face between them, and draw it forward for a kiss. The Mother's arms fly round her Son, and in a close embrace they cling.

The Mother kisses her Boy again and again; and together they stand, as though to part were impossible.

Suddenly the Boy turns as though he heard a call. The Mother clings closer. He seems to remonstrate tenderly; but the loving arms hold tighter, till with gentle force he tears himself away. The Mother takes a step forward, and holds out the thin hands trembling in an agony of grief. The Boy stops; to one knee he bends, then, dashing away his tears, he waves his cap, and hurries on, while once again the Mother sinks to her knees, and weeps.

And so, slowly, once again, the shadows of the Mother and the Child grown greater in the fulness of time, pass out through the Gate of Dread, and circle among the phantoms in the Procession of the Dead Past – the Mother following hard upon the speeding footsteps of her Son.

In the long pause that follows, whilst the Shadow Builder watches, all seems changed. Out from the Threshold comes a mist, such as hangs sometimes over the surface of a tropic sea.

By little and little the mist rolls away, and forth advances, black and great, the prow of a mighty vessel. The shadows of the great sails lie faintly in the cool depths of the sea, as the sails flap idly in the breezeless air. Over the bulwark lean listless figures waiting for a wind to come. The mist on the sea melts slowly away; and by the dark shadows of men sheltering from the sunny glare and fanning themselves with their broad sailor hats, it is plain that the heat is terrible.

Now from far off, behind the ship, comes up over the horizon a black cloud no bigger than a man's hand, but sweeping on with terrible speed. Also, from far away, before her course, rises the edge of a coral reef, scarcely seen above the glassy water, but darkling the depths below.

Those on board see neither of these things, for they shelter under their awnings, and sigh for cool breezes.

Quicker and quicker comes the dark cloud, sweeping faster and faster, and growing blacker and blacker and vaster and vaster as it comes.

Then those on board seem to know the danger. Hurried shadows fly along the decks; up the shadows of the ladders hurry shadows of men. The flapping of the great sails ceases as one by one the willing hands draw them in.

But quicker than the hands of men can work sweeps the tempest.

Onwards it rushes, and terrible things come close behind; black darkness – towering waves that break in fury and fly aloft – the spume of the sea swept heavenwards – the great clouds wheeling in fury – and in the centre of these flying, whirling, maddening shadows, rocks the shadow of the ship.

As the black darkness of the heavens encompasses all, the rush of shadowy storm sweeps through the Gate of Dread.

As he waits and looks and sees the cyclone whirling amongst the shadows in the Procession of the Dead Past, the Shadow Builder, even in his dead heart, feels a weight of pain for the brave Sailor Boy tossed on the deep, and the anxious Mother sitting lonely at home.

Again from the Threshold passes a shadow, growing deeper as it comes, but very, very faint at first; for here the sun is strong, and there is but little room for shadows on the bare rock which seems to rise from the glare and the glitter of the sea deeps round.

On the lonely rock a Sailor Boy stands; thin and gaunt he is, and his clothing is but a few rags. Sheltering his eyes with his hand, he looks out to sea, where, afar off, the cloudless sky sinks to meet the burning sea; but no speck over the horizon – no distant glitter of a white sail – gives him a ray of hope.

Long, long he peers, till, wearied out, he sits down on the rock and bows his head as if in despair for a time. As the sea falls, he gathers from the rock the shellfish which has come during the tide.

So the day wears on, and the night comes; and in the tropic sky the stars hang like lamps.

In the cool silence of the night the forlorn Sailor Boy rests – sleeps, and dreams. His dreams are of home – of loving arms stretched out to meet him – of banquets spread – of green fields and waving branches, and the sheltering happiness of his mother's love. For in his sleep the Shadow Builder summons his dreaming soul, and shows him all these blessings passing ceaselessly in the Procession of the Dead Past, and so comforts him lest he should despair and die.

Thus wear on many weary days; and the sailor-boy lingers on the lonely rock.

Afar off he can just see a hill that seems to rise over the Water. One morning when the blackening sky and the sultry air promise a storm, the distant mountain seems nearer; and he thinks that he will try to reach it by swimming.

Whilst he is thus resolving, the storm rushes up over the horizon and sweeps him from the lonely rock. He swims with a bold heart; but just as his strength is done, he is cast by the fury of the storm on a beach of soft sand. The storm passes on its way and the waves leave him high and dry. He goes inland, where, in a cave in the rock, he finds shelter, and sinks to sleep.

The Shadow Builder, as he sees all this happen in the shadows on the clouds, and land, and sea, rejoices in his dead heart that the lonely mother perhaps will not wait in vain.

So time wears on, and many, many weary days pass. The Boy becomes a young Man, living in the lonely island; his beard has grown, and he is clothed in a dress of leaves. All day long, save when he is not working to get food to eat, he watches from the mountain top for a ship to come. As he stands looking out over the sea, the sun casts his shadow down the hillside, so that at evening, as it sinks low in the waters, the shadow of the lonely Sailor grows longer and longer, till at the last it makes a dark streak down the hill side, even to the water's edge.

The lonely Man's heart grows heavier and heavier as he waits and watches, whilst the weary time passes and the countless days and nights come and go.

Time comes when he begins to get feebler and feebler. At last he grows sick to death, and lingers long a-dying.

Then these shadows pass away.

Out from the Threshold grows the shadow of an old woman, thin and worn, sitting in a lonely cottage on a jutting cliff. In the window a lamp burns in the night time to welcome the Lost One should he ever return, and to guide him to his Mother's home. By the lamp the Mother watches, till, wearied out, she sinks to sleep.

As she sleeps the Shadow Builder summons her sleeping soul with the wave of his spectral hand.

She stands beside him in the lonely abode, whilst round them through the misty walls passes onward the Procession of the Dead Past.

As she looks, the Shadow Builder lifts his spectral hand to point to the vision of her Son.

But the Mother's eyes are quicker than even the spectral hand that evokes all the shadows of the rushing storm, and ere the hand is raised she sees her Son among the Shadows of the Past. The Mother's heart is filled with unspeakable joy, as she sees him alive and hale, although a prisoner amongst the tropic seas.

But alas! she knows not that in the dim Procession pass only the things that have been; and that although in the past the lonely Sailor lived, in the present – even at the moment – he may be dying or dead.

The Mother stretches out her arms to her Boy; but even as she does, her sleeping soul loses sight of the dim Procession and vanishes from the Shadow Builder's lonely abode. For when she knows that her Boy is alive, there follows a great pain that he is lonely and waits and watches for help; and the quick heart of the Mother is overcome with grief, and she wakes with a bitter cry.

Then as she rises and looks past the dying lamp out into the dawn, the Mother feels that she has seen a vision of her son in sleep, and that he lives and waits for help; and her heart glows with a great resolve.

Quickly then from the Threshold float many shadows –

A lonely Mother speeding with flying feet to a distant city.

Grave men refusing, but not unkindly, a kneeling woman making an appeal with uplifted hands.

Hard men spurning a praying Mother from their doors.

A wild rabble of bad and thoughtless boys and girls hounding through the streets a hurrying woman.

A shadow of pain on a Mother's heart.

The upcoming of a black cloud of despair, but which hangs far off – for it cannot advance into the bright sunlight of the Mother's resolve.

Weary days with their own myriad shadows.

Lonely nights – black want – cold – hunger and pain; and through all these darkening shadows the swift moving shadow of the Mother's flying feet.

A long long line of such pictures come ever anigh in the Procession, till the dead heart of the Shadow Builder grows icy, and his burning eyes look out savagely on all who give pain and trial to the Mother's faithful heart.

And so all these shadows float out into a black mist, and are lost in the gloom of the Gate of Dread.

Another shadow grows out of the mist –

An Old Man sits in his armchair. The firelight flickering throws his image, quaintly dancing, on the wall of the room. He is old, for the great shoulders are bowed, and the grand strong face is lined with years. There is another shadow in the room; it is the Mother's – she is standing by the table, and is telling her story; her thin hands point away where in the distance she knows her Son is a prisoner in the lonely seas.

The Old Man rises; the enthusiasm of the Mother's heart has touched him, and back to his memory rush the old love and energy and valour of his youth. The great hand rises, closes, and strikes the table with a mighty blow, as though declaring a binding promise. The Mother sinks to her knees – she seizes the great hand and kisses it, and stands erect.

Other men come in – they receive orders – they hurry out.

Then come many shadows whose movement and swiftness and firm purpose mean life and hope.

At sunset, when the masts make long shadows on the harbour water, a big ship moves out on her journey to the tropic seas. Men's shadows quickly flit up and down the rigging and along the decks.

As the shadows wheel round the capstan bar the anchor rises; and into the sunset passes the great vessel.

In the bow, like a figure of Hope, stands the Mother, gazing with eager eyes on the far-off horizon.

Then this shadow fades.

A great ship sweeps along with white sails swelling to the breeze; at the bow stands the Mother, gazing ever out into the distance before her.

Storms come and the ship flies before the blast; but she swerves not, for the Mother, with outstretched hand, points the way, and the helmsman swaying beside his wheel obeys the hand.

So this shadow also passes.

The shadows of days and nights come on in quick succession; and the Mother seeks ever for her Son.

So the records of the prosperous journey melt into a faint, dim, misty shadow through which one figure alone stands clear – the watching Mother at the vessel's prow.

Now from the Threshold grow the shadows of the mountain island and of the ship drawing nigh. In the prow the Mother kneels, looking out and pointing. A boat is lowered. Men spring on board with eager feet; but before them all is the Mother. The boat nears the island; the water shallows, and on the hot white beach the men spring to land.

But in the boat's prow still the Mother sits. In her long anxious hours of agony she has seen in her dreams her Son standing afar off and watching; she has seen him wave his arms with a great joy as the ship rises over the horizon's edge; she has seen him standing on the beach waiting; she has seen him rushing through the surf so that the first thing that the lonely Sailor Boy should touch would be his Mother's loving hands.

But alas! for her dreams. No figure with joyous waving arms stands on the summit of the mountain – no eager figure stands at the water's edge or dashes to meet her through the surf. Her heart grows cold and chill with fear.

Has she indeed come too late?

The men leave the boat, comforting her as they go with shakings of the hand and kindly touches upon the shoulder. She motions them to haste and remains kneeling.

The time goes on. The men ascend the mountain; they search, but they find not the lost Sailor Boy, and with slow, halting feet they return to the boat.

The Mother hears them coming afar and rises to meet them. They hang their heads. The Mother's arms go up, tossed aloft in the anguish of despair, and she sinks swooning in the boat.

The Shadow Builder in an instant summons her spirit from her senseless clay, and points to a figure passing, without movement, in the Procession of the Dead Past.

Then quicker than light the Mother's soul flies back full of new-found joy.

She rises from the boat – she springs to land. The men follow wondering.

She rushes along the shore with flying feet; the sailors come close behind.

She stops opposite the entrance to a cave obscured with trailing brambles. Here, without turning, she motions to the men to wait. They pause and she passes within.

For a few moments grim darkness pours from the threshold; and then one sad, sad vision grows and passes –

A dim, dark cave – a worn man lying prone, and a Mother in anguish bending over the cold clay. On the icy breast she lays her hand; but alas! she cannot feel the beat of the heart she loves.

With a wild, heart-stricken gesture, she flings herself upon the body of her Son and holds it close, close – as though the clasp of a Mother were stronger than the grasp of Death.

The dead heart of the Shadow Builder is alive with pain as he turns away from the sad picture, and with anxious eyes looks where from behind the Gate of Dread, the Mother and Child must come to join the ever-swelling ranks of the Procession of the Dead Past.

Slowly, slowly comes the shadow of the clay cold Mariner passing on.

But swifter than light come the Mother's flying feet. The arms so strong with love are stretched out – the thin hands grasp the passing shadow of her Son and tear him back beyond the Gate of Dread – to life – and liberty – and love.

The lonely Shadow Builder knows now that the Mother's arms are stronger than the grasp of Death.

If you enjoyed this, you might also like...
'The Invisible Giant,' see page 38
'A Star Trap,' see page 400

The Castle of the King

WHEN THEY TOLD the poor Poet that the One he loved best was lying sick in the shadow of danger, he was nigh distraught.

For weeks past he had been alone; she, his Wife, having gone afar to her old home to see an aged grandsire ere he died.

The Poet's heart had for some days been oppressed with a strange sorrow. He did not know the cause of it; he only knew with the deep sympathy which is the poet's gift, that the One he loved was sick. Anxiously had he awaited tidings. When the news came, the shock, although he expected a sad message, was too much for him, and he became nigh distraught.

In his sadness and anxiety he went out into the garden which long years he had cultured for Her. There, amongst the bright flowers, where the old statues stood softly white against the hedges of yew, he lay down in the long uncut summer grass, and wept with his head buried low.

He thought of all the past – of how he had won his Wife and how they loved each other; and to him it seemed a sad and cruel thing that she was afar and in danger, and he not near to comfort her or even to share her pain.

Many many thoughts came back to him, telling the story of the weary years whose gloom and solitude he had forgotten in the brightness of his lovely home.

How in youth they twain had met and in a moment loved. How his poverty and her greatness had kept them apart. How he had struggled and toiled in the steep and rugged road to fame and fortune.

How all through the weary years he had striven with the single idea of winning such a place in the history of his time, that he should be able to come and to her say, "I love you," and to her proud relations, "I am worthy, for I too have become great."

How amid all this dreaming of a happy time which might come, he had kept silent as to his love. How he had never seen her or heard her voice, or even known her habitation, lest, knowing, he should fail in the purpose of his life.

How time – as it ever does to those who work with honesty and singleness of purpose – crowned the labours and the patience of his life.

How the world had come to know his name and reverence and love it as of one who had helped the weak and weary by his example; who had purified the thoughts of all who listened to his words; and who had swept away baseness before the grandeur and simpleness of his noble thoughts.

How success had followed in the wake of fame.

How at length even to his heart, timorous with the doubt of love, had been borne the thought that he had at last achieved the greatness which justified him in seeking the hand of her he loved.

How he had come back to his native place, and there found her still free.

How when he had dared to tell her of his love she had whispered to him that she, too, had waited all the years, for that she knew that he would come to claim her at the end.

How she had come with him as his bride into the home which he had been making for her all these years. How, there, they had lived happily; and had dared to look into the long years to come for joy and content without a bar.

How he thought that even then, when though somewhat enfeebled in strength by the ceaseless toil of years and the care of hoping, he might look to the happy time to come.

But, alas! for hope; for who knoweth what a day may bring forth? Only a little while ago his Dear One had left him hale, departing in the cause of duty; and now she lay sick and he not nigh to help her.

All the sunshine of his life seemed passing away. All the long years of waiting and the patient continuance in well-doing which had crowned their years with love, seemed as but a passing dream, and was all in vain – all, all in vain.

Now with the shadow hovering over his Beloved One, the cloud seemed to be above and around them, and to hold in its dim recesses the doom of them both.

"Why, oh why," asked the poor Poet to the viewless air, "did love come to us? Why came peace and joy and happiness, if the darkening wings of peril shadow the air around her, and leave me to weep alone?"

Thus he moaned, and raved, and wept; and the bitter hours went by him in his solitude.

* * *

As he lay in the garden with his face buried in the long grass, they came to him and told him with weeping, that tiding – sad, indeed – had come.

As they spoke he lifted his poor head and gazed at them; and they saw in the great, dark, tender eyes that now he was quite distraught. He smiled at them sadly, as though not quite understanding the import of their words. As tenderly as they could they tried to tell him that the One he loved best was dead.

They said:

"She has walked in the Valley of the Shadow;" but he seemed to understand them not.

They whispered:

"She has heard the Music of the Spheres," but still he comprehended not.

Then they spoke to him sorrowfully and said:

"She now abides in the Castle of the King."

He looked at them eagerly, as if to ask:

"What castle? What king?"

They bowed their heads; and as they turned away weeping they murmured to him softly:

"The Castle of the King of Death."

He spake no word; so they turned their weeping faces to him again. They found that he had risen and stood with a set purpose on his face. Then he said sweetly:

"I go to find her, that where she abideth, I too may there abide."

They said to him:

"You cannot go. Beyond the Portal she is, and in the Land of Death."

Set purpose shone in the Poet's earnest, loving eyes as he answered them for the last time:

"Where she has gone, there go I too. Through the Valley of the Shadow shall I wend my way. In these ears also shall ring the Music of the Spheres. I shall seek, and I shall find my Beloved in the Halls of the Castle of the King. I shall clasp her close – even before the dread face of the King of Death."

As they heard these words they bowed their heads again and wept, and said: "Alas! Alas!"

The poet turned and left them; and passed away. They fain would have followed; but he motioned them that they should not stir. So, alone, in his grief he went.

As he passed on he turned and waved his hand to them in farewell. Then for a while with uplifted hand he stood, and turned him slowly all around.

Suddenly his outstretched hand stopped and pointed. His friends looking with him saw, where, away beyond the Portal, the idle wilderness spread. There in the midst of desolation the mist from the marshes hung like a pall of gloom on the far off horizon.

As the Poet pointed there was a gleam of happiness – very very faint it was – in his poor sad eyes, distraught with loss, as if afar he beheld some sign or hope of the Lost One.

* * *

Swiftly and sadly the Poet fared on through the burning day.

The Rest Time came; but on he journeyed. He paused not for shade or rest. Never, even for an instant did he stop to cool his parched lips with an icy draught from the crystal springs.

The weary wayfarers resting in the cool shadows beside the fountains raised their tired heads and looked at him with sleepy eyes as he hurried. He heeded them not; but went ever onward with set purpose in his eyes, as though some gleam of hope bursting through the mists of the distant marshes urged him on.

So he fared on through all the burning day, and all the silent night. In the earliest dawn, when the promise of the still unrisen sun quickened the eastern sky into a pale light, he drew anigh the Portal. The horizon stood out blackly in the cold morning light.

There, as ever, stood the Angels who kept watch and ward, and oh, wondrous! although invisible to human eyes, they were seen of him.

As he drew nigh they gazed at him pityingly and swept their great wings out wide, as if to shelter him. He spake; and from his troubled heart the sad words came sweetly through the pale lips:

"Say, Ye who guard the Land, has my Beloved One passed hither on the journey to the Valley of the Shadow, to hear the Music of the Spheres, and to abide in the Castle of the King?"

The Angels at the Portal bowed their heads in token of assent; and they turned and looked outward from the Land to where, far off in the idle wilderness, the dank mists crept from the lifeless bosom of the marsh.

They knew well that the poor lonely Poet was in quest of his Beloved One; so they hindered him not, neither urged they him to stay. They pitied him much for that much he loved.

They parted wide, that through the Portal he might pass without let.

So, the Poet went onwards into the idle desert to look for his Beloved One in the Castle of the King.

For a time he went through gardens whose beauty was riper than the gardens of the Land. The sweetness of all things stole on the senses like the odours from the Isles of the Blest.

The subtlety of the King of Death, who rules in the Realms of Evil, is great. He has ordered that the way beyond the Portal be made full of charm. Thus those straying from the paths ordained for good see around them such beauty that in its joy the gloom and cruelty and guilt of the desert are forgotten.

But as the Poet passed onwards the beauty began to fade away.

The fair gardens looked as gardens do when the hand of care is taken off, and when the weeds in their hideous luxuriance choke, as they spring up, the choicer life of the flowers.

From cool alleys under spreading branches, and from crisp sward which touched as soft as velvet the Wanderer's aching feet, the way became a rugged stony path, full open to the burning glare. The flowers began to lose their odour, and to dwarf to stunted growth. Tall hemlocks rose on every side, infecting the air with their noisome odour.

Great fungi grew in the dark hollows where the pools of dank water lay. Tall trees, with branches like skeletons, rose-trees which had no leaves, and under whose shadow to pause were to die.

Then huge rocks barred the way. These were only passed by narrow, winding passages, overhung by the ponderous cliffs above, which ever threatened to fall and engulf the Sojourner.

Here the night began to fall; and the dim mist rising from the far-off marshes, took weird shapes of gloom. In the distant fastnesses of the mountains the wild beasts began to roar in their cavern lairs. The air became hideous with the fell sounds of the night season.

But the poor Poet heeded not ill sights or sounds of dread. Onward he went ever-unthinking of the terrors of the night. To him there was no dread of darkness – no fear of death – no consciousness of horror. He sought his Beloved One in the Castle of the King; and in that eager quest all natural terrors were forgot.

So fared he onward through the livelong night. Up the steep defiles he trod. Through the shadows of the huge rocks he passed unscathed. The wild animals came around him roaring fiercely – their great eyes flaming like fiery stars through the blackness of the night.

From the high rocks great pythons crawled and hung to seize their prey. From the crevices of the mountain steeps, and from cavernous rifts in the rocky way poisonous serpents glided and rose to strike.

But close though the noxious things came, they all refrained to attack; for they knew that the lonely Sojourner was bound for the Castle of their King.

Onward still, onward he went – unceasing – pausing not in his course – but pressing ever forward in his quest.

When daylight broke at last, the sun rose on a sorry sight. There toiling on the rocky way, the poor lonely Poet went ever onwards, unheeding of cold or hunger or pain.

His feet were bare, and his footsteps on the rock-strewn way were marked by blood. Around and behind him, and afar off keeping equal pace on the summits of the rocky ridges, came the wild beasts that looked on him as their prey, but that refrained from touching him because he sought the Castle of their King.

In the air wheeled the obscene birds who follow ever on the track of the dying and the lost. Hovered the bare-necked vultures with eager eyes, and hungry beaks. Their great wings flapped lazily in the idle air as they followed in the Wanderer's track. The vulture are a patient folk, and they await the falling of the prey.

From the cavernous recesses in the black mountain gorges crept, with silent speed, the serpents that there lurk. Came the python, with his colossal folds and endless coils, whence looked forth cunningly the small flat head. Came the boa and all his tribe, which seize their prey by force and crush it with the dread strictness of their embrace. Came the hooded snakes and all those which with their venom destroy their prey. Here, too, came those serpents most terrible of all to their quarry – which fascinate with eyes of weird magic and by the slow gracefulness of their approach.

Here came or lay in wait, subtle snakes, which take the colour of herb, or leaf, or dead branch, or slimy pool, amongst which they lurk, and so strike their prey unsuspecting.

Great serpents there were, nimble of body, which hang from rock or branch. These gripping tight to their distant hold, strike downward with the rapidity of light as they hurl their whip-like bodies from afar upon their prey.

Thus came forth all these noxious things to meet the Questing Man, and to assail him. But when they knew he was bound for the dread Castle of their King, and saw how he went onward without fear, they abstained from attack.

The deadly python and the boa towering aloft, with colossal folds, were passive, and for the nonce, became as stone. The hooded serpents drew in again their venomous fangs. The mild, deep earnest eyes of the fascinating snake became lurid with baffled spleen, as he felt his power to charm was without avail. In its deadly descent the hanging snake arrested its course, and hung a limp line from rock or branch.

Many followed the Wanderer onwards into the desert wilds, waiting and hoping for a chance to destroy.

Many other perils also were there for the poor Wanderer in the desert idleness. As he went onward the rocky way got steeper and darker. Lurid fogs and deadly chill mists arose.

Then in this path along the trackless wilderness were strange and terrible things.

Mandrakes – half plant, half man – shrieked at him with despairing cry, as, helpless for evil, they stretched out their ghastly arms in vain.

Giant thorns arose in the path; they pierced his suffering feet and tore his flesh as onward he trod. He felt the pain, but he heeded it not.

In all the long, terrible journey he had but one idea other than his eager search for his Beloved One. He thought that the children of men might learn much from the journey towards the Castle of the King, which began so fair, amidst the odorous gardens and under the cool shadow of the spreading trees. In his heart the Poet spake to the multitude of the children of men; and from his lips the words flowed like music, for he sang of the Golden Gate which the Angels call TRUTH.

> *"Pass not the Portal of the Sunset Land!*
> *Pause where the Angels at their vigil stand.*
> *Be warned! and press not though the gates lie wide,*
> *But rest securely on the hither side.*
> *Though odorous gardens and cool ways invite,*
> *Beyond are darkest valleys of the night.*
> *Rest! Rest contented – Pause whilst undefiled,*
> *Nor seek the horrors of the desert wild."*

Thus treading down all obstacles with his bleeding feet, passed ever onwards, the poor distraught Poet, to seek his Beloved One in the Castle of the King.

Even as onward he went the life that is of the animals seemed to die away behind him. The jackals and the more cowardly savage animals slunk away. The lions and tigers, and bears, and wolves, and all the braver of the fierce beasts of prey which followed on his track even after the others had stopped, now began to halt in their career.

They growled low and then roared loudly with uplifted heads; the bristles of their mouths quivered with passion, and the great white teeth champed angrily together in baffled rage. They went on a little further; and stopped again roaring and growling as before. Then one by one they ceased, and the poor Poet went on alone.

In the air the vultures wheeled and screamed, pausing and halting in their flight, as did the savage beasts. These too ceased at length to follow in air the Wanderer in his onward course.

Longest of all kept up the snakes. With many a writhe and stealthy onward glide, they followed hard upon the footsteps of the Questing Man. In the blood marks of his feet upon the flinty rocks they found a joy and hope, and they followed ever.

But time came when the awful aspect of the places where the Poet passed checked even the serpents in their track – the gloomy defiles whence issue the poisonous winds that sweep with desolation even the dens of the beasts of prey – the sterile fastnesses which march upon the valleys of desolation. Here even the stealthy serpents paused in their course; and they too fell away. They glided back, smiling with deadliest rancour, to their obscene clefts.

Then came places where plants and verdure began to cease. The very weeds became more and more stunted and inane. Farther on they declined into the sterility of lifeless rock. Then the most noxious herbs that grew in ghastly shapes of gloom and terror lost even the power to harm, which outlives their living growth. Dwarfed and stunted even of evil, they were compact of the dead rock. Here even the deadly Upas tree could strike no root into the pestiferous earth.

Then came places where, in the entrance to the Valley of the Shadow, even solid things lost their substance, and melted in the dank and cold mists which swept along.

As he passed, the distraught Poet could feel not solid earth under his bleeding feet. On shadows he walked, and amid them, onward through the Valley of the Shadow to seek his Beloved One in the Castle of the King.

The Valley of the Shadow seemed of endless expanse. Circled by the teeming mist, no eye could pierce to where rose the great mountains between which the Valley lay.

Yet they stood there – Mount Despair on the one hand, and the Hill of Fear upon the other.

Hitherto the poor bewildered brain of the Poet had taken no note of all the dangers, and horrors, and pains which surrounded him – save only for the lesson which they taught. But now, lost as he was in the shrouding vapour of the Valley of the Shadow, he could not but think of the terrors of the way. He was surrounded by grisly phantoms that ever and anon arose silent in the mist, and were lost again before he could catch to the full their dread import.

Then there flashed across his soul a terrible thought:

Could it be possible that hither his Beloved One had travelled? Had there come to her the pains which shook his own form with agony? Was it indeed necessary that she should have been appalled by all these surrounding horrors?

At the thought of her, his Beloved One, suffering such pain and dread, he gave forth one bitter cry that rang through the solitude – that cleft the vapour of the Valley, and echoed in the caverns of the mountains of Despair and Fear.

The wild cry prolonged with the agony of the Poet's soul rang through the Valley, till the shadows that peopled it woke for the moment into life-in-death. They flitted dimly along, now melting away and anon springing again into life – till all the Valley of the Shadow was for once peopled with quickened ghosts.

Oh, in that hour there was agony to the poor distraught Poet's soul.

But presently there came a calm. When the rush of his first agony passed, the Poet knew that to the Dead came not the horrors of the journey that he undertook. To the Quick alone is the horror of the passage to the Castle of the King. With the thought came to him such peace that even there – in the dark Valley of the Shadow – stole soft music that sounded in the desert gloom like the Music of the Spheres.

Then the poor Poet remembered what they had told him; that his Beloved One had walked through the Valley of the Shadow, that she had known the Music of the Spheres, and that she abode in the Castle of the King. So he thought that as he was now in the Valley of the Shadow, and as he heard the Music of the Spheres, that soon he should see the Castle of the King where his Beloved One abode. Thus he went on in hope.

But alas! That very hope was a new pain that ere this he wot not of.

Hitherto he had gone on blindly, recking not of where he went or what came a-nigh him, so long as he pressed onward on his quest; but now the darkness and the peril of the way had new terrors, for he thought of how they might arrest his course. Such thoughts made the way long indeed, for the moments seemed an age with hoping. Eagerly he sought for the end to come, when, beyond the Valley of the Shadow through which he fared, he should see rising the turrets of the Castle of the King.

Despair seemed to grow upon him; and as it grew there rang out, ever louder, the Music of the Spheres.

Onward, ever onward, hurried in mad haste the poor distraught Poet. The dim shadows that peopled the mist shrank back as he passed, extending towards him warning hands with long gloomy fingers of deadly cold. In the bitter silence of the moment, they seemed to say:

"Go back! Go back!"

Louder and louder rang now the Music of the Spheres. Faster and faster in mad, feverish haste rushed the Poet, amid the shrinking Shadows of the gloomy valley. The peopling shadows as they faded away before him, seemed to wail in sorrowful warning:

"Go back! Go back!"

Still in his ears rang ever the swelling tumult of the music.

Faster and faster he rushed onward; till, at last, wearied nature gave way and he fell prone to earth, senseless, bleeding, and alone.

After a time – how long he could not even guess – he awoke from his swoon.

For awhile he could not think where he was; and his scattered senses could not help him.

All was gloom and cold and sadness. A solitude reigned around him, more deadly than aught he had ever dreamt of. No breeze was in the air; no movement of a passing cloud.

No voice or stir of living thing in earth, or water, or air. No rustle of leaf or sway of branch – all was silent, dead, and deserted. Amid the eternal hills of gloom around, lay the valley devoid of aught that lived or grew.

The sweeping mists with their multitude of peopling shadows had gone by. The fearsome terrors of the desert even were not there. The Poet, as he gazed around him, in his utter loneliness, longed for the sweep of the storm or the roar of the avalanche to break the dread horror of the silent gloom.

Then the Poet knew that through the Valley of the Shadow had he come; that scared and maddened though he had been, he had heard the Music of the Spheres. He thought that now hard by the desolate Kingdom of Death he trod.

He gazed all around him, fearing lest he should see anywhere the dread Castle of the King, where his Beloved One abode; and he groaned as the fear of his heart found voice:

"Not here! Oh not here, amid this awful solitude."

Then amid the silence around, upon distant hills his words echoed:

"Not here! Oh not here," till with the echoing and re-echoing rock, the idle wilderness was peopled with voices.

Suddenly the echo voices ceased.

From the lurid sky broke the terrible sound of the thunder peal. Along the distant skies it rolled. Far away over the endless ring of the grey horizon it swept – going and returning – pealing – swelling – dying away. It traversed the aether, muttering now in ominous sound as of threats, and anon crashing with the voice of dread command.

In its roar came a sound as of a word:

"Onward."

To his knees the Poet sank and welcomed with tears of joy the sound of the thunder. It swept away as a Power from Above the silent desolation of the wilderness. It told him that in and above the Valley of the Shadow rolled the mighty tones of Heaven's command.

Then the Poet rose to his feet, and with new heart went onwards into the wilderness.

As he went the roll of the thunder died away, and again the silence of desolation reigned alone.

* * *

So time wore on; but never came rest to the weary feet. Onwards, still onwards he went, with but one memory to cheer him – the echo of the thunder roll in his ears, as it pealed out in the Valley of Desolation:

"Onward! Onward!"

Now the road became less and less rocky, as on his way he passed. The great cliffs sank and dwindled away, and the ooze of the fens crept upward to the mountain's feet.

At length the hills and hollows of the mountain fastnesses disappeared. The Wanderer took his way amid mere trackless wastes, where was nothing but quaking marsh and slime.

On, on he wandered; stumbling blindly with weary feet on the endless road.

Over his soul crept ever closer the blackness of despair. Whilst amid the mountain gorges he had been wandering, some small cheer came from the hope that at any moment some turn in the path might show him his journey's end. Some entry from a dark defile might expose to him, looming great in the distance – or even anigh him – the dread Castle of the King. But now with the flat desolation of the silent marsh around him, he knew that the Castle could not exist without his seeing it.

He stood for awhile erect, and turned him slowly round, so that the complete circuit of the horizon was swept by his eager eyes. Alas! Never a sight did he see. Nought was there but the black line of the horizon, where the sad earth lay against the level sky. All, all was compact of a silent gloom.

Still on he tottered. His breath came fast and laboured. His weary limbs quivered as they bore him feebly up. His strength – his life – was ebbing fast.

On, on, he hurried, ever on, with one idea desperately fixed in his poor distraught mind – that in the Castle of the King he should find his Beloved One.

He stumbled and fell. There was no obstacle to arrest his feet; only from his own weakness he declined.

Quickly he arose and went onward with flying feet. He dreaded that should he fall he might not be able to arise again.

Again he fell. Again he rose and went on his way desperately, with blind purpose.

So for a while went he onwards, stumbling and falling; but arising ever and pausing not on his way. His quest he followed, of his Beloved One abiding in the Castle of the King.

At last so weak he grew that when he sank he was unable to rise again.

Feebler and feebler he grew as he lay prone; and over his eager eyes came the film of death.

But even then came comfort; for he knew that his race was run, and that soon he would meet his Beloved One in the Halls of the Castle of the King.

To the wilderness his thoughts he spoke. His voice came forth with a feeble sound, like the moaning before a storm of the wind as it passes through reeds in the grey autumn:

"A little longer. Soon I shall meet her in the Halls of the King; and we shall part no more. For this it is worth to pass through the Valley of the Shadow and to listen to the Music of the Spheres with their painful hope. What boots it though the Castle be afar? Quickly speed the feet of the dead. To the fleeting spirit all distance is but a span. I fear not now to see the Castle of the King; for there, within its chiefest Hall, soon shall I meet my Beloved – to part no more."

Even as he spoke he felt that the end was nigh.

Forth from the marsh before him crept a still, spreading mist. It rose silently, higher – higher – enveloping the wilderness for far around. It took deeper and darker shades as it arose. It was as though the Spirit of Gloom were hid within, and grew mightier with the spreading vapour.

To the eyes of the dying Poet the creeping mist was as a shadowy castle. Arose the tall turrets and the frowning keep. The gateway with its cavernous recesses and its beetling towers took shape as a skull. The distant battlements towered aloft into the silent air. From the very ground whereon the stricken Poet lay, grew, dim and dark, a vast causeway leading into the gloom of the Castle gate.

The dying Poet raised his head and looked. His fast failing eyes, quickened by the love and hope of his spirit, pierced through the dark walls of the keep and the gloomy terrors of the gateway.

There, within the great Hall where the grim King of Terrors himself holds his court, he saw her whom he sought. She was standing in the ranks of those who wait in patience for their Beloved to follow them into the Land of Death.

The Poet knew that he had but a little while to wait, and he was patient – stricken though he lay, amongst the Eternal Solitudes. Afar off, beyond the distant horizon, came a faint light as of the dawn of a coming day.

As it grew brighter the Castle stood out more and more clearly; till in the quickening dawn it stood revealed in all its cold expanse.

The dying Poet knew that the end was at hand. With a last effort he raised himself to his feet, that standing erect and bold, as is the right of manhood, he might so meet face to face the grim King of Death before the eyes of his Beloved One.

The distant sun of the coming day rose over the horizon's edge.

A ray of light shot upward.

As it struck the summit of the Castle keep the Poet's Spirit in an instant of time swept along the causeway. Through the ghostly portal of the Castle it swept, and met with joy the kindred Spirit that it loved before the very face of the King of Death.

Quicker then than the lightning's flash the whole Castle melted into nothingness; and the sun of the coming day shone calmly down upon the Eternal Solitudes.

In the Land within the Portal rose the sun of the coming day. It shone calmly and brightly on a fair garden, where, among the long summer grass lay the Poet, colder than the marble statues around him.

If you enjoyed this, you might also like...
'The Man from Shorrox,' see page 320
'The Crystal Cup,' see page 373

A Star Trap

"WHEN I WAS APPRENTICED to theatrical carpentering my master was John Haliday, who was Master Machinist – we called men in his post 'Master Carpenter' in those days – of the old Victoria Theatre, Hulme. It wasn't called Hulme; but that name will do. It would only stir up painful memories if I were to give the real name. I daresay some of you – not the Ladies (this with a gallant bow all round) – will remember the case of a Harlequin as was killed in an accident in the pantomime. We needn't mention names; Mortimer will do for a name to call him by – Henry Mortimer. The cause of it was never found out. But I knew it; and I've kept silence for so long that I may speak now without hurting anyone. They're all dead long ago that was interested in the death of Henry Mortimer or the man who wrought that death."

"Any of you who know of the case will remember what a handsome, dapper, well-built man Mortimer was. To my own mind he was the handsomest man I ever saw."

The Tragedian's low, grumbling whisper, "That's a large order," sounded a warning note. Hempitch, however, did not seem to hear it, but went on:

"Of course, I was only a boy then, and I hadn't seen any of you gentlemen – Yer very good health, Mr. Wellesley Dovercourt, sir, and cetera. I needn't tell you, Ladies, how well a harlequin's dress sets off a nice slim figure. No wonder that in these days of suffragettes, women wants to be harlequins as well as columbines. Though I hope they won't make the columbine a man's part!"

"Mortimer was the nimblest chap at the traps I ever see. He was so sure of hisself that he would have extra weight put on so that when the counter weights fell he'd shoot up five or six feet higher than anyone else could even try to. Moreover, he had a way of drawing up his legs when in the air – the way a frog does when he is swimming – that made his jump look ever so much higher."

"I think the girls were all in love with him, the way they used to stand in the wings when the time was comin' for his entrance. That wouldn't have mattered much, for girls are always falling in love with some man or other, but it made trouble, as it always does when the married ones take the same start. There were several of these that was always after him, more shame for them, with husbands of their own. That was dangerous enough, and hard to stand for a man who might mean to be decent in any way. But the real trial – and the real trouble, too – was none other than the young wife of my own master, and she was more than flesh and blood could stand. She had come into the panto, the season before, as a high-kicker – and she could! She could kick higher than girls that was more than a foot taller than her; for she was a wee bit of a thing and as pretty as pie; a gold-haired, blue-eyed, slim thing with much the figure of a boy, except for...and they saved her from any mistaken idea of that kind. Jack Haliday went crazy over her, and when the notice was up, and there was no young spark with plenty of oof coming along to do the proper thing by her, she married him. It was, when they was joined, what you Ladies call a marriage of convenience; but after a bit they two got on very well, and we all thought she was beginning to like the old man – for Jack was old enough to be her father, with a bit to spare. In the summer, when the house was closed, he took her to the Isle of Man; and when they came back he made no secret of it that he'd had the happiest time of his life. She looked quite happy, too, and treated him affectionate; and we all began to think that that marriage had not been a failure at any rate."

"Things began to change, however, when the panto rehearsals began next year. Old Jack began to look unhappy, and didn't take no interest in his work. Loo – that was Mrs. Haliday's name – didn't seem over fond of him now, and was generally impatient when he was by. Nobody said anything about this, however, to us men; but the married women smiled and nodded their heads and whispered that perhaps there were reasons. One day on the stage, when the harlequinade rehearsal was beginning, someone mentioned as how perhaps Mrs. Haliday wouldn't be dancing that year, and they smiled as if they was all in the secret. Then Mrs. Jack ups and gives them Johnny-up-the-orchard for not minding their own business and telling a pack of lies, and such like as you Ladies like to express in your own ways when you get your back hair down. The rest of us tried to soothe her all we could, and she went off home."

"It wasn't long after that that she and Henry Mortimer left together after rehearsal was over, he saying he'd leave her at home. She didn't make no objections – I told you he was a very handsome man."

"Well, from that day on she never seemed to take her eyes from him during every rehearsal, right up to the night of the last rehearsal, which, of course, was full dress – 'Everybody and Everything.'"

"Jack Haliday never seemed to notice anything that was going on, like the rest of them did. True, his time was taken up with his own work, for I'm telling you that a Master Machinist hasn't got no loose time on his hands at the first dress rehearsal of a panto. And, of course, none of the company ever said a word or gave a look that would call his attention to it. Men and women are queer beings. They will be blind and deaf whilst danger is being run; and it's only after the scandal is beyond repair that they begin to talk – just the very time when most of all they should be silent."

"I saw all that went on, but I didn't understand it. I liked Mortimer myself and admired him – like I did Mrs. Haliday, too – and I thought he was a very fine fellow. I was only a boy, you know, and Haliday's apprentice, so naturally I wasn't looking for any trouble I could help, even if I'd seen it coming. It was when I looked back afterwards at the whole thing that I began to comprehend; so you will all understand now, I hope, that what I tell you is the result of much knowledge of what I saw and heard and was told of afterwards – all morticed and clamped up by thinking."

"The panto had been on about three weeks when one Saturday, between the shows, I heard two of our company talking. Both of them was among the extra girls that both sang and danced and had to make theirselves useful. I don't think either of them was better than she should be; they went out to too many champagne suppers with young men that had money to burn. That part doesn't matter in this affair – except that they was naturally enough jealous of women who was married – which was what they was aiming at – and what lived straighter than they did. Women of that kind like to see a good woman tumble down; it seems to make them all more even. Now real bad girls what have gone under altogether will try to save a decent one from following their road.

That is, so long as they're young; for a bad one what is long in the tooth is the limit. They'll help anyone down hill – so long as they get anything out of it."

"Well – no offence, you Ladies, as has growed up! – these two girls was enjoyin' themselves over Mrs. Haliday and the mash she had set up on Mortimer. They didn't see that I was sitting on a stage box behind a built-out piece of the Prologue of the panto, which was set ready for night. They were both in love with Mortimer, who wouldn't look at either of them, so they was miaw'n cruel, like cats on the tiles. Says one: 'The Old Man seems worse than blind; he won't see.'"

"'Don't you be too sure of that,' says the other. 'He don't mean to take no chances. I think you must be blind, too, Kissie.' That was her name – on the bills anyhow, Kissie Mountpelier. 'Don't he make a point of taking her home hisself every night after the play. You should know, for you're in the hall yourself waiting for your young man till he comes from his club.'"

"'Wot-ho, you bally geeser,' says the other – which her language was mostly coarse – 'don't you know there's two ends to everything? The Old Man looks to one end only!' Then they began to snigger and whisper; and presently the other one says: 'Then he thinks harm can be only done when work is over!'"

"'Jest so,' she answers. 'Her and him knows that the old man has to be down long before the risin' of the rag; but she doesn't come in till the Vision of Venus dance after half time; and he not till the harlequinade!'"

"Then I quit. I didn't want to hear any more of that sort."

"All that week things went on as usual. Poor old Haliday wasn't well. He looked worried and had a devil of a temper. I had reason to know that, for what worried him was his work. He was always a hard worker, and the panto season was a terror with him. He didn't ever seem to mind anything else outside his work. I thought at the time that that was how those two chattering girls made up their slanderous story; for, after all, a slander, no matter how false it may be, must have some sort of beginning. Something that seems, if there isn't something that is! But no matter how busy he might be, old Jack always made time to leave the wife at home."

"As the week went on he got more and more pale; and I began to think he was in for some sickness. He generally remained in the theatre between the shows on Saturday; that is, he didn't go home, but took a high tea in the coffee shop close to the theatre, so as to be handy in case there might be a hitch anywhere in the preparation for night. On that Saturday he went out as usual when the first scene was set, and the men were getting ready the packs for the rest of the scenes. By and bye there was some trouble – the usual Saturday kind – and I went off to tell him. When I went into the coffee shop I couldn't see him. I thought it best not to ask or to seem to take any notice, so I came back to the theatre, and heard that the trouble had settled itself as usual, by the men who had been quarrelling going off to have another drink. I hustled up those who remained, and we got things smoothed out in time for them all to have their tea. Then I had my own. I was just then beginning to feel the responsibility of my business, so I wasn't long over my food, but came back to look things over and see that all was right, especially the trap, for that was a thing Jack Haliday was most particular about. He would overlook a fault for anything else; but if it was along of a trap, the man had to go. He always told the men that that wasn't ordinary work; it was life or death."

"I had just got through my inspection when I saw old Jack coming in from the hall. There was no one about at that hour, and the stage was dark. But dark as it was I could see that the old man was ghastly pale. I didn't speak, for I wasn't near enough, and as he was moving very silently behind the scenes I thought that perhaps he wouldn't like anyone to notice that he had been away. I thought the best thing I could do would be to clear out of the way, so I went back and had another cup of tea."

"I came away a little before the men, who had nothing to think of except to be in their places when Haliday's whistle sounded.

I went to report myself to my master, who was in his own little glass-partitioned den at the back of the carpenter's shop. He was there bent over his own bench, and was filing away at something so intently that he did not seem to hear me; so I cleared out. I tell you, Ladies and Gents, that from an apprentice point of view it is not wise to be too obtrusive when your master is attending to some private matter of his own!"

"When the 'get-ready' time came and the lights went up, there was Haliday as usual at his post. He looked very white and ill – so ill that the stage manager, when he came in, said to him that if he liked to go home and rest he would see that all his work would be attended to. He thanked him, and said that he thought he would be able to stay. 'I do feel a little weak and ill, sir,' he said. 'I felt just now for a few moments as if I was going to faint. But that's gone by already, and I'm sure I shall be able to get through the work before us all right.'"

"Then the doors was opened, and the Saturday night audience came rushing and tumbling in. The Victoria was a great Saturday night house. No matter what other nights might be, that was sure to be good. They used to say in the perfesh that the Victoria lived on it, and that the management was on holiday for the rest of the week. The actors knew it, and no matter how slack they might be from Monday to Friday they was all taut and trim then. There was no walking through and no fluffing on Saturday nights – or else they'd have had the bird."

"Mortimer was one of the most particular of the lot in this way. He never was slack at any time – indeed, slackness is not a harlequin's fault, for if there's slackness there's no harlequin, that's all. But Mortimer always put on an extra bit on the Saturday night. When he jumped up through the star trap he always went then a couple of feet higher. To do this we had always to put on a lot more weight. This he always saw to himself; for, mind you, it's no joke being driven up through the trap as if you was shot out of a gun. The points of the star had to be kept free, and the hinges at their bases must be well oiled, or else there can be a disaster at any time. Moreover, 'tis the duty of someone appointed for the purpose to see that all is clear upon the stage. I remember hearing that once at New York, many years ago now, a harlequin was killed by a 'grip' – as the Yankees call a carpenter – what outsiders here call a scene-shifter – walking over the trap just as the stroke had been given to let go the counter-weights. It wasn't much satisfaction to the widow to know that the 'grip' was killed too."

"That night Mrs. Haliday looked prettier than ever, and kicked even higher than I had ever seen her do. Then, when she got dressed for home, she came as usual and stood in the wings for the beginning of the harlequinade. Old Jack came across the stage and stood beside her; I saw him from the back follow up the sliding ground-row that closed in on the Realms of Delight. I couldn't help noticing that he still looked ghastly pale. He kept turning his eyes on the star trap. Seeing this, I naturally looked at it too, for I feared lest something might have gone wrong. I had seen that it was in good order, and that the joints were properly oiled when the stage was set for the evening show, and as it wasn't used all night for anything else I was reassured.

Indeed, I thought I could see it shine a bit as the limelight caught the brass hinges. There was a spot light just above it on the bridge, which was intended to make a good show of harlequin and his big jump. The people used to howl with delight as he came rushing up through the trap and when in the air drew up his legs and spread them wide for an instant and then straightened them again as he came down – only bending his knees just as he touched the stage."

"When the signal was given the counter-weight worked properly. I knew, for the sound of it at that part was all right."

"But something was wrong. The trap didn't work smooth, and open at once as the harlequin's head touched it. There was a shock and a tearing sound, and the pieces of the star seemed torn about, and some of them were thrown about the stage. And in the middle of them came the coloured and spangled figure that we knew."

"But somehow it didn't come up in the usual way. It was erect enough, but there was not the usual elasticity. The legs never moved; and when it went up a fair height – though nothing like usual – it seemed to topple over and fall on the stage on its side. The audience shrieked, and the people in the wings – actors and staff all the same – closed in, some of them in their stage clothes, others dressed for going home. But the man in the spangles lay quite still."

"The loudest shriek of all was from Mrs. Haliday; and she was the first to reach the spot where he – it – lay. Old Jack was close behind her, and caught her as she fell. I had just time to see that, for I made it my business to look after the pieces of the trap; there was plenty of people to look after the corpse. And the pit was by now crossing the orchestra and climbing up on the stage."

"I managed to get the bits together before the rush came. I noticed that there were deep scratches on some of them, but I didn't have time for more than a glance. I put a stage box over the hole lest anyone should put a foot through it. Such would mean a broken leg at least; and if one fell through, it might mean worse. Amongst other things I found a queer-looking piece of flat steel with some bent points on it. I knew it didn't belong to the trap; but it came from somewhere, so I put it in my pocket."

"By this time there was a crowd where Mortimer's body lay. That he was stone dead nobody could doubt. The very attitude was enough. He was all straggled about in queer positions; one of the legs was doubled under him with the toes sticking out in the wrong way. But let that suffice! It doesn't do to go into details of a dead body...I wish someone would give me a drop of punch."

"There was another crowd round Mrs. Haliday, who was lying a little on one side nearer the wings where her husband had carried her and laid her down. She, too, looked like a corpse; for she was as white as one and as still, and looked as cold. Old Jack was kneeling beside her, chafing her hands. He was evidently frightened about her, for he, too, was deathly white. However, he kept his head, and called his men round him. He left his wife in care of Mrs. Homcroft, the Wardrobe Mistress, who had by this time hurried down. She was a capable woman, and knew how to act promptly. She got one of the men to lift Mrs. Haliday and carry her up to the wardrobe. I heard afterwards that when she got her there she turned out all the rest of them that followed up – the women as well as the men – and looked after her herself."

"I put the pieces of the broken trap on the top of the stage box, and told one of our chaps to mind them, and see that no one touched them, as they might be wanted. By this time the police who had been on duty in front had come round, and as they had at once telephoned to headquarters, more police kept coming in all the time. One of them took charge of the place where the broken trap was; and when he heard who put the box and the broken pieces there, sent for me. More of them took the body away to the property room, which was a large room with benches in it, and which could be locked up. Two of them stood at the door, and wouldn't let anyone go in without permission."

"The man who was in charge of the trap asked me if I had seen the accident. When I said I had, he asked me to describe it. I don't think he had much opinion of my powers of description, for he soon dropped that part of his questioning. Then he asked me to point out where I found the bits of the broken trap. I simply said:"

"'Lord bless you, sir, I couldn't tell. They was scattered all over the place. I had to pick them up between people's feet as they were rushing in from all sides.'"

"'All right, my boy,' he said, in quite a kindly way, for a policeman, 'I don't think they'll want to worry you. There are lots of men and women, I am told, who were standing by and saw the whole thing. They will be all subpoenaed.' I was a small-made lad in those days – I ain't a giant now! – and I suppose he thought it was no use having children for witnesses when they had plenty of grown-ups. Then he said something about me and an idiot asylum that was not kind – no, nor wise either, for I dried up and did not say another word."

"Gradually the public was got rid of. Some strolled off by degrees, going off to have a glass before the pubs closed, and talk it all over. The rest us and the police ballooned out. Then, when the police had taken charge of everything and put in men to stay all night, the coroner's officer came and took off the body to the city mortuary, where the police doctor made a post mortem. I was allowed to go home. I did so – and gladly – when I had seen the place settling down. Mr. Haliday took his wife home in a four-wheeler. It was perhaps just as well, for Mrs. Homcroft and some other kindly souls had poured so much whisky and brandy and rum and gin and beer and peppermint into her that I don't believe she could have walked if she had tried."

"When I was undressing myself something scratched my leg as I was taking off my trousers. I found it was the piece of flat steel which I had picked up on the stage. It was in the shape of a star fish, but the spikes of it were short. Some of the points were turned down, the rest were pulled out straight again. I stood with it in my hand wondering where it had come from and what it was for, but I couldn't remember anything in the whole theatre that it could have belonged to. I looked at it closely again, and saw that the edges were all filed and quite bright. But that did not help me, so I put it on the table and thought I would take it with me in the morning; perhaps one of the chaps might know. I turned out the gas and went to bed – and to sleep."

"I must have begun to dream at once, and it was, naturally enough, all about the terrible thing that had occurred. But, like all dreams, it was a bit mixed. They were all mixed. Mortimer with his spangles flying up the trap, it breaking, and the pieces scattering round. Old Jack Haliday looking on at one side of the stage with his wife beside him – he as pale as death, and she looking prettier than ever. And then Mortimer coming down all crooked and falling on the stage, Mrs. Haliday shrieking, and her and Jack running forward, and me picking up the pieces of the broken trap from between people's legs, and finding the steel star with the bent points."

"I woke in a cold sweat, saying to myself as I sat up in bed in the dark: 'That's it!'"

"And then my head began to reel about so that I lay down again and began to think it all over. And it all seemed clear enough then. It was Mr. Haliday who made that star and put it over the star trap where the points joined! That was what Jack Haliday was filing at when I saw him at his bench; and he had done it because Mortimer and his wife had been making love to each other. Those girls were right, after all. Of course, the steel points had prevented the trap opening, and when Mortimer was driven up against it his neck was broken."

"But then came the horrible thought that if Jack did it, it was murder, and he would be hung. And, after all, it was his wife that the harlequin had made love to – and old Jack loved her very much indeed himself and had been good to her – and she was his wife. And that bit of steel would hang him if it should be known. But no one but me – and whoever made it, and put it on the trap – even knew of its existence – and Mr. Haliday was my master – and the man was dead – and he was a villain!"

"I was living then at Quarry Place; and in the old quarry was a pond so deep that the boys used to say that far down the water was boiling hot, it was so near Hell."

"I softly opened the window, and, there in the dark, threw the bit of steel as far as I could into the quarry."

"No one ever knew, for I have never spoken a word of it till this very minute. I was not called at the inquest. Everyone was in a hurry; the coroner and the jury and the police. Our governor was in a hurry too, because we wanted to go on as usual at night; and too much talk of the tragedy would hurt business. So nothing was known; and all went on as usual. Except that after that Mrs. Haliday didn't stand in the wings during the harlequinade, and she was as loving to her old husband as a woman can be. It was him she used to watch now; and always with a sort of respectful adoration. She knew, though no one else did, except her husband – and me."

When he finished there was a big spell of silence. The company had all been listening intently, so that there was no change except the cessation of Hempitch's voice. The eyes of all were now fixed on Mr. Wellesley Dovercourt. It was the role of the Tragedian to deal with such an occasion. He was quite alive to the privileges of his status, and spoke at once:

"H'm! Very excellent indeed! You will have to join the ranks of our profession, Mr. Master Machinist – the lower ranks, of course. A very thrilling narrative yours, and distinctly true. There may be some errors of detail, such as that Mrs. Haliday never flirted again. I…I knew John Haliday under, of course, his real name. But I shall preserve the secret you so judiciously suppressed. A very worthy person. He was stage carpenter at the Duke's Theatre, Bolton, where I first dared histrionic triumphs in the year – ah H'm! I saw quite a good deal of Mrs. Haliday at that time. And you are wrong about her. Quite wrong! She was a most attractive little woman – very!"

The Wardrobe Mistress here whispered to the Second Old Woman:

"Well, ma'am, they all seem agoin' of it tonight. I think they must have ketched the infection from Mr. Bloze. There isn't a bally word of truth in all Hempitch has said. I was there when the accident occurred – for it was an accident when Jim Bungnose, the clown, was killed. For he was a clown, not a 'arlequin; an' there wasn't no lovemakin' with Mrs. 'Aliday. God 'elp the woman as would try to make love to Jim; which she was the Strong Woman in a Circus, and could put up her dooks like a man. Moreover, there wasn't no Mrs. 'Aliday. The carpenter at Grimsby, where it is he means, was Tom

Elrington, as he was my first 'usband. And as to Mr. Dovercourt rememberin'! He's a cure, he is; an' the Limit!"

The effect of the Master Machinist's story was so depressing that the M.C. tried to hurry things on; any change of sentiment would, he thought, be and advantage. So he bustled along:

"Now, Mr. Turner Smith, you are the next on the roster. It is a pity we have not an easel and a canvas and paint box here, or even some cartridge pager and charcoal, so that you might give us a touch of your art – what I may call a plastic diversion of the current of narrative genius which has been enlivening the snowy waste around us." The artistic audience applauded this flight of metaphor – all except the young man from Oxford, who contented himself by saying loudly, "Pip-pip!" He had heard something like it before at the Union. The Scene Painter saw coming danger, for the Tragedian had put down his pipe and was clearing his throat; so he at once began:

If you enjoyed this, you might also like...
'The Gipsy Prophecy,' see page 296
'The Coming of Abel Behenna,' see page 408

The Coming of Abel Behenna

THE LITTLE CORNISH PORT of Pencastle was bright in the early April, when the sun had seemingly come to stay after a long and bitter winter. Boldly and blackly the rock stood out against a background of shaded blue, where the sky fading into mist met the far horizon. The sea was of true Cornish hue – sapphire, save where it became deep emerald green in the fathomless depths under the cliffs, where the seal caves opened their grim jaws. On the slopes the grass was parched and brown. The spikes of furze bushes were ashy grey, but the golden yellow of their flowers streamed along the hillside, dipping out in lines as the rock cropped up, and lessening into patches and dots till finally it died away all together where the sea winds swept round the jutting cliffs and cut short the vegetation as though with an ever-working aerial shears. The whole hillside, with its body of brown and flashes of yellow, was just like a colossal yellow-hammer.

The little harbour opened from the sea between towering cliffs, and behind a lonely rock, pierced with many caves and blow-holes through which the sea in storm time sent its thunderous voice, together with a fountain of drifting spume. Hence, it wound westwards in a serpentine course, guarded at its entrance by two little curving piers to left and right. These were roughly built of dark slates placed endways and held together with great beams bound with iron bands. Thence, it flowed up the rocky bed of the stream whose winter torrents had of old cut out its way amongst the hills.

This stream was deep at first, with here and there, where it widened, patches of broken rock exposed at low water, full of holes where crabs and lobsters were to be found at the ebb of the tide. From amongst the rocks rose sturdy posts, used for warping in the little coasting vessels which frequented the port. Higher up, the stream still flowed deeply, for the tide ran far inland, but always calmly for all the force of the wildest storm was broken below. Some quarter mile inland the stream was deep at high water, but at low tide there were at each side patches of the same broken rock as lower down, through the chinks of which the sweet water of the natural stream trickled and murmured after the tide had ebbed away. Here, too, rose mooring posts for the fishermen's boats.

At either side of the river was a row of cottages down almost on the level of high tide. They were pretty cottages, strongly and snugly built, with trim narrow gardens in front, full of old-fashioned plants, flowering currants, coloured primroses, wallflower, and stonecrop. Over the fronts of many of them climbed clematis and wisteria. The window sides and door posts of all were as white as snow, and the little pathway to each was paved with light coloured stones. At some of the doors were tiny porches, whilst at others were rustic seats cut from tree trunks or from old barrels; in nearly every case the window ledges were filled with boxes or pots of flowers or foliage plants.

Two men lived in cottages exactly opposite each other across the stream. Two men, both young, both good-looking, both prosperous, and who had been companions and rivals from their boyhood. Abel Behenna was dark with the gypsy darkness which the Phoenician mining wanderers left in their track; Eric Sanson – which the local antiquarian said was a corruption of Sagamanson – was fair, with the ruddy hue which marked the path of the wild Norseman.

These two seemed to have singled out each other from the very beginning to work and strive together, to fight for each other and to stand back to back in all endeavours. They had now put the coping-stone on their Temple of Unity by falling in love with the same girl. Sarah Trefusis was certainly the prettiest girl in Pencastle, and there was many a young man who would gladly have tried his fortune with her, but that there were two to contend against, and each of these the strongest and most resolute man in the port – except the other. The average young man thought that this was very hard, and on account of it bore no good will to either of the three principals: whilst the average young woman who had, lest worse should befall, to put up with the grumbling of her sweetheart, and the sense of being only second best which it implied, did not either, be sure, regard Sarah with friendly eye.

Thus it came, in the course of a year or so, for rustic courtship is a slow process, that the two men and woman found themselves thrown much together. They were all satisfied, so it did not matter, and Sarah, who was vain and something frivolous, took care to have her revenge on both men and women in a quiet way. When a young woman in her 'walking out' can only boast one not-quite-satisfied young man, it is no particular pleasure to her to see her escort cast sheep's eyes at a better-looking girl supported by two devoted swains.

At length there came a time which Sarah dreaded, and which she had tried to keep distant – the time when she had to make her choice between the two men. She liked them both, and, indeed, either of them might have satisfied the ideas of even a more exacting girl. But her mind was so constituted that she thought more of what she might lose, than of what she might gain; and whenever she thought she had made up her mind she became instantly assailed with doubts as to the wisdom of her choice. Always the man whom she had presumably lost became endowed afresh with a newer and more bountiful crop of advantages than had ever arisen from the possibility of his acceptance. She promised each man that on her birthday she would give him his answer, and that day, the 11th of April, had now arrived. The promises had been given singly and confidentially, but each was given to a man who was not likely to forget.

Early in the morning she found both men hovering round her door. Neither had taken the other into his confidence, and each was simply seeking an early opportunity of getting his answer, and advancing his suit if necessary. Damon, as a rule, does not take Pythias with him when making a proposal; and in the heart of each man his own affairs had a claim far above any requirements of friendship. So, throughout the day, they kept seeing each other out. The position was doubtless somewhat embarrassing to Sarah, and though the satisfaction of her vanity that she should be thus adored was very pleasing, yet there were moments when she was annoyed with both men for being so persistent. Her only consolation at such moments was that she saw, through the elaborate smiles of the other girls when in passing they noticed her door thus doubly guarded, the jealousy which filled their hearts.

Sarah's mother was a person of commonplace and sordid ideas, and, seeing all along the state of affairs, her one intention, persistently expressed to her daughter in the plainest words, was to so arrange matters that Sarah should get all that was possible out of both men. With this purpose she had cunningly kept herself as far as possible in the background in the matter of her daughter's wooings, and watched in silence. At first Sarah had been indignant with her for her sordid views; but, as usual, her weak nature gave way before persistence, and she had now got to the stage of acceptance. She was not surprised when her mother whispered to her in the little yard behind the house:

"Go up the hillside for a while; I want to talk to these two. They're both red-hot for ye, and now's the time to get things fixed!" Sarah began a feeble remonstrance, but her mother cut her short.

"I tell ye, girl, that my mind is made up! Both these men want ye, and only one can have ye, but before ye choose it'll be so arranged that ye'll have all that both have got! Don't argy, child! Go up the hillside, and when ye come back I'll have it fixed – I see a way quite easy!" So Sarah went up the hillside through the narrow paths between the golden furze, and Mrs. Trefusis joined the two men in the living-room of the little house.

She opened the attack with the desperate courage which is in all mothers when they think for their children, howsoever mean the thoughts may be.

"Ye two men, ye're both in love with my Sarah!"

Their bashful silence gave consent to the barefaced proposition. She went on.

"Neither of ye has much!" Again they tacitly acquiesced in the soft impeachment.

"I don't know that either of ye could keep a wife!" Though neither said a word their looks and bearing expressed distinct dissent. Mrs. Trefusis went on:

"But if ye'd put what ye both have together ye'd make a comfortable home for one of ye – and Sarah!" She eyed the men keenly, with her cunning eyes half shut, as she spoke; then satisfied from her scrutiny that the idea was accepted she went on quickly, as if to prevent argument:

"The girl likes ye both, and mayhap it's hard for her to choose. Why don't ye toss up for her? First put your money together – ye've each got a bit put by, I know. Let the lucky man take the lot and trade with it a bit, and then come home and marry her. Neither of ye's afraid, I suppose! And neither of ye'll say that he won't do that much for the girl that ye both say ye love!"

Abel broke the silence:

"It don't seem the square thing to toss for the girl! She wouldn't like it herself, and it doesn't seem – seem respectful like to her –" Eric interrupted. He was conscious that his chance was not so good as Abel's in case Sarah should wish to choose between them:

"Are ye afraid of the hazard?"

"Not me!" said Abel, boldly. Mrs. Trefusis, seeing that her idea was beginning to work, followed up the advantage.

"It is settled that ye put yer money together to make a home for her, whether ye toss for her or leave it for her to choose?"

"Yes," said Eric quickly, and Abel agreed with equal sturdiness. Mrs. Trefusis' little cunning eyes twinkled. She heard Sarah's step in the yard, and said:

"Well! Here she comes, and I leave it to her." And she went out.

During her brief walk on the hillside Sarah had been trying to make up her mind. She was feeling almost angry with both men for being the cause of her difficulty, and as she came into the room said shortly:

"I want to have a word with you both – come to the Flagstaff Rock, where we can be alone." She took her hat and went out of the house up the winding path to the steep rock crowned with a high flagstaff, where once the wreckers' fire basket used to burn. This was the rock which formed the northern jaw of the little harbour. There was only room on the path for two abreast, and it marked the state of things pretty well when, by a sort of implied arrangement, Sarah went first, and the two men followed, walking abreast and keeping step. By this time, each man's heart was boiling with jealousy. When they came to the top of the rock, Sarah stood against the flagstaff, and the two young men stood opposite her. She had chosen her position with knowledge and intention, for there was no room for anyone to stand beside her. They were all silent for a while; then Sarah began to laugh and said:

"I promised the both of you to give you an answer today. I've been thinking and thinking and thinking, till I began to get angry with you both for plaguing me so; and even now I don't seem any nearer than ever I was to making up my mind." Eric said suddenly:

"Let us toss for it, lass!" Sarah showed no indignation whatever at the proposition; her mother's eternal suggestion had schooled her to the acceptance of something of the kind, and her weak nature made it easy to her to grasp at any way out of the difficulty. She stood with downcast eyes idly picking at the sleeve of her dress, seeming to have tacitly acquiesced in the proposal. Both men instinctively realising this pulled each a coin from his pocket, spun it in the air, and dropped his other hand over the palm on which it lay. For a few seconds they remained thus, all silent; then Abel, who was the more thoughtful of the men, spoke:

"Sarah! Is this good?" As he spoke he removed the upper hand from the coin and placed the latter back in his pocket. Sarah was nettled.

"Good or bad, it's good enough for me! Take it or leave it as you like," she said, to which he replied quickly:

"Nay lass! Aught that concerns you is good enow for me. I did but think of you lest you might have pain or disappointment hereafter. If you love Eric better nor me, in God's name say so, and I think I'm man enow to stand aside. Likewise, if I'm the one, don't make us both miserable for life!" Face to face with a difficulty, Sarah's weak nature proclaimed itself; she put her hands before her face and began to cry, saying:

"It was my mother. She keeps telling me!" The silence which followed was broken by Eric, who said hotly to Abel:

"Let the lass alone, can't you? If she wants to choose this way, let her. It's good enough for me – and for you, too! She's said it now, and must abide by it!" Hereupon Sarah turned upon him in sudden fury, and cried:

"Hold your tongue! What is it to you, at any rate?" and she resumed her crying. Eric was so flabbergasted that he had not a word to say, but stood looking particularly foolish, with his mouth open and his hands held out with the coin still between them. All were silent till Sarah, taking her hands from her face laughed hysterically and said:

"As you two can't make up your minds, I'm going home!" and she turned to go.

"Stop," said Abel, in an authoritative voice. "Eric, you hold the coin, and I'll cry. Now, before we settle it, let us clearly understand: the man who wins takes all the money that we both have got, brings it to Bristol and ships on a voyage and trades with it. Then he comes back and marries Sarah, and they two keep all, whatever there may be, as the result of the trading. Is this what we understand?"

"Yes," said Eric.

"I'll marry him on my next birthday," said Sarah. Having said it the intolerably mercenary spirit of her action seemed to strike her, and impulsively she turned away with a bright blush. Fire seemed to sparkle in the eyes of both men. Said Eric: "A year so be! The man that wins is to have one year."

"Toss!" cried Abel, and the coin spun in the air. Eric caught it, and again held it between his outstretched hands.

"Heads!" cried Abel, a pallor sweeping over his face as he spoke. As he leaned forward to look Sarah leaned forward too, and their heads almost touched. He could feel her hair blowing on his cheek, and it thrilled through him like fire. Eric lifted his upper hand; the coin lay with its head up. Abel stepped forward and took Sarah in his arms. With a curse Eric hurled the coin far into the sea. Then he leaned against the flagstaff and scowled at the others with his hands thrust deep into his pockets. Abel whispered wild words of passion and delight into Sarah's ears, and as she listened she began to believe that fortune had rightly interpreted the wishes of her secret heart, and that she loved Abel best.

Presently Abel looked up and caught sight of Eric's face as the last ray of sunset struck it. The red light intensified the natural ruddiness of his complexion, and he looked as though he were steeped in blood. Abel did not mind his scowl, for now that his own heart was at rest he could feel unalloyed pity for his friend. He stepped over meaning to comfort him, and held out his hand, saying:

"It was my chance, old lad. Don't grudge it me. I'll try to make Sarah a happy woman, and you shall be a brother to us both!"

"Brother be damned!" was all the answer Eric made, as he turned away. When he had gone a few steps down the rocky path he turned and came back. Standing before Abel and Sarah, who had their arms round each other, he said:

"You have a year. Make the most of it! And be sure you're in time to claim your wife! Be back to have your banns up in time to be married on the 11th April. If you're not, I tell you I shall have my banns up, and you may get back too late."

"What do you mean, Eric? You are mad!"

"No more mad than you are, Abel Behenna. You go, that's your chance! I stay, that's mine! I don't mean to let the grass grow under my feet. Sarah cared no more for you than for me five minutes ago, and she may come back to that five minutes after you're gone! You won by a point only – the game may change."

"The game won't change!" said Abel shortly. "Sarah, you'll be true to me? You won't marry till I return?"

"For a year!" added Eric, quickly, "That's the bargain."

"I promise for the year," said Sarah. A dark look came over Abel's face, and he was about to speak, but he mastered himself and smiled.

"I mustn't be too hard or get angry tonight! Come, Eric! we played and fought together. I won fairly. I played fairly all the game of our wooing! You know that as well as I do; and now when I am going away, I shall look to my old and true comrade to help me when I am gone!"

"I'll help you none," said Eric, "so help me God!"

"It was God helped me," said Abel simply.

"Then let Him go on helping you,' said Eric angrily. "The Devil is good enough for me!" and without another word he rushed down the steep path and disappeared behind the rocks.

When he had gone Abel hoped for some tender passage with Sarah, but the first remark she made chilled him.

"How lonely it all seems without Eric!" and this note sounded till he had left her at home – and after.

Early on the next morning Abel heard a noise at his door, and on going out saw Eric walking rapidly away: a small canvas bag full of gold and silver lay on the threshold; on a small slip of paper pinned to it was written:

> *Take the money and go. I stay. God for you! The Devil for me! Remember the 11th of April.*
> – *ERIC SANSON.*

That afternoon Abel went off to Bristol, and a week later sailed on the *Star of the Sea* bound for Pahang. His money – including that which had been Eric's – was on board in the shape of a venture of cheap toys. He had been advised by a shrewd old mariner of Bristol whom he knew, and who knew the ways of the Chersonese, who predicted that every penny invested would be returned with a shilling to boot.

As the year wore on Sarah became more and more disturbed in her mind. Eric was always at hand to make love to her in his own persistent, masterful manner, and to this she did not object. Only one letter came from Abel, to say that his venture had proved successful, and that he had sent some two hundred pounds to the bank at Bristol, and was trading with fifty pounds still remaining in goods for China, whither the *Star of the Sea* was bound and whence she would return to Bristol. He suggested that Eric's share of the venture should be returned to him with his share of the profits. This proposition was treated with anger by Eric, and as simply childish by Sarah's mother.

More than six months had since then elapsed, but no other letter had come, and Eric's hopes which had been dashed down by the letter from Pahang, began to rise again. He perpetually assailed Sarah with an 'if!' If Abel did not return, would she then marry him? If the 11th April went by without Abel being in the port, would she give him over? If Abel had taken his fortune, and married another girl on the head of it, would she marry him, Eric, as soon as the truth were known? And so on in an endless variety of possibilities.

The power of the strong will and the determined purpose over the woman's weaker nature became in time manifest. Sarah began to lose her faith in Abel and to regard Eric as a possible husband; and a possible husband is in a woman's eye different to all other men. A new affection for him began to arise in her breast, and the daily familiarities of permitted courtship furthered the growing affection. Sarah began to regard Abel as rather a rock in the road of her life, and had it not been for her mother's constantly reminding her of the good fortune already laid by in the Bristol Bank she would have tried to have shut her eyes altogether to the fact of Abel's existence.

The 11th April was Saturday, so that in order to have the marriage on that day it would be necessary that the banns should be called on Sunday, 22nd March. From the beginning of that month Eric kept perpetually on the subject of Abel's absence, and his outspoken opinion that the latter was either dead or married began to become a reality to the woman's mind. As the first half of the month wore on Eric became more jubilant, and after church on the 15th he took Sarah for a walk to the Flagstaff Rock. There he asserted himself strongly:

"I told Abel, and you too, that if he was not here to put up his banns in time for the eleventh, I would put up mine for the twelfth. Now the time has come when I mean to do it. He hasn't kept his word" – here Sarah struck in out of her weakness and indecision:

"He hasn't broken it yet!" Eric ground his teeth with anger.

"If you mean to stick up for him," he said, as he smote his hands savagely on the flagstaff, which sent forth a shivering murmur, "well and good. I'll keep my part of the bargain. On Sunday I shall give notice of the banns, and you can deny them in the church if you will. If Abel is in Pencastle on the eleventh, he can have them cancelled, and his own put up; but till then, I take my course, and woe to anyone who stands in my way!" With that he flung himself down the rocky pathway, and Sarah could not but admire his Viking strength and spirit, as, crossing the hill, he strode away along the cliffs towards Bude.

During the week no news was heard of Abel, and on Saturday Eric gave notice of the banns of marriage between himself and Sarah Trefusis. The clergyman would have remonstrated with him, for although nothing formal had been told to the neighbours, it had been understood since Abel's departure that on his return he was to marry Sarah; but Eric would not discuss the question.

"It is a painful subject, sir," he said with a firmness which the parson, who was a very young man, could not but be swayed by. "Surely there is nothing against Sarah or me. Why should there be any bones made about the matter?" The parson said no more, and on the next day he read out the banns for the first time amidst an audible buzz from the congregation. Sarah was present, contrary to custom, and though she blushed furiously enjoyed her triumph over the other girls whose banns had not yet come. Before the week was over she began to make her wedding dress. Eric used to come and look at her at work and the sight thrilled through him. He used to say all sorts of pretty things to her at such times, and there were to both delicious moments of love-making.

The banns were read a second time on the 29th, and Eric's hope grew more and more fixed though there were to him moments of acute despair when he realised that the cup of happiness might be dashed from his lips at any moment, right up to the last. At such times he was full of passion – desperate and remorseless – and he ground his teeth and clenched his hands in a wild way as though some taint of the old Berserker fury of his ancestors still lingered in his blood. On the Thursday of that week he looked in on Sarah and found her, amid a flood of sunshine, putting finishing touches to her white wedding gown. His own heart was full of gaiety, and the sight of the woman who was so soon to be his own so occupied, filled him with a joy unspeakable, and he felt faint with languorous ecstasy. Bending over he kissed Sarah on the mouth, and then whispered in her rosy ear:

"Your wedding dress, Sarah! And for me!" As he drew back to admire her she looked up saucily, and said to him:

"Perhaps not for you. There is more than a week yet for Abel!" and then cried out in dismay, for with a wild gesture and a fierce oath Eric dashed out of the house, banging the door behind him. The incident disturbed Sarah more than she could have thought possible, for it awoke all her fears and doubts and indecision afresh

She cried a little, and put by her dress, and to soothe herself went out to sit for a while on the summit of the Flagstaff Rock.

When she arrived she found there a little group anxiously discussing the weather. The sea was calm and the sun bright, but across the sea were strange lines of darkness and light, and close in to shore the rocks were fringed with foam, which spread out in great white curves and circles as the currents drifted. The wind had backed, and came in sharp, cold puffs. The blow-hole, which ran under the Flagstaff Rock, from the rocky bay without to the harbour within, was booming at intervals, and the seagulls were screaming ceaselessly as they wheeled about the entrance of the port.

"It looks bad," she heard an old fisherman say to the coastguard. "I seen it just like this once before, when the East Indiaman *Coromandel* went to pieces in Dizzard Bay!" Sarah did not wait to hear more. She was of a timid nature where danger was concerned, and could not bear to hear of wrecks and disasters. She went home and resumed the completion of her dress, secretly determined to appease Eric when she should meet him with a sweet apology – and to take the earliest opportunity of being even with him after her marriage. The old fisherman's weather prophecy was justified. That night at dusk a wild storm came on. The sea rose and lashed the western coasts from Skye to Scilly and left a tale of disaster everywhere. The sailors and fishermen of Pencastle all turned out on the rocks and cliffs and watched eagerly. Presently, by a flash of lightning, a ketch was seen drifting under only a jib about half-a-mile outside the port. All eyes and all glasses were concentrated on her, waiting for the next flash, and when it came a chorus went up that it was the *Lovely Alice*, trading between Bristol and Penzance, and touching at all the little ports between.

"God help them!" said the harbour-master, "For nothing in this world can save them when they are between Bude and Tintagel and the wind on shore!" The coastguards exerted themselves, and, aided by brave hearts and willing hands, they brought the rocket apparatus up on the summit of the Flagstaff Rock. Then they burned blue lights so that those on board might see the harbour opening in case they could make any effort to reach it. They worked gallantly enough on board; but no skill or strength of man could avail.

Before many minutes were over the *Lovely Alice* rushed to her doom on the great island rock that guarded the mouth of the port. The screams of those on board were faintly borne on the tempest as they flung themselves into the sea in a last chance for life. The blue lights were kept burning, and eager eyes peered into the depths of the waters in case any face could be seen; and ropes were held ready to fling out in aid. But never a face was seen, and the willing arms rested idle. Eric was there amongst his fellows. His old Icelandic origin was never more apparent than in that wild hour. He took a rope, and shouted in the ear of the harbour-master:

"I shall go down on the rock over the seal cave. The tide is running up, and someone may drift in there!"

"Keep back, man!" came the answer. "Are you mad? One slip on that rock and you are lost: and no man could keep his feet in the dark on such a place in such a tempest!"

"Not a bit," came the reply. "You remember how Abel Behenna saved me there on a night like this when my boat went on the Gull Rock. He dragged me up from the deep water in the seal cave, and now someone may drift in there again as I did," and he was gone into the darkness. The projecting rock hid the light on the Flagstaff Rock, but he knew his way too well to miss it. His boldness and sureness of foot standing to him, he shortly stood on the great round-topped rock cut away beneath by the action of the waves over the entrance of the seal cave, where the water was fathomless. There he stood in comparative safety, for the concave shape of the rock beat back the waves with their own force, and though the water below him seemed to boil like a seething cauldron, just beyond the spot there was a space of almost calm.

The rock, too, seemed here to shut off the sound of the gale, and he listened as well as watched. As he stood there ready, with his coil of rope poised to throw, he thought he heard below him, just beyond the whirl of the water, a faint, despairing cry. He echoed it with a shout that rang into the night. Then he waited for the flash of lightning, and as it passed flung his rope out into the darkness where he had seen a face rising through the swirl of the foam. The rope was caught, for he felt a pull on it, and he shouted again in his mighty voice:

"Tie it round your waist, and I shall pull you up." Then when he felt that it was fast he moved along the rock to the far side of the sea cave, where the deep water was something stiller, and where he could get foothold secure enough to drag the rescued man on the overhanging rock. He began to pull, and shortly he knew from the rope taken in that the man he was now rescuing must soon be close to the top of the rock. He steadied himself for a moment, and drew a long breath, that he might at the next effort complete the rescue. He had just bent his back to the work when a flash of lightning revealed to each other the two men – the rescuer and the rescued.

Eric Sanson and Abel Behenna were face to face – and none knew of the meeting save themselves; and God.

On the instant a wave of passion swept through Eric's heart. All his hopes were shattered, and with the hatred of Cain his eyes looked out. He saw in the instant of recognition the joy in Abel's face that his was the hand to succour him, and this intensified his hate. Whilst the passion was on him he started back, and the rope ran out between his hands. His moment of hate was followed by an impulse of his better manhood, but it was too late.

Before he could recover himself, Abel encumbered with the rope that should have aided him, was plunged with a despairing cry back into the darkness of the devouring sea.

Then, feeling all the madness and the doom of Cain upon him, Eric rushed back over the rocks, heedless of the danger and eager only for one thing – to be amongst other people whose living noises would shut out that last cry which seemed to ring still in his ears. When he regained the Flagstaff Rock the men surrounded him, and through the fury of the storm he heard the harbour-master say:

"We feared you were lost when we heard a cry! How white you are! Where is your rope? Was there anyone drifted in?"

"No one," he shouted in answer, for he felt that he could never explain that he had let his old comrade slip back into the sea, and at the very place and under the very circumstances in which that comrade had saved his own life. He hoped by one bold lie to set the matter at rest for ever. There was no one to bear witness – and if he should have to carry that still white face in his eyes and that despairing cry in his ears for evermore – at least none should know of it. "No one," he cried, more loudly still. "I slipped on the rock, and the rope fell into the sea!" So saying he left them and, rushing down the steep path, gained his own cottage and locked himself within.

The remainder of that night he passed lying on his bed – dressed and motionless – staring upwards, and seeming to see through the darkness a pale face gleaming we n the lightning, with its glad recognition turning to ghastly despair, and to hear a cry which never ceased to echo in his soul.

In the morning the storm was over and all was smiling again, except that the sea was still boisterous with its unspent fury. Great pieces of wreck drifted into the port, and the sea around the island rock was strewn with others. Two bodies also drifted into the harbour – one the master of the wrecked ketch, the other a strange seaman whom no one knew.

Sarah saw nothing of Eric till the evening, and then he only looked in for a minute. He did not come into the house, but simply put his head in through the open window.

"Well, Sarah," he called out in a loud voice, though to her it did not ring truly, "is the wedding dress done? Sunday week, mind! Sunday week!"

Sarah was glad to have the reconciliation so easy; but, womanlike, when she saw the storm was over and her own fears groundless, she at once repeated the cause of offence.

"Sunday so be it," she said without looking up, "if Abel isn't there on Saturday!" Then she looked up saucily, though her heart was full of fear of another outburst on the part of her impetuous lover. But the window was empty; Eric had taken himself off, and with a pout she resumed her work. She saw Eric no more till Sunday afternoon, after the banns had been called the third time, when he came up to her before all the people with an air of proprietorship which half-pleased and half-annoyed her.

"Not yet, mister!" she said, pushing him away, as the other girls giggled. "Wait till Sunday next, if you please – the day after Saturday!" she added, looking at him saucily. The girls giggled again, and the young men guffawed. They thought it was the snub that touched him so that he became as white as a sheet as he turned away. But Sarah, who knew more than they did, laughed, for she saw triumph through the spasm of pain that overspread his face.

The week passed uneventfully; however, as Saturday drew nigh Sarah had occasional moments of anxiety, and as to Eric he went about at night-time like a man possessed. He restrained himself when others were by, but now and again he went down amongst the rocks and caves and shouted aloud. This seemed to relieve him somewhat, and he was better able to restrain himself for some time after. All Saturday he stayed in his own house and never left it. As he was to be married on the morrow, the neighbours thought it was shyness on his part, and did not trouble or notice him. Only once was he disturbed, and that was when the chief boatman came to him and sat down, and after a pause said:

"Eric, I was over in Bristol yesterday. I was in the ropemaker's getting a coil to replace the one you lost the night of the storm, and there I saw Michael Heavens of this place, who is a salesman there. He told me that Abel Behenna had come home the week ere last on the *Star of the Sea* from Canton, and that he had lodged a sight of money in the Bristol Bank in the name of Sarah Behenna. He told Michael so himself – and that he had taken passage on the *Lovely Alice* to Pencastle. Bear up, man," for Eric had with a groan dropped his head on his knees, with his face between his hands. "He was your old comrade, I know, but you couldn't help him. He must have gone down with the rest that awful night. I thought I'd better tell you, lest it might come some other way, and you might keep Sarah Trefusis from being frightened. They were good friends once, and women take these things to heart. It would not do to let her be pained with such a thing on her wedding day!" Then he rose and went away, leaving Eric still sitting disconsolately with his head on his knees.

"Poor fellow!" murmured the chief boatman to himself; "He takes it to heart. Well, well Right enough! They were true comrades once, and Abel saved him!"

The afternoon of that day, when the children had left school, they strayed as usual or half-holidays along' the quay and the paths by the cliffs. Presently some of them came running in a state of great excitement to the harbour, where a few men were unloading a coal ketch, and a great many were superintending the operation. One of the children called out:

"There is a porpoise in the harbour mouth! We saw it come through the blow-hole It had a long tail, and was deep under the water!"

"It was no porpoise," said another; "it was a seal; but it had a long tail! It came ou' of the seal cave!" The other children bore various testimony, but on two points they were unanimous – it, whatever 'it' was, had come through the blow-hole deep under the water, and had a long, thin tail – a tail so long that they could not see the end of it. There was much unmerciful chaffing of the children by the men on this point, but as it wa: evident that they had seen something, quite a number of persons, young and old, male and female, went along the high paths on either side of the harbour mouth to catch a glimpse of this new addition to the fauna of the sea, a long-tailed porpoise or seal.

The tide was now coming in. There was a slight breeze, and the surface of the water was rippled so that it was only at moments that anyone could see clearly into the deep water. After a spell of watching a woman called out that she saw something moving up the channel, just below where she was standing. There was a stampede to the spot, but by the time the crowd had gathered the breeze had freshened, and it was impossible to see with any distinctness below the surface of the water. On being questioned the woman described what she had seen, but in such an incoherent way that the whole thing was put down as an effect of imagination; had it not been for the children's report she would not have been credited at all. Her semi-hysterical statement that what she saw was 'like a pig with the entrails out' was only thought anything of by an old coastguard, who shook his head but did not make any remark For the remainder of the daylight this man was seen always on the bank, looking into the water, but always with disappointment manifest on his face.

Eric arose early on the next morning – he had not slept all night, and it was relief to him to move about in the light. He shaved himself with a hand that did not tremble, and dressed himself in his wedding clothes. There was a haggard look on his face, and he seemed as though he had grown years older in the last few days Still there was a wild, uneasy light of triumph in his eyes, and he kept murmuring to himself over and over again:

"This is my wedding-day! Abel cannot claim her now – living or dead! Living or dead Living or dead!" He sat in his arm-chair, waiting with an uncanny quietness for the church hour to arrive. When the bell began to ring he arose and passed out of his house, closing the door behind him. He looked at the river and saw the tide had just turned. In the church he sat with Sarah and her mother, holding Sarah's hand tightly in his all the time as though he feared to lose her. When the service was over they stood up together, and were married in the presence of the entire congregation; for no one left the church Both made the responses clearly – Eric's being even on the defiant side. When the wedding was over Sarah took her husband's arm, and they walked away together, the boys and younger girls being cuffed by their elders into a decorous behaviour, for the would fain have followed close behind their heels.

The way from the church led down to the back of Eric's cottage, a narrow passage being between it and that of his next neighbour. When the bridal couple had passed through this the remainder of the congregation, who had followed them at a little distance, were startled by a long, shrill scream from the bride. They rushed through the passage and found her on the bank with wild eyes, pointing to the river bed opposite Eric Sanson's door.

The falling tide had deposited there the body of Abel Behenna stark upon the broken rocks. The rope trailing from its waist had been twisted by the current round the mooring post, and had held it back whilst the tide had ebbed away from it. The right elbow had fallen in a chink in the rock, leaving the hand outstretched toward Sarah, with the open palm upward as though it were extended to receive hers, the pale drooping fingers open to the clasp.

All that happened afterwards was never quite known to Sarah Sanson. Whenever she would try to recollect there would become a buzzing in her ears and a dimness in her eyes, and all would pass away. The only thing that she could remember of it all – and this she never forgot – was Eric's breathing heavily, with his face whiter than that of the dead man, as he muttered under his breath:

"Devil's help! Devil's faith! Devil's price!"

If you enjoyed this, you might also like...
'The Gipsy Prophecy,' see page 296
'The Castle of the King,' see page 390

The Lady of the Shroud
Chapters III–V

[Publisher's Note: Prior to the events of the following extract, the character Rupert Sent Leger has learnt that he has inherited a castle from his uncle – but only on the condition that he agrees to live in that very castle for a year. Once there he begins to encounter some strange events...]

Chapter III
The Coming of the Lady

Rupert Sent Leger's Journal
April 3, 1907

I HAVE WAITED till now – well into midday – before beginning to set down the details of the strange episode of last night. I have spoken with persons whom I know to be of normal type. I have breakfasted, as usual heartily, and have every reason to consider myself in perfect health and sanity. So that the record following may be regarded as not only true in substance, but exact as to details. I have investigated and reported on too many cases for the Psychical Research Society to be ignorant of the necessity for absolute accuracy in such matters of even the minutest detail.

Yesterday was Tuesday, the second day of April, 1907. I passed a day of interest with its fair amount of work of varying kinds. Aunt Janet and I lunched together, had a stroll round the gardens after tea – especially examining the site for the new Japanese garden, which we shall call 'Janet's Garden.' We went in mackintoshes, for the rainy season is in its full, the only sign of its not being a repetition of the Deluge being that breaks in the continuance are beginning. They are short at present but will doubtless enlarge themselves as the season comes towards an end. We dined together at seven. After dinner I had a cigar, and then joined Aunt Janet for an hour in her drawing room. I left her at half-past ten, when I went to my own room and wrote some letters. At ten minutes past eleven I wound my watch, so I know the time accurately.

Having prepared for bed, I drew back the heavy curtain in front of my window, which opens on the marble steps into the Italian garden. I had put out my light before drawing back the curtain, for I wanted to have a look at the scene before turning in. Aunt Janet has always had an old-fashioned idea of the need (or propriety, I hardly know which) of keeping windows closed and curtains drawn. I am gradually getting her to leave my room alone in this respect, but at present the change is in its fitful stage, and, of course I must not hurry matters or be too persistent, as it would hurt her feelings.

This night was one of those under the old régime. It was a delight to look out, for the scene was perfect of its own kind. The long spell of rain – the ceaseless downpour which had for the time flooded everywhere – had passed, and water in abnormal places rather trickled than ran. We were now beginning to be in the sloppy rather than the deluged stage. There was plenty of light to see by, for the moon had begun to show out fitfully through the masses of flying clouds. The uncertain light made weird shadows with the shrubs and statues in the garden. The long straight walk which leads from the marble steps is strewn with fine sand white from the quartz strand in the nook to the south of the Castle. Tall shrubs of white holly, yew, juniper, cypress, and variegated maple and spiraea, which stood at intervals along the walk and its branches, appeared ghost-like in the fitful moonlight. The many vases and statues and urns, always like phantoms in a half-light, were more than ever weird. Last night the moonlight was unusually effective, and showed not only the gardens down to the defending wall, but the deep gloom of the great forest-trees beyond; and beyond that, again, to where the mountain chain began, the forest running up their silvered slopes flamelike in form, deviated here and there by great crags and the outcropping rocky sinews of the vast mountains.

Whilst I was looking at this lovely prospect, I thought I saw something white flit, like a modified white flash, at odd moments from one to another of the shrubs or statues – anything which would afford cover from observation. At first I was not sure whether I really saw anything or did not. This was in itself a little disturbing to me, for I have been so long trained to minute observation of facts surrounding me, on which often depend not only my own life, but the lives of others, that I have become accustomed to trust my eyes; and anything creating the faintest doubt in this respect is a cause of more or less anxiety to me. Now, however, that my attention was called to myself, I looked more keenly, and in a very short time was satisfied that something was moving – something clad in white.

It was natural enough that my thoughts should tend towards something uncanny – the belief that this place is haunted, conveyed in a thousand ways of speech and inference. Aunt Janet's eerie beliefs, fortified by her books on occult subjects – and of late, in our isolation from the rest of the world, the subject of daily conversations – helped to this end. No wonder, then, that, fully awake and with senses all on edge, I waited for some further manifestation from this ghostly visitor – as in my mind I took it to be. It must surely be a ghost or spiritual manifestation of some kind which moved in this silent way. In order to see and hear better, I softly moved back the folding grille, opened the French window, and stepped out, bare-footed and pyjama-clad as I was, on the marble terrace. How cold the wet marble was! How heavy smelled the rain-laden garden! It was as though the night and the damp, and even the moonlight, were drawing the aroma from all the flowers that blossomed. The whole night seemed to exhale heavy, half-intoxicating odours! I stood at the head of the marble steps, and all immediately before me was ghostly in the extreme – the white marble terrace and steps, the white walks of quartz-sand glistening under the fitful moonlight; the shrubs of white or pale green or yellow – all looking dim and ghostly in the glamorous light; the white statues and vases. And amongst them, still flitting noiselessly, that mysterious elusive figure which I could not say was based on fact or imagination. I held my breath, listening intently for every sound; but sound there was none, save those of the night and its denizens. Owls hooted in the forest; bats, taking advantage of the cessation of the rain, flitted about silently, like shadows in the air. But there was no more sign of moving ghost or phantom, or whatever I had seen might have been – if, indeed, there had been anything except imagination.

So, after waiting awhile, I returned to my room, closed the window, drew the grille across again, and dragged the heavy curtain before the opening; then, having extinguished my candles, went to bed in the dark. In a few minutes I must have been asleep.

"What was that?" I almost heard the words of my own thought as I sat up in bed wide awake. To memory rather than present hearing the disturbing sound had seemed like the faint tapping at the window. For some seconds I listened, mechanically but intently, with bated breath and that quick beating of the heart which in a timorous person speaks for fear, and for expectation in another. In the stillness the sound came again – this time a very, very faint but unmistakable tapping at the glass door.

I jumped up, drew back the curtain, and for a moment stood appalled.

There, outside on the balcony, in the now brilliant moonlight, stood a woman, wrapped in white grave-clothes saturated with water, which dripped on the marble floor, making a pool which trickled slowly down the wet steps. Attitude and dress and circumstance all conveyed the idea that, though she moved and spoke, she was not quick, but dead. She was young and very beautiful, but pale, like the grey pallor of death. Through the still white of her face, which made her look as cold as the wet marble she stood on, her dark eyes seemed to gleam with a strange but enticing lustre. Even in the unsearching moonlight, which is after all rather deceptive than illuminative, I could not but notice one rare quality of her eyes. Each had some quality of refraction which made it look as though it contained a star.

At every movement she made, the stars exhibited new beauties, of more rare and radiant force. She looked at me imploringly as the heavy curtain rolled back, and in eloquent gestures implored me to admit her. Instinctively I obeyed; I rolled back the steel grille, and threw open the French window. I noticed that she shivered and trembled as the glass door fell open. Indeed, she seemed so overcome with cold as to seem almost unable to move. In the sense of her helplessness all idea of the strangeness of the situation entirely disappeared. It was not as if my first idea of death taken from her cerements was negatived. It was simply that I did not think of it at all; I was content to accept things as they were – she was a woman, and in some dreadful trouble; that was enough.

I am thus particular about my own emotions, as I may have to refer to them again in matters of comprehension or comparison. The whole thing is so vastly strange and abnormal that the least thing may afterwards give some guiding light or clue to something otherwise not understandable. I have always found that in recondite matters first impressions are of more real value than later conclusions. We humans place far too little reliance on instinct as against reason; and yet instinct is the great gift of Nature to all animals for their protection and the fulfilment of their functions generally.

When I stepped out on the balcony, not thinking of my costume, I found that the woman was benumbed and hardly able to move. Even when I asked her to enter, and supplemented my words with gestures in case she should not understand my language, she stood stock-still, only rocking slightly to and fro as though she had just strength enough left to balance herself on her feet. I was afraid, from the condition in which she was, that she might drop down dead at any moment. So I took her by the hand to lead her in. But she seemed too weak to even make the attempt. When I pulled her slightly forward, thinking to help her, she tottered, and would have fallen had I not caught her in my arms. Then, half lifting her, I moved her forwards. Her feet, relieved of her weight, now seemed able to make the necessary effort; and so, I almost carrying her, we moved into the room. She was at the very end of her strength; I had to lift her over the sill. In obedience to her motion, I closed the French window and bolted it. I supposed the warmth of the room – though cool, it was warmer than the damp air without – affected her quickly, for on the instant she seemed to begin to recover herself. In a few seconds, as though she had reacquired her strength, she herself pulled the heavy curtain across the window. This left us in darkness, through which I heard her say in English:

"Light. Get a light!"

I found matches, and at once lit a candle. As the wick flared, she moved over to the door of the room, and tried if the lock and bolt were fastened. Satisfied as to this, she moved towards me, her wet shroud leaving a trail of moisture on the green carpet. By this time the wax of the candle had melted sufficiently to let me see her clearly. She was shaking and quivering as though in an ague; she drew the wet shroud around her piteously. Instinctively I spoke:

"Can I do anything for you?"

She answered, still in English, and in a voice of thrilling, almost piercing sweetness, which seemed somehow to go straight to my heart, and affected me strangely: "Give me warmth."

I hurried to the fireplace. It was empty; there was no fire laid. I turned to her, and said:

"Wait just a few minutes here. I shall call someone, and get help – and fire."

Her voice seemed to ring with intensity as she answered without a pause:

"No, no! Rather would I be" – here she hesitated for an instant, but as she caught sight of her cerements went on hurriedly – "as I am. I trust you – not others; and you must not betray my trust." Almost instantly she fell into a frightful fit of shivering, drawing again her death-clothes close to her, so piteously that it wrung my heart. I suppose I am a practical man. At any rate, I am accustomed to action. I took from its place beside my bed a thick Jaeger dressing-gown of dark brown – it was, of course, of extra length – and held it out to her as I said:

"Put that on. It is the only warm thing here which would be suitable. Stay; you must remove that wet – wet" – I stumbled about for a word that would not be offensive – "that frock – dress – costume – whatever it is." I pointed to where, in the corner of the room, stood a chintz-covered folding-screen which fences in my cold sponge bath, which is laid ready for me overnight, as I am an early riser.

She bowed gravely, and taking the dressing-gown in a long, white, finely-shaped hand, bore it behind the screen. There was a slight rustle, and then a hollow 'flop' as the wet garment fell on the floor; more rustling and rubbing, and a minute later she emerged wrapped from head to foot in the long Jaeger garment, which trailed on the floor behind her, though she was a tall woman. She was still shivering painfully, however. I took a flask of brandy and a glass from a cupboard, and offered her some; but with a motion of her hand she refused it, though she moaned grievously.

"Oh, I am so cold – so cold!" Her teeth were chattering. I was pained at her sad condition, and said despairingly, for I was at my wits' end to know what to do:

"Tell me anything that I can do to help you, and I will do it. I may not call help; there is no fire – nothing to make it with; you will not take some brandy. What on earth can I do to give you warmth?"

Her answer certainly surprised me when it came, though it was practical enough – so practical that I should not have dared to say it. She looked me straight in the face for a few seconds before speaking. Then, with an air of girlish innocence which disarmed suspicion and convinced me at once of her simple faith, she said in a voice that at once thrilled me and evoked all my pity:

"Let me rest for a while, and cover me up with rugs. That may give me warmth. I am dying of cold. And I have a deadly fear upon me – a deadly fear. Sit by me, and let me hold your hand. You are big and strong, and you look brave. It will reassure me. I am not myself a coward, but tonight fear has got me by the throat. I can hardly breathe. Do let me stay till I am warm. If you only knew what I have gone through, and have to go through still, I am sure you would pity me and help me."

To say that I was astonished would be a mild description of my feelings. I was not shocked. The life which I have led was not one which makes for prudery. To travel in strange places amongst strange peoples with strange views of their own is to have odd experiences and peculiar adventures now and again; a man without human passions is not the type necessary for an adventurous life, such as I myself have had. But even a man of passions and experiences can, when he respects a woman, be shocked – even prudish – where his own opinion of her is concerned. Such must bring to her guarding any generosity which he has, and any self-restraint also. Even should she place herself in a doubtful position, her honour calls to his honour. This is a call which may not be – *must* not be – unanswered. Even passion must pause for at least a while at sound of such a trumpet-call.

This woman I did respect – much respect. Her youth and beauty; her manifest ignorance of evil; her superb disdain of convention, which could only come through hereditary dignity; her terrible fear and suffering – for there must be more in her unhappy condition than meets the eye – would all demand respect, even if one did not hasten to yield it. Nevertheless, I thought it necessary to enter a protest against her embarrassing suggestion. I certainly did feel a fool when making it, also a cad. I can truly say it was made only for her good, and out of the best of me, such as I am. I felt impossibly awkward; and stuttered and stumbled before I spoke:

"But surely – the convenances! Your being here alone at night! Mrs. Grundy – convention – the –"

She interrupted me with an incomparable dignity – a dignity which had the effect of shutting me up like a clasp-knife and making me feel a decided inferior – and a poor show at that. There was such a gracious simplicity and honesty in it, too, such self-respecting knowledge of herself and her position, that I could be neither angry nor hurt. I could only feel ashamed of myself, and of my own littleness of mind and morals. She seemed in her icy coldness – now spiritual as well as bodily – like an incarnate figure of Pride as she answered:

"What are convenances or conventions to me! If you only knew where I have come from – the existence (if it can be called so) which I have had – the loneliness – the horror! And besides, it is for me to *make* conventions, not to yield my personal freedom of action to them. Even as I am – even here and in this garb – I am above convention. Convenances do not trouble me or hamper me. That, at least, I have won by what I have gone through, even if it had never come to me through any other way. Let me stay." She said the last words, in spite of all her pride, appealingly. But still, there was a note of high pride in all this – in all she said and did, in her attitude and movement, in the tones of her voice, in the loftiness of her carriage and the steadfast look of her open, starlit eyes. Altogether, there was something so rarely lofty in herself and all that clad her that, face to face with it and with her, my feeble attempt at moral precaution seemed puny, ridiculous, and out of place. Without a word in the doing, I took from an old chiffonier chest an armful of blankets, several of which I threw over her as she lay, for in the meantime, having replaced the coverlet, she had lain down at length on the bed. I took a chair, and sat down beside her. When she stretched out her hand from beneath the pile of wraps, I took it in mine, saying:

"Get warm and rest. Sleep if you can. You need not fear; I shall guard you with my life."

She looked at me gratefully, her starry eyes taking a new light more full of illumination than was afforded by the wax candle, which was shaded from her by my body.... She was horribly cold, and her teeth chattered so violently that I feared lest she should have incurred some dangerous evil from her wetting and the cold that followed it. I felt, however, so awkward that I could find no words to express my fears; moreover, I hardly dared say anything at all regarding herself after the haughty way in which she had received my well-meant protest. Manifestly I was but to her as a sort of refuge and provider of heat, altogether impersonal, and not to be regarded in any degree as an individual. In these humiliating circumstances what could I do but sit quiet – and wait developments?

Little by little the fierce chattering of her teeth began to abate as the warmth of her surroundings stole through her. I also felt, even in this strangely awakening position, the influence of the quiet; and sleep began to steal over me. Several times I tried to fend it off, but, as I could not make any overt movement without alarming my strange and beautiful companion, I had to yield myself to drowsiness. I was still in such an overwhelming stupor of surprise that I could not even think freely. There was nothing for me but to control myself and wait. Before I could well fix my thoughts I was asleep.

I was recalled to consciousness by hearing, even through the pall of sleep that bound me, the crowing of a cock in some of the out-offices of the castle. At the same instant the figure, lying deathly still but for the gentle heaving of her bosom, began to struggle wildly. The sound had won through the gates of her sleep also. With a swift, gliding motion she slipped from the bed to the floor, saying in a fierce whisper as she pulled herself up to her full height:

"Let me out! I must go! I must go!"

By this time I was fully awake, and the whole position of things came to me in an instant which I shall never – can never – forget: the dim light of the candle, now nearly burned down to the socket, all the dimmer from the fact that the first grey gleam of morning was stealing in round the edges of the heavy curtain; the tall, slim figure in the brown dressing-gown whose over-length trailed on the floor, the black hair showing glossy in the light, and increasing by contrast the marble whiteness of the face, in which the black eyes sent through their stars fiery gleams. She appeared quite in a frenzy of haste; her eagerness was simply irresistible.

I was so stupefied with amazement, as well as with sleep, that I did not attempt to stop her, but began instinctively to help her by furthering her wishes. As she ran behind the screen, and, as far as sound could inform me – began frantically to disrobe herself of the warm dressing-gown and to don again the ice-cold wet shroud, I pulled back the curtain from the window, and drew the bolt of the glass door. As I did so she was already behind me, shivering. As I threw open the door she glided out with a swift silent movement, but trembling in an agonized way. As she passed me, she murmured in a low voice, which was almost lost in the chattering of her teeth:

"Oh, thank you – thank you a thousand times! But I must go. I *must*! I *must*! I shall come again, and try to show my gratitude. Do not condemn me as ungrateful – till then." And she was gone.

I watched her pass the length of the white path, flitting from shrub to shrub or statue as she had come. In the cold grey light of the undeveloped dawn she seemed even more ghostly than she had done in the black shadow of the night.

When she disappeared from sight in the shadow of the wood, I stood on the terrace for a long time watching, in case I should be afforded another glimpse of her, for there was now no doubt in my mind that she had for me some strange attraction. I felt even then that the look in those glorious starry eyes would be with me always so long as I might live. There was some fascination which went deeper than my eyes or my flesh or my heart – down deep into the very depths of my soul. My mind was all in a whirl, so that I could hardly think coherently. It all was like a dream; the reality seemed far away. It was not possible to doubt that the phantom figure which had been so close to me during the dark hours of the night was actual flesh and blood. Yet she was so cold, so cold! Altogether I could not fix my mind to either proposition: that it was a living woman who had held my hand, or a dead body reanimated for the time or the occasion in some strange manner.

The difficulty was too great for me to make up my mind upon it, even had I wanted to. But, in any case, I did not want to. This would, no doubt, come in time. But till then I wished to dream on, as anyone does in a dream which can still be blissful though there be pauses of pain, or ghastliness, or doubt, or terror.

So I closed the window and drew the curtain again, feeling for the first time the cold in which I had stood on the wet marble floor of the terrace when my bare feet began to get warm on the soft carpet. To get rid of the chill feeling I got into the bed on which *she* had lain, and as the warmth restored me tried to think coherently. For a short while I was going over the facts of the night – or what seemed as facts to my remembrance. But as I continued to think, the possibilities of any result seemed to get less, and I found myself vainly trying to reconcile with the logic of life the grim episode of the night. The effort proved to be too much for such concentration as was left to me; moreover, interrupted sleep was clamant, and would not be denied. What I dreamt of – if I dreamt at all – I know not. I only know that I was ready for waking when the time came. It came with a violent knocking at my door. I sprang from bed, fully awake in a second, drew the bolt, and slipped back to bed. With a hurried "May I come in?" Aunt Janet entered. She seemed relieved when she saw me, and gave without my asking an explanation of her perturbation:

"Oh, laddie, I hae been so uneasy aboot ye all the nicht. I hae had dreams an' veesions an' a' sorts o' uncanny fancies. I fear that –" She was by now drawing back the curtain, and as her eyes took in the marks of wet all over the floor the current of her thoughts changed:

"Why, laddie, whatever hae ye been doin' wi' yer baith? Oh, the mess ye hae made! 'Tis sinful to gie sic trouble an' waste..." And so she went on. I was glad to hear the tirade, which was only what a good housewife, outraged in her sentiments of order, would have made. I listened in patience – with pleasure when I thought of what she would have thought (and said) had she known the real facts. I was well pleased to have got off so easily.

* * *

April 10, 1907.

FOR SOME DAYS after what I call 'the episode' I was in a strange condition of mind. I did not take anyone – not even Aunt Janet – into confidence. Even she dear, and open-hearted and liberal-minded as she is, might not have understood well enough to be just and tolerant; and I did not care to hear any adverse comment on my strange visitor. Somehow I could not bear the thought of anyone finding fault with her or in her, though, strangely enough, I was eternally defending her to myself; for, despite my wishes, embarrassing thoughts *would* come again and again, and again in all sorts and variants of queries difficult to answer. I found myself defending her, sometimes as a woman hard pressed by spiritual fear and physical suffering, sometimes as not being amenable to laws that govern the Living. Indeed, I could not make up my mind whether I looked on her as a living human being or as one with some strange existence in another world, and having only a chance foothold in our own. In such doubt imagination began to work, and thoughts of evil, of danger, of doubt, even of fear, began to crowd on me with such persistence and in such varied forms that I found my instinct of reticence growing into a settled purpose. The value of this instinctive precaution was promptly shown by Aunt Janet's state of mind, with consequent revelation of it. She became full of gloomy prognostications and what I thought were morbid fears. For the first time in my life I discovered that Aunt Janet had nerves! I had long had a secret belief that she was gifted, to some degree at any rate, with Second Sight, which quality, or whatever it is, skilled in the powers if not the lore of superstition, manages to keep at stretch not only the mind of its immediate pathic, but of others relevant to it. Perhaps this natural quality had received a fresh impetus from the arrival of some cases of her books sent on by Sir Colin. She appeared to read and reread these works, which were chiefly on occult subjects, day and night, except when she was imparting to me choice excerpts of the most baleful and fearsome kind. Indeed, before a week was over I found myself to be an expert in the history of the cult, as well as in its manifestations, which latter I had been versed in for a good many years.

The result of all this was that it set me brooding. Such, at least, I gathered was the fact when Aunt Janet took me to task for it. She always speaks out according to her convictions, so that her thinking I brooded was to me a proof that I did; and after a personal examination I came – reluctantly – to the conclusion that she was right, so far, at any rate, as my outer conduct was concerned. The state of mind I was in, however, kept me from making any acknowledgment of it – the real cause of my keeping so much to myself and of being so *distrait*. And so I went on, torturing myself as before with introspective questioning; and she, with her mind set on my actions, and endeavouring to find a cause for them, continued and expounded her beliefs and fears.

Her nightly chats with me when we were alone after dinner – for I had come to avoid her questioning at other times – kept my imagination at high pressure.

Despite myself, I could not but find new cause for concern in the perennial founts of her superstition. I had thought, years ago, that I had then sounded the depths of this branch of psychicism; but this new phase of thought, founded on the really deep hold which the existence of my beautiful visitor and her sad and dreadful circumstances had taken upon me, brought me a new concern in the matter of self-importance. I came to think that I must reconstruct my self-values, and begin a fresh understanding of ethical beliefs. Do what I would, my mind would keep turning on the uncanny subjects brought before it. I began to apply them one by one to my own late experience, and unconsciously to try to fit them in turn to the present case.

The effect of this brooding was that I was, despite my own will, struck by the similarity of circumstances bearing on my visitor, and the conditions apportioned by tradition and superstition to such strange survivals from earlier ages as these partial existences which are rather Undead than Living – still walking the earth, though claimed by the world of the Dead. Amongst them are the Vampire, or the Wehr-Wolf. To this class also might belong in a measure the Doppelgänger – one of whose dual existences commonly belongs to the actual world around it. So, too, the denizens of the world of Astralism. In any of these named worlds there is a material presence – which must be created, if only for a single or periodic purpose. It matters not whether a material presence already created can be receptive of a disembodied soul, or a soul unattached can have a body built up for it or around it; or, again, whether the body of a dead person can be made seeming quick through some diabolic influence manifested in the present, or an inheritance or result of some baleful use of malefic power in the past. The result is the same in each case, though the ways be widely different: a soul and a body which are not in unity but brought together for strange purposes through stranger means and by powers still more strange.

Through much thought and a process of exclusions the eerie form which seemed to be most in correspondence with my adventure, and most suitable to my fascinating visitor, appeared to be the Vampire. Doppelgänger, Astral creations, and all such-like, did not comply with the conditions of my night experience. The Wehr-Wolf is but a variant of the Vampire, and so needed not to be classed or examined at all. Then it was that, thus focussed, the Lady of the Shroud (for so I came to hold her in my mind) began to assume a new force. Aunt Janet's library afforded me clues which I followed with avidity. In my secret heart I hated the quest, and did not wish to go on with it. But in this I was not my own master. Do what I would – brush away doubts never so often, new doubts and imaginings came in their stead. The circumstance almost repeated the parable of the Seven Devils who took the place of the exorcised one. Doubts I could stand. Imaginings I could stand. But doubts and imaginings together made a force so fell that I was driven to accept any reading of the mystery which might presumably afford a foothold for satisfying thought. And so I came to accept tentatively the Vampire theory – accept it, at least, so far as to examine it as judicially as was given me to do. As the days wore on, so the conviction grew. The more I read on the subject, the more directly the evidences pointed towards this view. The more I thought, the more obstinate became the conviction. I ransacked Aunt Janet's volumes again and again to find anything to the contrary; but in vain. Again, no matter how obstinate were my convictions at any given time, unsettlement came with fresh thinking over the argument, so that I was kept in a harassing state of uncertainty.

Briefly, the evidence in favour of accord between the facts of the case and the Vampire theory were:

Her coming was at night – the time the Vampire is according to the theory, free to move at will.

She wore her shroud – a necessity of coming fresh from grave or tomb; for there is nothing occult about clothing which is not subject to astral or other influences.

She had to be helped into my room – in strict accordance with what one sceptical critic of occultism has called 'the Vampire etiquette.'

She made violent haste in getting away at cock-crow.

She seemed preternaturally cold; her sleep was almost abnormal in intensity, and yet the sound of the cock-crowing came through it.

These things showed her to be subject to *some* laws, though not in exact accord within those which govern human beings. Under the stress of such circumstances as she must have gone through, her vitality seemed more than human – the quality of vitality which could outlive ordinary burial. Again, such purpose as she had shown in donning, under stress of some compelling direction, her ice-cold wet shroud, and, wrapt in it, going out again into the night, was hardly normal for a woman.

But if so, and if she was indeed a Vampire, might not whatever it may be that holds such beings in thrall be by some means or other exorcised? To find the means must be my next task. I am actually pining to see her again. Never before have I been stirred to my depths by anyone. Come it from Heaven or Hell, from the Earth or the Grave, it does not matter; I shall make it my task to win her back to life and peace. If she be indeed a Vampire, the task may be hard and long; if she be not so, and if it be merely that circumstances have so gathered round her as to produce that impression, the task may be simpler and the result more sweet. No, not more sweet; for what can be more sweet than to restore the lost or seemingly lost soul of the woman you love! There, the truth is out at last! I suppose that I have fallen in love with her. If so, it is too late for me to fight against it. I can only wait with what patience I can till I see her again. But to that end I can do nothing. I know absolutely nothing about her – not even her name. Patience!

* * *

April 16, 1907.

THE ONLY RELIEF I have had from the haunting anxiety regarding the Lady of the Shroud has been in the troubled state of my adopted country. There has evidently been something up which I have not been allowed to know. The mountaineers are troubled and restless; are wandering about, singly and in parties, and holding meetings in strange places. This is what I gather used to be in old days when intrigues were on foot with Turks, Greeks, Austrians, Italians, Russians. This concerns me vitally, for my mind has long been made up to share the fortunes of the Land of the Blue Mountains. For good or ill I mean to stay here: *J'y suis, j'y reste.* I share henceforth the lot of the Blue Mountaineers; and not Turkey, nor Greece, nor Austria, nor Italy, nor Russia – no, not France nor Germany either; not man nor God nor Devil shall drive me from my purpose. With these patriots I throw in my lot! My only difficulty seemed at first to be with the men themselves. They are so proud that at the beginning I feared they would not even accord me the honour of being one of them! However, things always move on somehow, no matter what difficulties there be at the beginning. Never mind! When one looks back at an accomplished fact the beginning is not to be seen – and if it were it would not matter. It is not of any account, anyhow.

I heard that there was going to be a great meeting near here yesterday afternoon, and I attended it. I think it was a success. If such is any proof, I felt elated as well as satisfied when I came away. Aunt Janet's Second Sight on the subject was comforting, though grim, and in a measure disconcerting. When I was saying good-night she asked me to bend down my head. As I did so, she laid her hands on it and passed them all over it. I heard her say to herself:

"Strange! There's nothing there; yet I could have sworn I saw it!" I asked her to explain, but she would not. For once she was a little obstinate, and refused point blank to even talk of the subject. She was not worried nor unhappy; so I had no cause for concern. I said nothing, but I shall wait and see. Most mysteries become plain or disappear altogether in time. But about the meeting – lest I forget!

When I joined the mountaineers who had assembled, I really think they were glad to see me; though some of them seemed adverse, and others did not seem over well satisfied. However, absolute unity is very seldom to be found. Indeed, it is almost impossible; and in a free community is not altogether to be desired. When it is apparent, the gathering lacks that sense of individual feeling which makes for the real consensus of opinion – which is the real unity of purpose. The meeting was at first, therefore, a little cold and distant. But presently it began to thaw, and after some fiery harangues I was asked to speak. Happily, I had begun to learn the Balkan language as soon as ever Uncle Roger's wishes had been made known to me, and as I have some facility of tongues and a great deal of experience, I soon began to know something of it. Indeed, when I had been here a few weeks, with opportunity of speaking daily with the people themselves, and learned to understand the intonations and vocal inflexions, I felt quite easy in speaking it. I understood every word which had up to then been spoken at the meeting, and when I spoke myself I felt that they understood. That is an experience which every speaker has in a certain way and up to a certain point. He knows by some kind of instinct if his hearers are with him; if they respond, they must certainly have understood. Last night this was marked. I felt it every instant I was talking and when I came to realize that the men were in strict accord with my general views, I took them into confidence with regard to my own personal purpose. It was the beginning of a mutual trust; so for peroration I told them that I had come to the conclusion that what they wanted most for their own protection and the security and consolidation of their nation was arms – arms of the very latest pattern. Here they interrupted me with wild cheers, which so strung me up that I went farther than I intended, and made a daring venture. "Ay," I repeated, "the security and consolidation of your country – of *our* country, for I have come to live amongst you. Here is my home whilst I live. I am with you heart and soul. I shall live with you, fight shoulder to shoulder with you, and, if need be, shall die with you!" Here the shouting was terrific, and the younger men raised their guns to fire a salute in Blue Mountain fashion. But on the instant the Vladika held up his hands and motioned them to desist. In the immediate silence he spoke, sharply at first, but later ascending to a high pitch of single-minded, lofty eloquence. His words rang in my ears long after the meeting was over and other thoughts had come between them and the present.

"Silence!" he thundered. "Make no echoes in the forest or through the hills at this dire time of stress and threatened danger to our land. Bethink ye of this meeting, held here and in secret, in order that no whisper of it may be heard afar. Have ye all, brave men of the Blue Mountains, come hither through the forest like shadows that some of you, thoughtless, may enlighten your enemies as to our secret purpose? The thunder of your guns would doubtless sound well in the ears of those who wish us ill and try to work us wrong. Fellow-countrymen, know ye not that the Turk is awake once more for our harming? The Bureau of Spies has risen from the torpor which came on it when the purpose against our Teuta roused our mountains to such anger that the frontiers blazed with passion, and were swept with fire and sword. Moreover, there is a traitor somewhere in the land, or else incautious carelessness has served the same base purpose. Something of our needs – our doing, whose secret we have tried to hide, has gone out. The myrmidons of the Turk are close on our borders, and it may be that some of them have passed our guards and are amidst us unknown. So it behoves us doubly to be discreet. Believe me that I share with you, my brothers, our love for the gallant Englishman who has come amongst us to share our sorrows and ambitions – and I trust it may be our joys. We are all united in the wish to do him honour – though not in the way by which danger might be carried on the wings of love. My brothers, our newest brother comes to us from the Great Nation which amongst the nations has been our only friend, and which has ere now helped us in our direst need – that mighty Britain whose hand has ever been raised in the cause of freedom. We of the Blue Mountains know her best as she stands with sword in hand face to face with our foes. And this, her son and now our brother, brings further to our need the hand of a giant and the heart of a lion. Later on, when danger does not ring us round, when silence is no longer our outer guard; we shall bid him welcome in true fashion of our land. But till then he will believe – for he is great-hearted – that our love and thanks and welcome are not to be measured by sound. When the time comes, then shall be sound in his honour – not of rifles alone, but bells and cannon and the mighty voice of a free people shouting as one. But now we must be wise and silent, for the Turk is once again at our gates. Alas! The cause of his former coming may not be, for she whose beauty and nobility and whose place in our nation and in our hearts tempted him to fraud and violence is not with us to share even our anxiety."

Here his voice broke, and there arose from all a deep wailing sound, which rose and rose till the woods around us seemed broken by a mighty and long-sustained sob. The orator saw that his purpose was accomplished, and with a short sentence finished his harangue: "But the need of our nation still remains!" Then, with an eloquent gesture to me to proceed, he merged in the crowd and disappeared.

How could I even attempt to follow such a speaker with any hope of success? I simply told them what I had already done in the way of help, saying:

"As you needed arms, I have got them. My agent sends me word through the code between us that he has procured for me – for us – fifty thousand of the newest-pattern rifles, the French Ingis-Malbron, which has surpassed all others, and sufficient ammunition to last for a year of war. The first section is in hand, and will soon be ready for consignment. There are other war materials, too, which, when they arrive, will enable every man and woman – even the children – of our land to take a part in its defence should such be needed. My brothers, I am with you in all things, for good or ill!"

It made me very proud to hear the mighty shout which arose. I had felt exalted before, but now this personal development almost unmanned me. I was glad of the long-sustained applause to recover my self-control.

I was quite satisfied that the meeting did not want to hear any other speaker, for they began to melt away without any formal notification having been given. I doubt if there will be another meeting soon again. The weather has begun to break, and we are in for another spell of rain. It is disagreeable, of course; but it has its own charm. It was during a spell of wet weather that the Lady of the Shroud came to me. Perhaps the rain may bring her again. I hope so, with all my soul.

* * *

April 23, 1907.

THE RAIN HAS CONTINUED for four whole days and nights, and the low-lying ground is like a quagmire in places. In the sunlight the whole mountains glisten with running streams and falling water. I feel a strange kind of elation, but from no visible cause. Aunt Janet rather queered it by telling me, as she said good-night, to be very careful of myself, as she had seen in a dream last night a figure in a shroud. I fear she was not pleased that I did not take it with all the seriousness that she did. I would not wound her for the world if I could help it, but the idea of a shroud gets too near the bone to be safe, and I had to fend her off at all hazards. So when I doubted if the Fates regarded the visionary shroud as of necessity appertaining to me, she said, in a way that was, for her, almost sharp:

"Take care, laddie. 'Tis ill jesting wi' the powers o' time Unknown."

Perhaps it was that her talk put the subject in my mind. The woman needed no such aid; she was always there; but when I locked myself into my room that night, I half expected to find her in the room. I was not sleepy, so I took a book of Aunt Janet's and began to read. The title was *On the Powers and Qualities of Disembodied Spirits*. "Your grammar," said I to the author, "is hardly attractive, but I may learn something which might apply to her. I shall read your book." Before settling down to it, however, I thought I would have a look at the garden. Since the night of the visit the garden seemed to have a new attractiveness for me: a night seldom passed without my having a last look at it before turning in. So I drew the great curtain and looked out.

The scene was beautiful, but almost entirely desolate. All was ghastly in the raw, hard gleams of moonlight coming fitfully through the masses of flying cloud. The wind was rising, and the air was damp and cold. I looked round the room instinctively, and noticed that the fire was laid ready for lighting, and that there were small-cut logs of wood piled beside the hearth. Ever since that night I have had a fire laid ready. I was tempted to light it, but as I never have a fire unless I sleep in the open, I hesitated to begin. I went back to the window, and, opening the catch, stepped out on the terrace. As I looked down the white walk and let my eyes range over the expanse of the garden, where everything glistened as the moonlight caught the wet, I half expected to see some white figure flitting amongst the shrubs and statues. The whole scene of the former visit came back to me so vividly that I could hardly believe that any time had passed since then. It was the same scene, and again late in the evening. Life in Vissarion was primitive, and early hours prevailed – though not so late as on that night.

As I looked I thought I caught a glimpse of something white far away. It was only a ray of moonlight coming through the rugged edge of a cloud. But all the same it set me in a strange state of perturbation. Somehow I seemed to lose sight of my own identity. It was as though I was hypnotized by the situation or by memory, or perhaps by some occult force. Without thinking of what I was doing, or being conscious of any reason for it, I crossed the room and set light to the fire. Then I blew out the candle and came to the window again. I never thought it might be a foolish thing to do – to stand at a window with a light behind me in this country, where every man carries a gun with him always. I was in my evening clothes, too, with my breast well marked by a white shirt. I opened the window and stepped out on the terrace. There I stood for many minutes, thinking. All the time my eyes kept ranging over the garden. Once I thought I saw a white figure moving, but it was not followed up, so, becoming conscious that it was again beginning to rain, I stepped back into the room, shut the window, and drew the curtain. Then I realized the comforting appearance of the fire, and went over and stood before it.

Hark! Once more there was a gentle tapping at the window. I rushed over to it and drew the curtain.

There, out on the rain-beaten terrace, stood the white shrouded figure, more desolate-appearing than ever. Ghastly pale she looked, as before, but her eyes had an eager look which was new. I took it that she was attracted by the fire, which was by now well ablaze, and was throwing up jets of flame as the dry logs crackled. The leaping flames threw fitful light across the room, and every gleam threw the white-clad figure into prominence, showing the gleam of the black eyes, and fixing the stars that lay in them.

Without a word I threw open the window, and, taking the white hand extended to me, drew into the room the Lady of the Shroud.

As she entered and felt the warmth of the blazing fire, a glad look spread over her face. She made a movement as if to run to it. But she drew back an instant after, looking round with instinctive caution. She closed the window and bolted it, touched the lever which spread the grille across the opening, and pulled close the curtain behind it. Then she went swiftly to the door and tried if it was locked. Satisfied as to this, she came quickly over to the fire, and, kneeling before it, stretched out her numbed hands to the blaze. Almost on the instant her wet shroud began to steam. I stood wondering. The precautions of secrecy in the midst of her suffering – for that she did suffer was only too painfully manifest – must have presupposed some danger. Then and there my mind was made up that there should no harm assail her that I by any means could fend off. Still, the present must be attended to; pneumonia and other ills stalked behind such a chill as must infallibly come on her unless precautions were taken. I took again the dressing-gown which she had worn before and handed it to her, motioning as I did so towards the screen which had made a dressing-room for her on the former occasion. To my surprise she hesitated. I waited. She waited, too, and then laid down the dressing-gown on the edge of the stone fender. So I spoke:

"Won't you change as you did before? Your – your frock can then be dried. Do! It will be so much safer for you to be dry clad when you resume your own dress."

"How can I whilst you are here?"

Her words made me stare, so different were they from her acts of the other visit. I simply bowed – speech on such a subject would be at least inadequate – and walked over to the window. Passing behind the curtain, I opened the window. Before stepping out on to the terrace, I looked into the room and said:

"Take your own time. There is no hurry. I dare say you will find there all you may want. I shall remain on the terrace until you summon me." With that I went out on the terrace, drawing close the glass door behind me.

I stood looking out on the dreary scene for what seemed a very short time, my mind in a whirl. There came a rustle from within, and I saw a dark brown figure steal round the edge of the curtain. A white hand was raised, and beckoned me to come in. I entered, bolting the window behind me. She had passed across the room, and was again kneeling before the fire with her hands outstretched. The shroud was laid in partially opened folds on one side of the hearth, and was steaming heavily. I brought over some cushions and pillows, and made a little pile of them beside her.

"Sit there," I said, "and rest quietly in the heat." It may have been the effect of the glowing heat, but there was a rich colour in her face as she looked at me with shining eyes. Without a word, but with a courteous little bow, she sat down at once. I put a thick rug across her shoulders, and sat down myself on a stool a couple of feet away.

For fully five or six minutes we sat in silence. At last, turning her head towards me she said in a sweet, low voice:

"I had intended coming earlier on purpose to thank you for your very sweet and gracious courtesy to me, but circumstances were such that I could not leave my – my" – she hesitated before saying – "my abode. I am not free, as you and others are, to do what I will. My existence is sadly cold and stern, and full of horrors that appal. But I *do* thank you. For myself I am not sorry for the delay, for every hour shows me more clearly how good and understanding and sympathetic you have been to me. I only hope that some day you may realize how kind you have been, and how much I appreciate it."

"I am only too glad to be of any service," I said, feebly I felt, as I held out my hand. She did not seem to see it. Her eyes were now on the fire, and a warm blush dyed forehead and cheek and neck. The reproof was so gentle that no one could have been offended. It was evident that she was something coy and reticent, and would not allow me to come at present more close to her, even to the touching of her hand. But that her heart was not in the denial was also evident in the glance from her glorious dark starry eyes. These glances – veritable lightning flashes coming through her pronounced reserve – finished entirely any wavering there might be in my own purpose. I was aware now to the full that my heart was quite subjugated. I knew that I was in love – veritably so much in love as to feel that without this woman, be she what she might, by my side my future must be absolutely barren.

It was presently apparent that she did not mean to stay as long on this occasion as on the last. When the castle clock struck midnight she suddenly sprang to her feet with a bound, saying:

"I must go! There is midnight!" I rose at once, the intensity of her speech having instantly obliterated the sleep which, under the influence of rest and warmth, was creeping upon me. Once more she was in a frenzy of haste, so I hurried towards the window, but as I looked back saw her, despite her haste, still standing. I motioned towards the screen, and slipping behind the curtain, opened the window and went out on the terrace. As I was disappearing behind the curtain I saw her with the tail of my eye lifting the shroud, now dry, from the hearth.

She was out through the window in an incredibly short time, now clothed once more in that dreadful wrapping. As she sped past me barefooted on the wet, chilly marble which made her shudder, she whispered:

"Thank you again. You *are* good to me. You can understand."

Once again I stood on the terrace, saw her melt like a shadow down the steps, and disappear behind the nearest shrub. Thence she flitted away from point to point with exceeding haste. The moonlight had now disappeared behind heavy banks of cloud, so there was little light to see by. I could just distinguish a pale gleam here and there as she wended her secret way.

For a long time I stood there alone thinking, as I watched the course she had taken, and wondering where might be her ultimate destination. As she had spoken of her 'abode,' I knew there was some definitive objective of her flight.

It was no use wondering. I was so entirely ignorant of her surroundings that I had not even a starting-place for speculation. So I went in, leaving the window open. It seemed that this being so made one barrier the less between us. I gathered the cushions and rugs from before the fire, which was no longer leaping, but burning with a steady glow, and put them back in their places. Aunt Janet might come in the morning, as she had done before, and I did not wish to set her thinking. She is much too clever a person to have treading on the heels of a mystery – especially one in which my own affections are engaged. I wonder what she would have said had she seen me kiss the cushion on which my beautiful guest's head had rested?

When I was in bed, and in the dark save for the fading glow of the fire, my thoughts became fixed that whether she came from Earth or Heaven or Hell, my lovely visitor was already more to me than aught else in the world. This time she had, on going, said no word of returning. I had been so much taken up with her presence, and so upset by her abrupt departure, that I had omitted to ask her. And so I am driven, as before, to accept the chance of her returning – a chance which I fear I am or may be unable to control.

Surely enough Aunt Janet did come in the morning, early. I was still asleep when she knocked at my door. With that purely physical subconsciousness which comes with habit I must have realized the cause of the sound, for I woke fully conscious of the fact that Aunt Janet had knocked and was waiting to come in. I jumped from bed, and back again when I had unlocked the door. When Aunt Janet came in she noticed the cold of the room.

"Save us, laddie, but ye'll get your death o' cold in this room." Then, as she looked round and noticed the ashes of the extinct fire in the grate:

"Eh, but ye're no that daft after a'; ye've had the sense to light yer fire. Glad I am that we had the fire laid and a wheen o' dry logs ready to yer hand." She evidently felt the cold air coming from the window, for she went over and drew the curtain. When she saw the open window, she raised her hands in a sort of dismay, which to me, knowing how little base for concern could be within her knowledge, was comic. Hurriedly she shut the window, and then, coming close over to my bed, said:

"Yon has been a fearsome nicht again, laddie, for yer poor auld aunty."

"Dreaming again, Aunt Janet?" I asked – rather flippantly as it seemed to me. She shook her head:

"Not so, Rupert, unless it be that the Lord gies us in dreams what we in our spiritual darkness think are veesions." I roused up at this. When Aunt Janet calls me Rupert, as she always used to do in my dear mother's time, things are serious with her. As I was back in childhood now, recalled by her word, I thought the best thing I could do to cheer her would be to bring her back there too – if I could. So I patted the edge of the bed as I used to do when I was a wee kiddie and wanted her to comfort me, and said:

"Sit down, Aunt Janet, and tell me." She yielded at once, and the look of the happy old days grew over her face as though there had come a gleam of sunshine. She sat down, and I put out my hands as I used to do, and took her hand between them. There was a tear in her eye as she raised my hand and kissed it as in old times. But for the infinite pathos of it, it would have been comic:

Aunt Janet, old and grey-haired, but still retaining her girlish slimness of figure, petite, dainty as a Dresden figure, her face lined with the care of years, but softened and ennobled by the unselfishness of those years, holding up my big hand, which would outweigh her whole arm; sitting dainty as a pretty old fairy beside a recumbent giant – for my bulk never seems so great as when I am near this real little good fairy of my life – seven feet beside four feet seven.

So she began as of old, as though she were about to soothe a frightened child with a fairy tale:

"'Twas a veesion, I think, though a dream it may hae been. But whichever or whatever it was, it concerned my little boy, who has grown to be a big giant, so much that I woke all of a tremble. Laddie dear, I thought that I saw ye being married." This gave me an opening, though a small one, for comforting her, so I took it at once:

"Why, dear, there isn't anything to alarm you in that, is there? It was only the other day when you spoke to me about the need of my getting married, if it was only that you might have children of your boy playing around your knees as their father used to do when he was a helpless wee child himself."

"That is so, laddie," she answered gravely. "But your weddin' was none so merry as I fain would see. True, you seemed to lo'e her wi' all yer hairt. Yer eyes shone that bright that ye might ha' set her afire, for all her black locks and her winsome face. But, laddie, that was not all – no, not though her black een, that had the licht o' all the stars o' nicht in them, shone in yours as though a hairt o' love an' passion, too, dwelt in them. I saw ye join hands, an' heard a strange voice that talked stranger still, but I saw none ither. Your eyes an' her eyes, an' your hand an' hers, were all I saw. For all else was dim, and the darkness was close around ye twa. And when the benison was spoken – I knew that by the voices that sang, and by the gladness of her een, as well as by the pride and glory of yours – the licht began to glow a wee more, an' I could see yer bride. She was in a veil o' wondrous fine lace. And there were orange-flowers in her hair, though there were twigs, too, and there was a crown o' flowers on head wi' a golden band round it. And the heathen candles that stood on the table wi' the Book had some strange effect, for the reflex o' it hung in the air o'er her head like the shadow of a crown. There was a gold ring on her finger and a silver one on yours." Here she paused and trembled, so that, hoping to dispel her fears, I said, as like as I could to the way I used to when I was a child:

"Go on, Aunt Janet."

She did not seem to recognize consciously the likeness between past and present; but the effect was there, for she went on more like her old self, though there was a prophetic gravity in her voice, more marked than I had ever heard from her:

"All this I've told ye was well; but, oh, laddie, there was a dreadful lack o' livin' joy such as I should expect from the woman whom my boy had chosen for his wife – and at the marriage coupling, too! And no wonder, when all is said; for though the marriage veil o' love was fine, an' the garland o' flowers was fresh-gathered, underneath them a' was nane ither than a ghastly shroud. As I looked in my veesion – or maybe dream – I expectit to see the worms crawl round the flagstane at her feet. If 'twas not Death, laddie dear, that stood by ye, it was the shadow o' Death that made the darkness round ye, that neither the light o' candles nor the smoke o' heathen incense could pierce. Oh, laddie, laddie, wae is me that I hae seen sic a veesion – waking or sleeping, it matters not! I was sair distressed – so sair that I woke wi' a shriek on my lips and bathed in cold sweat. I would hae come doon to ye to see if you were hearty or no – or even to listen at your door for any sound o' yer being quick, but that I feared to alarm ye till morn should come. I've counted the hours and the minutes since midnight, when I saw the veesion, till I came hither just the now."

"Quite right, Aunt Janet," I said, "and I thank you for your kind thought for me in the matter, now and always." Then I went on, for I wanted to take precautions against the possibility of her discovery of my secret. I could not bear to think that she might run my precious secret to earth in any well-meant piece of bungling. That would be to me disaster unbearable. She might frighten away altogether my beautiful visitor, even whose name or origin I did not know, and I might never see her again:

"You must never do that, Aunt Janet. You and I are too good friends to have sense of distrust or annoyance come between us – which would surely happen if I had to keep thinking that you or anyone else might be watching me."

* * *

April 27, 1907.

AFTER A SPELL OF LONELINESS which has seemed endless I have something to write. When the void in my heart was becoming the receptacle for many devils of suspicion and distrust I set myself a task which might, I thought, keep my thoughts in part, at any rate, occupied – to explore minutely the neighbourhood round the Castle. This might, I hoped, serve as an anodyne to my pain of loneliness, which grew more acute as the days, the hours, wore on, even if it should not ultimately afford me some clue to the whereabouts of the woman whom I had now grown to love so madly.

My exploration soon took a systematic form, as I intended that it should be exhaustive. I would take every day a separate line of advance from the Castle, beginning at the south and working round by the east to the north. The first day only took me to the edge of the creek, which I crossed in a boat, and landed at the base of the cliff opposite. I found the cliffs alone worth a visit. Here and there were openings to caves which I made up my mind to explore later. I managed to climb up the cliff at a spot less beetling than the rest, and continued my journey. It was, though very beautiful, not a specially interesting place. I explored that spoke of the wheel of which Vissarion was the hub, and got back just in time for dinner.

The next day I took a course slightly more to the eastward. I had no difficulty in keeping a straight path, for, once I had rowed across the creek, the old church of St. Sava rose before me in stately gloom. This was the spot where many generations of the noblest of the Land of the Blue Mountains had from time immemorial been laid to rest, amongst them the Vissarions. Again, I found the opposite cliffs pierced here and there with caves, some with wide openings – others the openings of which were partly above and partly below water. I could, however, find no means of climbing the cliff at this part, and had to make a long detour, following up the line of the creek till further on I found a piece of beach from which ascent was possible.

Here I ascended, and found that I was on a line between the Castle and the southern side of the mountains. I saw the church of St. Sava away to my right, and not far from the edge of the cliff. I made my way to it at once, for as yet I had never been near it. Hitherto my excursions had been limited to the Castle and its many gardens and surroundings. It was of a style with which I was not familiar – with four wings to the points of the compass. The great doorway, set in a magnificent frontage of carved stone of manifestly ancient date, faced west, so that, when one entered, he went east. To my surprise – for somehow I expected the contrary – I found the door open. Not wide open, but what is called ajar – manifestly not locked or barred, but not sufficiently open for one to look in. I entered, and after passing through a wide vestibule, more like a section of a corridor than an ostensible entrance, made my way through a spacious doorway into the body of the church. The church itself was almost circular, the openings of the four naves being spacious enough to give the appearance of the interior as a whole, being a huge cross. It was strangely dim, for the window openings were small and high-set, and were, moreover, filled with green or blue glass, each window having a colour to itself. The glass was very old, being of the thirteenth or fourteenth century. Such appointments as there were – for it had a general air of desolation – were of great beauty and richness – especially so to be in a place – even a church – where the door lay open, and no one was to be seen. It was strangely silent even for an old church on a lonesome headland. There reigned a dismal solemnity which seemed to chill me, accustomed as I have been to strange and weird places. It seemed abandoned, though it had not that air of having been neglected which is so often to be noticed in old churches. There was none of the everlasting accumulation of dust which prevails in places of higher cultivation and larger and more strenuous work.

In the church itself or its appending chambers I could find no clue or suggestion which could guide me in any way in my search for the Lady of the Shroud. Monuments there were in profusion – statues, tablets, and all the customary memorials of the dead. The families and dates represented were simply bewildering. Often the name of Vissarion was given, and the inscription which it held I read through carefully, looking to find some enlightenment of any kind. But all in vain: there was nothing to see in the church itself. So I determined to visit the crypt. I had no lantern or candle with me, so had to go back to the Castle to secure one.

It was strange, coming in from the sunlight, here overwhelming to one so recently accustomed to northern skies, to note the slender gleam of the lantern which I carried, and which I had lit inside the door. At my first entry to the church my mind had been so much taken up with the strangeness of the place, together with the intensity of wish for some sort of clue, that I had really no opportunity of examining detail. But now detail became necessary, as I had to find the entrance to the crypt. My puny light could not dissipate the semi-Cimmerian gloom of the vast edifice; I had to throw the feeble gleam into one after another of the dark corners.

At last I found, behind the great screen, a narrow stone staircase which seemed to wind down into the rock. It was not in any way secret, but being in the narrow space behind the great screen, was not visible except when close to it. I knew I was now close to my objective, and began to descend. Accustomed though I have been to all sorts of mysteries and dangers, I felt awed and almost overwhelmed by a sense of loneliness and desolation as I descended the ancient winding steps. These were many in number, roughly hewn of old in the solid rock on which the church was built.

I met a fresh surprise in finding that the door of the crypt was open. After all, this was different from the church-door being open; for in many places it is a custom to allow all comers at all times to find rest and comfort in the sacred place. But I did expect that at least the final resting-place of the historic dead would be held safe against casual intrusion. Even I, on a quest which was very near my heart, paused with an almost overwhelming sense of decorum before passing through that open door. The crypt was a huge place, strangely lofty for a vault. From its formation, however, I soon came to the conclusion that it was originally a natural cavern altered to its present purpose by the hand of man. I could hear somewhere near the sound of running water, but I could not locate it. Now and again at irregular intervals there was a prolonged booming, which could only come from a wave breaking in a confined place. The recollection then came to me of the proximity of the church to the top of the beetling cliff, and of the half-sunk cavern entrances which pierced it.

With the gleam of my lamp to guide me, I went through and round the whole place. There were many massive tombs, mostly rough-hewn from great slabs or blocks of stone. Some of them were marble, and the cutting of all was ancient. So large and heavy were some of them that it was a wonder to me how they could ever have been brought to this place, to which the only entrance was seemingly the narrow, tortuous stairway by which I had come. At last I saw near one end of the crypt a great chain hanging. Turning the light upward, I found that it depended from a ring set over a wide opening, evidently made artificially. It must have been through this opening that the great sarcophagi had been lowered.

Directly underneath the hanging chain, which did not come closer to the ground than some eight or ten feet, was a huge tomb in the shape of a rectangular coffer or sarcophagus. It was open, save for a huge sheet of thick glass which rested above it on two thick balks of dark oak, cut to exceeding smoothness, which lay across it, one at either end. On the far side from where I stood each of these was joined to another oak plank, also cut smooth, which sloped gently to the rocky floor. Should it be necessary to open the tomb, the glass could be made to slide along the supports and descend by the sloping planks.

Naturally curious to know what might be within such a strange receptacle, I raised the lantern, depressing its lens so that the light might fall within.

Then I started back with a cry, the lantern slipping from my nerveless hand and falling with a ringing sound on the great sheet of thick glass.

Within, pillowed on soft cushions, and covered with a mantle woven of white natural fleece sprigged with tiny sprays of pine wrought in gold, lay the body of a woman – none other than my beautiful visitor. She was marble white, and her long black eyelashes lay on her white cheeks as though she slept.

Without a word or a sound, save the sounds made by my hurrying feet on the stone flooring, I fled up the steep steps, and through the dim expanse of the church, out into the bright sunlight. I found that I had mechanically raised the fallen lamp, and had taken it with me in my flight.

My feet naturally turned towards home. It was all instinctive. The new horror had – for the time, at any rate – drowned my mind in its mystery, deeper than the deepest depths of thought or imagination.

Chapter IV
Under the Flagstaff

May 1, 1907.

FOR SOME DAYS after the last adventure I was in truth in a half-dazed condition, unable to think sensibly, hardly coherently. Indeed, it was as much as I could do to preserve something of my habitual appearance and manner. However, my first test happily came soon, and when I was once through it I reacquired sufficient self-confidence to go through with my purpose. Gradually the original phase of stupefaction passed, and I was able to look the situation in the face. I knew the worst now, at any rate; and when the lowest point has been reached things must begin to mend. Still, I was wofully sensitive regarding anything which might affect my Lady of the Shroud, or even my opinion of her. I even began to dread Aunt Janet's Second-Sight visions or dreams. These had a fatal habit of coming so near to fact that they always made for a danger of discovery. I had to realize now that the Lady of the Shroud might indeed be a Vampire – one of that horrid race that survives death and carries on a life-in-death existence eternally and only for evil. Indeed, I began to expect that Aunt Janet would ere long have some prophetic insight to the matter. She had been so wonderfully correct in her prophetic surmises with regard to both the visits to my room that it was hardly possible that she could fail to take cognizance of this last development.

But my dread was not justified; at any rate, I had no reason to suspect that by any force or exercise of her occult gift she might cause me concern by the discovery of my secret. Only once did I feel that actual danger in that respect was close to me. That was when she came early one morning and rapped at my door. When I called out, "Who is that? What is it?" she said in an agitated way:

"Thank God, laddie, you are all right! Go to sleep again."

Later on, when we met at breakfast, she explained that she had had a nightmare in the grey of the morning. She thought she had seen me in the crypt of a great church close beside a stone coffin; and, knowing that such was an ominous subject to dream about, came as soon as she dared to see if I was all right. Her mind was evidently set on death and burial, for she went on:

"By the way, Rupert, I am told that the great church on time top of the cliff across the creek is St. Sava's, where the great people of the country used to be buried. I want you to take me there some day. We shall go over it, and look at the tombs and monuments together. I really think I should be afraid to go alone, but it will be all right if you are with me." This was getting really dangerous, so I turned it aside:

"Really, Aunt Janet, I'm afraid it won't do. If you go off to weird old churches, and fill yourself up with a fresh supply of horrors, I don't know what will happen. You'll be dreaming dreadful things about me every night and neither you nor I shall get any sleep." It went to my heart to oppose her in any wish; and also this kind of chaffy opposition might pain her. But I had no alternative; the matter was too serious to be allowed to proceed. Should Aunt Janet go to the church, she would surely want to visit the crypt. Should she do so, and there notice the glass-covered tomb – as she could not help doing – the Lord only knew what would happen. She had already Second-Sighted a woman being married to me, and before I myself knew that I had such a hope. What might she not reveal did she know where the woman came from? It may have been that her power of Second Sight had to rest on some basis of knowledge or belief, and that her vision was but some intuitive perception of my own subjective thought. But whatever it was it should be stopped – at all hazards.

This whole episode set me thinking introspectively, and led me gradually but imperatively to self-analysis – not of powers, but of motives. I found myself before long examining myself as to what were my real intentions. I thought at first that this intellectual process was an exercise of pure reason; but soon discarded this as inadequate – even impossible. Reason is a cold manifestation; this feeling which swayed and dominated me is none other than passion, which is quick, hot, and insistent.

As for myself, the self-analysis could lead to but one result – the expression to myself of the reality and definiteness of an already-formed though unconscious intention. I wished to do the woman good – to serve her in some way – to secure her some benefit by any means, no matter how difficult, which might be within my power. I knew that I loved her – loved her most truly and fervently; there was no need for self-analysis to tell me that. And, moreover, no self-analysis, or any other mental process that I knew of, could help my one doubt: whether she was an ordinary woman (or an extraordinary woman, for the matter of that) in some sore and terrible straits; or else one who lay under some dreadful condition, only partially alive, and not mistress of herself or her acts. Whichever her condition might be, there was in my own feeling a superfluity of affection for her. The self-analysis taught me one thing, at any rate – that I had for her, to start with, an infinite pity which had softened towards her my whole being, and had already mastered merely selfish desire. Out of it I began to find excuses for her every act. In the doing so I knew now, though perhaps I did not at the time the process was going on, that my view in its true inwardness was of her as a living woman – the woman I loved.

In the forming of our ideas there are different methods of work, as though the analogy with material life holds good. In the building of a house, for instance, there are many persons employed; men of different trades and occupations – architect, builder, masons, carpenters, plumbers, and a host of others – and all these with the officials of each guild or trade. So in the world of thought and feelings: knowledge and understanding come through various agents, each competent to its task.

How far pity reacted with love I knew not; I only knew that whatever her state might be, were she living or dead, I could find in my heart no blame for the Lady of the Shroud. It could not be that she was dead in the real conventional way; for, after all, the Dead do not walk the earth in corporal substance, even if there be spirits which take the corporal form. This woman was of actual form and weight. How could I doubt that, at all events – I, who had held her in my arms? Might it not be that she was not quite dead, and that it had been given to me to restore her to life again? Ah! that would be, indeed, a privilege well worth the giving my life to accomplish. That such a thing may be is possible. Surely the old myths were not absolute inventions; they must have had a basis somewhere in fact. May not the world-old story of Orpheus and Eurydice have been based on some deep-lying principle or power of human nature? There is not one of us but has wished at some time to bring back the dead. Ay, and who has not felt that in himself or herself was power in the deep love for our dead to make them quick again, did we but know the secret of how it was to be done?

For myself, I have seen such mysteries that I am open to conviction regarding things not yet explained. These have been, of course, amongst savages or those old-world people who have brought unchecked traditions and beliefs – ay, and powers too – down the ages from the dim days when the world was young; when forces were elemental, and Nature's handiwork was experimental rather than completed. Some of these wonders may have been older still than the accepted period of our own period of creation. May we not have today other wonders, different only in method, but not more susceptible of belief? Obi-ism and Fantee-ism have been exercised in my own presence, and their results proved by the evidence of my own eyes and other senses. So, too, have stranger rites, with the same object and the same success, in the far Pacific Islands. So, too, in India and China, in Thibet and in the Golden Chersonese. On all and each of these occasions there was, on my own part, enough belief to set in motion the powers of understanding; and there were no moral scruples to stand in the way of realization. Those whose lives are so spent that they achieve the reputation of not fearing man or God or devil are not deterred in their doing or thwarted from a set purpose by things which might deter others not so equipped for adventure. Whatever may be before them – pleasant or painful, bitter or sweet, arduous or facile, enjoyable or terrible, humorous or full of awe and horror – they must accept, taking them in the onward course as a good athlete takes hurdles in his stride. And there must be no hesitating, no looking back. If the explorer or the adventurer has scruples, he had better give up that special branch of effort and come himself to a more level walk in life. Neither must there be regrets. There is no need for such; savage life has this advantage: it begets a certain toleration not to be found in conventional existence.

* * *

May 2, 1907.

I had heard long ago that Second Sight is a terrible gift, even to its possessor. I am now inclined not only to believe, but to understand it. Aunt Janet has made such a practice of it of late that I go in constant dread of discovery of my secret. She seems to parallel me all the time, whatever I may do. It is like a sort of dual existence to her; for she is her dear old self all the time, and yet some other person with a sort of intellectual kit of telescope and notebook, which are eternally used on me. I know they are for me, too – for what she considers my good. But all the same it makes an embarrassment. Happily Second Sight cannot speak as clearly as it sees, or, rather, as it understands. For the translation of the vague beliefs which it inculcates is both nebulous and uncertain – a sort of Delphic oracle which always says things which no one can make out at the time, but which can be afterwards read in any one of several ways. This is all right, for in my case it is a kind of safety; but, then, Aunt Janet is a very clever woman, and some time she herself may be able to understand. Then she may begin to put two and two together. When she does that, it will not be long before she knows more than I do of the facts of the whole affair. And her reading of them and of the Lady of the Shroud, round whom they circle, may not be the same as mine. Well, that will be all right too. Aunt Janet loves me – God knows I have good reason to know that all through these years – and whatever view she may take, her acts will be all I could wish. But I shall come in for a good lot of scolding, I am sure. By the way, I ought to think of that; if Aunt Janet scolds me, it is a pretty good proof that I ought to be scolded. I wonder if I dare tell her all. No! It is too strange. She is only a woman, after all: and if she knew I loved...I wish I knew her name, and thought – as I might myself do, only that I resist it – that she is not alive at all. Well, what she would either think or do beats me. I suppose she would want to slipper me as she used to do when I was a wee kiddie – in a different way, of course.

* * *

May 3, 1907.

I really could not go on seriously last night. The idea of Aunt Janet giving me a licking as in the dear old days made me laugh so much that nothing in the world seemed serious then. Oh, Aunt Janet is all right whatever comes. That I am sure of, so I needn't worry over it. A good thing too; there will be plenty to worry about without that. I shall not check her telling me of her visions, however; I may learn something from them.

For the last four-and-twenty hours I have, whilst awake, been looking over Aunt Janet's books, of which I brought a wheen down here. Gee whizz! No wonder the old dear is superstitious, when she is filled up to the back teeth with that sort of stuff! There may be some truth in some of those yarns; those who wrote them may believe in them, or some of them, at all events. But as to coherence or logic, or any sort of reasonable or instructive deduction, they might as well have been written by so many hens! These occult book-makers seem to gather only a lot of bare, bald facts, which they put down in the most uninteresting way possible. They go by quantity only. One story of the kind, well examined and with logical comments, would be more convincing to a third party than a whole hecatomb of them.

* * *

May 4, 1907.

There is evidently something up in the country. The mountaineers are more uneasy than they have been as yet. There is constant going to and fro amongst them, mostly at night and in the grey of the morning. I spend many hours in my room in the eastern tower, from which I can watch the woods, and gather from signs the passing to and fro. But with all this activity no one has said to me a word on the subject.

It is undoubtedly a disappointment to me. I had hoped that the mountaineers had come to trust me; that gathering at which they wanted to fire their guns for me gave me strong hopes. But now it is apparent that they do not trust me in full – as yet, at all events. Well, I must not complain. It is all only right and just. As yet I have done nothing to prove to them the love and devotion that I feel to the country. I know that such individuals as I have met trust me, and I believe like me. But the trust of a nation is different. That has to be won and tested; he who would win it must justify, and in a way that only troublous times can allow. No nation will – can – give full meed of honour to a stranger in times of peace. Why should it? I must not forget that I am here a stranger in the land, and that to the great mass of people even my name is unknown. Perhaps they will know me better when Rooke comes back with that store of arms and ammunition that he has bought, and the little warship he has got from South America. When they see that I hand over the whole lot to the nation without a string on them, they may begin to believe. In the meantime all I can do is to wait. It will all come right in time, I have no doubt. And if it doesn't come right, well, we can only die once!

Is that so? What about my Lady of the Shroud? I must not think of that or of her in this gallery. Love and war are separate, and may not mix – cannot mix, if it comes to that. I must be wise in the matter; and if I have got the hump in any degree whatever, must not show it.

But one thing is certain: something is up, and it must be the Turks. From what the Vladika said at that meeting they have some intention of an attack on the Blue Mountains. If that be so, we must be ready; and perhaps I can help there. The forces must be organized; we must have some method of communication. In this country, where are neither roads nor railways nor telegraphs, we must establish a signalling system of some sort. That I can begin at once. I can make a code, or adapt one that I have used elsewhere already. I shall rig up a semaphore on the top of the Castle which can be seen for an enormous distance around. I shall train a number of men to be facile in signalling. And then, should need come, I may be able to show the mountaineers that I am fit to live in their hearts....

And all this work may prove an anodyne to pain of another kind. It will help, at any rate, to keep my mind occupied whilst I am waiting for another visit from my Lady of the Shroud.

* * *

May 18, 1907.

The two weeks that have passed have been busy, and may, as time goes on, prove eventful. I really think they have placed me in a different position with the Blue Mountaineers – certainly so far as those in this part of the country are concerned. They are no longer suspicious of me – which is much; though they have not yet received me into their confidence. I suppose this will come in time, but I must not try to hustle them. Already they are willing, so far as I can see, to use me to their own ends. They accepted the signalling idea very readily, and are quite willing to drill as much as I like. This can be (and I think is, in its way) a pleasure to them. They are born soldiers, every man of them; and practice together is only a realization of their own wishes and a further development of their powers. I think I can understand the trend of their thoughts, and what ideas of public policy lie behind them. In all that we have attempted together as yet they are themselves in absolute power. It rests with them to carry out any ideas I may suggest, so they do not fear any assumption of power or governance on my part. Thus, so long as they keep secret from me both their ideas of high policy and their immediate intentions, I am powerless to do them ill, and I may be of service should occasion arise. Well, all told, this is much. Already they accept me as an individual, not merely one of the mass. I am pretty sure that they are satisfied of my personal bona fides. It is policy and not mistrust that hedges me in. Well, policy is a matter of time. They are a splendid people, but if they knew a little more than they do they would understand that the wisest of all policies is trust – when it can be given. I must hold myself in check, and never be betrayed into a harsh thought towards them. Poor souls! with a thousand years behind them of Turkish aggression, strenuously attempted by both force and fraud, no wonder they are suspicious. Likewise every other nation with whom they have ever come in contact – except one, my own – has deceived or betrayed them. Anyhow, they are fine soldiers, and before long we shall have an army that cannot be ignored. If I can get so that they trust me, I shall ask Sir Colin to come out here. He would be a splendid head for their army. His great military knowledge and tactical skill would come in well. It makes me glow to think of what an army he would turn out of this splendid material, and one especially adapted for the style of fighting which would be necessary in this country.

If a mere amateur like myself, who has only had experience of organizing the wildest kind of savages, has been able to advance or compact their individual style of fighting into systematic effort, a great soldier like MacKelpie will bring them to perfection as a fighting machine. Our Highlanders, when they come out, will foregather with them, as mountaineers always do with each other. Then we shall have a force which can hold its own against any odds. I only hope that Rooke will be returning soon. I want to see those Ingis-Malbron rifles either safely stored in the Castle or, what is better, divided up amongst the mountaineers – a thing which will be done at the very earliest moment that I can accomplish it. I have a conviction that when these men have received their arms and ammunition from me they will understand me better, and not keep any secrets from me.

All this fortnight when I was not drilling or going about amongst the mountaineers, and teaching them the code which I have now got perfected, I was exploring the side of the mountain nearest to here. I could not bear to be still. It is torture to me to be idle in my present condition of mind regarding my Lady of the Shroud…. Strange I do not mind mentioning the word to myself now. I used to at first; but that bitterness has all gone away.

* * *

May 19, 1907.

I was so restless early this morning that before daylight I was out exploring on the mountain-side. By chance I came across a secret place just as the day was breaking. Indeed, it was by the change of light as the first sun-rays seemed to fall down the mountain-side that my attention was called to an opening shown by a light behind it. It was, indeed, a secret place – so secret that I thought at first I should keep it to myself. In such a place as this either to hide in or to be able to prevent anyone else hiding in might on occasion be an asset of safety.

When, however, I saw indications rather than traces that someone had already used it to camp in, I changed my mind, and thought that whenever I should get an opportunity I would tell the Vladika of it, as he is a man on whose discretion I can rely. If we ever have a war here or any sort of invasion, it is just such places that may be dangerous. Even in my own case it is much too near the Castle to be neglected.

The indications were meagre – only where a fire had been on a little shelf of rock; and it was not possible, through the results of burning vegetation or scorched grass, to tell how long before the fire had been alight. I could only guess. Perhaps the mountaineers might be able to tell or even to guess better than I could. But I am not so sure of this. I am a mountaineer myself, and with larger and more varied experience than any of them. For myself, though I could not be certain, I came to the conclusion that whoever had used the place had done so not many days before. It could not have been quite recently; but it may not have been very long ago. Whoever had used it had covered up his tracks well. Even the ashes had been carefully removed, and the place where they had lain was cleaned or swept in some way, so that there was no trace on the spot. I applied some of my West African experience, and looked on the rough bark of the trees to leeward, to where the agitated air, however directed, must have come, unless it was wanted to call attention to the place by the scattered wood-ashes, however fine. I found traces of it, but they were faint. There had not been rain for several days; so the dust must have been blown there since the rain had fallen, for it was still dry.

The place was a tiny gorge, with but one entrance, which was hidden behind a barren spur of rock – just a sort of long fissure, jagged and curving, in the rock, like a fault in the stratification. I could just struggle through it with considerable effort, holding my breath here and there, so as to reduce my depth of chest. Within it was tree-clad, and full of possibilities of concealment.

As I came away I marked well its direction and approaches, noting any guiding mark which might aid in finding it by day or night. I explored every foot of ground around it – in front, on each side, and above. But from nowhere could I see an indication of its existence. It was a veritable secret chamber wrought by the hand of Nature itself. I did not return home till I was familiar with every detail near and around it. This new knowledge added distinctly to my sense of security.

Later in the day I tried to find the Vladika or any mountaineer of importance, for I thought that such a hiding-place which had been used so recently might be dangerous, and especially at a time when, as I had learned at the meeting where they did not fire their guns that there may have been spies about or a traitor in the land.

Even before I came to my own room tonight I had fully made up my mind to go out early in the morning and find some proper person to whom to impart the information, so that a watch might be kept on the place. It is now getting on for midnight, and when I have had my usual last look at the garden I shall turn in. Aunt Janet was uneasy all day, and especially so this evening. I think it must have been my absence at the usual breakfast-hour which got on her nerves; and that unsatisfied mental or psychical irritation increased as the day wore on.

* * *

May 20, 1907.

The clock on the mantelpiece in my room, which chimes on the notes of the clock at St. James's Palace, was striking midnight when I opened the glass door on the terrace. I had put out my lights before I drew the curtain, as I wished to see the full effect of the moonlight. Now that the rainy season is over, the moon is quite as beautiful as it was in the wet, and a great deal more comfortable. I was in evening dress, with a smoking-jacket in lieu of a coat, and I felt the air mild and mellow on the warm side, as I stood on the terrace.

But even in that bright moonlight the further corners of the great garden were full of mysterious shadows. I peered into them as well as I could – and my eyes are pretty good naturally, and are well trained. There was not the least movement. The air was as still as death, the foliage as still as though wrought in stone.

I looked for quite a long time in the hope of seeing something of my Lady. The quarters chimed several times, but I stood on unheeding. At last I thought I saw far off in the very corner of the old defending wall a flicker of white. It was but momentary, and could hardly have accounted in itself for the way my heart beat. I controlled myself, and stood as though I, too, were a graven image. I was rewarded by seeing presently another gleam of white. And then an unspeakable rapture stole over me as I realized that my Lady was coming as she had come before. I would have hurried out to meet her, but that I knew well that this would not be in accord with her wishes. So, thinking to please her, I drew back into the room. I was glad I had done so when, from the dark corner where I stood, I saw her steal up the marble steps and stand timidly looking in at the door. Then, after a long pause, came a whisper as faint and sweet as the music of a distant Aeolian harp:

"Are you there? May I come in? Answer me! I am lonely and in fear!" For answer I emerged from my dim corner so swiftly that she was startled. I could hear from the quivering intake of her breath that she was striving – happily with success – to suppress a shriek.

"Come in," I said quietly. "I was waiting for you, for I felt that you would come. I only came in from the terrace when I saw you coming, lest you might fear that anyone might see us. That is not possible, but I thought you wished that I should be careful."

"I did – I do," she answered in a low, sweet voice, but very firmly. "But never avoid precaution. There is nothing that may not happen here. There may be eyes where we least expect – or suspect them." As she spoke the last words solemnly and in a low whisper, she was entering the room. I closed the glass door and bolted it, rolled back the steel grille, and pulled the heavy curtain. Then, when I had lit a candle, I went over and put a light to the fire. In a few seconds the dry wood had caught, and the flames were beginning to rise and crackle. She had not objected to my closing the window and drawing the curtain; neither did she make any comment on my lighting the fire. She simply acquiesced in it, as though it was now a matter of course. When I made the pile of cushions before it as on the occasion of her last visit, she sank down on them, and held out her white, trembling hands to the warmth.

She was different tonight from what she had been on either of the two former visits. From her present bearing I arrived at some gauge of her self-concern, her self-respect. Now that she was dry, and not overmastered by wet and cold, a sweet and gracious dignity seemed to shine from her, enwrapping her, as it were, with a luminous veil. It was not that she was by this made or shown as cold or distant, or in any way harsh or forbidding. On the contrary, protected by this dignity, she seemed much more sweet and genial than before. It was as though she felt that she could afford to stoop now that her loftiness was realized – that her position was recognized and secure. If her inherent dignity made an impenetrable nimbus round her, this was against others; she herself was not bound by it, or to be bound. So marked was this, so entirely and sweetly womanly did she appear, that I caught myself wondering in flashes of thought, which came as sharp periods of doubting judgment between spells of unconscious fascination, how I had ever come to think she was aught but perfect woman. As she rested, half sitting and half lying on the pile of cushions, she was all grace, and beauty, and charm, and sweetness – the veritable perfect woman of the dreams of a man, be he young or old. To have such a woman sit by his hearth and hold her holy of holies in his heart might well be a rapture to any man. Even an hour of such entrancing joy might be well won by a lifetime of pain, by the balance of a long life sacrificed, by the extinction of life itself. Quick behind the record of such thoughts came the answer to the doubt they challenged: if it should turn out that she was not living at all, but one of the doomed and pitiful Un-Dead, then so much more on account of her very sweetness and beauty would be the winning of her back to Life and Heaven – even were it that she might find happiness in the heart and in the arms of another man.

Once, when I leaned over the hearth to put fresh logs on the fire, my face was so close to hers that I felt her breath on my cheek. It thrilled me to feel even the suggestion of that ineffable contact. Her breath was sweet – sweet as the breath of a calf, sweet as the whiff of a summer breeze across beds of mignonette. How could anyone believe for a moment that such sweet breath could come from the lips of the dead – the dead in esse or in posse – that corruption could send forth fragrance so sweet and pure? It was with satisfied happiness that, as I looked at her from my stool, I saw the dancing of the flames from the beech-logs reflected in her glorious black eyes, and the stars that were hidden in them shine out with new colours and new lustre as they gleamed, rising and falling like hopes and fears. As the light leaped, so did smiles of quiet happiness flit over her beautiful face, the merriment of the joyous flames being reflected in ever-changing dimples.

At first I was a little disconcerted whenever my eyes took note of her shroud, and there came a momentary regret that the weather had not been again bad, so that there might have been compulsion for her putting on another garment – anything lacking the loathsomeness of that pitiful wrapping. Little by little, however, this feeling disappeared, and I found no matter for even dissatisfaction in her wrapping. Indeed, my thoughts found inward voice before the subject was dismissed from my mind:

"One becomes accustomed to anything – even a shroud!" But the thought was followed by a submerging wave of pity that she should have had such a dreadful experience.

By-and-by we seemed both to forget everything – I know I did – except that we were man and woman, and close together. The strangeness of the situation and the circumstances did not seem of moment – not worth even a passing thought. We still sat apart and said little, if anything. I cannot recall a single word that either of us spoke whilst we sat before the fire, but other language than speech came into play; the eyes told their own story, as eyes can do, and more eloquently than lips whilst exercising their function of speech. Question and answer followed each other in this satisfying language, and with an unspeakable rapture I began to realize that my affection was returned. Under these circumstances it was unrealizable that there should be any incongruity in the whole affair. I was not myself in the mood of questioning. I was diffident with that diffidence which comes alone from true love, as though it were a necessary emanation from that delightful and overwhelming and commanding passion. In her presence there seemed to surge up within me that which forbade speech. Speech under present conditions would have seemed to me unnecessary, imperfect, and even vulgarly overt. She, too, was silent. But now that I am alone, and memory is alone with me, I am convinced that she also had been happy. No, not that exactly. 'Happiness' is not the word to describe either her feeling or my own. Happiness is more active, a more conscious enjoyment. We had been content. That expresses our condition perfectly; and now that I can analyze my own feeling, and understand what the word implies, I am satisfied of its accuracy. 'Content' has both a positive and negative meaning or antecedent condition. It implies an absence of disturbing conditions as well as of wants; also it implies something positive which has been won or achieved, or which has accrued. In our state of mind – for though it may be presumption on my part, I am satisfied that our ideas were mutual – it meant that we had reached an understanding whence all that might come must be for good. God grant that it may be so!

As we sat silent, looking into each other's eyes, and whilst the stars in hers were now full of latent fire, perhaps from the reflection of the flames, she suddenly sprang to her feet, instinctively drawing the horrible shroud round her as she rose to her full height in a voice full of lingering emotion, as of one who is acting under spiritual compulsion rather than personal will, she said in a whisper:

"I must go at once. I feel the morning drawing nigh. I must be in my place when the light of day comes."

She was so earnest that I felt I must not oppose her wish; so I, too, sprang to my feet and ran towards the window. I pulled the curtain aside sufficiently far for me to press back the grille and reach the glass door, the latch of which I opened. I passed behind the curtain again, and held the edge of it back so that she could go through. For an instant she stopped as she broke the long silence:

"You are a true gentleman, and my friend. You understand all I wish. Out of the depth of my heart I thank you." She held out her beautiful high-bred hand. I took it in both mine as I fell on my knees, and raised it to my lips. Its touch made me quiver. She, too, trembled as she looked down at me with a glance which seemed to search my very soul. The stars in her eyes, now that the firelight was no longer on them, had gone back to their own mysterious silver. Then she drew her hand from mine very, very gently, as though it would fain linger; and she passed out behind the curtain with a gentle, sweet, dignified little bow which left me on my knees.

When I heard the glass door pulled-to gently behind her, I rose from my knees and hurried without the curtain, just in time to watch her pass down the steps. I wanted to see her as long as I could. The grey of morning was just beginning to war with the night gloom, and by the faint uncertain light I could see dimly the white figure flit between shrub and statue till finally it merged in the far darkness.

I stood for a long time on the terrace, sometimes looking into the darkness in front of me, in case I might be blessed with another glimpse of her; sometimes with my eyes closed, so that I might recall and hold in my mind her passage down the steps. For the first time since I had met her she had thrown back at me a glance as she stepped on the white path below the terrace. With the glamour over me of that look, which was all love and enticement, I could have dared all the powers that be.

When the grey dawn was becoming apparent through the lightening of the sky I returned to my room. In a dazed condition – half hypnotized by love – I went to bed, and in dreams continued to think, all happily, of my Lady of the Shroud.

* * *

May 27, 1907.

A whole week has gone since I saw my Love! There it is; no doubt whatever is left in my mind about it now! Since I saw her my passion has grown and grown by leaps and bounds, as novelists put it. It has now become so vast as to overwhelm me, to wipe out all thought of doubt or difficulty. I suppose it must be what men suffered – suffering need not mean pain – under enchantments in old times. I am but as a straw whirled in the resistless eddies of a whirlpool. I feel that I must see her again, even if it be but in her tomb in the crypt. I must, I suppose, prepare myself for the venture, for many things have to be thought of. The visit must not be at night, for in such case I might miss her, did she come to me again here....

The morning came and went, but my wish and intention still remained; and so in the full tide of noon, with the sun in all its fiery force, I set out for the old church of St. Sava. I carried with me a lantern with powerful lens. I had wrapped it up secretly, for I had a feeling that I should not like anyone to know that I had such a thing with me.

On this occasion I had no misgivings. On the former visit I had for a moment been overwhelmed at the unexpected sight of the body of the woman I thought I loved – I knew it now – lying in her tomb. But now I knew all, and it was to see this woman, though in her tomb, that I came.

When I had lit my lantern, which I did as soon as I had pushed open the great door, which was once again unlocked, I turned my steps to the steps of the crypt, which lay behind the richly carven wood screen. This I could see, with the better light, was a noble piece of work of priceless beauty and worth. I tried to keep my heart in full courage with thoughts of my Lady, and of the sweetness and dignity of our last meeting; but, despite all, it sank down, down, and turned to water as I passed with uncertain feet down the narrow, tortuous steps. My concern, I am now convinced, was not for myself, but that she whom I adored should have to endure such a fearful place. As anodyne to my own pain I thought what it would be, and how I should feel, when I should have won for her a way out of that horror, at any rate. This thought reassured me somewhat, and restored my courage. It was in something of the same fashion which has hitherto carried me out of tight places as well as into them that at last I pushed open the low, narrow door at the foot of the rock-hewn staircase and entered the crypt.

Without delay I made my way to the glass-covered tomb set beneath the hanging chain. I could see by the flashing of the light around me that my hand which held the lantern trembled. With a great effort I steadied myself, and raising the lantern, turned its light down into the sarcophagus.

Once again the fallen lantern rang on the tingling glass, and I stood alone in the darkness, for an instant almost paralyzed with surprised disappointment.

The tomb was empty! Even the trappings of the dead had been removed.

I knew not what happened till I found myself groping my way up the winding stair. Here, in comparison with the solid darkness of the crypt, it seemed almost light. The dim expanse of the church sent a few straggling rays down the vaulted steps, and as I could see, be it never so dimly, I felt I was not in absolute darkness. With the light came a sense of power and fresh courage, and I groped my way back into the crypt again. There, by now and again lighting matches, I found my way to the tomb and recovered my lantern. Then I took my way slowly – for I wished to prove, if not my own courage, at least such vestiges of self-respect as the venture had left me – through the church, where I extinguished my lantern, and out through the great door into the open sunlight. I seemed to have heard, both in the darkness of the crypt and through the dimness of the church, mysterious sounds as of whispers and suppressed breathing; but the memory of these did not count for much when once I was free. I was only satisfied of my own consciousness and identity when I found myself on the broad rock terrace in front of the church, with the fierce sunlight beating on my upturned face, and, looking downward, saw far below me the rippled blue of the open sea.

* * *

June 3, 1907.

Another week has elapsed – a week full of movement of many kinds and in many ways – but as yet I have had no tale or tidings of my Lady of the Shroud. I have not had an opportunity of going again in daylight to St. Sava's as I should have liked to have done. I felt that I must not go at night. The night is her time of freedom, and it must be kept for her – or else I may miss her, or perhaps never see her again.

The days have been full of national movement. The mountaineers have evidently been organizing themselves, for some reason which I cannot quite understand, and which they have hesitated to make known to me. I have taken care not to manifest any curiosity, whatever I may have felt. This would certainly arouse suspicion, and might ultimately cause disaster to my hopes of aiding the nation in their struggle to preserve their freedom.

These fierce mountaineers are strangely – almost unduly – suspicious, and the only way to win their confidence is to begin the trusting. A young American attaché of the Embassy at Vienna, who had made a journey through the Land of the Blue Mountains, once put it to me in this form:

"Keep your head shut, and they'll open theirs. If you don't, they'll open it for you – down to the chine!"

It was quite apparent to me that they were completing some fresh arrangements for signalling with a code of their own. This was natural enough, and in no way inconsistent with the measure of friendliness already shown to me. Where there are neither telegraphs, railways, nor roads, any effective form of communication must – can only be purely personal. And so, if they wish to keep any secret amongst themselves, they must preserve the secret of their code. I should have dearly liked to learn their new code and their manner of using it, but as I want to be a helpful friend to them – and as this implies not only trust, but the appearance of it – I had to school myself to patience.

This attitude so far won their confidence that before we parted at our last meeting, after most solemn vows of faith and secrecy, they took me into the secret. This was, however, only to the extent of teaching me the code and method; they still withheld from me rigidly the fact or political secret, or whatever it was that was the mainspring of their united action.

When I got home I wrote down, whilst it was fresh in my memory, all they told me. This script I studied until I had it so thoroughly by heart that I could not forget it. Then I burned the paper. However, there is now one gain at least: with my semaphore I can send through the Blue Mountains from side to side, with expedition, secrecy, and exactness, a message comprehensible to all.

* * *

June 6, 1907.

Last night I had a new experience of my Lady of the Shroud – in so far as form was concerned, at any rate. I was in bed, and just falling asleep, when I heard a queer kind of scratching at the glass door of the terrace. I listened acutely, my heart beating hard. The sound seemed to come from low down, close to the floor. I jumped out of bed, ran to the window, and, pulling aside the heavy curtains, looked out.

The garden looked, as usual, ghostly in the moonlight, but there was not the faintest sign of movement anywhere, and no one was on or near the terrace. I looked eagerly down to where the sound had seemed to come from.

There, just inside the glass door, as though it had been pushed under the door, lay a paper closely folded in several laps. I picked it up and opened it. I was all in a tumult, for my heart told me whence it came. Inside was written in English, in a large, sprawling hand, such as might be from an English child of seven or eight:

"Meet me at the Flagstaff on the Rock!"

I knew the place, of course. On the farthermost point of the rock on which the Castle stands is set a high flagstaff, whereon in old time the banner of the Vissarion family flew. At some far-off time, when the Castle had been liable to attack, this point had been strongly fortified. Indeed, in the days when the bow was a martial weapon it must have been quite impregnable.

A covered gallery, with loopholes for arrows, had been cut in the solid rock, running right round the point, quite surrounding the flagstaff and the great boss of rock on whose centre it was reared. A narrow drawbridge of immense strength had connected – in peaceful times, and still remained – the outer point of rock with an entrance formed in the outer wall, and guarded with flanking towers and a portcullis. Its use was manifestly to guard against surprise. From this point only could be seen the line of the rocks all round the point. Thus, any secret attack by boats could be made impossible.

Having hurriedly dressed myself, and taking with me both hunting-knife and revolver, I went out on the terrace, taking the precaution, unusual to me, of drawing the grille behind me and locking it. Matters around the Castle are in far too disturbed a condition to allow the taking of any foolish chances, either in the way of being unarmed or of leaving the private entrance to the Castle open. I found my way through the rocky passage, and climbed by the Jacob's ladder fixed on the rock – a device of convenience in time of peace – to the foot of the flagstaff.

I was all on fire with expectation, and the time of going seemed exceeding long; so I was additionally disappointed by the contrast when I did not see my Lady there when I arrived. However, my heart beat freely again – perhaps more freely than ever – when I saw her crouching in the shadow of the Castle wall. From where she was she could not be seen from any point save that alone which I occupied; even from there it was only her white shroud that was conspicuous through the deep gloom of the shadow. The moonlight was so bright that the shadows were almost unnaturally black.

I rushed over towards her, and when close was about to say impulsively, "Why did you leave your tomb?" when it suddenly struck me that the question would be malapropos and embarrassing in many ways. So, better judgment prevailing, I said instead:

"It has been so long since I saw you! It has seemed an eternity to me!" Her answer came as quickly as even I could have wished; she spoke impulsively and without thought:

"It has been long to me too! Oh, so long! so long! I have asked you to come out here because I wanted to see you so much that I could not wait any longer. I have been heart-hungry for a sight of you!"

Her words, her eager attitude, the ineffable something which conveys the messages of the heart, the longing expression in her eyes as the full moonlight fell on her face, showing the stars as living gold – for in her eagerness she had stepped out towards me from the shadow – all set me on fire. Without a thought or a word – for it was Nature speaking in the language of Love, which is a silent tongue – I stepped towards her and took her in my arms. She yielded with that sweet unconsciousness which is the perfection of Love, as if it was in obedience to some command uttered before the beginning of the world. Probably without any conscious effort on either side – I know there was none on mine – our mouths met in the first kiss of love.

At the time nothing in the meeting struck me as out of the common. But later in the night, when I was alone and in darkness, whenever I thought of it all – its strangeness and its stranger rapture – I could not but be sensible of the bizarre conditions for a love meeting. The place lonely, the time night, the man young and strong, and full of life and hope and ambition; the woman, beautiful and ardent though she was, a woman seemingly dead, clothed in the shroud in which she had been wrapped when lying in her tomb in the crypt of the old church.

Whilst we were together, anyhow, there was little thought of the kind; no reasoning of any kind on my part. Love has its own laws and its own logic. Under the flagstaff, where the Vissarion banner was wont to flap in the breeze, she was in my arms; her sweet breath was on my face; her heart was beating against my own. What need was there for reason at all? Inter arma silent leges – the voice of reason is silent in the stress of passion. Dead she may be, or Un-dead – a Vampire with one foot in Hell and one on earth. But I love her; and come what may, here or hereafter, she is mine. As my mate, we shall fare along together, whatsoever the end may be, or wheresoever our path may lead. If she is indeed to be won from the nethermost Hell, then be mine the task!

But to go back to the record. When I had once started speaking to her in words of passion I could not stop. I did not want to – if I could; and she did not appear to wish it either. Can there be a woman – alive or dead – who would not want to hear the rapture of her lover expressed to her whilst she is enclosed in his arms?

There was no attempt at reticence on my part now; I took it for granted that she knew all that I surmised, and, as she made neither protest nor comment, that she accepted my belief as to her indeterminate existence. Sometimes her eyes would be closed, but even then the rapture of her face was almost beyond belief. Then, when the beautiful eyes would open and gaze on me, the stars that were in them would shine and scintillate as though they were formed of living fire. She said little, very little; but though the words were few, every syllable was fraught with love, and went straight to the very core of my heart.

By-and-by, when our transport had calmed to joy, I asked when I might next see her, and how and where I might find her when I should want to. She did not reply directly, but, holding me close in her arms, whispered in my ear with that breathless softness which is a lover's rapture of speech:

"I have come here under terrible difficulties, not only because I love you – and that would be enough – but because, as well as the joy of seeing you, I wanted to warn you."

"To warn me! Why?" I queried. Her reply came with a bashful hesitation, with something of a struggle in it, as of one who for some ulterior reason had to pick her words:

"There are difficulties and dangers ahead of you. You are beset with them; and they are all the greater because they are, of grim necessity, hidden from you. You cannot go anywhere, look in any direction, do anything, say anything, but it may be a signal for danger. My dear, it lurks everywhere – in the light as well as in the darkness; in the open as well as in the secret places; from friends as well as foes; when you are least prepared; when you may least expect it. Oh, I know it, and what it is to endure; for I share it for you – for your dear sake!"

"My darling!" was all I could say, as I drew her again closer to me and kissed her. After a bit she was calmer; seeing this, I came back to the subject that she had – in part, at all events – come to me to speak about:

"But if difficulty and danger hedge me in so everlastingly, and if I am to have no indication whatever of its kind or purpose, what can I do? God knows I would willingly guard myself – not on my own account, but for your dear sake. I have now a cause to live and be strong, and to keep all my faculties, since it may mean much to you. If you may not tell me details, may you not indicate to me some line of conduct, of action, that would be most in accord with your wishes – or, rather, with your idea of what would be best?"

She looked at me fixedly before speaking – a long, purposeful, loving look which no man born of woman could misunderstand. Then she spoke slowly, deliberately, emphatically:

"Be bold, and fear not. Be true to yourself, to me – it is the same thing. These are the best guards you can use. Your safety does not rest with me. Ah, I wish it did! I wish to God it did!" In my inner heart it thrilled me not merely to hear the expression of her wish, but to hear her use the name of God as she did. I understand now, in the calm of this place and with the sunlight before me, that my belief as to her being all woman – living woman – was not quite dead: but though at the moment my heart did not recognize the doubt, my brain did. And I made up my mind that we should not part this time until she knew that I had seen her, and where; but, despite my own thoughts, my outer ears listened greedily as she went on.

"As for me, you may not find me, but I shall find you, be sure! And now we must say 'Good-night,' my dear, my dear! Tell me once again that you love me, for it is a sweetness that one does not wish to forego – even one who wears such a garment as this – and rests where I must rest." As she spoke she held up part of her cerements for me to see. What could I do but take her once again in my arms and hold her close, close. God knows it was all in love; but it was passionate love which surged through my every vein as I strained her dear body to mine. But yet this embrace was not selfish; it was not all an expression of my own passion. It was based on pity – the pity which is twin-born with true love. Breathless from our kisses, when presently we released each other, she stood in a glorious rapture, like a white spirit in the moonlight, and as her lovely, starlit eyes seemed to devour me, she spoke in a languorous ecstasy:

"Oh, how you love me! how you love me! It is worth all I have gone through for this, even to wearing this terrible drapery." And again she pointed to her shroud.

Here was my chance to speak of what I knew, and I took it. "I know, I know. Moreover, I know that awful resting-place."

I was interrupted, cut short in the midst of my sentence, not by any word, but by the frightened look in her eyes and the fear-mastered way in which she shrank away from me. I suppose in reality she could not be paler than she looked when the colour-absorbing moonlight fell on her; but on the instant all semblance of living seemed to shrink and fall away, and she looked with eyes of dread as if in I some awful way held in thrall. But for the movement of the pitiful glance, she would have seemed of soulless marble, so deadly cold did she look.

The moments that dragged themselves out whilst I waited for her to speak seemed endless. At length her words came in an awed whisper, so faint that even in that stilly night I could hardly hear it:

"You know – you know my resting-place! How – when was that?" There was nothing to do now but to speak out the truth:

"I was in the crypt of St. Sava. It was all by accident. I was exploring all around the Castle, and I went there in my course. I found the winding stair in the rock behind the screen, and went down. Dear, I loved you well before that awful moment, but then, even as the lantern fell tingling on the glass, my love multiplied itself, with pity as a factor." She was silent for a few seconds. When she spoke, there was a new tone in her voice:

"But were you not shocked?"

"Of course I was," I answered on the spur of the moment, and I now think wisely. "Shocked is hardly the word. I was horrified beyond anything that words can convey that you – you should have to so endure! I did not like to return, for I feared lest my doing so might set some barrier between us. But in due time I did return on another day."

"Well?" Her voice was like sweet music.

"I had another shock that time, worse than before, for you were not there. Then indeed it was that I knew to myself how dear you were – how dear you are to me. Whilst I live, you – living or dead – shall always be in my heart." She breathed hard. The elation in her eyes made them outshine the moonlight, but she said no word. I went on:

"My dear, I had come into the crypt full of courage and hope, though I knew what dreadful sight should sear my eyes once again. But we little know what may be in store for us, no matter what we expect. I went out with a heart like water from that dreadful desolation."

"Oh, how you love me, dear!" Cheered by her words, and even more by her tone, I went on with renewed courage. There was no halting, no faltering in my intention now:

"You and I, my dear, were ordained for each other. I cannot help it that you had already suffered before I knew you. It may be that there may be for you still suffering that I may not prevent, endurance that I may not shorten; but what a man can do is yours. Not Hell itself will stop me, if it be possible that I may win through its torments with you in my arms!"

"Will nothing stop you, then?" Her question was breathed as softly as the strain of an Aeolian harp.

"Nothing!" I said, and I heard my own teeth snap together. There was something speaking within me stronger than I had ever known myself to be. Again came a query, trembling, quavering, quivering, as though the issue was of more than life or death:

"Not this?" She held up a corner of the shroud, and as she saw my face and realized the answer before I spoke, went on: "With all it implies?"

"Not if it were wrought of the cerecloths of the damned!" There was a long pause. Her voice was more resolute when she spoke again. It rang. Moreover, there was in it a joyous note, as of one who feels new hope:

"But do you know what men say? Some of them, that I am dead and buried; others, that I am not only dead and buried, but that I am one of those unhappy beings that may not die the common death of man. Who live on a fearful life-in-death, whereby they are harmful to all. Those unhappy Un-dead whom men call Vampires – who live on the blood of the living, and bring eternal damnation as well as death with the poison of their dreadful kisses!

"I know what men say sometimes," I answered. "But I know also what my own heart says; and I rather choose to obey its calling than all the voices of the living or the dead. Come what may, I am pledged to you. If it be that your old life has to be rewon for you out of the very jaws of Death and Hell, I shall keep the faith I have pledged, and that here I pledge again!" As I finished speaking I sank on my knees at her feet, and, putting my arms round her, drew her close to me. Her tears rained down on my face as she stroked my hair with her soft, strong hand and whispered to me:

"This is indeed to be one. What more holy marriage can God give to any of His creatures?" We were both silent for a time.

I think I was the first to recover my senses. That I did so was manifest by my asking her: "When may we meet again?" – a thing I had never remembered doing at iny of our former partings. She answered with a rising and falling of the voice that was just above a whisper, as soft and cooing as the voice of a pigeon:

"That will be soon – as soon as I can manage it, be sure. My dear, my dear!" The last four words of endearment she spoke in a low but prolonged and piercing tone which made me thrill with delight.

"Give me some token," I said, "that I may have always close to me to ease my aching heart till we meet again, and ever after, for love's sake!" Her mind seemed to leap to understanding, and with a purpose all her own. Stooping for an instant, she tore off with swift, strong fingers a fragment of her shroud. This, having kissed it, she handed to me, whispering:

"It is time that we part. You must leave me now. Take this, and keep it for ever. I shall be less unhappy in my terrible loneliness whilst it lasts if I know that this my gift, which for good or ill is a part of me as you know me, is close to you. It may be, my very dear, that some day you may be glad and even proud of this hour, as I am." She kissed me as I took it.

"For life or death, I care not which, so long as I am with you!" I said, as I moved off. Descending the Jacob's ladder, I made my way down the rock-hewn passage.

The last thing I saw was the beautiful face of my Lady of the Shroud as she leaned over the edge of the opening. Her eyes were like glowing stars as her looks followed me. That look shall never fade from my memory.

After a few agitating moments of thought I half mechanically took my way down to the garden. Opening the grille, I entered my lonely room, which looked all the more lonely for the memory of the rapturous moments under the Flagstaff. I went to bed as one in a dream. There I lay till sunrise – awake and thinking.

Chapter V
A Ritual at Midnight

Rupert's Journal – Continued
June 20, 1907.

THE TIME HAS GONE as quickly as work can effect since I saw my Lady. As I told the mountaineers, Rooke, whom I had sent on the service, had made a contract for fifty thousand Ingis-Malbron rifles, and as many tons of ammunition as the French experts calculated to be a full supply for a year of warfare. I heard from him by our secret telegraph code that the order had been completed, and that the goods were already on the way. The morning after the meeting at the Flagstaff I had word that at night the vessel – one chartered by Rooke for the purpose – would arrive at Vissarion during the night. We were all expectation. I had always now in the Castle a signalling party, the signals being renewed as fast as the men were sufficiently expert to proceed with their practice alone or in groups. We hoped that every fighting-man in the country would in time become an expert signaller. Beyond these, again, we have always a few priests. The Church of the country is a militant Church; its priests are soldiers, its Bishops commanders. But they all serve wherever the battle most needs them. Naturally they, as men of brains, are quicker at learning than the average mountaineers; with the result that they learnt the code and the signalling almost by instinct. We have now at least one such expert in each community of them, and shortly the priests alone will be able to signal, if need be, for the nation; thus releasing for active service the merely fighting-man. The men at present with me I took into confidence as to the vessel's arrival, and we were all ready for work when the man on the lookout at the Flagstaff sent word that a vessel without lights was creeping in towards shore. We all assembled on the rocky edge of the creek, and saw her steal up the creek and gain the shelter of the harbour. When this had been effected, we ran out the boom which protects the opening, and after that the great armoured sliding-gates which Uncle Roger had himself had made so as to protect the harbour in case of need.

We then came within and assisted in warping the steamer to the side of the dock.

Rooke looked fit, and was full of fire and vigour. His responsibility and the mere thought of warlike action seemed to have renewed his youth.

When we had arranged for the unloading of the cases of arms and ammunition, I took Rooke into the room which we call my 'office,' where he gave me an account of his doings. He had not only secured the rifles and the ammunition for them, but he had purchased from one of the small American Republics an armoured yacht which had been especially built for war service. He grew quite enthusiastic, even excited, as he told me of her:

"She is the last word in naval construction – a torpedo yacht. A small cruiser, with turbines up to date, oil-fuelled, and fully armed with the latest and most perfect weapons and explosives of all kinds. The fastest boat afloat today. Built by Thorneycroft, engined by Parsons, armoured by Armstrong, armed by Crupp. If she ever comes into action, it will be bad for her opponent, for she need not fear to tackle anything less than a Dreadnought."

He also told me that from the same Government, whose nation had just established an unlooked-for peace, he had also purchased a whole park of artillery of the very latest patterns, and that for range and accuracy the guns were held to be supreme. These would follow before long, and with them their proper ammunition, with a shipload of the same to follow shortly after.

When he had told me all the rest of his news, and handed me the accounts, we went out to the dock to see the debarkation of the war material. Knowing that it was arriving, I had sent word in the afternoon to the mountaineers to tell them to come and remove it. They had answered the call, and it really seemed to me that the whole of the land must that night have been in motion.

They came as individuals, grouping themselves as they came within the defences of the Castle; some had gathered at fixed points on the way. They went secretly and in silence, stealing through the forests like ghosts, each party when it grouped taking the place of that which had gone on one of the routes radiating round Vissarion. Their coming and going was more than ghostly. It was, indeed, the outward manifestation of an inward spirit – a whole nation dominated by one common purpose.

The men in the steamer were nearly all engineers, mostly British, well conducted, and to be depended upon. Rooke had picked them separately, and in the doing had used well his great experience of both men and adventurous life. These men were to form part of the armoured yacht's crew when she should come into the Mediterranean waters. They and the priests and fighting-men in the Castle worked well together, and with a zeal that was beyond praise. The heavy cases seemed almost of their own accord to leave the holds, so fast came the procession of them along the gangways from deck to dock-wall. It was a part of my design that the arms should be placed in centres ready for local distribution. In such a country as this, without railways or even roads, the distribution of war material in any quantity is a great labour, for it has to be done individually, or at least from centres.

But of this work the great number of mountaineers who were arriving made little account. As fast as the ship's company, with the assistance of the priests and fighting-men, placed the cases on the quay, the engineers opened them and laid the contents ready for portage. The mountaineers seemed to come in a continuous stream; each in turn shouldered his burden and passed out, the captain of his section giving him as he passed his instruction where to go and in what route. The method had been already prepared in my office ready for such a distribution when the arms should arrive, and descriptions and quantities had been noted by the captains. The whole affair was treated by all as a matter of the utmost secrecy. Hardly a word was spoken beyond the necessary directions, and these were given in whispers. All night long the stream of men went and came, and towards dawn the bulk of the imported material was lessened by half. On the following night the remainder was removed, after my own men had stored in the Castle the rifles and ammunition reserved for its defence if necessary. It was advisable to keep a reserve supply in case it should ever be required. The following night Rooke went away secretly in the chartered vessel. He had to bring back with him the purchased cannon and heavy ammunition, which had been in the meantime stored on one of the Greek islands. The second morning, having had secret word that the steamer was on the way, I had given the signal for the assembling of the mountaineers.

A little after dark the vessel, showing no light, stole into the creek. The barrier gates were once again closed, and when a sufficient number of men had arrived to handle the guns, we began to unload. The actual deportation was easy enough, for the dock had all necessary appliances quite up to date, including a pair of shears for gun-lifting which could be raised into position in a very short time.

The guns were well furnished with tackle of all sorts, and before many hours had passed a little procession of them disappeared into the woods in ghostly silence. A number of men surrounded each, and they moved as well as if properly supplied with horses.

In the meantime, and for a week after the arrival of the guns, the drilling went on without pause. The gun-drill was wonderful. In the arduous work necessary for it the great strength and stamina of the mountaineers showed out wonderfully. They did not seem to know fatigue any more than they knew fear.

For a week this went on, till a perfect discipline and management was obtained. They did not practise the shooting, for this would have made secrecy impossible. It was reported all along the Turkish frontier that the Sultan's troops were being massed, and though this was not on a war footing, the movement was more or less dangerous. The reports of our own spies, although vague as to the purpose and extent of the movement, were definite as to something being on foot. And Turkey does not do something without a purpose that bodes ill to someone. Certainly the sound of cannon, which is a far-reaching sound, would have given them warning of our preparations, and would so have sadly minimized their effectiveness.

When the cannon had all been disposed of – except, of course, those destined for defence of the Castle or to be stored there – Rooke went away with the ship and crew. The ship he was to return to the owners; the men would be shipped on the war-yacht, of whose crew they would form a part. The rest of them had been carefully selected by Rooke himself, and were kept in secrecy at Cattaro, ready for service the moment required. They were all good men, and quite capable of whatever work they might be set to. So Rooke told me, and he ought to know. The experience of his young days as a private made him an expert in such a job.

* * *

June 24, 1907.

Last night I got from my Lady a similar message to the last, and delivered in a similar way. This time, however, our meeting was to be on the leads of the Keep.

I dressed myself very carefully before going on this adventure, lest by any chance of household concern, any of the servants should see me; for if this should happen, Aunt Janet would be sure to hear of it, which would give rise to endless surmises and questionings – a thing I was far from desiring.

I confess that in thinking the matter over during the time I was making my hurried preparations I was at a loss to understand how any human body, even though it be of the dead, could go or be conveyed to such a place without some sort of assistance, or, at least, collusion, on the part of some of the inmates. At the visit to the Flagstaff circumstances were different. This spot was actually outside the Castle, and in order to reach it I myself had to leave the Castle privately, and from the garden ascend to the ramparts. But here was no such possibility. The Keep was an imperium in imperio. It stood within the Castle, though separated from it, and it had its own defences against intrusion. The roof of it was, so far as I knew, as little approachable as the magazine.

The difficulty did not, however, trouble me beyond a mere passing thought. In the joy of the coming meeting and the longing rapture at the mere thought of it, all difficulties disappeared. Love makes its own faith, and I never doubted that my Lady would be waiting for me at the place designated. When I had passed through the little arched passages, and up the doubly-grated stairways contrived in the massiveness of the walls, I let myself out on the leads. It was well that as yet the times were sufficiently peaceful not to necessitate guards or sentries at all such points.

There, in a dim corner where the moonlight and the passing clouds threw deep shadows, I saw her, clothed as ever in her shroud. Why, I know not. I felt somehow that the situation was even more serious than ever. But I was steeled to whatever might come. My mind had been already made up. To carry out my resolve to win the woman I loved I was ready to face death. But now, after we had for a few brief moments held each other in our arms, I was willing to accept death – or more than death. Now, more than before, was she sweet and dear to me. Whatever qualms there might have been at the beginning of our love-making, or during the progress of it, did not now exist. We had exchanged vows and confidences, and acknowledged our loves. What, then, could there be of distrust, or even doubt, that the present might not set at naught? But even had there been such doubts or qualms, they must have disappeared in the ardour of our mutual embrace. I was by now mad for her, and was content to be so mad. When she had breath to speak after the strictness of our embrace, she said:

"I have come to warn you to be more than ever careful." It was, I confess, a pang to me, who thought only of love, to hear that anything else should have been the initiative power of her coming, even though it had been her concern for my own safety. I could not but notice the bitter note of chagrin in my voice as I answered:

"It was for love's sake that I came." She, too, evidently felt the undercurrent of pain, for she said quickly:

"Ah, dearest, I, too, came for love's sake. It is because I love you that I am so anxious about you. What would the world – ay, or heaven – be to me without you?"

There was such earnest truth in her tone that the sense and realization of my own harshness smote me. In the presence of such love as this even a lover's selfishness must become abashed. I could not express myself in words, so simply raised her slim hand in mine and kissed it. As it lay warm in my own I could not but notice, as well as its fineness, its strength and the firmness of its clasp. Its warmth and fervour struck into my heart – and my brain. Thereupon I poured out to her once more my love for her, she listening all afire. When passion had had its say, the calmer emotions had opportunity of expression.

When I was satisfied afresh of her affection, I began to value her care for my safety, and so I went back to the subject. Her very insistence, based on personal affection, gave me more solid ground for fear. In the moment of love transports I had forgotten, or did not think, of what wonderful power or knowledge she must have to be able to move in such strange ways as she did. Why, at this very moment she was within my own gates. Locks and bars, even the very seal of death itself, seemed unable to make for her a prison-house. With such freedom of action and movement, going when she would into secret places, what might she not know that was known to others? How could anyone keep secret from such an one even an ill intent? Such thoughts, such surmises, had often flashed through my mind in moments of excitement rather than of reflection, but never long enough to become fixed into belief. But yet the consequences, the convictions, of them were with me, though unconsciously, though the thoughts themselves were perhaps forgotten or withered before development.

"And you?" I asked her earnestly. "What about danger to you?" She smiled, her little pearl-white teeth gleaming in the moonlight, as she spoke:

"There is no danger for me. I am safe. I am the safest person, perhaps the only safe person, in all this land." The full significance of her words did not seem to come to me all at once. Some base for understanding such an assertion seemed to be wanting. It was not that I did not trust or believe her, but that I thought she might be mistaken. I wanted to reassure myself, so in my distress I asked unthinkingly:

"How the safest? What is your protection?" For several moments that spun themselves out endlessly she looked me straight in the face, the stars in her eyes seeming to glow like fire; then, lowering her head, she took a fold of her shroud and held it up to me.

"This!"

The meaning was complete and understandable now. I could not speak at once for the wave of emotion which choked me. I dropped on my knees, and taking her in my arms, held her close to me. She saw that I was moved, and tenderly stroked my hair, and with delicate touch pressed down my head on her bosom, as a mother might have done to comfort a frightened child.

Presently we got back to the realities of life again. I murmured:

"Your safety, your life, your happiness are all-in-all to me. When will you let them be my care?" She trembled in my arms, nestling even closer to me. Her own arms seemed to quiver with delight as she said:

"Would you indeed like me to be always with you? To me it would be a happiness unspeakable; and to you, what would it be?"

I thought that she wished to hear me speak my love to her, and that, woman-like, she had led me to the utterance, and so I spoke again of the passion that now raged in me, she listening eagerly as we strained each other tight in our arms. At last there came a pause, a long, long pause, and our hearts beat consciously in unison as we stood together. Presently she said in a sweet, low, intense whisper, as soft as the sighing of summer wind:

"It shall be as you wish; but oh, my dear, you will have to first go through an ordeal which may try you terribly! Do not ask me anything! You must not ask, because I may not answer, and it would be pain to me to deny you anything. Marriage with such an one as I am has its own ritual, which may not be foregone. It may..." I broke passionately into her speaking:

"There is no ritual that I fear, so long as it be that it is for your good, and your lasting happiness. And if the end of it be that I may call you mine, there is no horror in life or death that I shall not gladly face. Dear, I ask you nothing. I am content to leave myself in your hands. You shall advise me when the time comes, and I shall be satisfied, content to obey. Content! It is but a poor word to express what I long for! I shall shirk nothing which may come to me from this or any other world, so long as it is to make you mine!" Once again her murmured happiness was music to my ears:

"Oh, how you love me! how you love me, dear, dear!" She took me in her arms, and for a few seconds we hung together. Suddenly she tore herself apart from me, and stood drawn up to the full height, with a dignity I cannot describe or express. Her voice had a new dominance, as with firm utterance and in staccato manner she said:

"Rupert Sent Leger, before we go a step further I must say something to you, ask you something, and I charge you, on your most sacred honour and belief, to answer me truly. Do you believe me to be one of those unhappy beings who may not die, but have to live in shameful existence between earth and the nether world, and whose hellish mission is to destroy, body and soul, those who love them till they fall to their level? You are a gentleman, and a brave one. I have found you fearless. Answer me in sternest truth, no matter what the issue may be!"

She stood there in the glamorous moonlight with a commanding dignity which seemed more than human. In that mystic light her white shroud seemed diaphanous, and she appeared like a spirit of power. What was I to say? How could I admit to such a being that I had actually had at moments, if not a belief, a passing doubt? It was a conviction with me that if I spoke wrongly I should lose her for ever. I was in a desperate strait. In such a case there is but one solid ground which one may rest on – the Truth.

I really felt I was between the devil and the deep sea. There was no avoiding the issue, and so, out of this all-embracing, all-compelling conviction of truth, I spoke.

For a fleeting moment I felt that my tone was truculent, and almost hesitated; but as I saw no anger or indignation on my Lady's face, but rather an eager approval, I was reassured. A woman, after all, is glad to see a man strong, for all belief in him must be based on that.

"I shall speak the truth. Remember that I have no wish to hurt your feelings, but as you conjure me by my honour, you must forgive me if I pain. It is true that I had at first – ay, and later, when I came to think matters over after you had gone, when reason came to the aid of impression – a passing belief that you are a Vampire. How can I fail to have, even now, though I love you with all my soul, though I have held you in my arms and kissed you on the mouth, a doubt, when all the evidences seem to point to one thing? Remember that I have only seen you at night, except that bitter moment when, in the broad noonday of the upper world, I saw you, clad as ever in a shroud, lying seemingly dead in a tomb in the crypt of St. Sava's Church.... But let that pass. Such belief as I have is all in you. Be you woman or Vampire, it is all the same to me. It is you whom I love! Should it be that you are – you are not woman, which I cannot believe, then it will be my glory to break your fetters, to open your prison, and set you free. To that I consecrate my life." For a few seconds I stood silent, vibrating with the passion which had been awakened in me. She had by now lost the measure of her haughty isolation, and had softened into womanhood again. It was really like a realization of the old theme of Pygmalion's statue. It was with rather a pleading than a commanding voice that she said:

"And shall you always be true to me?"

"Always – so help me, God!" I answered, and I felt that there could be no lack of conviction in my voice.

Indeed, there was no cause for such lack. She also stood for a little while stone-still, and I was beginning to expand to the rapture which was in store for me when she should take me again in her arms.

But there was no such moment of softness. All at once she started as if she had suddenly wakened from a dream, and on the spur of the moment said:

"Now go, go!" I felt the conviction of necessity to obey, and turned at once. As I moved towards the door by which I had entered, I asked:

"When shall I see you again?"

"Soon!" came her answer. "I shall let you know soon – when and where. Oh, go, go!" She almost pushed me from her.

When I had passed through the low doorway and locked and barred it behind me, I felt a pang that I should have had to shut her out like that; but I feared lest there should arise some embarrassing suspicion if the door should be found open. Later came the comforting thought that, as she had got to the roof though the door had been shut, she would be able to get away by the same means. She had evidently knowledge of some secret way into the Castle. The alternative was that she must have some supernatural quality or faculty which gave her strange powers. I did not wish to pursue that train of thought, and so, after an effort, shut it out from my mind.

When I got back to my room I locked the door behind me, and went to sleep in the dark. I did not want light just then – could not bear it.

This morning I woke, a little later than usual, with a kind of apprehension which I could not at once understand. Presently, however, when my faculties became fully awake and in working order, I realized that I feared, half expected, that Aunt Janet would come to me in a worse state of alarm than ever apropos of some new Second-Sight experience of more than usual ferocity.

But, strange to say, I had no such visit. Later on in the morning, when, after breakfast, we walked together through the garden, I asked her how she had slept, and if she had dreamt. She answered me that she had slept without waking, and if she had had any dreams, they must have been pleasant ones, for she did not remember them. "And you know, Rupert," she added, "that if there be anything bad or fearsome or warning in dreams, I always remember them."

Later still, when I was by myself on the cliff beyond the creek, I could not help commenting on the absence of her power of Second Sight on the occasion. Surely, if ever there was a time when she might have had cause of apprehension, it might well have been when I asked the Lady whom she did not know to marry me – the Lady of whose identity I knew nothing, even whose name I did not know – whom I loved with all my heart and soul – my Lady of the Shroud.

I have lost faith in Second Sight.

* * *

July 1, 1907.

Another week gone. I have waited patiently, and I am at last rewarded by another letter. I was preparing for bed a little while ago, when I heard the same mysterious sound at the door as on the last two occasions. I hurried to the glass door, and there found another close-folded letter. But I could see no sign of my Lady, or of any other living being. The letter, which was without direction, ran as follows:

"If you are still of the same mind, and feel no misgivings, meet me at the Church of St. Sava beyond the Creek tomorrow night at a quarter before midnight. If you come, come in secret, and, of course, alone. Do not come at all unless you are prepared for a terrible ordeal. But if you love me, and have neither doubts nor fears, come. Come!"

Needless to say, I did not sleep last night. I tried to, but without success. It was no morbid happiness that kept me awake, no doubting, no fear. I was simply overwhelmed with the idea of the coming rapture when I should call my Lady my very, very own. In this sea of happy expectation all lesser things were submerged. Even sleep, which is an imperative force with me, failed in its usual effectiveness, and I lay still, calm, content.

With the coming of the morning, however, restlessness began. I did not know what to do, how to restrain myself, where to look for an anodyne. Happily the latter came in the shape of Rooke, who turned up shortly after breakfast. He had a satisfactory tale to tell me of the armoured yacht, which had lain off Cattaro on the previous night, and to which he had brought his contingent of crew which had waited for her coming. He did not like to take the risk of going into any port with such a vessel, lest might be detained or otherwise hampered by forms, and had gone out upon the open sea before daylight. There was on board the yacht a tiny torpedo-boat, for which provision was made both for hoisting on deck and housing there. This last would run into the creek at ten o'clock that evening, at which time it would be dark. The yacht would then run to near Otranto, to which she would send a boat to get any message I might send. This was to be in a code, which we arranged, and would convey instructions as to what night and approximate hour the yacht would come to the creek.

The day was well on before we had made certain arrangements for the future; and not till then did I feel again the pressure of my personal restlessness. Rooke, like a wise commander, took rest whilst he could. Well he knew that for a couple of days and nights at least there would be little, if any, sleep for him.

For myself, the habit of self-control stood to me, and I managed to get through the day somehow without exciting the attention of anyone else. The arrival of the torpedo-boat and the departure of Rooke made for me a welcome break in my uneasiness. An hour ago I said good-night to Aunt Janet, and shut myself up alone here. My watch is on the table before me, so that I may make sure of starting to the moment. I have allowed myself half an hour to reach St. Sava. My skiff is waiting, moored at the foot of the cliff on the hither side, where the zigzag comes close to the water. It is now ten minutes past eleven.

I shall add the odd five minutes to the time for my journey so as to make safe. I go unarmed and without a light.

I shall show no distrust of anyone or anything this night.

* * *

July 2, 1907.

When I was outside the church, I looked at my watch in the bright moonlight, and found I had one minute to wait. So I stood in the shadow of the doorway and looked out at the scene before me. Not a sign of life was visible around me, either on land or sea. On the broad plateau on which the church stands there was no movement of any kind. The wind, which had been pleasant in the noontide, had fallen completely, and not a leaf was stirring. I could see across the creek and note the hard line where the battlements of the Castle cut the sky, and where the keep towered above the line of black rock, which in the shadow of the land made an ebon frame for the picture. When I had seen the same view on former occasions, the line where the rock rose from the sea was a fringe of white foam. But then, in the daylight, the sea was sapphire blue; now it was an expanse of dark blue – so dark as to seem almost black. It had not even the relief of waves or ripples – simply a dark, cold, lifeless expanse, with no gleam of light anywhere, of lighthouse or ship; neither was there any special sound to be heard that one could distinguish – nothing but the distant hum of the myriad voices of the dark mingling in one ceaseless inarticulate sound. It was well I had not time to dwell on it, or I might have reached some spiritually-disturbing melancholy.

Let me say here that ever since I had received my Lady's message concerning this visit to St. Sava's I had been all on fire – not, perhaps, at every moment consciously or actually so, but always, as it were, prepared to break out into flame. Did I want a simile, I might compare myself to a well-banked furnace, whose present function it is to contain heat rather than to create it; whose crust can at any moment be broken by a force external to itself, and burst into raging, all-compelling heat. No thought of fear really entered my mind. Every other emotion there was, coming and going as occasion excited or lulled, but not fear. Well I knew in the depths of my heart the purpose which that secret quest was to serve. I knew not only from my Lady's words, but from the teachings of my own senses and experiences, that some dreadful ordeal must take place before happiness of any kind could be won. And that ordeal, though method or detail was unknown to me, I was prepared to undertake. This was one of those occasions when a man must undertake, blindfold, ways that may lead to torture or death, or unknown terrors beyond. But, then, a man – if, indeed, he have the heart of a man – can always undertake; he can at least make the first step, though it may turn out that through the weakness of mortality he may be unable to fulfil his own intent, or justify his belief in his own powers. Such, I take it, was the intellectual attitude of the brave souls who of old faced the tortures of the Inquisition.

But though there was no immediate fear, there was a certain doubt. For doubt is one of those mental conditions whose calling we cannot control. The end of the doubting may not be a reality to us, or be accepted as a possibility. These things cannot forego the existence of the doubt. "For even if a man," says Victor Cousin, "doubt everything else, at least he cannot doubt that he doubts." The doubt had at times been on me that my Lady of the Shroud was a Vampire. Much that had happened seemed to point that way, and here, on the very threshold of the Unknown, when, through the door which I was pushing open, my eyes met only an expanse of absolute blackness, all doubts which had ever been seemed to surround me in a legion. I have heard that, when a man is drowning, there comes a time when his whole life passes in review during the space of time which cannot be computed as even a part of a second. So it was to me in the moment of my body passing into the church. In that moment came to my mind all that had been, which bore on the knowledge of my Lady; and the general tendency was to prove or convince that she was indeed a Vampire. Much that had happened, or become known to me, seemed to justify the resolving of doubt into belief. Even my own reading of the books in Aunt Janet's little library, and the dear lady's comments on them, mingled with her own uncanny beliefs, left little opening for doubt. My having to help my Lady over the threshold of my house on her first entry was in accord with Vampire tradition; so, too, her flying at cock-crow from the warmth in which she revelled on that strange first night of our meeting; so, too, her swift departure at midnight on the second. Into the same category came the facts of her constant wearing of her Shroud, even her pledging herself, and me also, on the fragment torn from it, which she had given to me as a souvenir; her lying still in the glass-covered tomb; her coming alone to the most secret places in a fortified Castle where every aperture was secured by unopened locks and bolts; her very movements, though all of grace, as she flitted noiselessly through the gloom of night.

All these things, and a thousand others of lesser import, seemed, for the moment, to have consolidated an initial belief. But then came the supreme recollections of how she had lain in my arms; of her kisses on my lips; of the beating of her heart against my own; of her sweet words of belief and faith breathed in my ear in intoxicating whispers; of.... I paused. No! I could not accept belief as to her being other than a living woman of soul and sense, of flesh and blood, of all the sweet and passionate instincts of true and perfect womanhood.

And so, in spite of all – in spite of all beliefs, fixed or transitory, with a mind whirling amid contesting forces and compelling beliefs – I stepped into the church overwhelmed with that most receptive of atmospheres – doubt.

In one thing only was I fixed: here at least was no doubt or misgiving whatever. I intended to go through what I had undertaken. Moreover, I felt that I was strong enough to carry out my intention, whatever might be of the Unknown – however horrible, however terrible.

When I had entered the church and closed the heavy door behind me, the sense of darkness and loneliness in all their horror enfolded me round. The great church seemed a living mystery, and served as an almost terrible background to thoughts and remembrances of unutterable gloom. My adventurous life has had its own schooling to endurance and upholding one's courage in trying times; but it has its contra in fulness of memory.

I felt my way forward with both hands and feet. Every second seemed as if it had brought me at last to a darkness which was actually tangible. All at once, and with no heed of sequence or order, I was conscious of all around me, the knowledge or perception of which – or even speculation on the subject – had never entered my mind. They furnished the darkness with which I was encompassed with all the crowded phases of a dream. I knew that all around me were memorials of the dead – that in the Crypt deep-wrought in the rock below my feet lay the dead themselves. Some of them, perhaps – one of them I knew – had even passed the grim portals of time Unknown, and had, by some mysterious power or agency, come back again to material earth. There was no resting-place for thought when I knew that the very air which I breathed might be full of denizens of the spirit-world. In that impenetrable blackness was a world of imagining whose possibilities of horror were endless.

I almost fancied that I could see with mortal eyes down through that rocky floor to where, in the lonely Crypt, lay, in her tomb of massive stone and under that bewildering coverlet of glass, the woman whom I love. I could see her beautiful face, her long black lashes, her sweet mouth – which I had kissed – relaxed in the sleep of death. I could note the voluminous shroud – a piece of which as a precious souvenir lay even then so close to my heart – the snowy woollen coverlet wrought over in gold with sprigs of pine, the soft dent in the cushion on which her head must for so long have lain. I could see myself – within my eyes the memory of that first visit – coming once again with glad step to renew that dear sight – dear, though it scorched my eyes and harrowed my heart – and finding the greater sorrow, the greater desolation of the empty tomb!

There! I felt that I must think no more of that lest the thought should unnerve me when I should most want all my courage. That way madness lay! The darkness had already sufficient terrors of its own without bringing to it such grim remembrances and imaginings...And I had yet to go through some ordeal which, even to her who had passed and repassed the portals of death, was full of fear.

It was a merciful relief to me when, in groping my way forwards through the darkness, I struck against some portion of the furnishing of the church. Fortunately I was all strung up to tension, else I should never have been able to control instinctively, as I did, the shriek which was rising to my lips.

I would have given anything to have been able to light even a match. A single second of light would, I felt, have made me my own man again. But I knew that this would be against the implied condition of my being there at all, and might have had disastrous consequences to her whom I had come to save. It might even frustrate my scheme, and altogether destroy my opportunity. At that moment it was borne upon me more strongly than ever that this was not a mere fight for myself or my own selfish purposes – not merely an adventure or a struggle for only life and death against unknown difficulties and dangers. It was a fight on behalf of her I loved, not merely for her life, but perhaps even for her soul.

And yet this very thinking – understanding – created a new form of terror. For in that grim, shrouding darkness came memories of other moments of terrible stress.

Of wild, mystic rites held in the deep gloom of African forests, when, amid scenes of revolting horror, Obi and the devils of his kind seemed to reveal themselves to reckless worshippers, surfeited with horror, whose lives counted for naught; when even human sacrifice was an episode, and the reek of old deviltries and recent carnage tainted the air, till even I, who was, at the risk of my life, a privileged spectator who had come through dangers without end to behold the scene, rose and fled in horror.

Of scenes of mystery enacted in rock-cut temples beyond the Himalayas, whose fanatic priests, cold as death and as remorseless, in the reaction of their phrenzy of passion, foamed at the mouth and then sank into marble quiet, as with inner eyes they beheld the visions of the hellish powers which they had invoked.

Of wild, fantastic dances of the Devil-worshippers of Madagascar, where even the very semblance of humanity disappeared in the fantastic excesses of their orgies.

Of strange doings of gloom and mystery in the rock-perched monasteries of Thibet.

Of awful sacrifices, all to mystic ends, in the innermost recesses of Cathay.

Of weird movements with masses of poisonous snakes by the medicine-men of the Zuni and Mochi Indians in the far south-west of the Rockies, beyond the great plains.

Of secret gatherings in vast temples of old Mexico, and by dim altars of forgotten cities in the heart of great forests in South America.

Of rites of inconceivable horror in the fastnesses of Patagonia.

Of.... Here I once more pulled myself up. Such thoughts were no kind of proper preparation for what I might have to endure. My work that night was to be based on love, on hope, on self-sacrifice for the woman who in all the world was the closest to my heart, whose future I was to share, whether that sharing might lead me to Hell or Heaven. The hand which undertook such a task must have no trembling.

Still, those horrible memories had, I am bound to say, a useful part in my preparation for the ordeal. They were of fact which I had seen, of which I had myself been in part a sharer, and which I had survived. With such experiences behind me, could there be aught before me more dreadful?...

Moreover, if the coming ordeal was of supernatural or superhuman order, could it transcend in living horror the vilest and most desperate acts of the basest men?...

With renewed courage I felt my way before me, till my sense of touch told me that I was at the screen behind which lay the stair to the Crypt.

There I waited, silent, still.

My own part was done, so far as I knew how to do it. Beyond this, what was to come was, so far as I knew, beyond my own control. I had done what I could; the rest must come from others. I had exactly obeyed my instructions, fulfilled my warranty to the utmost in my knowledge and power. There was, therefore, left for me in the present nothing but to wait.

It is a peculiarity of absolute darkness that it creates its own reaction. The eye, wearied of the blackness, begins to imagine forms of light. How far this is effected by imagination pure and simple I know not. It may be that nerves have their own senses that bring thought to the depository common to all the human functions, but, whatever may be the mechanism or the objective, the darkness seems to people itself with luminous entities.

So was it with me as I stood lonely in the dark, silent church. Here and there seemed to flash tiny points of light.

In the same way the silence began to be broken now and again by strange muffled sounds – the suggestion of sounds rather than actual vibrations. These were all at first of the minor importance of movement – rustlings, creakings, faint stirrings, fainter breathings. Presently, when I had somewhat recovered from the sort of hypnotic trance to which the darkness and stillness had during the time of waiting reduced me, I looked around in wonder.

The phantoms of light and sound seemed to have become real. There were most certainly actual little points of light in places – not enough to see details by, but quite sufficient to relieve the utter gloom. I thought – though it may have been a mingling of recollection and imagination – that I could distinguish the outlines of the church; certainly the great altar-screen was dimly visible. Instinctively I looked up – and thrilled. There, hung high above me, was, surely enough, a great Greek Cross, outlined by tiny points of light.

I lost myself in wonder, and stood still, in a purely receptive mood, unantagonistic to aught, willing for whatever might come, ready for all things, in rather a negative than a positive mood – a mood which has an aspect of spiritual meekness. This is the true spirit of the neophyte, and, though I did not think of it at the time, the proper attitude for what is called by the Church in whose temple I stood a 'neo-nymph.'

As the light grew a little in power, though never increasing enough for distinctness, I saw dimly before me a table on which rested a great open book, whereon were laid two rings – one of sliver, the other of gold – and two crowns wrought of flowers, bound at the joining of their stems with tissue – one of gold, the other of silver. I do not know much of the ritual of the old Greek Church, which is the religion of the Blue Mountains, but the things which I saw before me could be none other than enlightening symbols. Instinctively I knew that I had been brought hither, though in this grim way, to be married. The very idea of it thrilled me to the heart's core. I thought the best thing I could do would be to stay quite still, and not show surprise at anything that might happen; but be sure I was all eyes and ears.

I peered anxiously around me in every direction, but I could see no sign of her whom I had come to meet.

Incidentally, however, I noticed that in the lighting, such as it was, there was no flame, no 'living' light. Whatever light there was came muffled, as though through some green translucent stone. The whole effect was terribly weird and disconcerting.

Presently I started, as, seemingly out of the darkness beside me, a man's hand stretched out and took mine. Turning, I found close to me a tall man with shining black eyes and long black hair and beard. He was clad in some kind of gorgeous robe of cloth of gold, rich with variety of adornment. His head was covered with a high, over-hanging hat draped closely with a black scarf, the ends of which formed a long, hanging veil on either side. These veils, falling over the magnificent robes of cloth of gold, had an extraordinarily solemn effect.

I yielded myself to the guiding hand, and shortly found myself, so far as I could see, at one side of the sanctuary.

In the floor close to my feet was a yawning chasm, into which, from so high over my head that in the uncertain light I could not distinguish its origin, hung a chain. At the sight a strange wave of memory swept over me. I could not but remember the chain which hung over the glass-covered tomb in the Crypt, and I had an instinctive feeling that the grim chasm in the floor of the sanctuary was but the other side of the opening in the roof of the crypt from which the chain over the sarcophagus depended.

There was a creaking sound – the groaning of a windlass and the clanking of a chain. There was heavy breathing close to me somewhere. I was so intent on what was going on that I did not see that one by one, seeming to grow out of the surrounding darkness, several black figures in monkish garb appeared with the silence of ghosts. Their faces were shrouded in black cowls, wherein were holes through which I could see dark gleaming eyes. My guide held me tightly by the hand. This gave me a feeling of security in the touch which helped to retain within my breast some semblance of calm.

The strain of the creaking windlass and the clanking chain continued for so long that the suspense became almost unendurable. At last there came into sight an iron ring, from which as a centre depended four lesser chains spreading wide. In a few seconds more I could see that these were fixed to the corners of the great stone tomb with the covering of glass, which was being dragged upward. As it arose it filled closely the whole aperture. When its bottom had reached the level of the floor it stopped, and remained rigid. There was no room for oscillation. It was at once surrounded by a number of black figures, who raised the glass covering and bore it away into the darkness. Then there stepped forward a very tall man, black-bearded, and with head-gear like my guide, but made in triple tiers, he also was gorgeously arrayed in flowing robes of cloth of gold richly embroidered. He raised his hand, and forthwith eight other black-clad figures stepped forward, and bending over the stone coffin, raised from it the rigid form of my Lady, still clad in her Shroud, and laid it gently on the floor of the sanctuary.

I felt it a grace that at that instant the dim lights seemed to grow less, and finally to disappear – all save the tiny points that marked the outline of the great Cross high overhead. These only gave light enough to accentuate the gloom. The hand that held mine now released it, and with a sigh I realized that I was alone. After a few moments more of the groaning of the winch and clanking of the chain there was a sharp sound of stone meeting stone; then there was silence. I listened acutely, but could not hear near me the slightest sound. Even the cautious, restrained breathing around me, of which up to then I had been conscious, had ceased. Not knowing, in the helplessness of my ignorance, what I should do, I remained as I was, still and silent, for a time that seemed endless. At last, overcome by some emotion which I could not at the moment understand, I slowly sank to my knees and bowed my head. Covering my face with my hands, I tried to recall the prayers of my youth. It was not, I am certain, that fear in any form had come upon me, or that I hesitated or faltered in my intention. That much I know now; I knew it even then. It was, I believe, that the prolonged impressive gloom and mystery had at last touched me to the quick. The bending of the knees was but symbolical of the bowing of the spirit to a higher Power. When I had realized that much, I felt more content than I had done since I had entered the church, and with the renewed consciousness of courage, took my hands from my face, and lifted again my bowed head.

Impulsively I sprang to my feet and stood erect – waiting. All seemed to have changed since I had dropped on my knees. The points of light about time church, which had been eclipsed, had come again, and were growing in power to a partial revealing of the dim expanse. Before me was the table with the open book, on which were laid the gold and silver rings and the two crowns of flowers. There were also two tall candles, with tiniest flames of blue – the only living light to be seen.

Out of the darkness stepped the same tall figure in the gorgeous robes and the triple hat. He led by the hand my Lady, still clad in her Shroud; but over it, descending from the crown of her head, was a veil of very old and magnificent lace of astonishing fineness. Even in that dim light I could note the exquisite beauty of the fabric. The veil was fastened with a bunch of tiny sprays of orange-blossom mingled with cypress and laurel – a strange combination. In her hand she carried a great bouquet of the same. Its sweet intoxicating odour floated up to my nostrils. It and the sentiment which its very presence evoked made me quiver.

Yielding to the guiding of the hand which held hers, she stood at my left side before the table. Her guide then took his place behind her. At either end of the table, to right and left of us, stood a long-bearded priest in splendid robes, and wearing the hat with depending veil of black. One of them, who seemed to be the more important of the two, and took the initiative, signed to us to put our right hands on the open book. My Lady, of course, understood the ritual, and knew the words which the priest was speaking, and of her own accord put out her hand. My guide at the same moment directed my hand to the same end. It thrilled me to touch my Lady's hand, even under such mysterious conditions.

After the priest had signed us each thrice on the forehead with the sign of the Cross, he gave to each of us a tiny lighted taper brought to him for the purpose. The lights were welcome, not so much for the solace of the added light, great as that was, but because it allowed us to see a little more of each other's faces. It was rapture to me to see the face of my Bride; and from the expression of her face I was assured that she felt as I did. It gave me an inexpressible pleasure when, as her eyes rested on me, there grew a faint blush over the grey pallor of her cheeks.

The priest then put in solemn voice to each of us in turn, beginning with me, the questions of consent which are common to all such rituals. I answered as well as I could, following the murmured words of my guide. My Lady answered out proudly in a voice which, though given softly, seemed to ring. It was a concern – even a grief – to me that I could not, in the priest's questioning, catch her name, of which, strangely enough – I was ignorant. But, as I did not know the language, and as the phrases were not in accord literally with our own ritual, I could not make out which word was the name.

After some prayers and blessings, rhythmically spoken or sung by an invisible choir, the priest took the rings from the open book, and, after signing my forehead thrice with the gold one as he repeated the blessing in each case, placed it on my right hand; then he gave my Lady the silver one, with the same ritual thrice repeated. I suppose it was the blessing which is the effective point in making two into one.

After this, those who stood behind us exchanged our rings thrice, taking them from one finger and placing them on the other, so that at the end my wife wore the gold ring and I the silver one.

Then came a chant, during which the priest swung the censer himself, and my wife and I held our tapers. After that he blessed us, the responses coming from the voices of the unseen singers in the darkness.

After a long ritual of prayer and blessing, sung in triplicate, the priest took the crowns of flowers, and put one on the head of each, crowning me first, and with the crown tied with gold. Then he signed and blessed us each thrice. The guides, who stood behind us, exchanged our crowns thrice, as they had exchanged the rings; so that at the last, as I was glad to see, my wife wore the crown of gold, and I that of silver.

Then there came, if it is possible to describe such a thing, a hush over even that stillness, as though some form of added solemnity were to be gone through. I was not surprised, therefore, when the priest took in his hands the great golden chalice. Kneeling, my wife and I partook together thrice.

When we had risen from our knees and stood for a little while, the priest took my left hand in his right, and I, by direction of my guide, gave my right hand to my wife. And so in a line, the priest leading, we circled round the table in rhythmic measure. Those who supported us moved behind us, holding the crowns over our heads, and replacing them when we stopped.

After a hymn, sung through the darkness, the priest took off our crowns. This was evidently the conclusion of the ritual, for the priest placed us in each other's arms to embrace each other. Then he blessed us, who were now man and wife!

The lights went out at once, some as if extinguished, others slowly fading down to blackness.

Left in the dark, my wife and I sought each other's arms again, and stood together for a few moments heart to heart, tightly clasping each other, and kissed each other fervently.

Instinctively we turned to the door of the church, which was slightly open, so that we could see the moonlight stealing in through the aperture. With even steps, she holding me tightly by the left arm – which is the wife's arm, we passed through the old church and out into the free air.

Despite all that the gloom had brought me, it was sweet to be in the open air and together – this quite apart from our new relations to each other. The moon rode high, and the full light, coming after the dimness or darkness in the church, seemed as bright as day. I could now, for the first time, see my wife's face properly. The glamour of the moonlight may have served to enhance its ethereal beauty, but neither moonlight nor sunlight could do justice to that beauty in its living human splendour. As I gloried in her starry eyes I could think of nothing else; but when for a moment my eyes, roving round for the purpose of protection, caught sight of her whole figure, there was a pang to my heart. The brilliant moonlight showed every detail in terrible effect, and I could see that she wore only her Shroud. In the moment of darkness, after the last benediction, before she returned to my arms, she must have removed her bridal veil. This may, of course, have been in accordance with the established ritual of her church; but, all the same, my heart was sore. The glamour of calling her my very own was somewhat obscured by the bridal adornment being shorn. But it made no difference in her sweetness to me. Together we went along the path through the wood, she keeping equal step with me in wifely way.

When we had come through the trees near enough to see the roof of the Castle, now gilded with the moonlight, she stopped, and looking at me with eyes full of love, said:

"Here I must leave you!"

"What?" I was all aghast, and I felt that my chagrin was expressed in the tone of horrified surprise in my voice. She went on quickly:

"Alas! It is impossible that I should go farther – at present!"

"But what is to prevent you?" I queried. "You are now my wife. This is our wedding-night; and surely your place is with me!" The wail in her voice as she answered touched me to the quick:

"Oh, I know, I know! There is no dearer wish in my heart – there can be none – than to share my husband's home. Oh, my dear, my dear, if you only knew what it would be to me to be with you always! But indeed I may not – not yet! I am not free! If you but knew how much that which has happened tonight has cost me – or how much cost to others as well as to myself may be yet to come – you would understand. Rupert" – it was the first time she had ever addressed me by name, and naturally it thrilled me through and through – "Rupert, my husband, only that I trust you with all the faith which is in perfect love – mutual love, I dare not have done what I have done this night. But, dear, I know that you will bear me out; that your wife's honour is your honour, even as your honour is mine. My honour is given to this; and you can help me – the only help I can have at present – by trusting me. Be patient, my beloved, be patient! Oh, be patient for a little longer! It shall not be for long. So soon as ever my soul is freed I shall come to you, my husband; and we shall never part again. Be content for a while! Believe me that I love you with my very soul; and to keep away from your dear side is more bitter for me than even it can be for you! Think, my dear one, I am not as other women are, as some day you shall clearly understand. I am at the present, and shall be for a little longer, constrained by duties and obligations put upon me by others, and for others, and to which I am pledged by the most sacred promises – given not only by myself, but by others – and which I must not forgo. These forbid me to do as I wish. Oh, trust me, my beloved – my husband!"

She held out her hands appealingly. The moonlight, falling through the thinning forest, showed her white cerements. Then the recollection of all she must have suffered – the awful loneliness in that grim tomb in the Crypt, the despairing agony of one who is helpless against the unknown – swept over me in a wave of pity. What could I do but save her from further pain? And this could only be by showing her my faith and trust. If she was to go back to that dreadful charnel-house, she would at least take with her the remembrance that one who loved her and whom she loved – to whom she had been lately bound in the mystery of marriage – trusted her to the full. I loved her more than myself – more than my own soul; and I was moved by pity so great that all possible selfishness was merged in its depths. I bowed my head before her – my Lady and my Wife – as I said:

"So be it, my beloved. I trust you to the full, even as you trust me. And that has been proven this night, even to my own doubting heart. I shall wait; and as I know you wish it, I shall wait as patiently as I can. But till you come to me for good and all, let me see you or hear from you when you can. The time, dear wife, must go heavily with me as I think of you suffering and lonely. So be good to me, and let not too long a time elapse between my glimpses of hope. And, sweetheart, when you do come to me, it shall be for ever!" There was something in the intonation of the last sentence – I felt its sincerity myself – some implied yearning for a promise, that made her beautiful eyes swim. The glorious stars in them were blurred as she answered with a fervour which seemed to me as more than earthly:

"For ever! I swear it!"

With one long kiss, and a straining in each others arms, which left me tingling for long after we had lost sight of each other, we parted. I stood and watched her as her white figure, gliding through the deepening gloom, faded as the forest thickened. It surely was no optical delusion or a phantom of the mind that her shrouded arm was raised as though in blessing or farewell before the darkness swallowed her up.

The complete and unabridged text is available
online, *from flametreepublishing.com/extras*

If you enjoyed this, you might also like...
'Crooken Sands,' see page 59
Dracula (chapters I–IV), see page 81

Biographies

Bram Stoker

Abraham 'Bram' Stoker (1847–1912) was born in Dublin, Ireland. Often ill during his childhood, he spent a lot of time in bed listening to his mother's grim stories, sparking his imagination. Striking up a friendship as an adult with the actor Henry Irving, Stoker eventually came to work and live in London, meeting notable authors such as Arthur Conan Doyle and Oscar Wilde. Stoker is best-known for his gothic masterpiece *Dracula* which has left an enduring and powerful impact on the genre, creating one of the most iconic figures that horror fiction has ever seen. He wrote many other novels and short stories, several of which had a horror, and often supernatural, theme.

Dr. Catherine Wynne

Foreword: Bram Stoker Horror Stories

Dr. Catherine Wynne is Senior Lecturer in English at the University of Hull. She is author of *Bram Stoker, Dracula and the Victorian Gothic Stage* (Palgrave, 2013) and has edited two volumes of Bram Stoker's theatrical writings, *Bram Stoker and the Stage: Reviews, Reminiscences, Essays and Fiction* (Pickering and Chatto, 2012). She has also edited *Stoker and the Gothic: Formations to Transformations* (Palgrave, 2015), a collection of essays on Stoker. In 2012 she organized the *Bram Stoker Centenary Conference* (Hull and Whitby). She has contributed to documentaries on Stoker for radio and television and has spoken about Stoker at the British Library.

Sources

Supernatural Foes

The Chain of Destiny
Originally Published in *The Shamrock*, May 1875

The Invisible Giant
Originally Published in *Under the Sunset*, Sampson Low, Marston, Searle & Rivington, London, 1881

The Judge's House
Originally Published in *Holly Leaves*, December 1891

Crooken Sands
Originally Published in *Holly Leaves*, December 1894

Dracula's Guest
Originally Published in *Dracula's Guest and Other Weird Stories*, George Routledge & Sons, 1914. (Widely believed to have been written as the first chapter of *Dracula*, but then omitted from the published book, possibly for reasons of length.)

Dracula (chapters I–IV)
Originally Published by Archibald Constable & Co., London, 1897

The Jewel of Seven Stars
Originally Published by William Heinemann, London, 1903

The Lair of the White Worm (chapter V; chapters XIX–XXVIII)
Originally Published by William Rider & Son Ltd., London, 1911

Murder & Revenge

The Gipsy Prophecy
Originally Published in *The Spirit of the Times*, December 1885

The Secret of the Growing Gold
Originally Published in *Black and White*, January 1892

The Squaw
Originally Published in *Holly Leaves*, December 1893

The Man from Shorrox
Originally Published in *The Pall Mall Magazine*, February 1894

A Dream of Red Hands
Originally Published in *The Sketch: A Journal of Art and Actuality*, July 1894

The Red Stockade
Originally Published in *The Cosmopolitan*, September 1894

The Burial of the Rats
Originally Published in *Lloyd's Weekly Newspaper*, London, January–February 1896 and *The Boston Herald*, January–February 1896

The Dualitists
Originally Published in *The Theatre Annual: Containing Stories, Reminiscences and Verses*, November 1886

Love & Tragedy

The Crystal Cup
Originally Published in *London Society*, September 1872

The Shadow Builder
Originally Published in *Under the Sunset*, Sampson Low, Marston, Searle & Rivington, London, 1881

The Castle of the King
Originally Published in *Under the Sunset*, Sampson Low, Marston, Searle & Rivington, London, 1881

A Star Trap [a.k.a. Death in the Wings]
Originally Published in *Colliers*, November 1888

The Coming of Abel Behenna
Originally Published in *Lloyd's Weekly Newspaper*, London, March–April 1893 and *The New Haven Register*, Connecticut, March 1893

The Lady of the Shroud (chapters III–V)
Originally Published by William Heinemann, London, 1909

FLAME TREE PUBLISHING
Short Story Series
New & Classic Writing

Flame Tree's Gothic Fantasy books offer a carefully curated series of new titles, each with combinations of original and classic writing:

Chilling Horror Short Stories
Chilling Ghost Short Stories
Science Fiction Short Stories
Murder Mayhem Short Stories
Crime & Mystery Short Stories
Swords & Steam Short Stories
Dystopia Utopia Short Stories
Supernatural Horror Short Stories
Lost Worlds Short Stories
Time Travel Short Stories
Heroic Fantasy Short Stories
Pirates & Ghosts Short Stories
Agents & Spies Short Stories
Endless Apocalypse Short Stories
Alien Invasion Short Stories

as well as new companion titles which offer rich collections of classic fiction from masters of the gothic fantasy genres:

H.G. Wells Short Stories
Lovecraft Short Stories
Sherlock Holmes Collection
Edgar Allan Poe Collection

Available from all good bookstores, worldwide, and online at
flametreepublishing.com

...and coming soon:

FLAME TREE PRESS | FICTION WITHOUT FRONTIERS
New and original writing in Horror, Crime, SF and Fantasy

GOTHIC FANTASY

For our books, calendars, blog
and latest special offers please see:
flametreepublishing.com